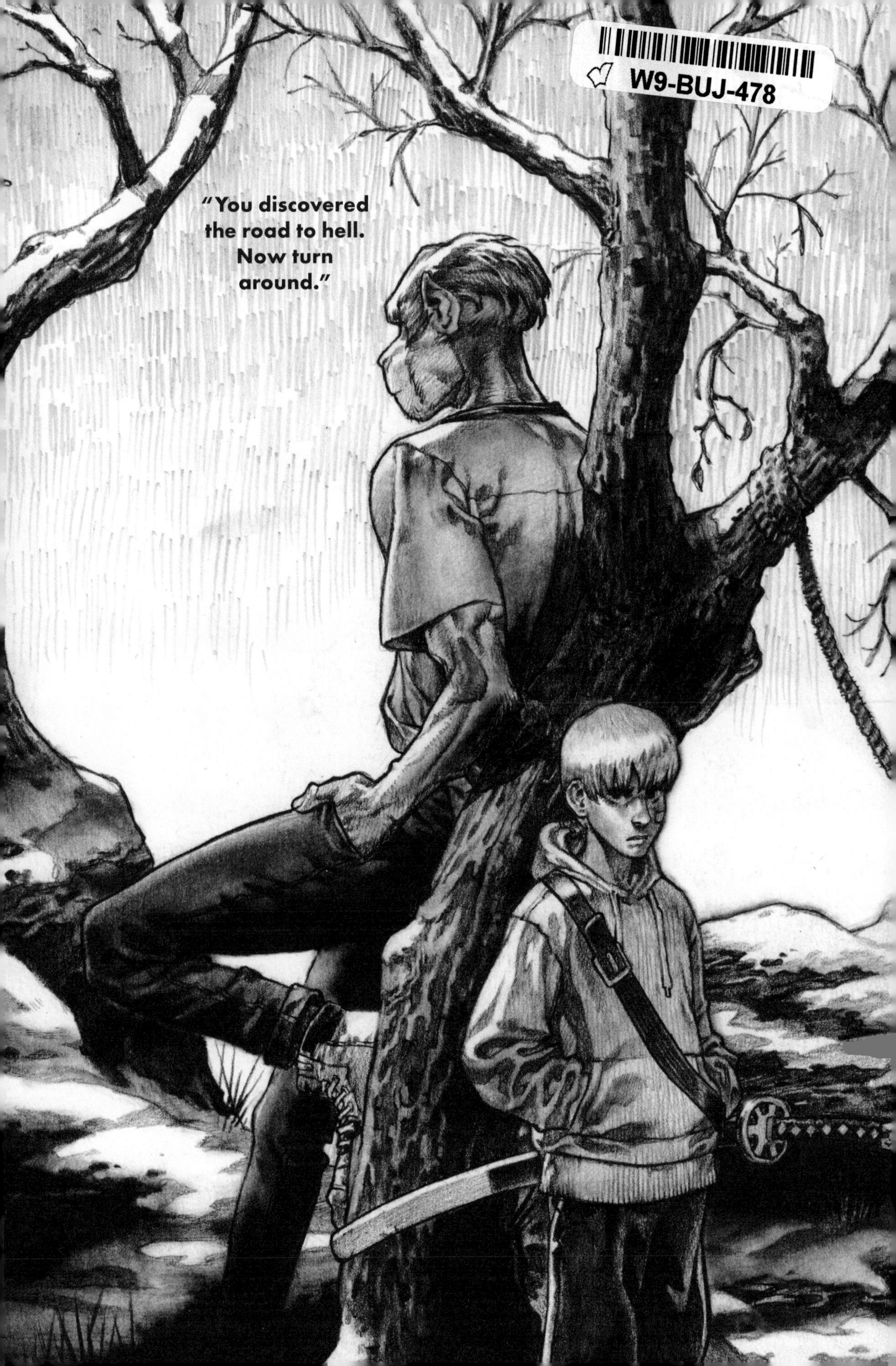
"You discovered the road to hell. Now turn around."

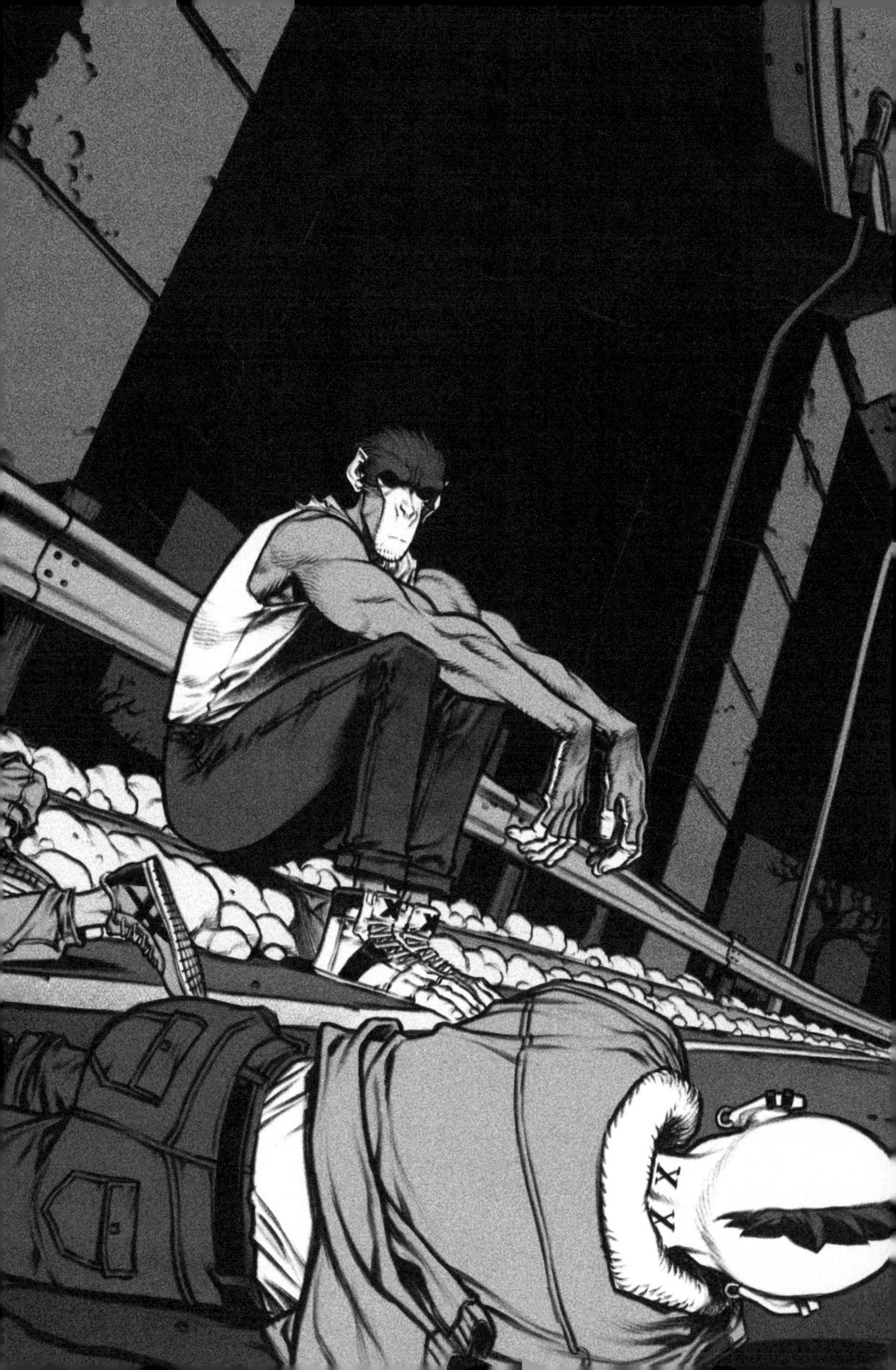

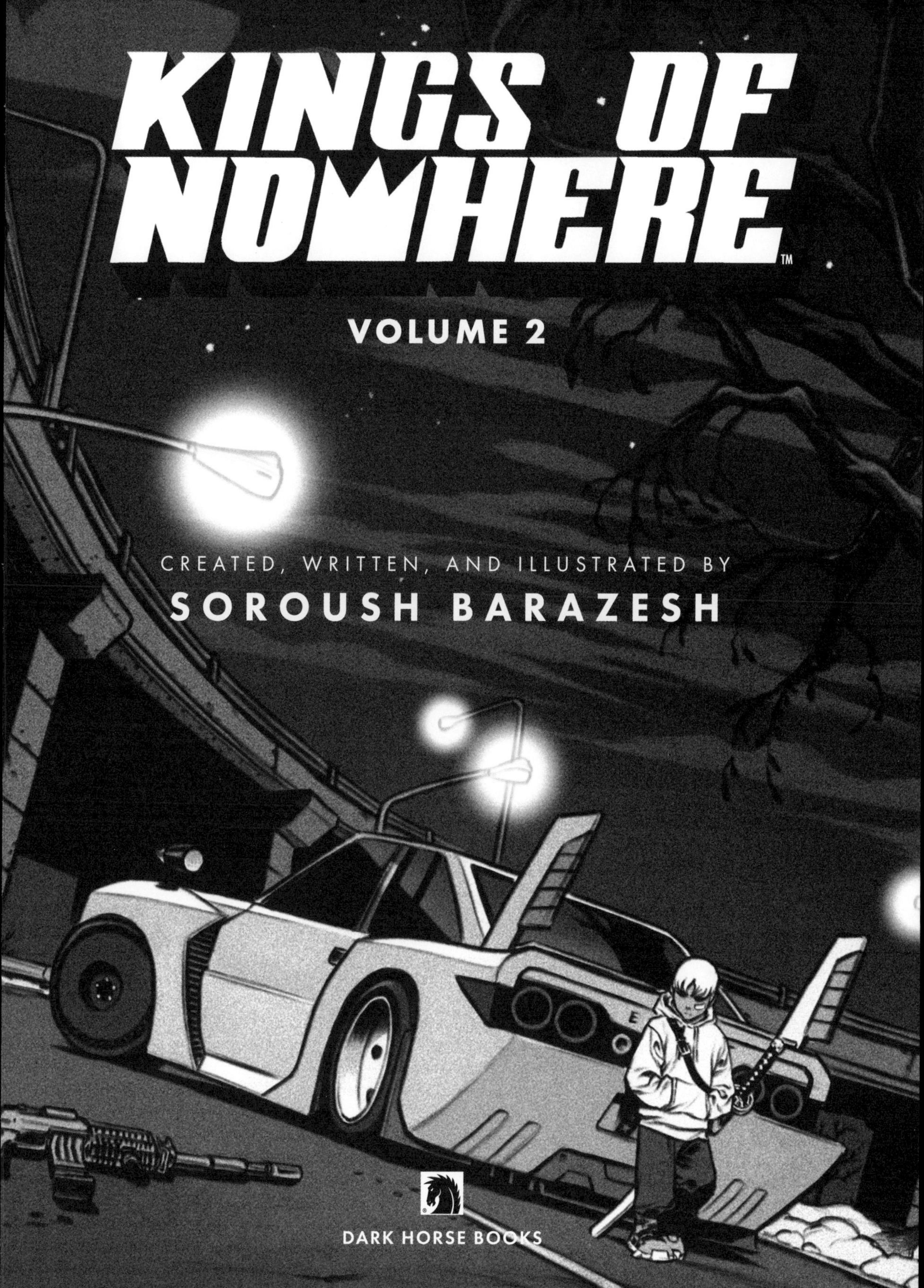

KINGS OF NOWHERE™

VOLUME 2

CREATED, WRITTEN, AND ILLUSTRATED BY

SOROUSH BARAZESH

DARK HORSE BOOKS

PRÉSIDENT & PUBLISHER
MIKE RICHARDSON

COLLECTION EDITOR
JUDY KHUU

COLLECTION DESIGNER
JUSTIN COUCH

COLLECTION ASSISTANT EDITOR
ROSE WEITZ

DIGITAL ART TECHNICIAN
ADAM PRUETT

Neil Hankerson, Executive Vice President; Tom Weddle, Chief Financial Officer; Dale LaFountain, Chief Information Officer; Tim Wiesch, Vice President of Licensing; Vanessa Todd-Holmes, Vice President of Production and Scheduling; Mark Bernardi, Vice President of Book Trade and Digital Sales; Randy Lahrman, Vice President of Product Development and Sales; Ken Lizzi, General Counsel; Dave Marshall, Editor in Chief; Davey Estrada, Editorial Director; Chris Warner, Senior Books Editor; Cara O'Neil, Senior Director of Marketing; Cary Grazzini, Director of Specialty Projects; Lia Ribacchi, Art Director; Michael Gombos, Senior Director of Licensed Publications; Kari Yadro, Director of Custom Programs; Kari Torson, Director of International Licensing; Christina Niece, Director of Scheduling

KINGS OF NOWHERE VOLUME 2

PUBLISHED BY DARK HORSE BOOKS
A division of Dark Horse Comics LLC
10956 SE Main Street, Milwaukie, OR 97222

DARKHORSE.COM
To find a comics shop in your area, visit comicshoplocator.com

First edition: March 2023
Ebook ISBN 978-1-50673-325-8
Trade Paperback ISBN 978-1-50673-329-6

10 9 8 7 6 5 4 3 2 1
Printed in China

LIBRARY OF CONGRESS CATALOGING-IN-PUBLICATION DATA

Names: Barazesh, Soroush, writer, artist.
Title: Kings of nowhere / Soroush Barazesh.
Description: Milwaukie, OR : Dark Horse Books, 2022-
Identifiers: LCCN 2022011814 (print) | LCCN 2022011815 (ebook) | ISBN 9781506733289 (v. 1 ; trade paperback) | ISBN 9781506733241 (v. 1 ; ebook)
Subjects: LCSH: Shapeshifting--Comic books, strips, etc. | Revenge--Comic books, strips, etc. | LCGFT: Action and adventure comics. | Fantasy comics. | Graphic novels.
Classification: LCC PN6733.B27 K56 2022 (print) | LCC PN6733.B27 (ebook) | DDC 741.5/971--dc23/eng/20220426
LC record available at https://lccn.loc.gov/2022011814
LC ebook record available at https://lccn.loc.gov/2022011815

THE YEAR IS 3991, twenty-four years after the turbulent events that took place in Lo Divino. No, we are not in the distant future, nor are we on Earth. We are on a planet vaguely similar to ours called Gaia, located in a long-forgotten dimension. Our adventures take us far north of Lo Divino to the city of T'Karanto, where rival gang disputes are impacting the lives of the locals.

KINGS OF NOWHERE

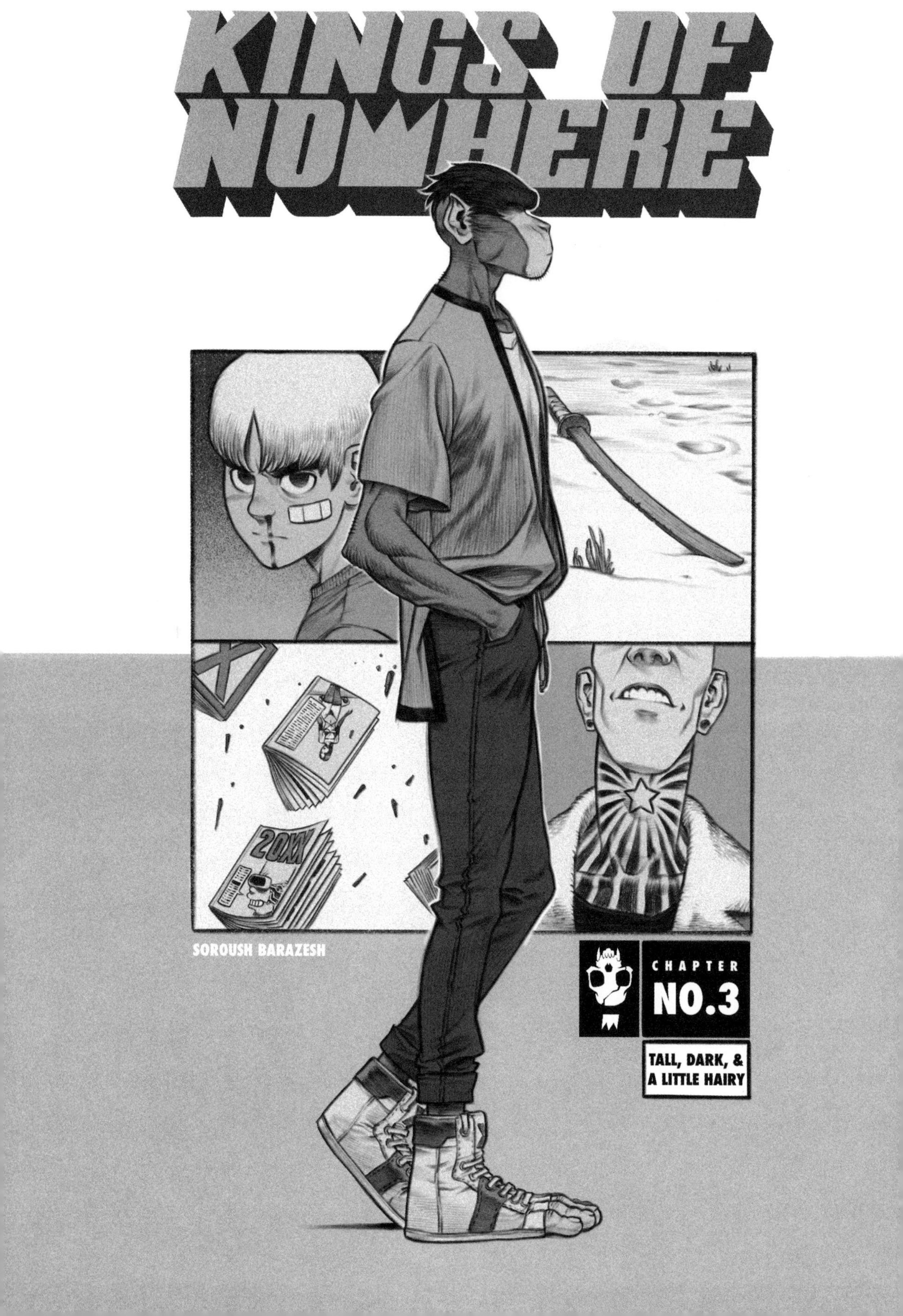
20XX

SOROUSH BARAZESH

CHAPTER
NO.3

TALL, DARK, & A LITTLE HAIRY

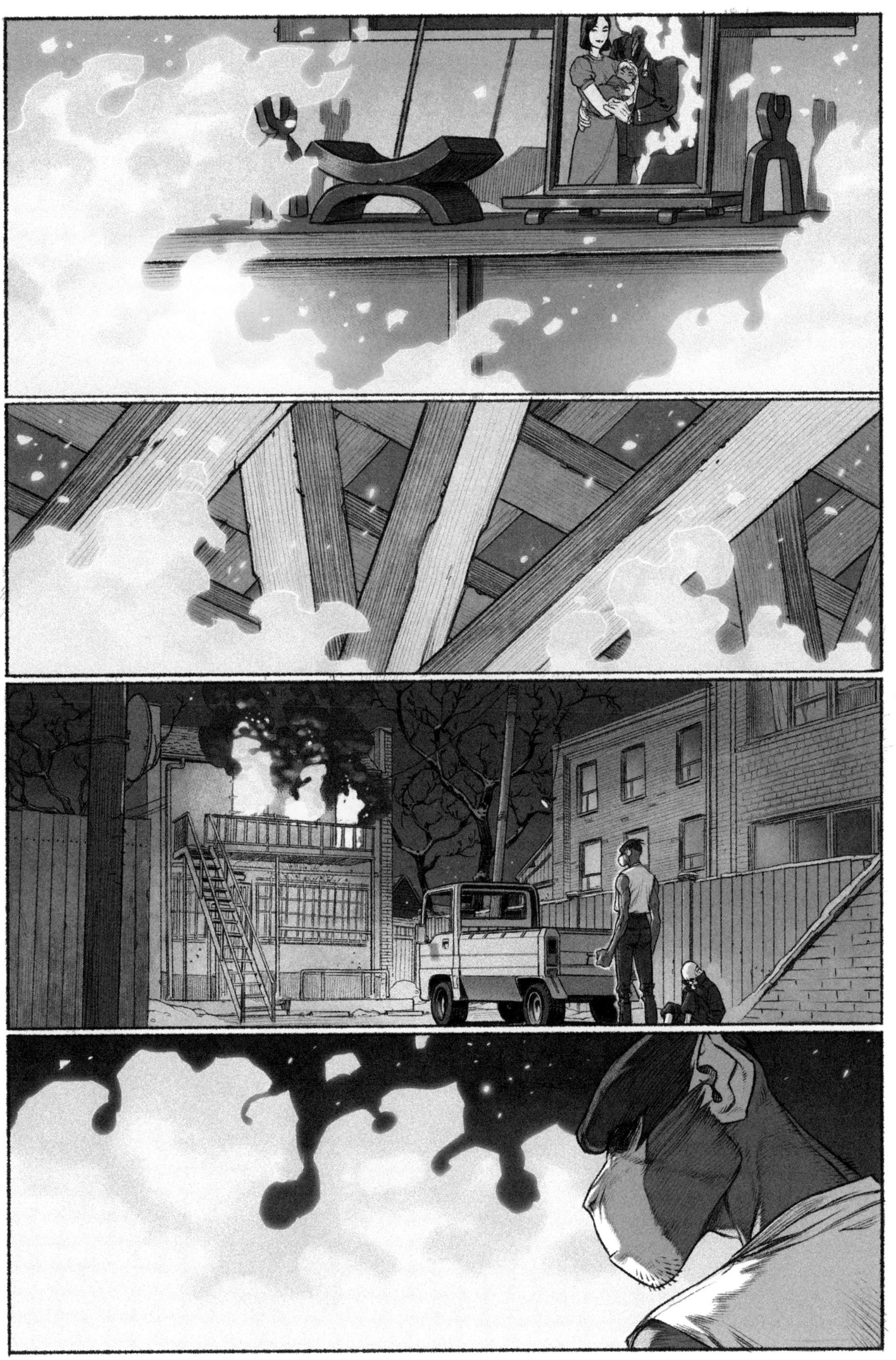

KON VOL.2

CHAPTER NO. 3

TALL, DARK, & A LITTLE HAIRY

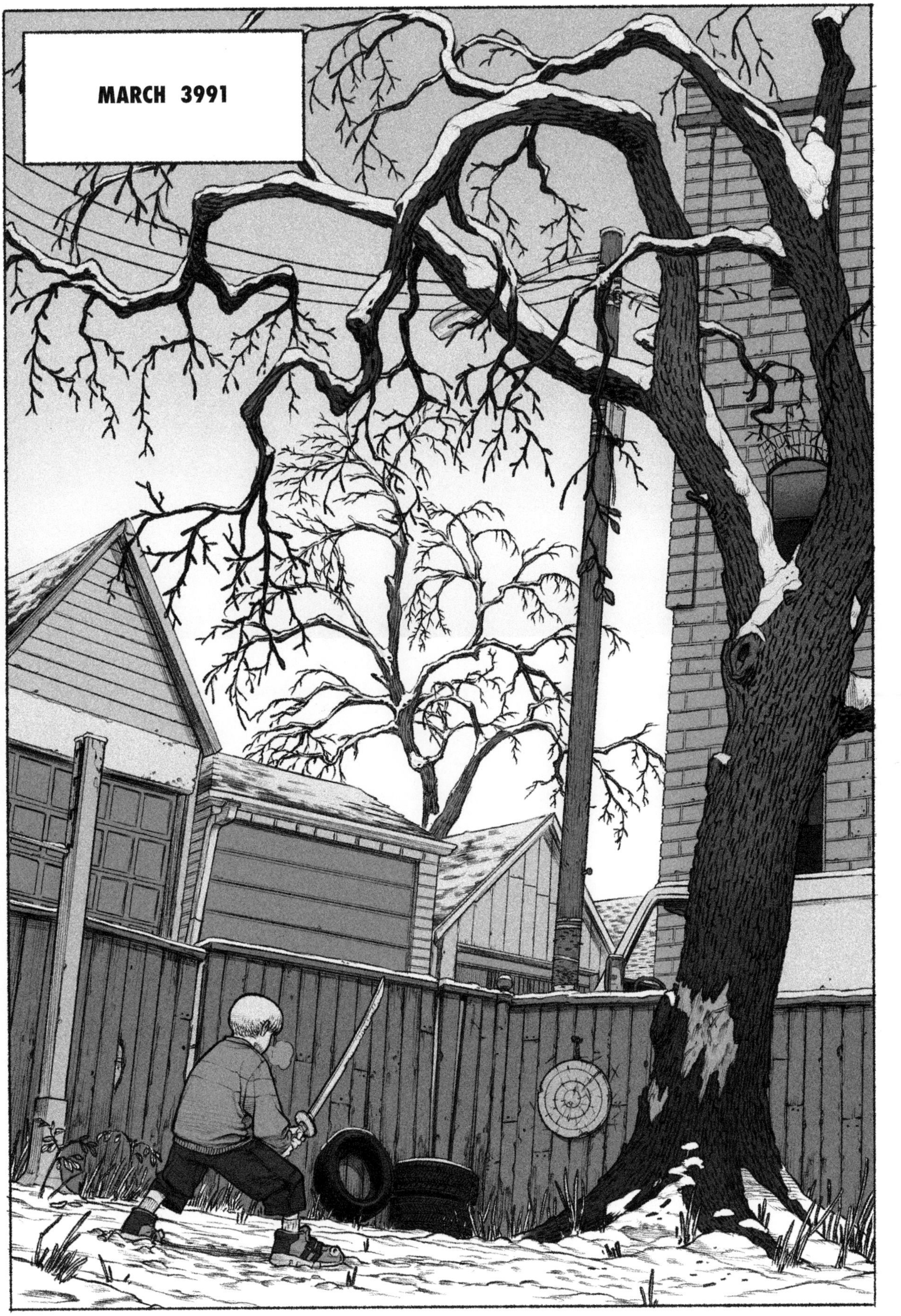
MARCH 3991

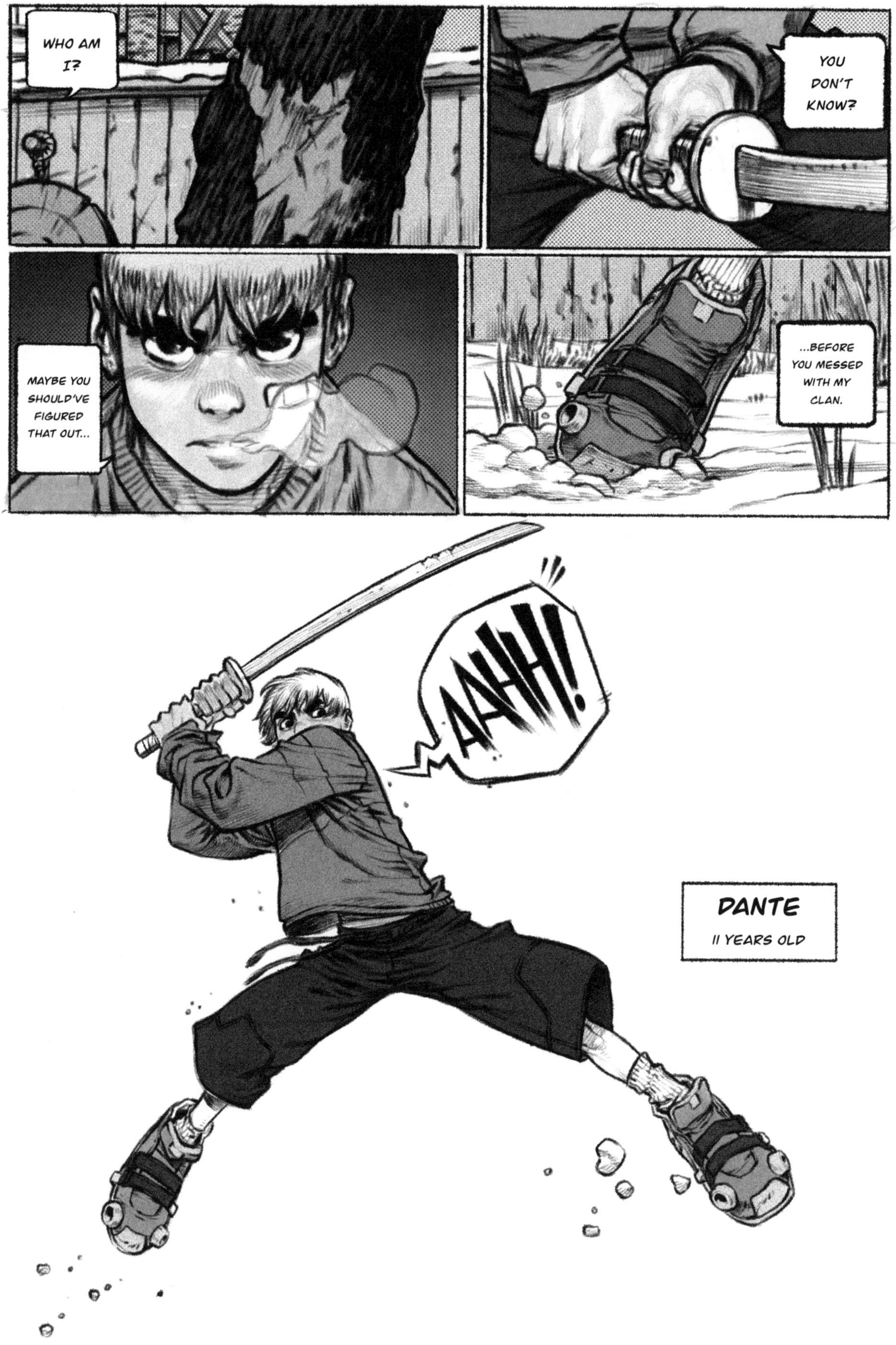
WHO AM I?
YOU DON'T KNOW?
MAYBE YOU SHOULD'VE FIGURED THAT OUT...
...BEFORE YOU MESSED WITH MY CLAN.
AAHH!
DANTE
11 YEARS OLD

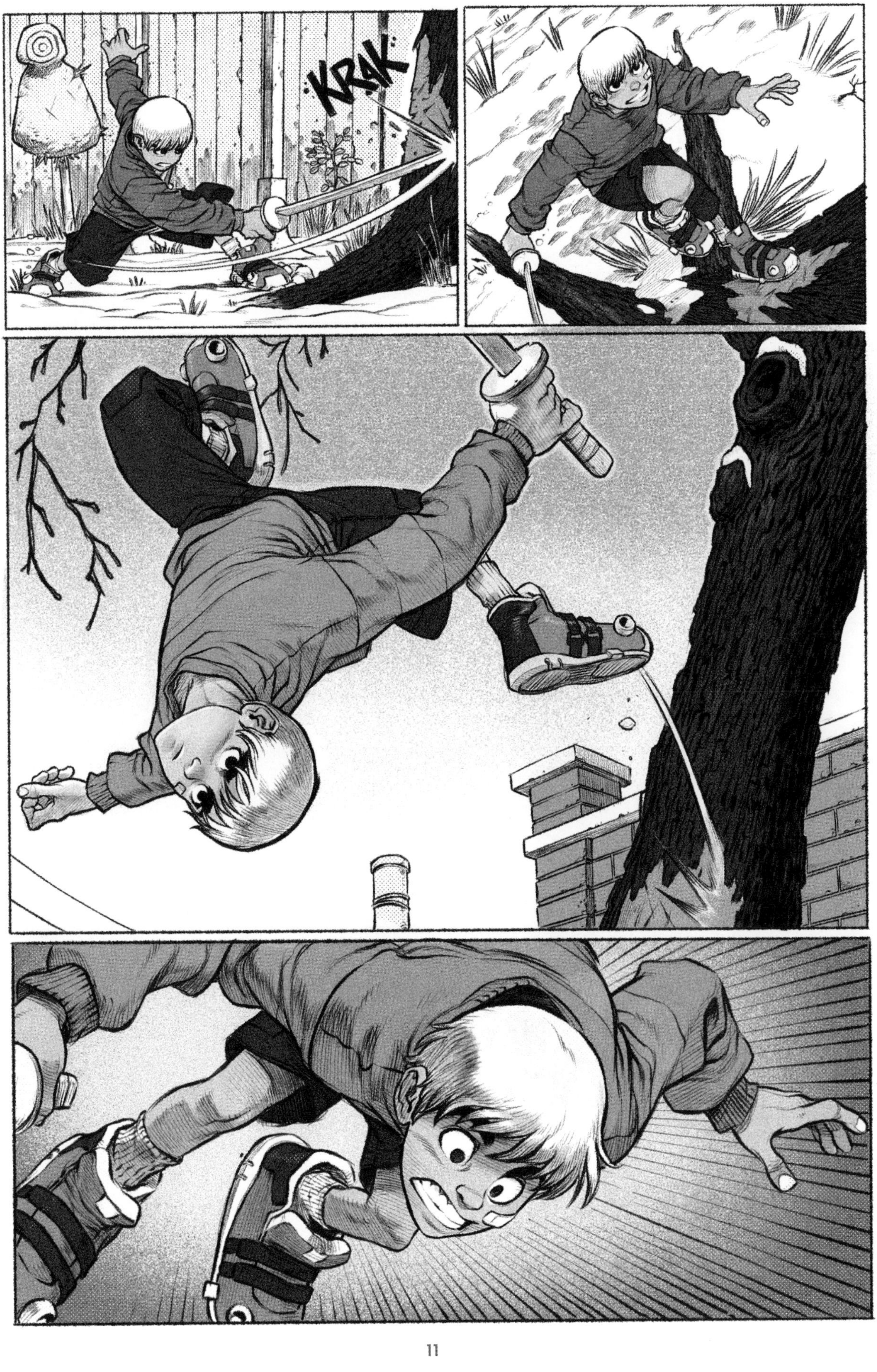
KRAK

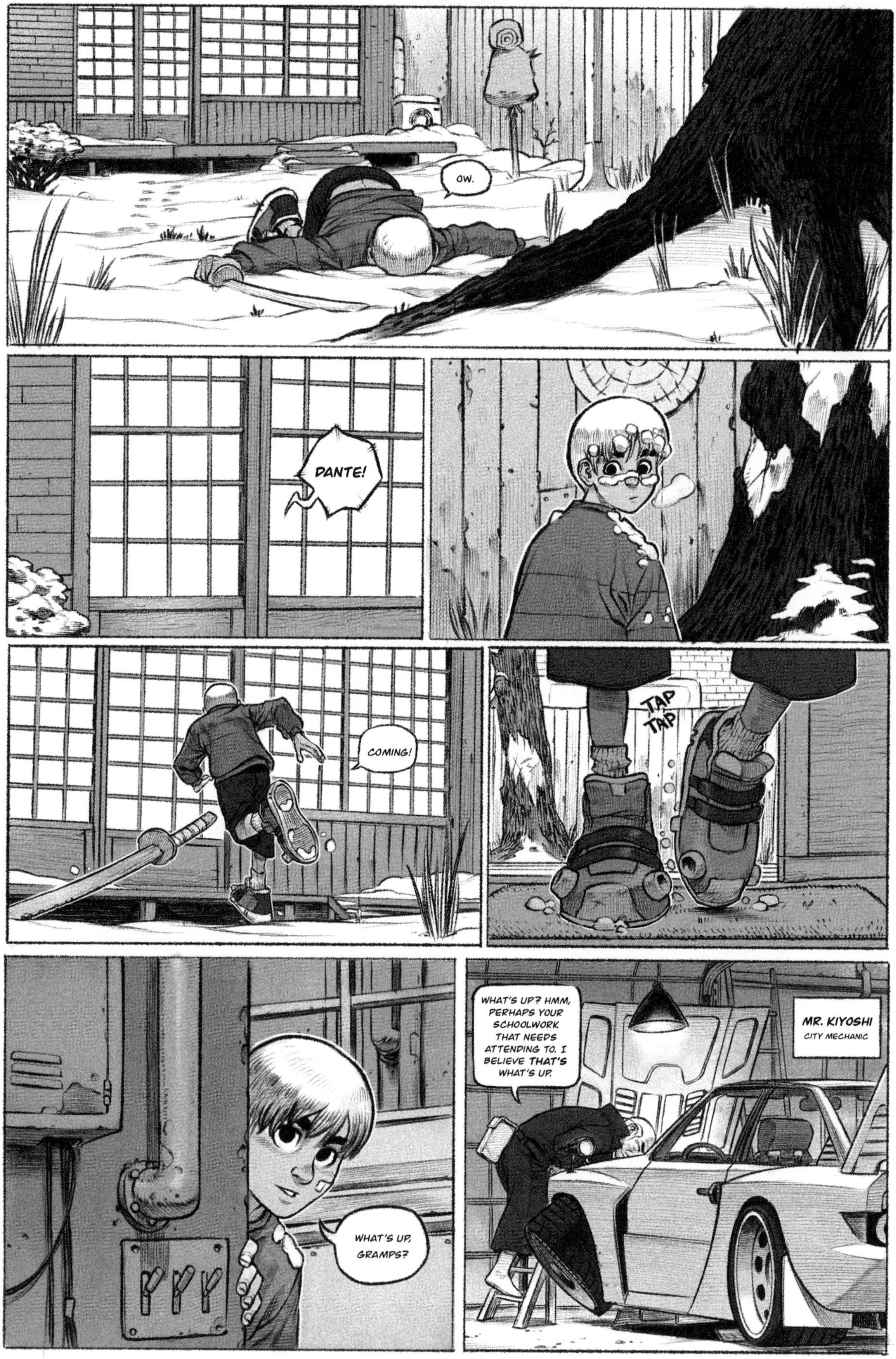
OW.
DANTE!
COMING!
TAP
TAP
WHAT'S UP, GRAMPS?
MR. KIYOSHI
CITY MECHANIC
WHAT'S UP? HMM, PERHAPS YOUR SCHOOLWORK THAT NEEDS ATTENDING TO. I BELIEVE THAT'S WHAT'S UP.

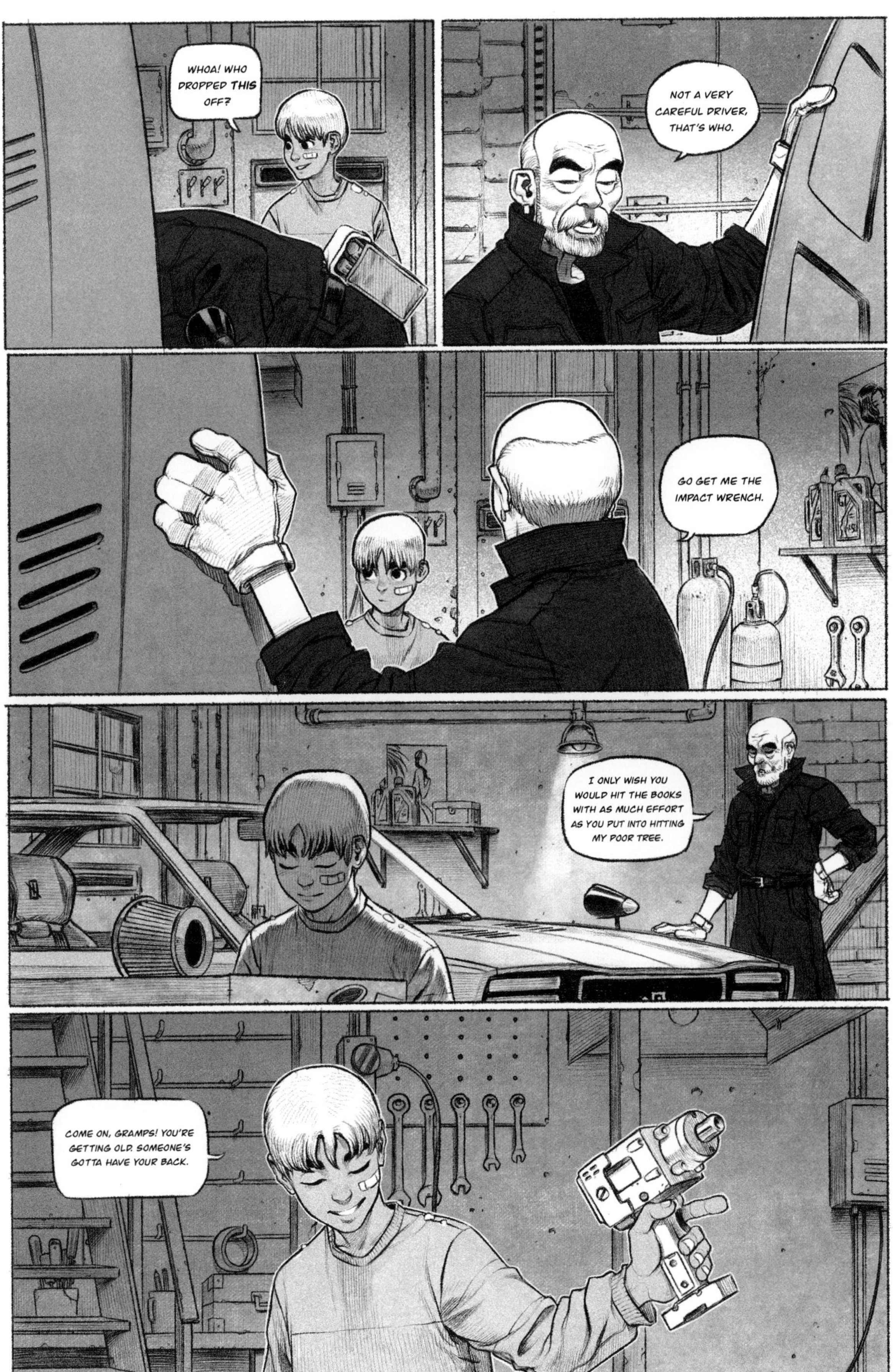
WHOA! WHO DROPPED THIS OFF?
NOT A VERY CAREFUL DRIVER, THAT'S WHO.
GO GET ME THE IMPACT WRENCH.
I ONLY WISH YOU WOULD HIT THE BOOKS WITH AS MUCH EFFORT AS YOU PUT INTO HITTING MY POOR TREE.
COME ON, GRAMPS! YOU'RE GETTING OLD. SOMEONE'S GOTTA HAVE YOUR BACK.

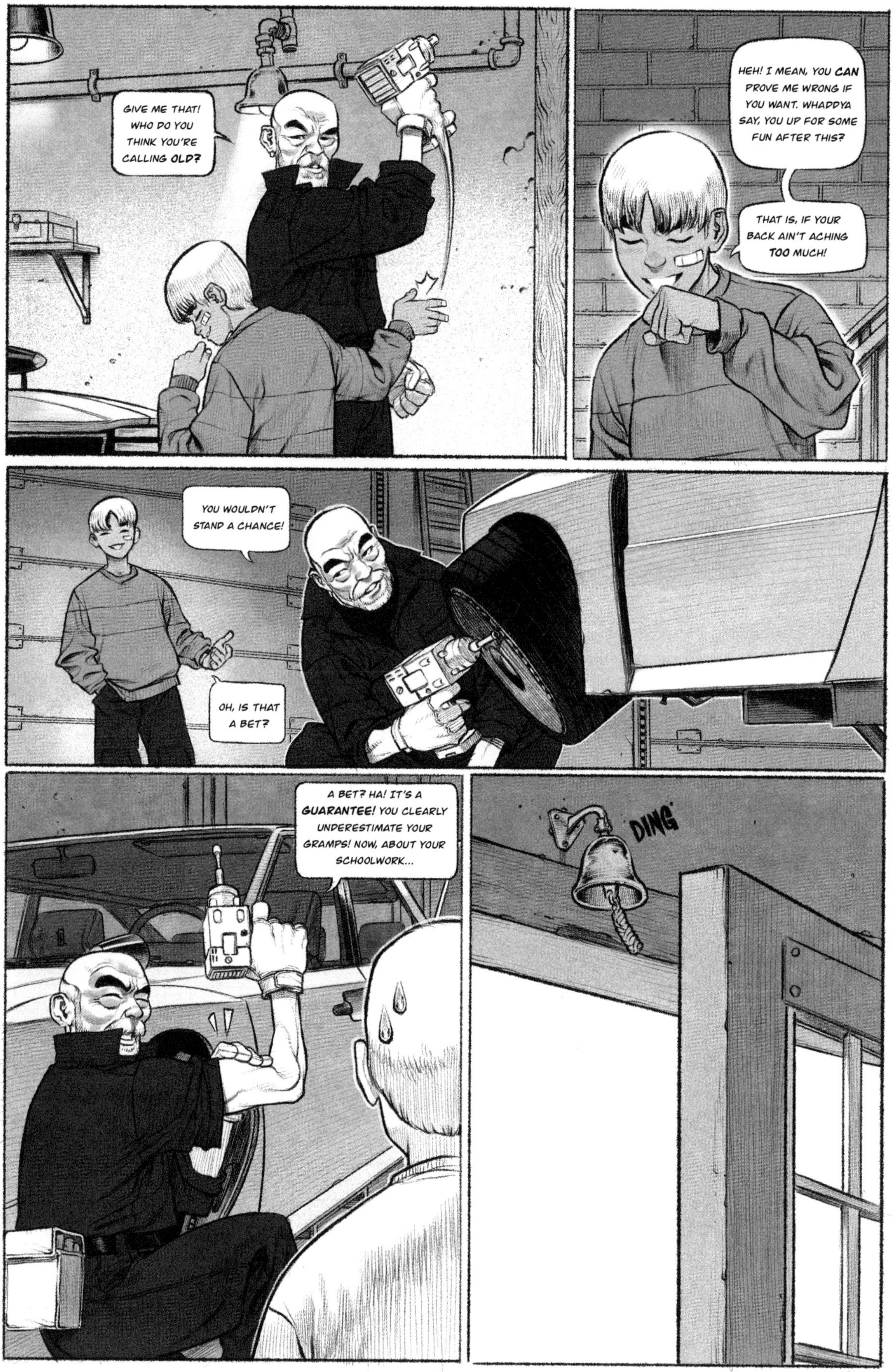
GIVE ME THAT! WHO DO YOU THINK YOU'RE CALLING **OLD?**
HEH! I MEAN, YOU **CAN** PROVE ME WRONG IF YOU WANT. WHADDYA SAY, YOU UP FOR SOME FUN AFTER THIS?
THAT IS, IF YOUR BACK AIN'T ACHING **TOO** MUCH!
YOU WOULDN'T STAND A CHANCE!
OH, IS THAT A BET?
A BET? HA! IT'S A **GUARANTEE!** YOU CLEARLY UNDERESTIMATE YOUR GRAMPS! NOW, ABOUT YOUR SCHOOLWORK...
DING

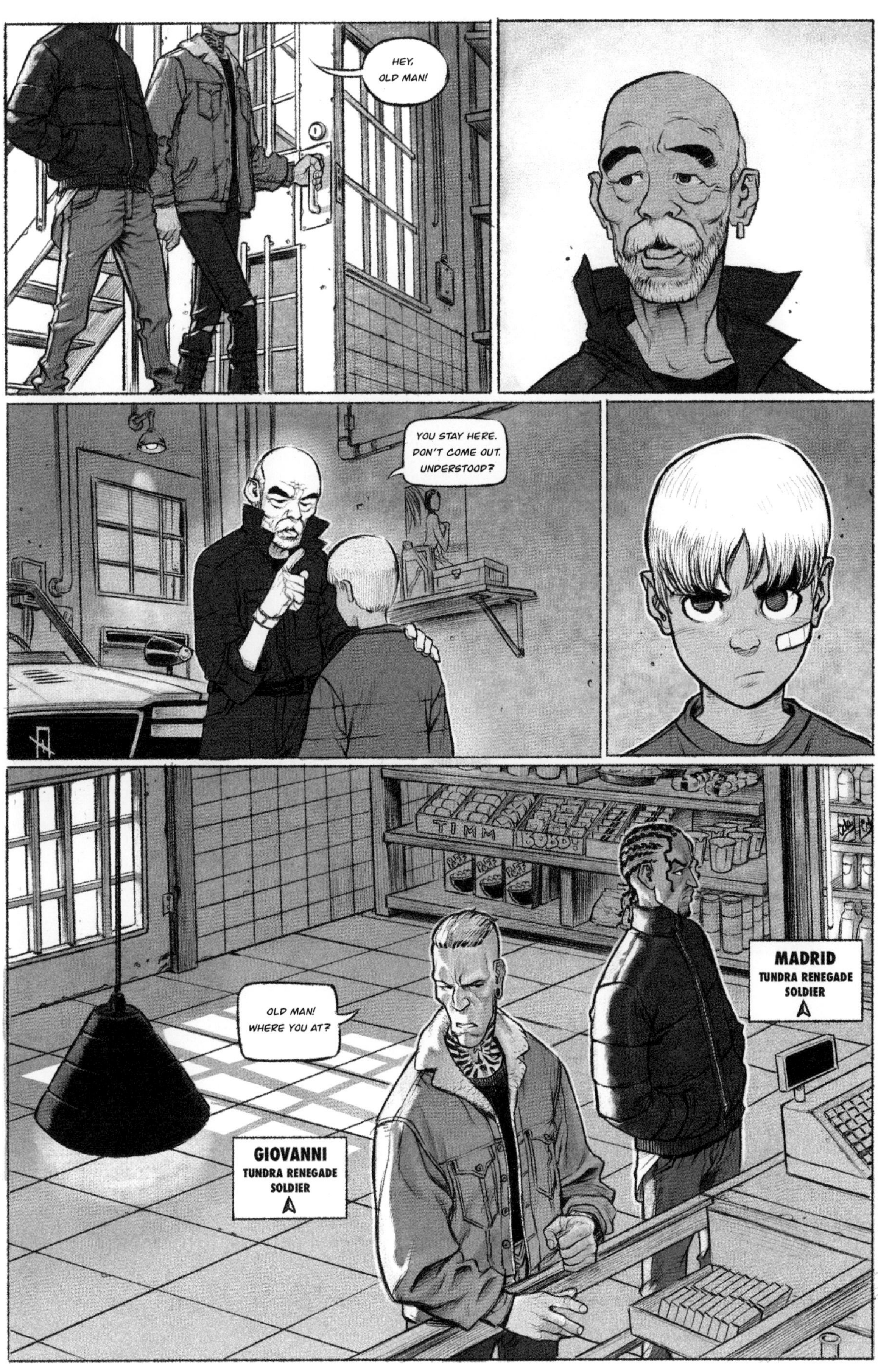
HEY, OLD MAN!
YOU STAY HERE. DON'T COME OUT. UNDERSTOOD?
TIMM
OLD MAN! WHERE YOU AT?
MADRID
TUNDRA RENEGADE SOLDIER
GIOVANNI
TUNDRA RENEGADE SOLDIER

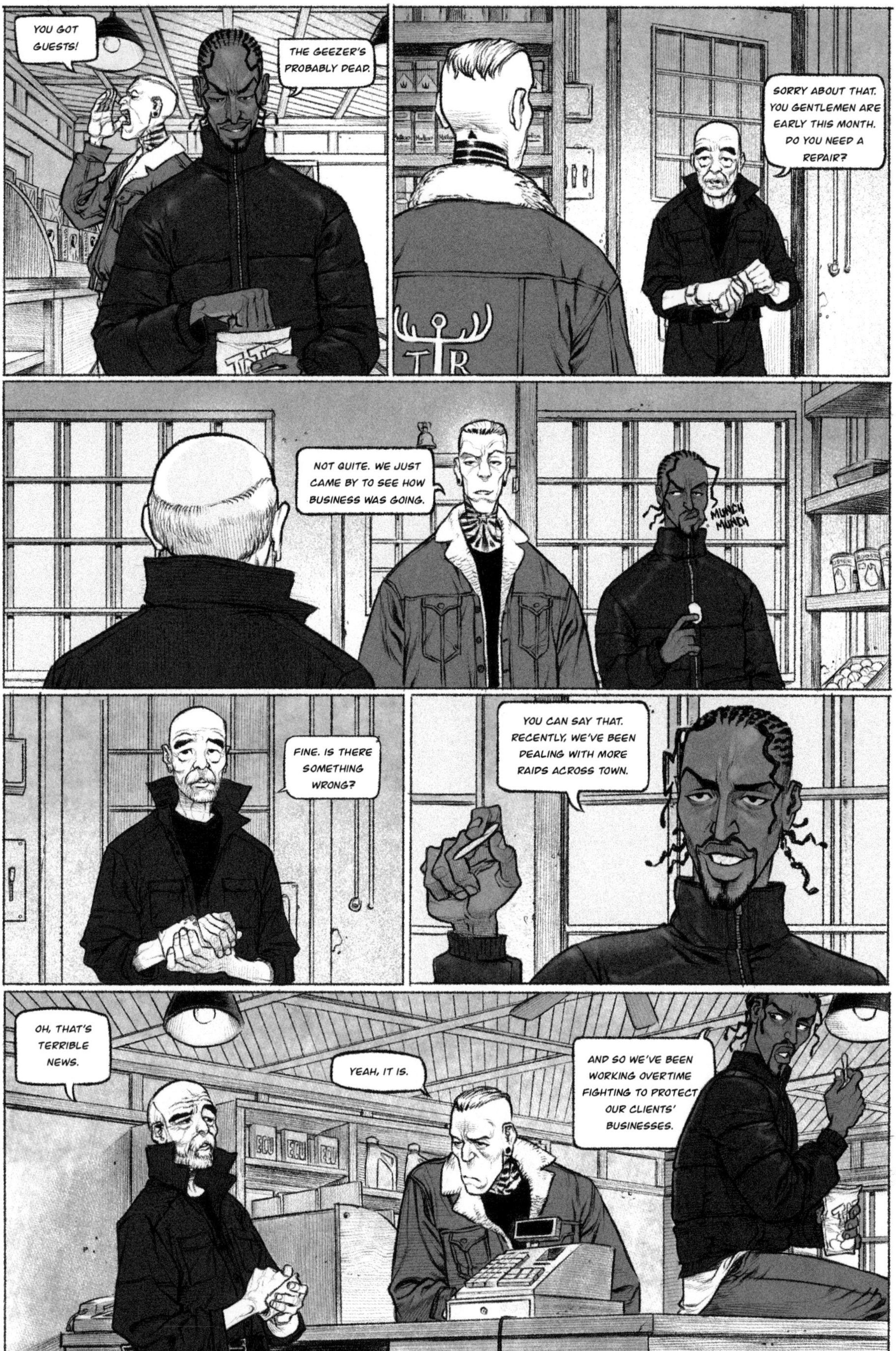
YOU GOT GUESTS!
THE GEEZER'S PROBABLY DEAD.
SORRY ABOUT THAT. YOU GENTLEMEN ARE EARLY THIS MONTH. DO YOU NEED A REPAIR?
NOT QUITE. WE JUST CAME BY TO SEE HOW BUSINESS WAS GOING.
MUNCH MUNCH
FINE. IS THERE SOMETHING WRONG?
YOU CAN SAY THAT. RECENTLY, WE'VE BEEN DEALING WITH MORE RAIDS ACROSS TOWN.
OH, THAT'S TERRIBLE NEWS.
YEAH, IT IS.
AND SO WE'VE BEEN WORKING OVERTIME FIGHTING TO PROTECT OUR CLIENTS' BUSINESSES.

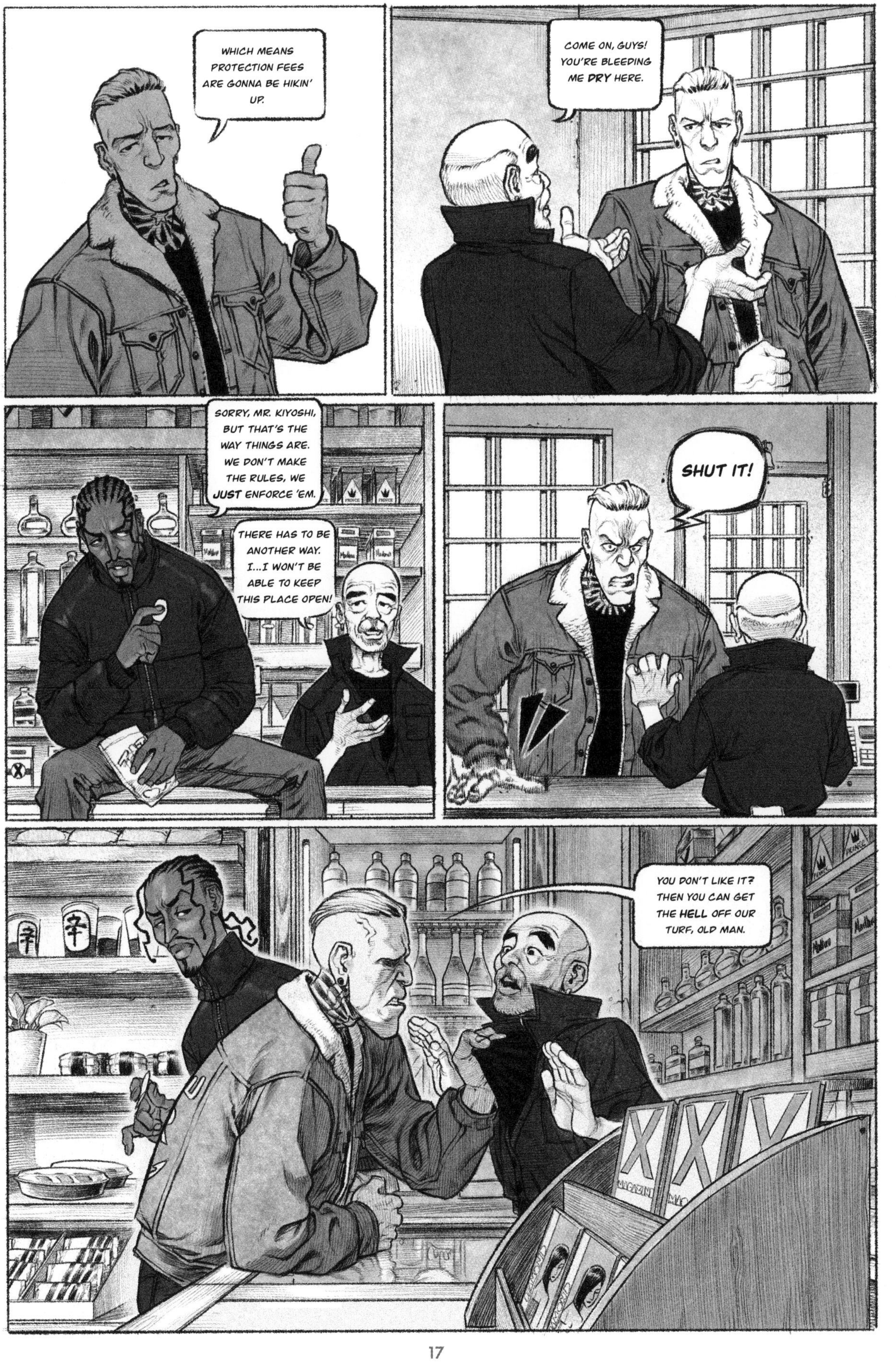
WHICH MEANS PROTECTION FEES ARE GONNA BE HIKIN' UP.
COME ON, GUYS! YOU'RE BLEEDING ME DRY HERE.
SORRY, MR. KIYOSHI, BUT THAT'S THE WAY THINGS ARE. WE DON'T MAKE THE RULES, WE JUST ENFORCE 'EM.
THERE HAS TO BE ANOTHER WAY. I...I WON'T BE ABLE TO KEEP THIS PLACE OPEN!
SHUT IT!
YOU DON'T LIKE IT? THEN YOU CAN GET THE HELL OFF OUR TURF, OLD MAN.

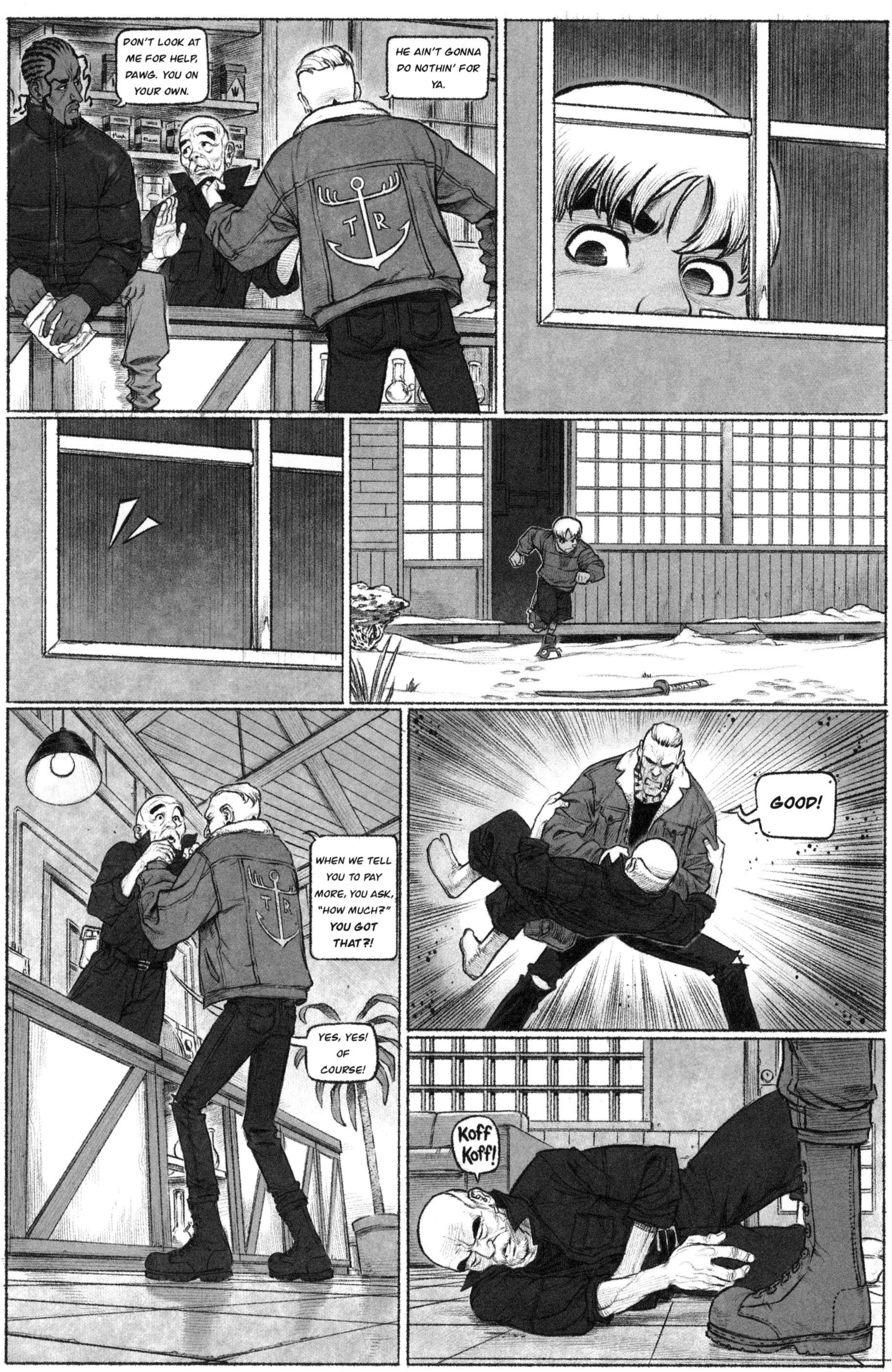
DON'T LOOK AT ME FOR HELP, DAWG. YOU ON YOUR OWN.
HE AIN'T GONNA DO NOTHIN' FOR YA.
WHEN WE TELL YOU TO PAY MORE, YOU ASK, "HOW MUCH?" YOU GOT THAT?!
YES, YES! OF COURSE!
GOOD!
KOFF KOFF!

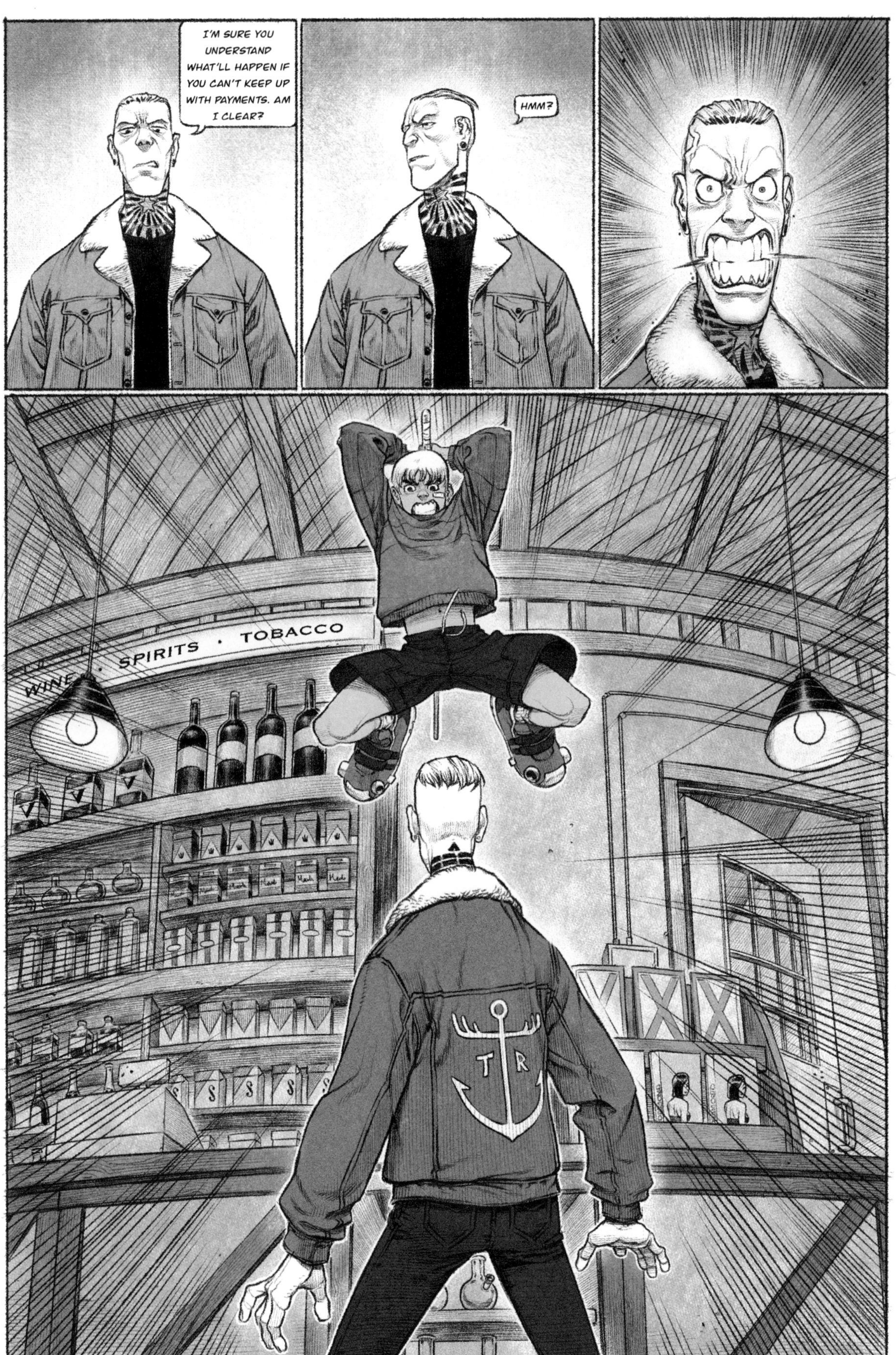
I'M SURE YOU UNDERSTAND WHAT'LL HAPPEN IF YOU CAN'T KEEP UP WITH PAYMENTS. AM I CLEAR?
HMM?
WINE · SPIRITS · TOBACCO
T R

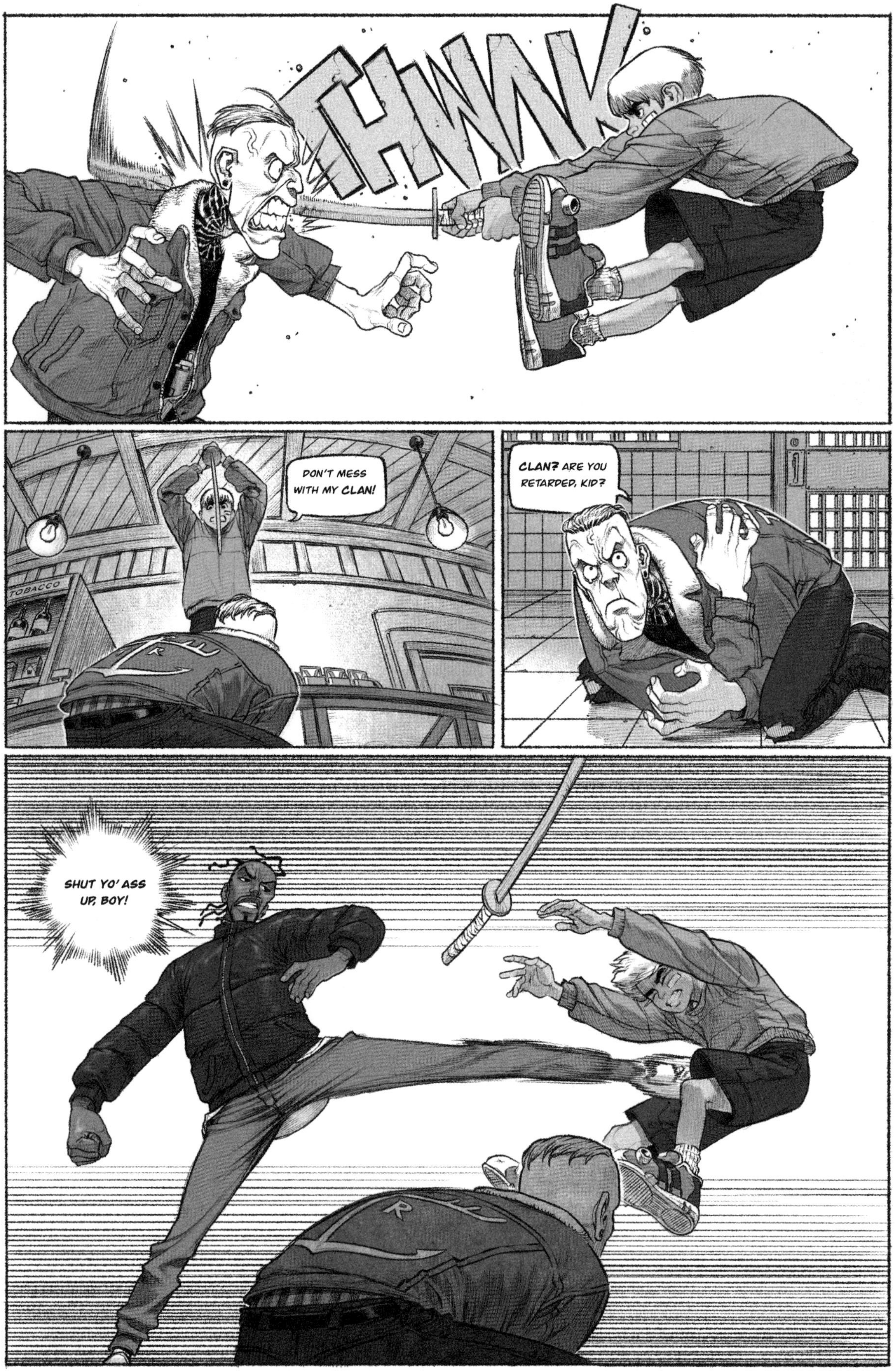
THWAK
DON'T MESS WITH MY CLAN!
CLAN? ARE YOU RETARDED, KID?
SHUT YO' ASS UP, BOY!

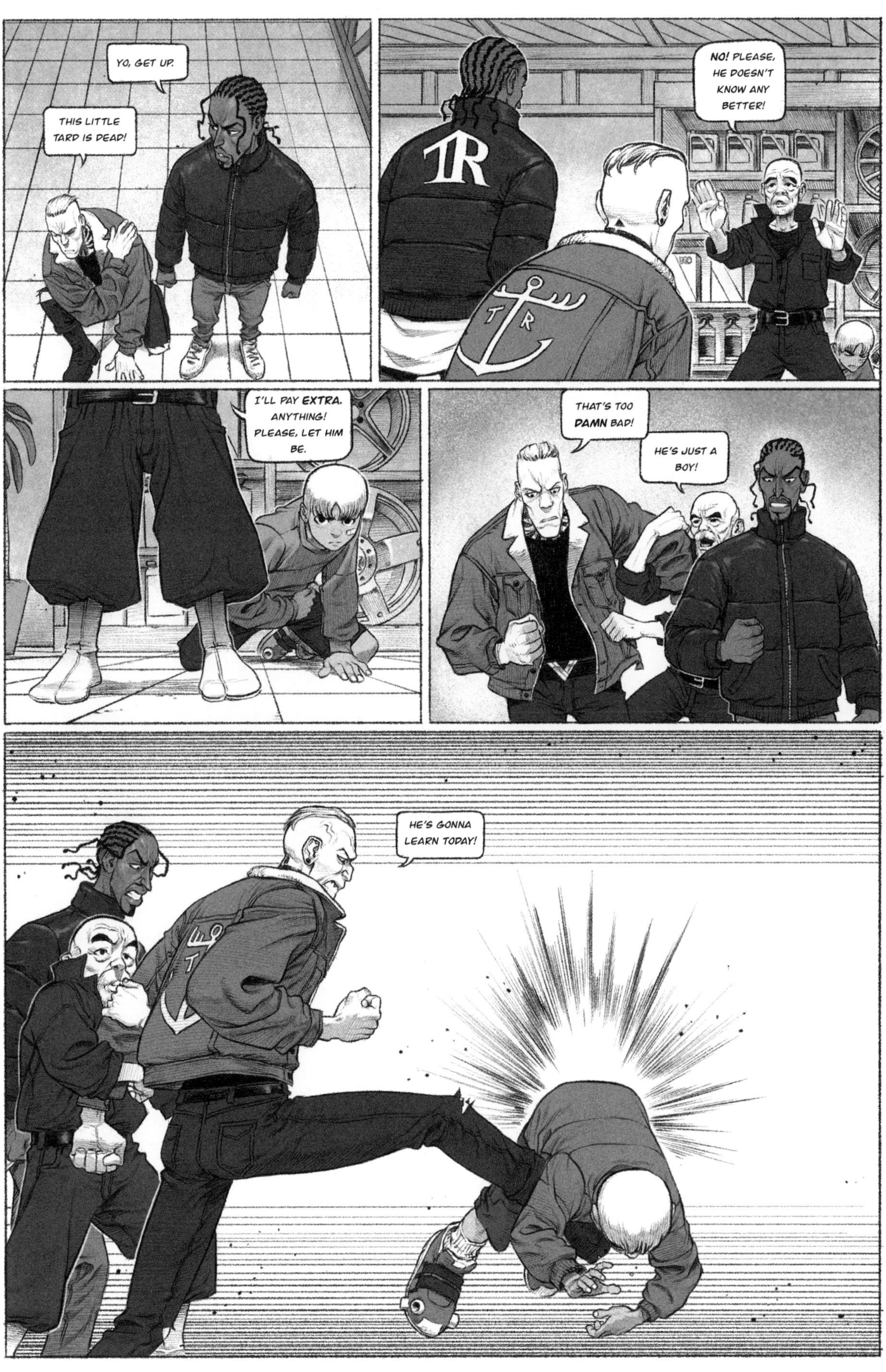
YO, GET UP.
THIS LITTLE TARD IS DEAD!
NO! PLEASE, HE DOESN'T KNOW ANY BETTER!
I'LL PAY EXTRA. ANYTHING! PLEASE, LET HIM BE.
THAT'S TOO DAMN BAD!
HE'S JUST A BOY!
HE'S GONNA LEARN TODAY!

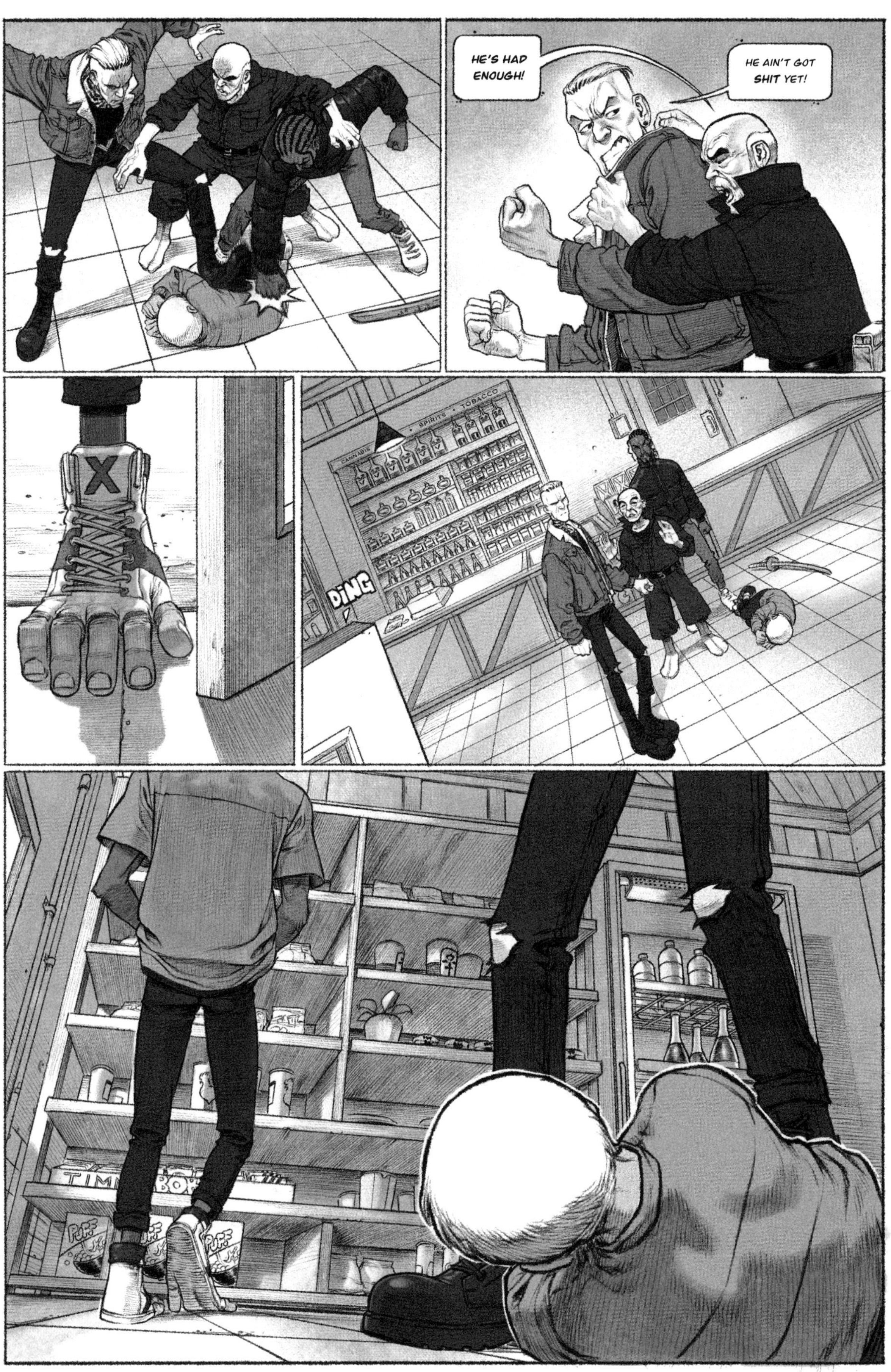
HE'S HAD ENOUGH!
HE AIN'T GOT **SHIT** YET!
CANNABIS • SPIRITS • TOBACCO
DING

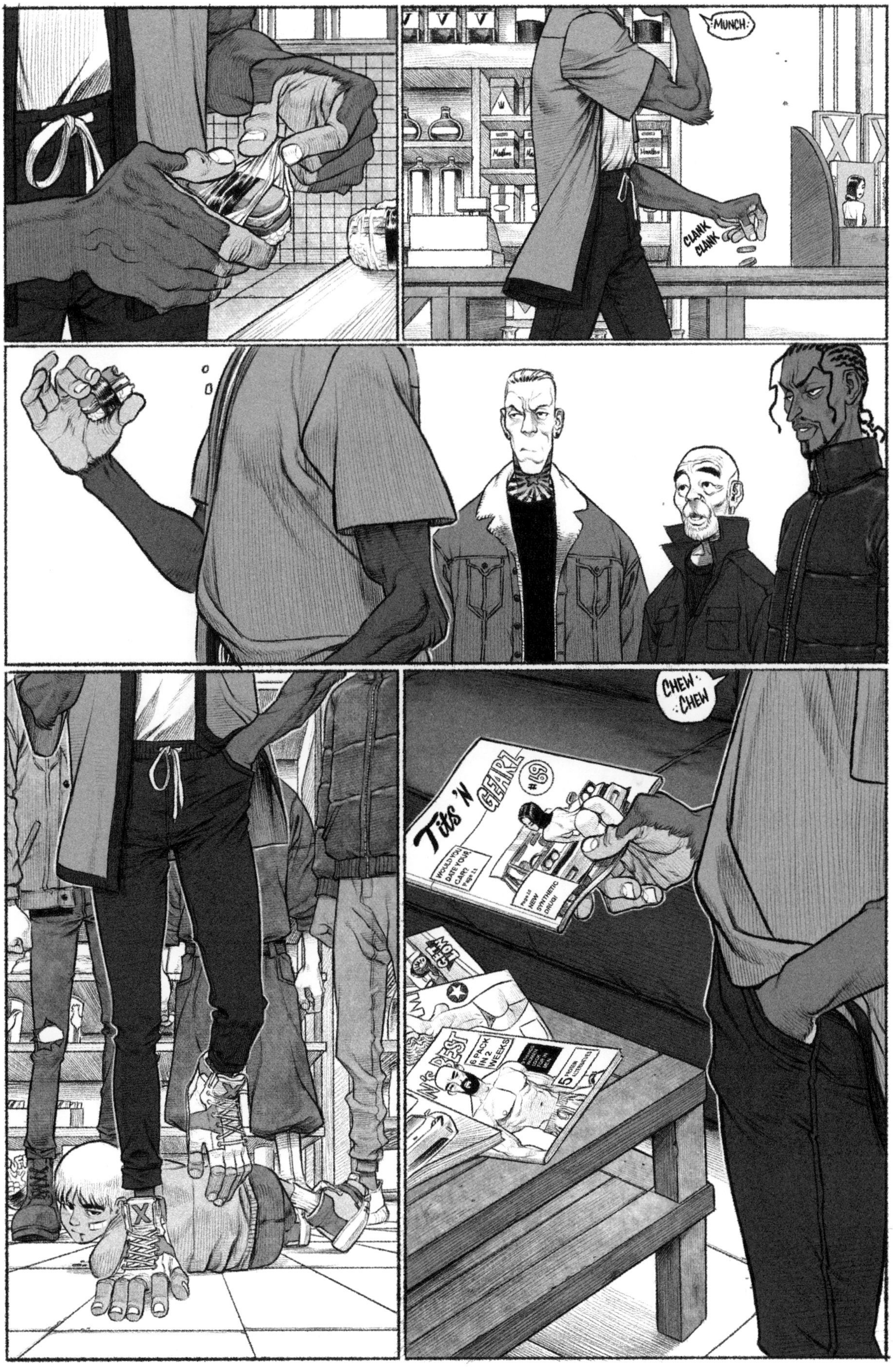
MUNCH
CLANK CLANK
CHEW CHEW
Tits 'N GEARZ
#69
WOULD YOU DATE YOUR CAR? Page 11
Page 15 NEW SYNTHETIC DRUG!
6 PACK IN 2 WEEKS
5 PROTEIN ALTERNATIVES

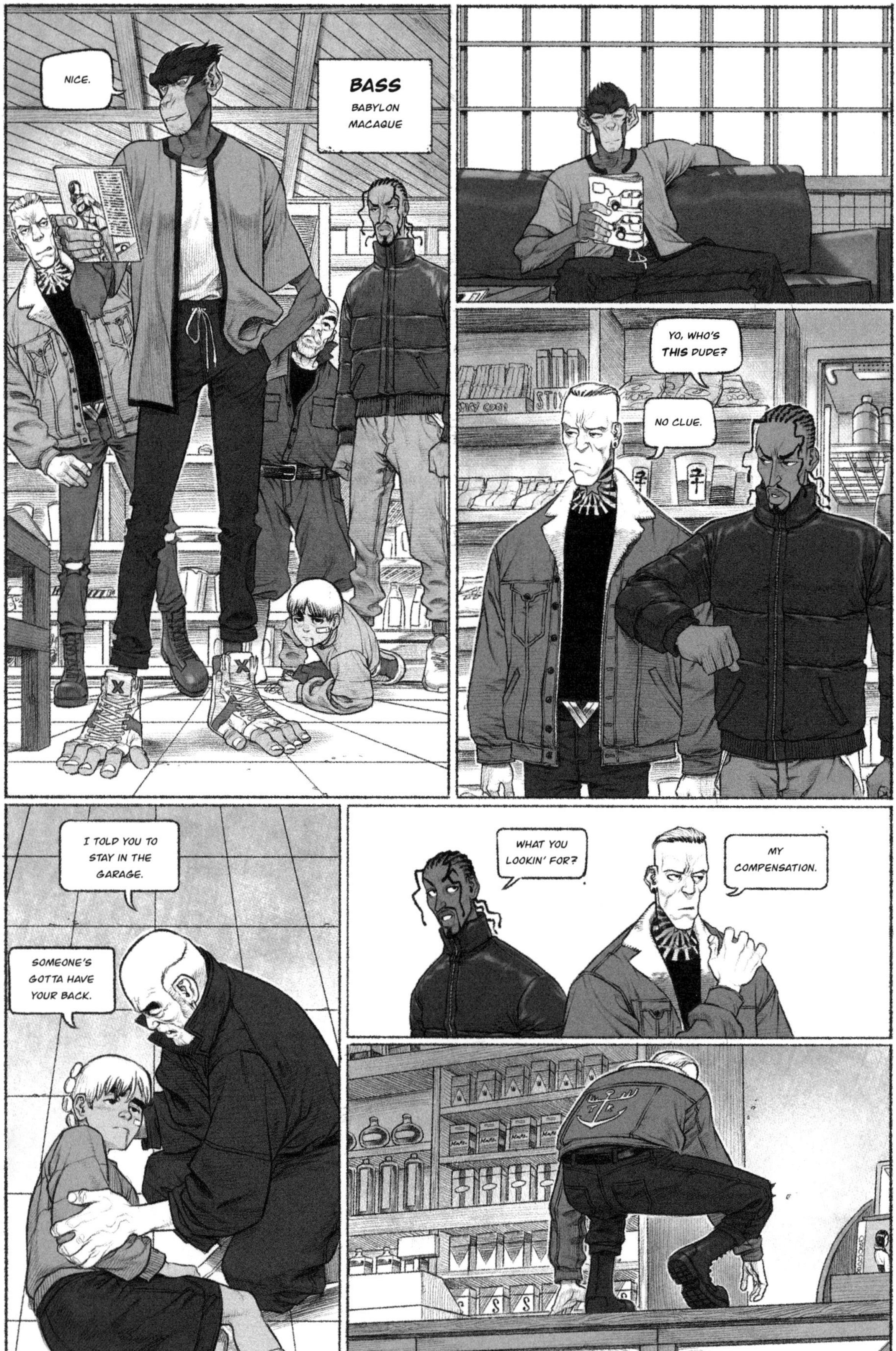
NICE.
BASS
BABYLON
MACAQUE
YO, WHO'S THIS DUDE?
NO CLUE.
I TOLD YOU TO STAY IN THE GARAGE.
SOMEONE'S GOTTA HAVE YOUR BACK.
WHAT YOU LOOKIN' FOR?
MY COMPENSATION.

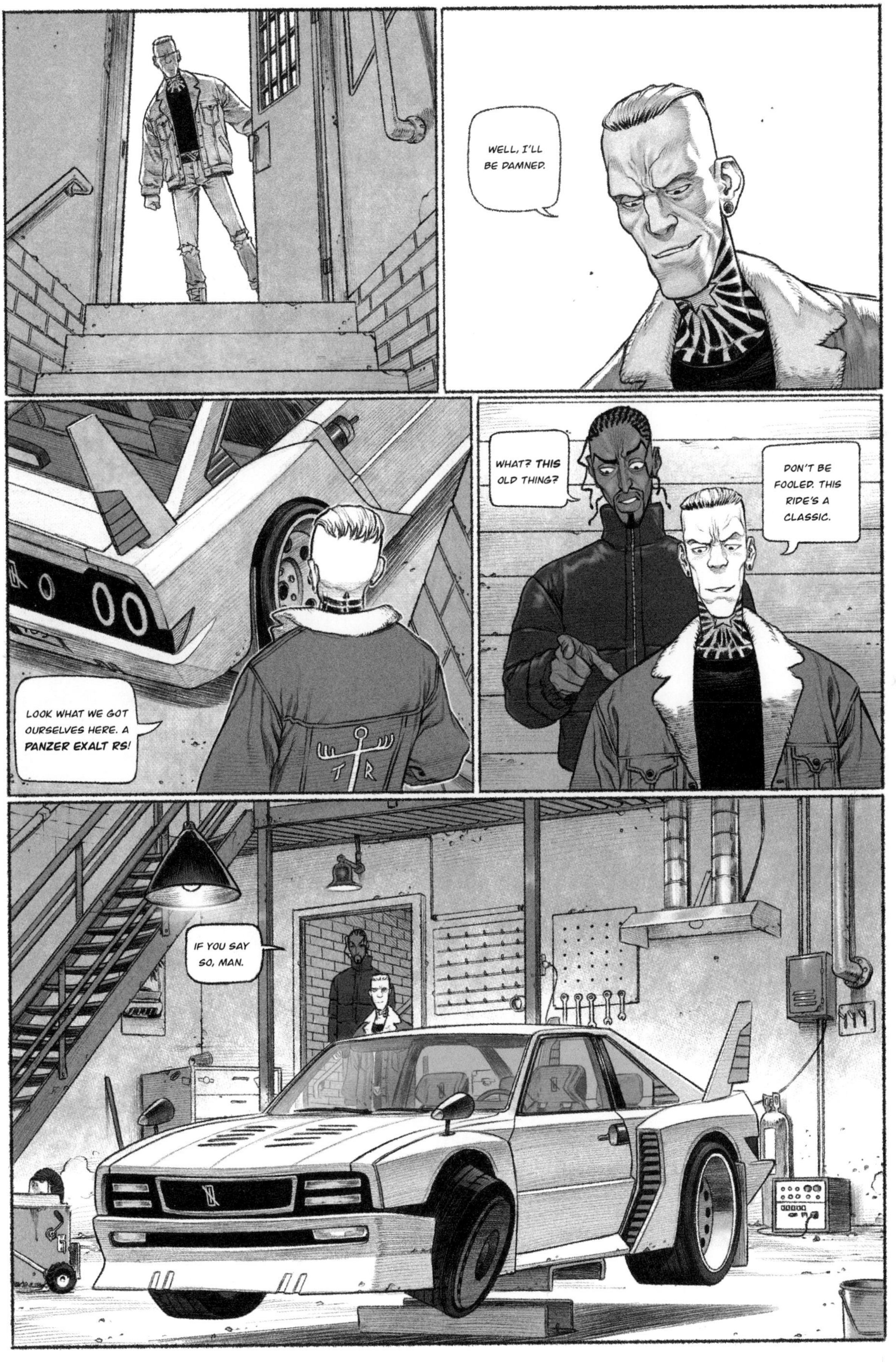
WELL, I'LL BE DAMNED.
LOOK WHAT WE GOT OURSELVES HERE. A **PANZER EXALT RS!**
WHAT? **THIS** OLD THING?
DON'T BE FOOLED. THIS RIDE'S A CLASSIC.
IF YOU SAY SO, MAN.

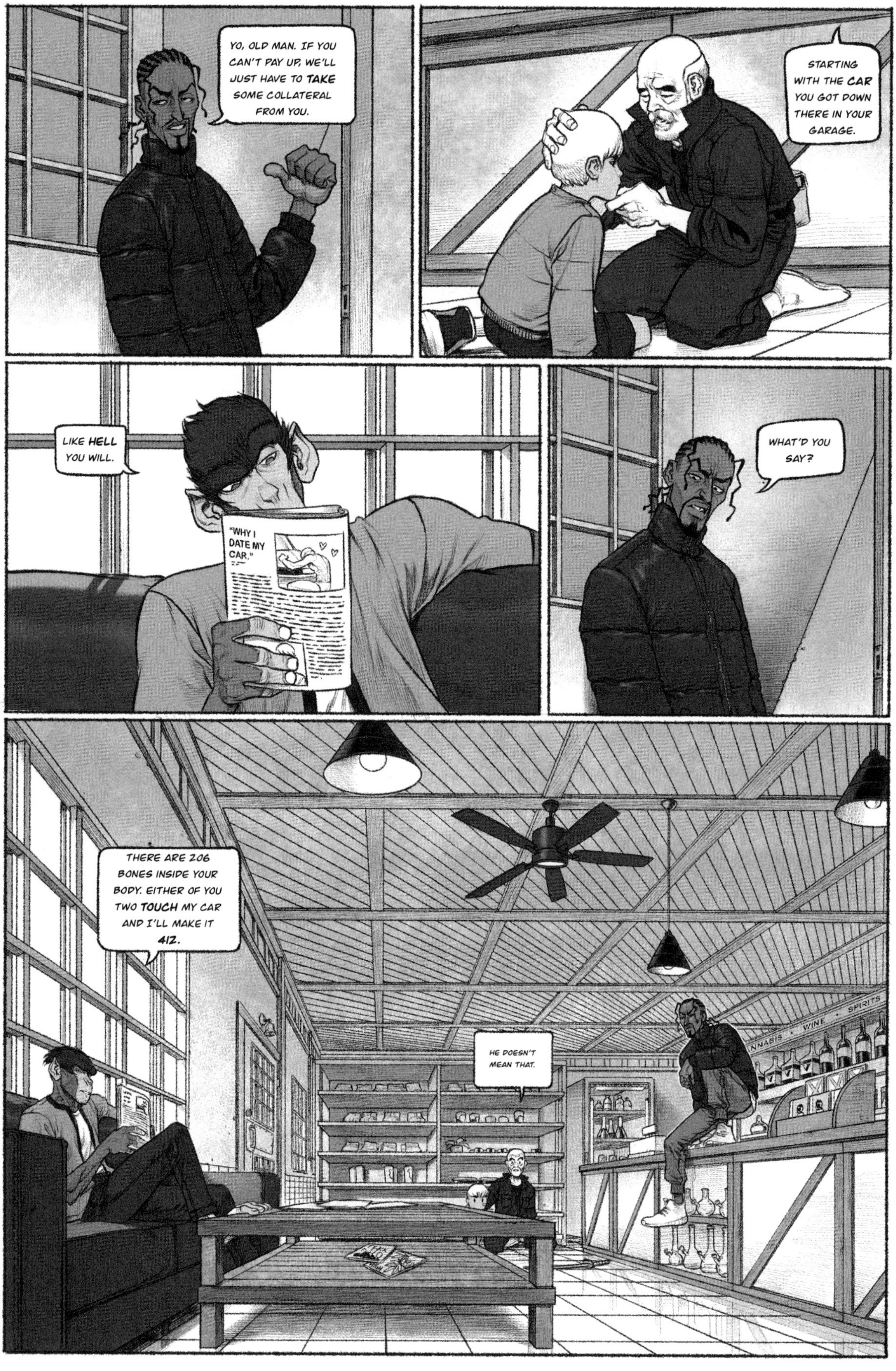
YO, OLD MAN. IF YOU CAN'T PAY UP, WE'LL JUST HAVE TO **TAKE** SOME COLLATERAL FROM YOU.
STARTING WITH THE **CAR** YOU GOT DOWN THERE IN YOUR GARAGE.
LIKE **HELL** YOU WILL.
"WHY I DATE MY CAR."
WHAT'D YOU SAY?
THERE ARE 206 BONES INSIDE YOUR BODY. EITHER OF YOU TWO **TOUCH** MY CAR AND I'LL MAKE IT **412**.
WINE · SPIRITS
HE DOESN'T MEAN THAT.

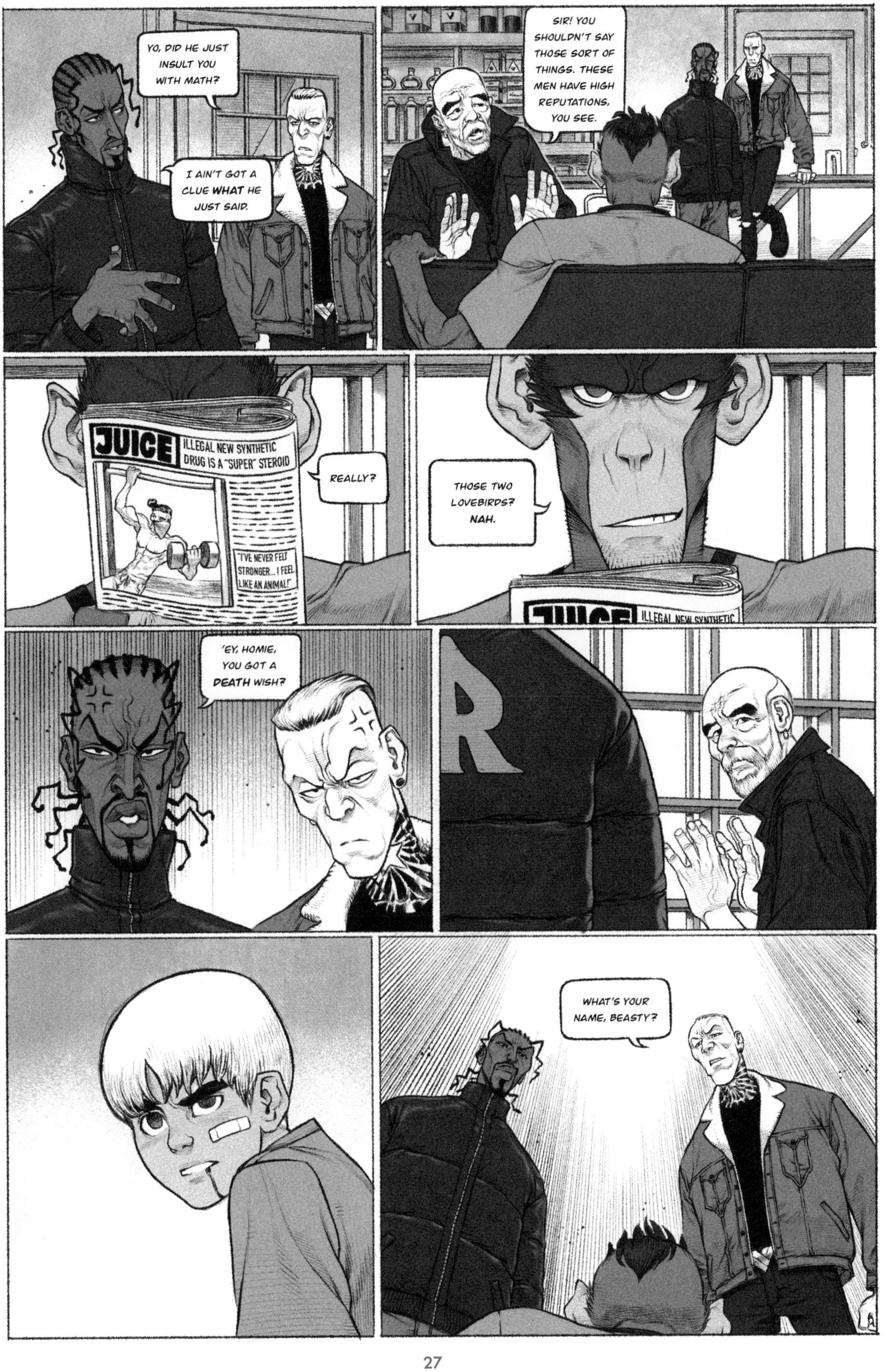
YO, DID HE JUST INSULT YOU WITH MATH?
I AIN'T GOT A CLUE WHAT HE JUST SAID.
SIR! YOU SHOULDN'T SAY THOSE SORT OF THINGS. THESE MEN HAVE HIGH REPUTATIONS, YOU SEE.
JUICE
ILLEGAL NEW SYNTHETIC DRUG IS A "SUPER" STEROID
"I'VE NEVER FELT STRONGER... I FEEL LIKE AN ANIMAL!"
REALLY?
THOSE TWO LOVEBIRDS? NAH.
JUICE ILLEGAL NEW SYNTHETIC
'EY, HOMIE, YOU GOT A DEATH WISH?
WHAT'S YOUR NAME, BEASTY?

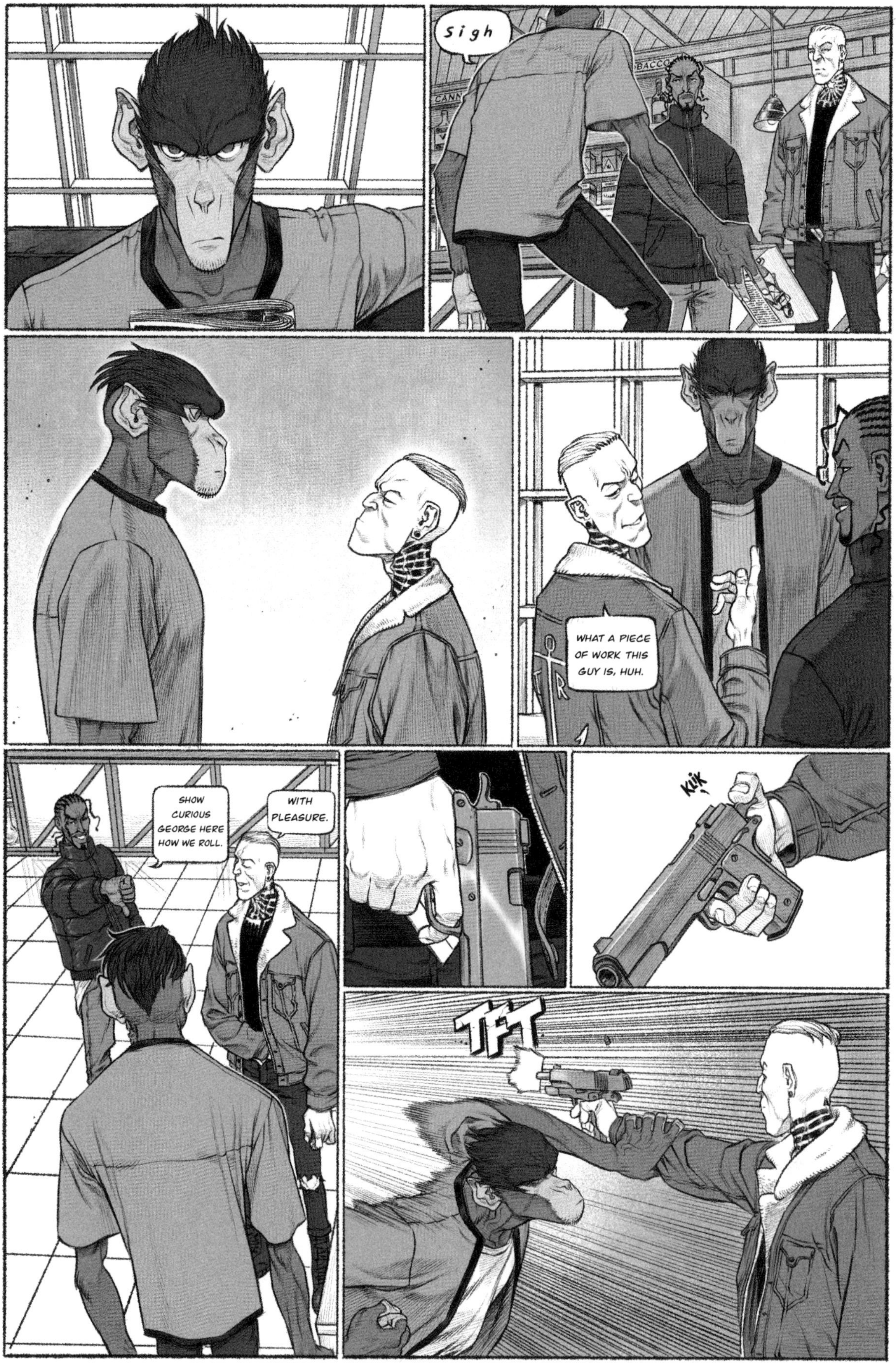
Sigh
WHAT A PIECE OF WORK THIS GUY IS, HUH.
SHOW CURIOUS GEORGE HERE HOW WE ROLL.
WITH PLEASURE.
KLIK
TFT

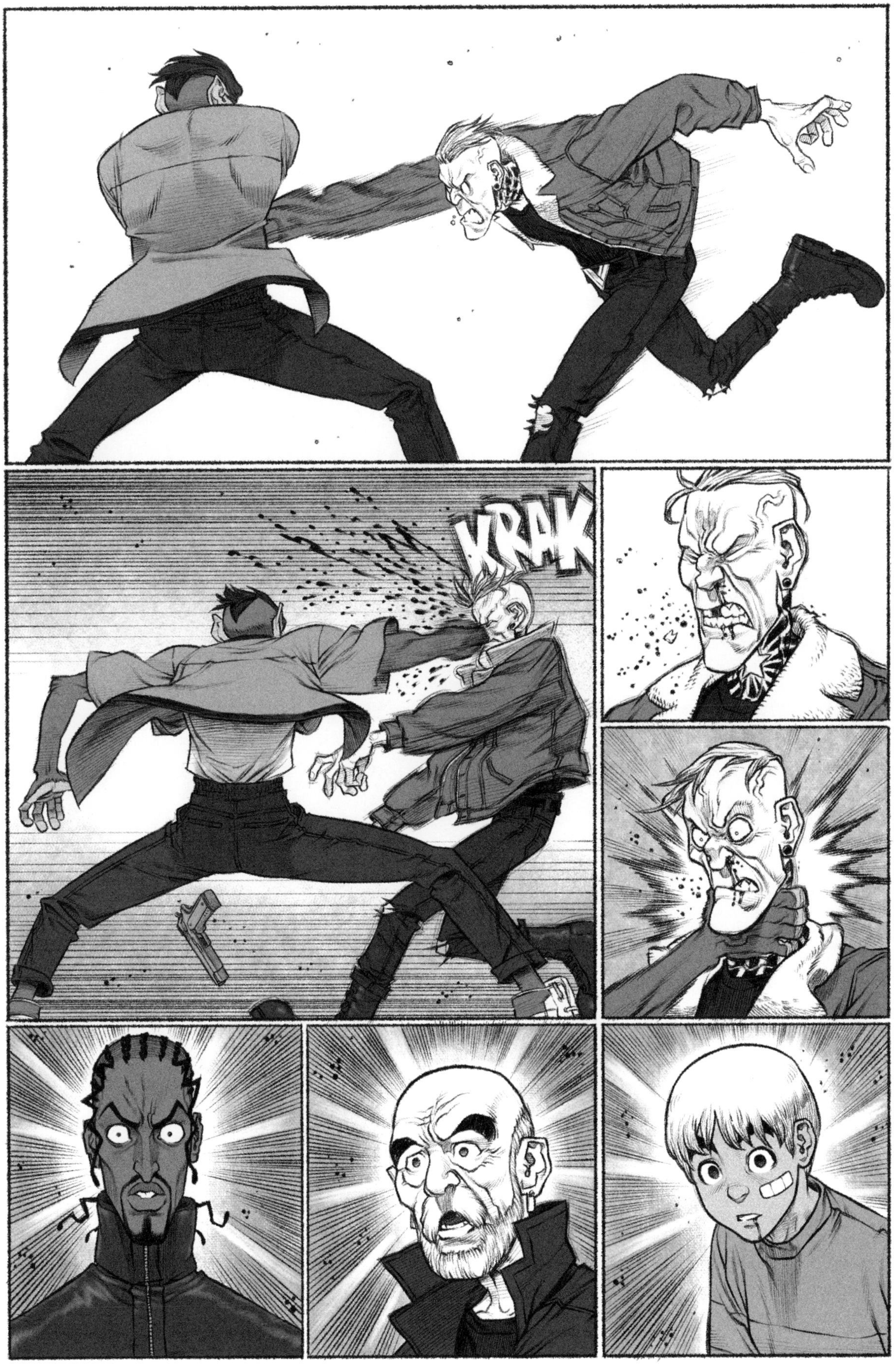
KRAK

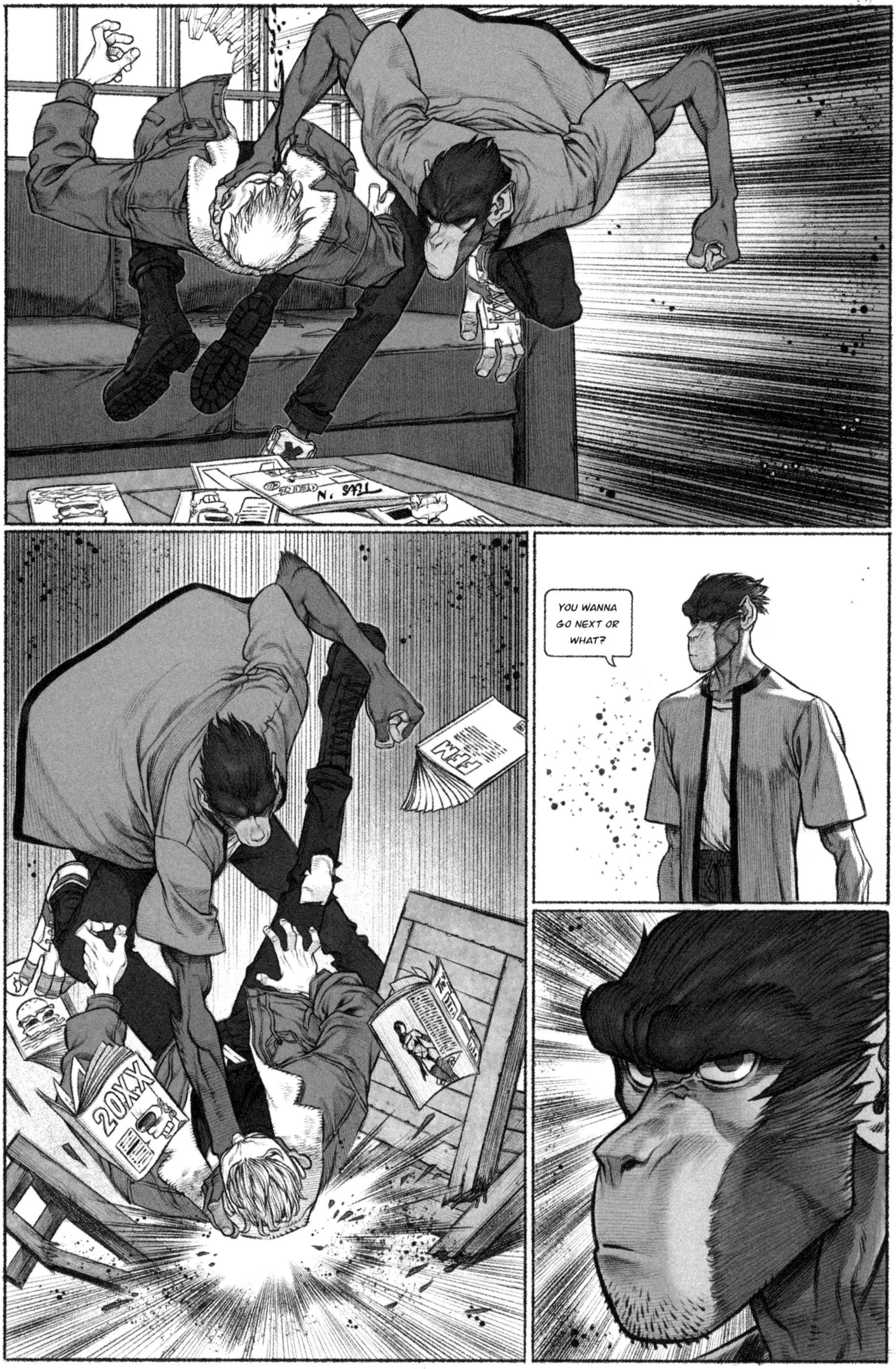
YOU WANNA GO NEXT OR WHAT?
FEM
20XX

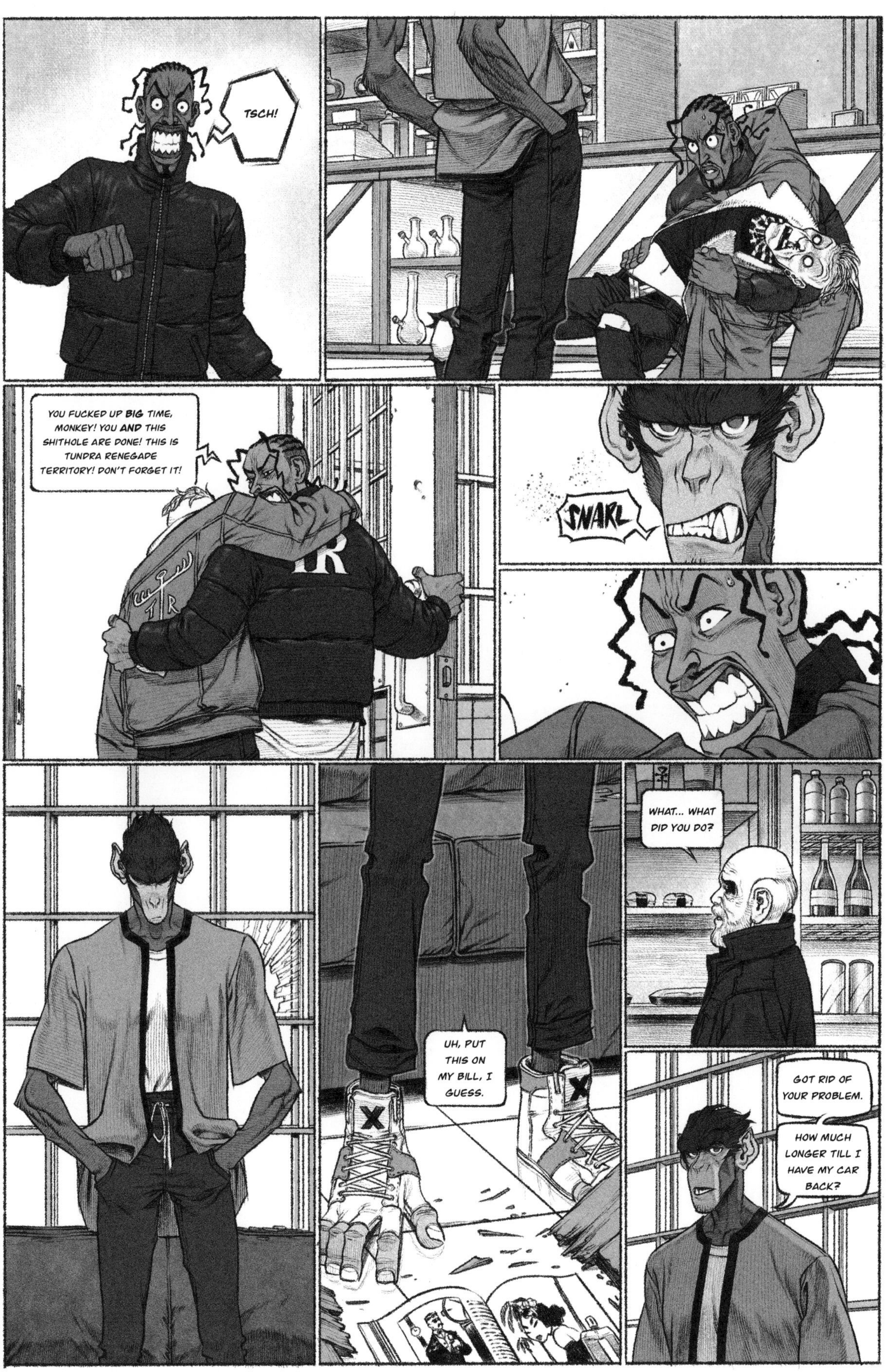
TSCH!
YOU FUCKED UP BIG TIME, MONKEY! YOU AND THIS SHITHOLE ARE DONE! THIS IS TUNDRA RENEGADE TERRITORY! DON'T FORGET IT!
SNARL
UH, PUT THIS ON MY BILL, I GUESS.
WHAT... WHAT DID YOU DO?
GOT RID OF YOUR PROBLEM.
HOW MUCH LONGER TILL I HAVE MY CAR BACK?

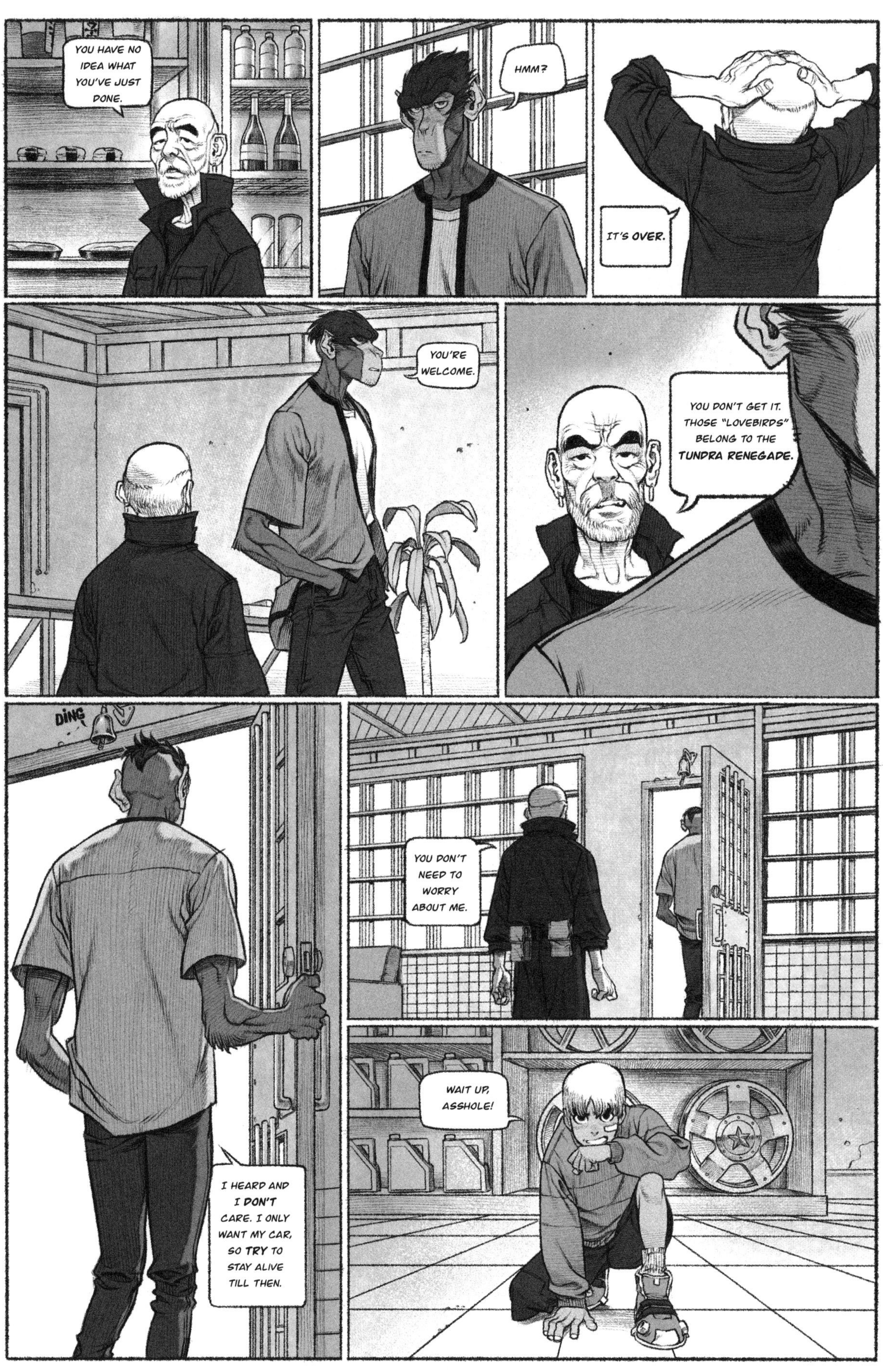
YOU HAVE NO IDEA WHAT YOU'VE JUST DONE.
HMM?
IT'S OVER.
YOU'RE WELCOME.
YOU DON'T GET IT. THOSE "LOVEBIRDS" BELONG TO THE TUNDRA RENEGADE.
DING
I HEARD AND I DON'T CARE. I ONLY WANT MY CAR, SO TRY TO STAY ALIVE TILL THEN.
YOU DON'T NEED TO WORRY ABOUT ME.
WAIT UP, ASSHOLE!

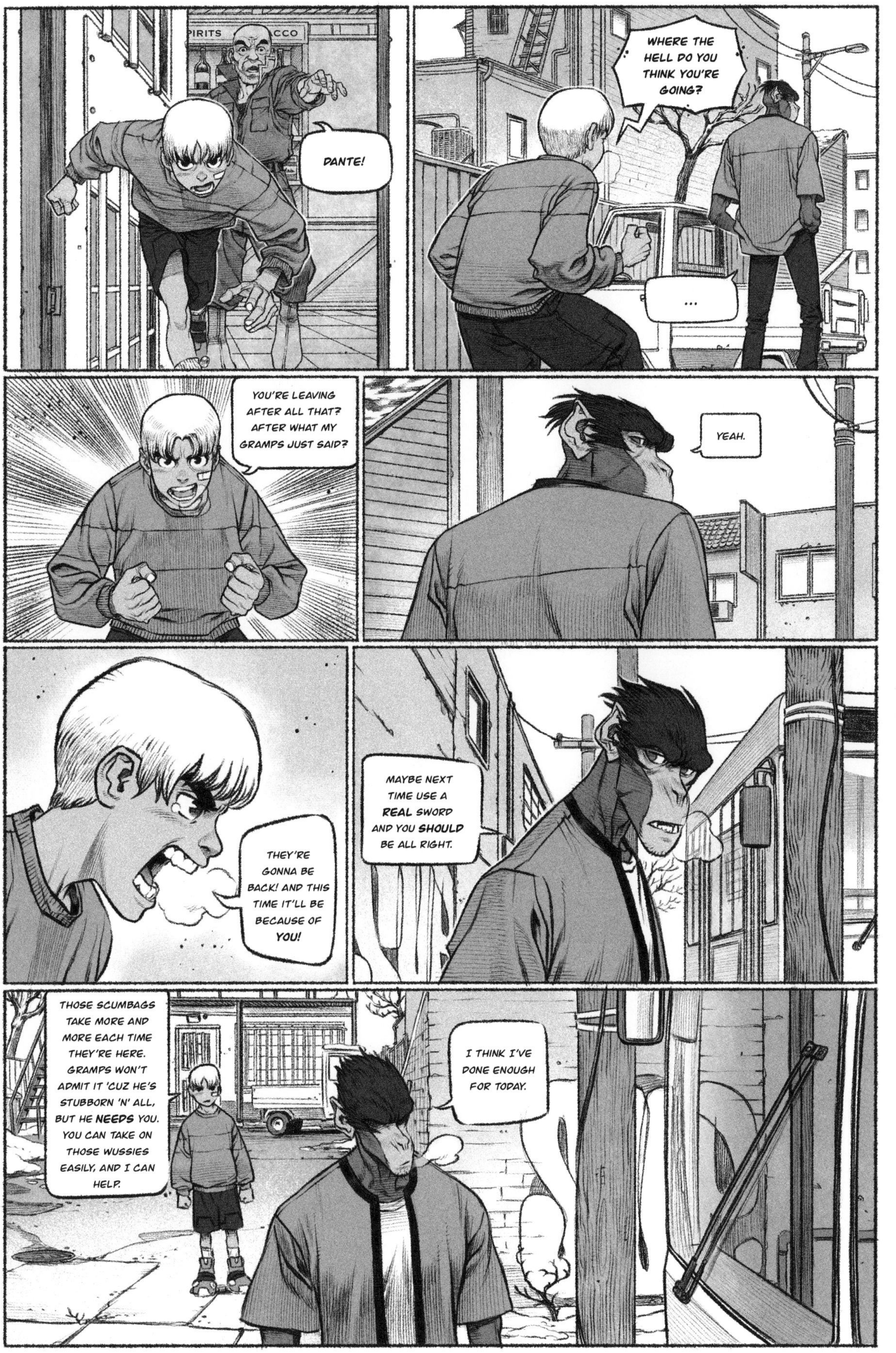
SPIRITS ACCO
DANTE!
WHERE THE HELL DO YOU THINK YOU'RE GOING?
...
YOU'RE LEAVING AFTER ALL THAT? AFTER WHAT MY GRAMPS JUST SAID?
YEAH.
THEY'RE GONNA BE BACK! AND THIS TIME IT'LL BE BECAUSE OF YOU!
MAYBE NEXT TIME USE A REAL SWORD AND YOU SHOULD BE ALL RIGHT.
THOSE SCUMBAGS TAKE MORE AND MORE EACH TIME THEY'RE HERE. GRAMPS WON'T ADMIT IT 'CUZ HE'S STUBBORN 'N' ALL, BUT HE NEEDS YOU. YOU CAN TAKE ON THOSE WUSSIES EASILY, AND I CAN HELP.
I THINK I'VE DONE ENOUGH FOR TODAY.

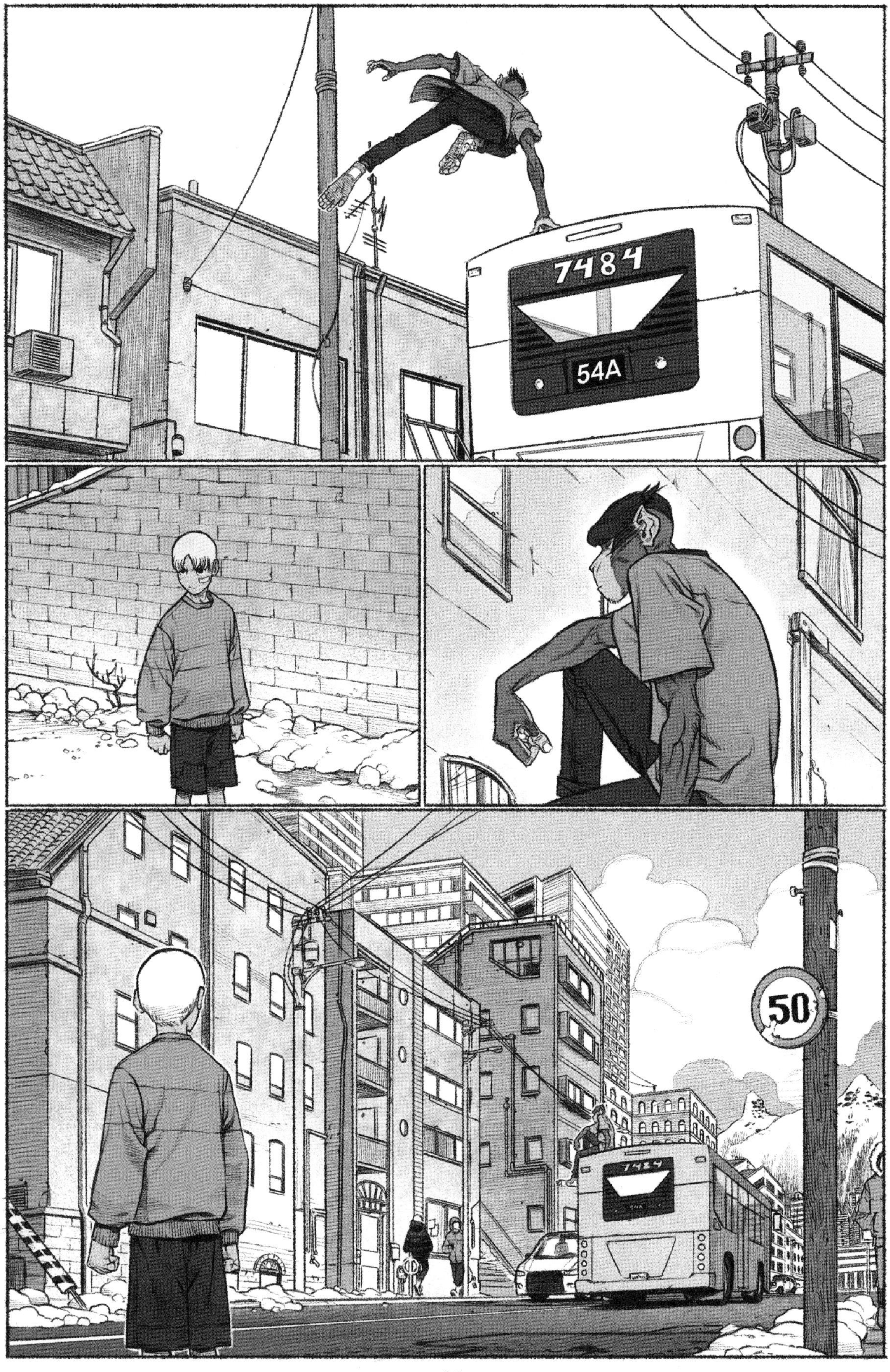
7484
54A
50
7484

KINGS OF NOWHERE

GET OUT

SOROUSH BARAZESH

CHAPTER

NO.4

WRONGFUL RETRIBUTION

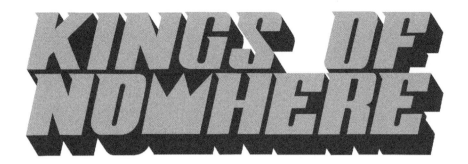

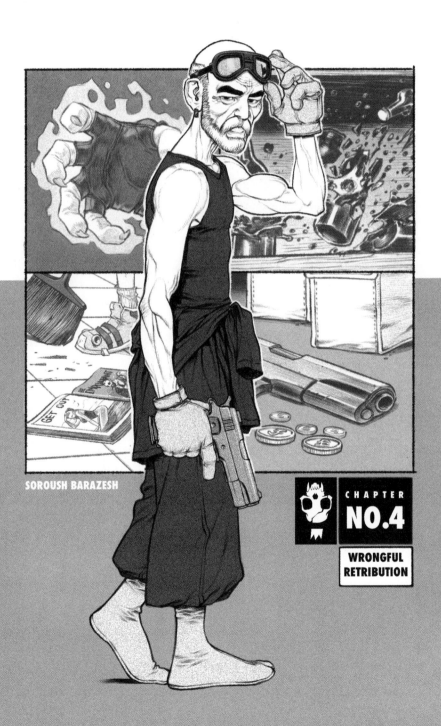

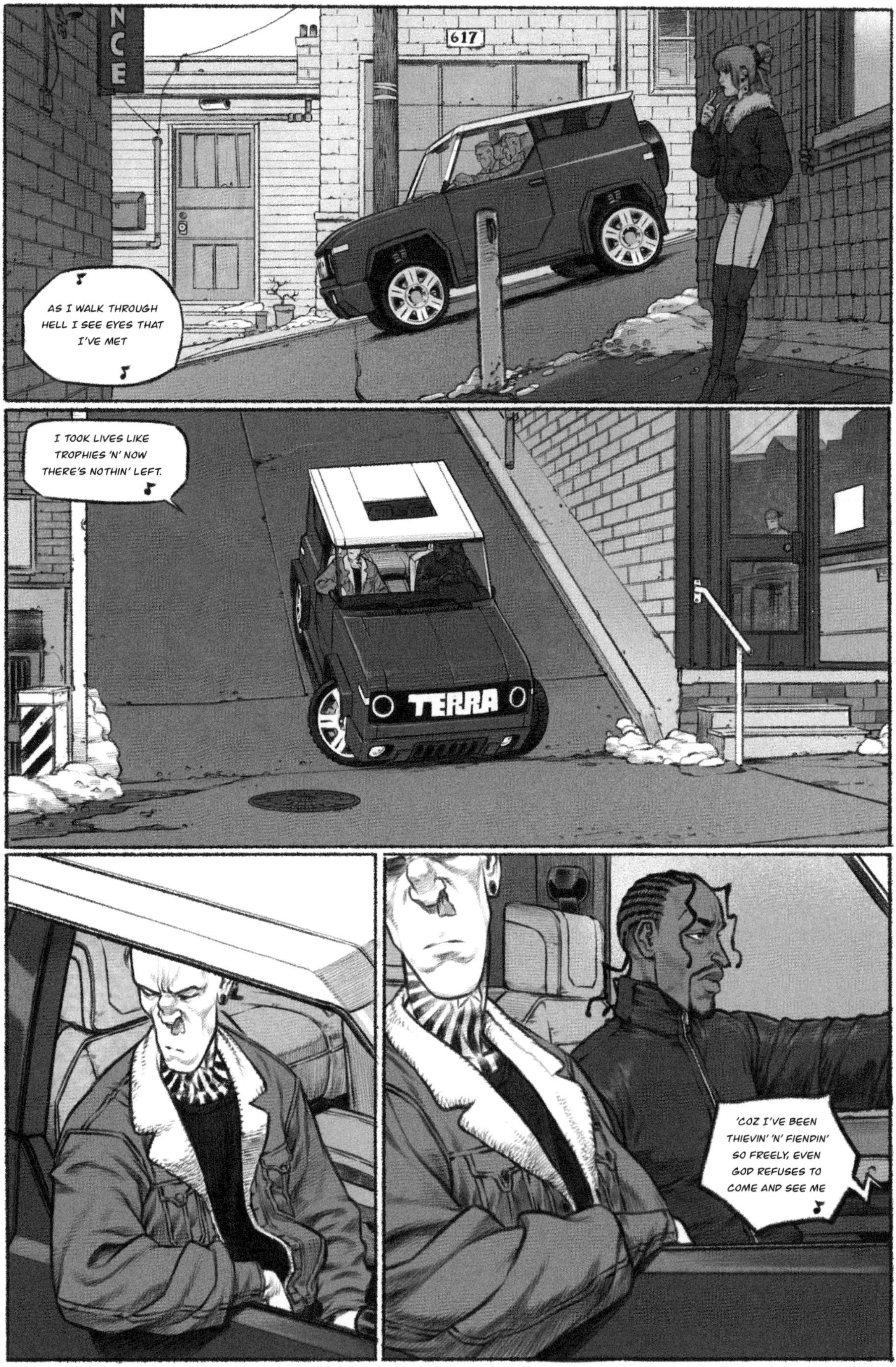
NCE
617
AS I WALK THROUGH HELL I SEE EYES THAT I'VE MET
I TOOK LIVES LIKE TROPHIES 'N' NOW THERE'S NOTHIN' LEFT.
TERRA
'COZ I'VE BEEN THIEVIN' 'N' FIENDIN' SO FREELY, EVEN GOD REFUSES TO COME AND SEE ME

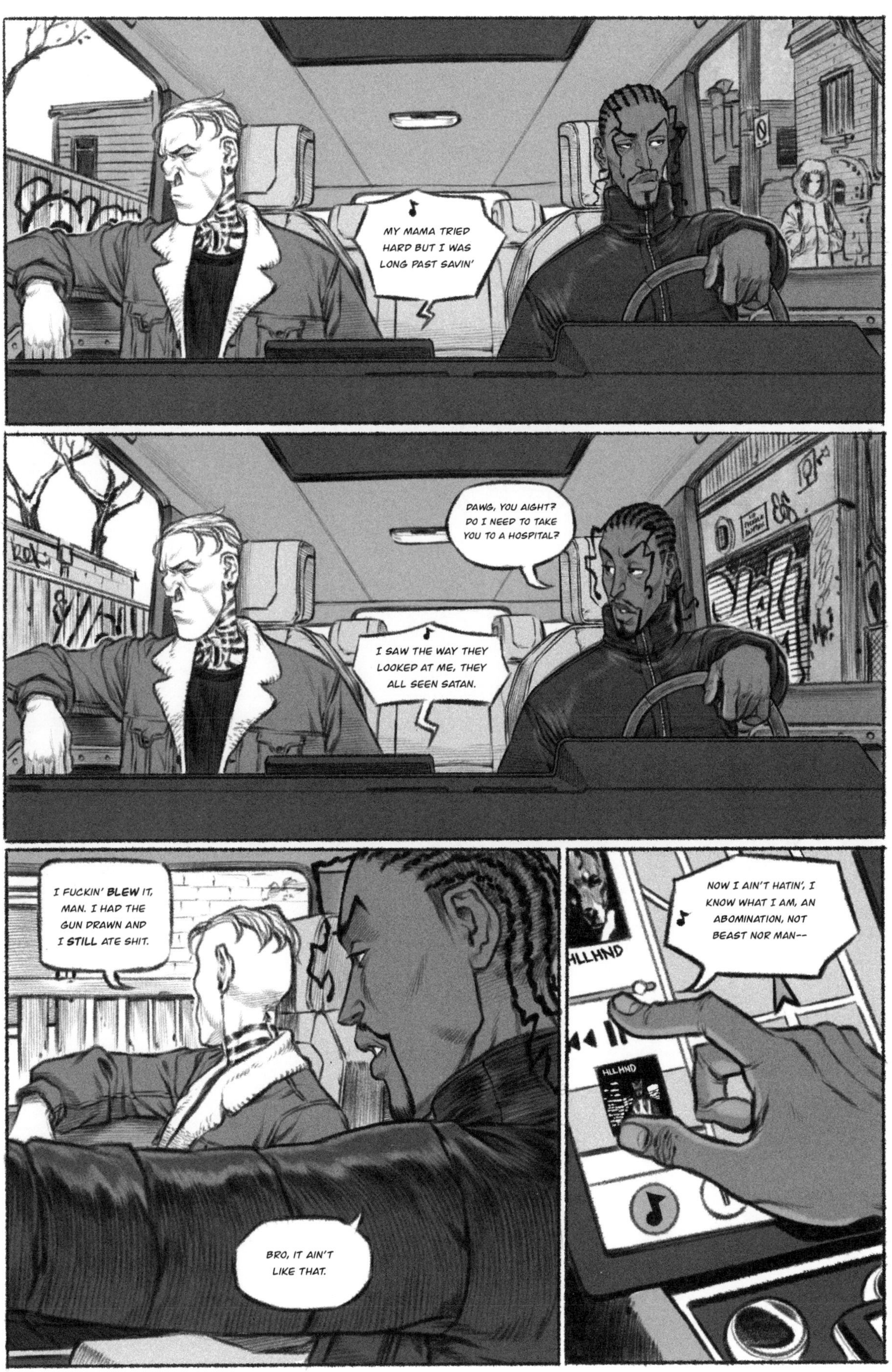

MY MAMA TRIED HARD BUT I WAS LONG PAST SAVIN'
DAWG, YOU AIGHT? DO I NEED TO TAKE YOU TO A HOSPITAL?
I SAW THE WAY THEY LOOKED AT ME, THEY ALL SEEN SATAN.
I FUCKIN' **BLEW** IT, MAN. I HAD THE GUN DRAWN AND I **STILL** ATE SHIT.
BRO, IT AIN'T LIKE THAT.
NOW I AIN'T HATIN', I KNOW WHAT I AM, AN ABOMINATION, NOT BEAST NOR MAN--
HLLHND
HLLHND

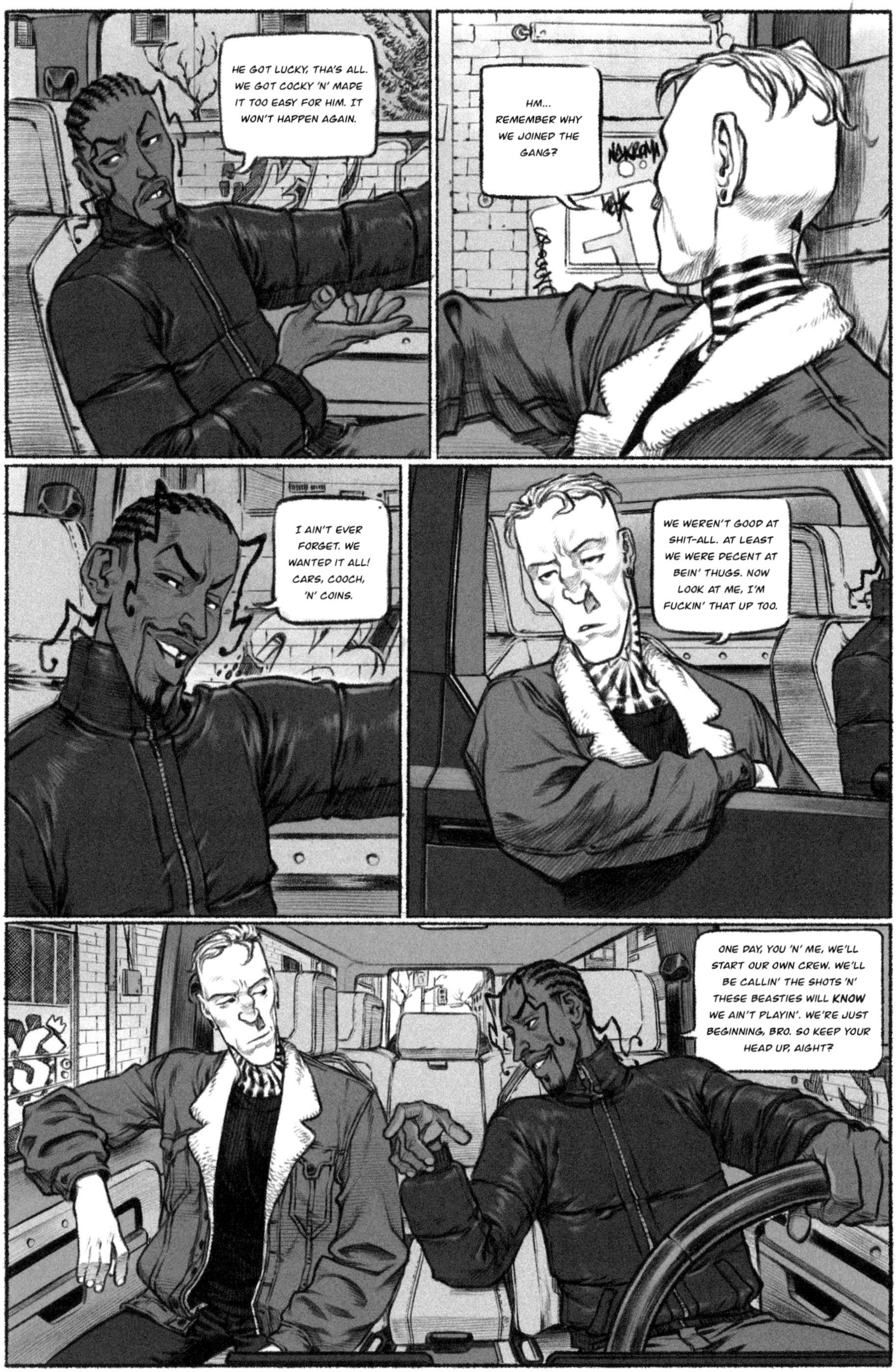
HE GOT LUCKY, THA'S ALL. WE GOT COCKY 'N' MADE IT TOO EASY FOR HIM. IT WON'T HAPPEN AGAIN.
HM... REMEMBER WHY WE JOINED THE GANG?
I AIN'T EVER FORGET. WE WANTED IT ALL! CARS, COOCH, 'N' COINS.
WE WEREN'T GOOD AT SHIT-ALL. AT LEAST WE WERE DECENT AT BEIN' THUGS. NOW LOOK AT ME, I'M FUCKIN' THAT UP TOO.
ONE DAY, YOU 'N' ME, WE'LL START OUR OWN CREW. WE'LL BE CALLIN' THE SHOTS 'N' THESE BEASTIES WILL **KNOW** WE AIN'T PLAYIN'. WE'RE JUST BEGINNING, BRO. SO KEEP YOUR HEAD UP, AIGHT?

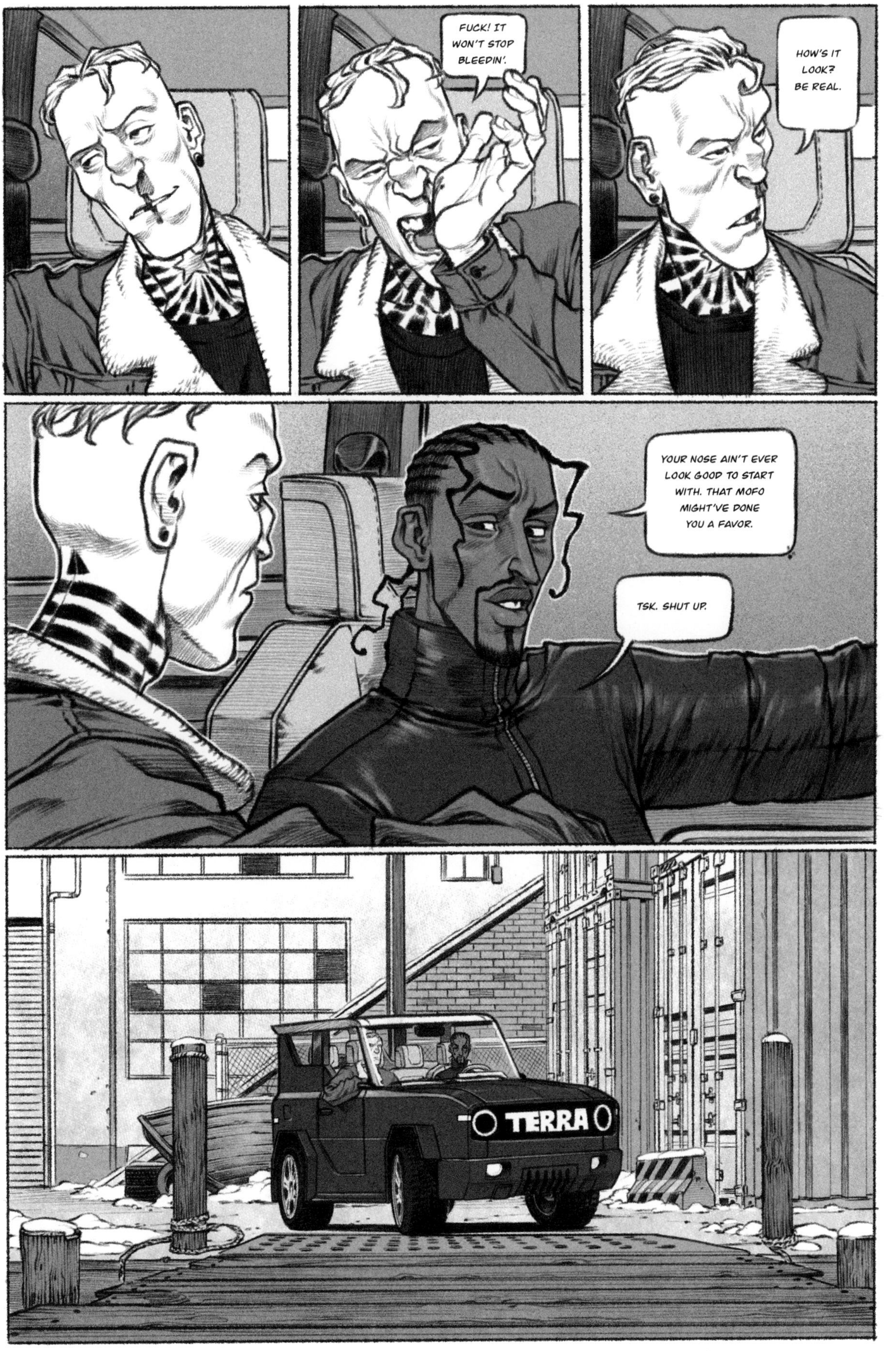
FUCK! IT WON'T STOP BLEEDIN'.
HOW'S IT LOOK? BE REAL.
YOUR NOSE AIN'T EVER LOOK GOOD TO START WITH. THAT MOFO MIGHT'VE DONE YOU A FAVOR.
TSK. SHUT UP.
TERRA

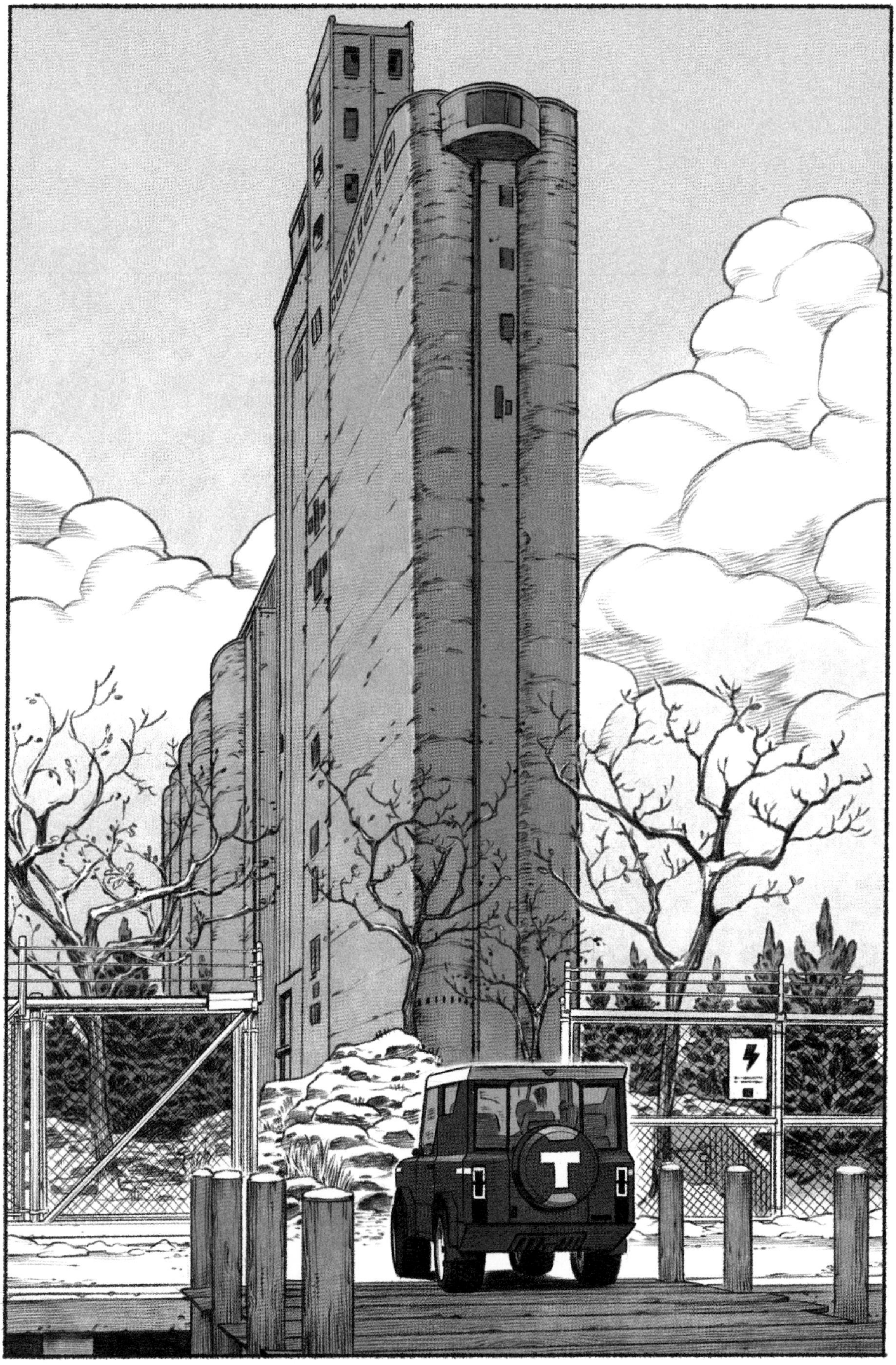

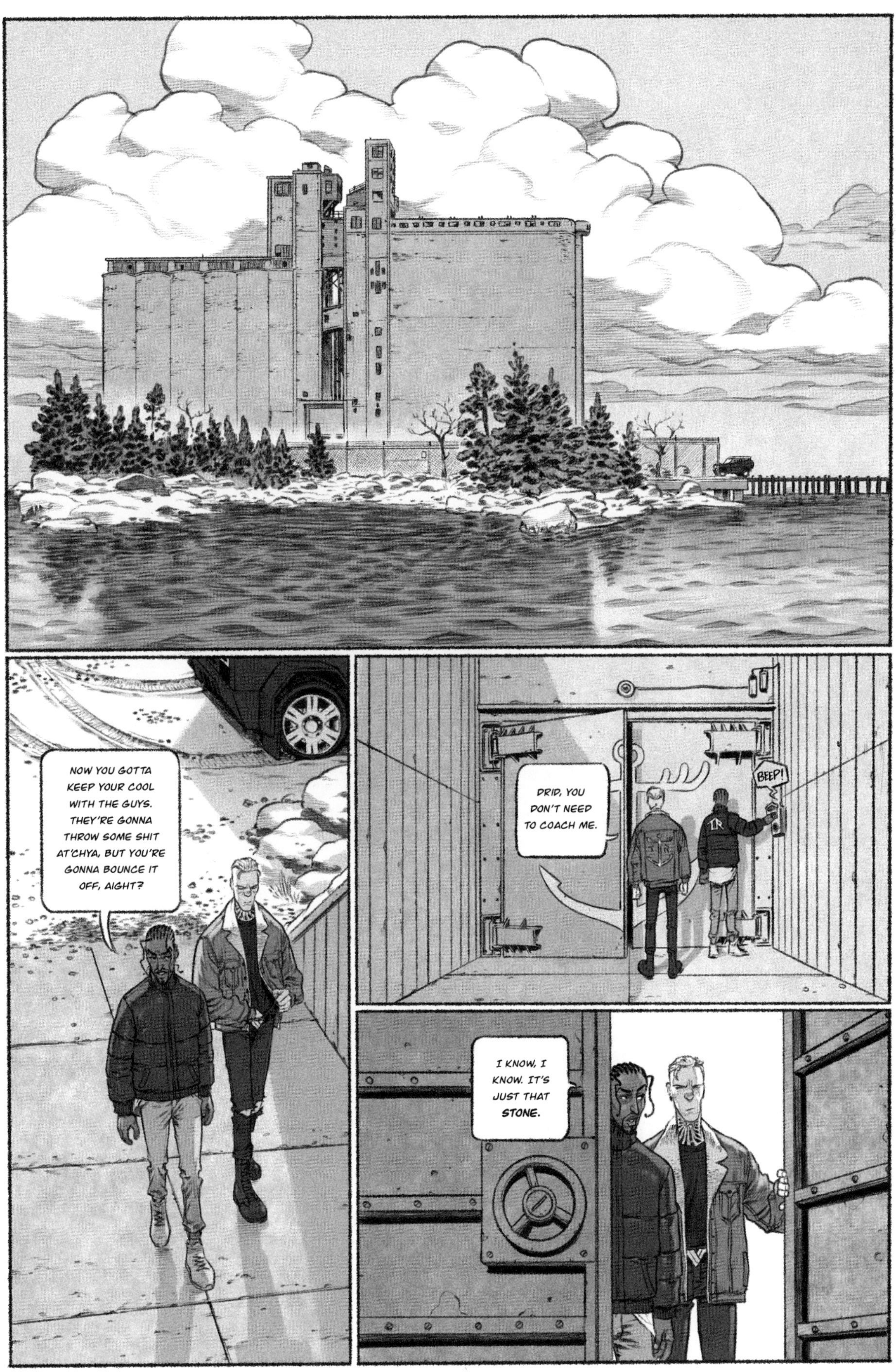
NOW YOU GOTTA KEEP YOUR COOL WITH THE GUYS. THEY'RE GONNA THROW SOME SHIT AT'CHYA, BUT YOU'RE GONNA BOUNCE IT OFF, AIGHT?
DRID, YOU DON'T NEED TO COACH ME.
BEEP!
I KNOW, I KNOW. IT'S JUST THAT STONE.

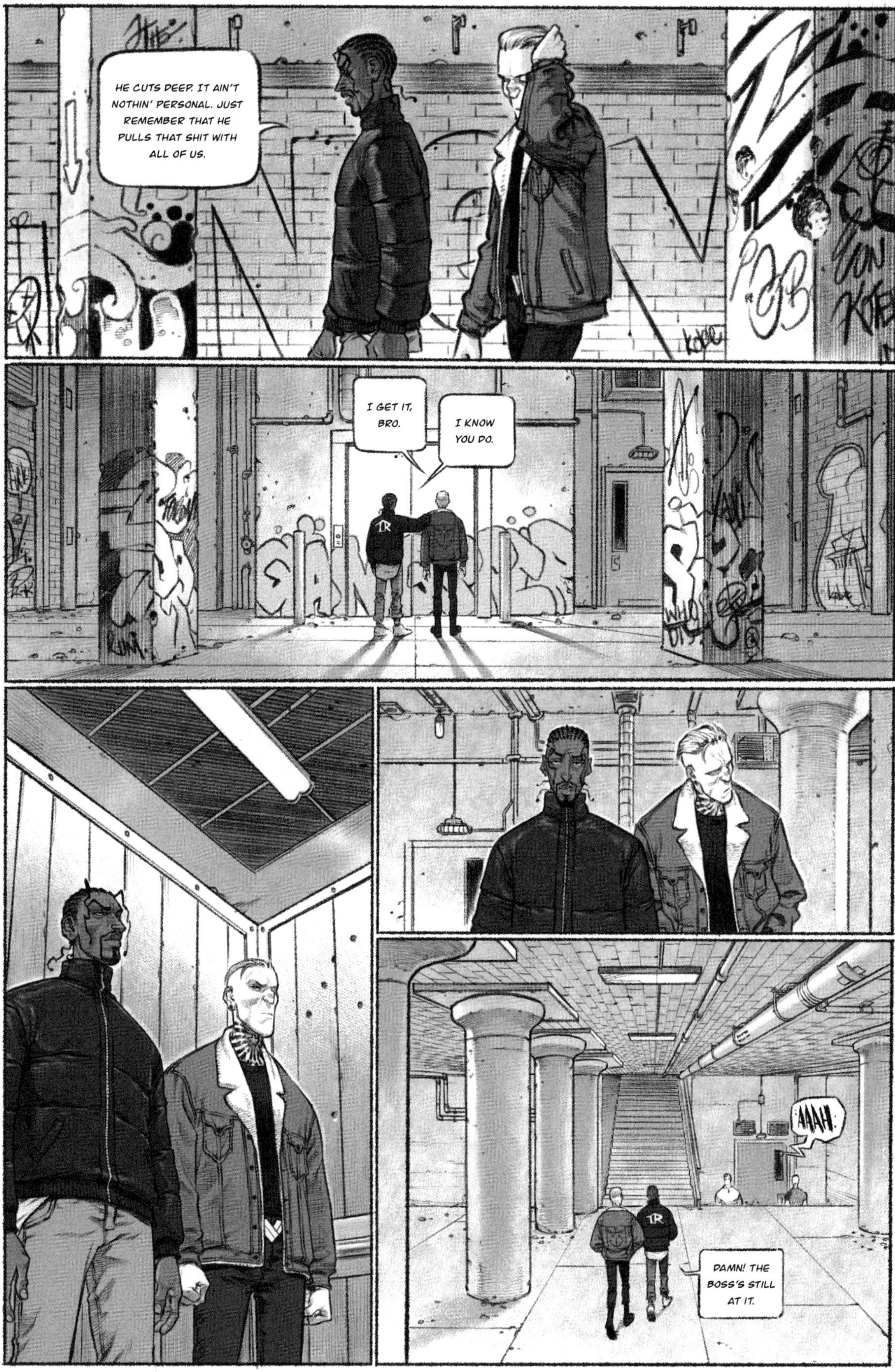
HE CUTS DEEP. IT AIN'T NOTHIN' PERSONAL. JUST REMEMBER THAT HE PULLS THAT SHIT WITH ALL OF US.
I GET IT, BRO.
I KNOW YOU DO.
AAAH.
DAMN! THE BOSS'S STILL AT IT.

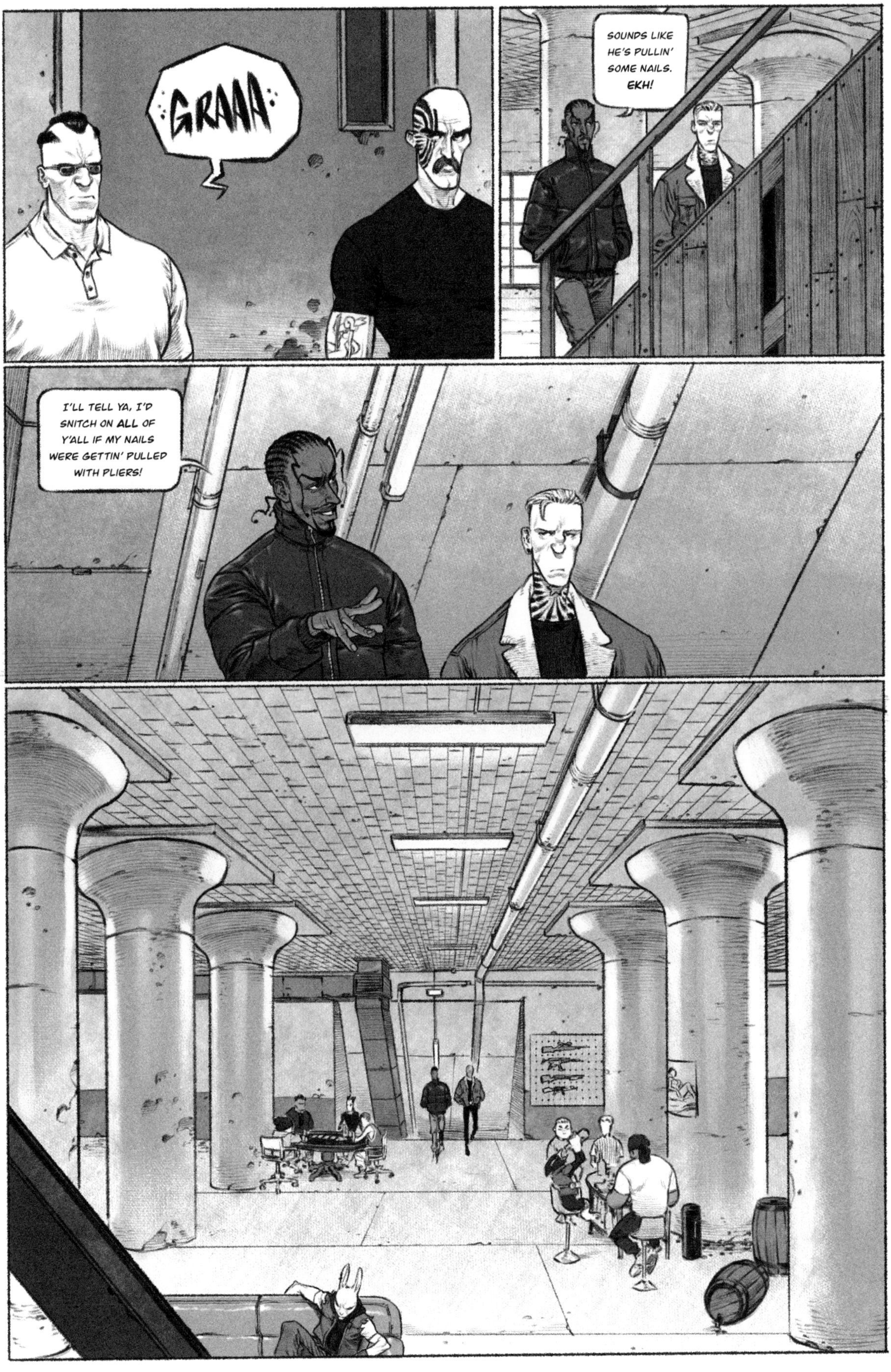
GRAAA
SOUNDS LIKE HE'S PULLIN' SOME NAILS. EKH!
I'LL TELL YA, I'D SNITCH ON ALL OF Y'ALL IF MY NAILS WERE GETTIN' PULLED WITH PLIERS!

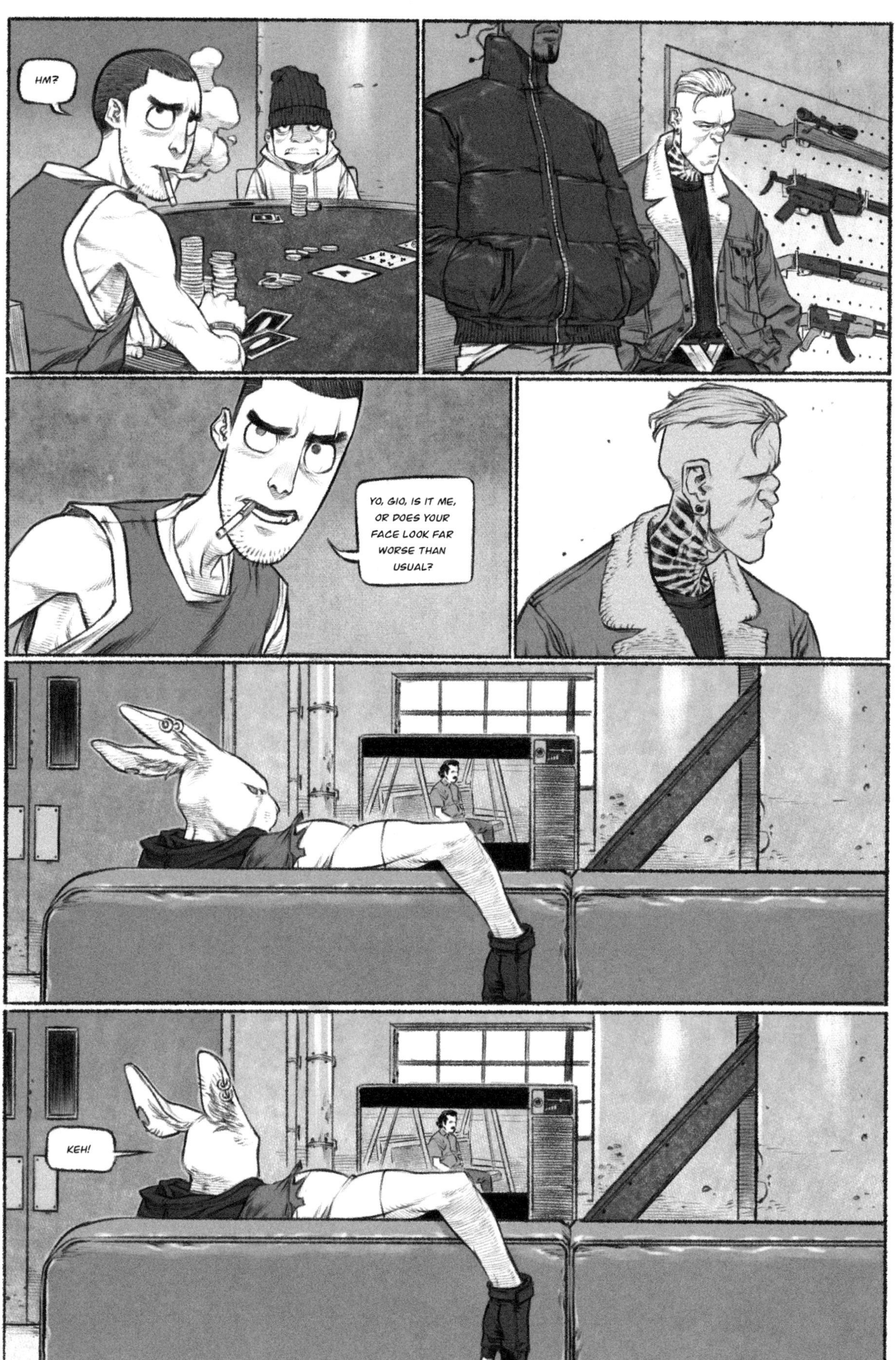
HM?
YO, GIO, IS IT ME, OR DOES YOUR FACE LOOK FAR WORSE THAN USUAL?
KEH!

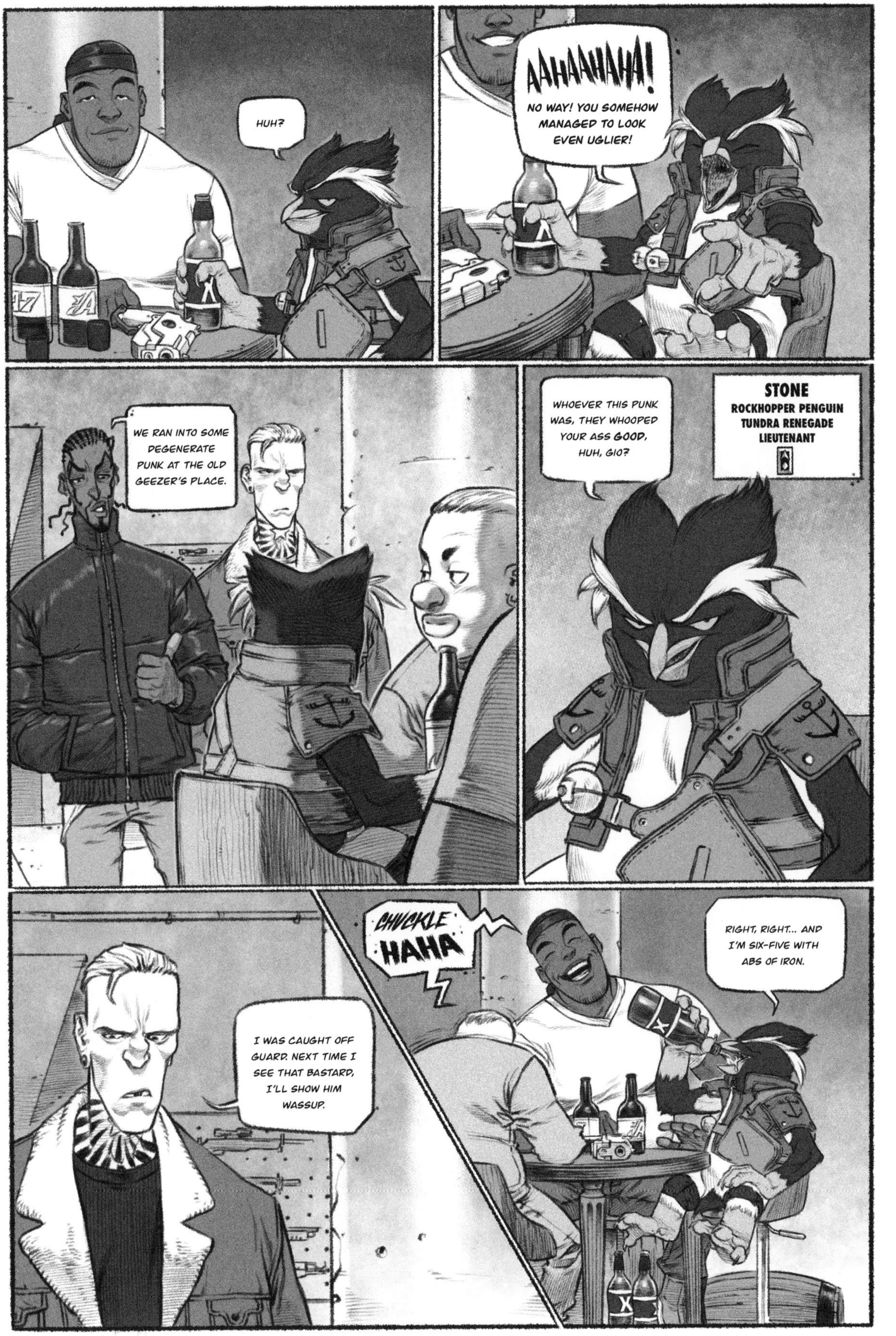
HUH?
AAHAAHAHA!
NO WAY! YOU SOMEHOW MANAGED TO LOOK EVEN UGLIER!
WE RAN INTO SOME DEGENERATE PUNK AT THE OLD GEEZER'S PLACE.
WHOEVER THIS PUNK WAS, THEY WHOOPED YOUR ASS GOOD, HUH, GIO?
STONE
ROCKHOPPER PENGUIN
TUNDRA RENEGADE
LIEUTENANT
I WAS CAUGHT OFF GUARD. NEXT TIME I SEE THAT BASTARD, I'LL SHOW HIM WASSUP.
CHUCKLE
HAHA
RIGHT, RIGHT... AND I'M SIX-FIVE WITH ABS OF IRON.

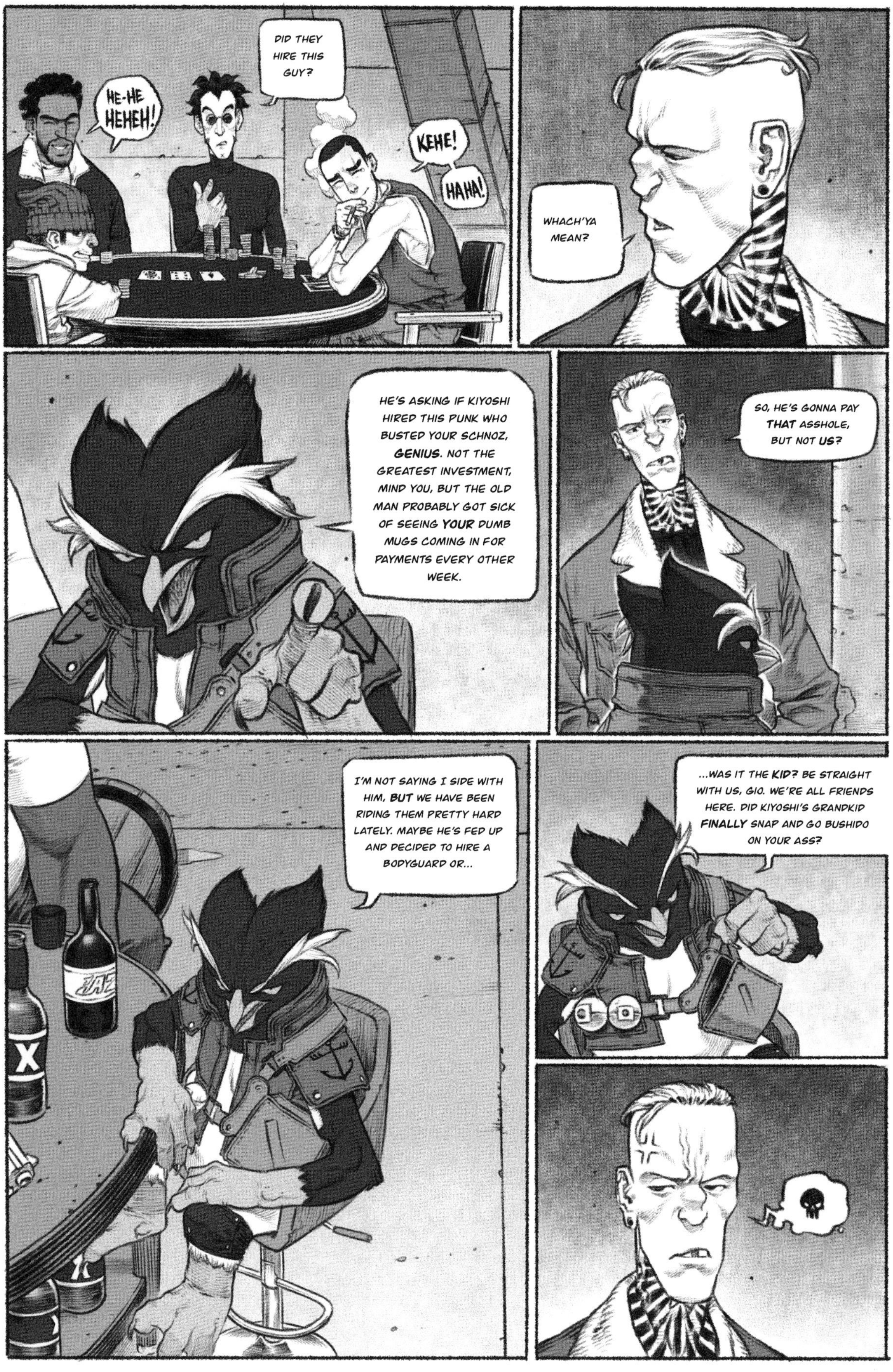
HE-HE HEHEH!
DID THEY HIRE THIS GUY?
KEHE!
HAHA!
WHACH'YA MEAN?
HE'S ASKING IF KIYOSHI HIRED THIS PUNK WHO BUSTED YOUR SCHNOZ, GENIUS. NOT THE GREATEST INVESTMENT, MIND YOU, BUT THE OLD MAN PROBABLY GOT SICK OF SEEING YOUR DUMB MUGS COMING IN FOR PAYMENTS EVERY OTHER WEEK.
SO, HE'S GONNA PAY THAT ASSHOLE, BUT NOT US?
I'M NOT SAYING I SIDE WITH HIM, BUT WE HAVE BEEN RIDING THEM PRETTY HARD LATELY. MAYBE HE'S FED UP AND DECIDED TO HIRE A BODYGUARD OR...
...WAS IT THE KID? BE STRAIGHT WITH US, GIO. WE'RE ALL FRIENDS HERE. DID KIYOSHI'S GRANDKID FINALLY SNAP AND GO BUSHIDO ON YOUR ASS?

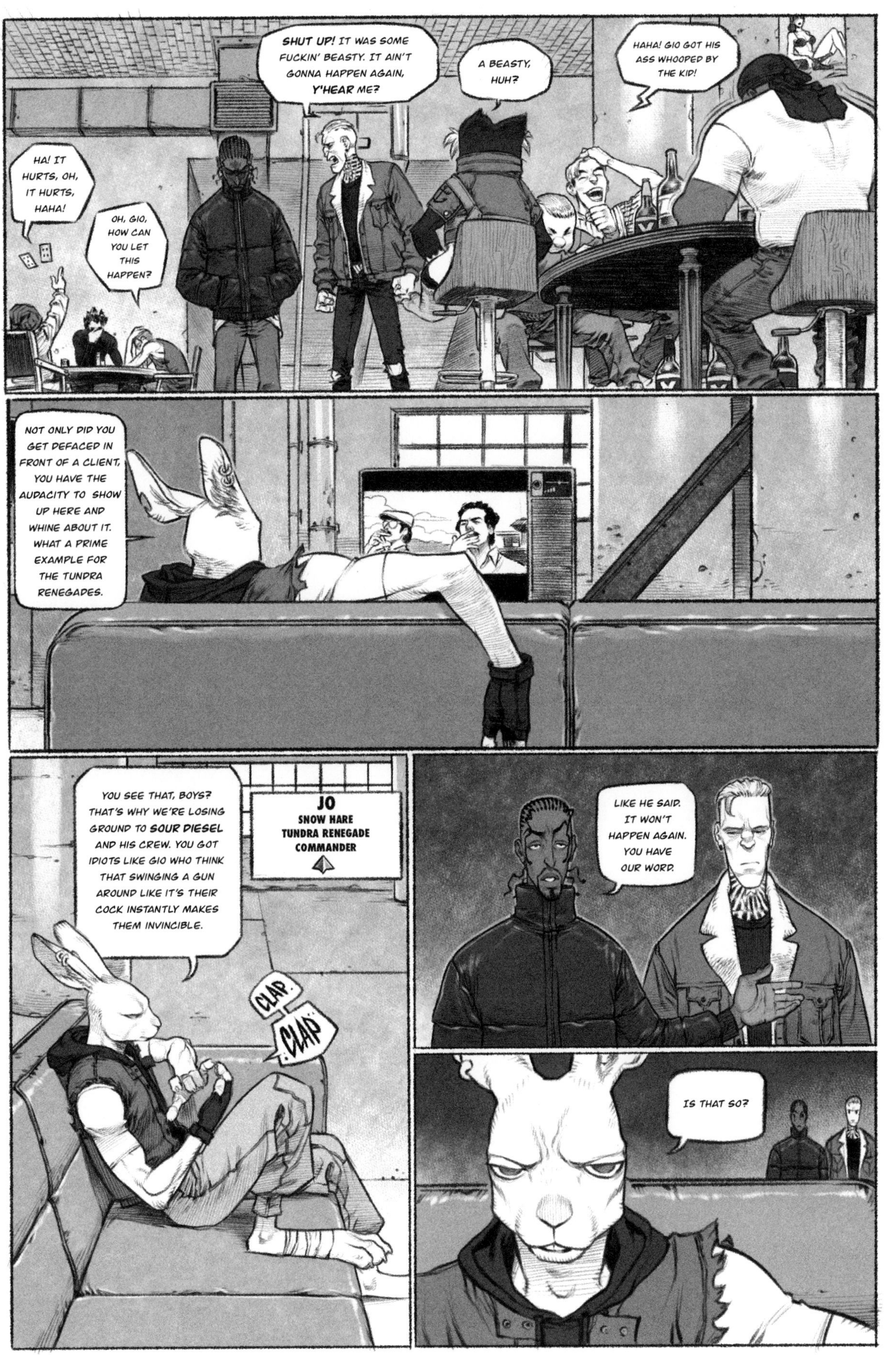
SHUT UP! IT WAS SOME FUCKIN' BEASTY. IT AIN'T GONNA HAPPEN AGAIN, Y'HEAR ME?
A BEASTY, HUH?
HAHA! GIO GOT HIS ASS WHOOPED BY THE KID!
HA! IT HURTS, OH, IT HURTS, HAHA!
OH, GIO, HOW CAN YOU LET THIS HAPPEN?
NOT ONLY DID YOU GET DEFACED IN FRONT OF A CLIENT, YOU HAVE THE AUDACITY TO SHOW UP HERE AND WHINE ABOUT IT. WHAT A PRIME EXAMPLE FOR THE TUNDRA RENEGADES.
YOU SEE THAT, BOYS? THAT'S WHY WE'RE LOSING GROUND TO SOUR DIESEL AND HIS CREW. YOU GOT IDIOTS LIKE GIO WHO THINK THAT SWINGING A GUN AROUND LIKE IT'S THEIR COCK INSTANTLY MAKES THEM INVINCIBLE.
JO
SNOW HARE
TUNDRA RENEGADE
COMMANDER
CLAP.
CLAP
LIKE HE SAID. IT WON'T HAPPEN AGAIN. YOU HAVE OUR WORD.
IS THAT SO?

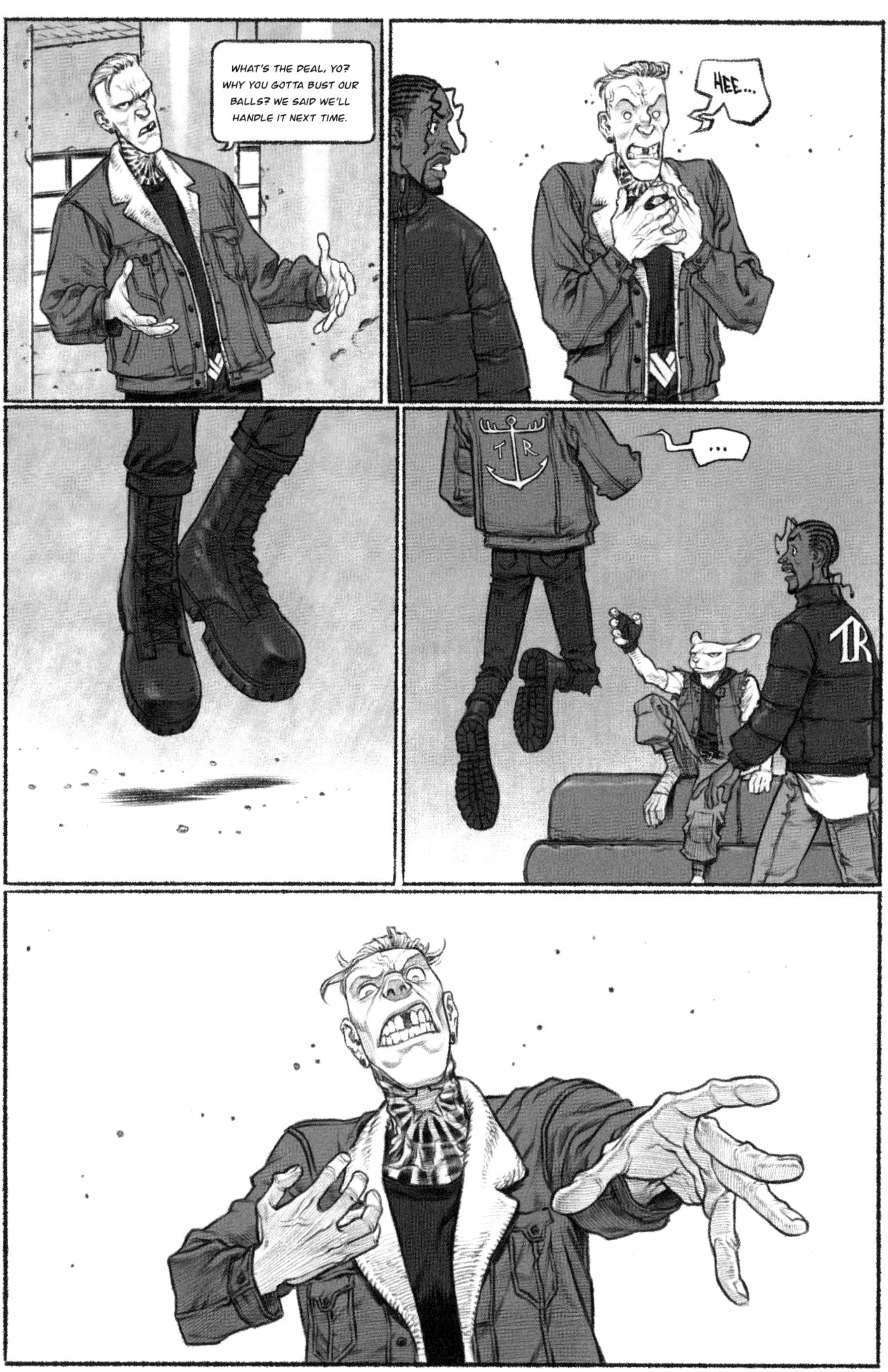
WHAT'S THE DEAL, YO? WHY YOU GOTTA BUST OUR BALLS? WE SAID WE'LL HANDLE IT NEXT TIME.
HEE...
...

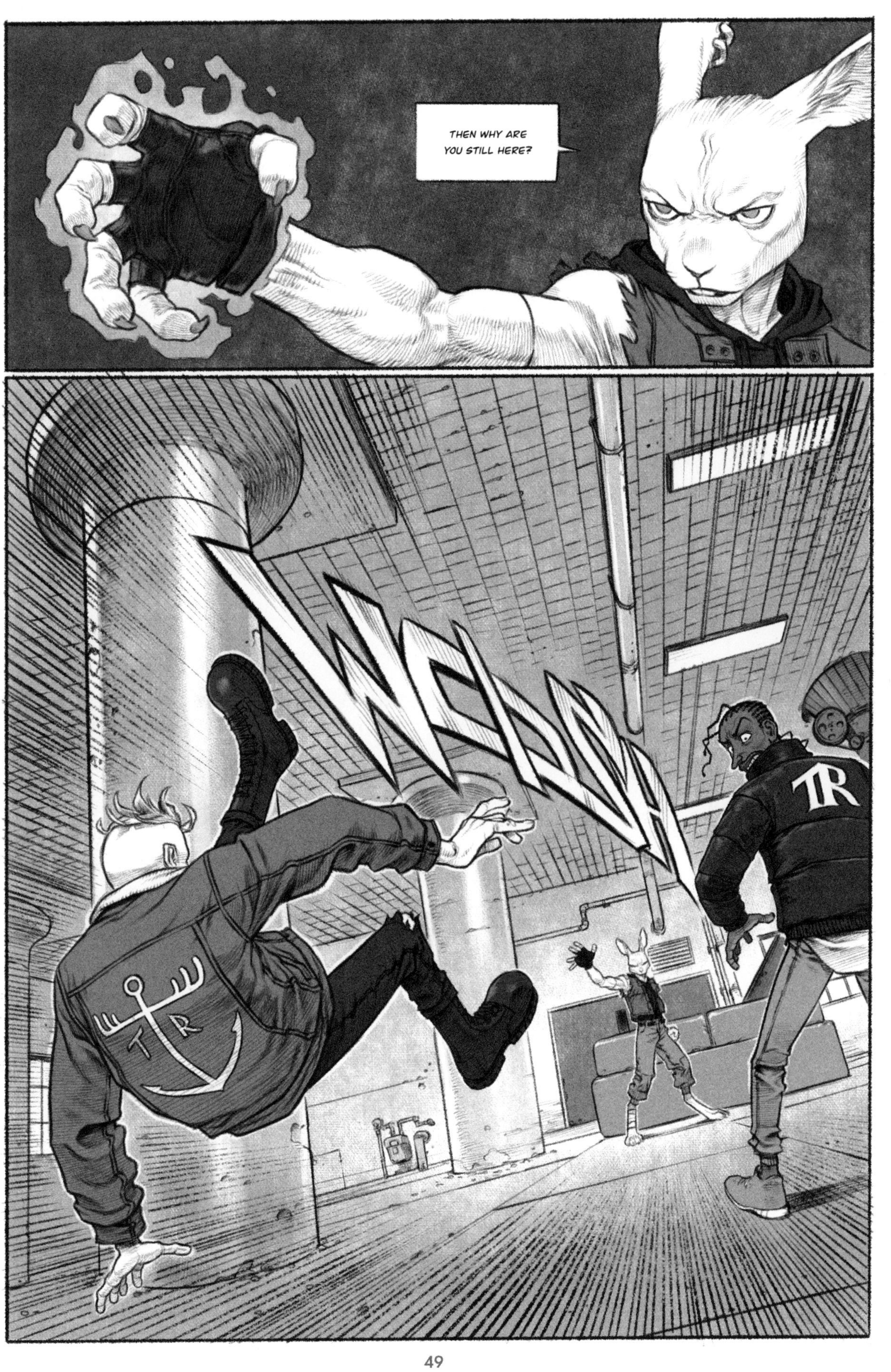
THEN WHY ARE
YOU STILL HERE?
TR
T R

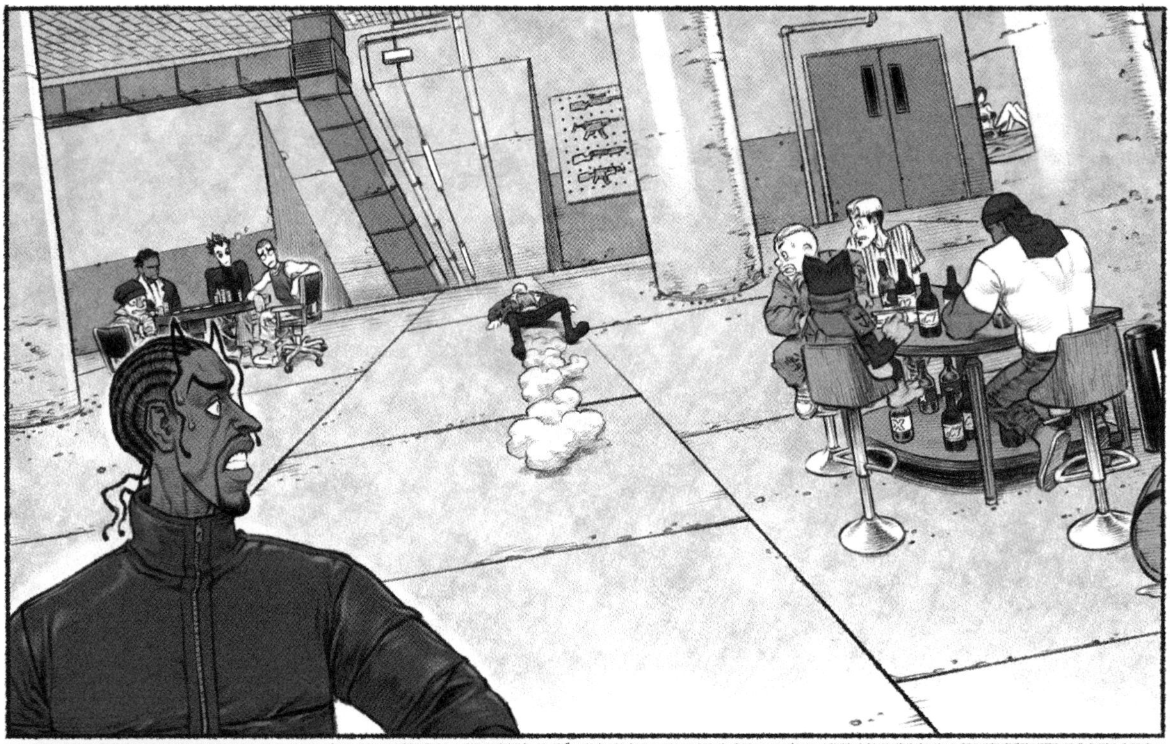

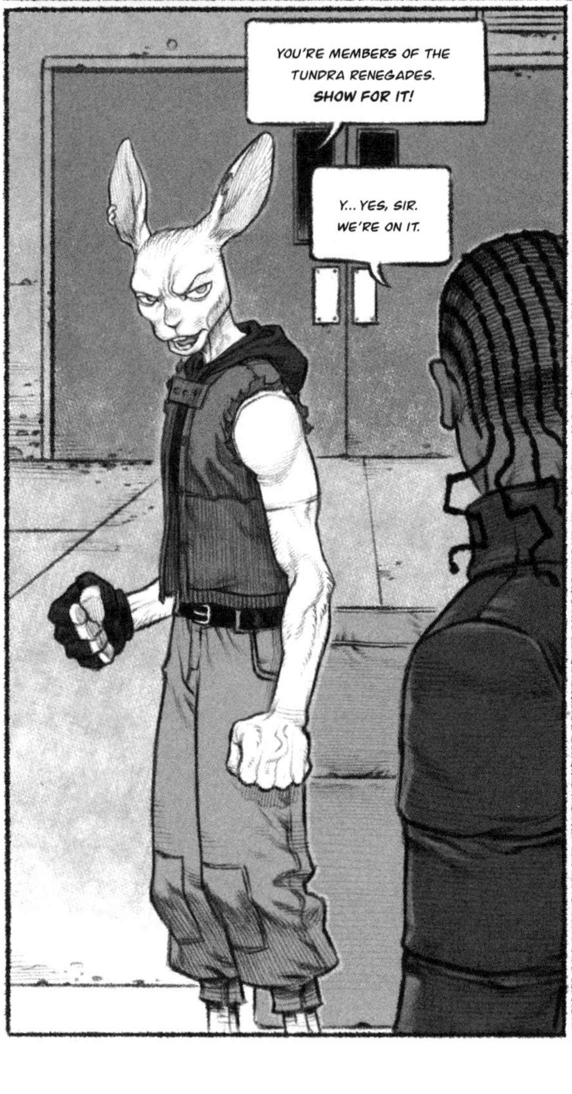
YOU'RE MEMBERS OF THE TUNDRA RENEGADES. SHOW FOR IT!
Y... YES, SIR. WE'RE ON IT.

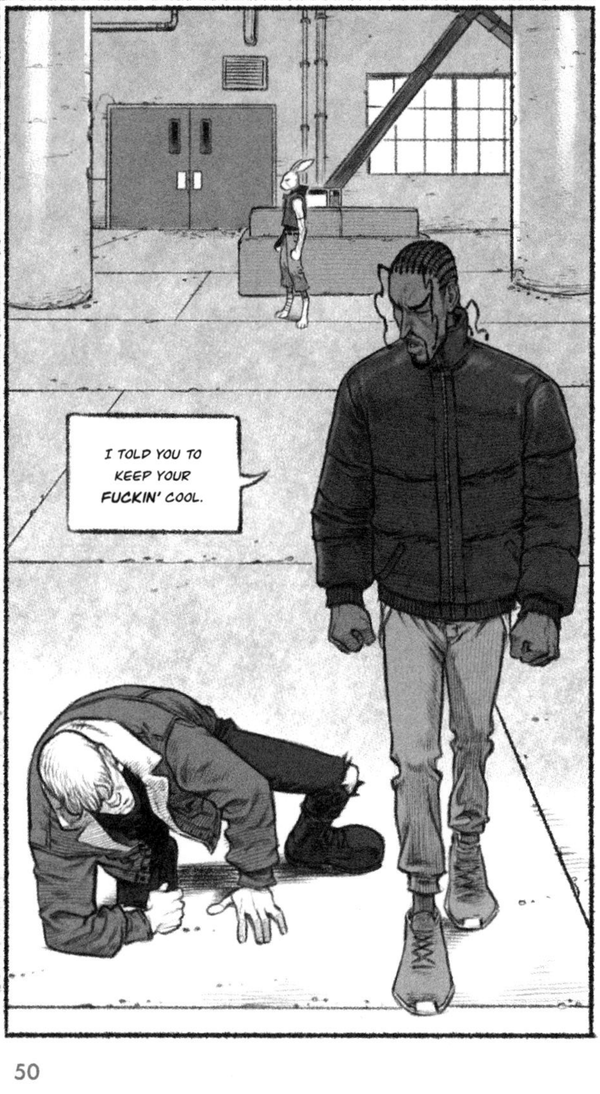
I TOLD YOU TO KEEP YOUR FUCKIN' COOL.

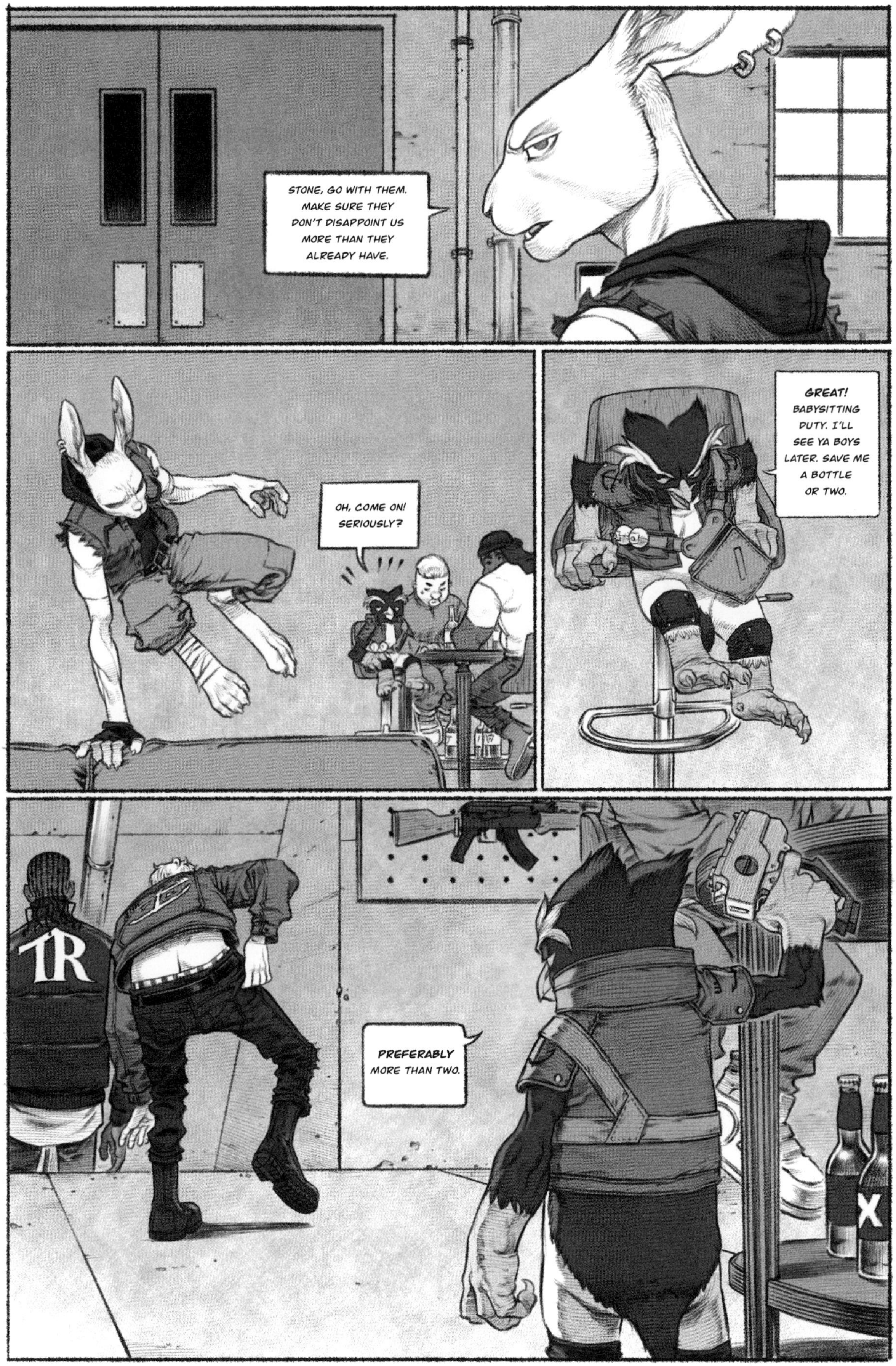
STONE, GO WITH THEM. MAKE SURE THEY DON'T DISAPPOINT US MORE THAN THEY ALREADY HAVE.
OH, COME ON! SERIOUSLY?
GREAT! BABYSITTING DUTY. I'LL SEE YA BOYS LATER. SAVE ME A BOTTLE OR TWO.
TR
PREFERABLY MORE THAN TWO.

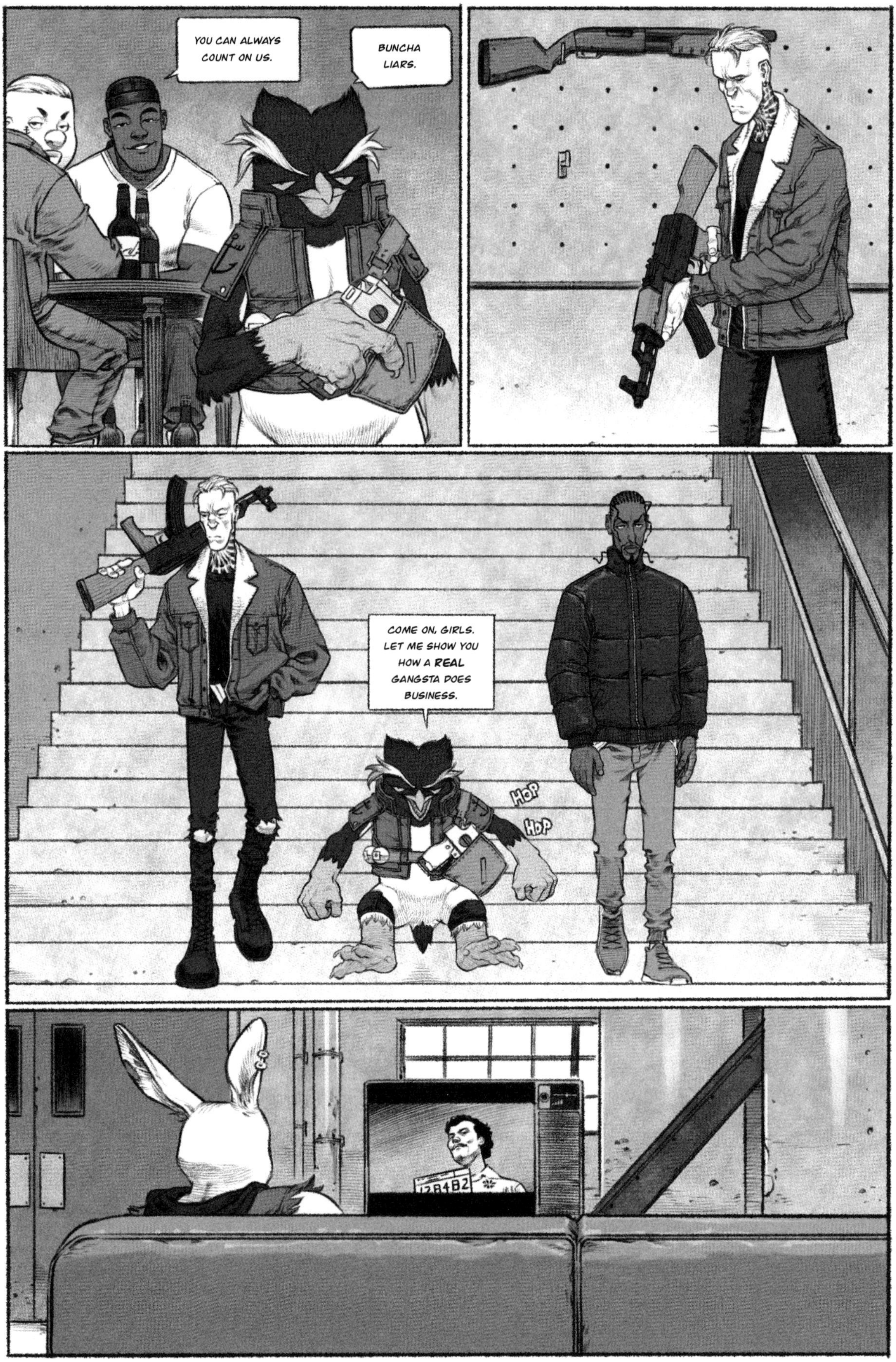
YOU CAN ALWAYS COUNT ON US.
BUNCHA LIARS.
COME ON, GIRLS. LET ME SHOW YOU HOW A **REAL** GANGSTA DOES BUSINESS.
HOP
HOP

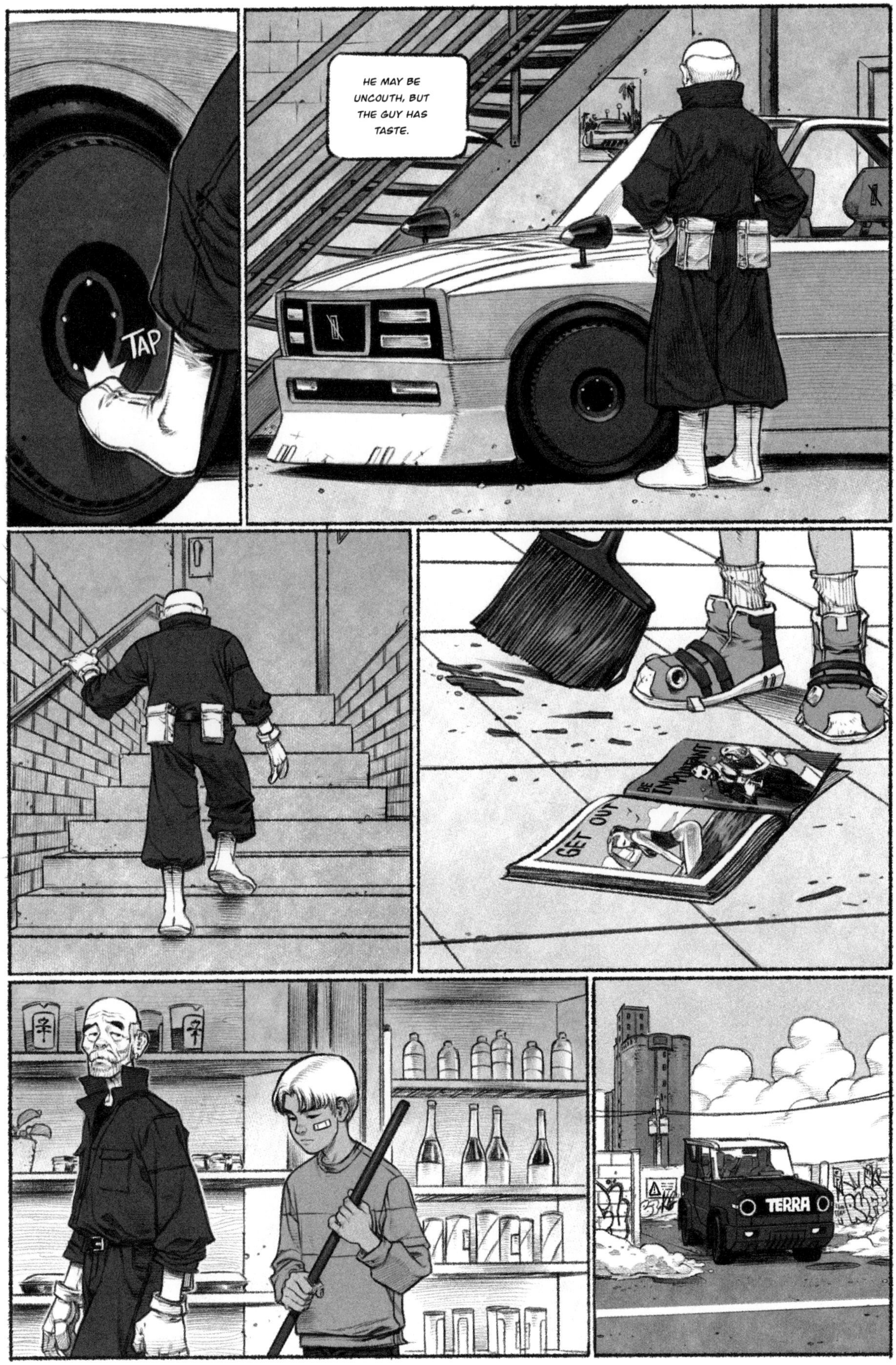
TAP
HE MAY BE UNCOUTH, BUT THE GUY HAS TASTE.
BE IMPORTANT
GET OUT
TERRA

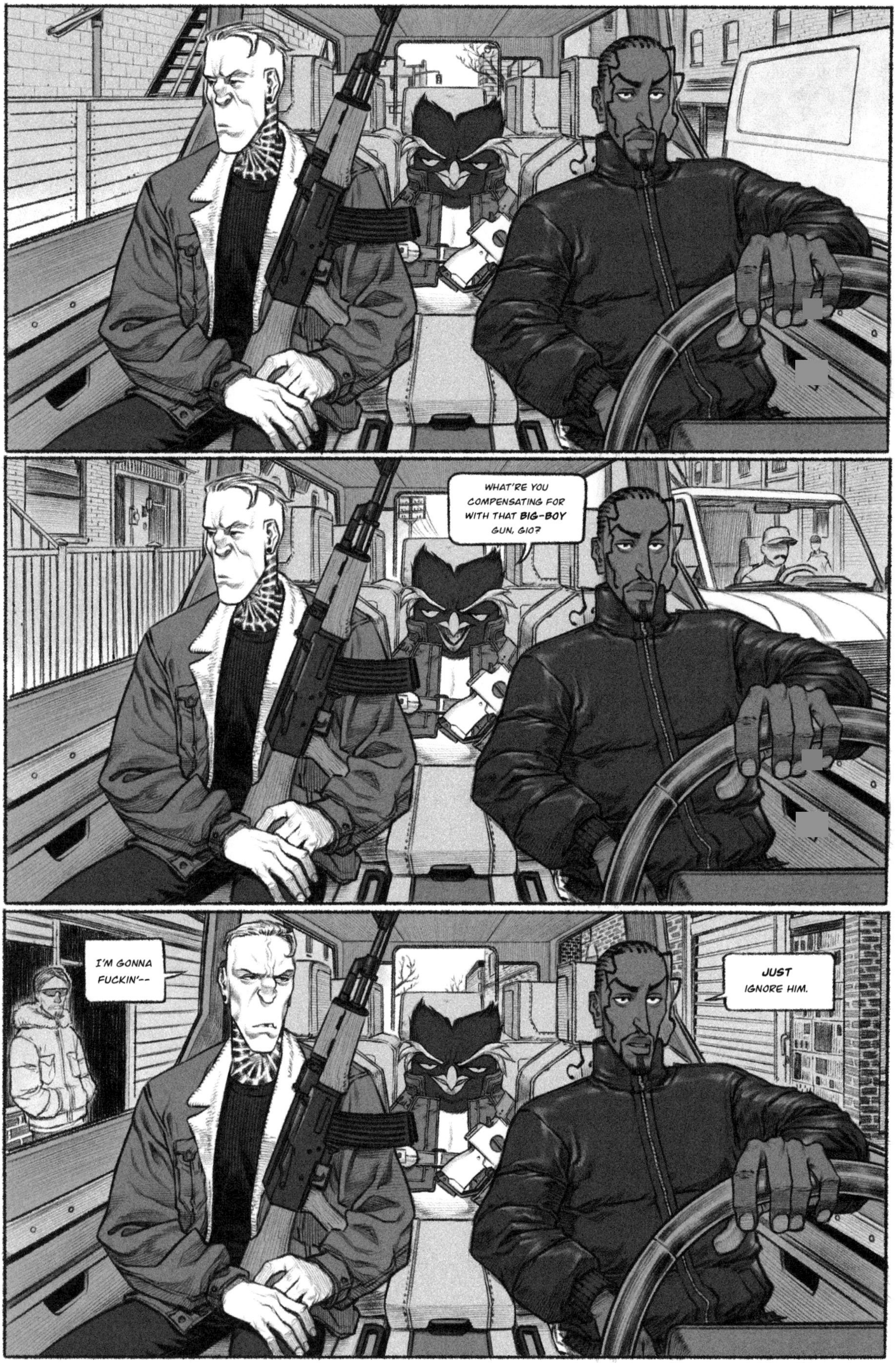
WHAT'RE YOU COMPENSATING FOR WITH THAT BIG-BOY GUN, GIO?
I'M GONNA FUCKIN'--
JUST IGNORE HIM.

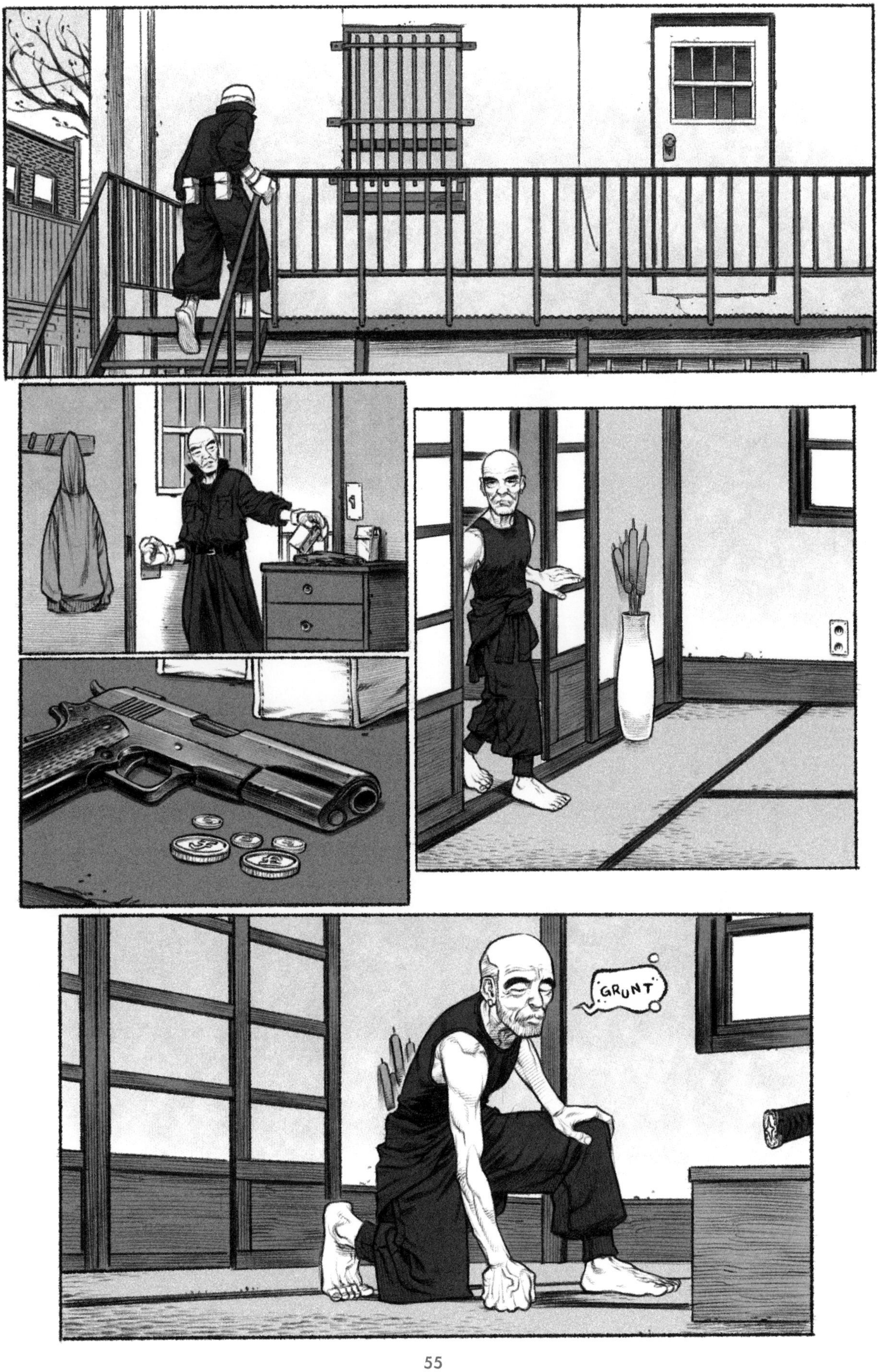
GRUNT

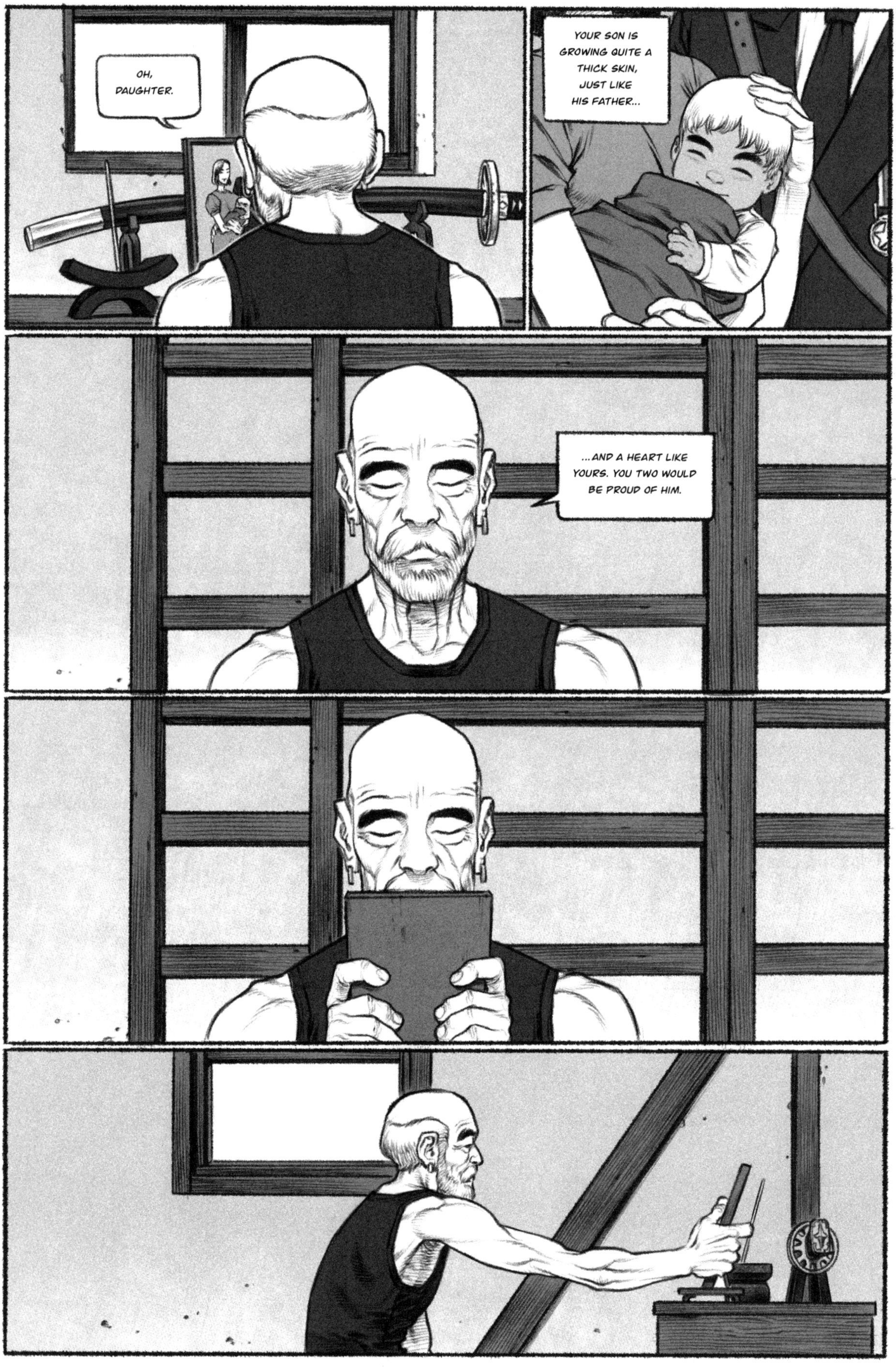
OH, DAUGHTER.
YOUR SON IS GROWING QUITE A THICK SKIN, JUST LIKE HIS FATHER...
...AND A HEART LIKE YOURS. YOU TWO WOULD BE PROUD OF HIM.

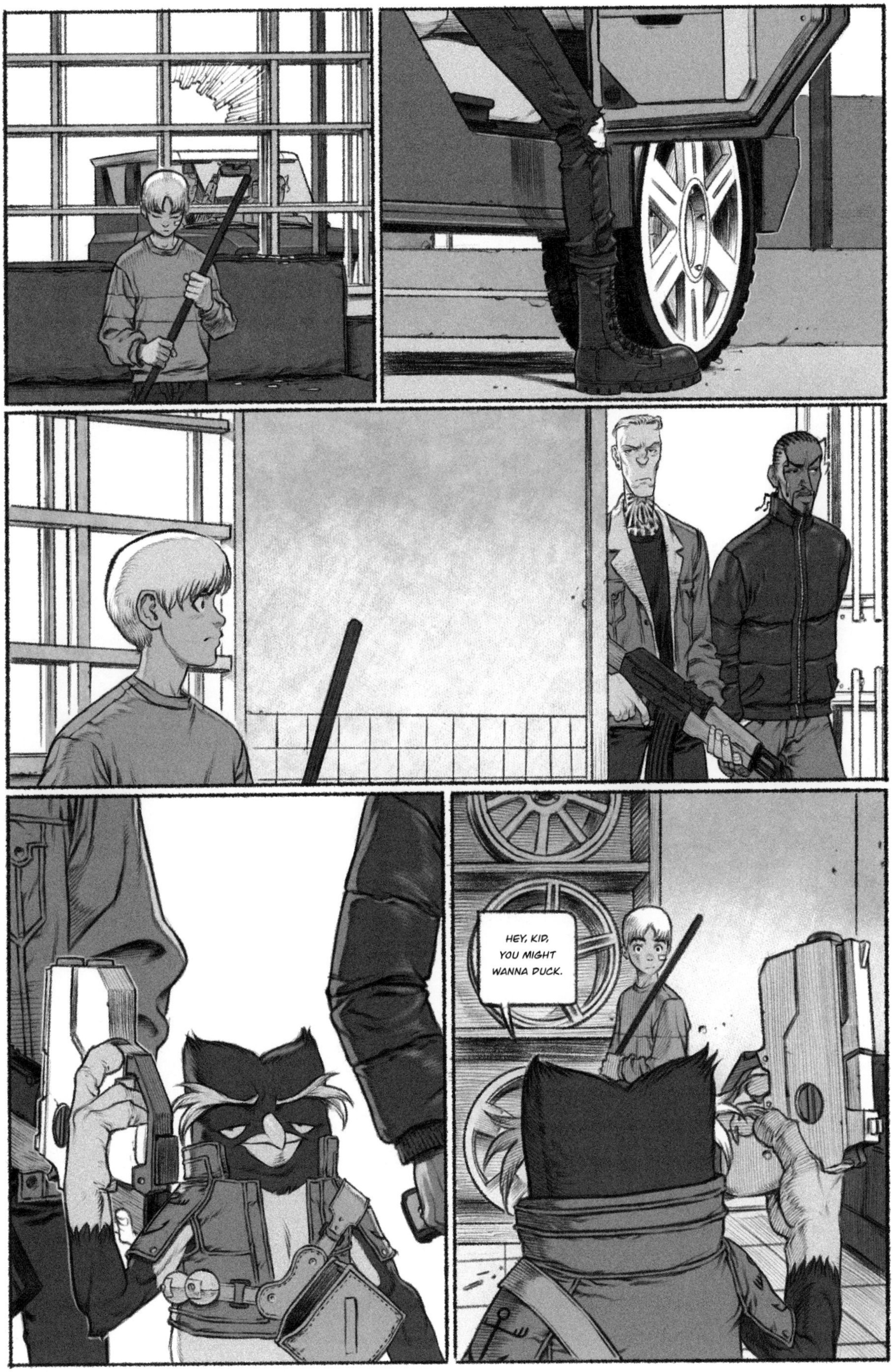
HEY, KID, YOU MIGHT WANNA DUCK.

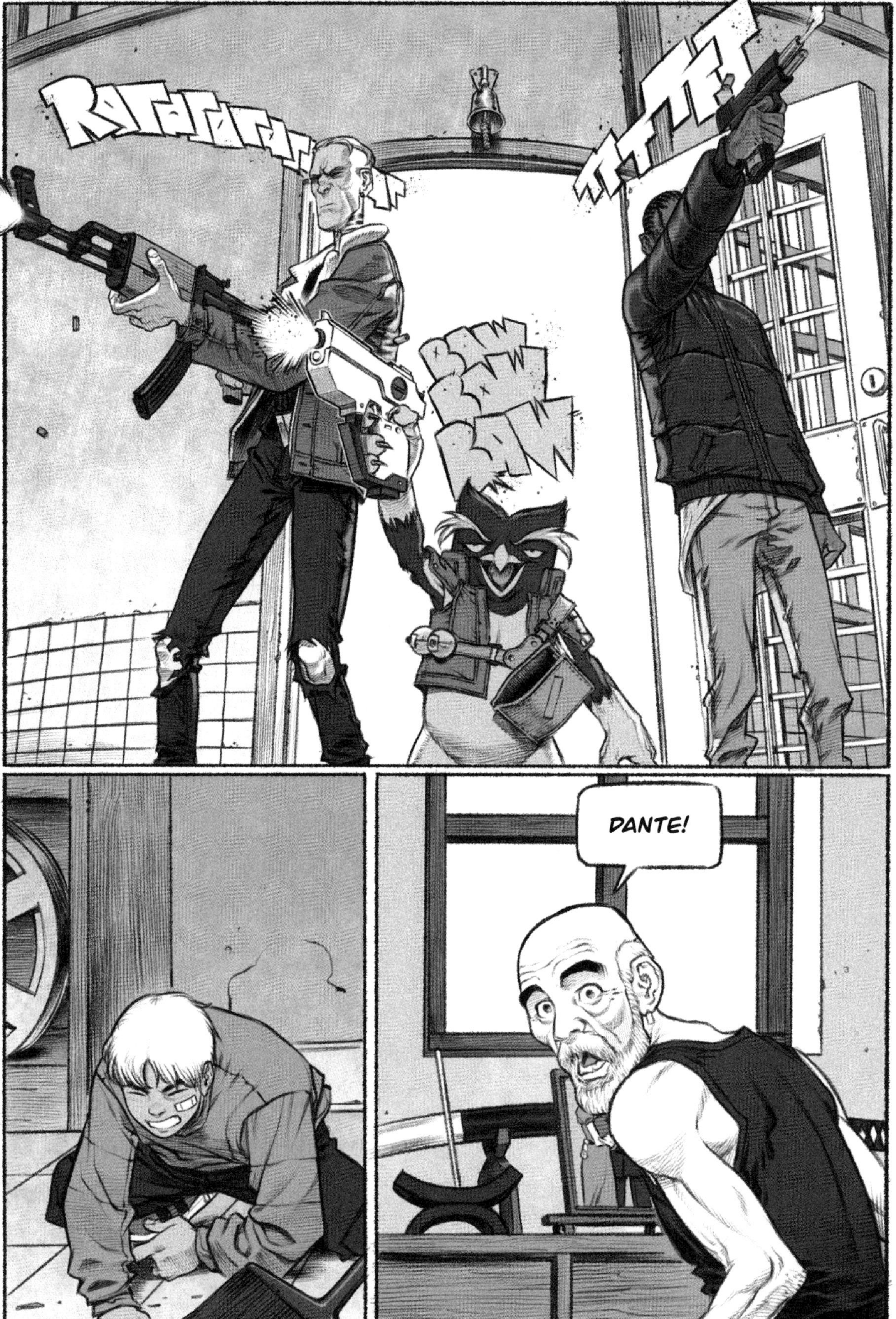
BAW BAW BAW
DANTE!

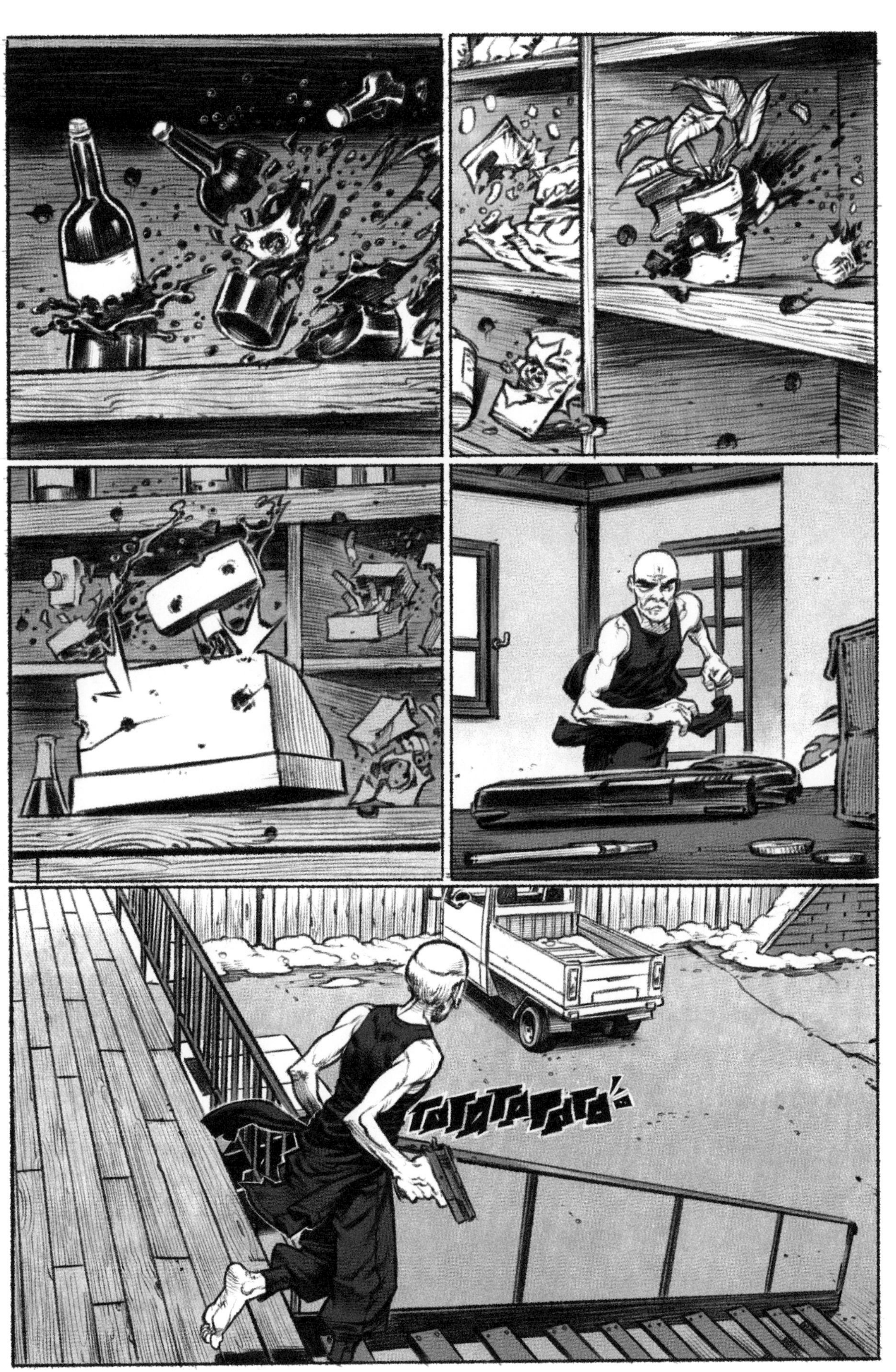

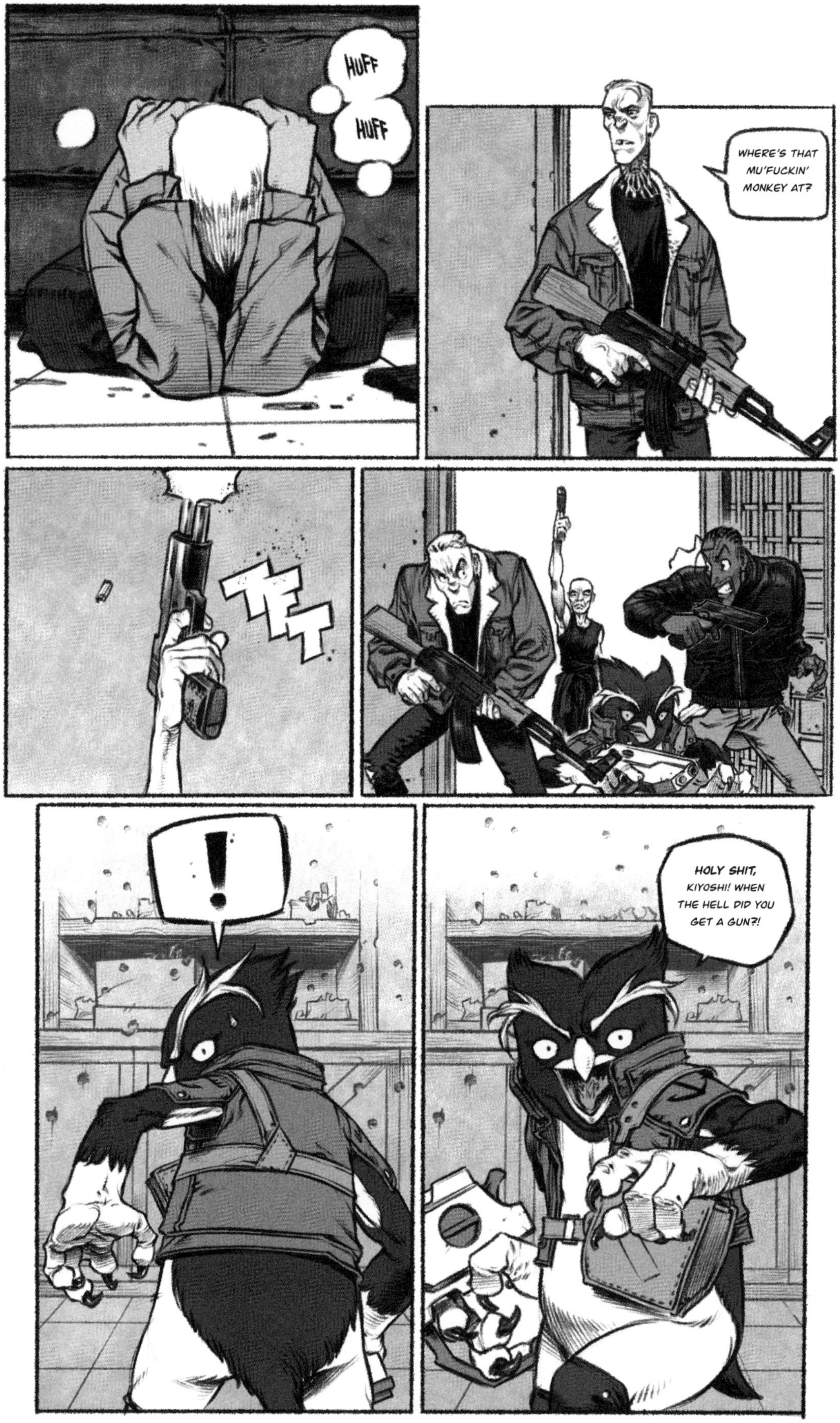
HUFF
HUFF
WHERE'S THAT MU'FUCKIN' MONKEY AT?
TET
!
HOLY SHIT, KIYOSHI! WHEN THE HELL DID YOU GET A GUN?!

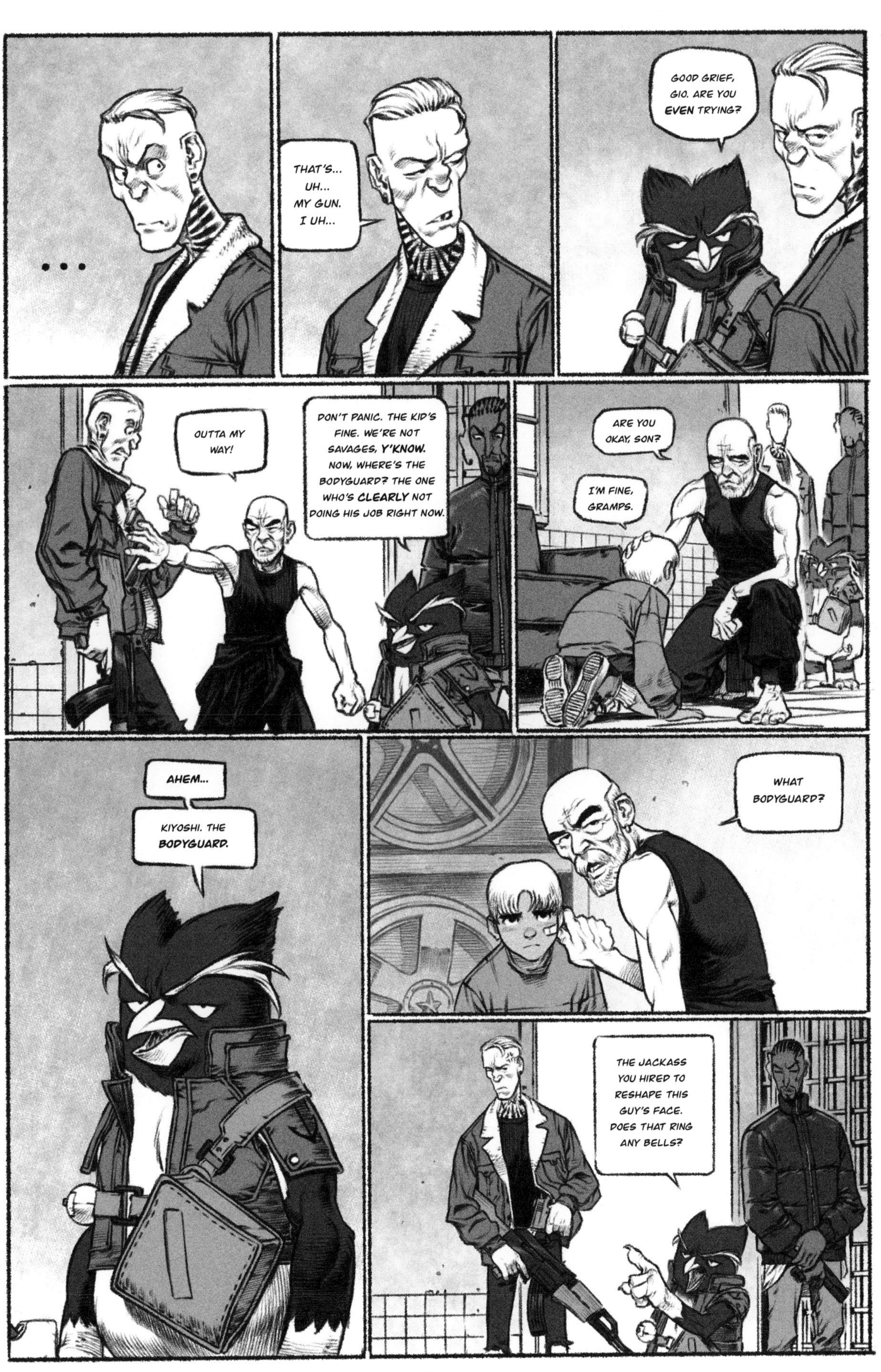
• • •
THAT'S... UH... MY GUN. I UH...
GOOD GRIEF, GIO. ARE YOU EVEN TRYING?
OUTTA MY WAY!
DON'T PANIC. THE KID'S FINE. WE'RE NOT SAVAGES, Y'KNOW. NOW, WHERE'S THE BODYGUARD? THE ONE WHO'S CLEARLY NOT DOING HIS JOB RIGHT NOW.
ARE YOU OKAY, SON?
I'M FINE, GRAMPS.
AHEM...
KIYOSHI. THE BODYGUARD.
WHAT BODYGUARD?
THE JACKASS YOU HIRED TO RESHAPE THIS GUY'S FACE. DOES THAT RING ANY BELLS?

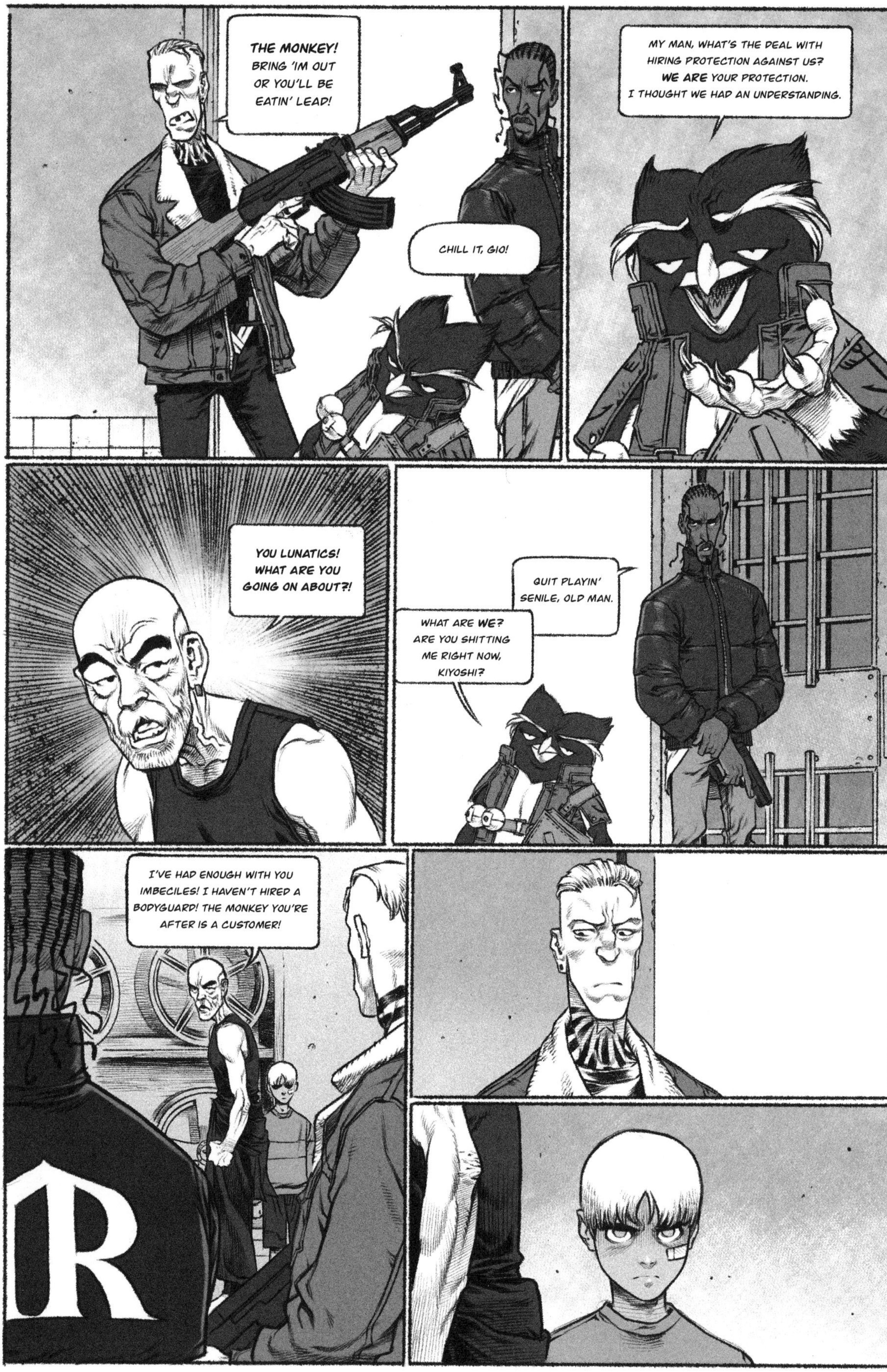
THE MONKEY! BRING 'IM OUT OR YOU'LL BE EATIN' LEAD!
CHILL IT, GIO!
MY MAN, WHAT'S THE DEAL WITH HIRING PROTECTION AGAINST US? WE ARE YOUR PROTECTION. I THOUGHT WE HAD AN UNDERSTANDING.
YOU LUNATICS! WHAT ARE YOU GOING ON ABOUT?!
QUIT PLAYIN' SENILE, OLD MAN.
WHAT ARE WE? ARE YOU SHITTING ME RIGHT NOW, KIYOSHI?
I'VE HAD ENOUGH WITH YOU IMBECILES! I HAVEN'T HIRED A BODYGUARD! THE MONKEY YOU'RE AFTER IS A CUSTOMER!
R

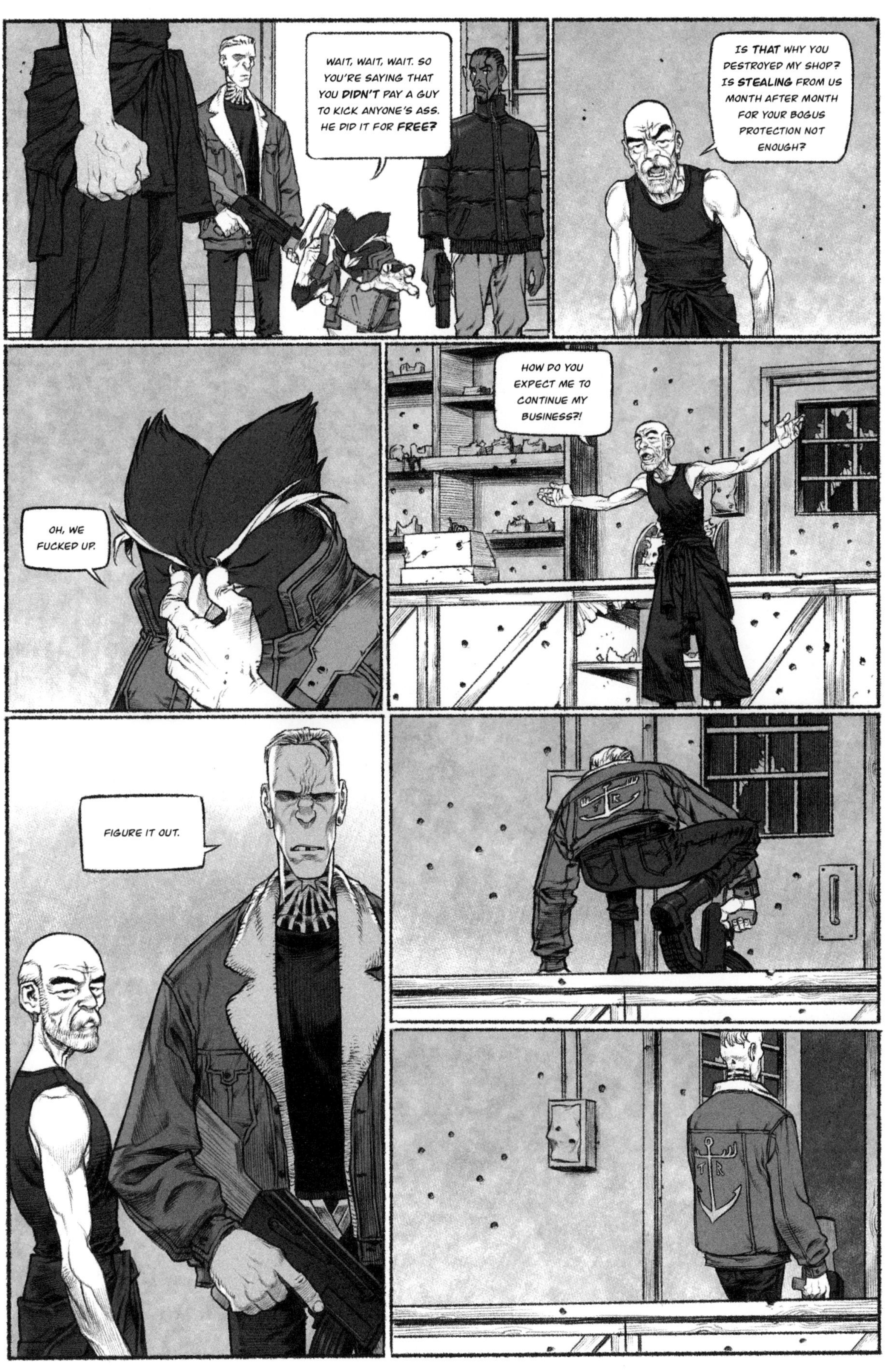
WAIT, WAIT, WAIT. SO YOU'RE SAYING THAT YOU DIDN'T PAY A GUY TO KICK ANYONE'S ASS. HE DID IT FOR FREE?
IS THAT WHY YOU DESTROYED MY SHOP? IS STEALING FROM US MONTH AFTER MONTH FOR YOUR BOGUS PROTECTION NOT ENOUGH?
OH, WE FUCKED UP.
HOW DO YOU EXPECT ME TO CONTINUE MY BUSINESS?!
FIGURE IT OUT.

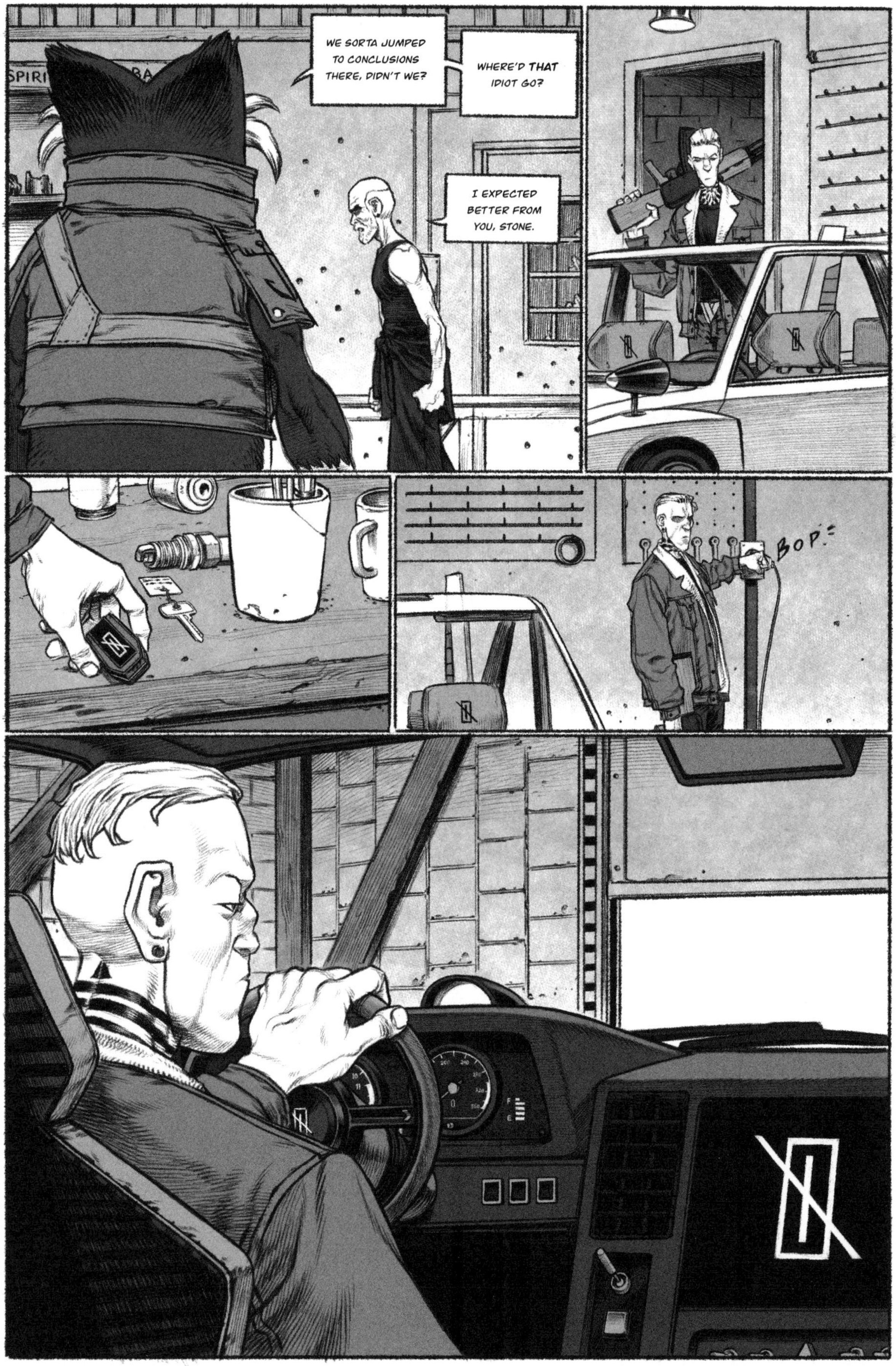

We sorta jumped to conclusions there, didn't we?
Where'd THAT idiot go?
I expected better from you, Stone.
BOP=

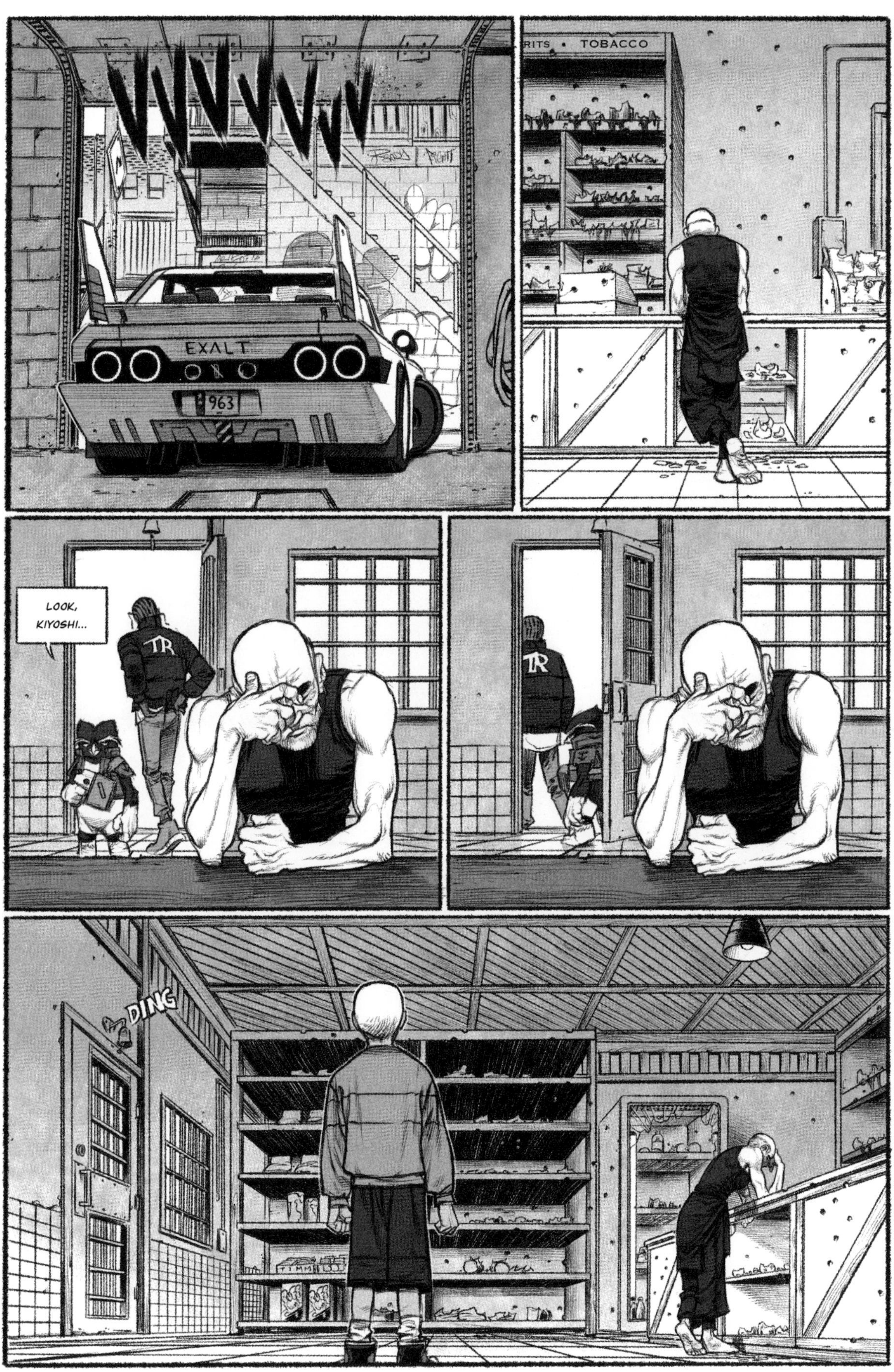
RITS • TOBACCO
EXALT
963
LOOK, KIYOSHI...
DING

KINGS OF NOWHERE

BFT
BLUB BLUB
CLICK

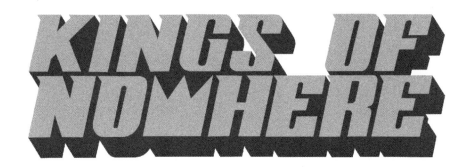

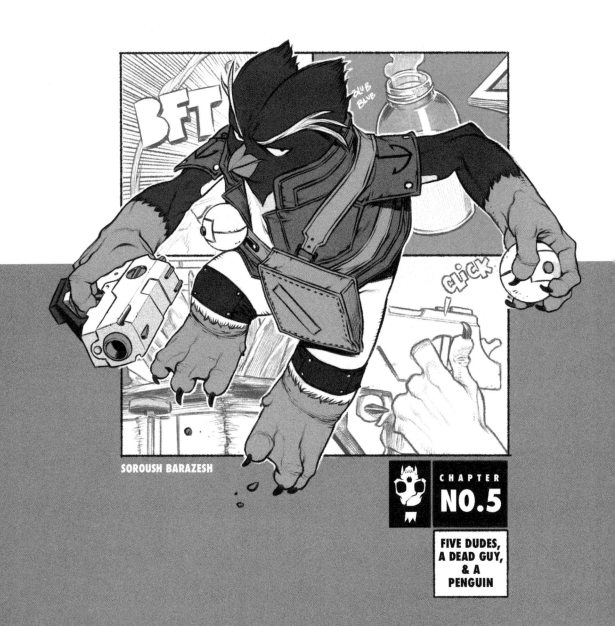

SOROUSH BARAZESH

CHAPTER

NO.5

FIVE DUDES, A DEAD GUY, & A PENGUIN

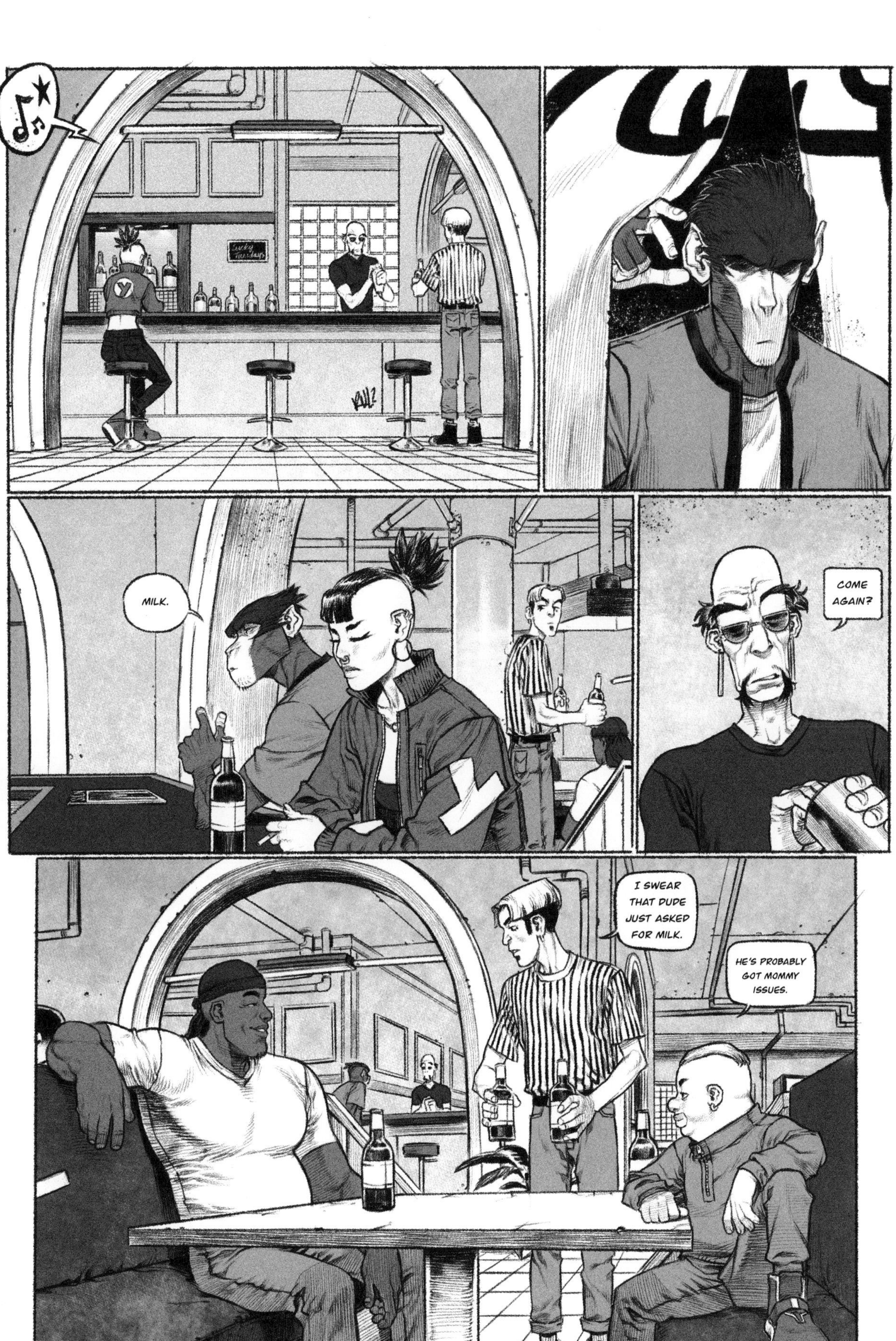
MILK.
COME AGAIN?
I SWEAR THAT DUDE JUST ASKED FOR MILK.
HE'S PROBABLY GOT MOMMY ISSUES.

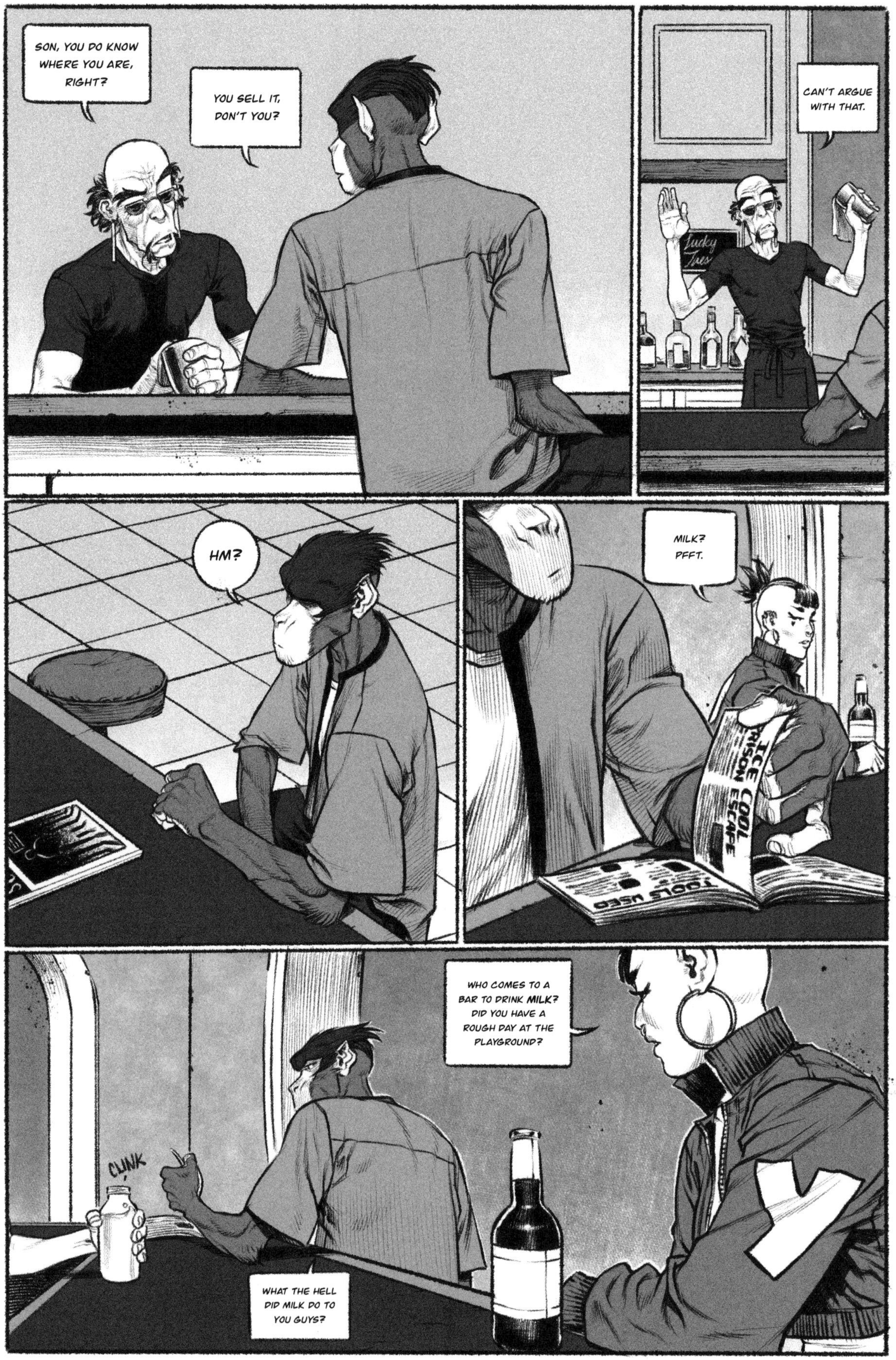
SON, YOU DO KNOW WHERE YOU ARE, RIGHT?
YOU SELL IT, DON'T YOU?
CAN'T ARGUE WITH THAT.
HM?
MILK? PFFT.
ICE COOL
TOOLS USED
WHO COMES TO A BAR TO DRINK MILK? DID YOU HAVE A ROUGH DAY AT THE PLAYGROUND?
CLINK
WHAT THE HELL DID MILK DO TO YOU GUYS?

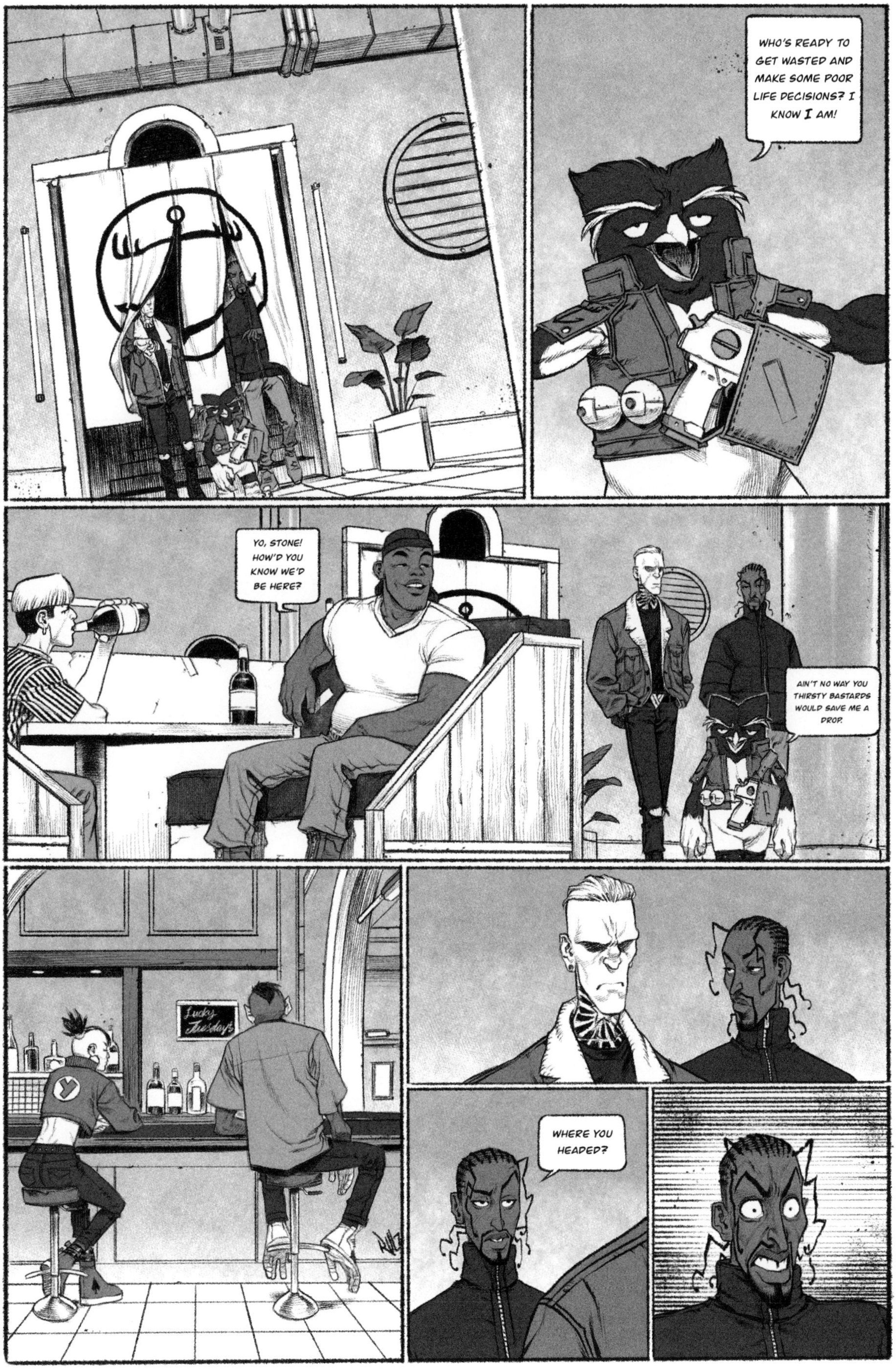
WHO'S READY TO GET WASTED AND MAKE SOME POOR LIFE DECISIONS? I KNOW I AM!
YO, STONE! HOW'D YOU KNOW WE'D BE HERE?
AIN'T NO WAY YOU THIRSTY BASTARDS WOULD SAVE ME A DROP.
WHERE YOU HEADED?

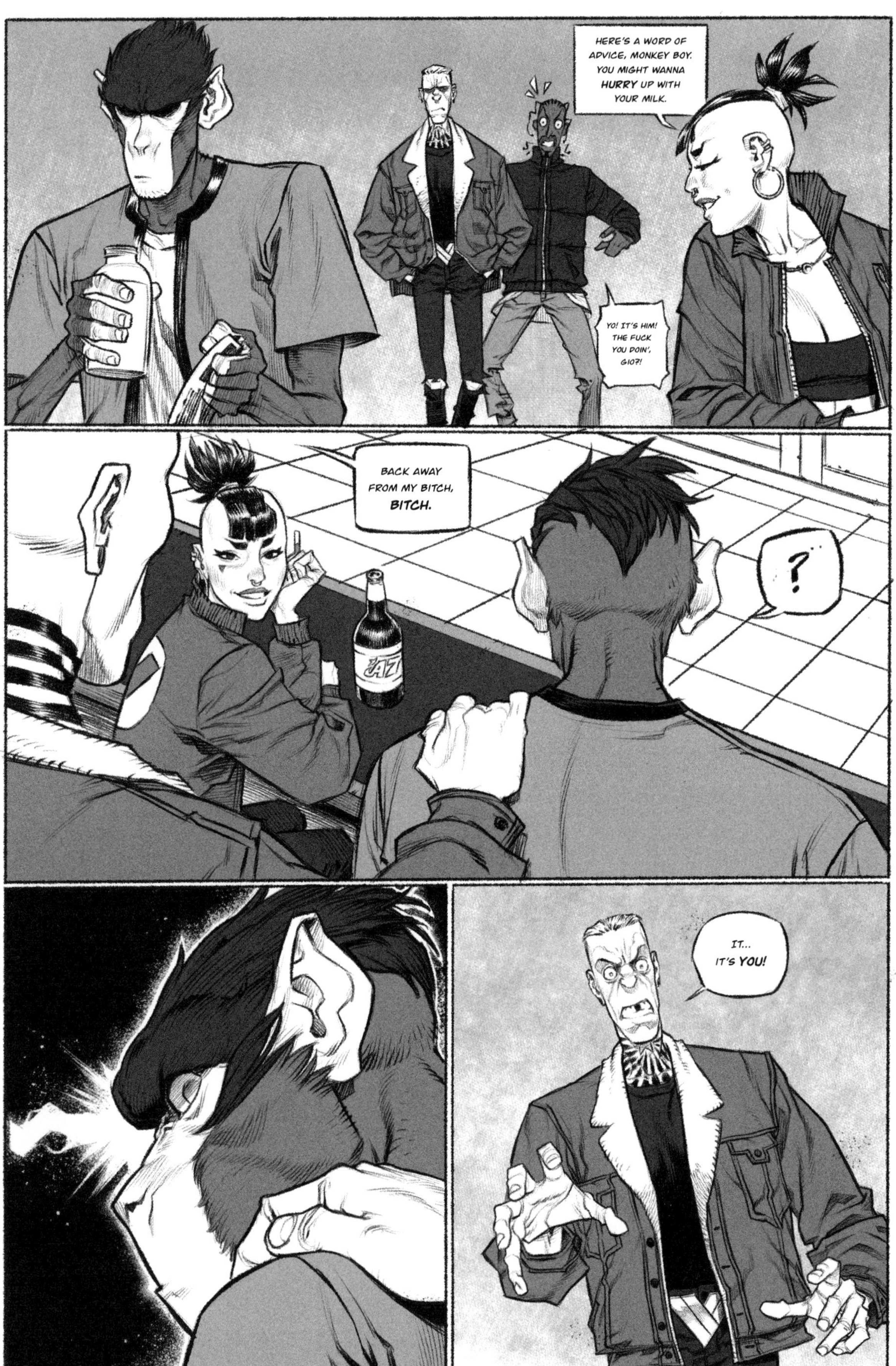
HERE'S A WORD OF ADVICE, MONKEY BOY. YOU MIGHT WANNA HURRY UP WITH YOUR MILK.
YO! IT'S HIM! THE FUCK YOU DOIN', GIO?!
BACK AWAY FROM MY BITCH, BITCH.
?
IT... IT'S YOU!

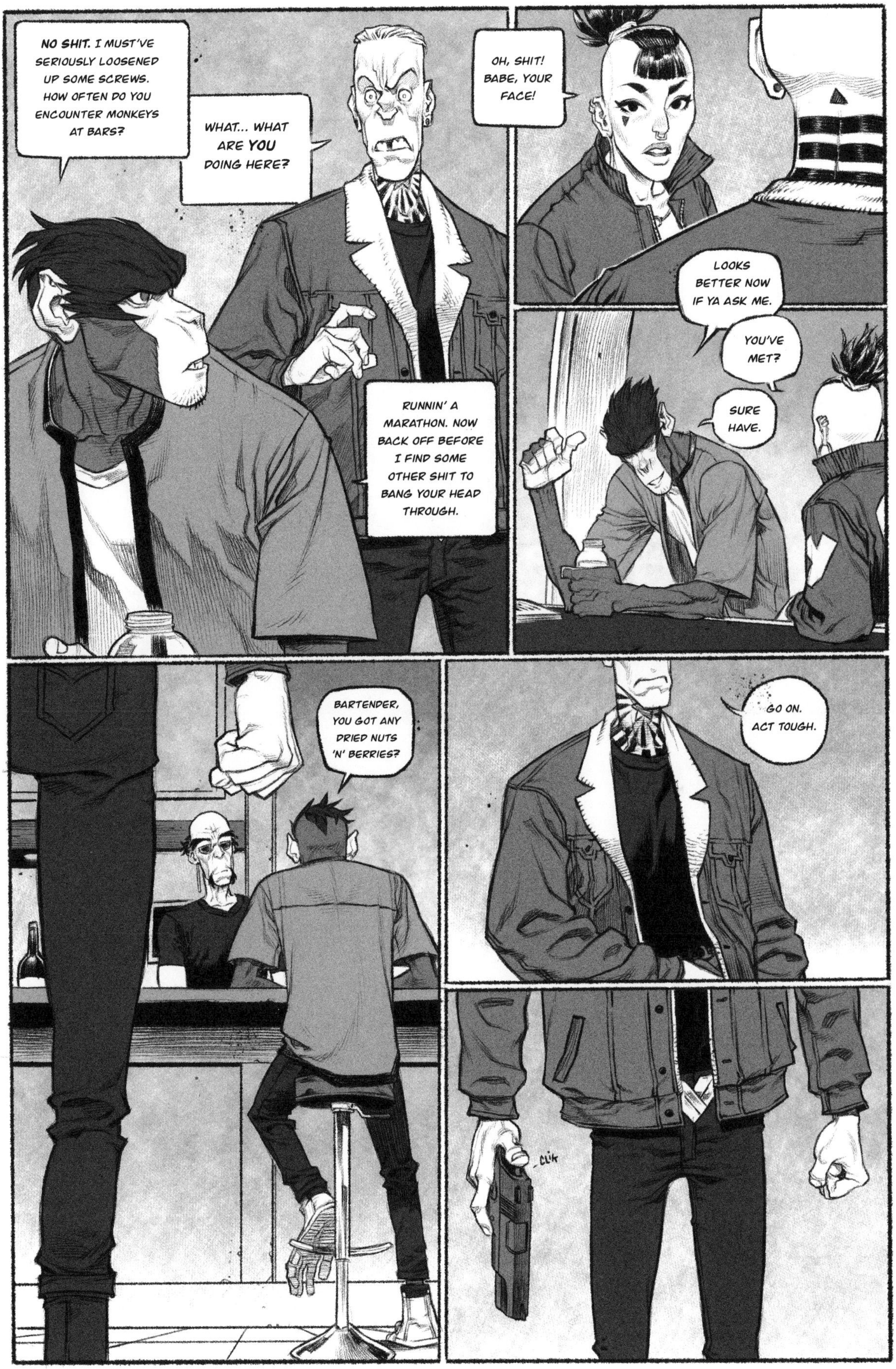
NO SHIT. I MUST'VE SERIOUSLY LOOSENED UP SOME SCREWS. HOW OFTEN DO YOU ENCOUNTER MONKEYS AT BARS?
WHAT... WHAT ARE YOU DOING HERE?
RUNNIN' A MARATHON. NOW BACK OFF BEFORE I FIND SOME OTHER SHIT TO BANG YOUR HEAD THROUGH.
OH, SHIT! BABE, YOUR FACE!
LOOKS BETTER NOW IF YA ASK ME.
YOU'VE MET?
SURE HAVE.
BARTENDER, YOU GOT ANY DRIED NUTS 'N' BERRIES?
GO ON. ACT TOUGH.
CLIK

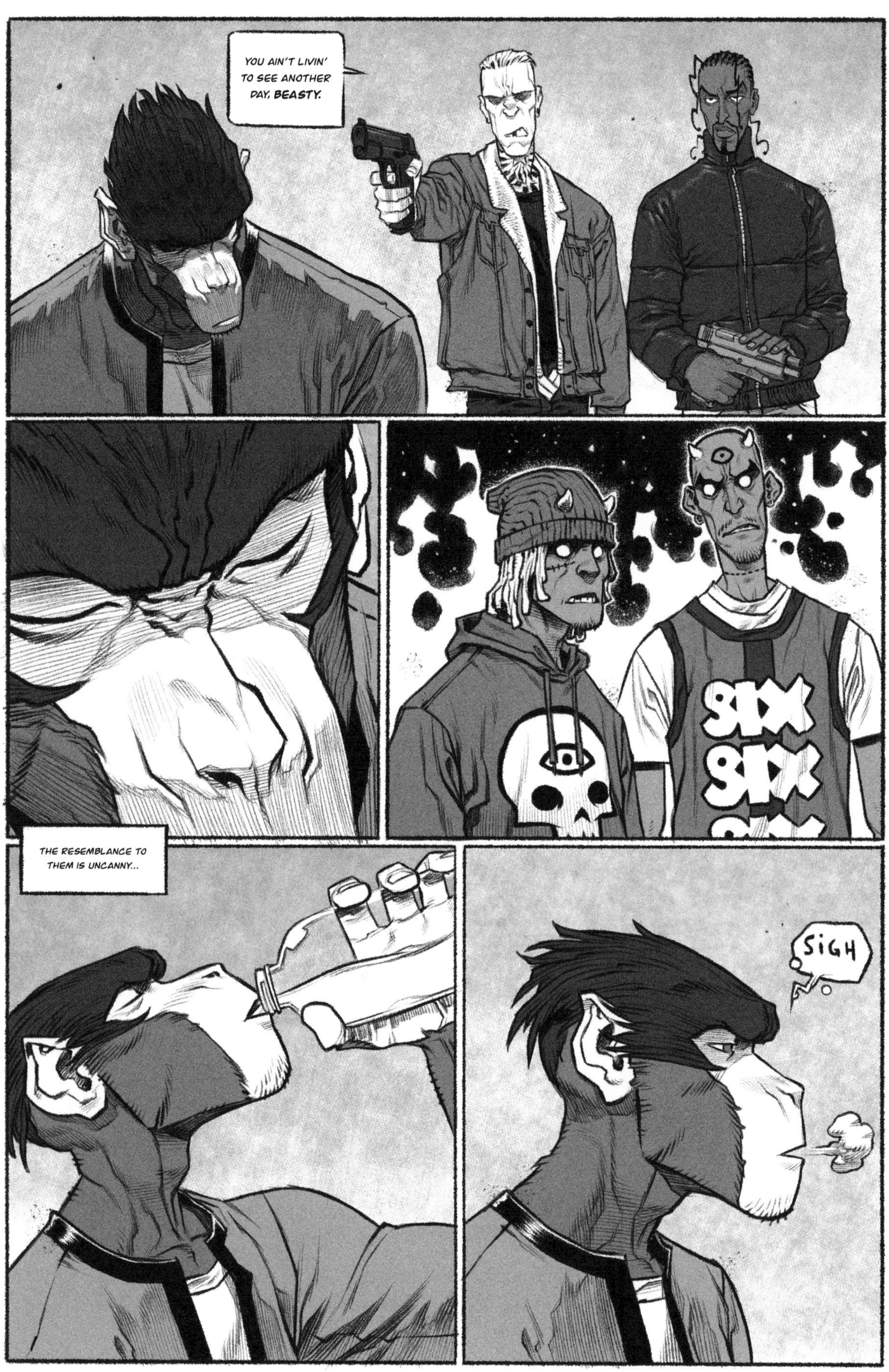
YOU AIN'T LIVIN' TO SEE ANOTHER DAY, **BEASTY.**
SIX
SIX
THE RESEMBLANCE TO THEM IS UNCANNY...
SIGH

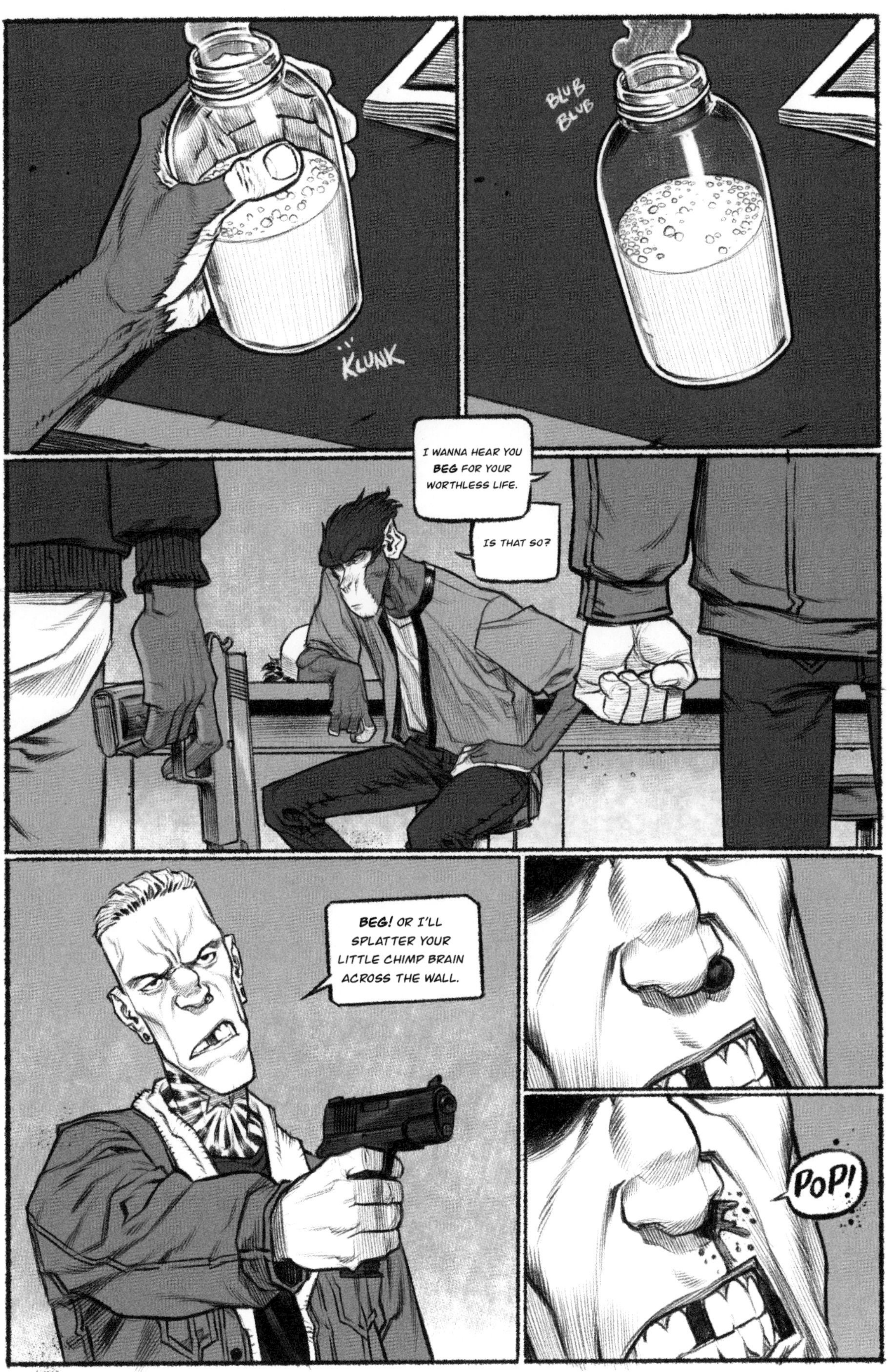
KLUNK
BLUB BLUB
I WANNA HEAR YOU BEG FOR YOUR WORTHLESS LIFE.
IS THAT SO?
BEG! OR I'LL SPLATTER YOUR LITTLE CHIMP BRAIN ACROSS THE WALL.
POP!

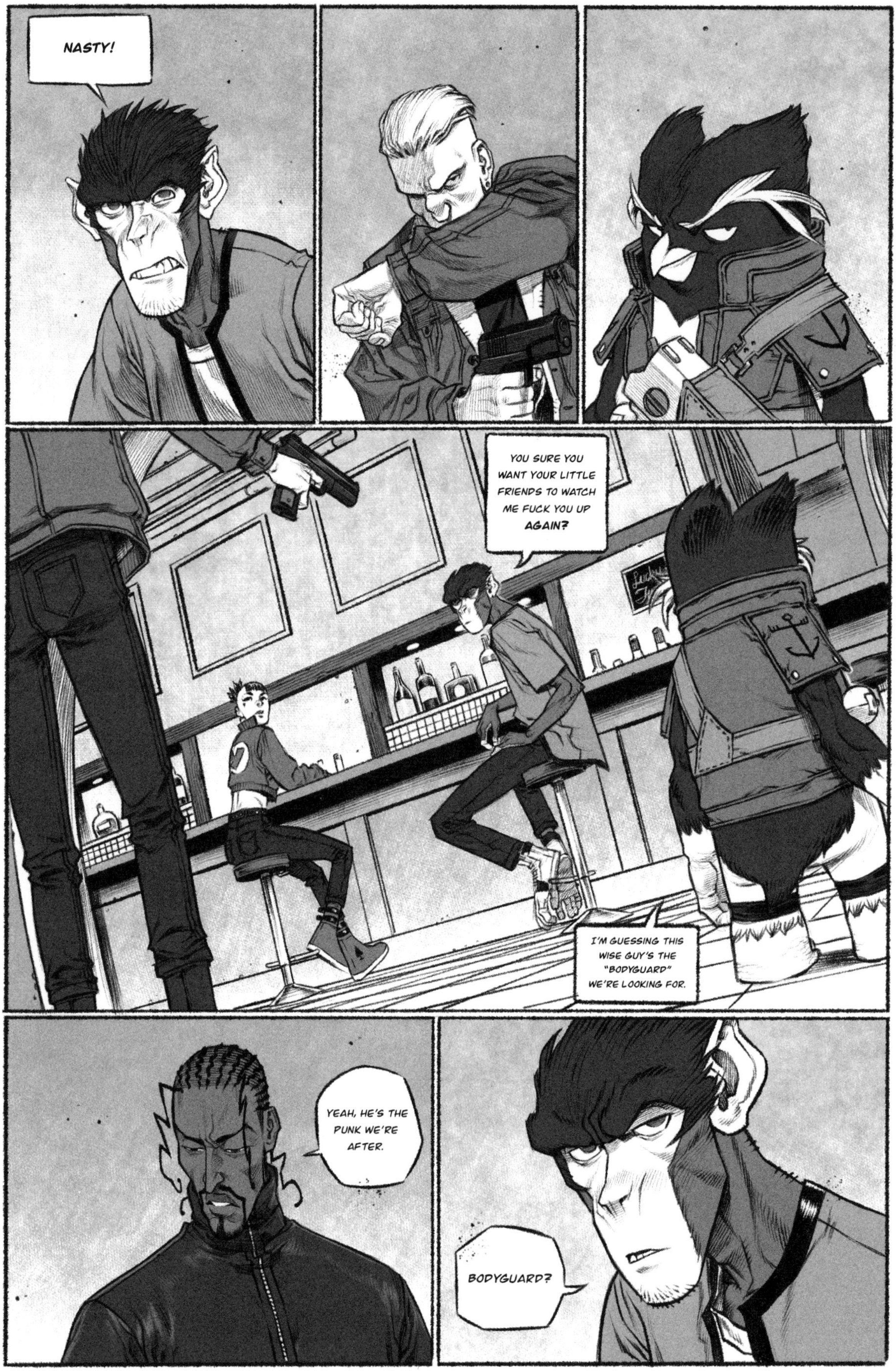
NASTY!
YOU SURE YOU WANT YOUR LITTLE FRIENDS TO WATCH ME FUCK YOU UP AGAIN?
I'M GUESSING THIS WISE GUY'S THE "BODYGUARD" WE'RE LOOKING FOR.
YEAH, HE'S THE PUNK WE'RE AFTER.
BODYGUARD?

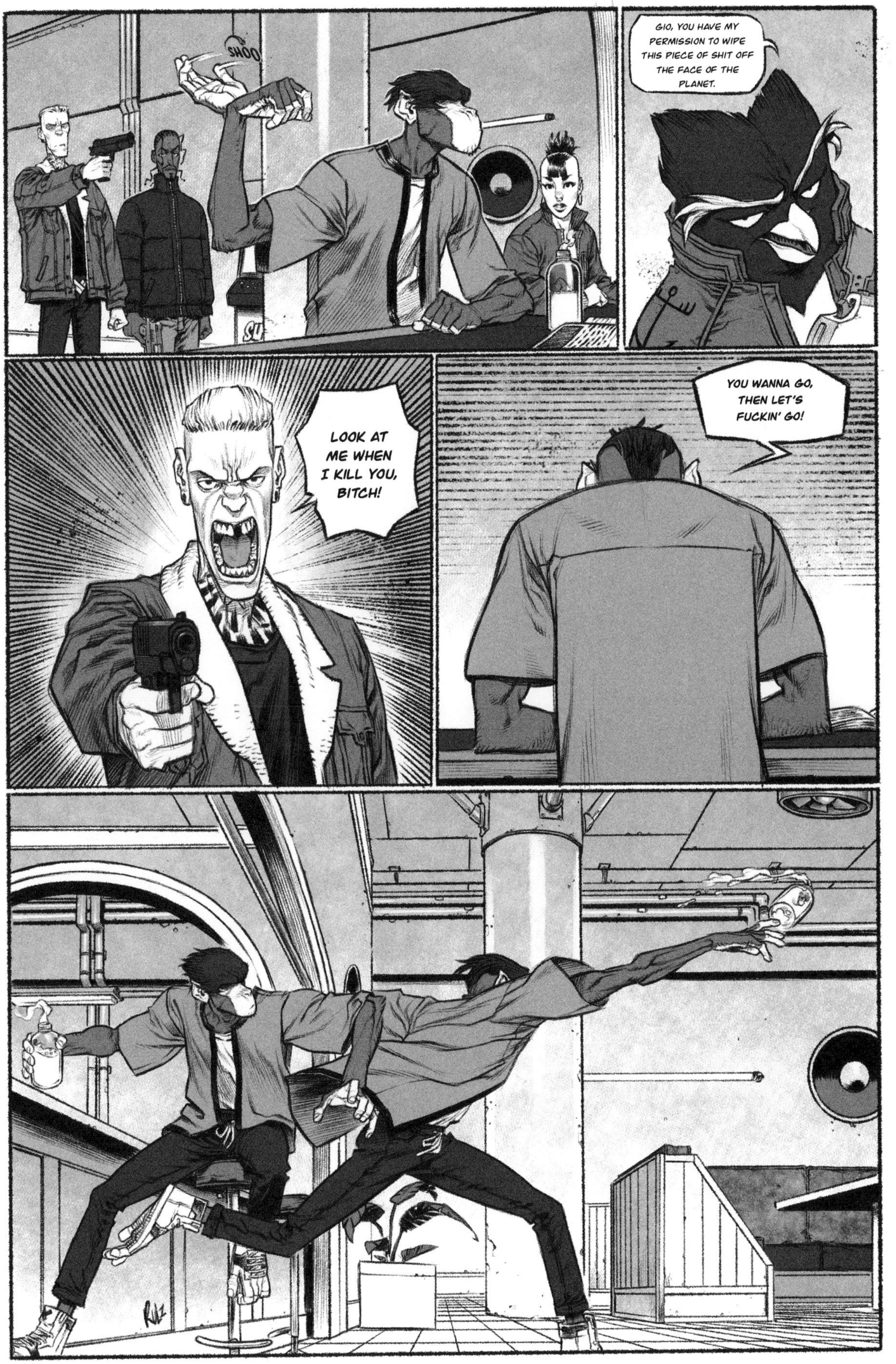
SHOOO
GIO, YOU HAVE MY PERMISSION TO WIPE THIS PIECE OF SHIT OFF THE FACE OF THE PLANET.
LOOK AT ME WHEN I KILL YOU, BITCH!
YOU WANNA GO, THEN LET'S FUCKIN' GO!

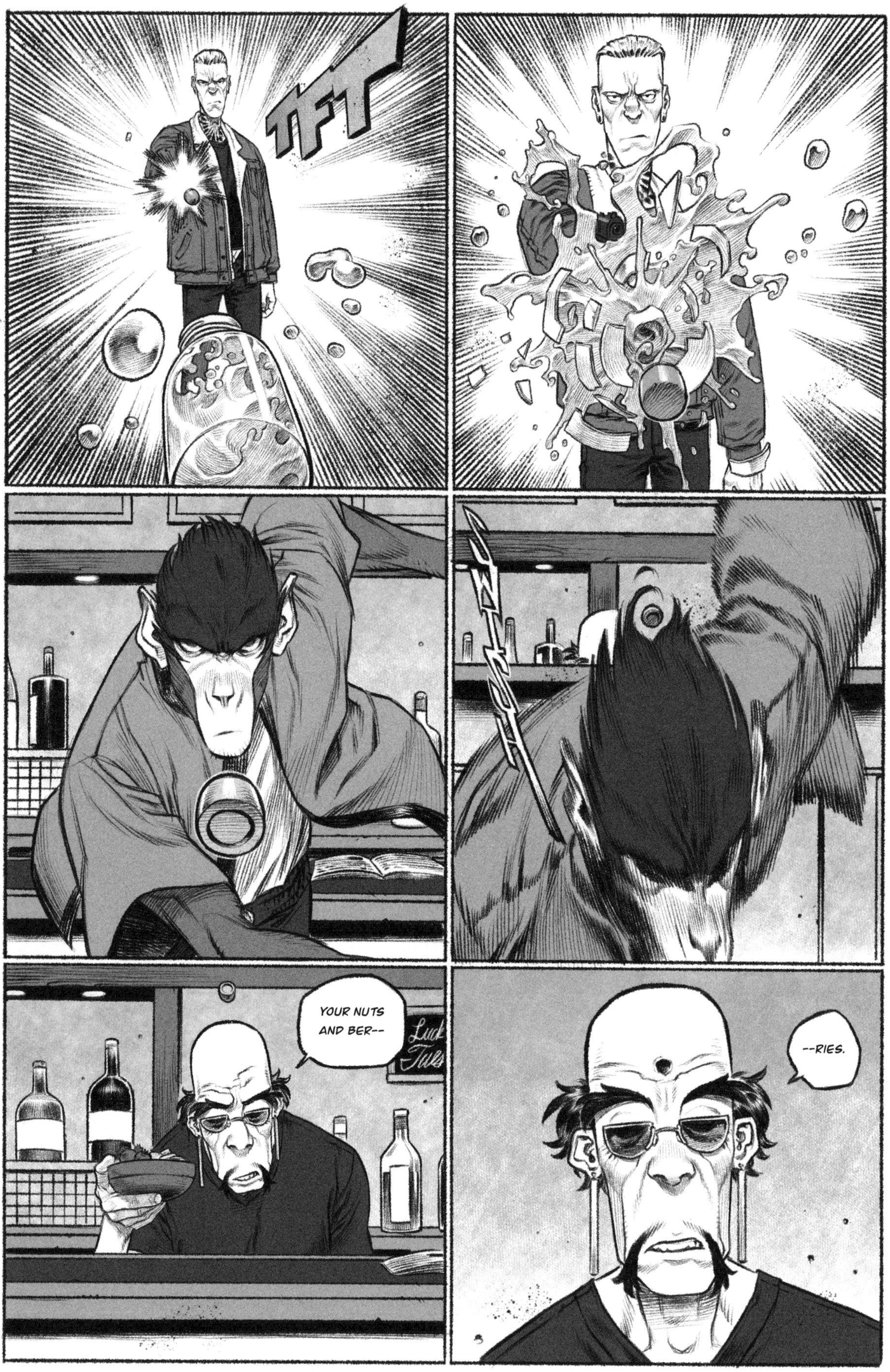
TFT
YOUR NUTS AND BER--
--RIES.

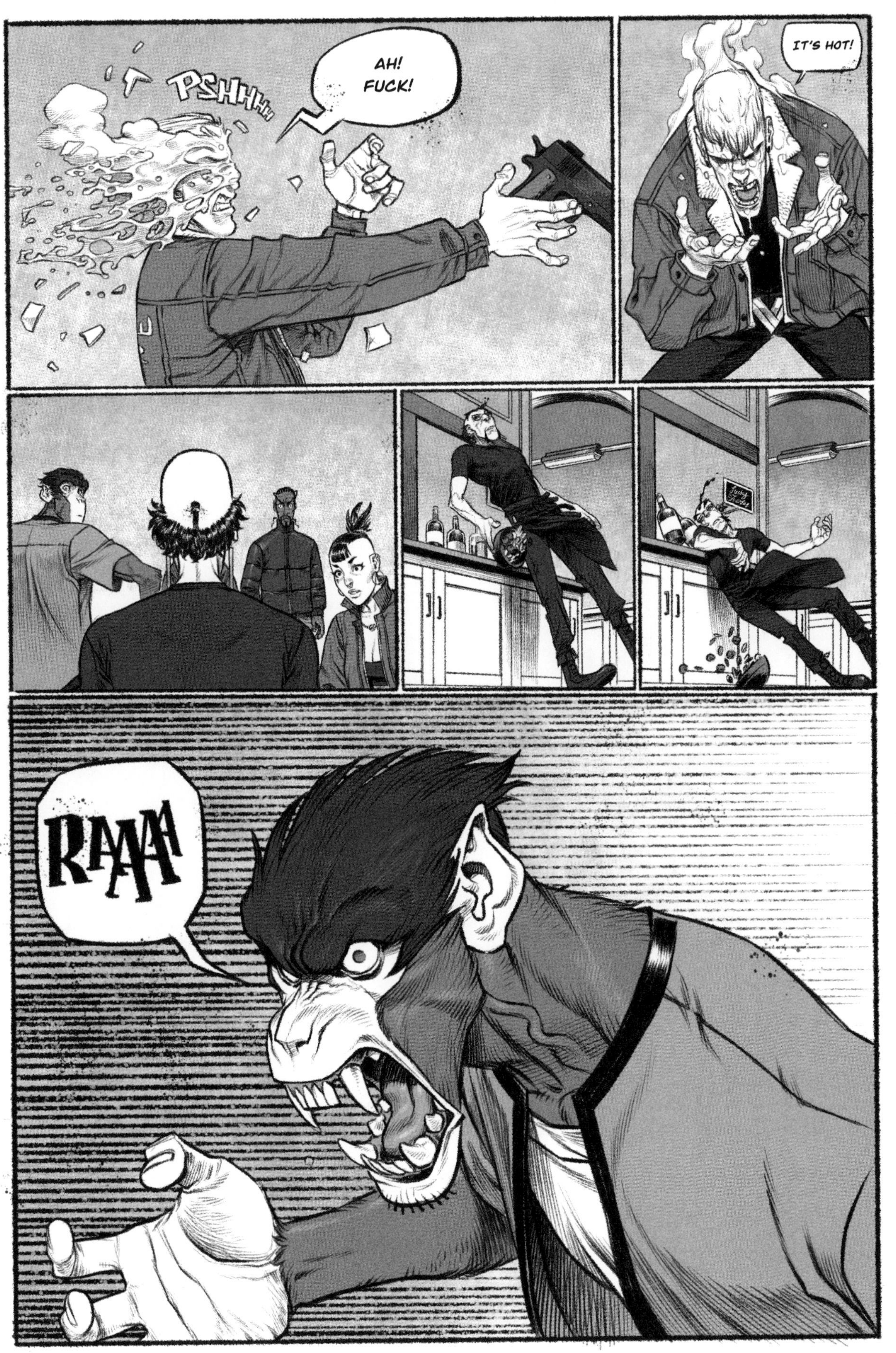
PSHHHHH
AH! FUCK!
IT'S HOT!
RAAAA

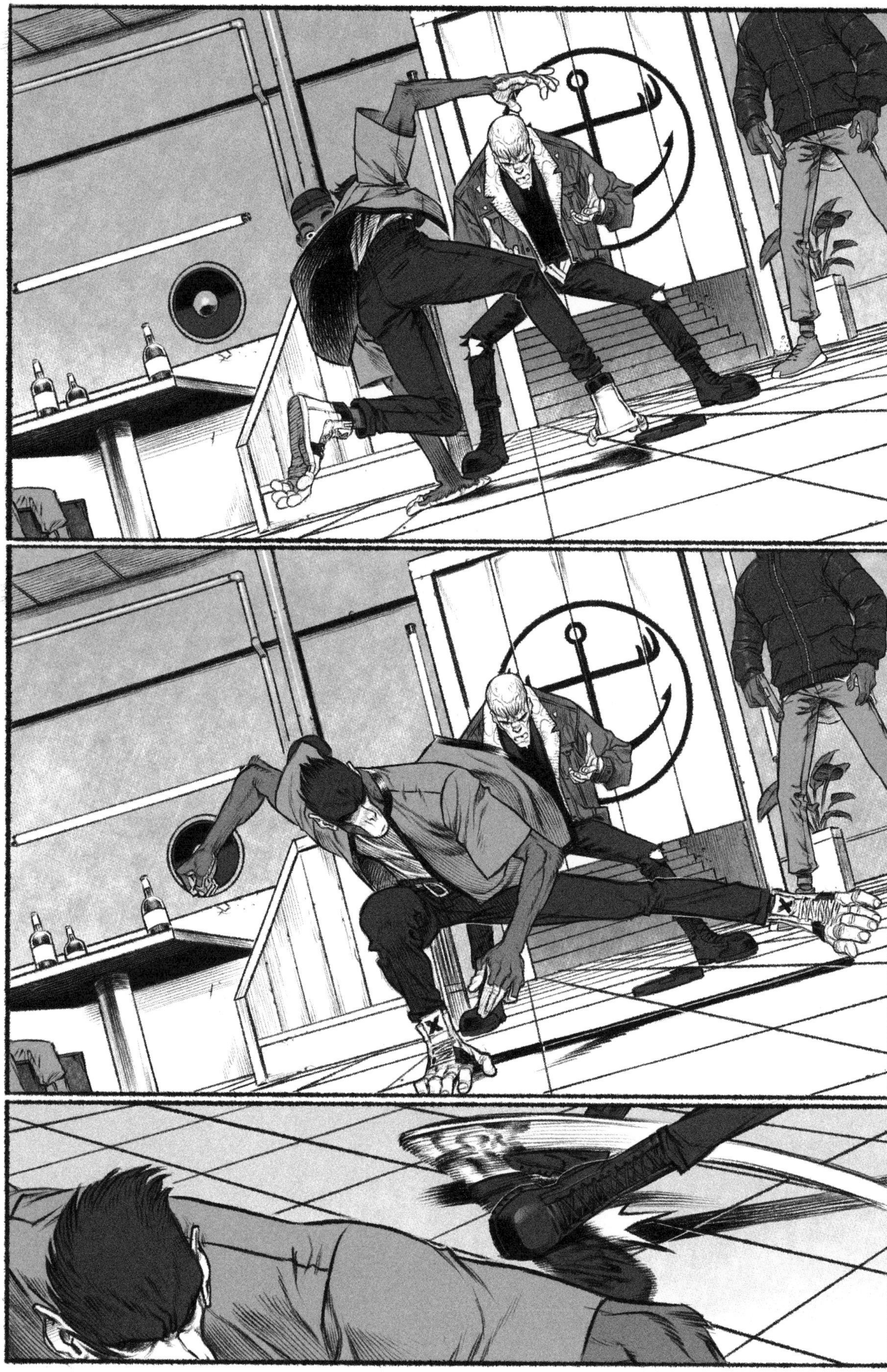

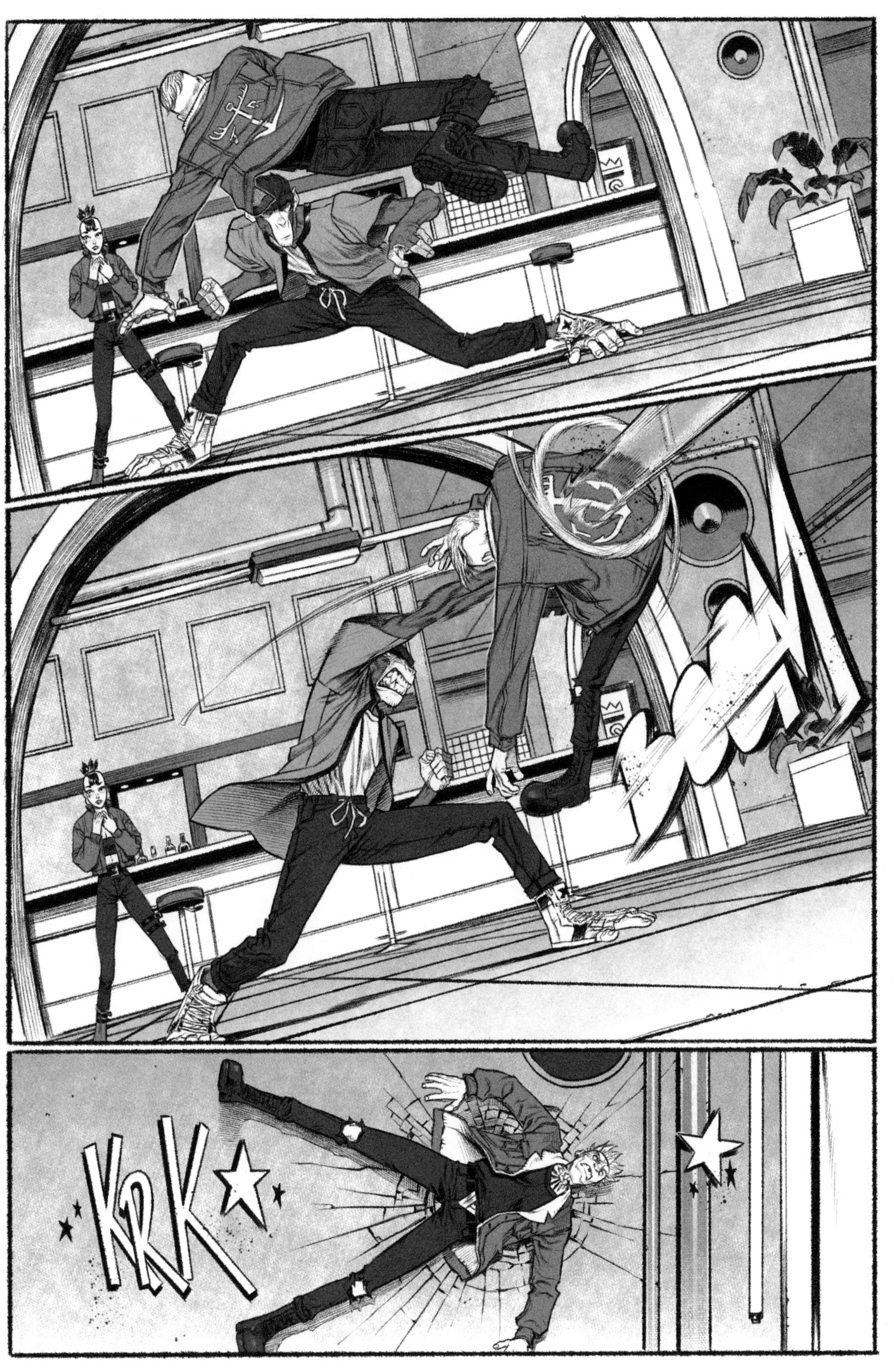
KRK

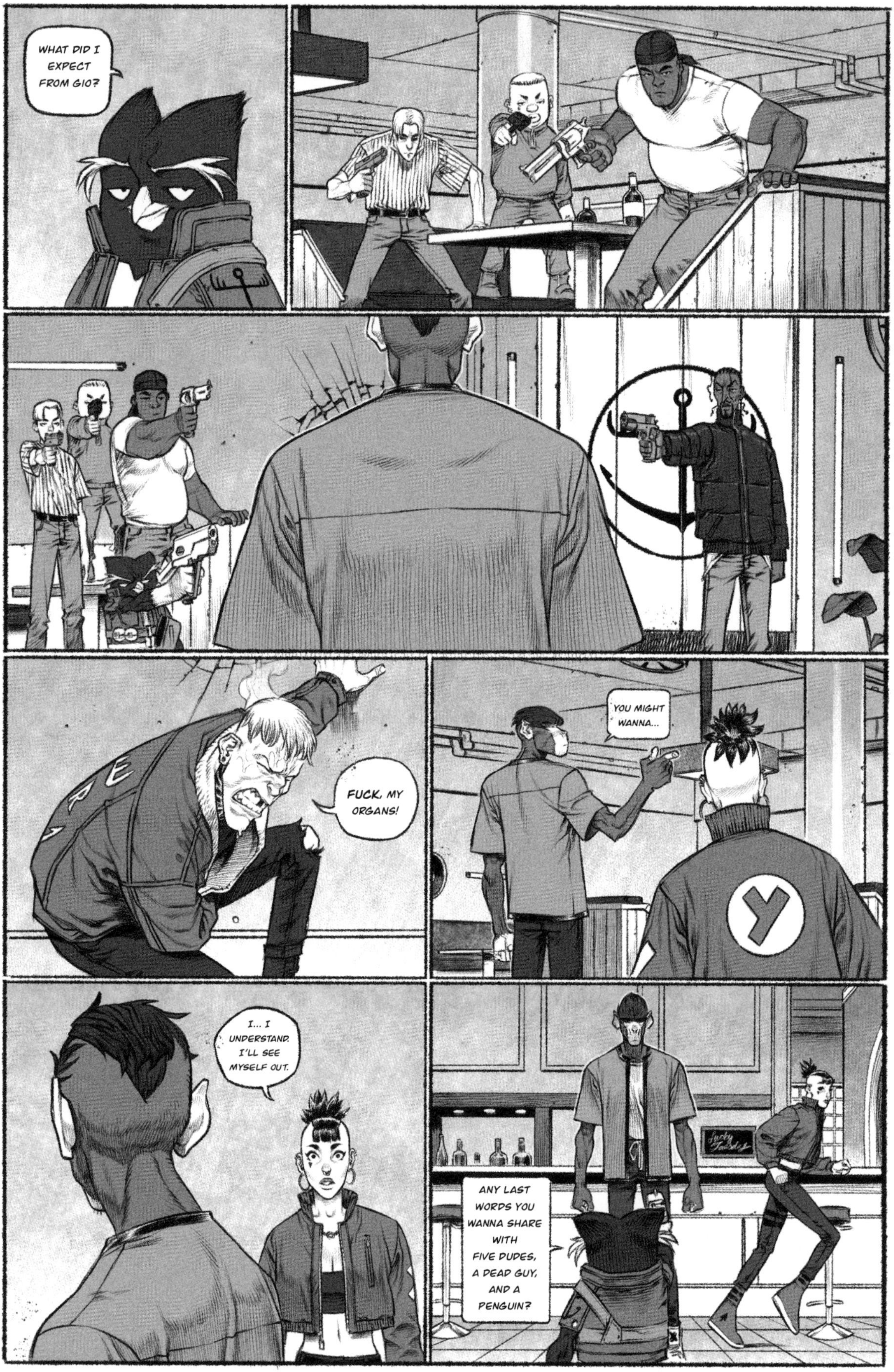
WHAT DID I EXPECT FROM GIO?
FUCK, MY ORGANS!
YOU MIGHT WANNA...
I... I UNDERSTAND. I'LL SEE MYSELF OUT.
ANY LAST WORDS YOU WANNA SHARE WITH FIVE DUDES, A DEAD GUY, AND A PENGUIN?

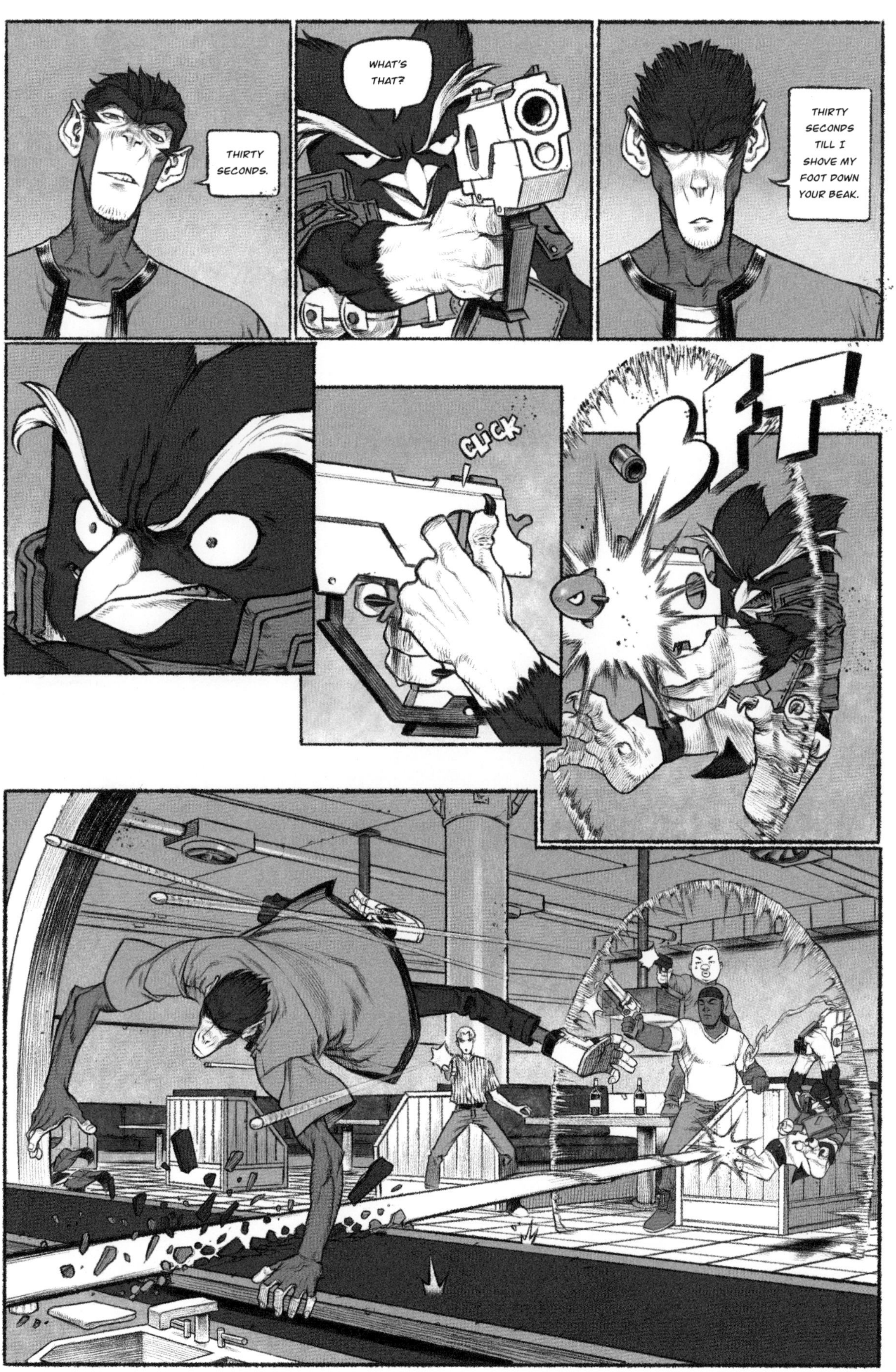
THIRTY SECONDS.
WHAT'S THAT?
THIRTY SECONDS TILL I SHOVE MY FOOT DOWN YOUR BEAK.
CLICK

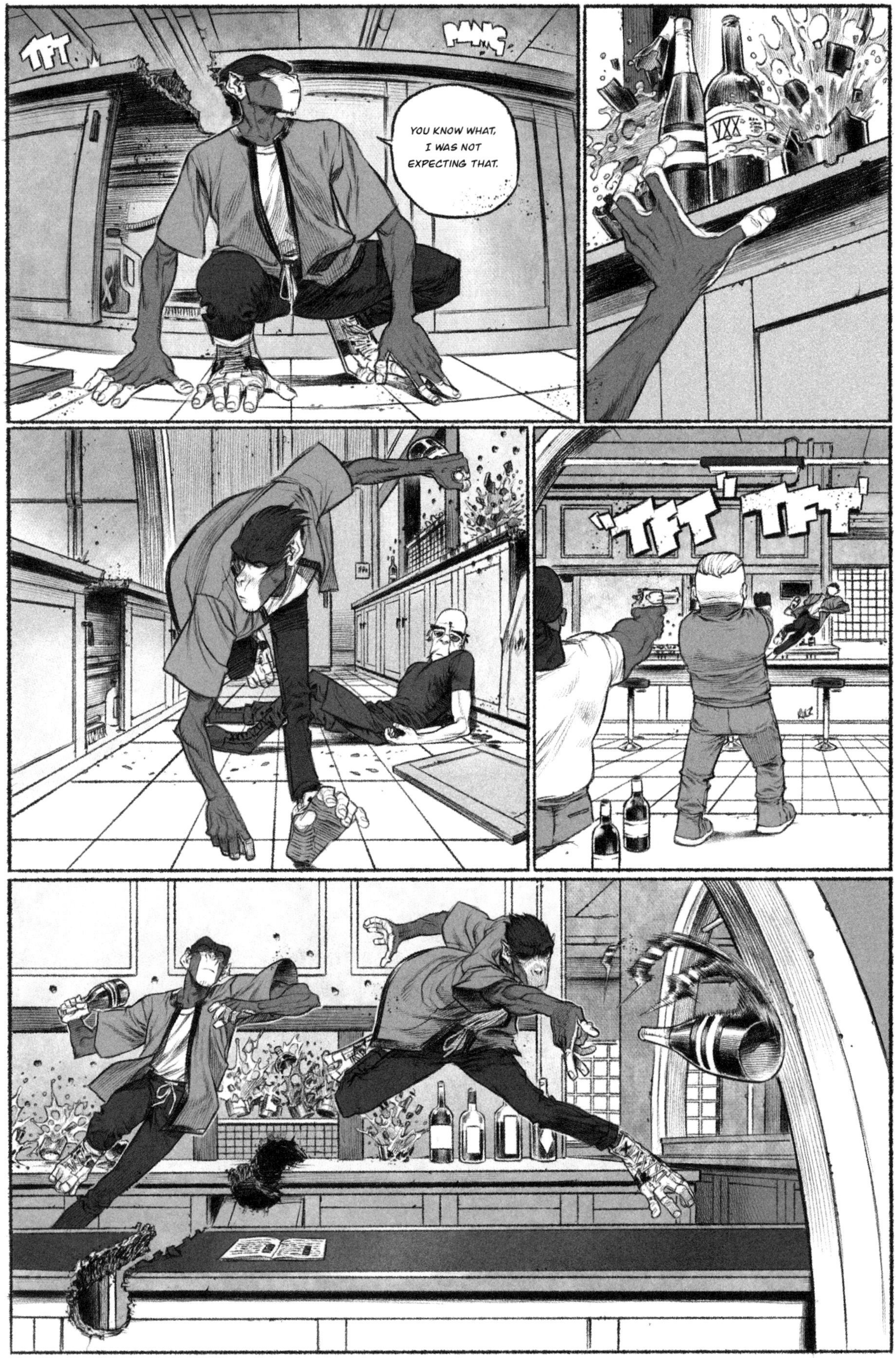
TFT
BANG
YOU KNOW WHAT, I WAS NOT EXPECTING THAT.
TFT TFT

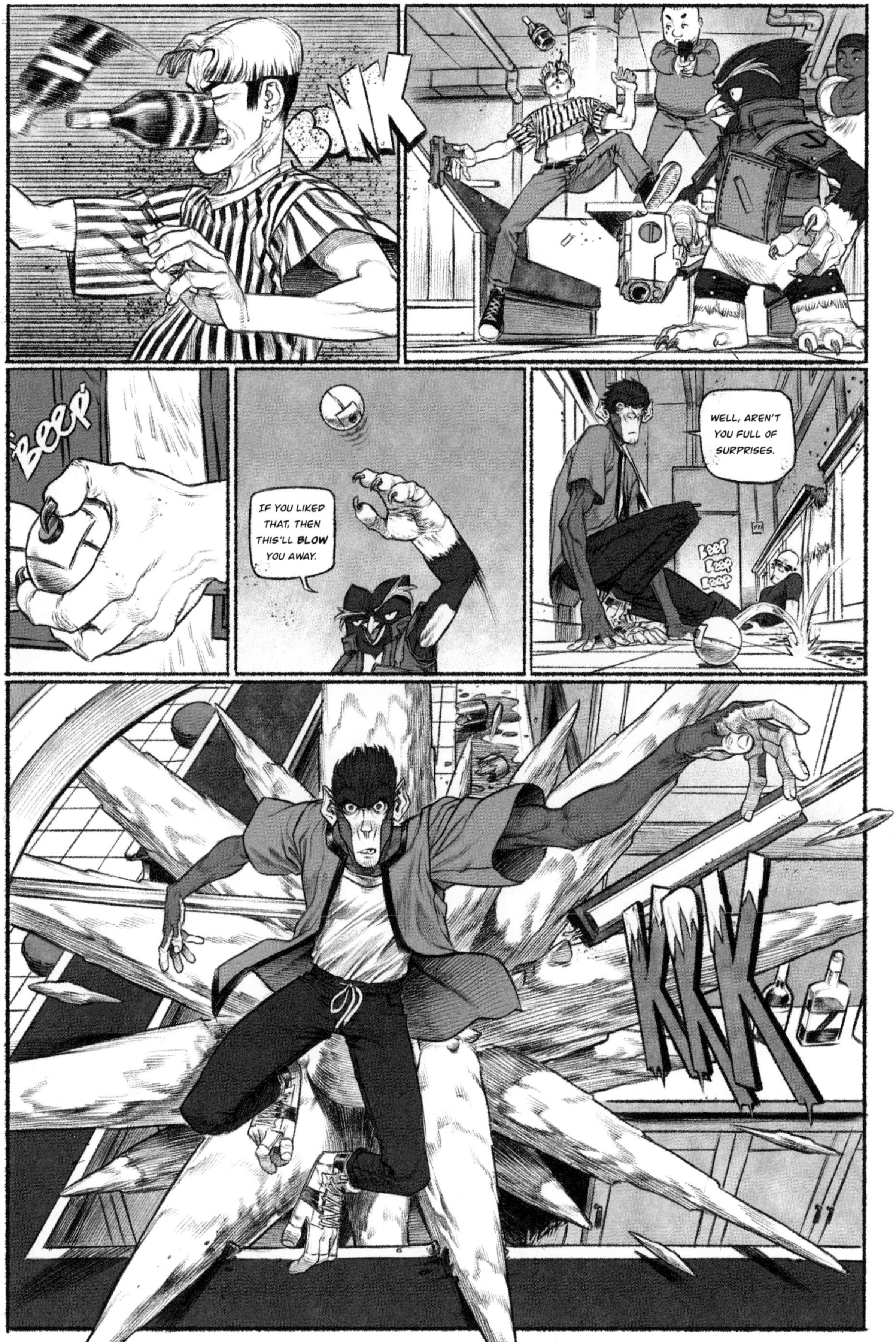
BEEP
IF YOU LIKED THAT, THEN THIS'LL **BLOW** YOU AWAY.
WELL, AREN'T YOU FULL OF SURPRISES.
BEEP BEEP BEEP

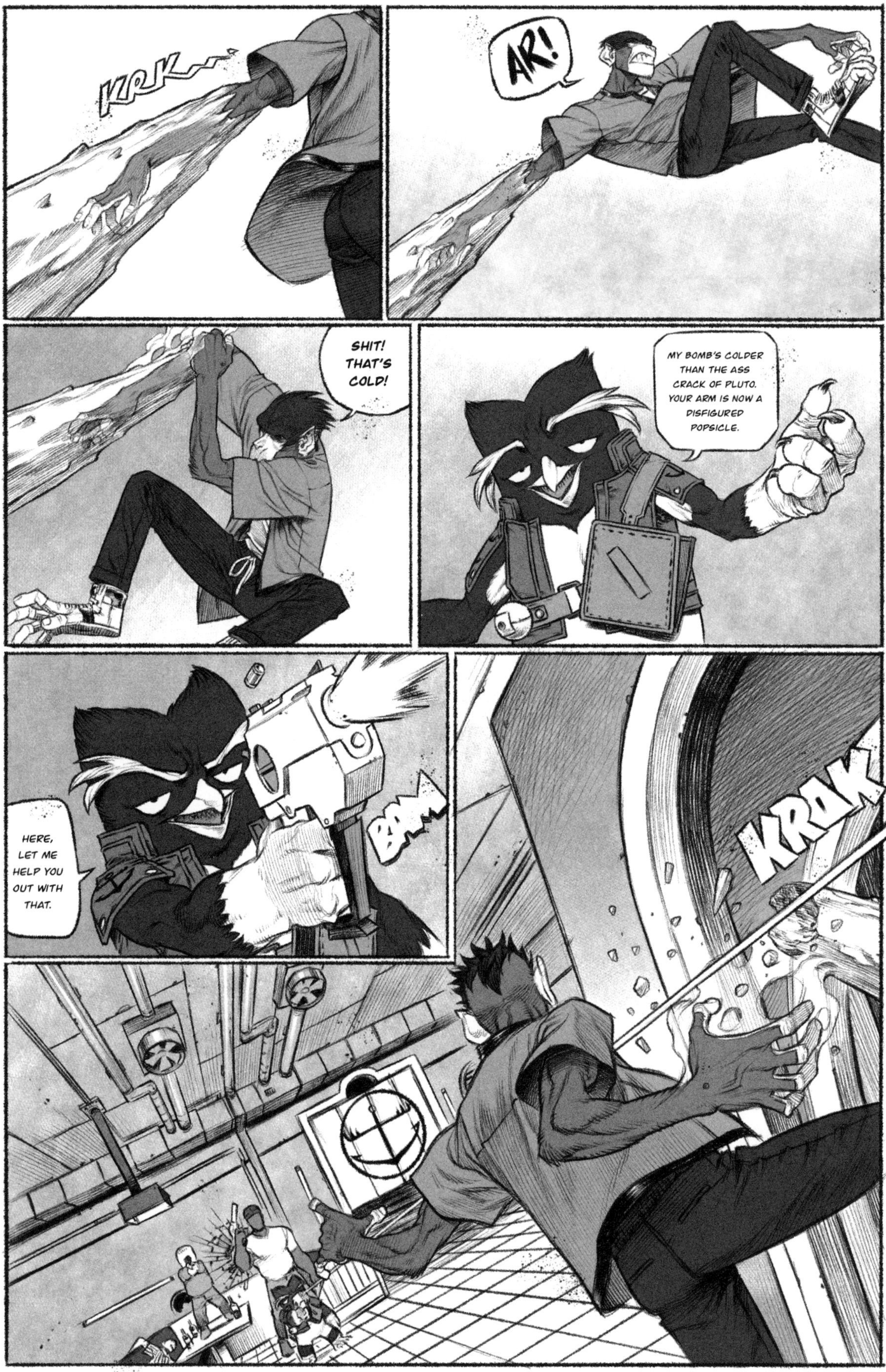
KRK
AR!
SHIT! THAT'S COLD!
MY BOMB'S COLDER THAN THE ASS CRACK OF PLUTO. YOUR ARM IS NOW A DISFIGURED POPSICLE.
HERE, LET ME HELP YOU OUT WITH THAT.
BAM
KRAK

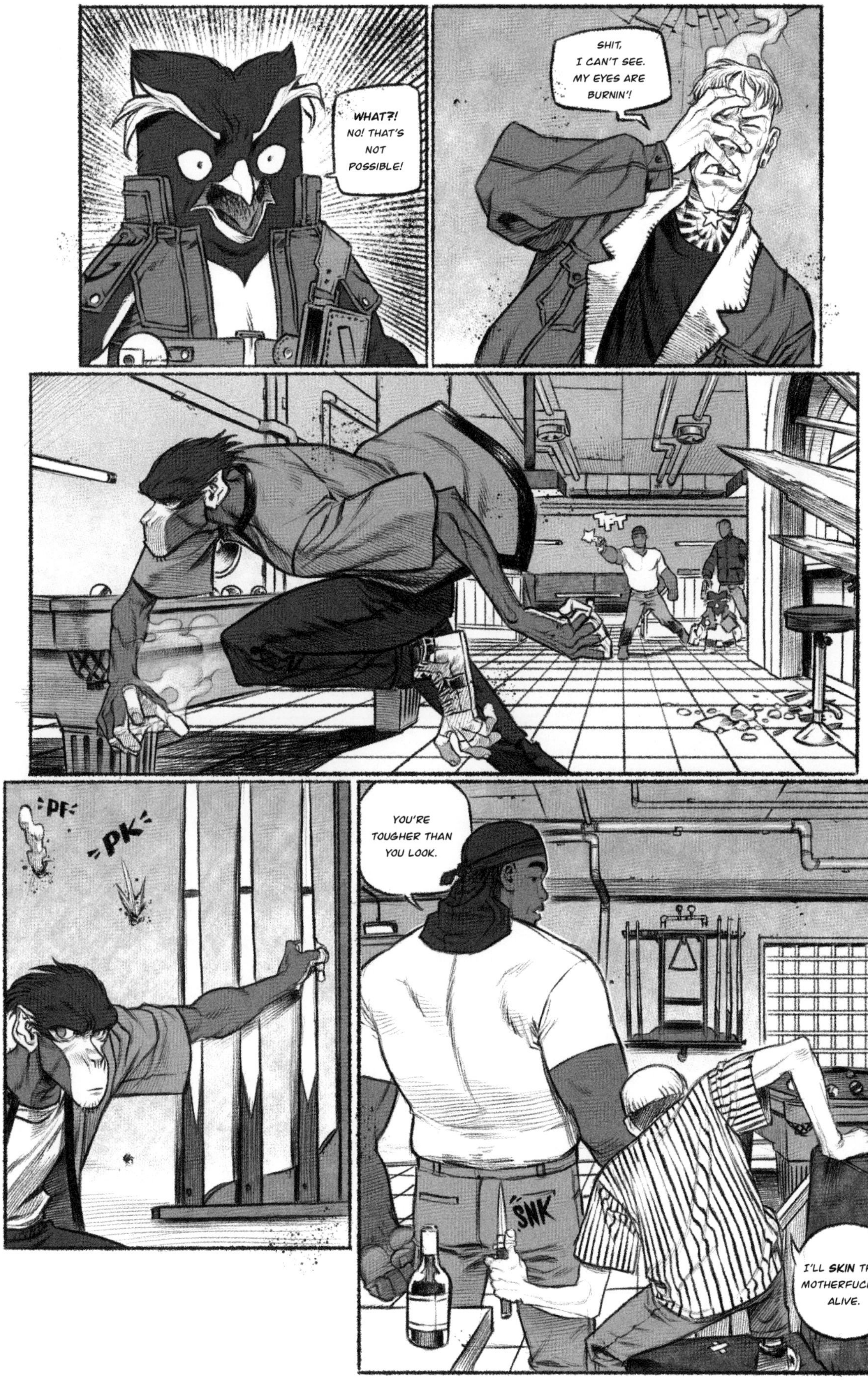
WHAT?! NO! THAT'S NOT POSSIBLE!
SHIT, I CAN'T SEE. MY EYES ARE BURNIN'!
TFT
PF
PK
YOU'RE TOUGHER THAN YOU LOOK.
SNK
I'LL SKIN THAT MOTHERFUCKER ALIVE.

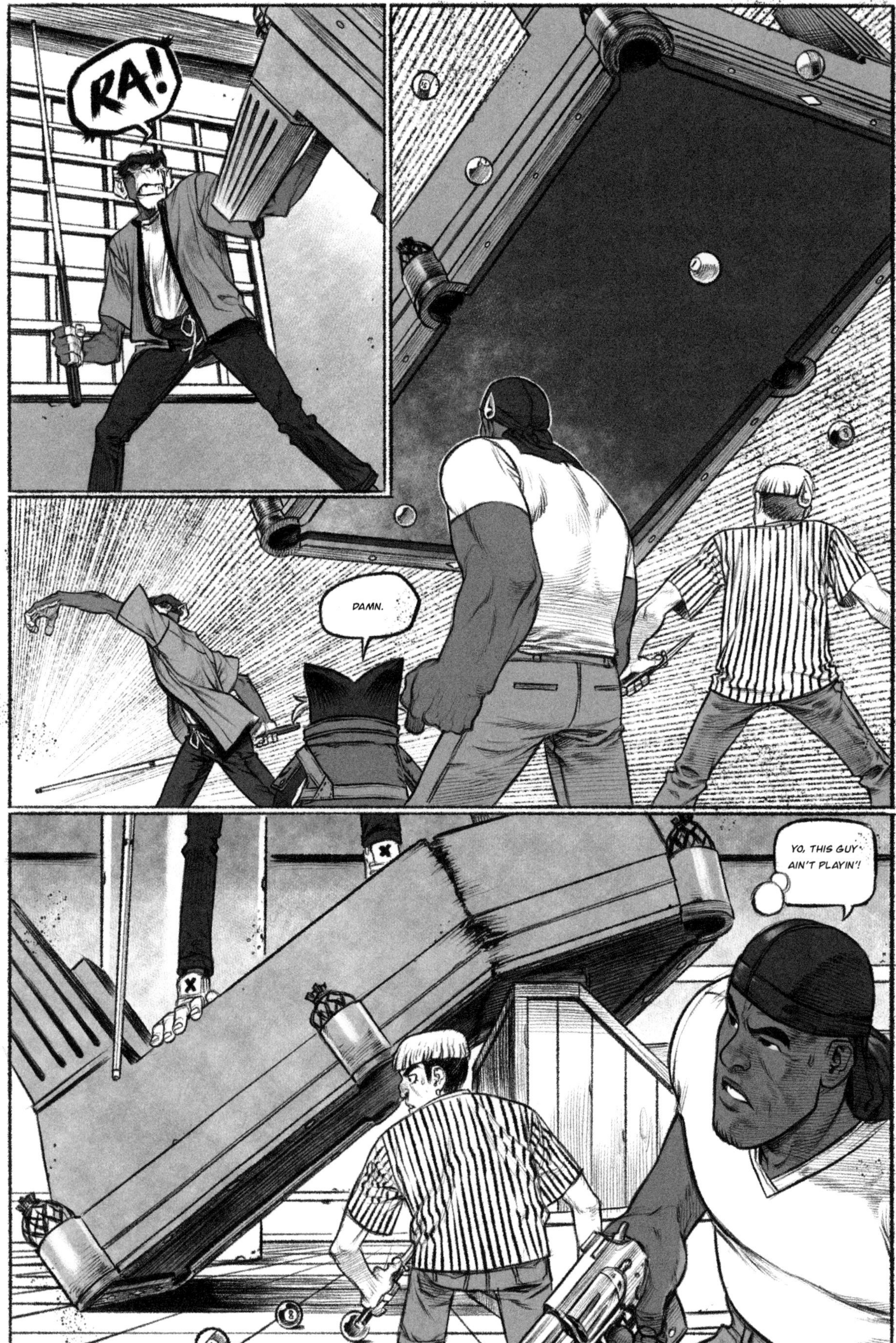
RA!
DAMN.
YO, THIS GUY AIN'T PLAYIN'!

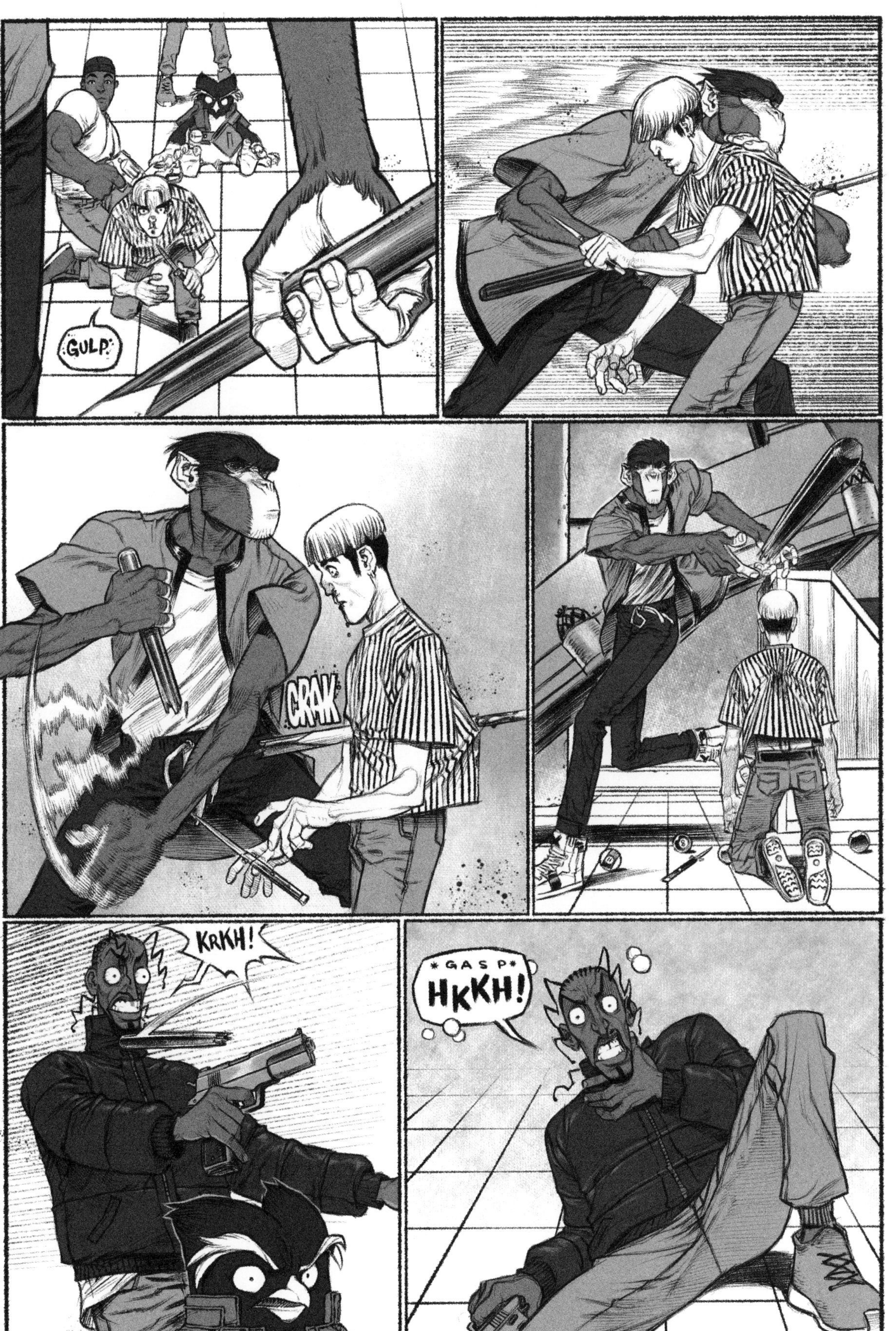
GULP
CRAK
KRKH!
GASP
HKKH!

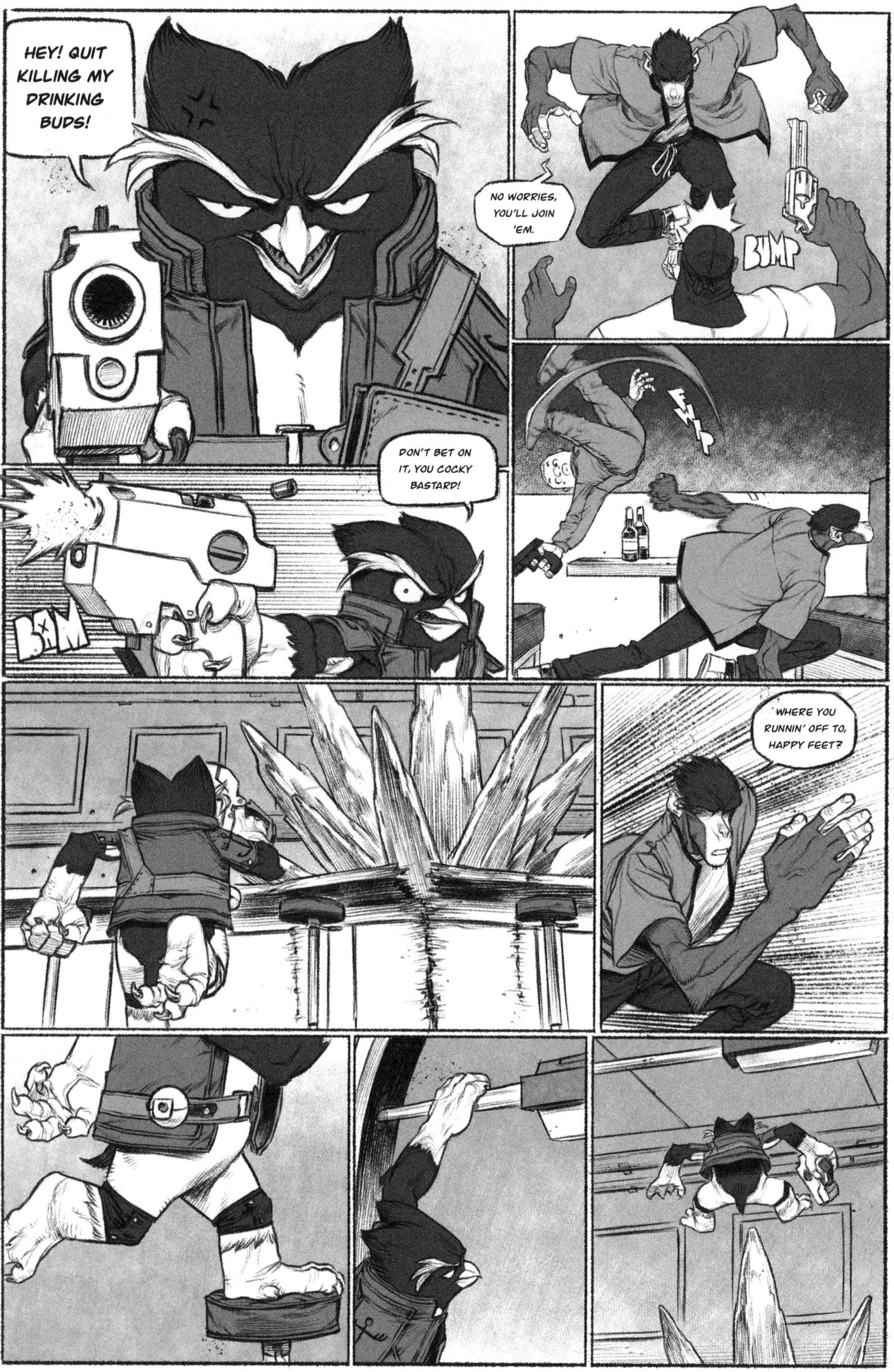
HEY! QUIT KILLING MY DRINKING BUDS!
NO WORRIES, YOU'LL JOIN 'EM.
BUMP
FWIP
DON'T BET ON IT, YOU COCKY BASTARD!
BAM
WHERE YOU RUNNIN' OFF TO, HAPPY FEET?

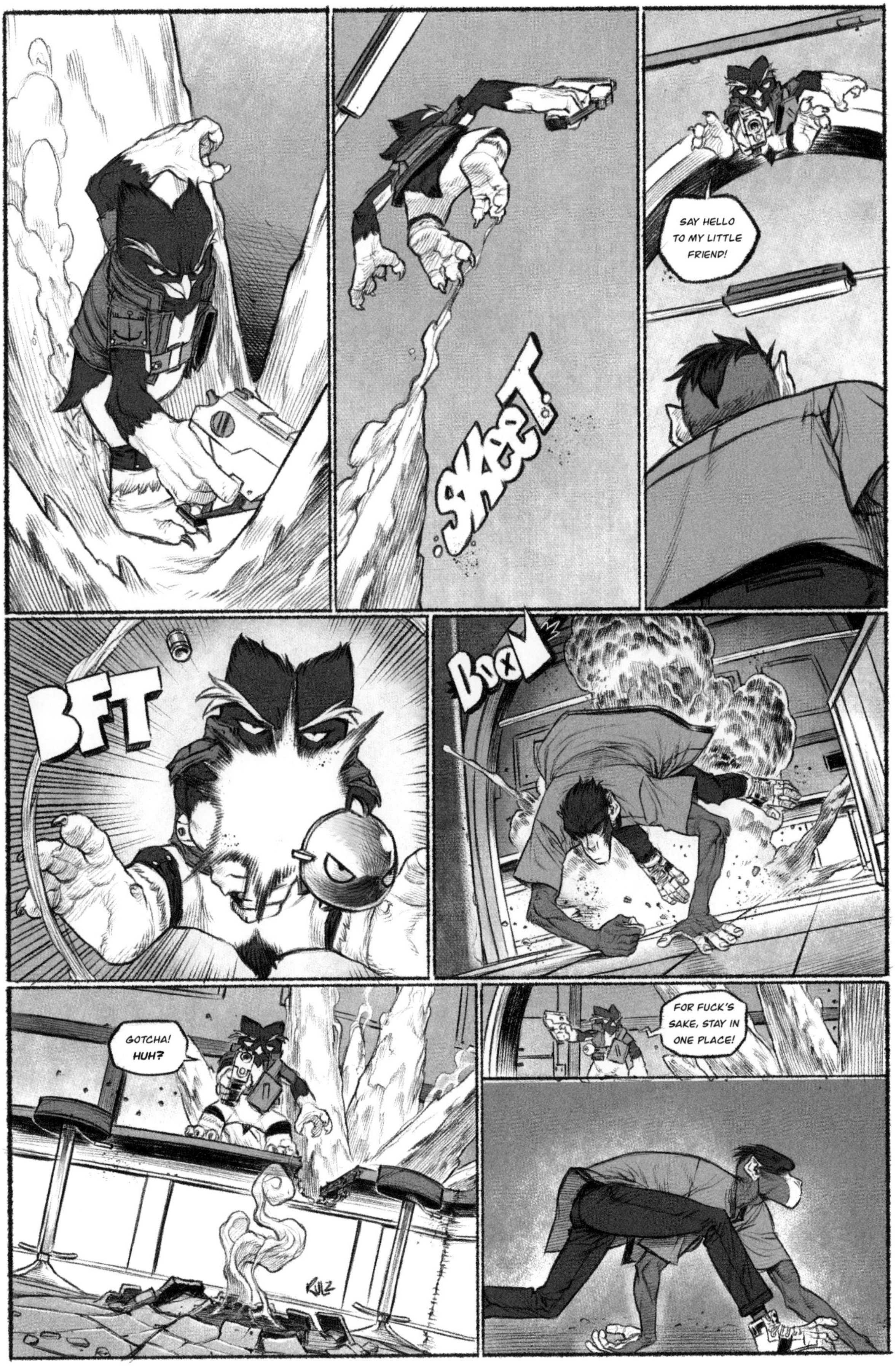
SKEET!
SAY HELLO TO MY LITTLE FRIEND!
BFT
BOOM
GOTCHA! HUH?
FOR FUCK'S SAKE, STAY IN ONE PLACE!

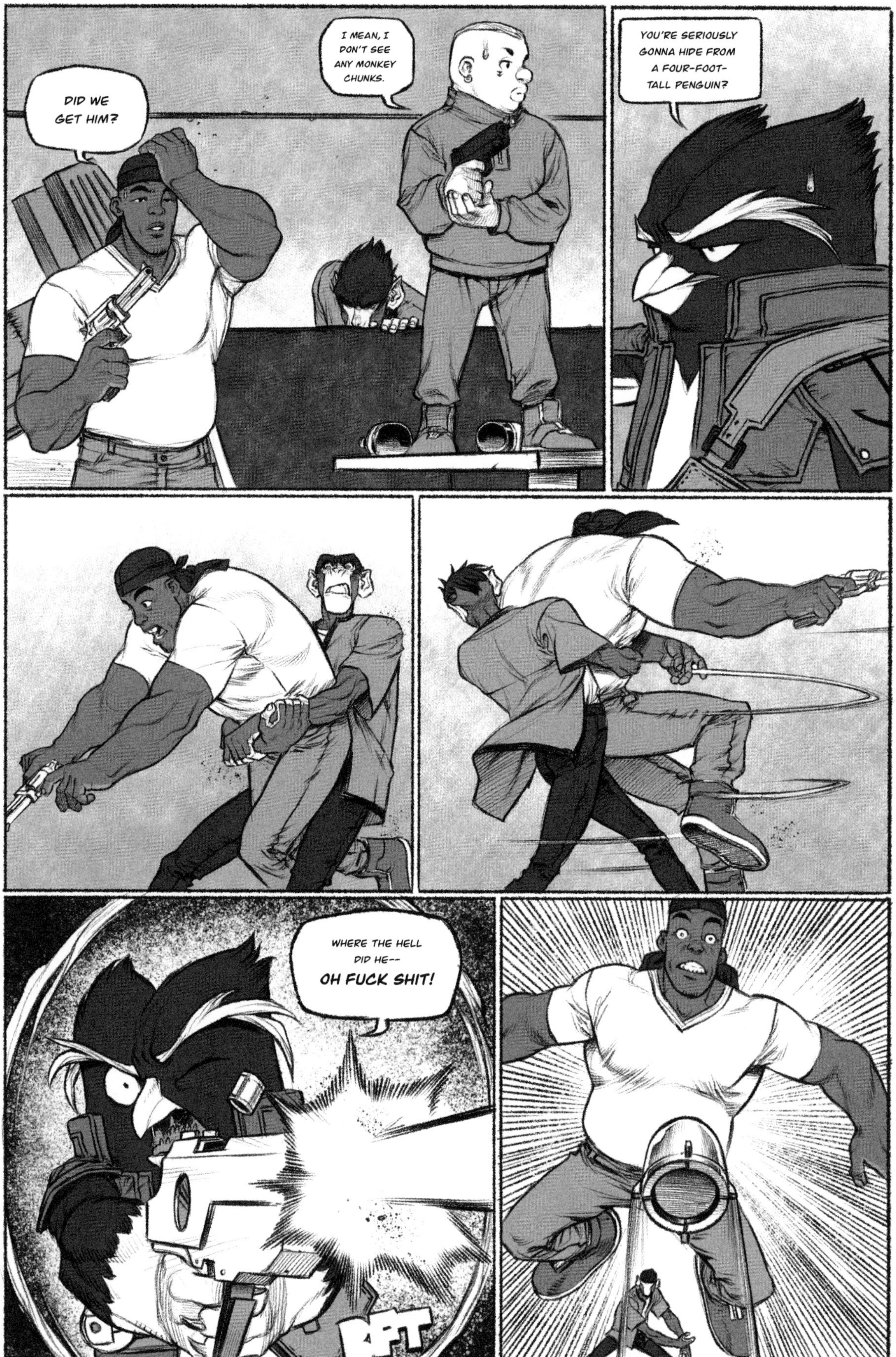
DID WE GET HIM?
I MEAN, I DON'T SEE ANY MONKEY CHUNKS.
YOU'RE SERIOUSLY GONNA HIDE FROM A FOUR-FOOT-TALL PENGUIN?
WHERE THE HELL DID HE-- OH FUCK SHIT!
BFFT

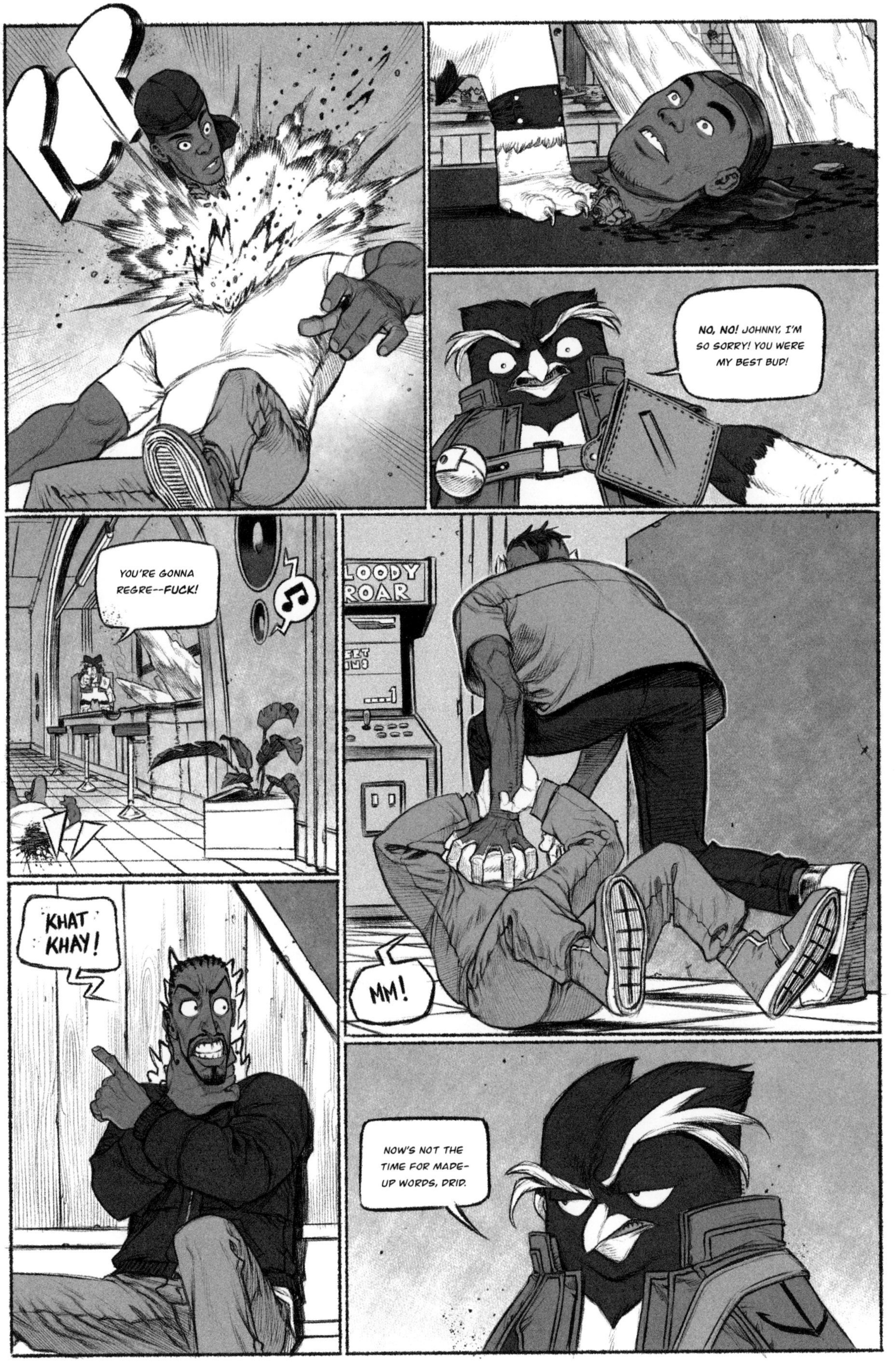
NO, NO! JOHNNY, I'M SO SORRY! YOU WERE MY BEST BUD!
YOU'RE GONNA REGRE--FUCK!
LOODY ROAR
MM!
KHAT KHAY!
NOW'S NOT THE TIME FOR MADE-UP WORDS, DRID.

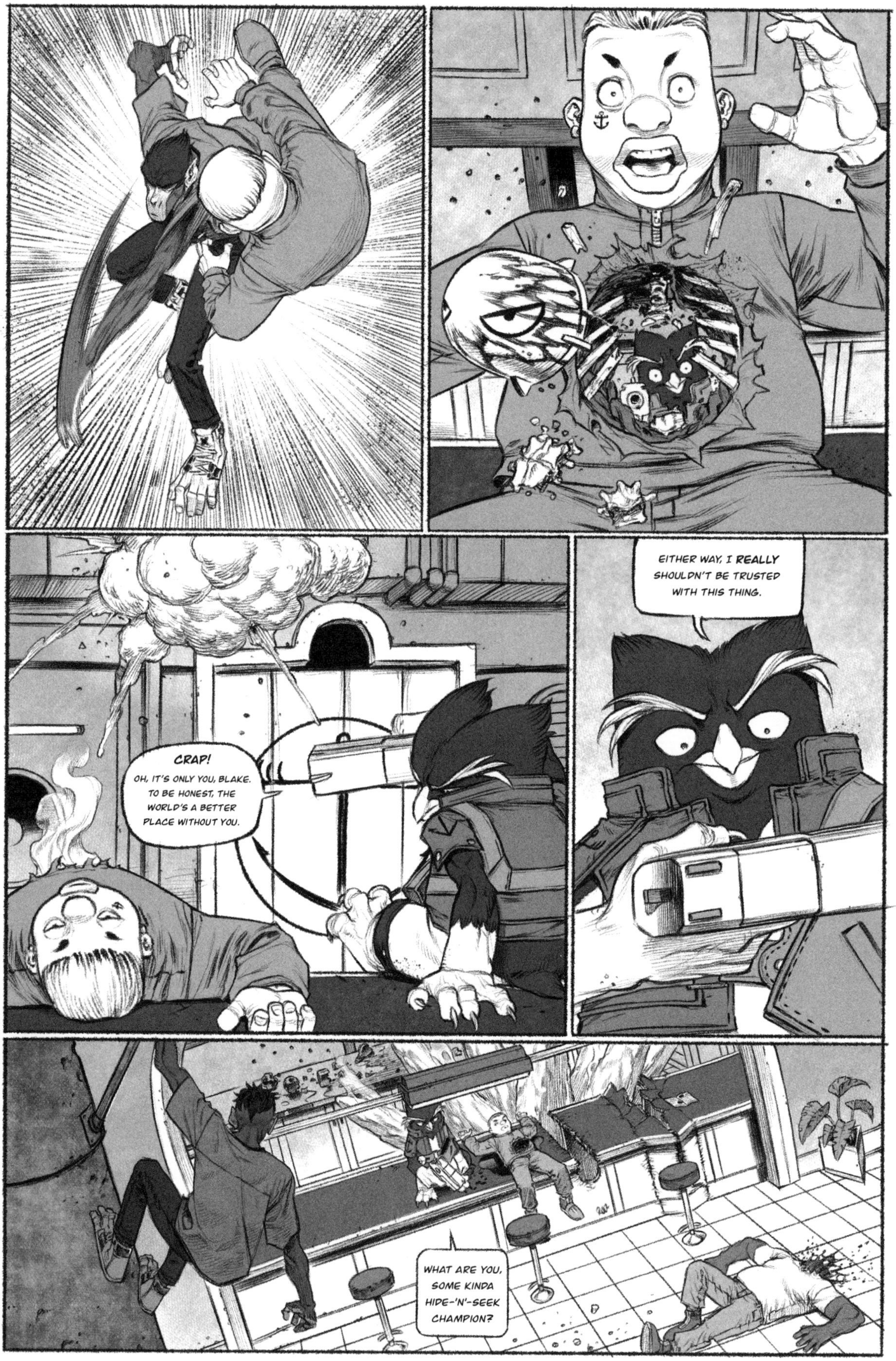
CRAP!
OH, IT'S ONLY YOU, BLAKE. TO BE HONEST, THE WORLD'S A BETTER PLACE WITHOUT YOU.
EITHER WAY, I REALLY SHOULDN'T BE TRUSTED WITH THIS THING.
WHAT ARE YOU, SOME KINDA HIDE-'N'-SEEK CHAMPION?

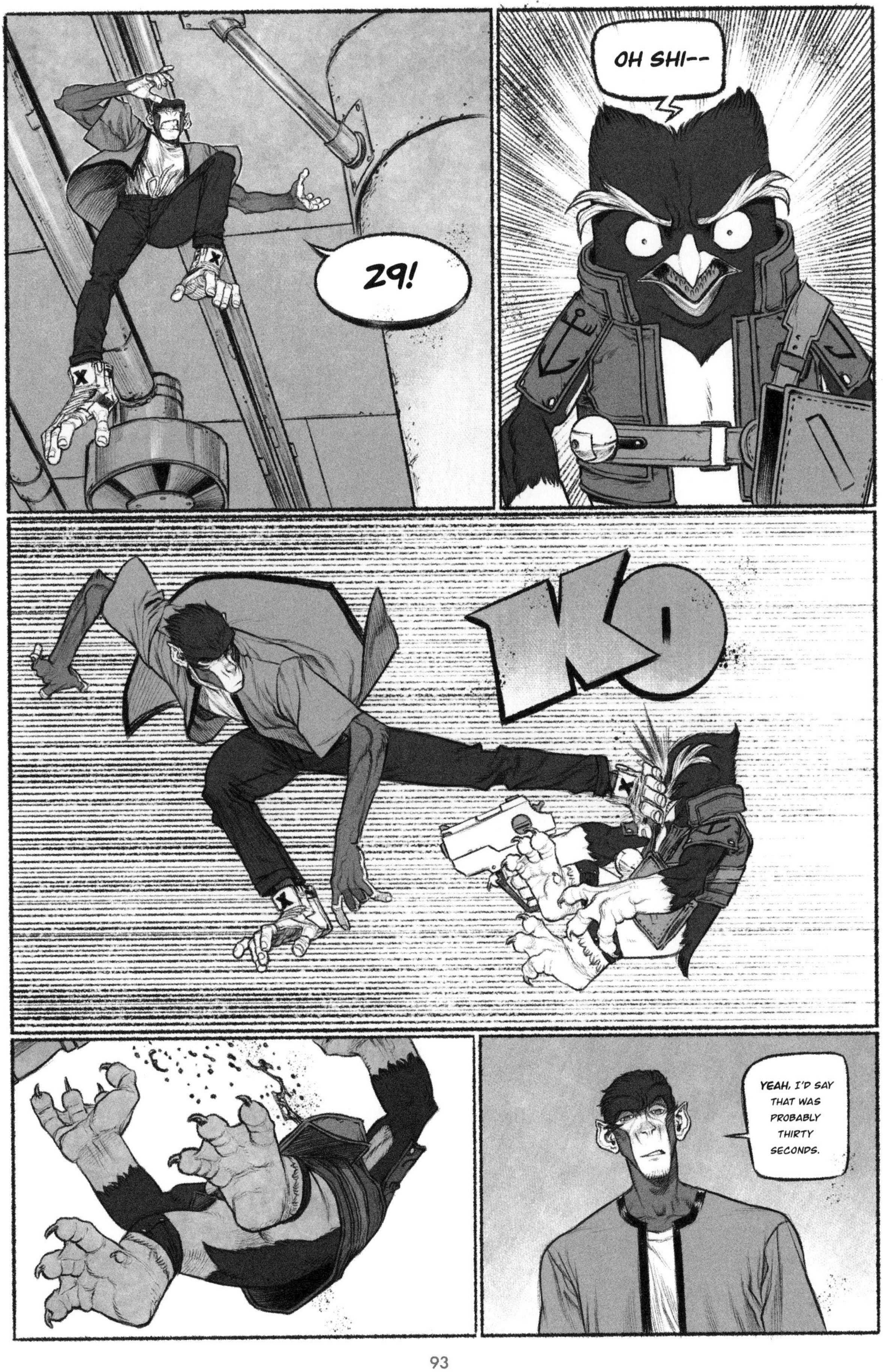
29!
OH SHI--
KO
YEAH, I'D SAY THAT WAS PROBABLY THIRTY SECONDS.

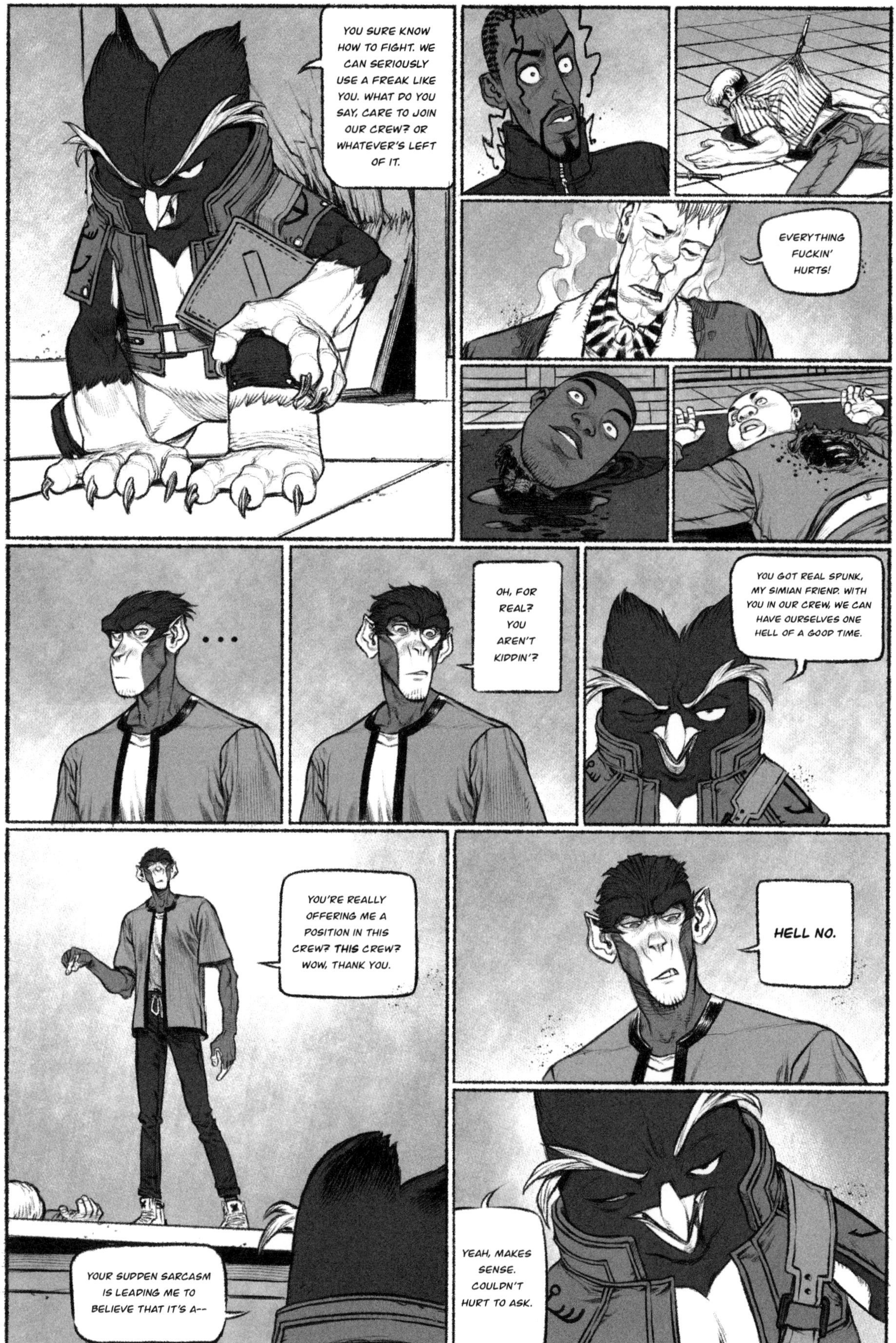

YOU SURE KNOW HOW TO FIGHT. WE CAN SERIOUSLY USE A FREAK LIKE YOU. WHAT DO YOU SAY, CARE TO JOIN OUR CREW? OR WHATEVER'S LEFT OF IT.
EVERYTHING FUCKIN' HURTS!
...
OH, FOR REAL? YOU AREN'T KIDDIN'?
YOU GOT REAL SPUNK, MY SIMIAN FRIEND. WITH YOU IN OUR CREW, WE CAN HAVE OURSELVES ONE HELL OF A GOOD TIME.
YOU'RE REALLY OFFERING ME A POSITION IN THIS CREW? THIS CREW? WOW, THANK YOU.
YOUR SUDDEN SARCASM IS LEADING ME TO BELIEVE THAT IT'S A--
HELL NO.
YEAH, MAKES SENSE. COULDN'T HURT TO ASK.

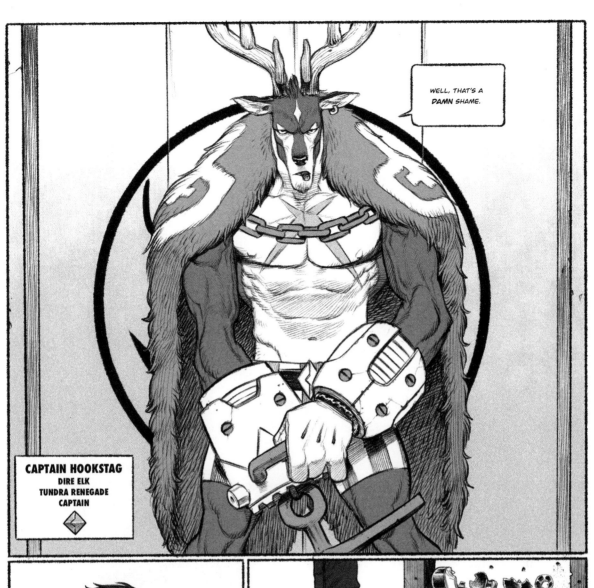

WELL, THAT'S A **DAMN** SHAME.

CAPTAIN HOOKSTAG
DIRE ELK
TUNDRA RENEGADE
CAPTAIN

HM?

PECK

WHAT THE?!

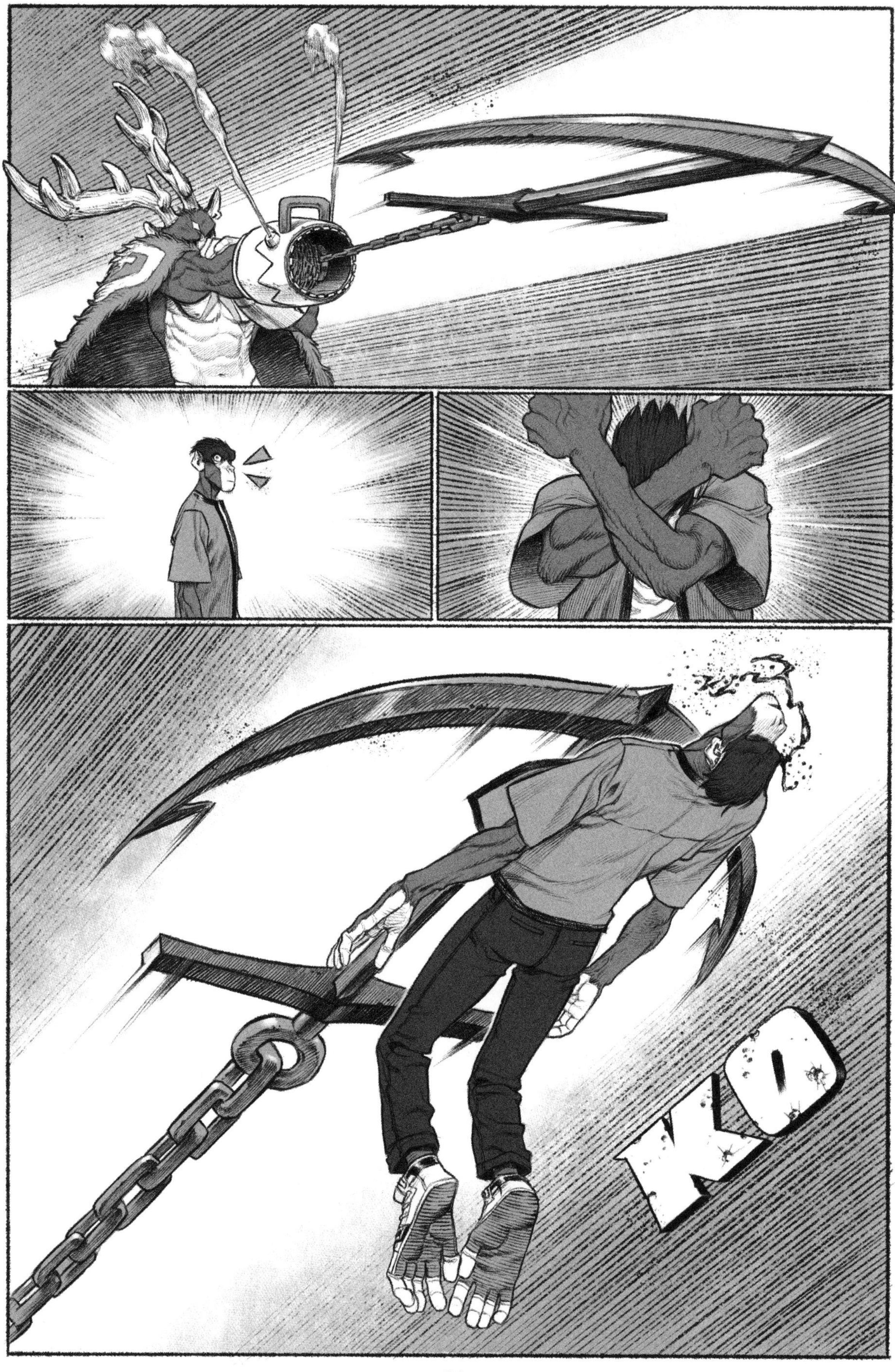
KO

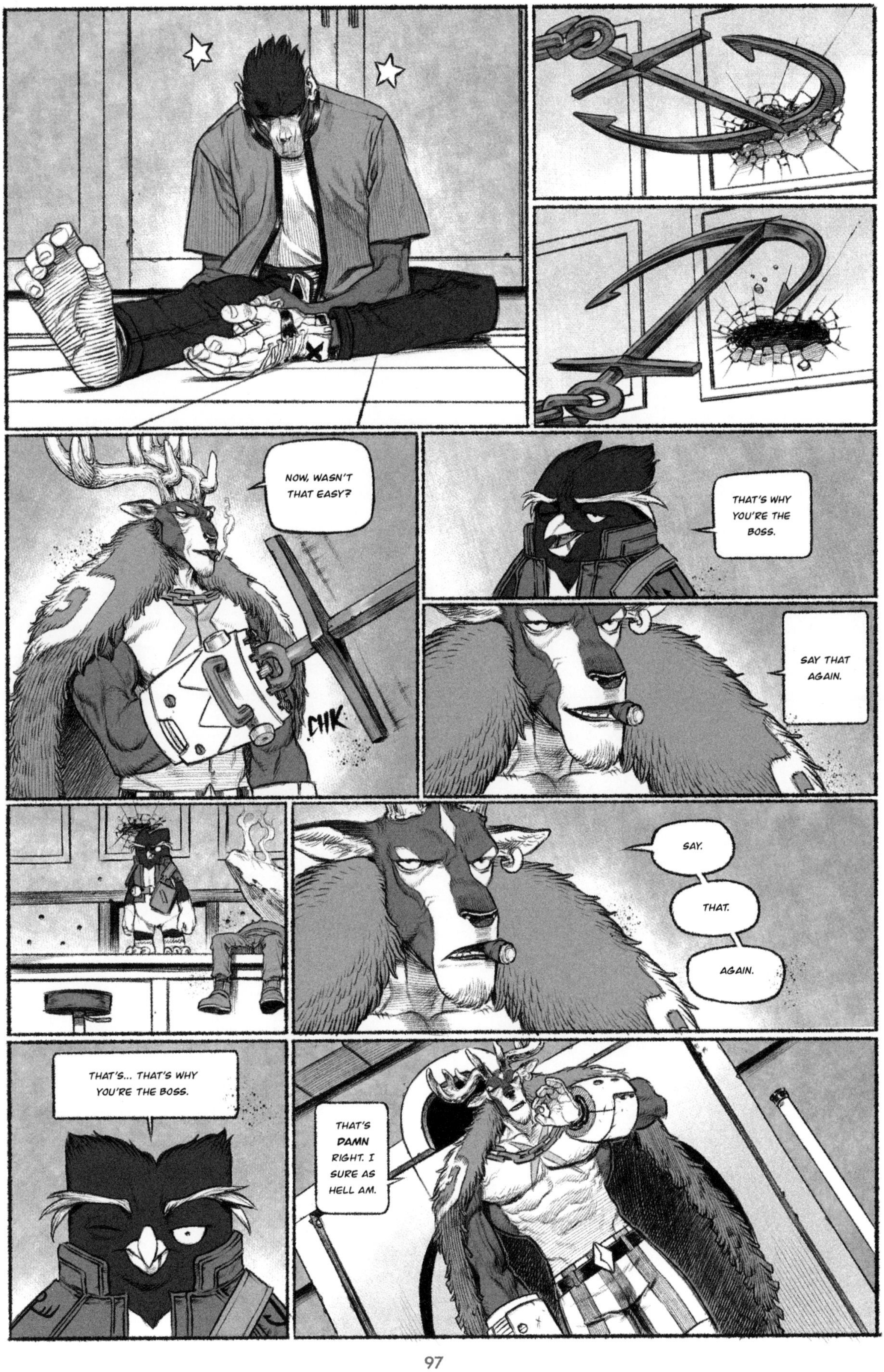
NOW, WASN'T THAT EASY?
CHK
THAT'S WHY YOU'RE THE BOSS.
SAY THAT AGAIN.
SAY.
THAT.
AGAIN.
THAT'S... THAT'S WHY YOU'RE THE BOSS.
THAT'S **DAMN** RIGHT. I SURE AS HELL AM.

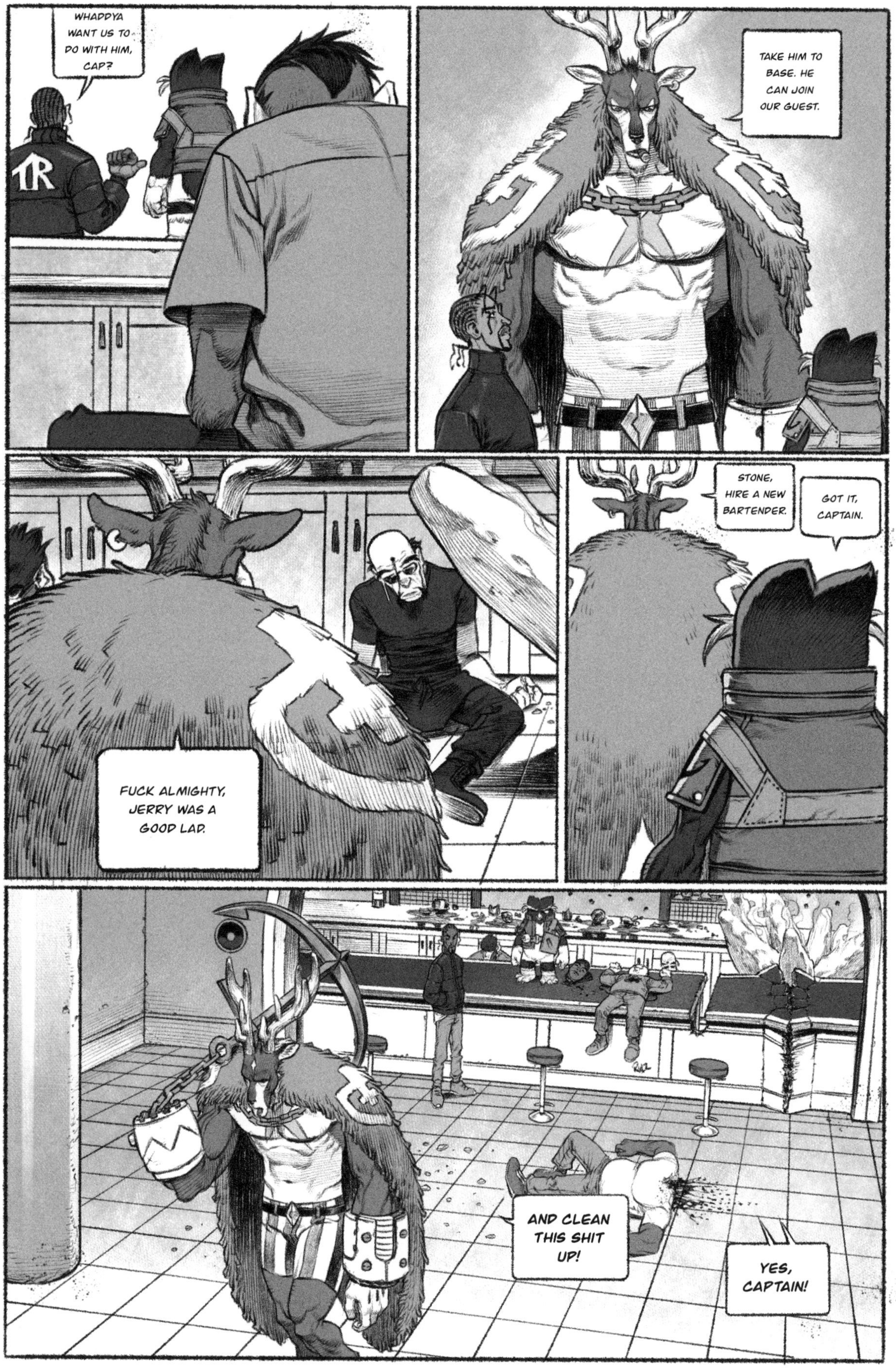
WHADDYA WANT US TO DO WITH HIM, CAP?
TAKE HIM TO BASE. HE CAN JOIN OUR GUEST.
FUCK ALMIGHTY, JERRY WAS A GOOD LAD.
STONE, HIRE A NEW BARTENDER.
GOT IT, CAPTAIN.
AND CLEAN THIS SHIT UP!
YES, CAPTAIN!

KINGS OF NOWHERE

Club
NUDE GIRLS
KRK

SOROUSH BARAZESH

CHAPTER
NO.6

JUVENILE DAMNATION

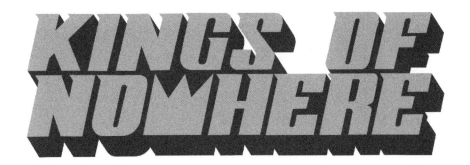

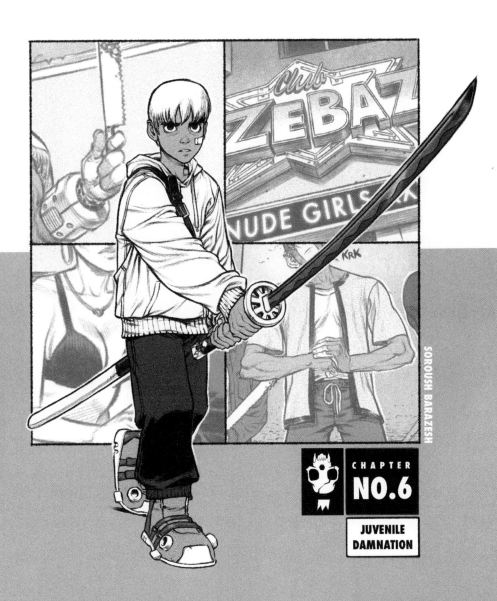

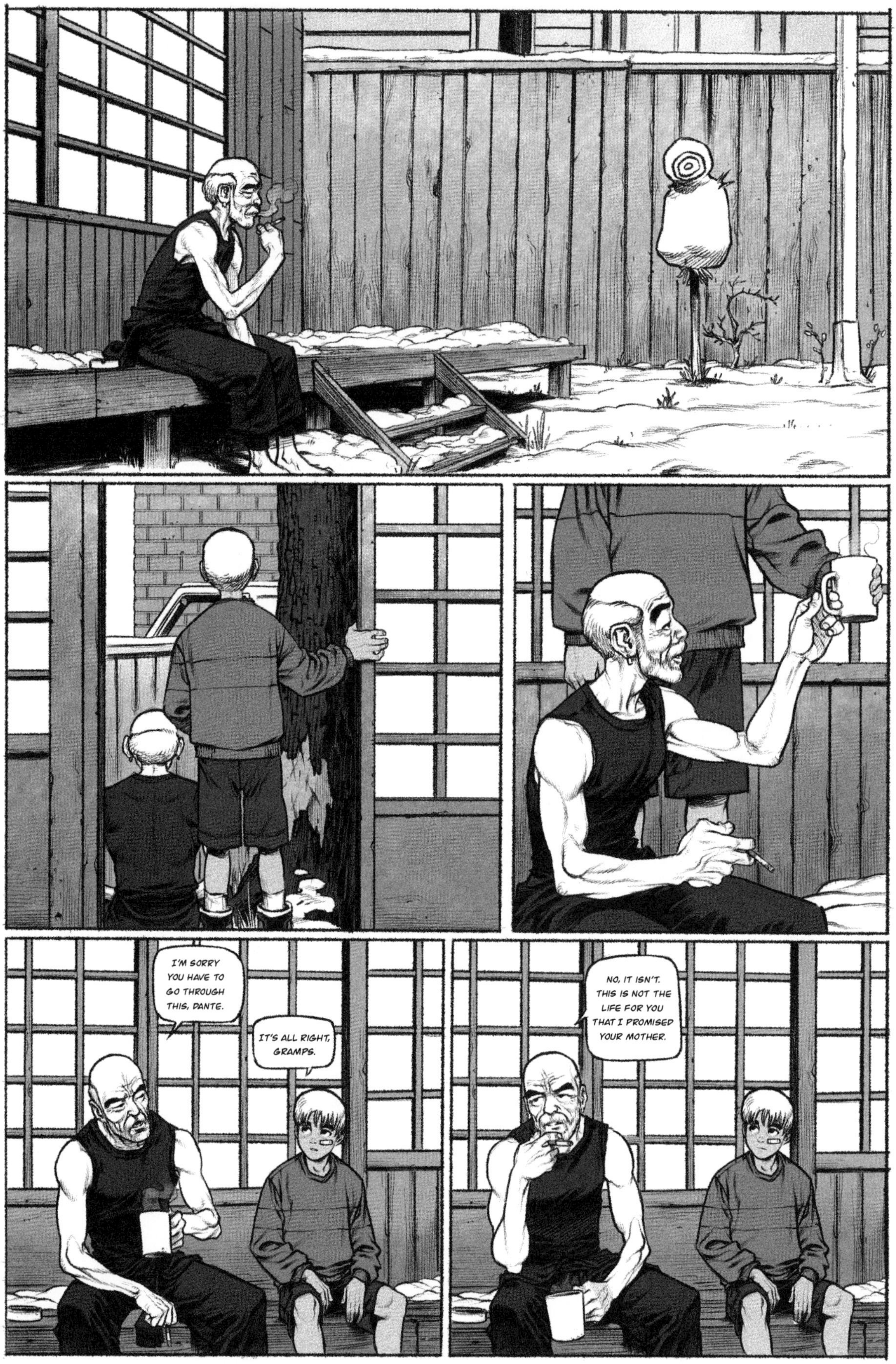

I'M SORRY YOU HAVE TO GO THROUGH THIS, DANTE.
IT'S ALL RIGHT, GRAMPS.
NO, IT ISN'T. THIS IS NOT THE LIFE FOR YOU THAT I PROMISED YOUR MOTHER.

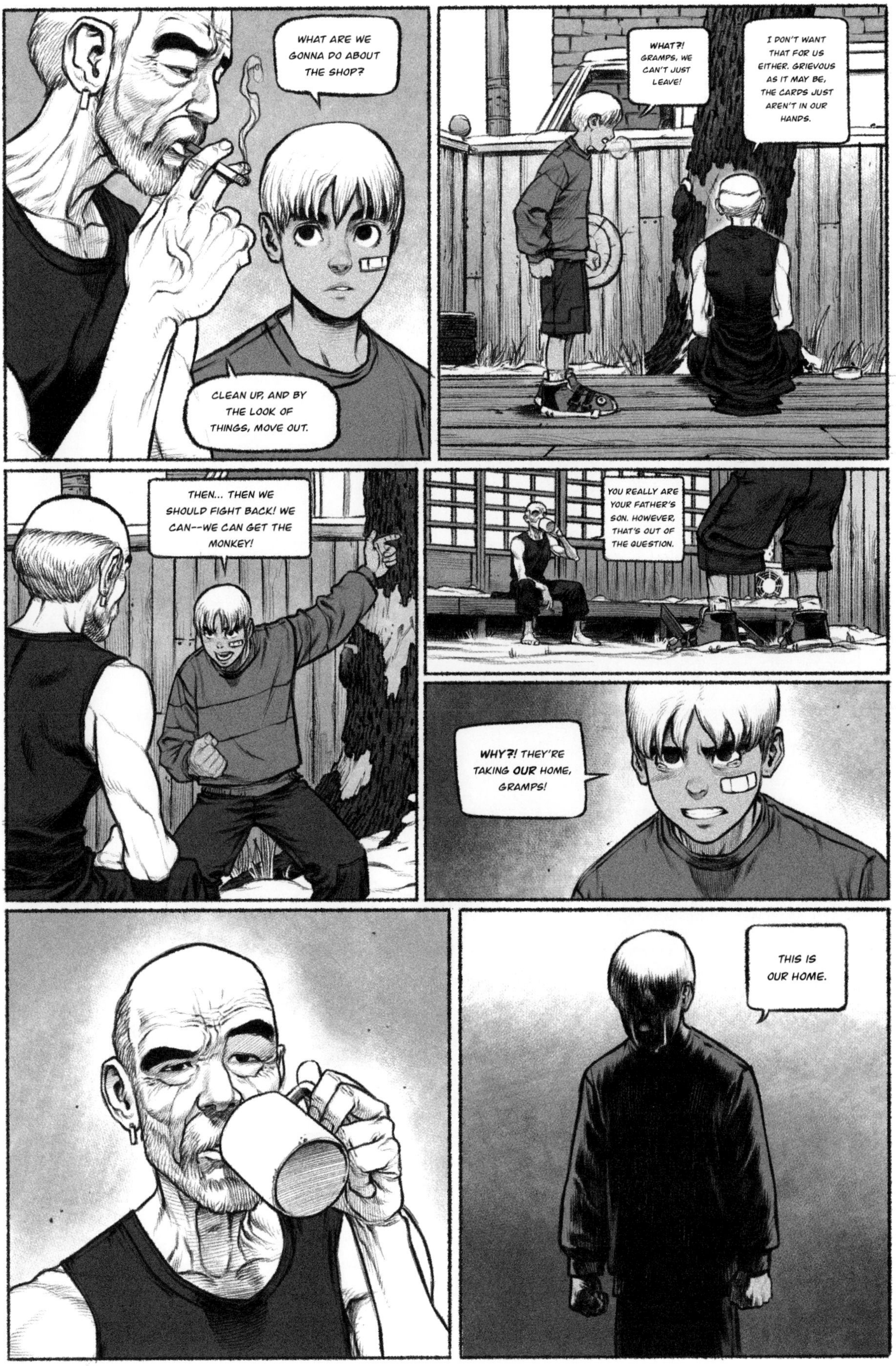
WHAT ARE WE GONNA DO ABOUT THE SHOP?
CLEAN UP, AND BY THE LOOK OF THINGS, MOVE OUT.
WHAT?! GRAMPS, WE CAN'T JUST LEAVE!
I DON'T WANT THAT FOR US EITHER. GRIEVOUS AS IT MAY BE, THE CARDS JUST AREN'T IN OUR HANDS.
THEN... THEN WE SHOULD FIGHT BACK! WE CAN--WE CAN GET THE MONKEY!
YOU REALLY ARE YOUR FATHER'S SON. HOWEVER, THAT'S OUT OF THE QUESTION.
WHY?! THEY'RE TAKING OUR HOME, GRAMPS!
THIS IS OUR HOME.

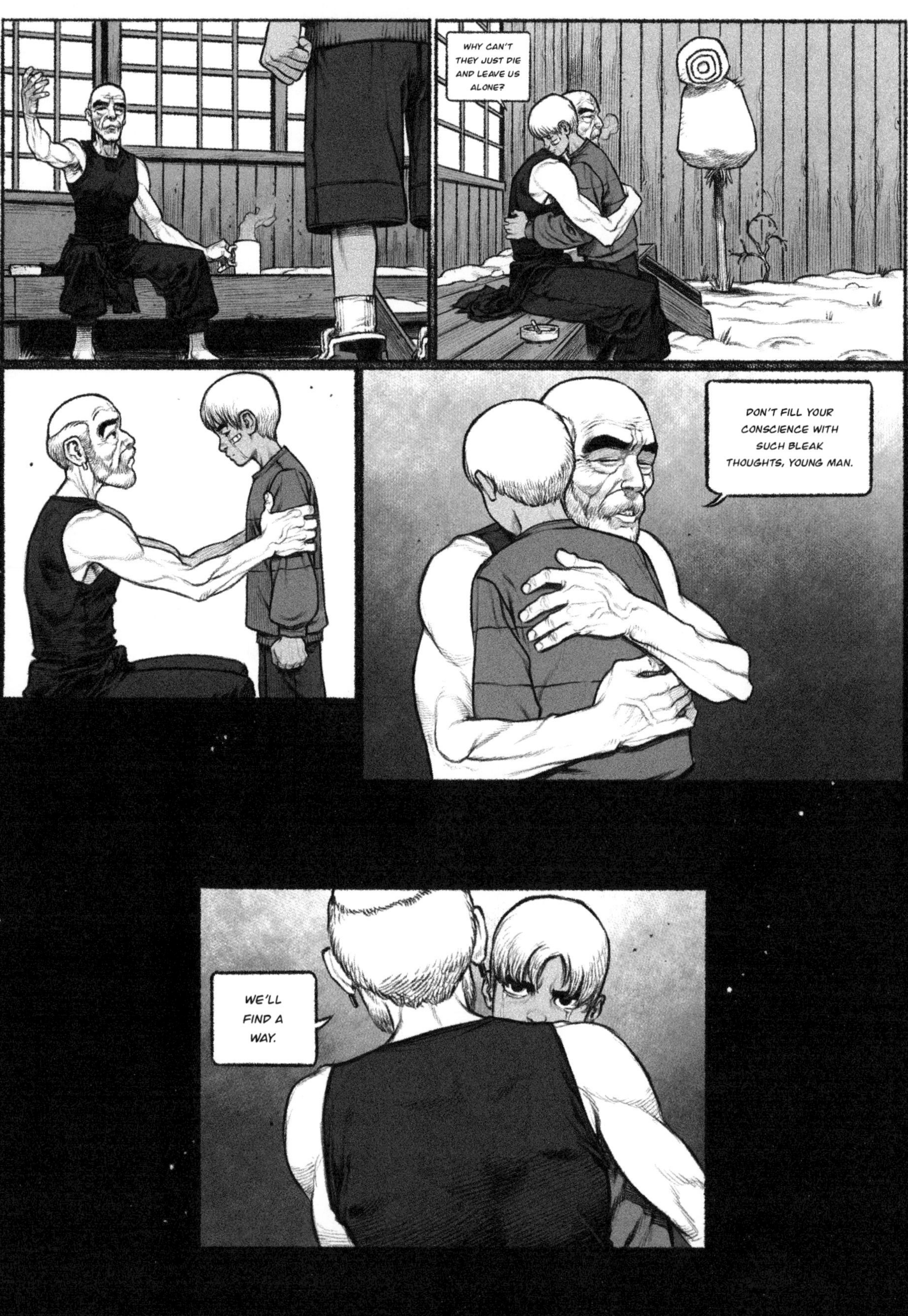
WHY CAN'T THEY JUST DIE AND LEAVE US ALONE?
DON'T FILL YOUR CONSCIENCE WITH SUCH BLEAK THOUGHTS, YOUNG MAN.
WE'LL FIND A WAY.

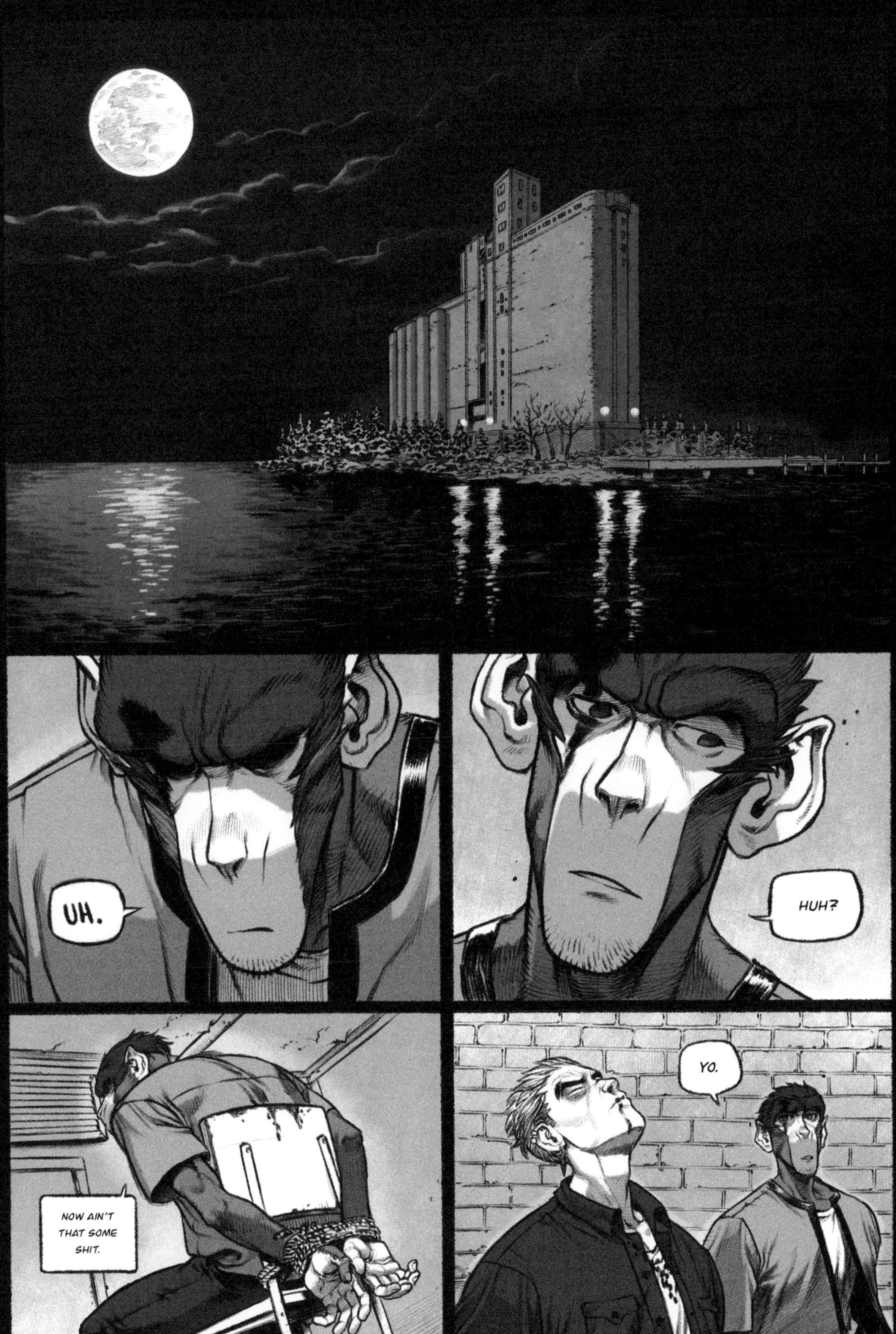
UH.
HUH?
NOW AIN'T THAT SOME SHIT.
YO.

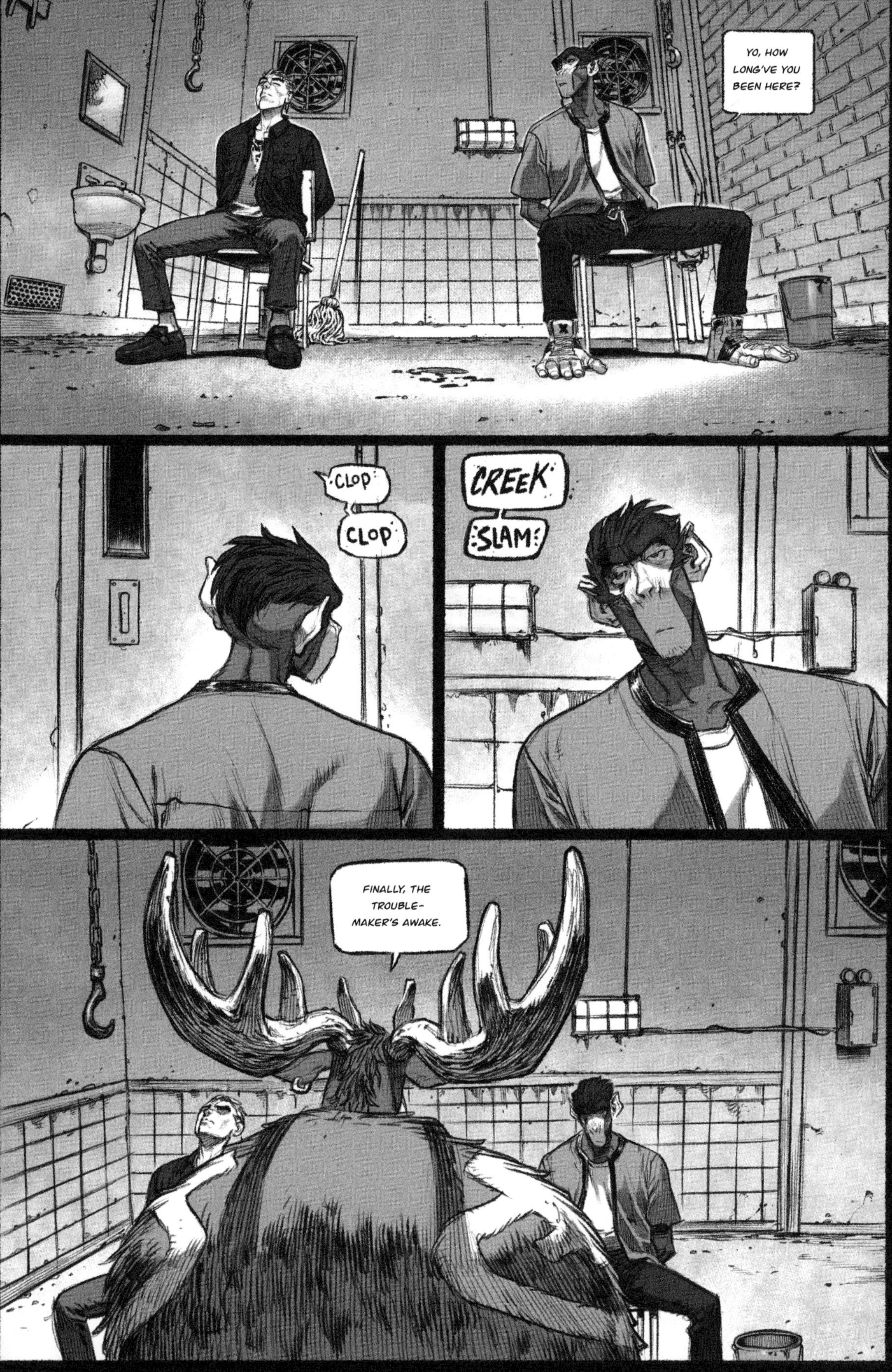
YO, HOW LONG'VE YOU BEEN HERE?
CLOP
CLOP
CREEK
SLAM
FINALLY, THE TROUBLE-MAKER'S AWAKE.

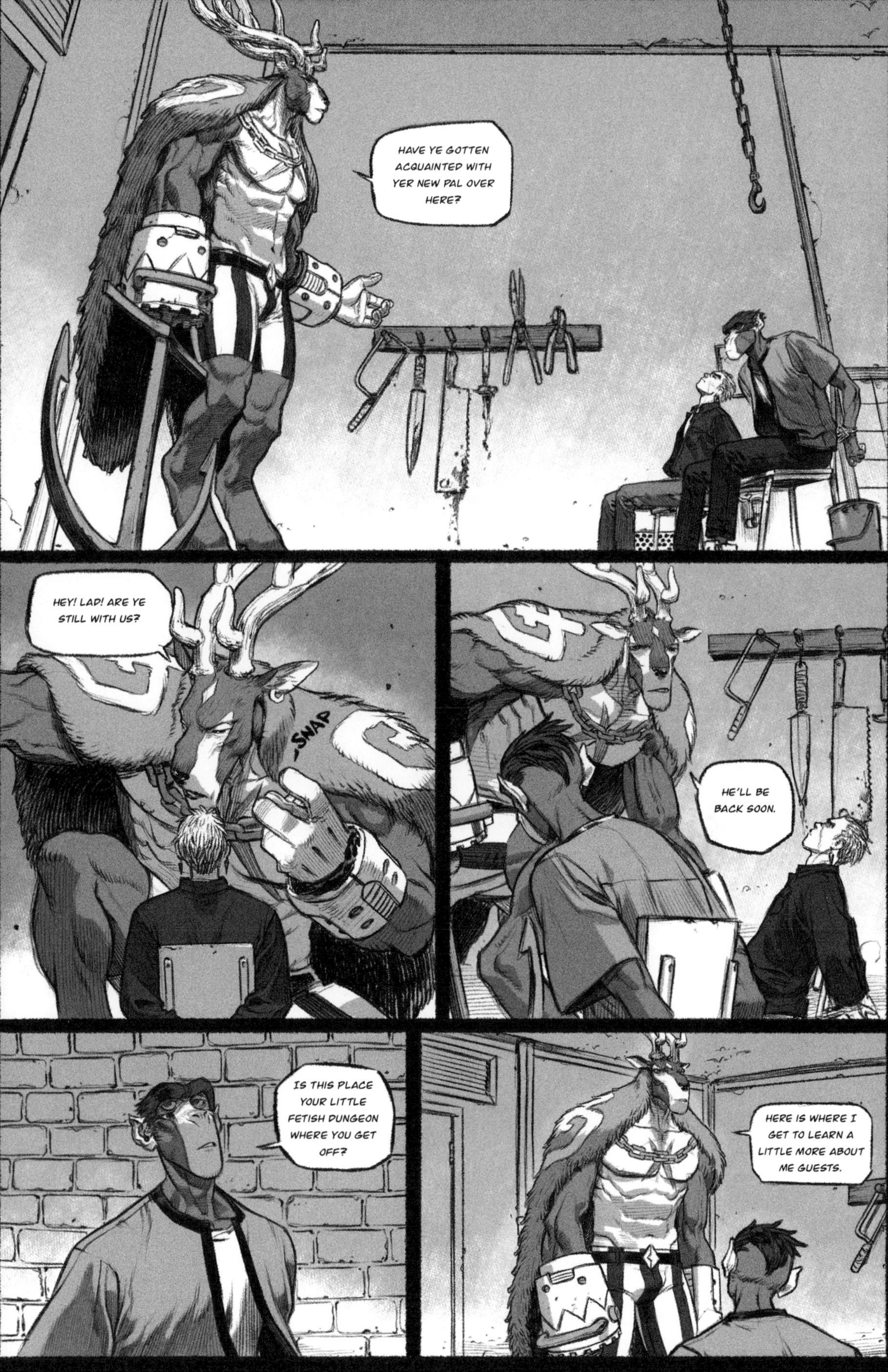

HAVE YE GOTTEN ACQUAINTED WITH YER NEW PAL OVER HERE?
HEY! LAD! ARE YE STILL WITH US?
SNAP
HE'LL BE BACK SOON.
IS THIS PLACE YOUR LITTLE FETISH DUNGEON WHERE YOU GET OFF?
HERE IS WHERE I GET TO LEARN A LITTLE MORE ABOUT ME GUESTS.

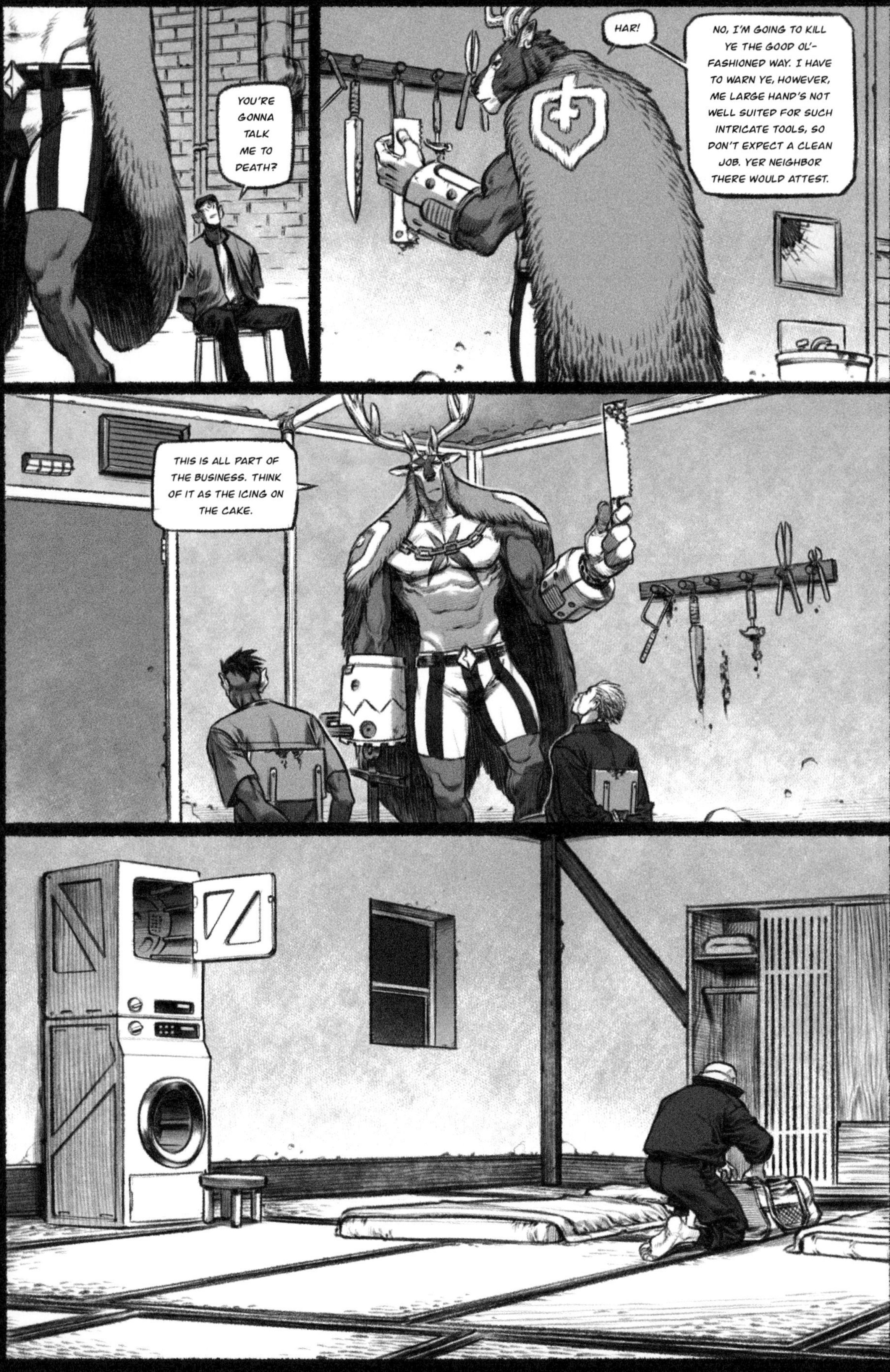

YOU'RE GONNA TALK ME TO DEATH?
HAR!
NO, I'M GOING TO KILL YE THE GOOD OL'-FASHIONED WAY. I HAVE TO WARN YE, HOWEVER, ME LARGE HAND'S NOT WELL SUITED FOR SUCH INTRICATE TOOLS, SO DON'T EXPECT A CLEAN JOB. YER NEIGHBOR THERE WOULD ATTEST.
THIS IS ALL PART OF THE BUSINESS. THINK OF IT AS THE ICING ON THE CAKE.

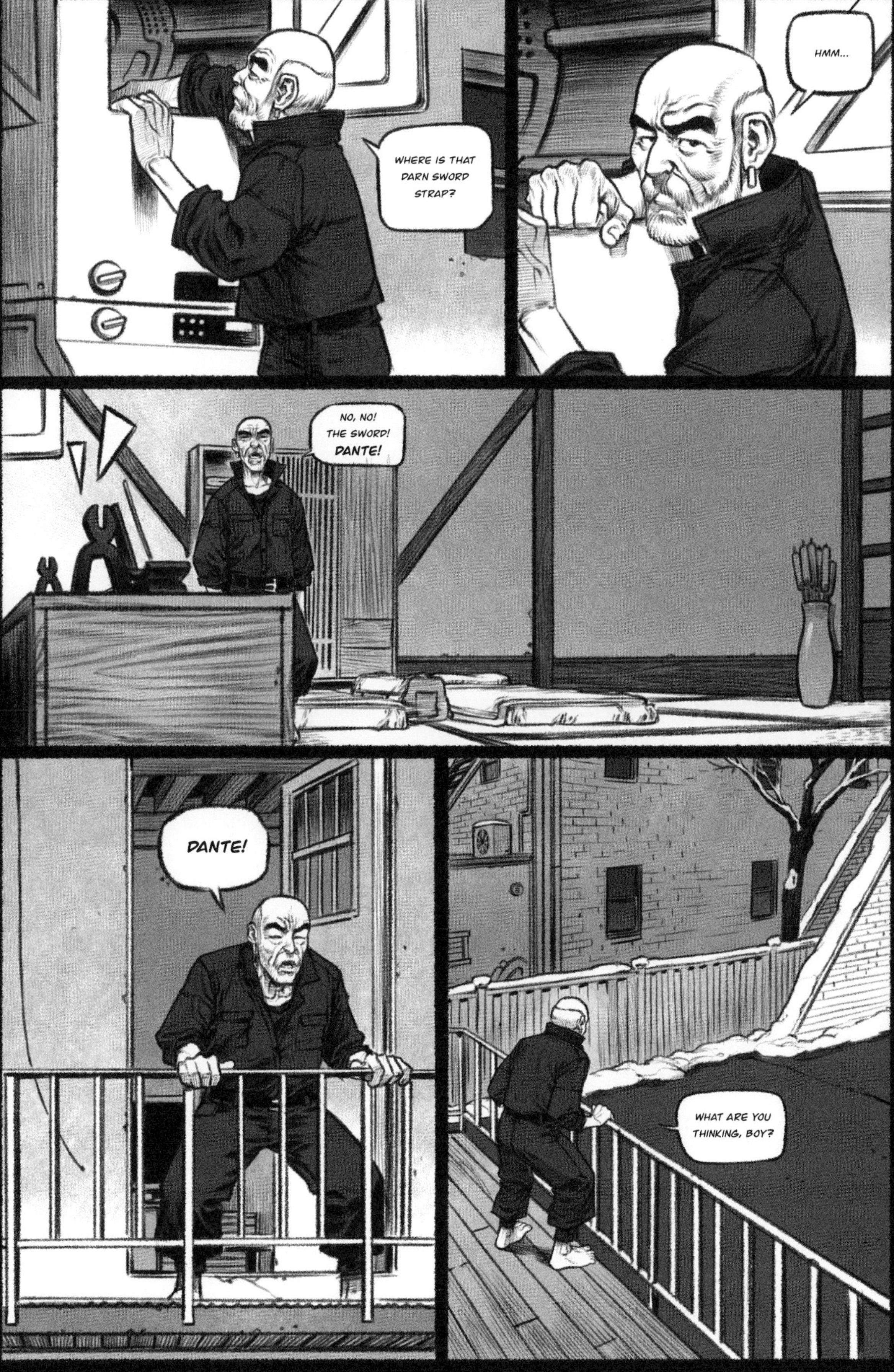
WHERE IS THAT DARN SWORD STRAP?
HMM...
NO, NO! THE SWORD! DANTE!
DANTE!
WHAT ARE YOU THINKING, BOY?

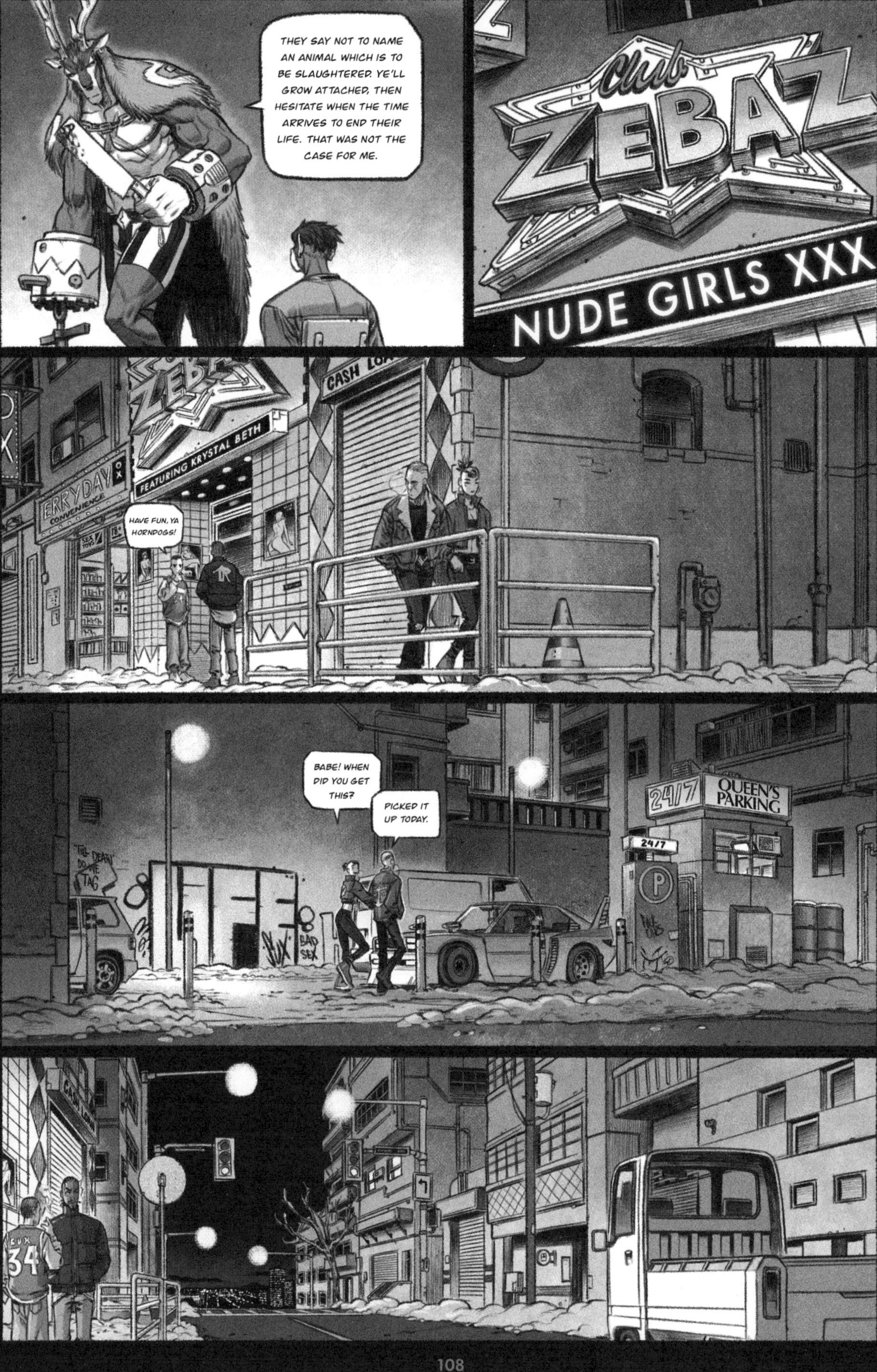
THEY SAY NOT TO NAME AN ANIMAL WHICH IS TO BE SLAUGHTERED. YE'LL GROW ATTACHED, THEN HESITATE WHEN THE TIME ARRIVES TO END THEIR LIFE. THAT WAS NOT THE CASE FOR ME.
Club ZEBAZ
NUDE GIRLS XXX
FEATURING KRYSTAL BETH
CASH LOA
ERRYDAY
CONVENIENCE
HAVE FUN, YA HORNDOGS!
BABE! WHEN DID YOU GET THIS?
PICKED IT UP TODAY.
24/7
QUEEN'S PARKING
24/7
P
BAD SEX
34

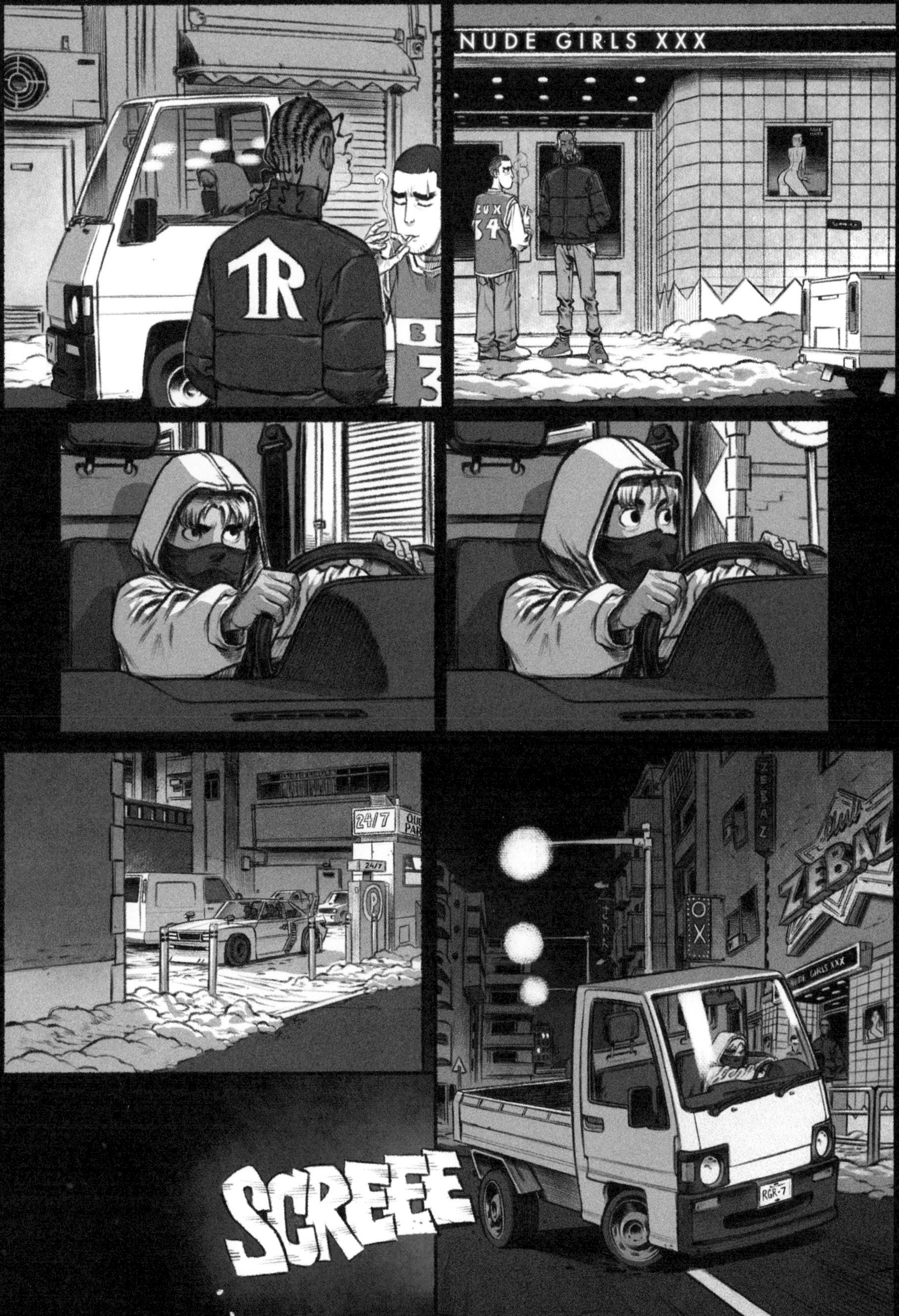

NUDE GIRLS XXX
BUX
34
24/7
SCREEE
RGR-7

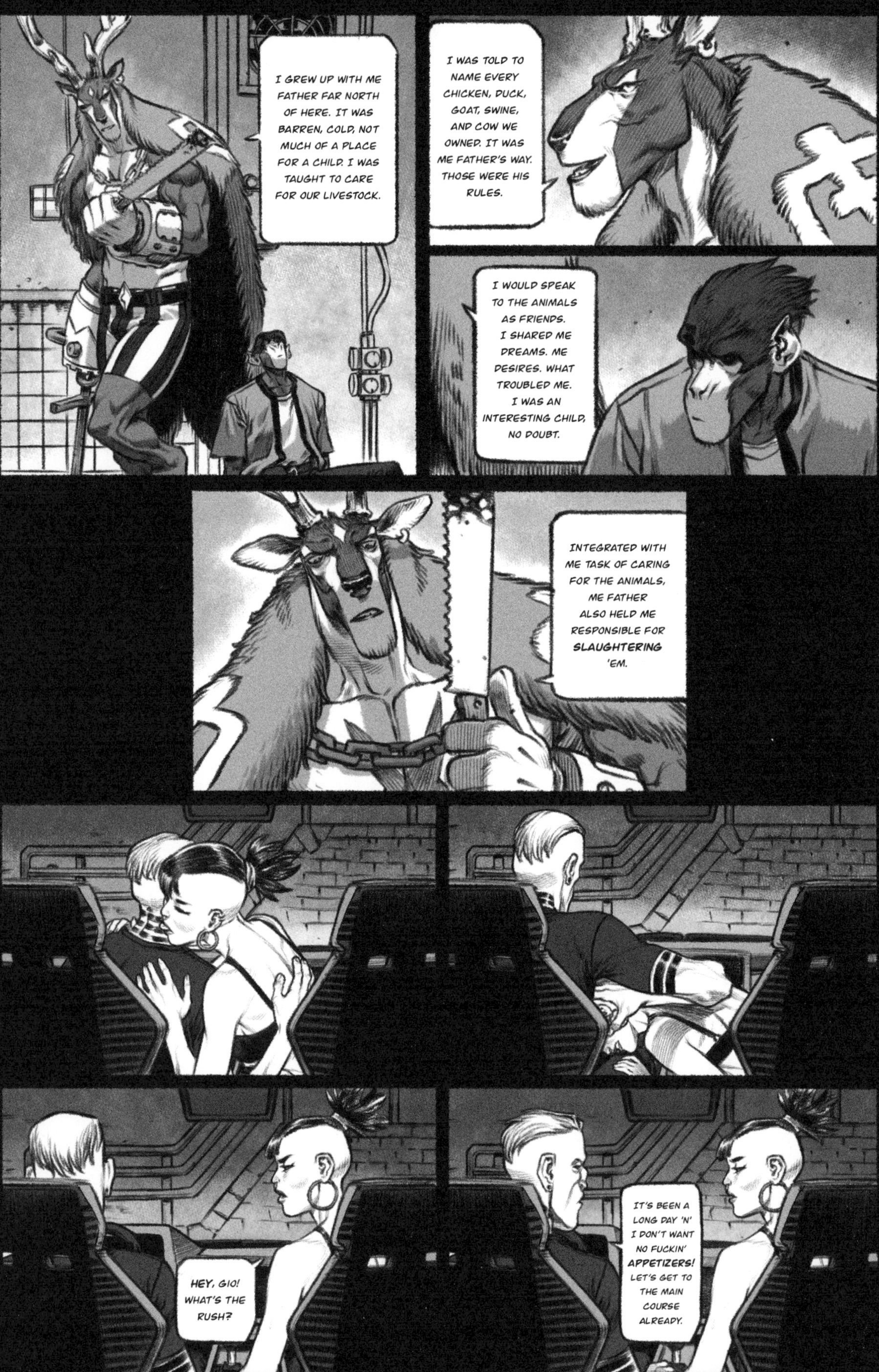
I GREW UP WITH ME FATHER FAR NORTH OF HERE. IT WAS BARREN, COLD, NOT MUCH OF A PLACE FOR A CHILD. I WAS TAUGHT TO CARE FOR OUR LIVESTOCK.
I WAS TOLD TO NAME EVERY CHICKEN, DUCK, GOAT, SWINE, AND COW WE OWNED. IT WAS ME FATHER'S WAY. THOSE WERE HIS RULES.
I WOULD SPEAK TO THE ANIMALS AS FRIENDS. I SHARED ME DREAMS. ME DESIRES. WHAT TROUBLED ME. I WAS AN INTERESTING CHILD, NO DOUBT.
INTEGRATED WITH ME TASK OF CARING FOR THE ANIMALS, ME FATHER ALSO HELD ME RESPONSIBLE FOR **SLAUGHTERING** 'EM.
HEY, GIO! WHAT'S THE RUSH?
IT'S BEEN A LONG DAY 'N' I DON'T WANT NO FUCKIN' **APPETIZERS!** LET'S GET TO THE MAIN COURSE ALREADY.

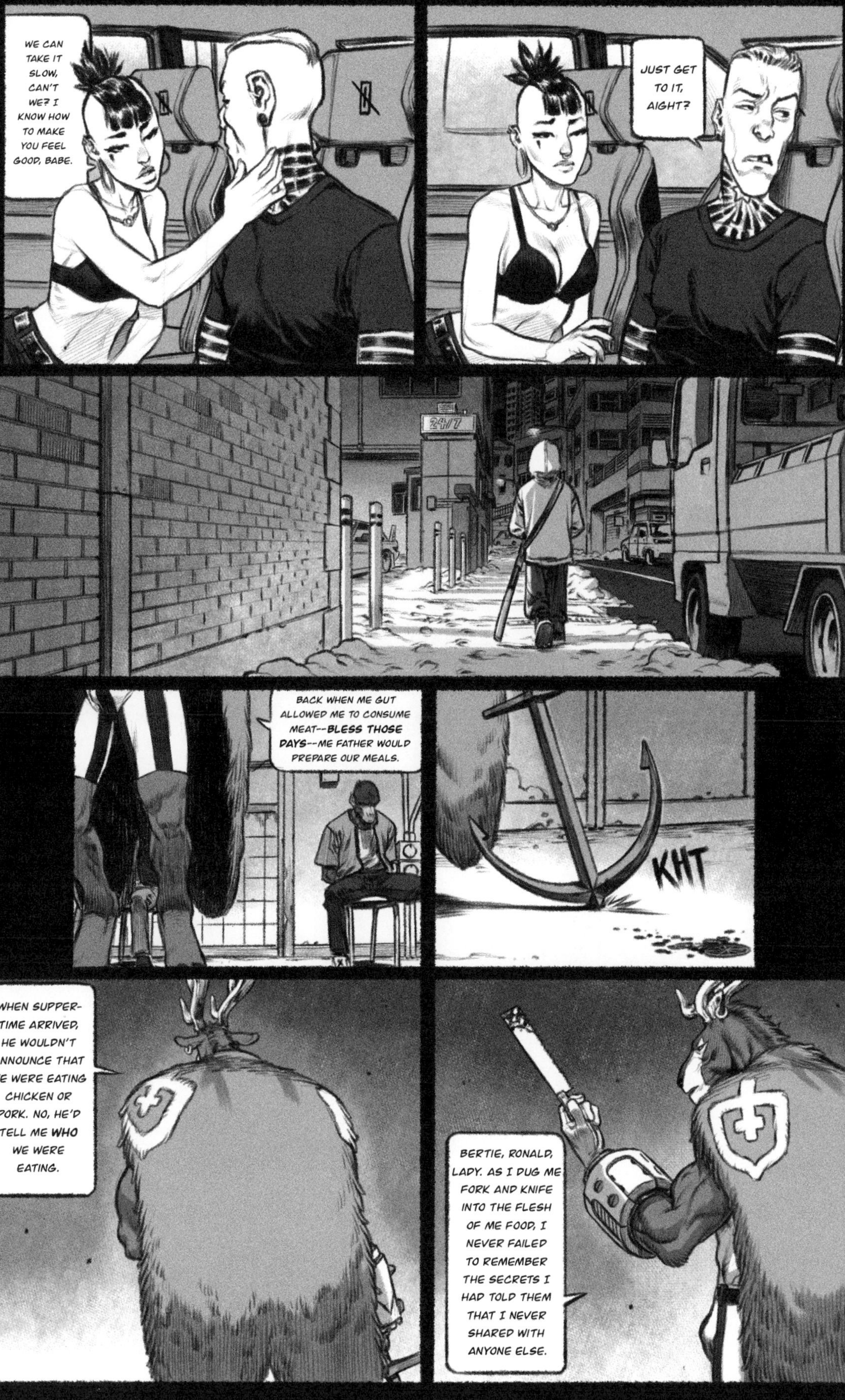
WE CAN TAKE IT SLOW, CAN'T WE? I KNOW HOW TO MAKE YOU FEEL GOOD, BABE.
JUST GET TO IT, AIGHT?
24/7
BACK WHEN ME GUT ALLOWED ME TO CONSUME MEAT--**BLESS THOSE DAYS**--ME FATHER WOULD PREPARE OUR MEALS.
KHT
WHEN SUPPER-TIME ARRIVED, HE WOULDN'T ANNOUNCE THAT WE WERE EATING CHICKEN OR PORK. NO, HE'D TELL ME **WHO** WE WERE EATING.
BERTIE, RONALD, LADY. AS I DUG ME FORK AND KNIFE INTO THE FLESH OF ME FOOD, I NEVER FAILED TO REMEMBER THE SECRETS I HAD TOLD THEM THAT I NEVER SHARED WITH ANYONE ELSE.

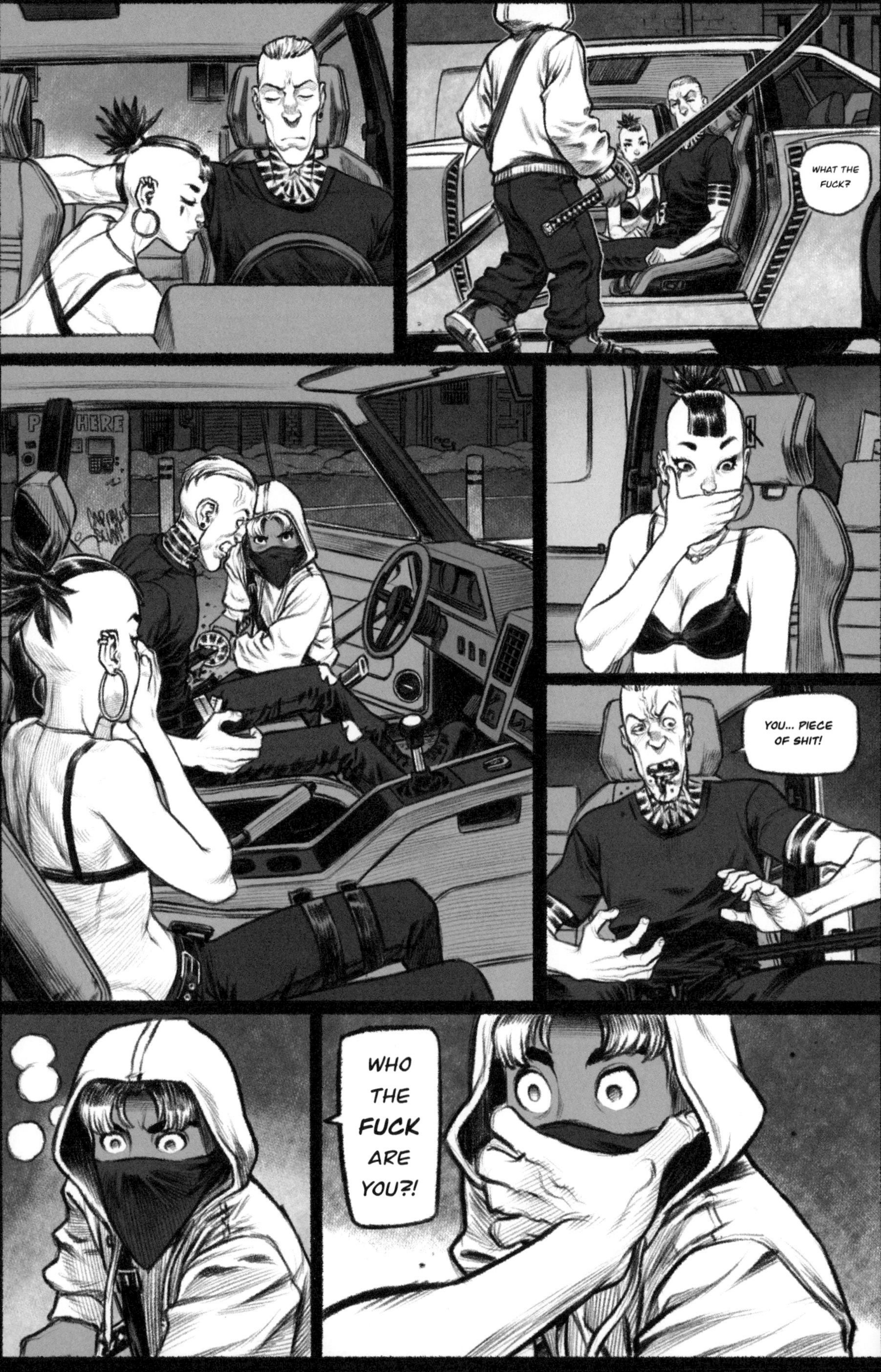
WHAT THE FUCK?
YOU... PIECE OF SHIT!
WHO THE FUCK ARE YOU?!

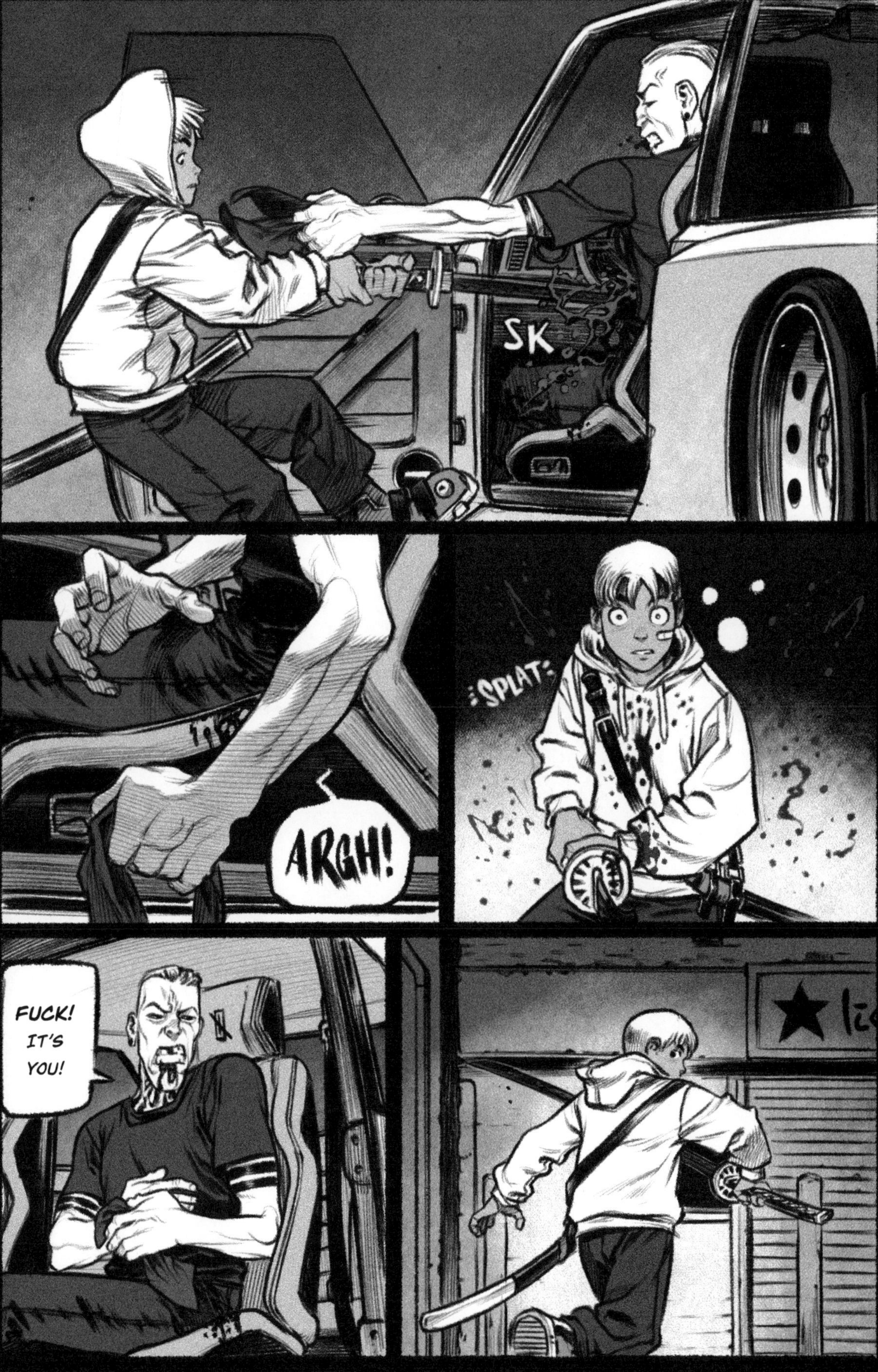
SK
ARGH!
SPLAT
FUCK! IT'S YOU!

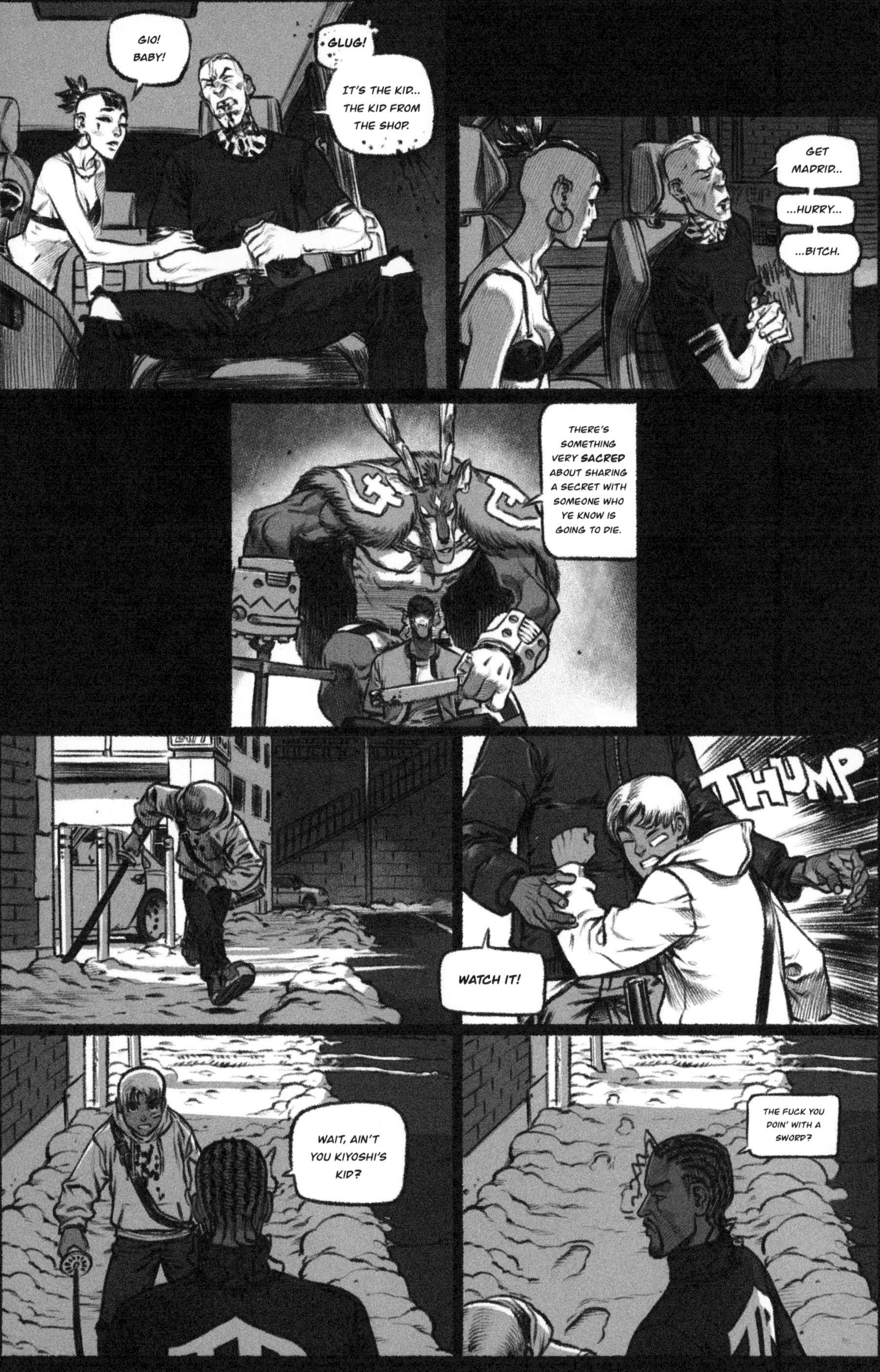
GIO! BABY!
GLUG!
IT'S THE KID... THE KID FROM THE SHOP.
GET MADRID...
...HURRY...
...BITCH.
THERE'S SOMETHING VERY SACRED ABOUT SHARING A SECRET WITH SOMEONE WHO YE KNOW IS GOING TO DIE.
THUMP
WATCH IT!
WAIT, AIN'T YOU KIYOSHI'S KID?
THE FUCK YOU DOIN' WITH A SWORD?

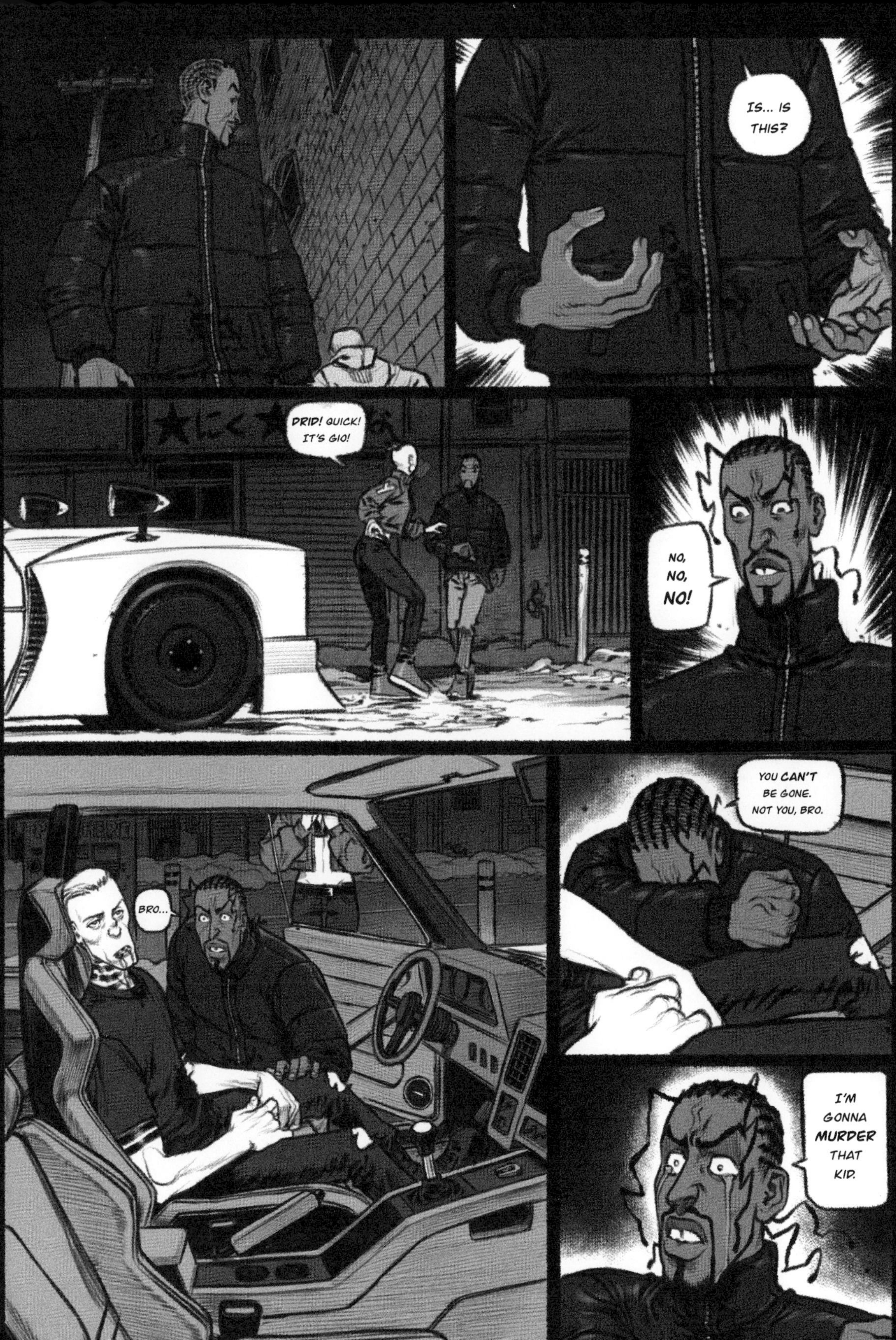
IS... IS THIS?
DRID! QUICK! IT'S GIO!
NO, NO, NO!
BRO...
YOU CAN'T BE GONE. NOT YOU, BRO.
I'M GONNA MURDER THAT KID.

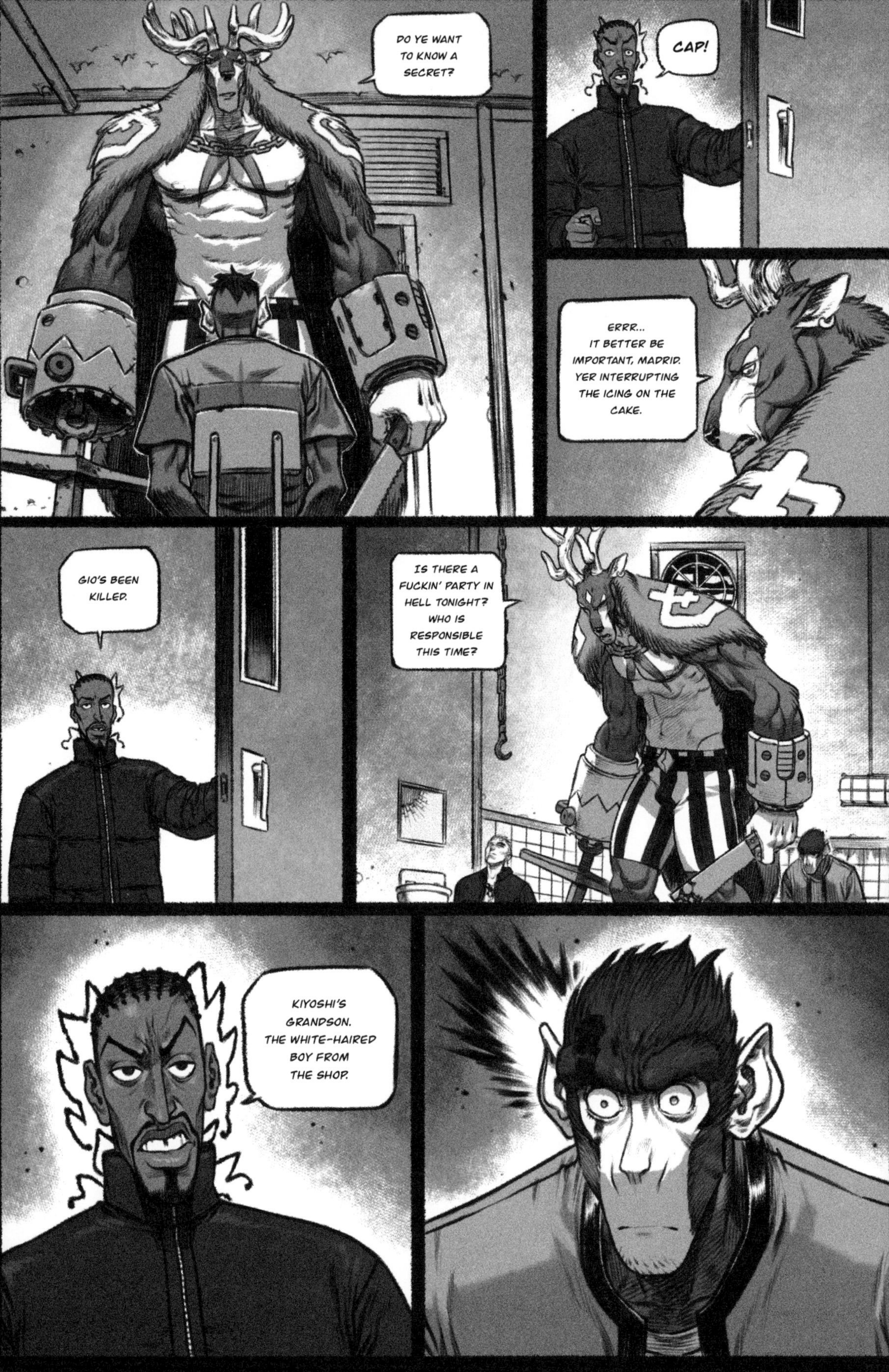
DO YE WANT TO KNOW A SECRET?
CAP!
ERRR... IT BETTER BE IMPORTANT, MADRID. YER INTERRUPTING THE ICING ON THE CAKE.
GIO'S BEEN KILLED.
IS THERE A FUCKIN' PARTY IN HELL TONIGHT? WHO IS RESPONSIBLE THIS TIME?
KIYOSHI'S GRANDSON. THE WHITE-HAIRED BOY FROM THE SHOP.

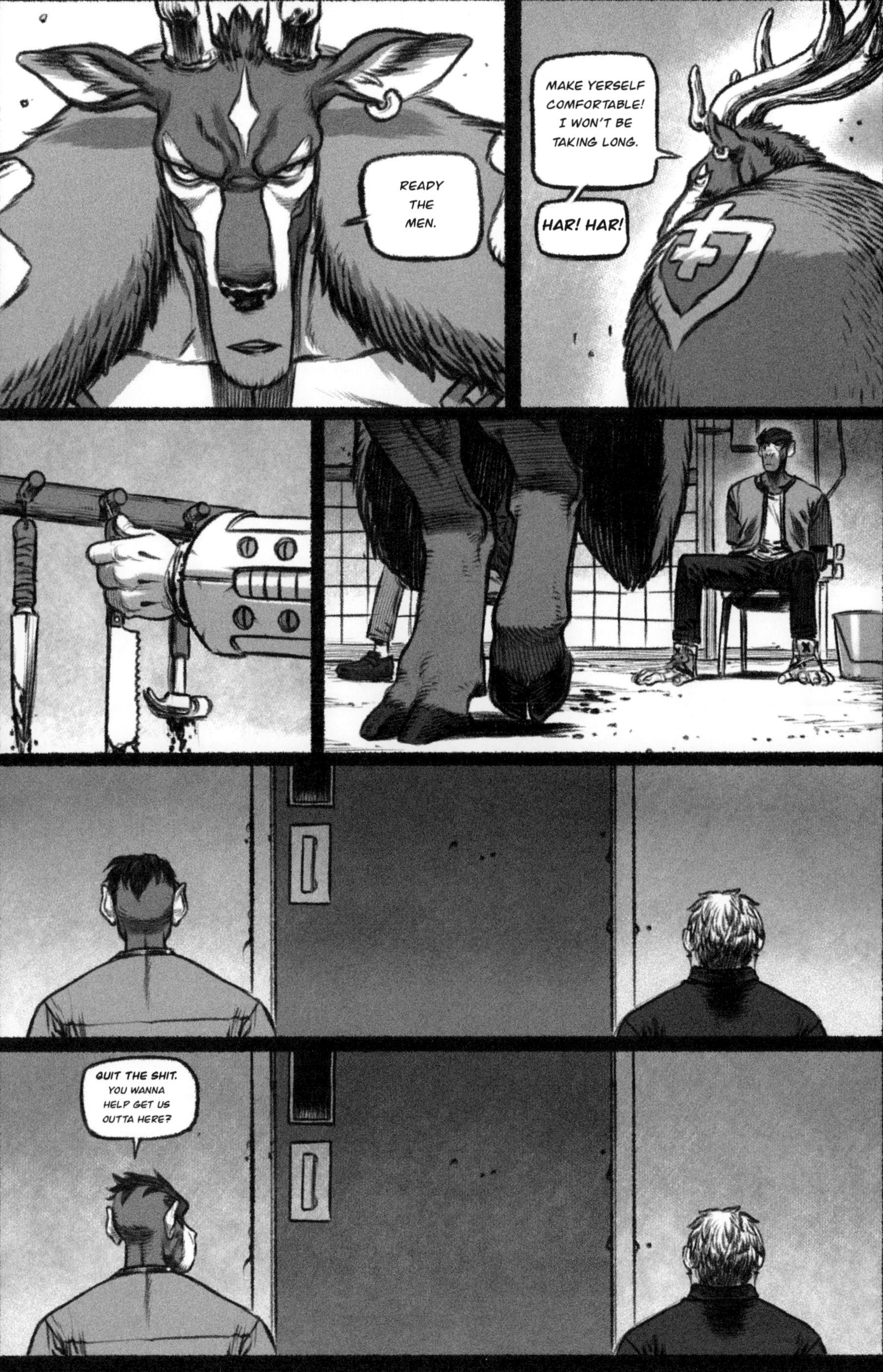
READY THE MEN.
MAKE YERSELF COMFORTABLE! I WON'T BE TAKING LONG.
HAR! HAR!
QUIT THE SHIT. YOU WANNA HELP GET US OUTTA HERE?

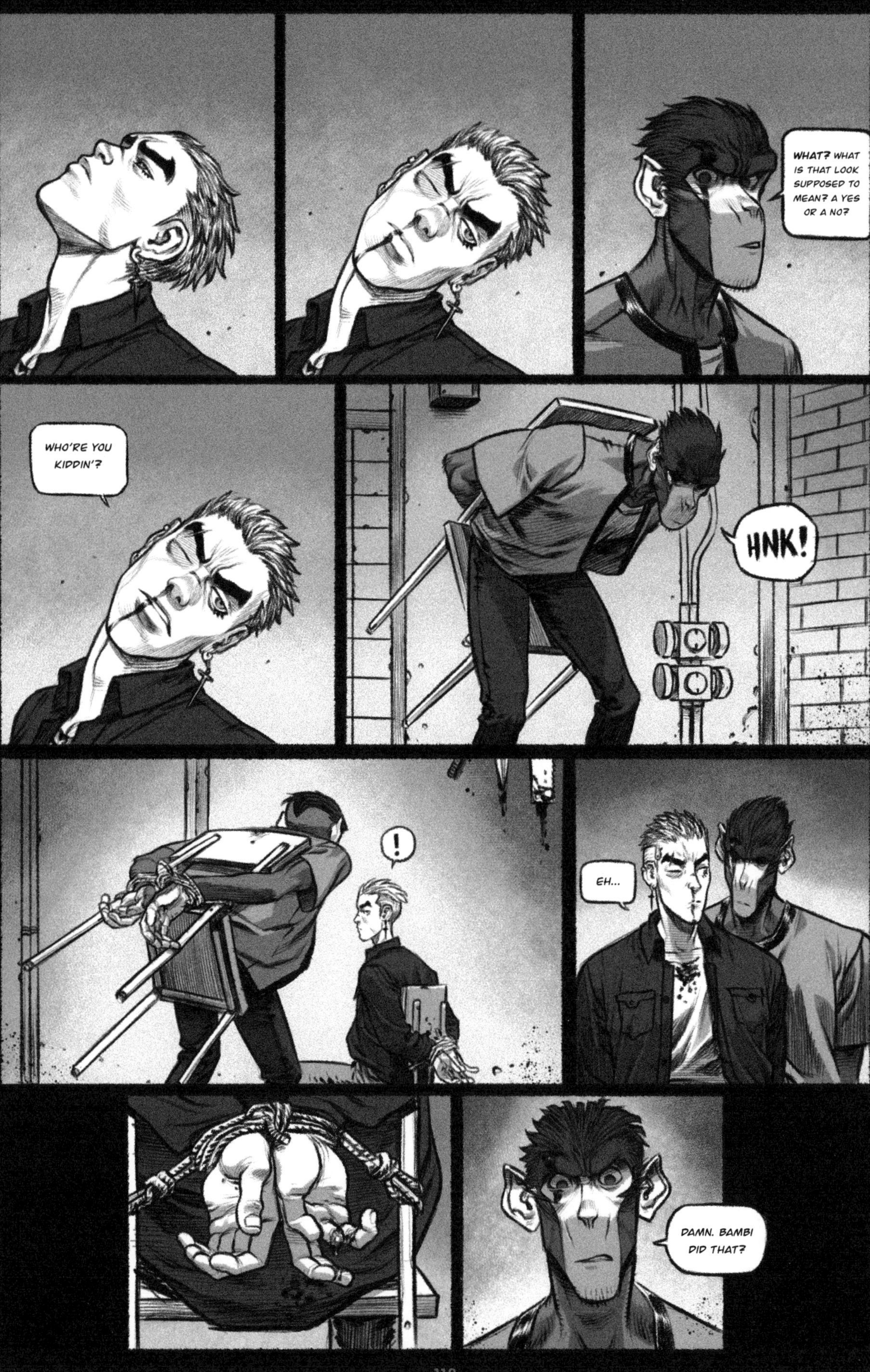
WHAT? WHAT IS THAT LOOK SUPPOSED TO MEAN? A YES OR A NO?
WHO'RE YOU KIDDIN'?
HNK!
!
EH...
DAMN. BAMBI DID THAT?

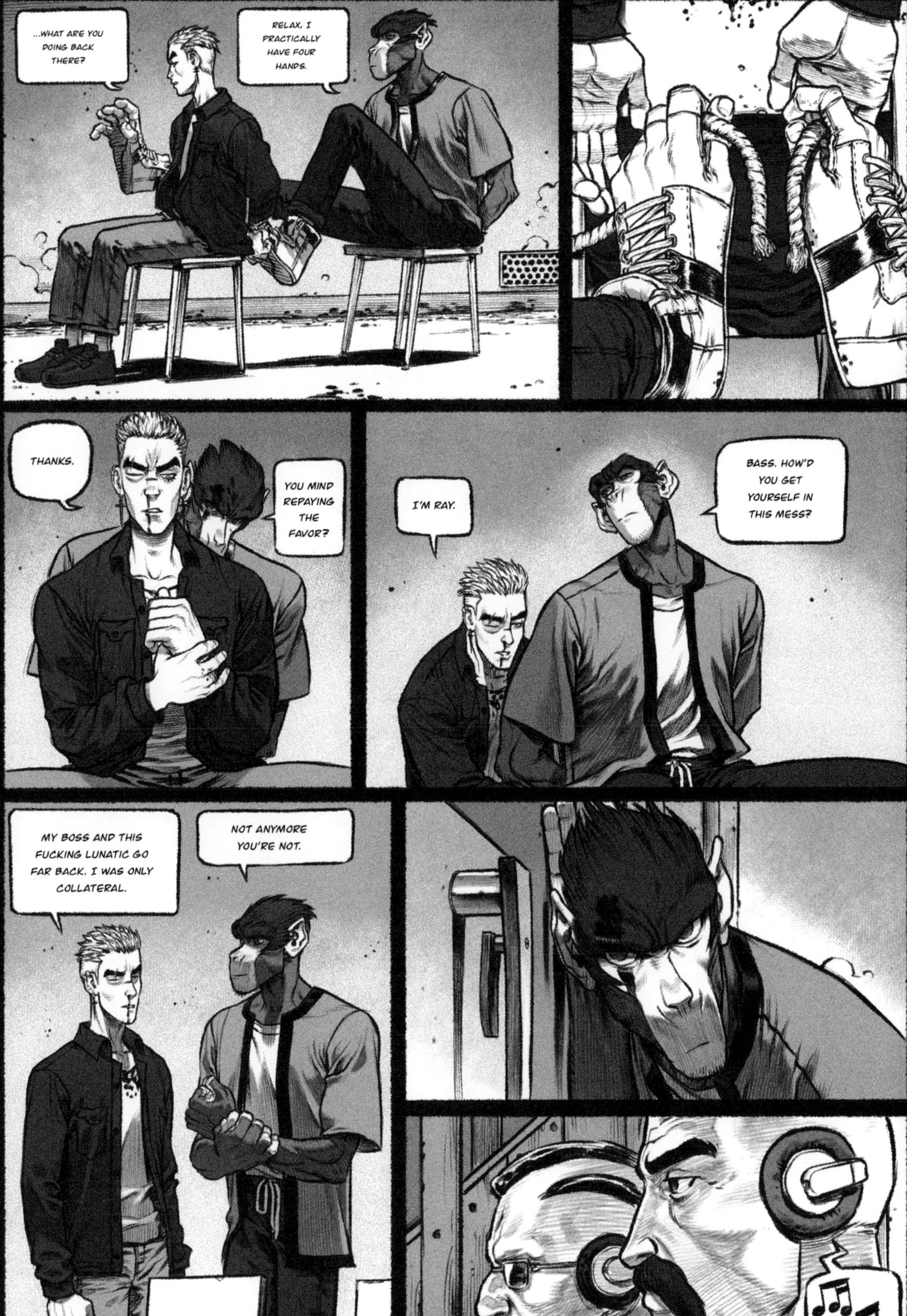
...WHAT ARE YOU DOING BACK THERE?
RELAX, I PRACTICALLY HAVE FOUR HANDS.
THANKS.
YOU MIND REPAYING THE FAVOR?
I'M RAY.
BASS. HOW'D YOU GET YOURSELF IN THIS MESS?
MY BOSS AND THIS FUCKING LUNATIC GO FAR BACK. I WAS ONLY COLLATERAL.
NOT ANYMORE YOU'RE NOT.

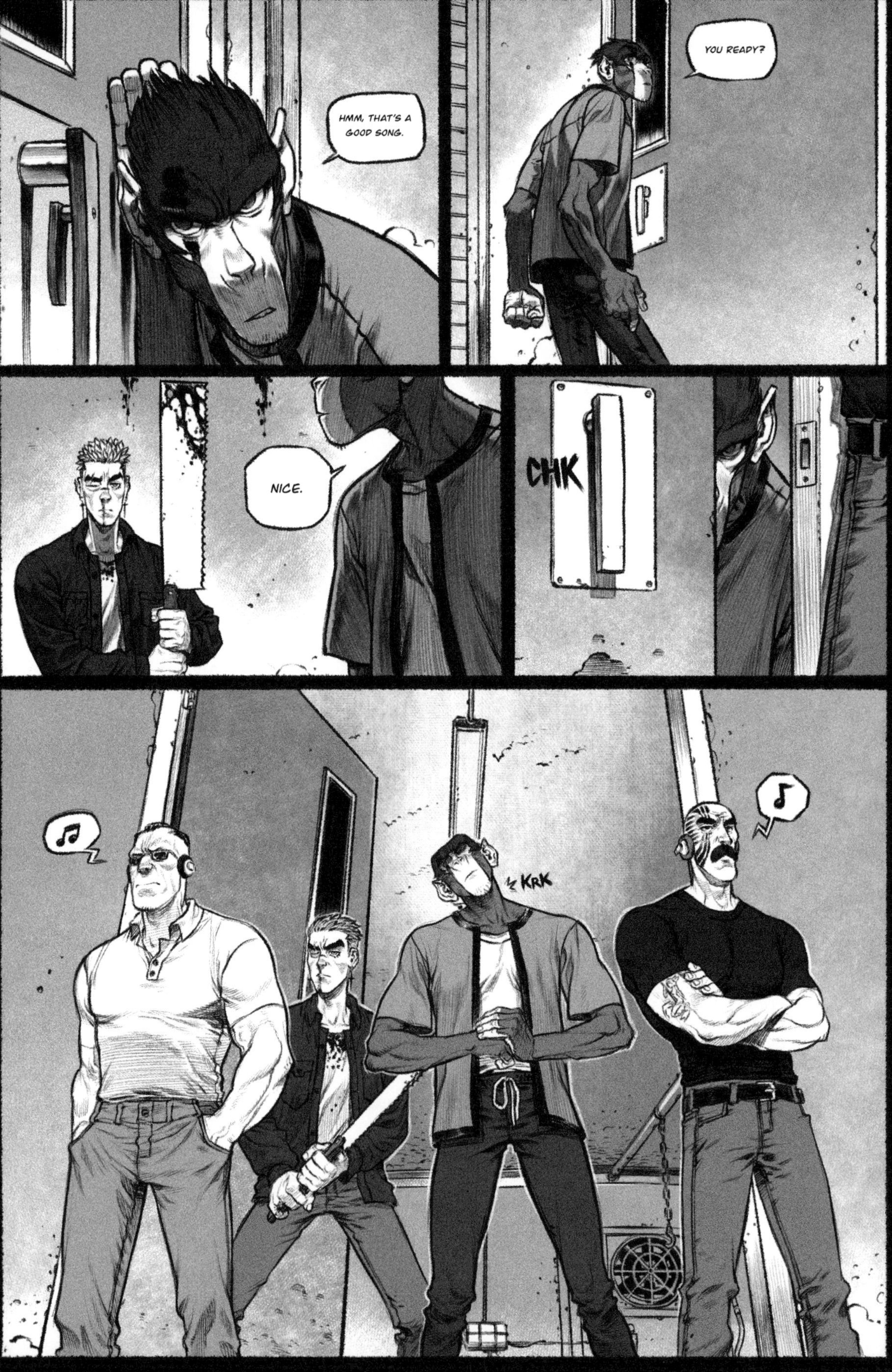
HMM, THAT'S A GOOD SONG.
YOU READY?
NICE.
CHK
♫
KRK
♪

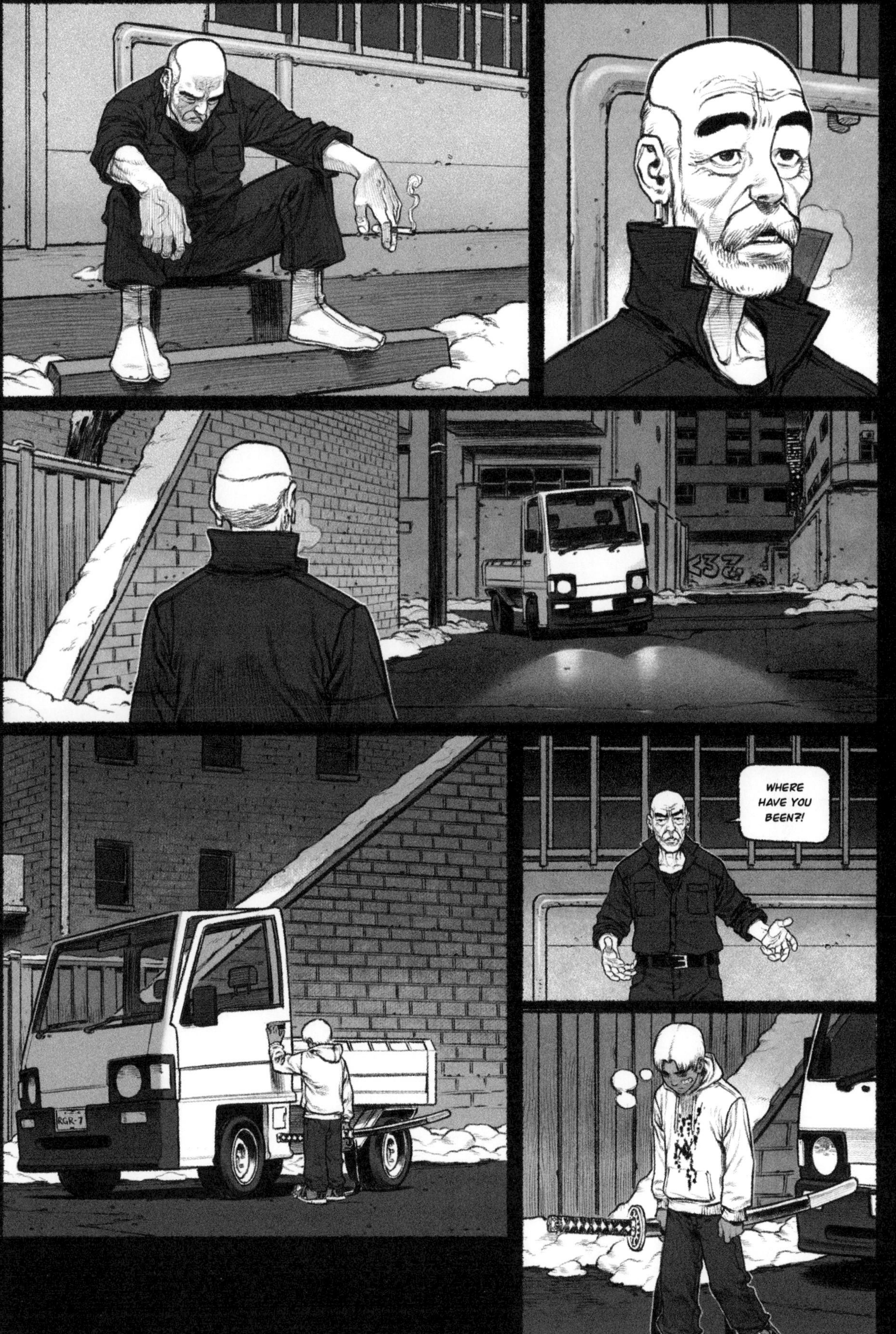
WHERE HAVE YOU BEEN?!
RGR-7

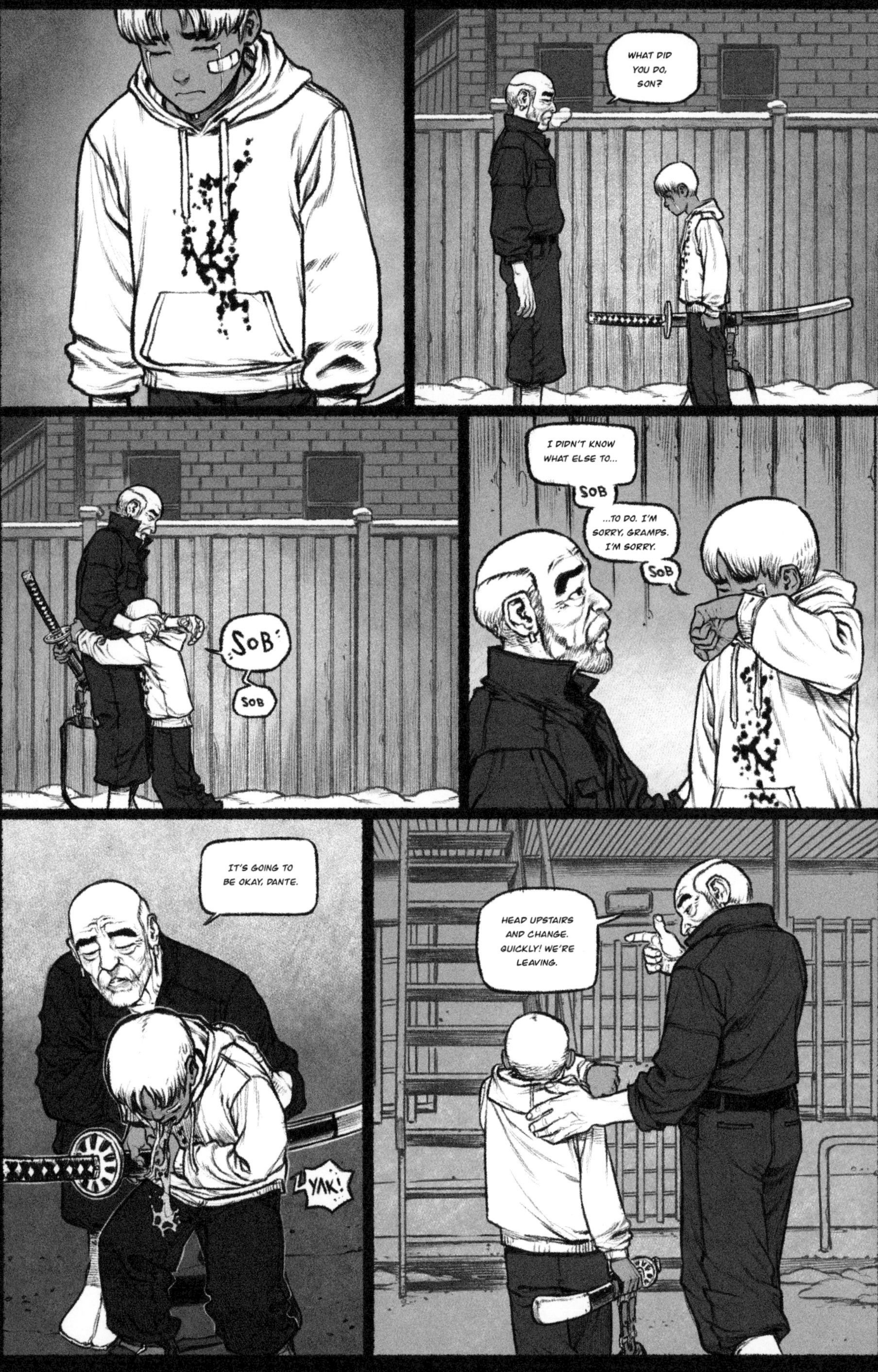
WHAT DID YOU DO, SON?
I DIDN'T KNOW WHAT ELSE TO...
SOB
...TO DO. I'M SORRY, GRAMPS. I'M SORRY.
SOB
SOB
SOB
IT'S GOING TO BE OKAY, DANTE.
YAK!
HEAD UPSTAIRS AND CHANGE. QUICKLY! WE'RE LEAVING.

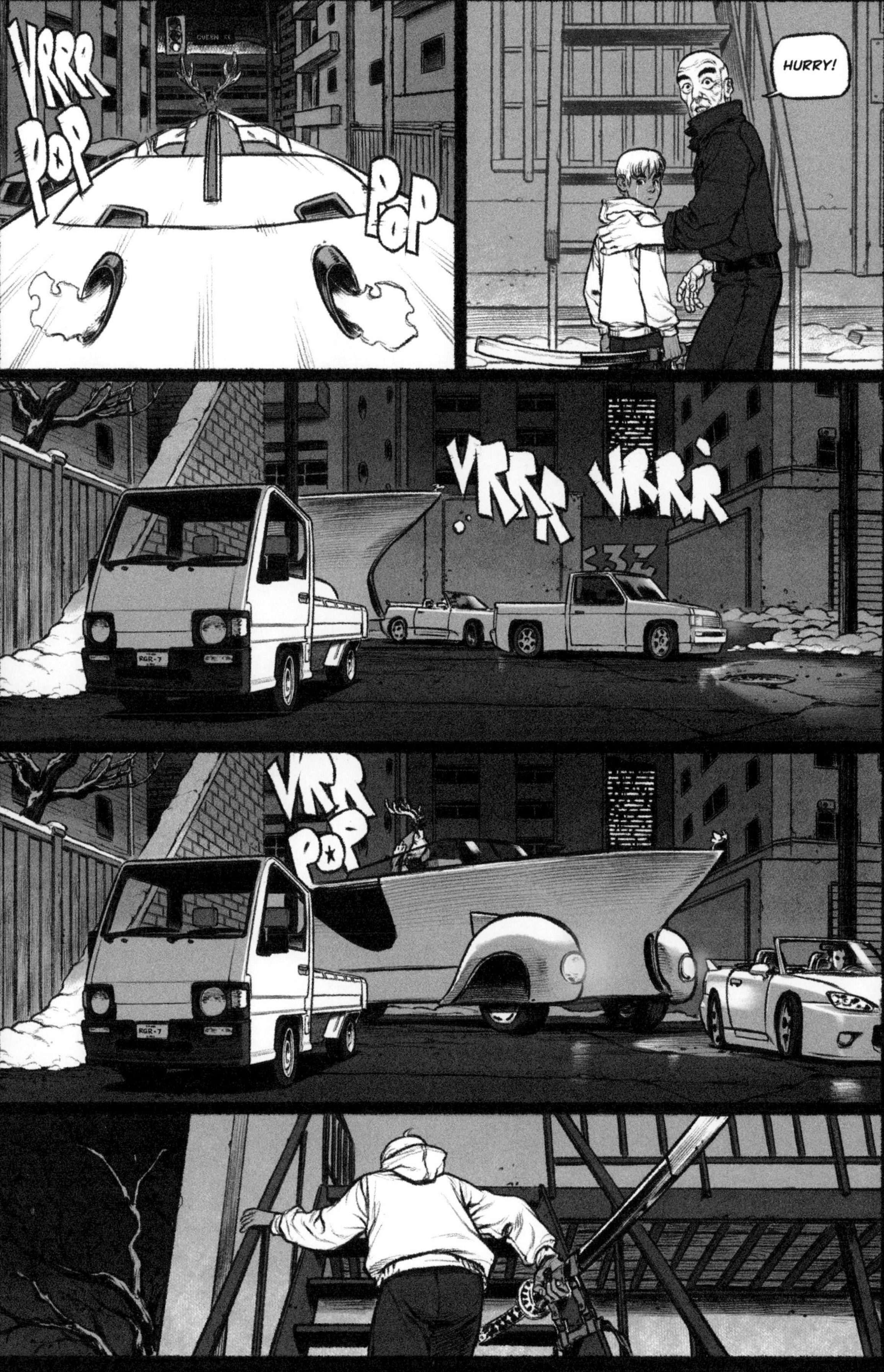
VRRR
POP
POP
HURRY!
VRRR
VRRR
RGR-7
VRR
POP
RGR-7

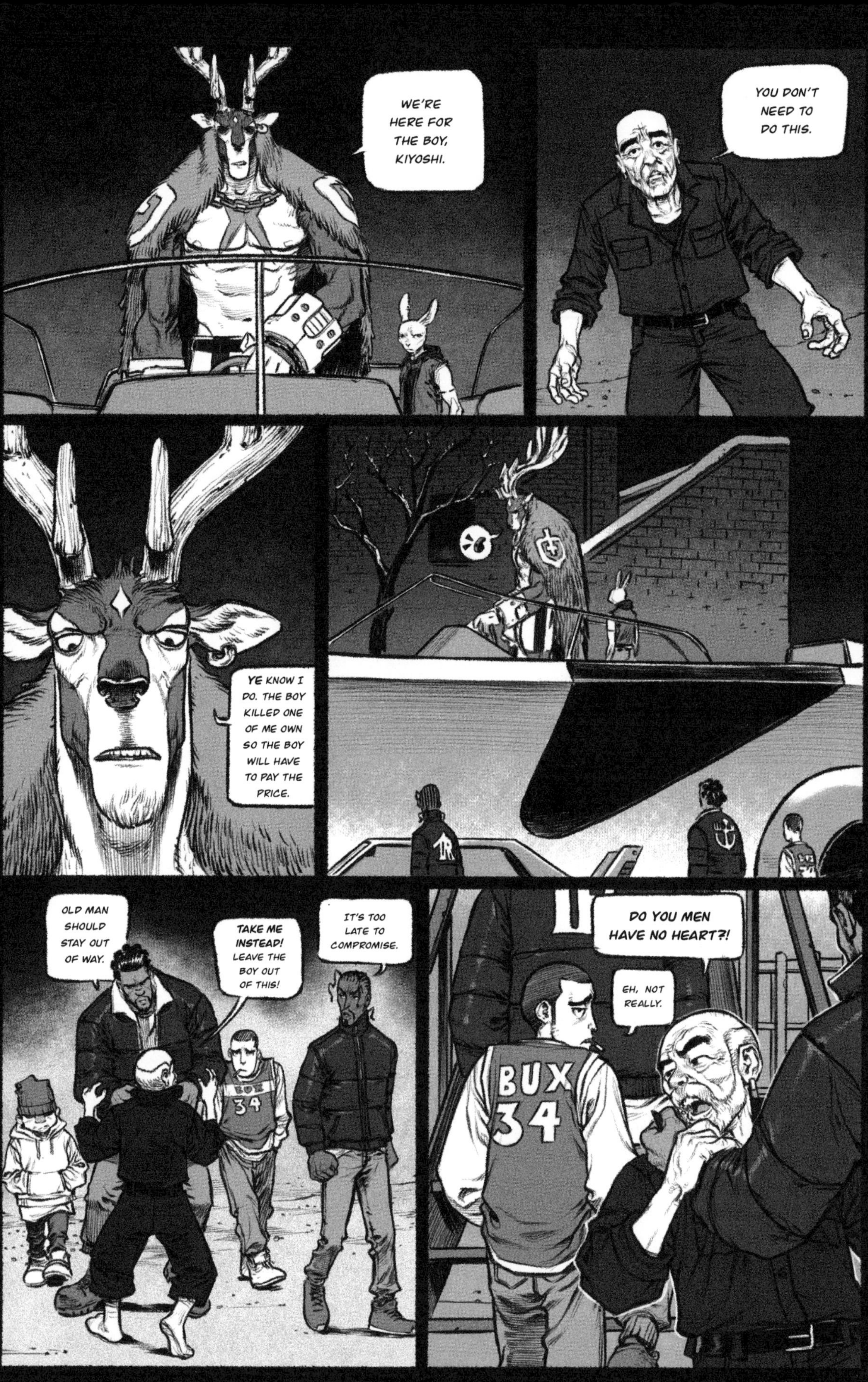
WE'RE HERE FOR THE BOY, KIYOSHI.
YOU DON'T NEED TO DO THIS.
YE KNOW I DO. THE BOY KILLED ONE OF ME OWN SO THE BOY WILL HAVE TO PAY THE PRICE.
OLD MAN SHOULD STAY OUT OF WAY.
TAKE ME INSTEAD! LEAVE THE BOY OUT OF THIS!
IT'S TOO LATE TO COMPROMISE.
DO YOU MEN HAVE NO HEART?!
EH, NOT REALLY.
BUX 34

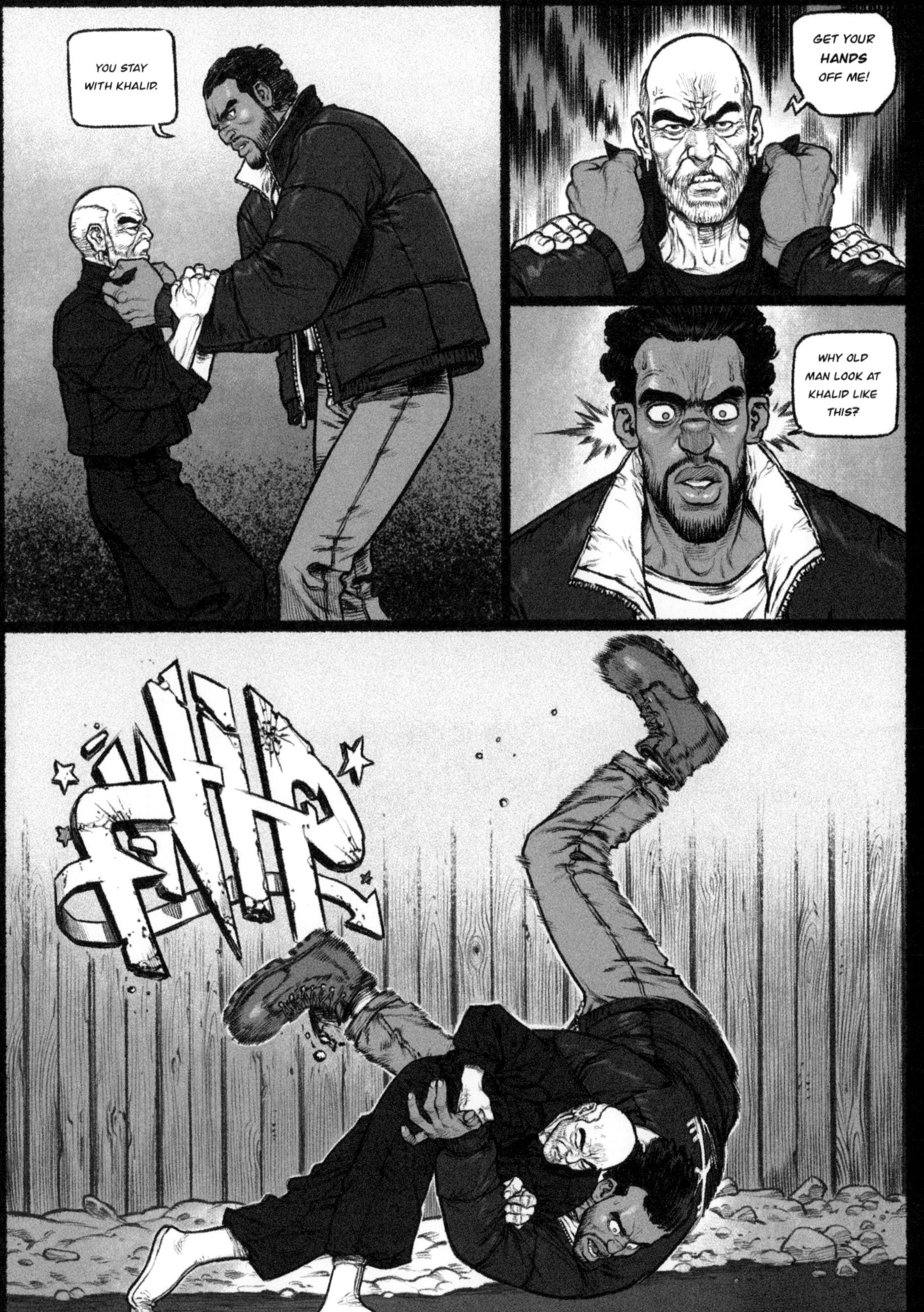
YOU STAY WITH KHALID.
GET YOUR HANDS OFF ME!
WHY OLD MAN LOOK AT KHALID LIKE THIS?

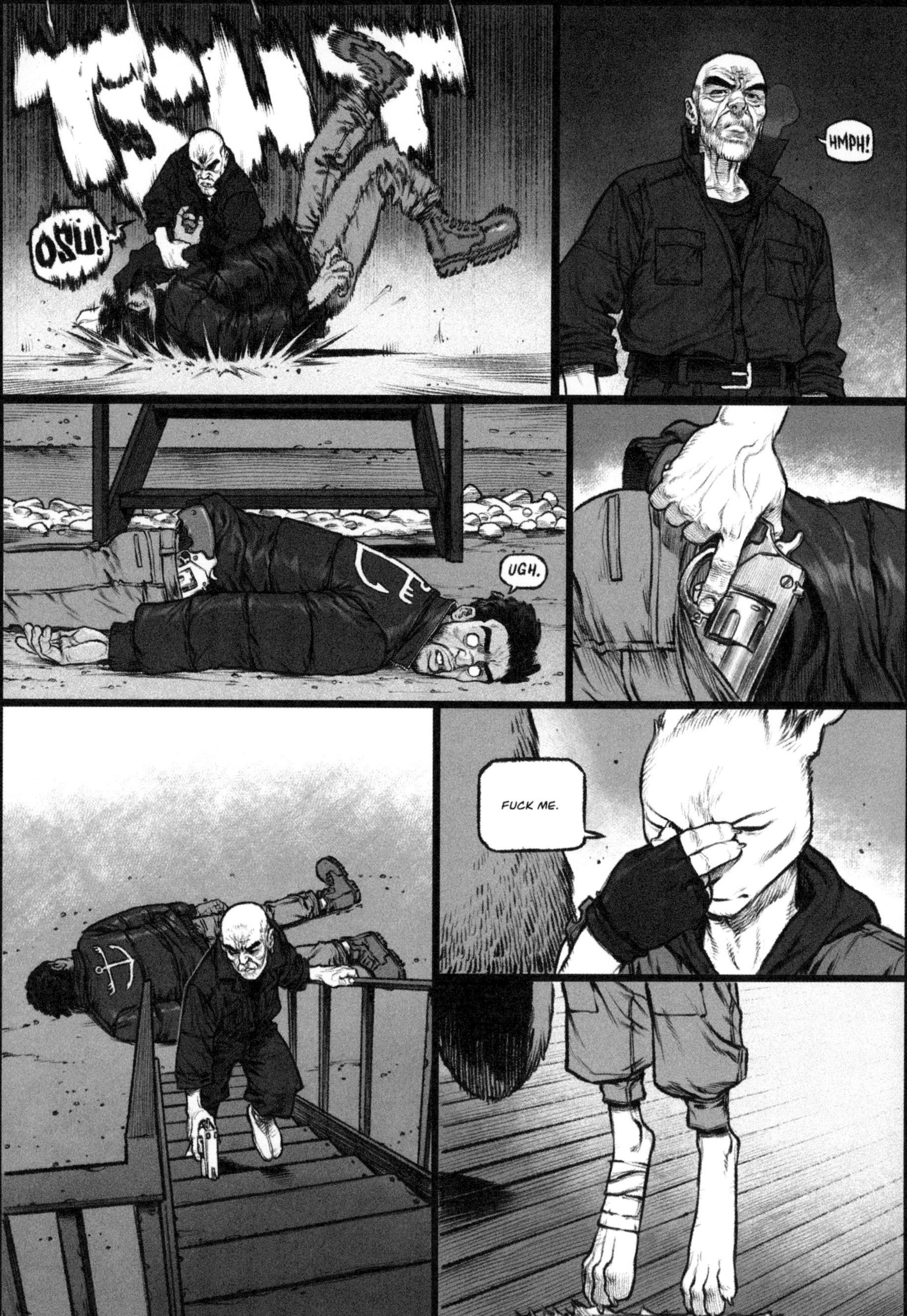
TSHT
OSU!
HMPH!
UGH.
FUCK ME.

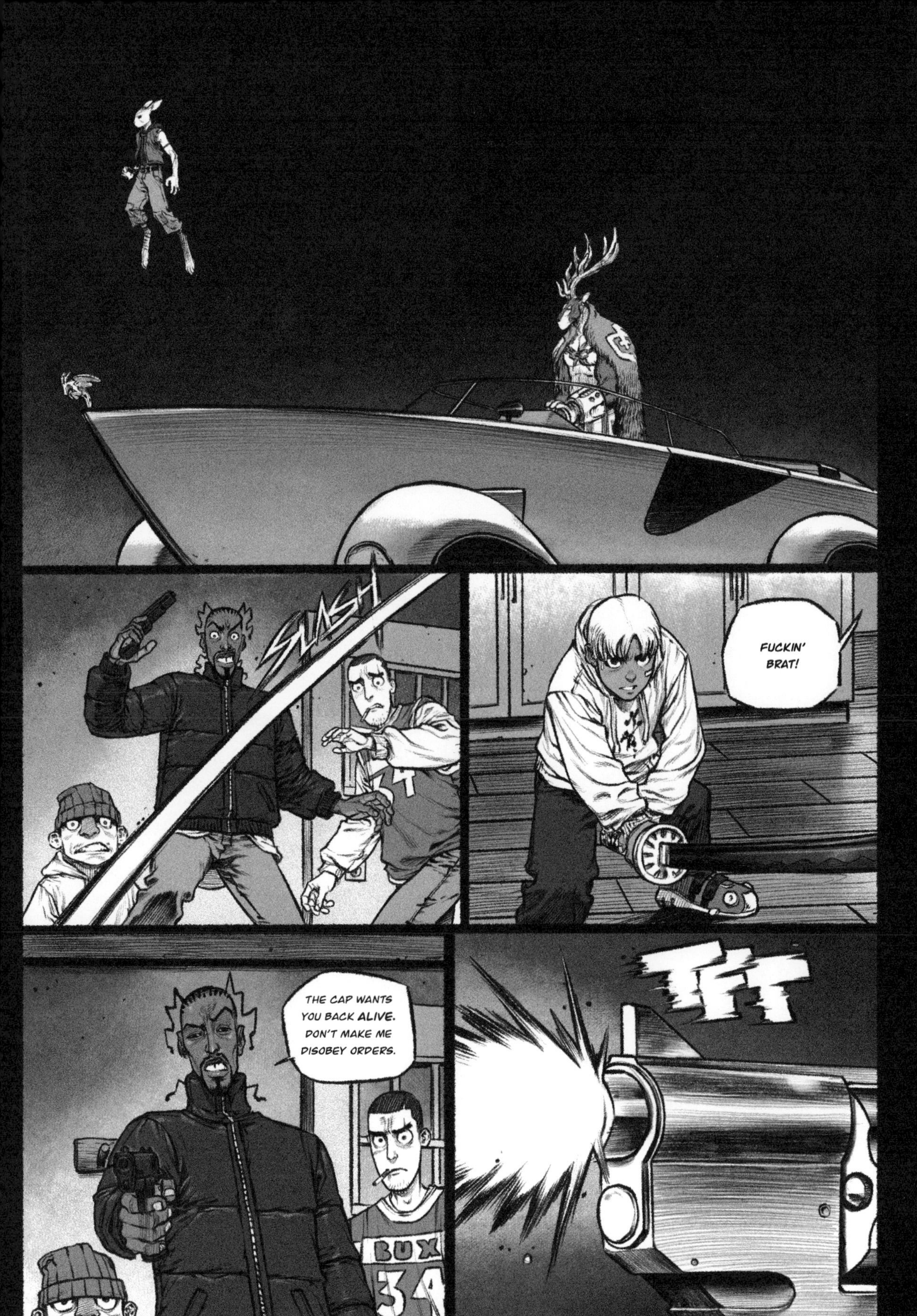
SLASH
FUCKIN' BRAT!
THE CAP WANTS YOU BACK ALIVE. DON'T MAKE ME DISOBEY ORDERS.
TFT

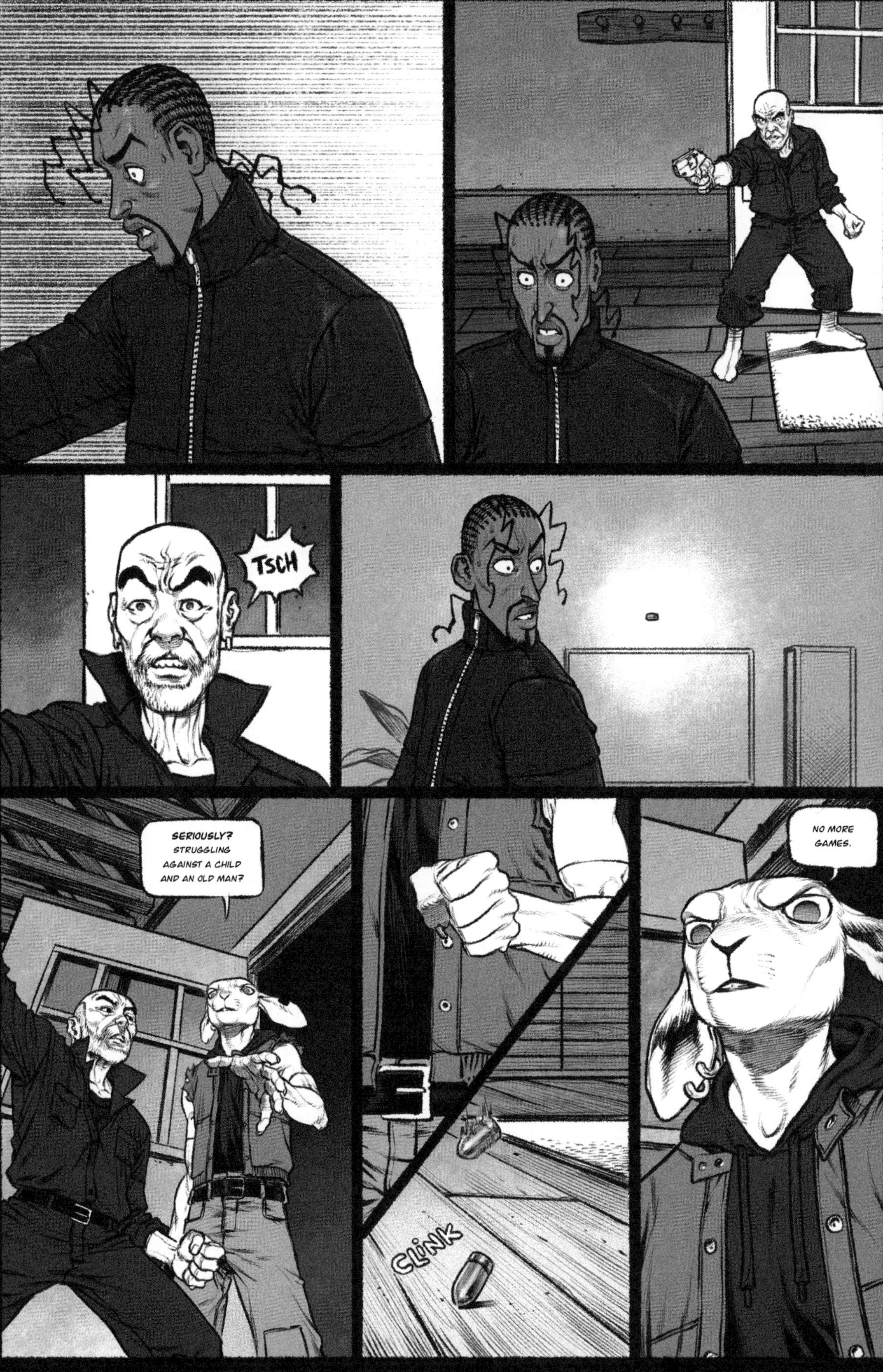
TSCH
SERIOUSLY? STRUGGLING AGAINST A CHILD AND AN OLD MAN?
CLINK
NO MORE GAMES.

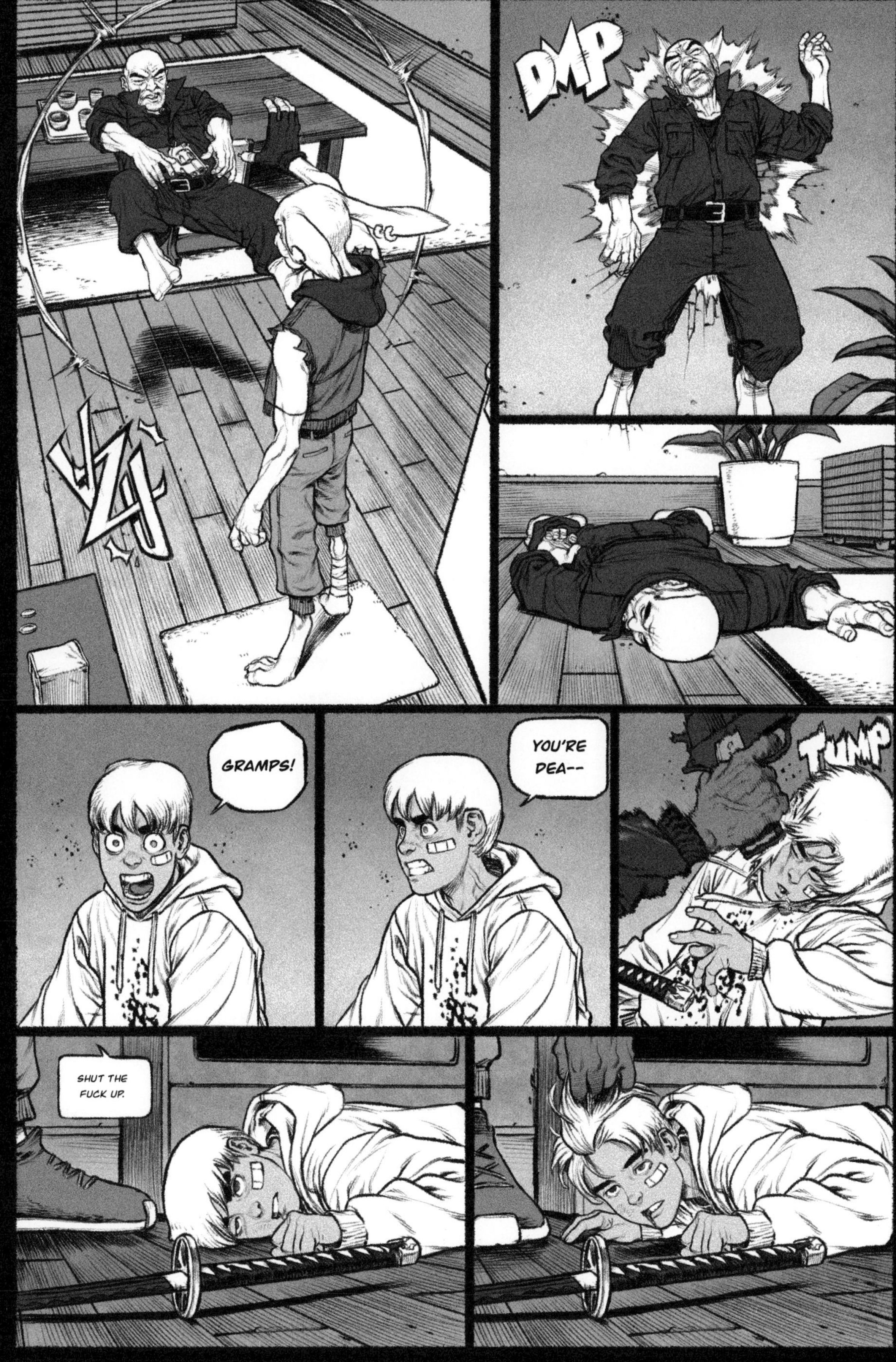
ZZT
DMP
GRAMPS!
YOU'RE DEA--
TUMP
SHUT THE FUCK UP.

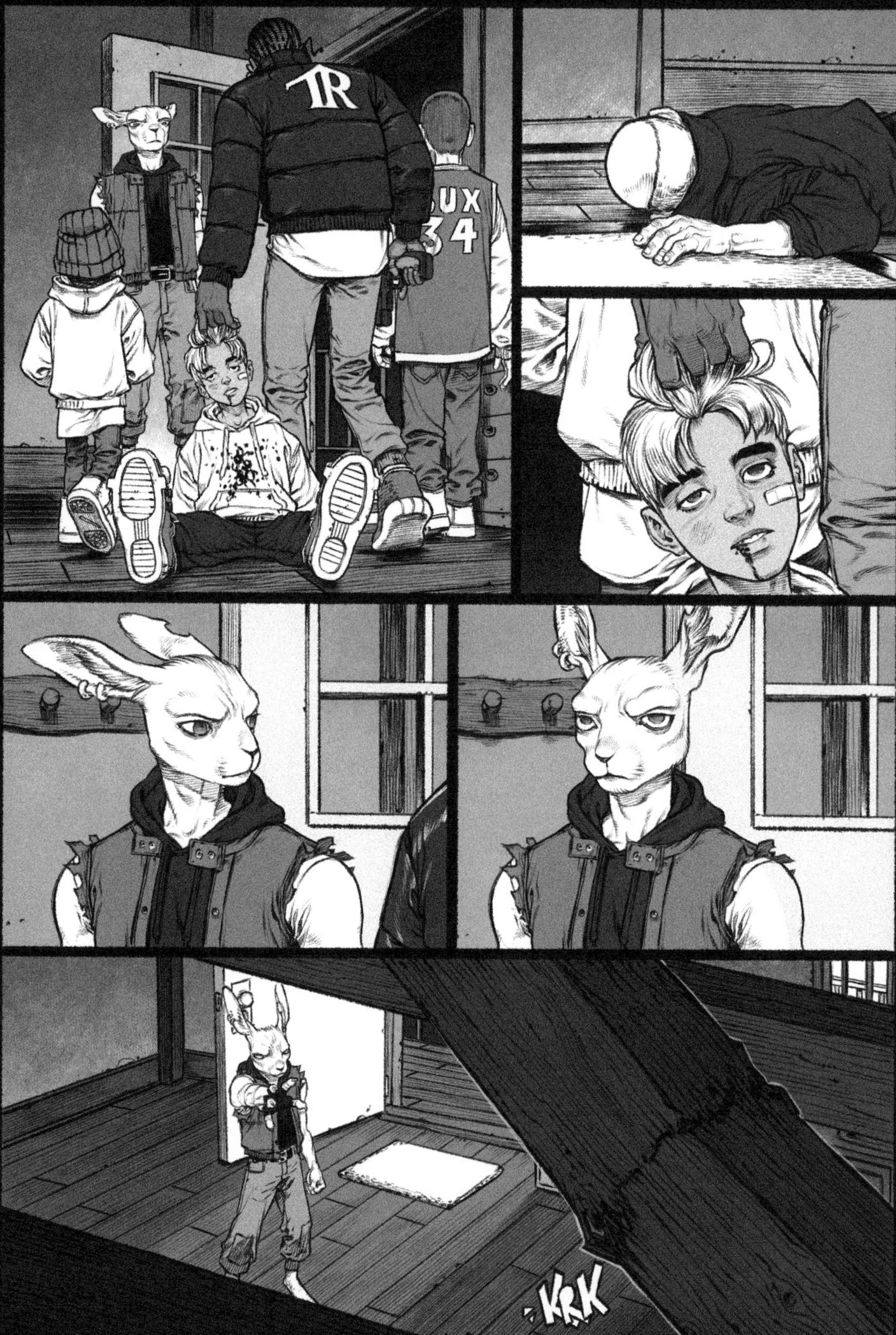

TR
UX
34
KRK

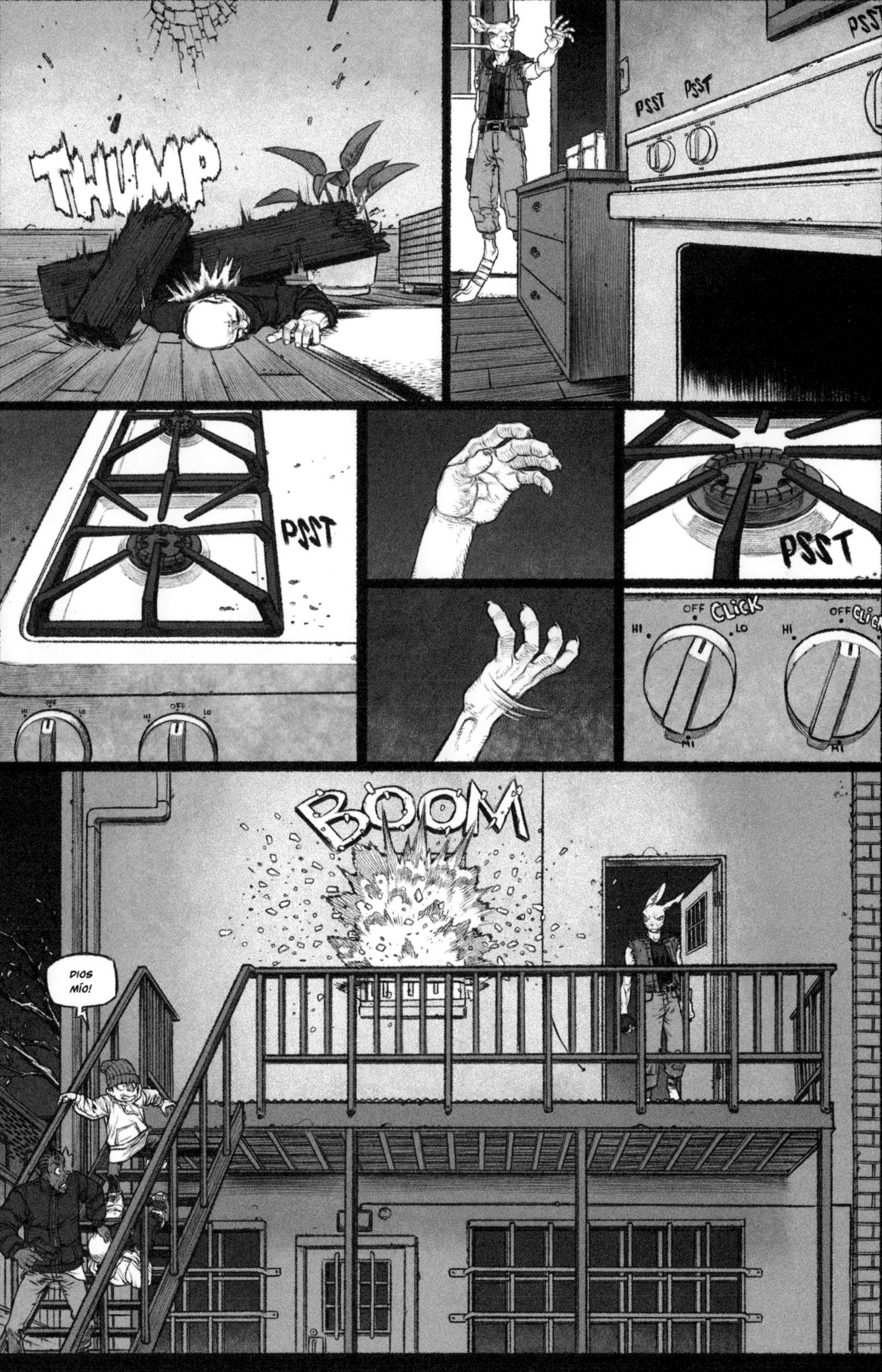
THUMP
PSST
PSST PSST
PSST
PSST
OFF CLICK
HI LO
OFF CLICK
HI
BOOM
DIOS MÍO!

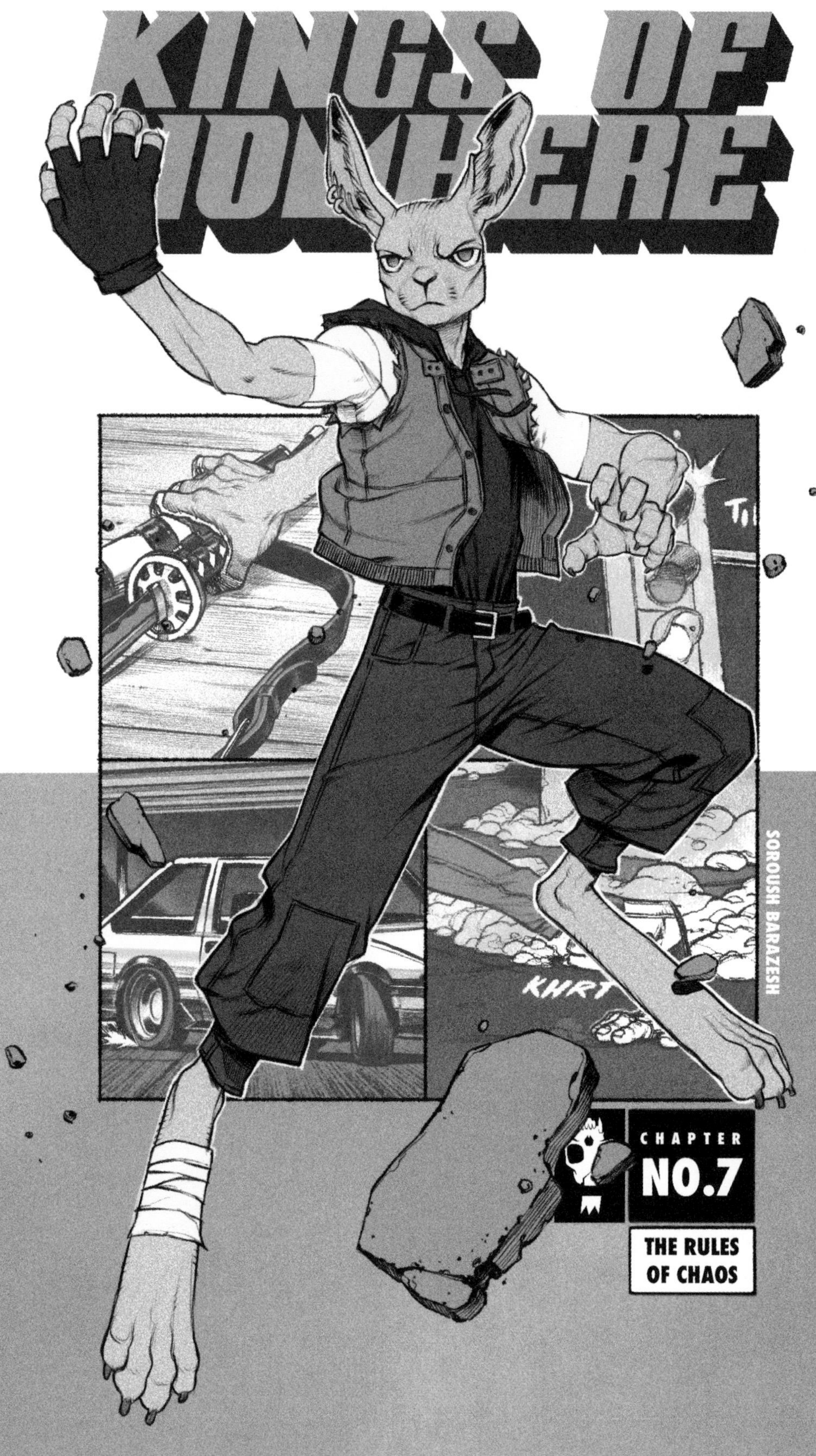
KINGS OF
KHRT
SOROUSH BARAZESH
CHAPTER
NO.7
THE RULES OF CHAOS

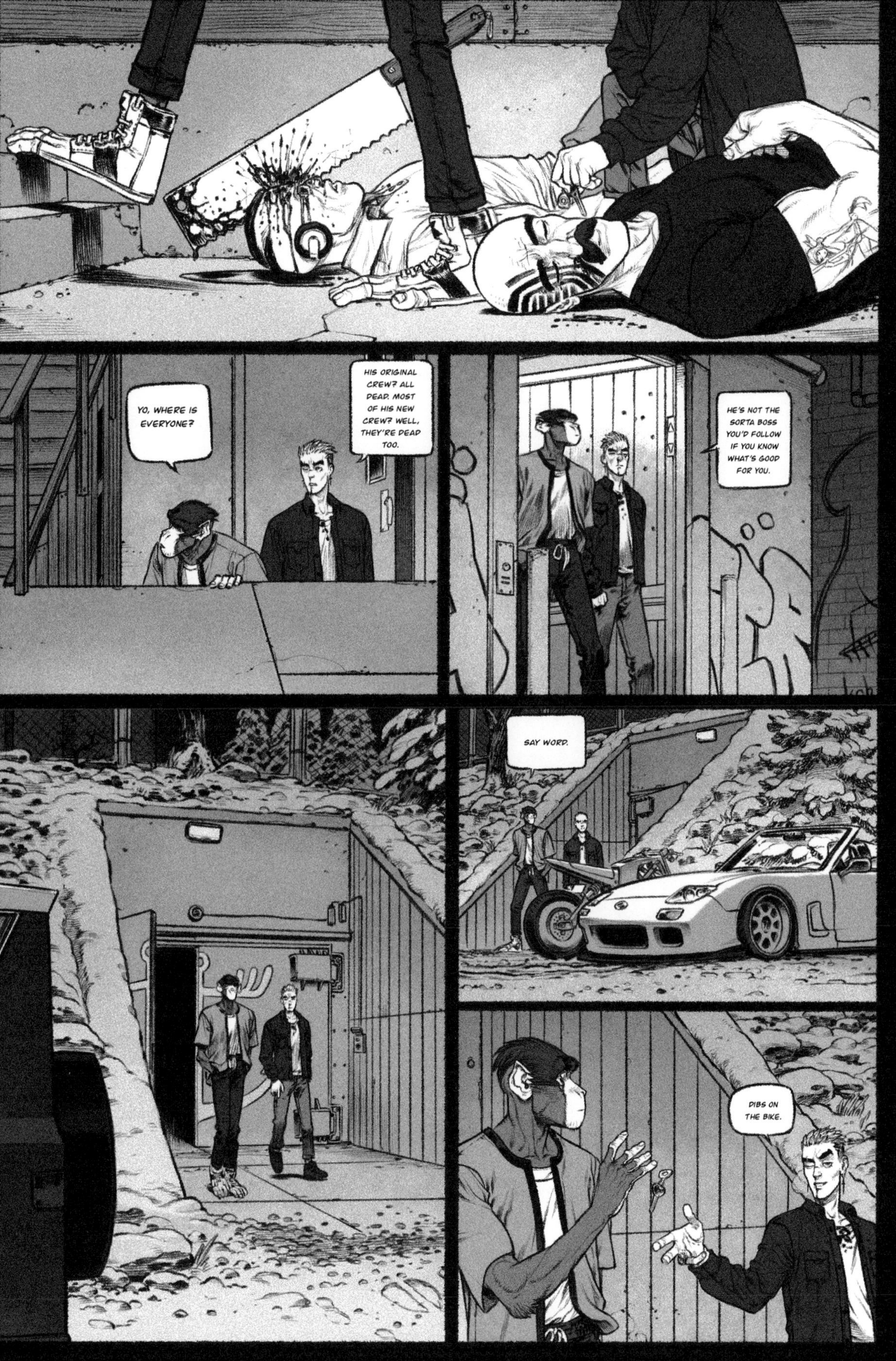
YO, WHERE IS EVERYONE?
HIS ORIGINAL CREW? ALL DEAD. MOST OF HIS NEW CREW? WELL, THEY'RE DEAD TOO.
HE'S NOT THE SORTA BOSS YOU'D FOLLOW IF YOU KNOW WHAT'S GOOD FOR YOU.
SAY WORD.
DIBS ON THE BIKE.

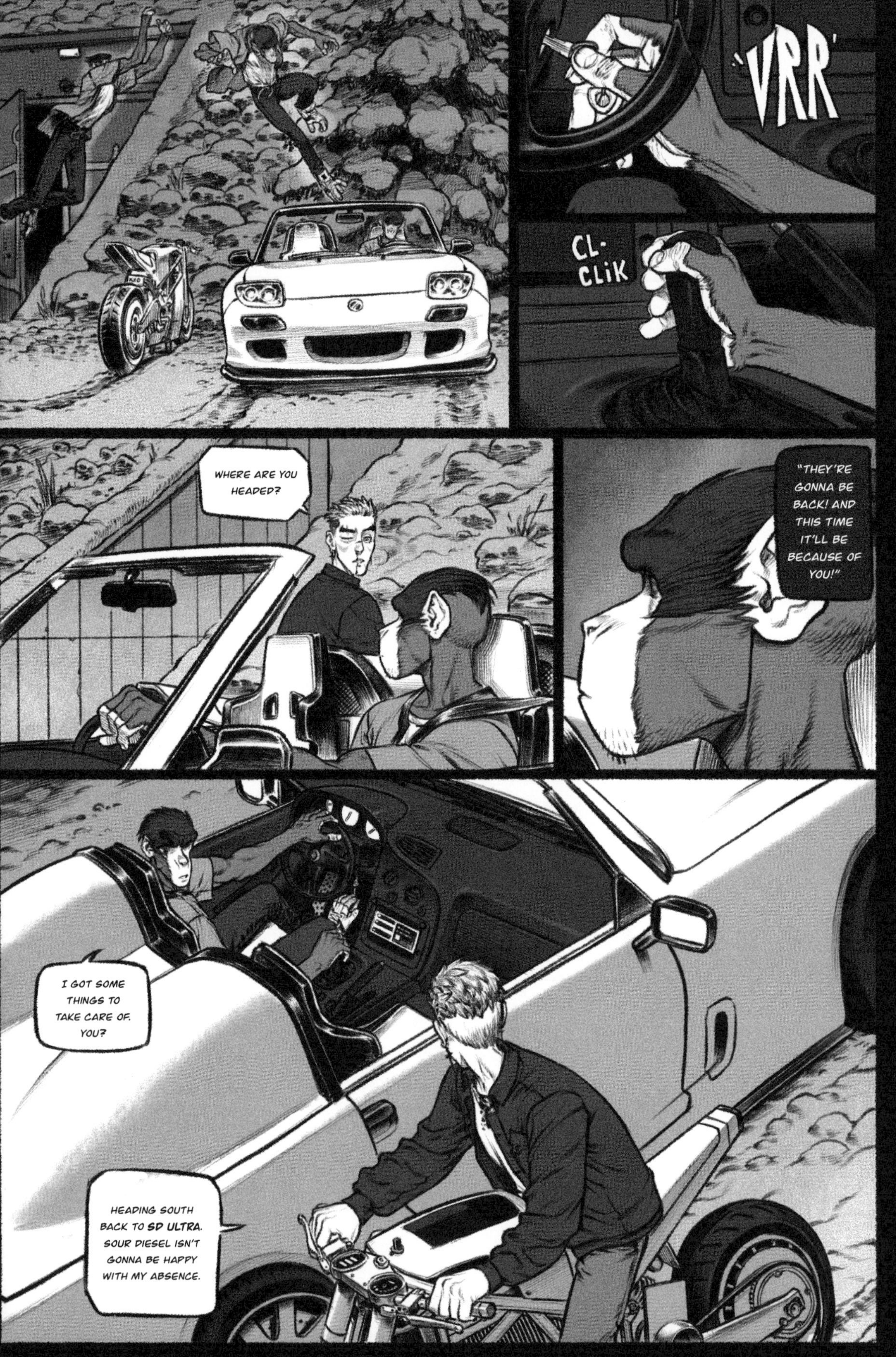
VRR
CL-CLIK
WHERE ARE YOU HEADED?
"THEY'RE GONNA BE BACK! AND THIS TIME IT'LL BE BECAUSE OF YOU!"
I GOT SOME THINGS TO TAKE CARE OF. YOU?
HEADING SOUTH BACK TO **SD ULTRA**. SOUR DIESEL ISN'T GONNA BE HAPPY WITH MY ABSENCE.

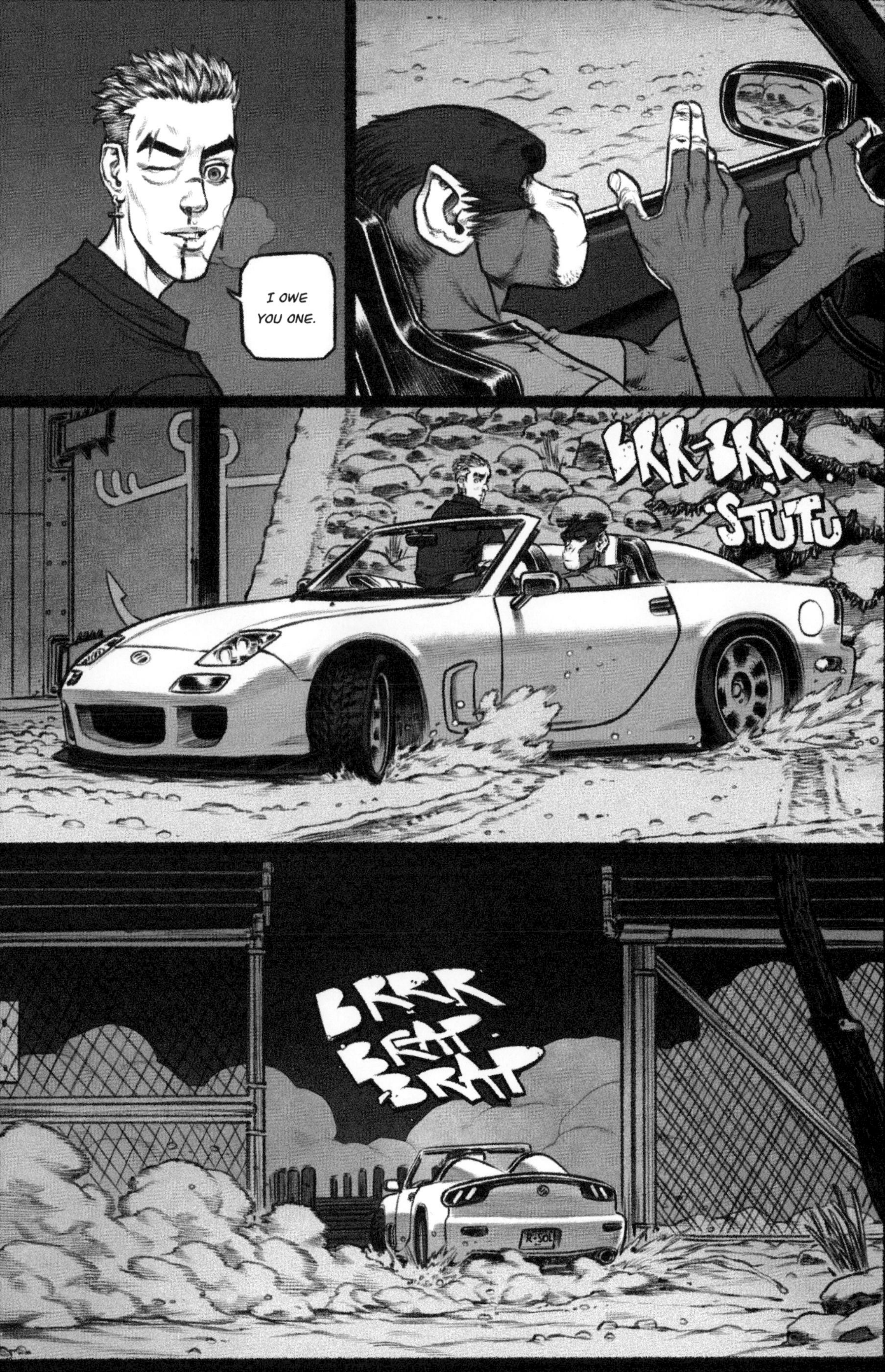
I OWE YOU ONE.
BRR-BRR
STUTU
BRRR
BRAT
BRAT
R-SOL

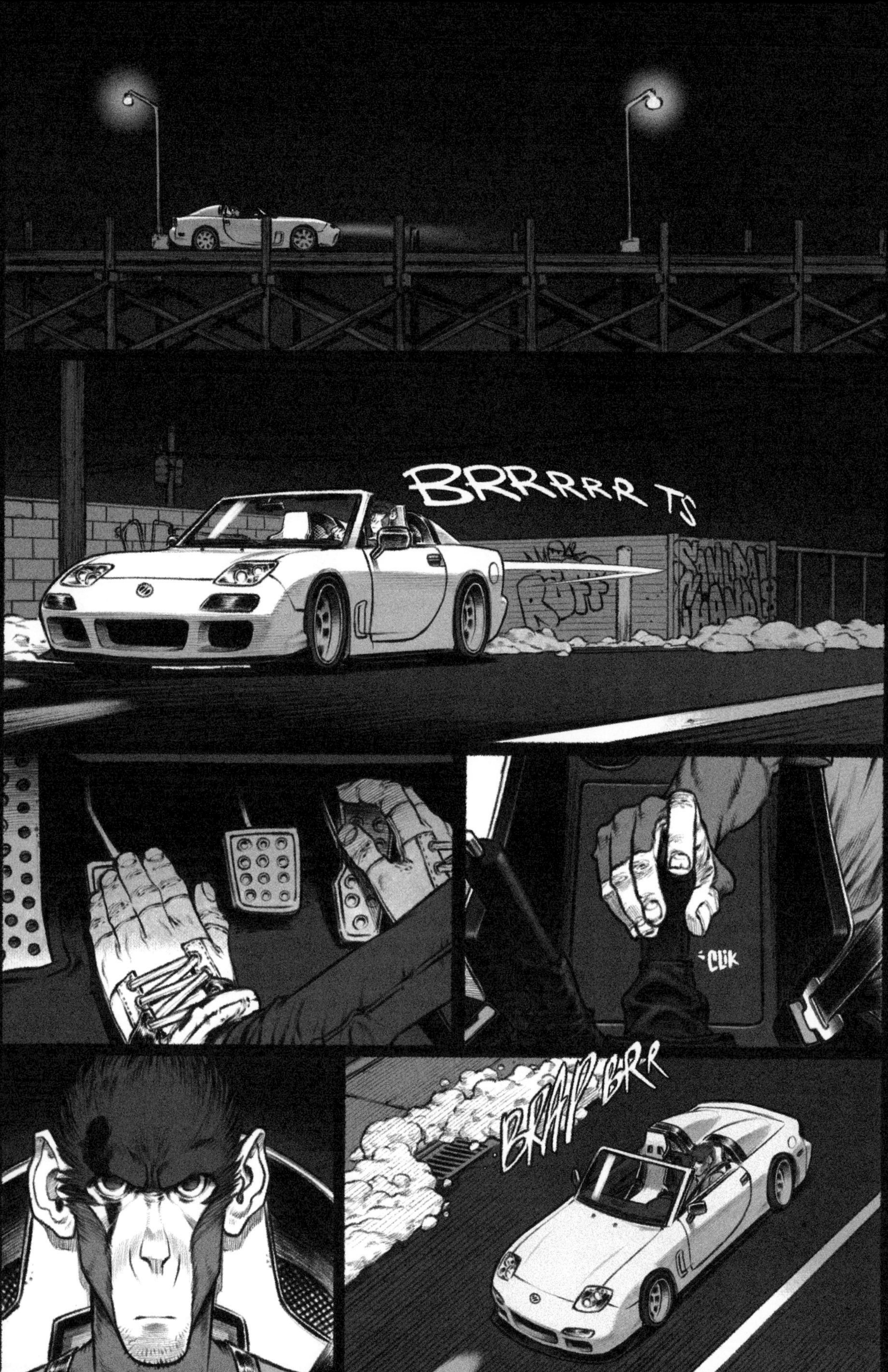
BRRRRRR TS
CLIK
BRAAP BR-R

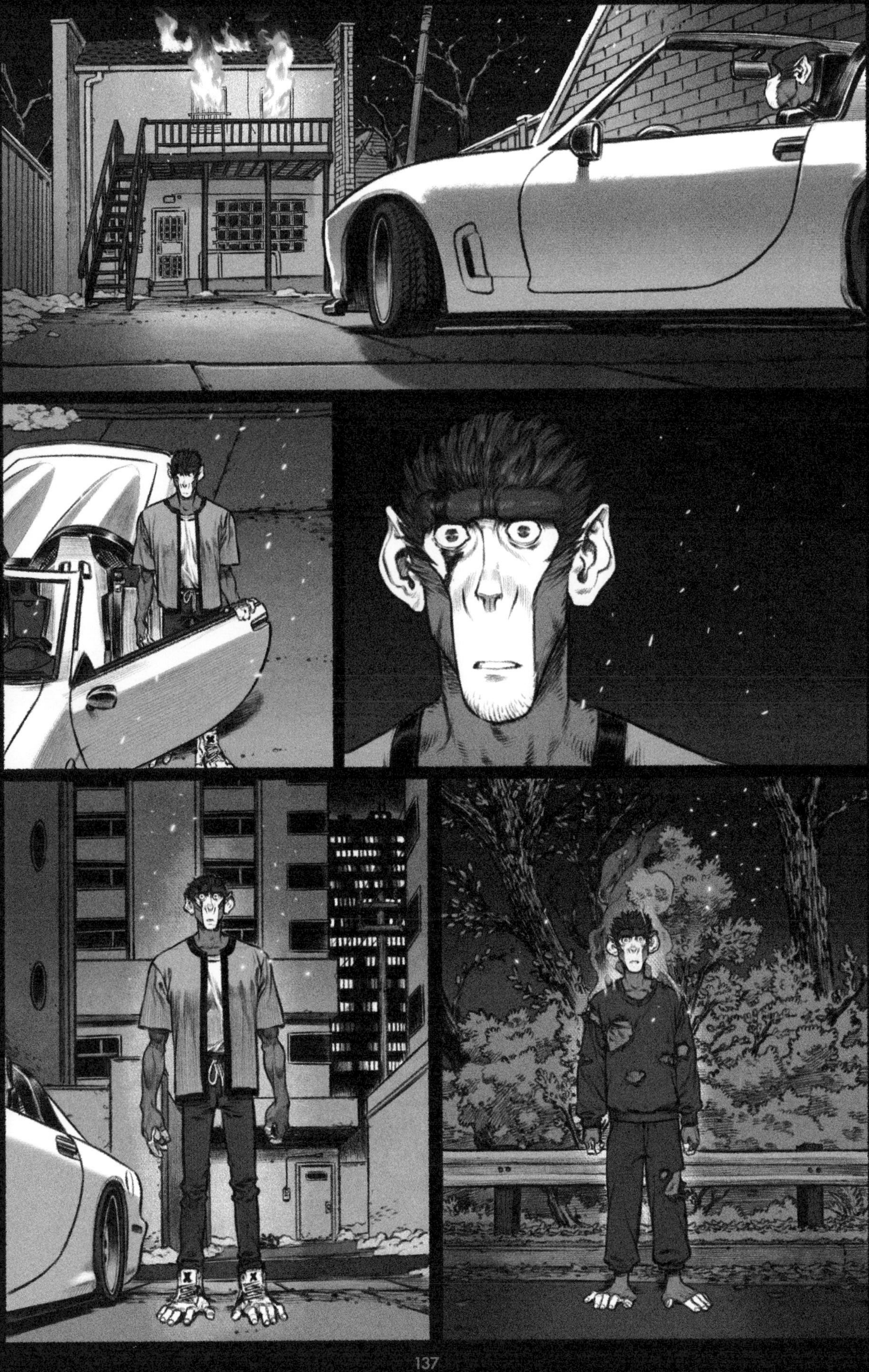

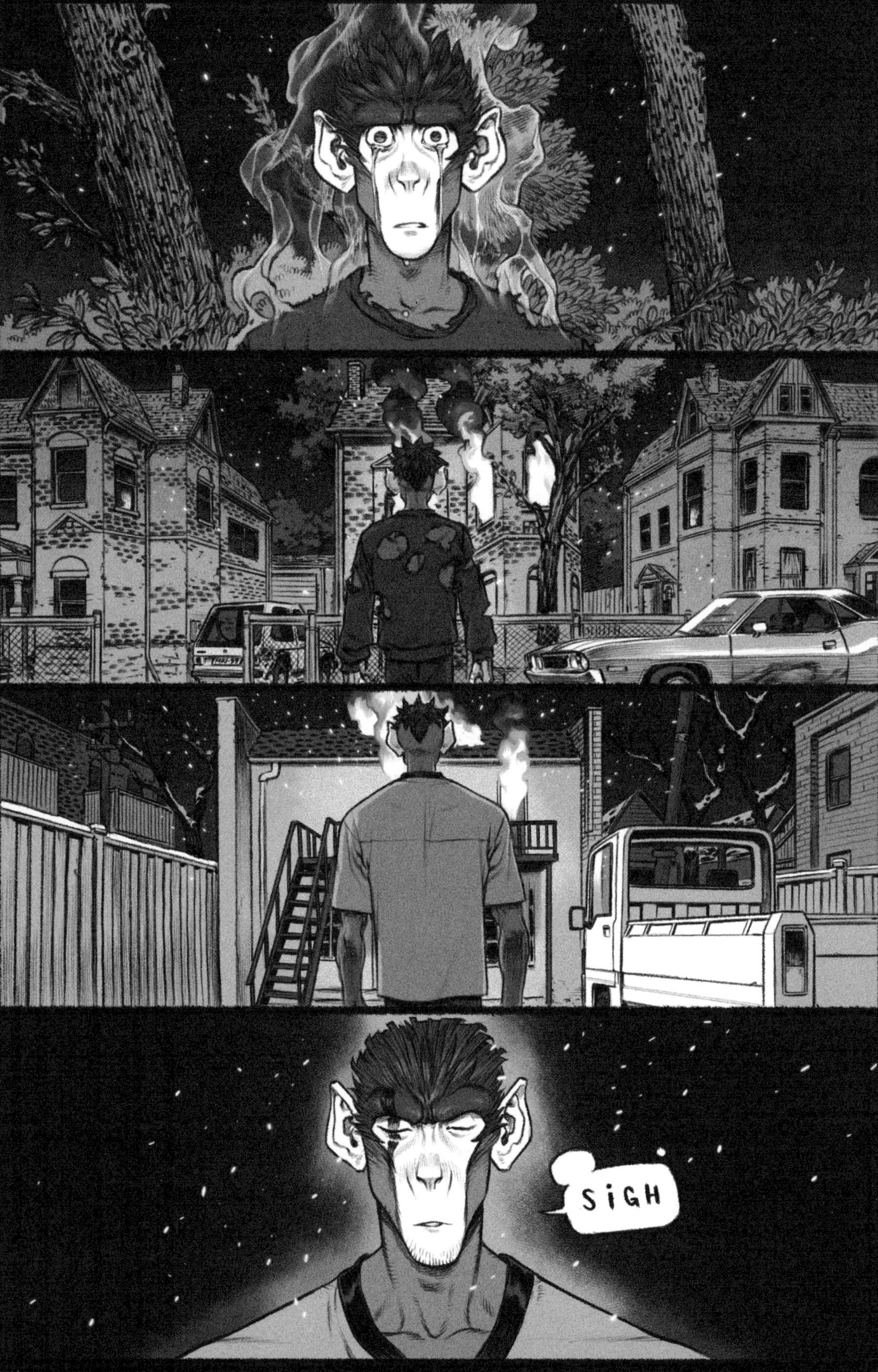
SIGH

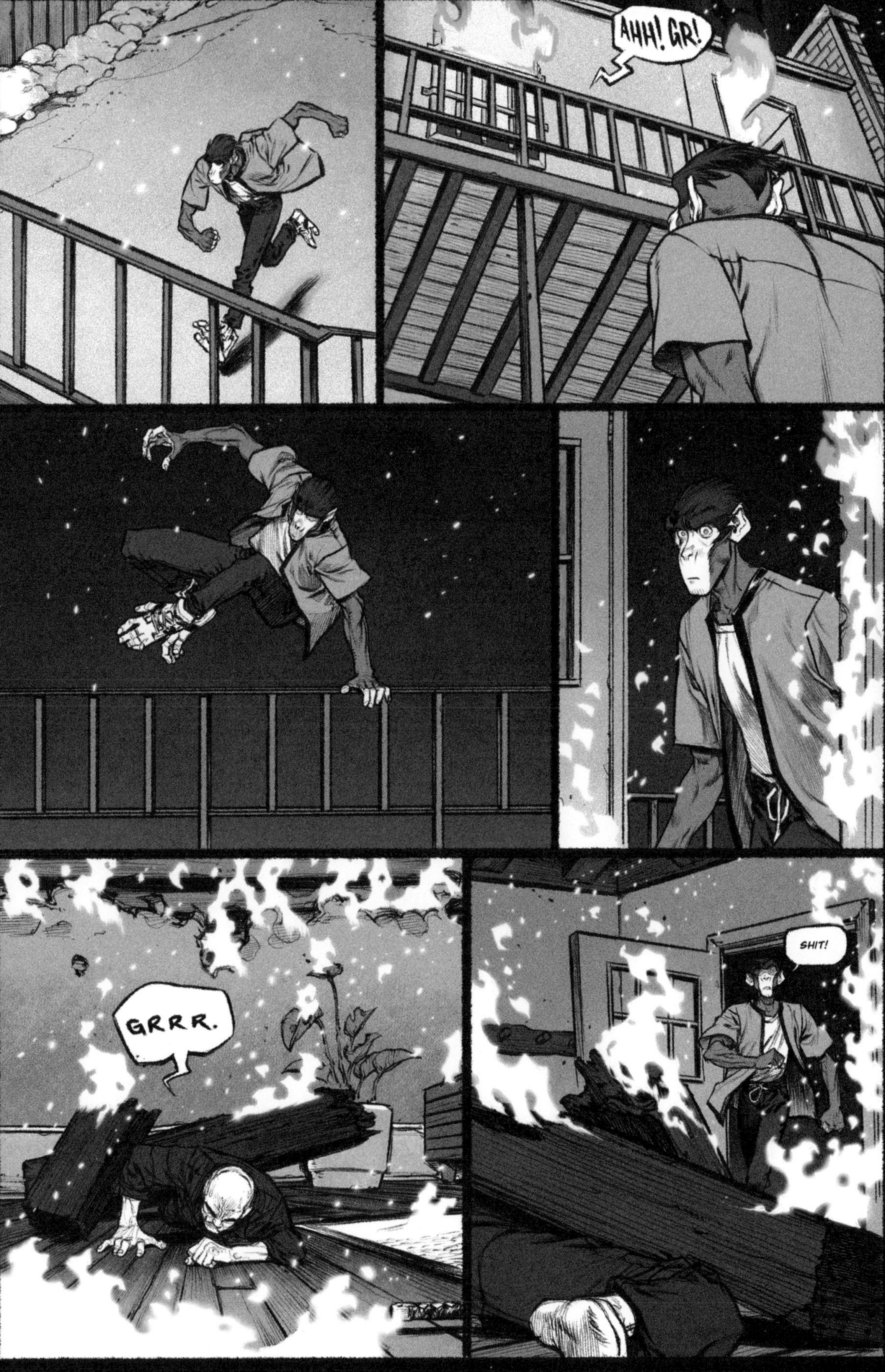
AHH! GR!
GRRR.
SHIT!

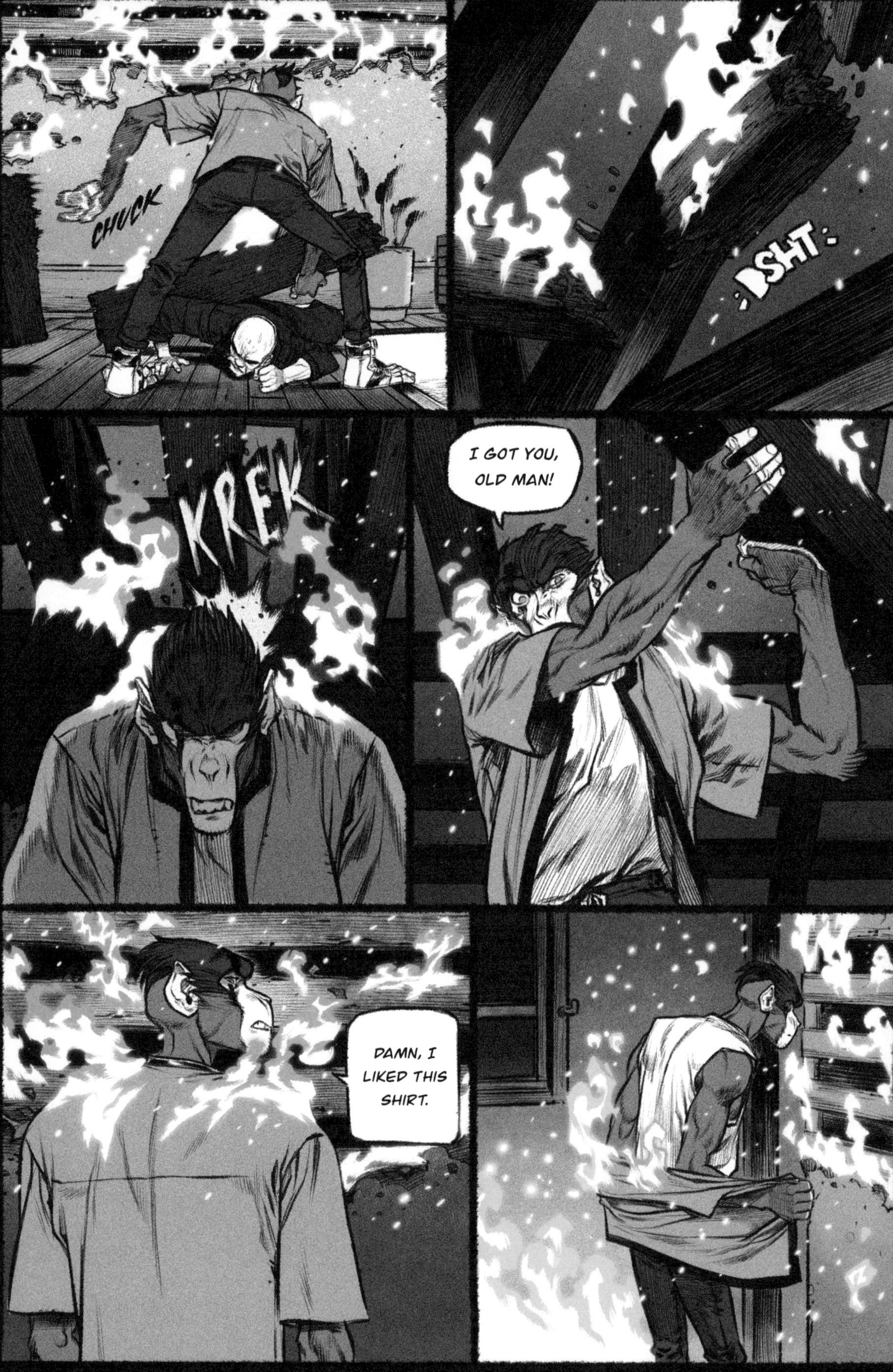
CHUCK
DSHT
KREK
I GOT YOU, OLD MAN!
DAMN, I LIKED THIS SHIRT.

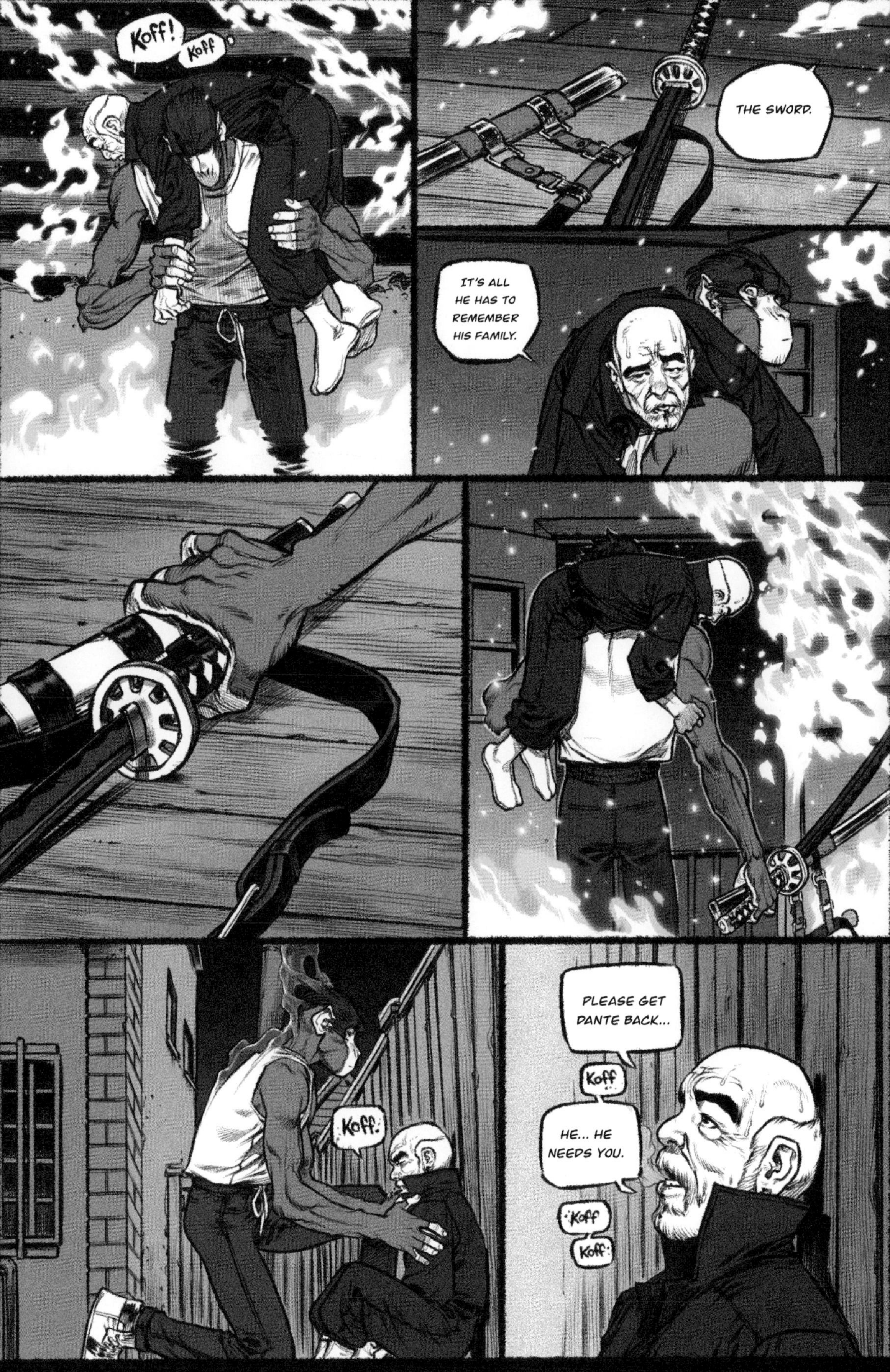
Koff!
Koff
THE SWORD.
IT'S ALL HE HAS TO REMEMBER HIS FAMILY.
Koff.
PLEASE GET DANTE BACK...
Koff
HE... HE NEEDS YOU.
Koff
Koff

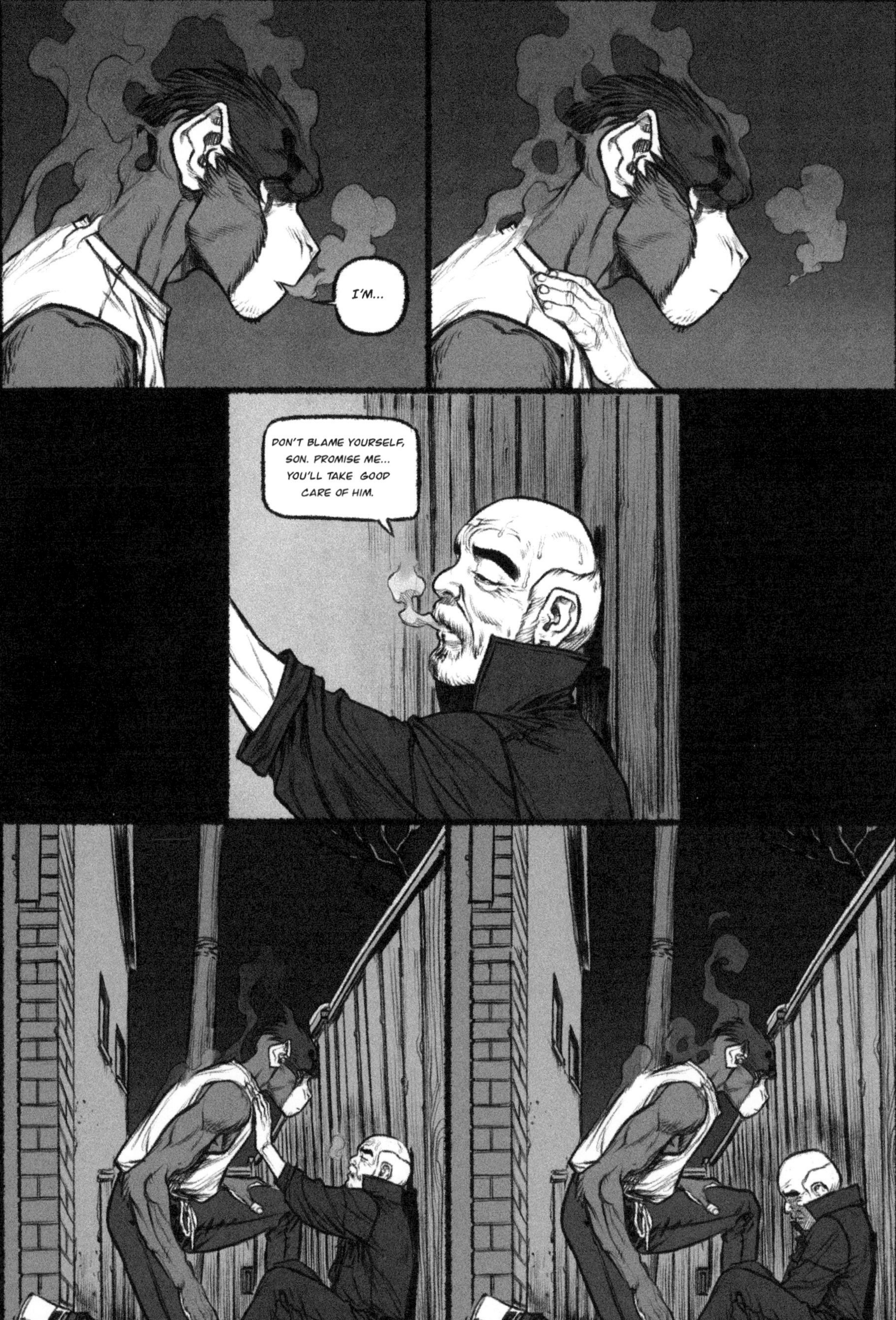
I'M...
DON'T BLAME YOURSELF, SON. PROMISE ME... YOU'LL TAKE GOOD CARE OF HIM.

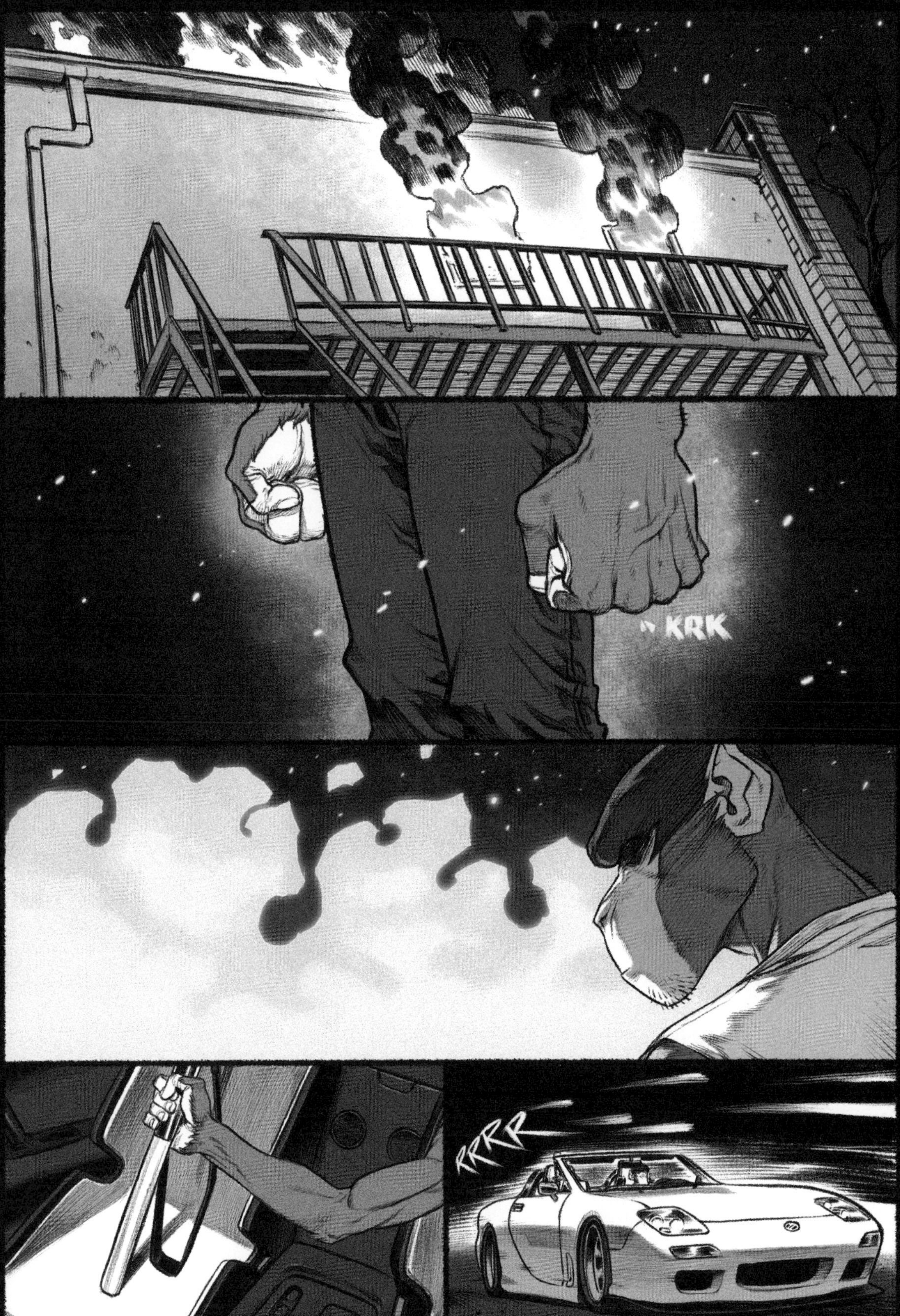
KRK
RRRR

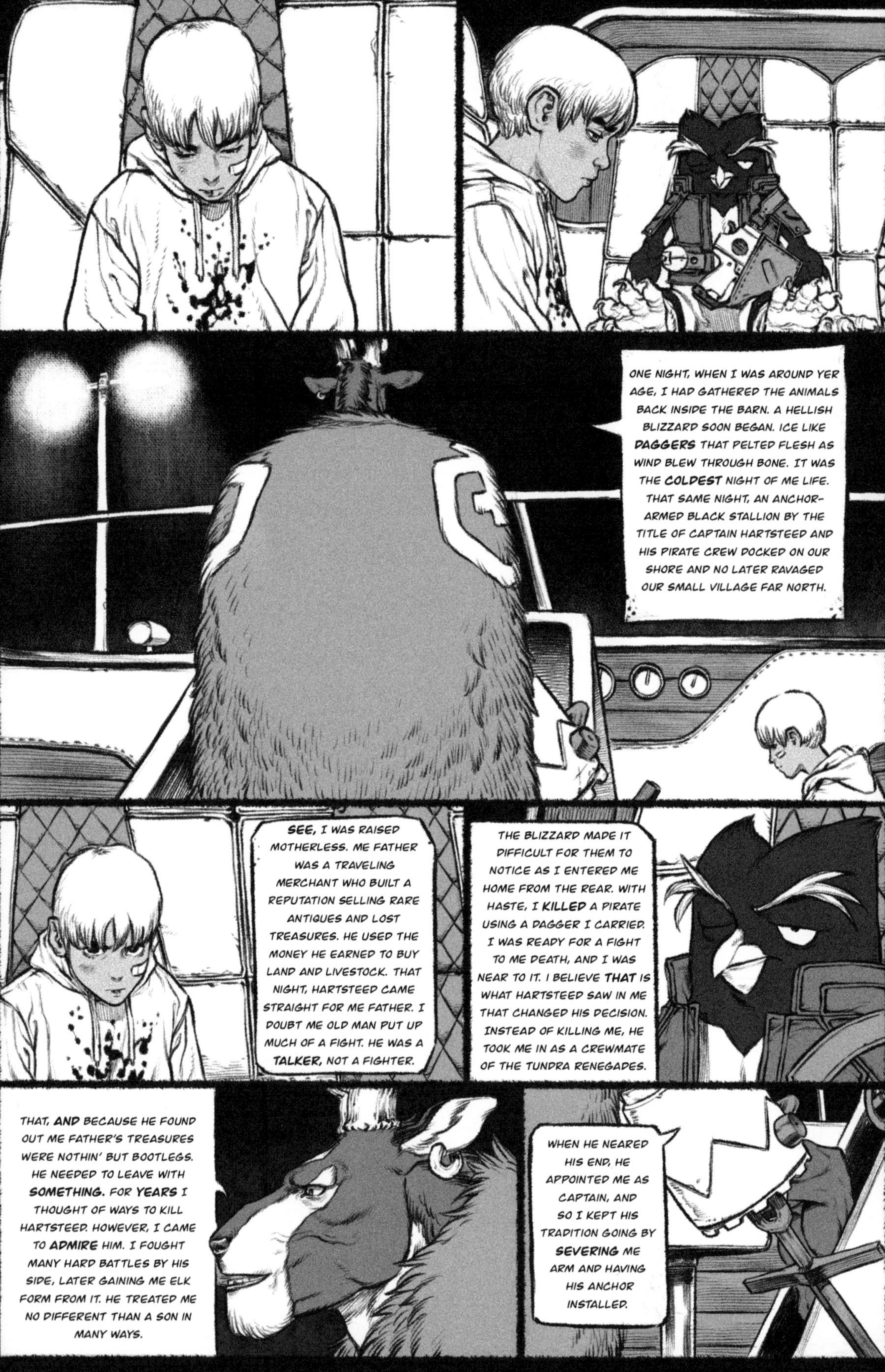

ONE NIGHT, WHEN I WAS AROUND YER AGE, I HAD GATHERED THE ANIMALS BACK INSIDE THE BARN. A HELLISH BLIZZARD SOON BEGAN. ICE LIKE DAGGERS THAT PELTED FLESH AS WIND BLEW THROUGH BONE. IT WAS THE COLDEST NIGHT OF ME LIFE. THAT SAME NIGHT, AN ANCHOR-ARMED BLACK STALLION BY THE TITLE OF CAPTAIN HARTSTEED AND HIS PIRATE CREW DOCKED ON OUR SHORE AND NO LATER RAVAGED OUR SMALL VILLAGE FAR NORTH.
SEE, I WAS RAISED MOTHERLESS. ME FATHER WAS A TRAVELING MERCHANT WHO BUILT A REPUTATION SELLING RARE ANTIQUES AND LOST TREASURES. HE USED THE MONEY HE EARNED TO BUY LAND AND LIVESTOCK. THAT NIGHT, HARTSTEED CAME STRAIGHT FOR ME FATHER. I DOUBT ME OLD MAN PUT UP MUCH OF A FIGHT. HE WAS A TALKER, NOT A FIGHTER.
THE BLIZZARD MADE IT DIFFICULT FOR THEM TO NOTICE AS I ENTERED ME HOME FROM THE REAR. WITH HASTE, I KILLED A PIRATE USING A DAGGER I CARRIED. I WAS READY FOR A FIGHT TO ME DEATH, AND I WAS NEAR TO IT. I BELIEVE THAT IS WHAT HARTSTEED SAW IN ME THAT CHANGED HIS DECISION. INSTEAD OF KILLING ME, HE TOOK ME IN AS A CREWMATE OF THE TUNDRA RENEGADES.
THAT, AND BECAUSE HE FOUND OUT ME FATHER'S TREASURES WERE NOTHIN' BUT BOOTLEGS. HE NEEDED TO LEAVE WITH SOMETHING. FOR YEARS I THOUGHT OF WAYS TO KILL HARTSTEED. HOWEVER, I CAME TO ADMIRE HIM. I FOUGHT MANY HARD BATTLES BY HIS SIDE, LATER GAINING ME ELK FORM FROM IT. HE TREATED ME NO DIFFERENT THAN A SON IN MANY WAYS.
WHEN HE NEARED HIS END, HE APPOINTED ME AS CAPTAIN, AND SO I KEPT HIS TRADITION GOING BY SEVERING ME ARM AND HAVING HIS ANCHOR INSTALLED.

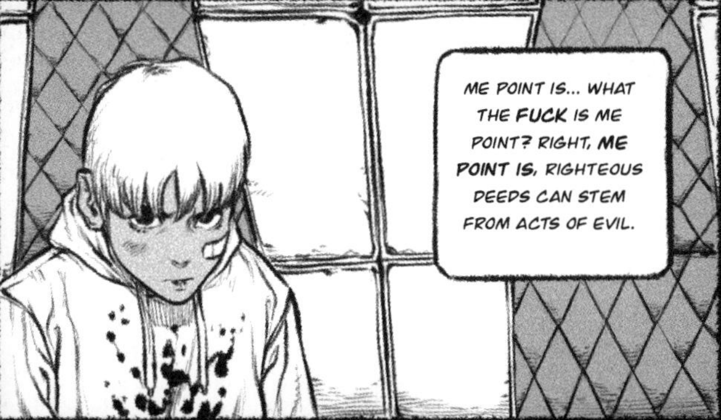
ME POINT IS... WHAT THE FUCK IS ME POINT? RIGHT, ME POINT IS, RIGHTEOUS DEEDS CAN STEM FROM ACTS OF EVIL.

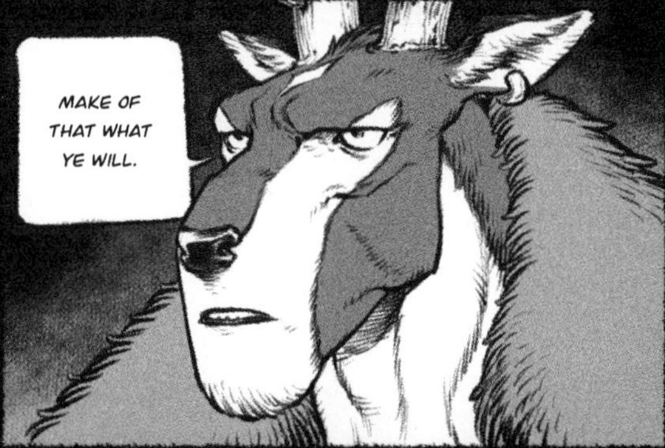
MAKE OF THAT WHAT YE WILL.

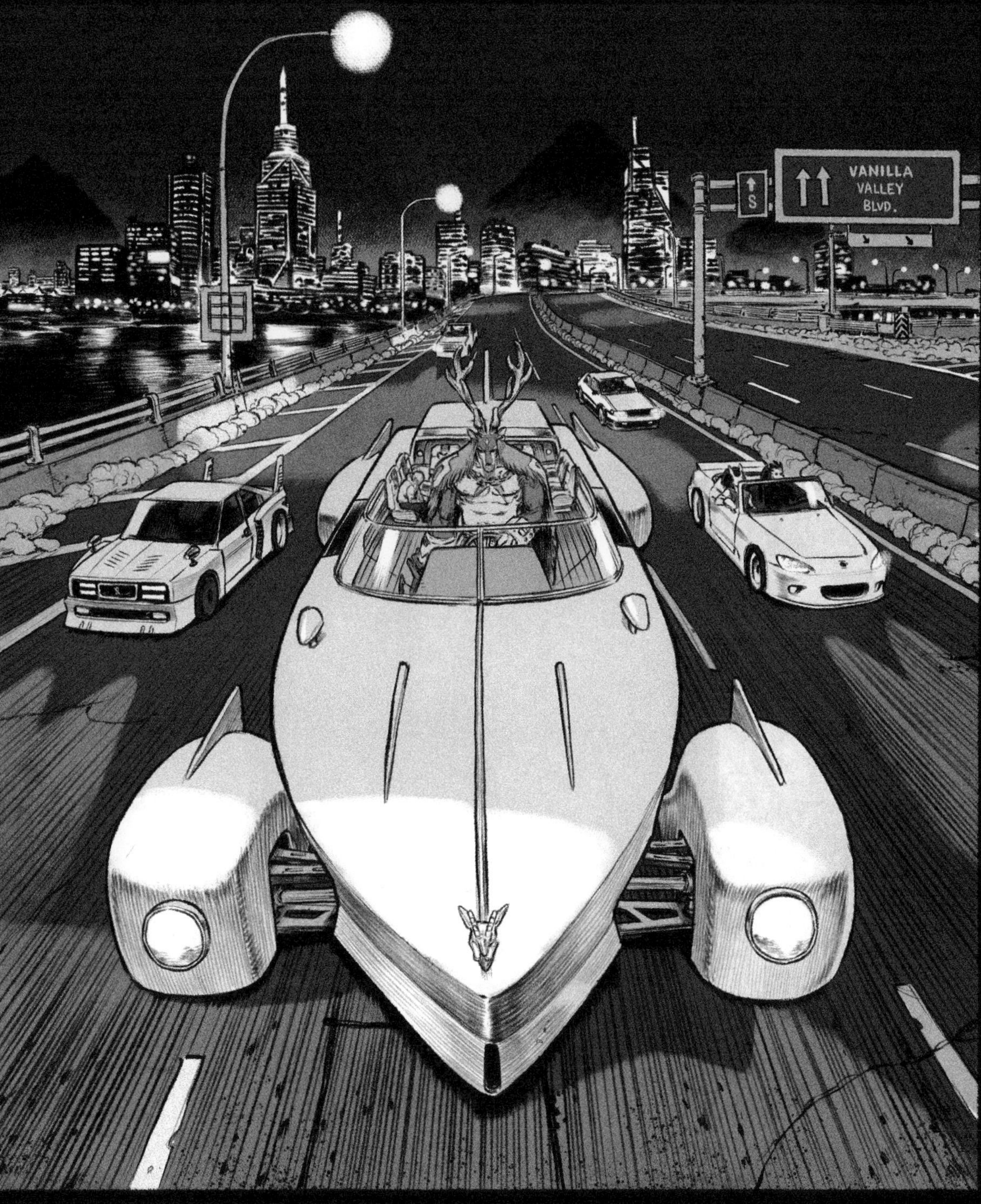
VANILLA
VALLEY
BLVD.
S

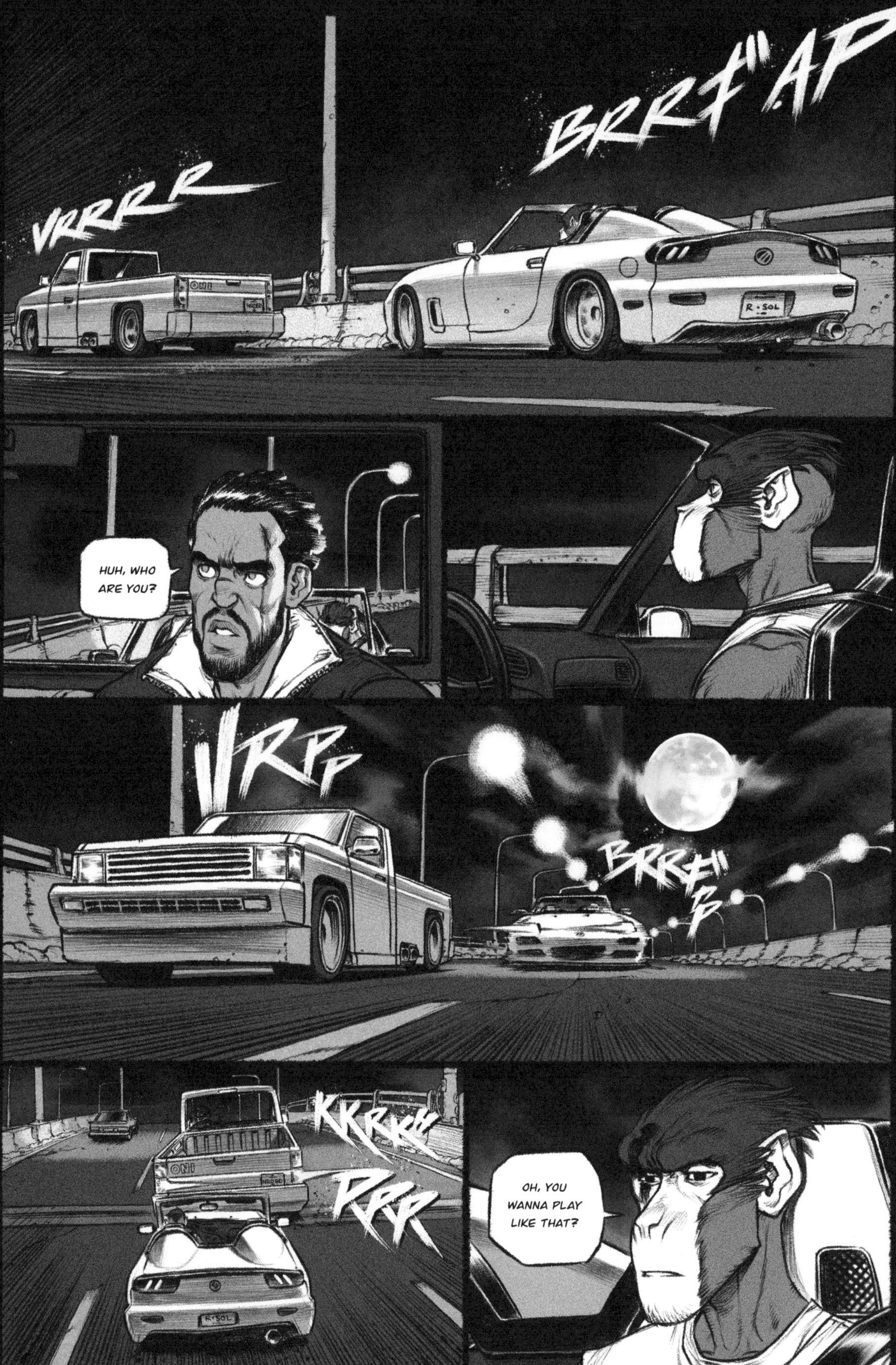
VRRRR
BRRF"AP
HUH, WHO ARE YOU?
VRPP
BRRF"PP
KKRKK"
DPP
OH, YOU WANNA PLAY LIKE THAT?

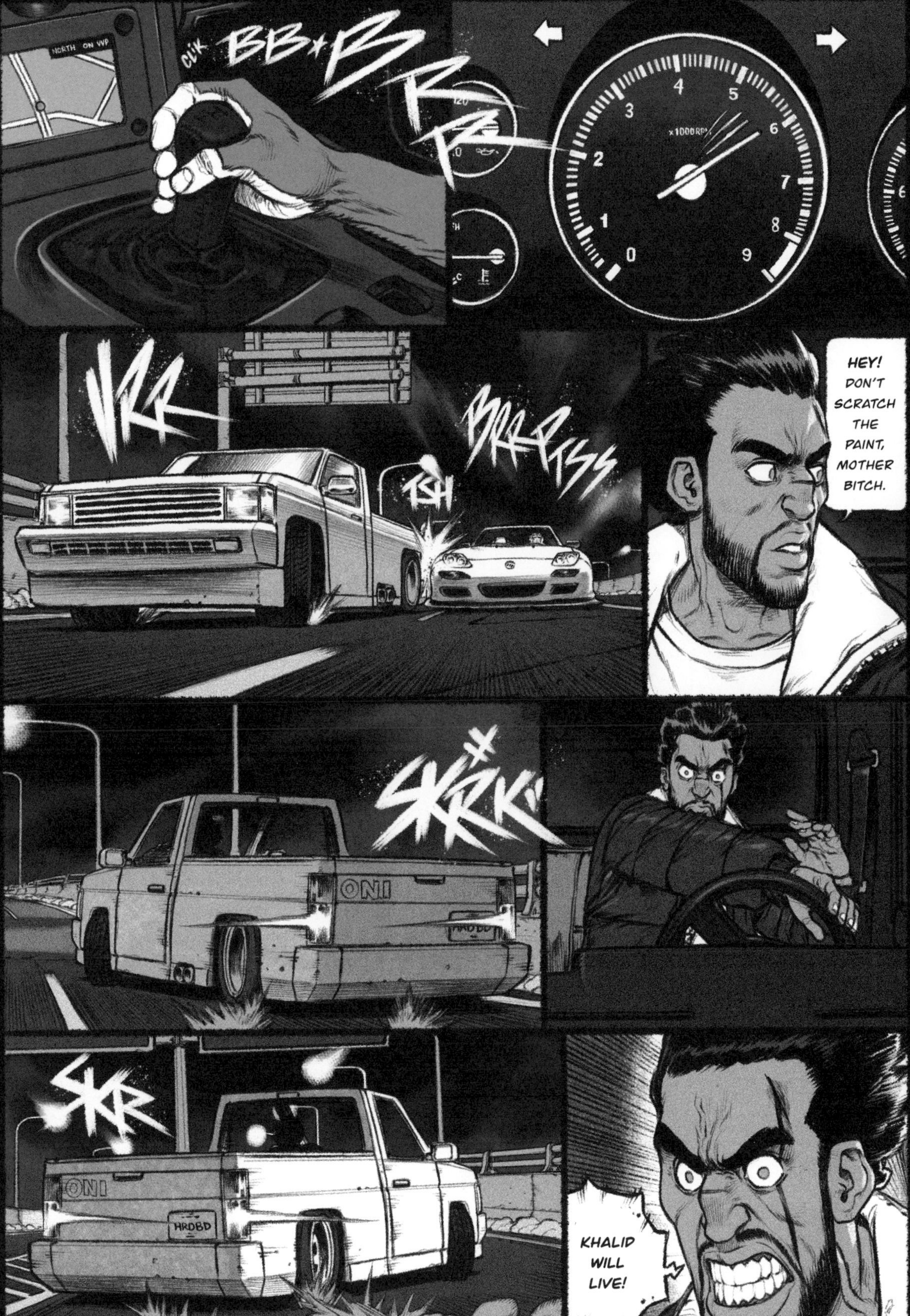
NORTH ON VVP
CLIK
BB*BRR
VRR
TSH
BRRRTSS
HEY! DON'T SCRATCH THE PAINT, MOTHER BITCH.
SKRK
ONI
SKR
ONI
HRDBD
KHALID WILL LIVE!

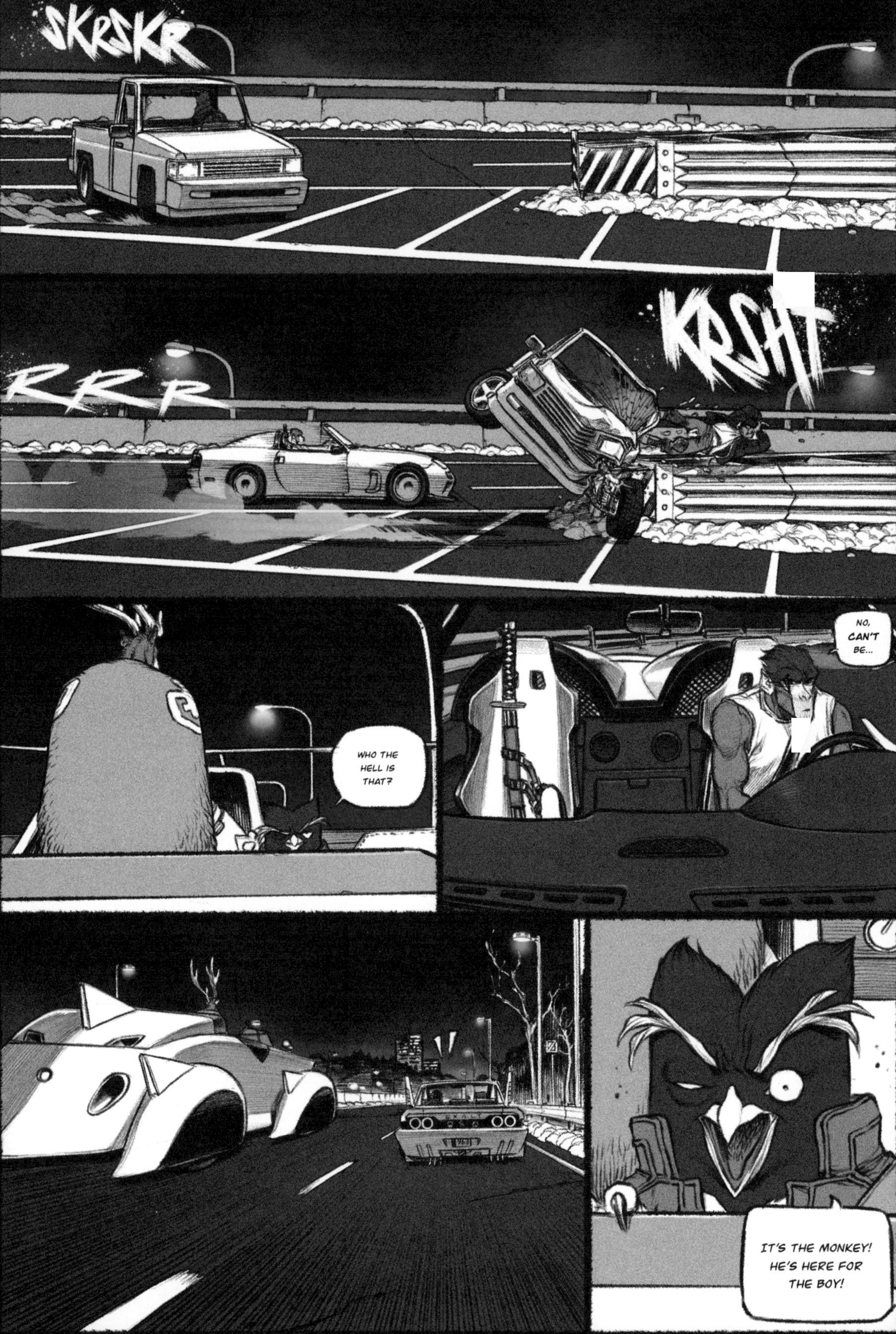
SKRSKR
RRR
KRSHT
WHO THE HELL IS THAT?
NO, CAN'T BE...
IT'S THE MONKEY! HE'S HERE FOR THE BOY!

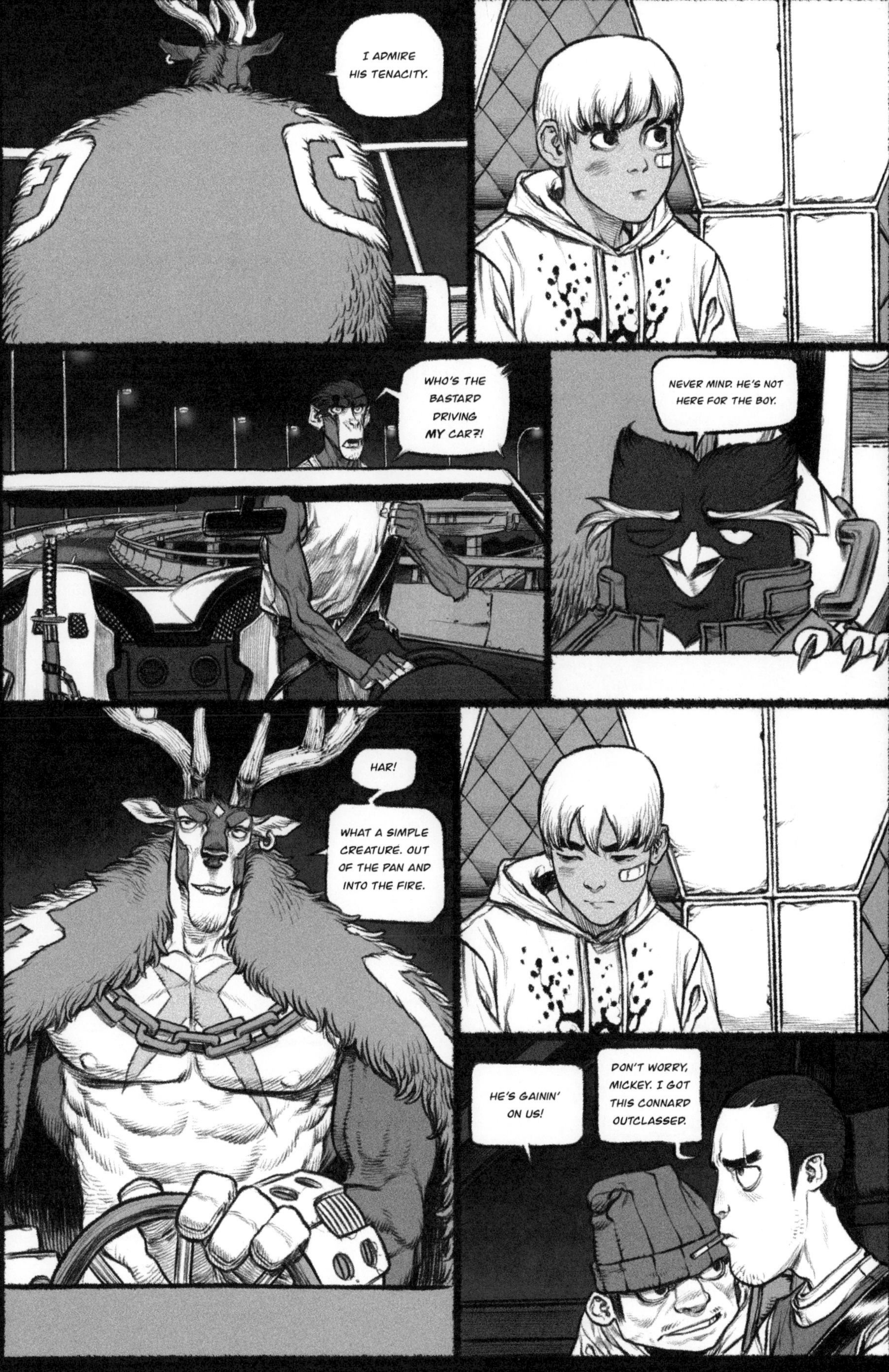

I ADMIRE HIS TENACITY.
WHO'S THE BASTARD DRIVING MY CAR?!
NEVER MIND. HE'S NOT HERE FOR THE BOY.
HAR!
WHAT A SIMPLE CREATURE. OUT OF THE PAN AND INTO THE FIRE.
HE'S GAININ' ON US!
DON'T WORRY, MICKEY. I GOT THIS CONNARD OUTCLASSED.

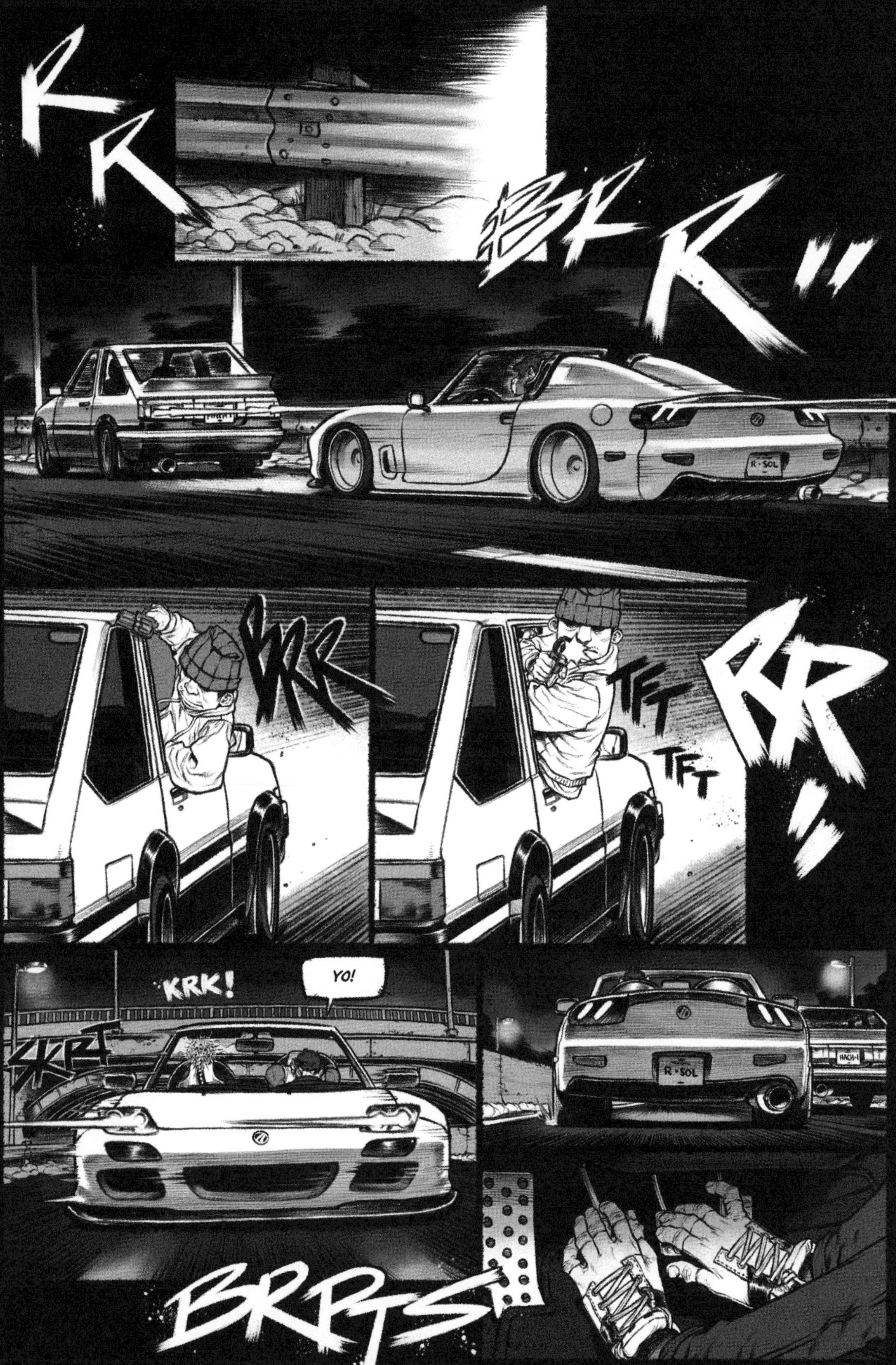
KRK!
YO!
SKRT
R-SOL
HACH-I
BRRTS

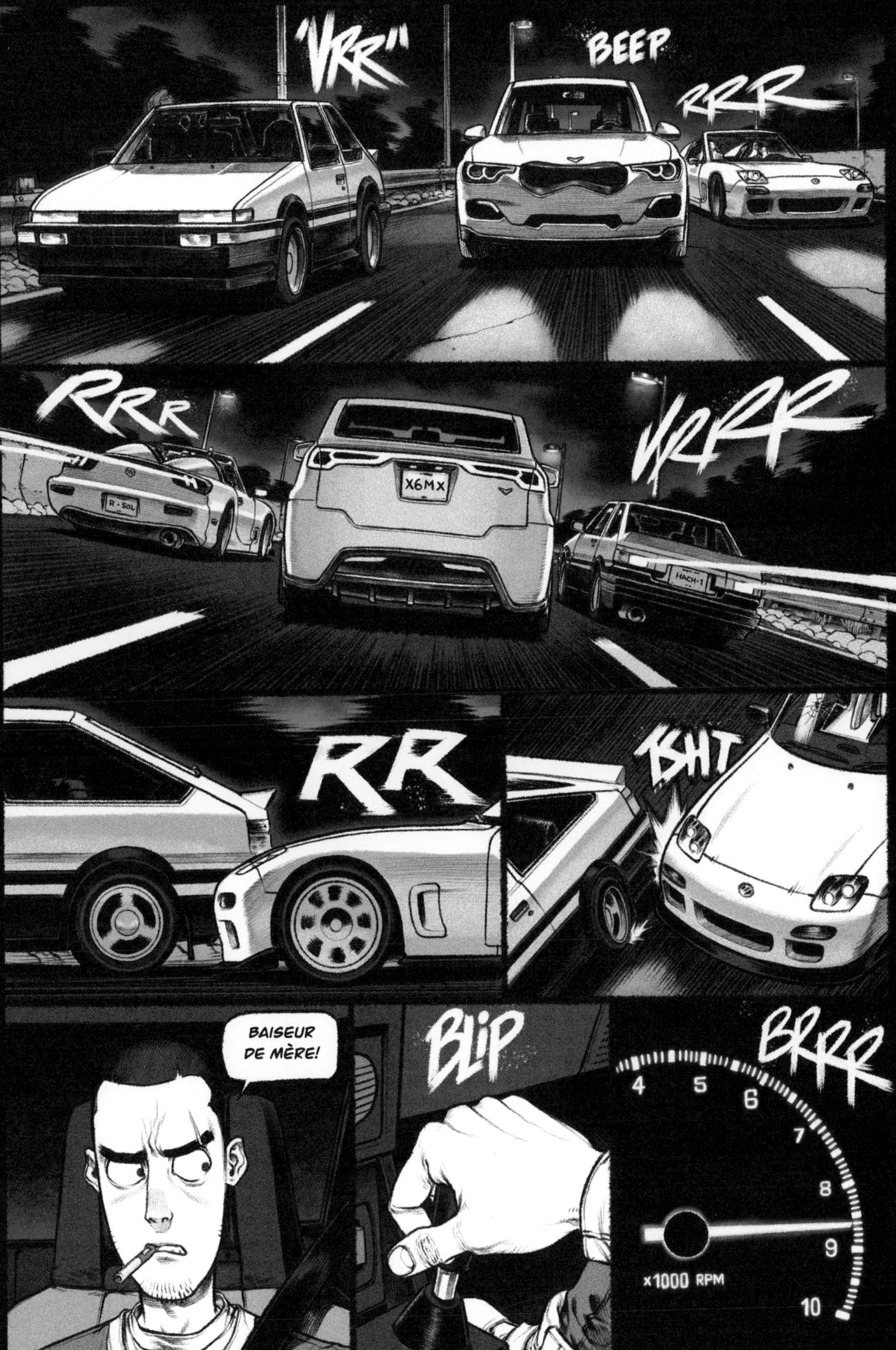
"VRR"
BEEP
RRR
RRR
X6MX
R-SOL
VRRR
HACH-1
RR
TSHT
BAISEUR DE MÈRE!
BLIP
BRRR
4
5
6
7
8
9
10
x1000 RPM

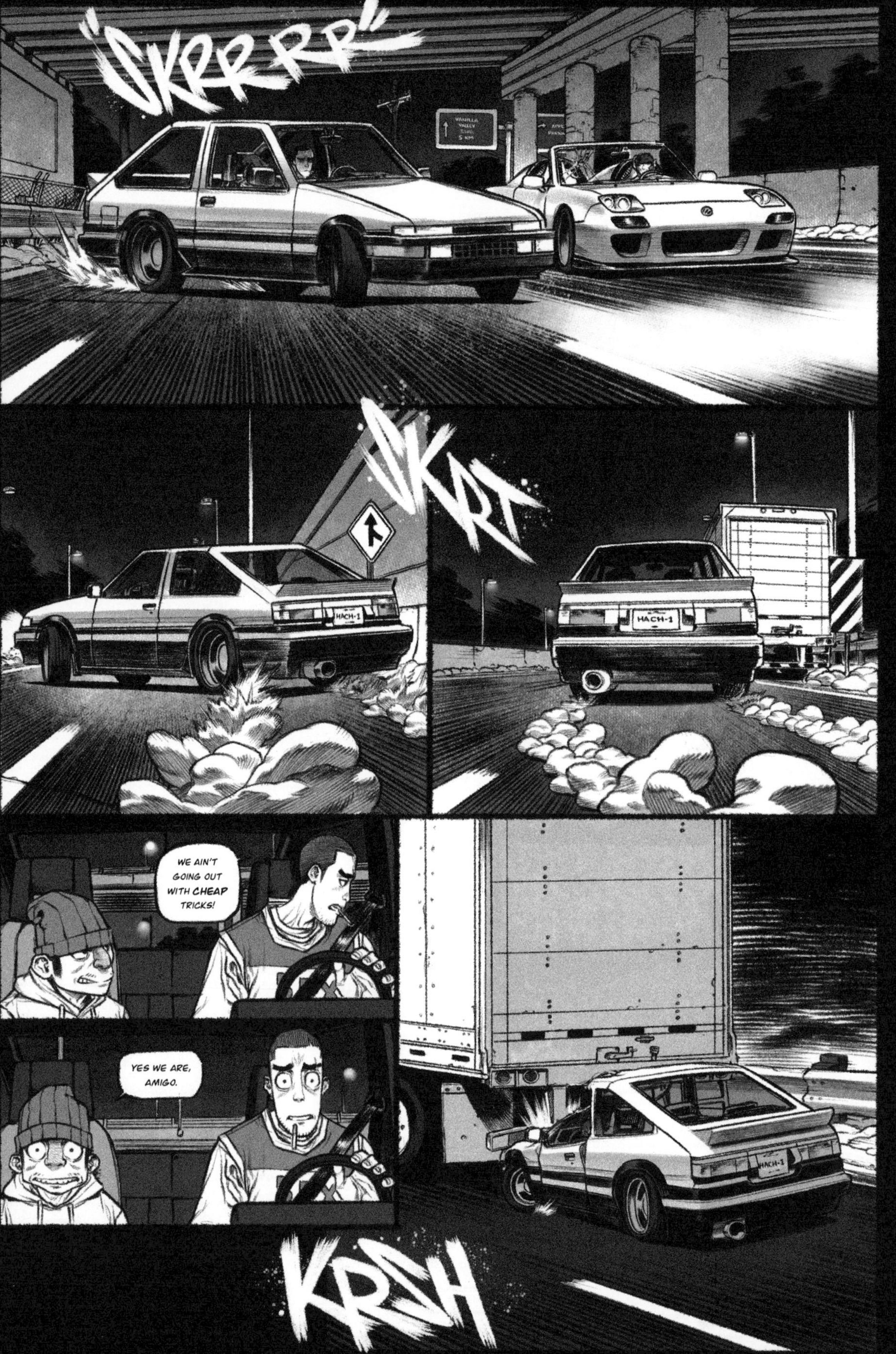
SKRRRR
VANILLA VALLEY 5 KM
SKRT
HACH-1
WE AIN'T GOING OUT WITH CHEAP TRICKS!
YES WE ARE, AMIGO.
KRSH

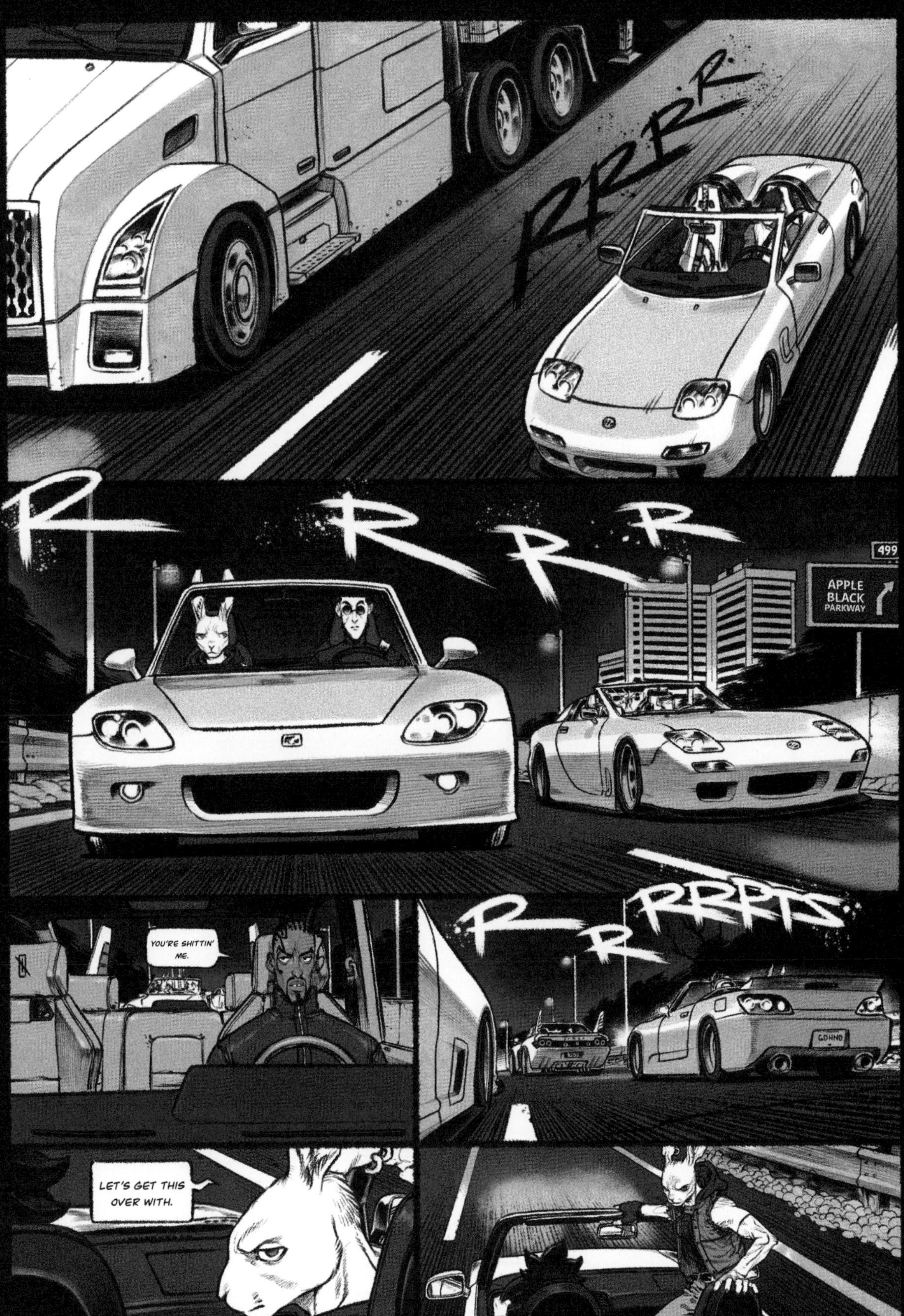

RRRR
R R R R
499
APPLE
BLACK
PARKWAY
YOU'RE SHITTIN' ME.
R R RRRPTS
LET'S GET THIS OVER WITH.

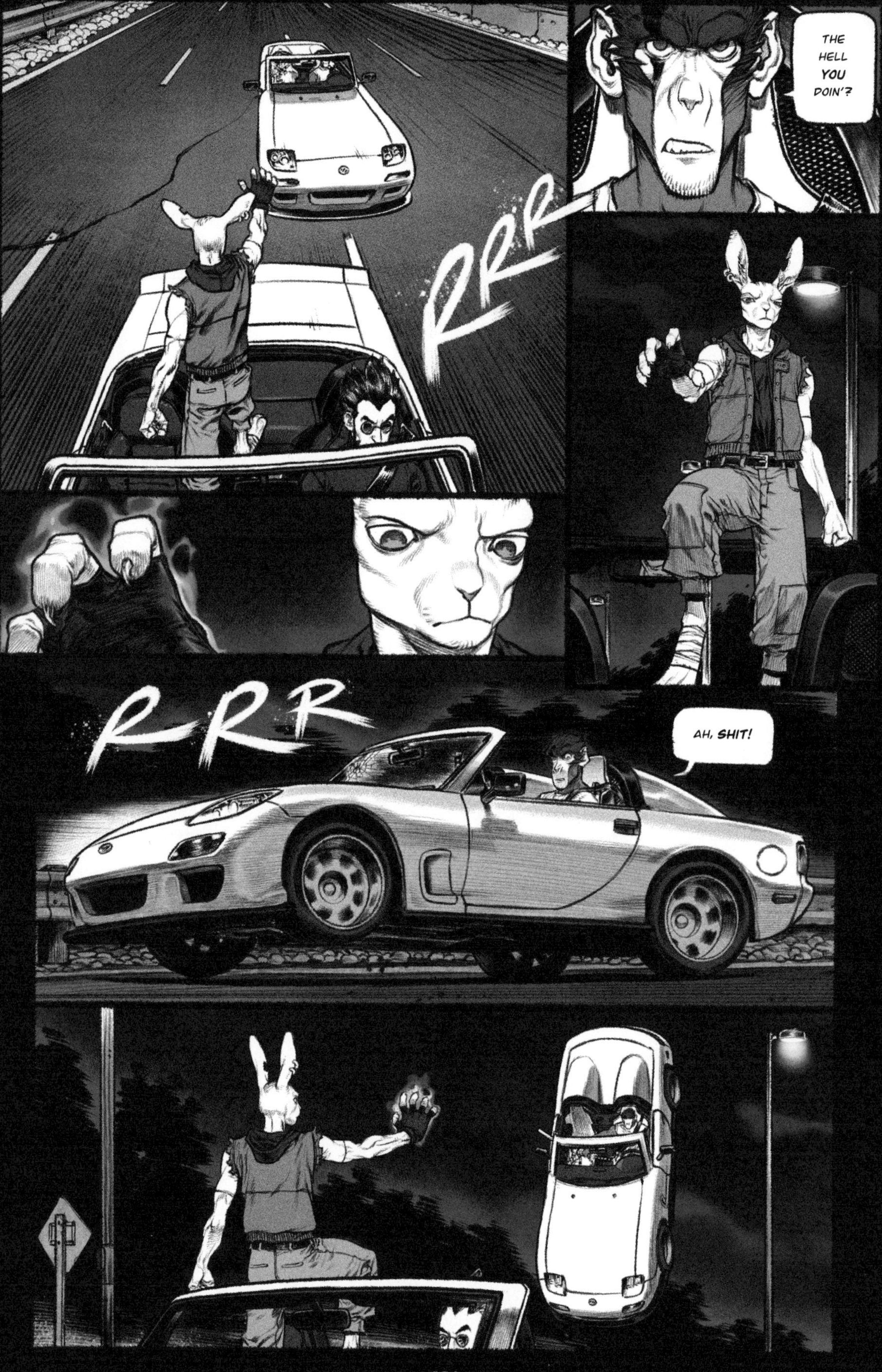
RRR
THE HELL YOU DOIN'?
RRR
AH, SHIT!

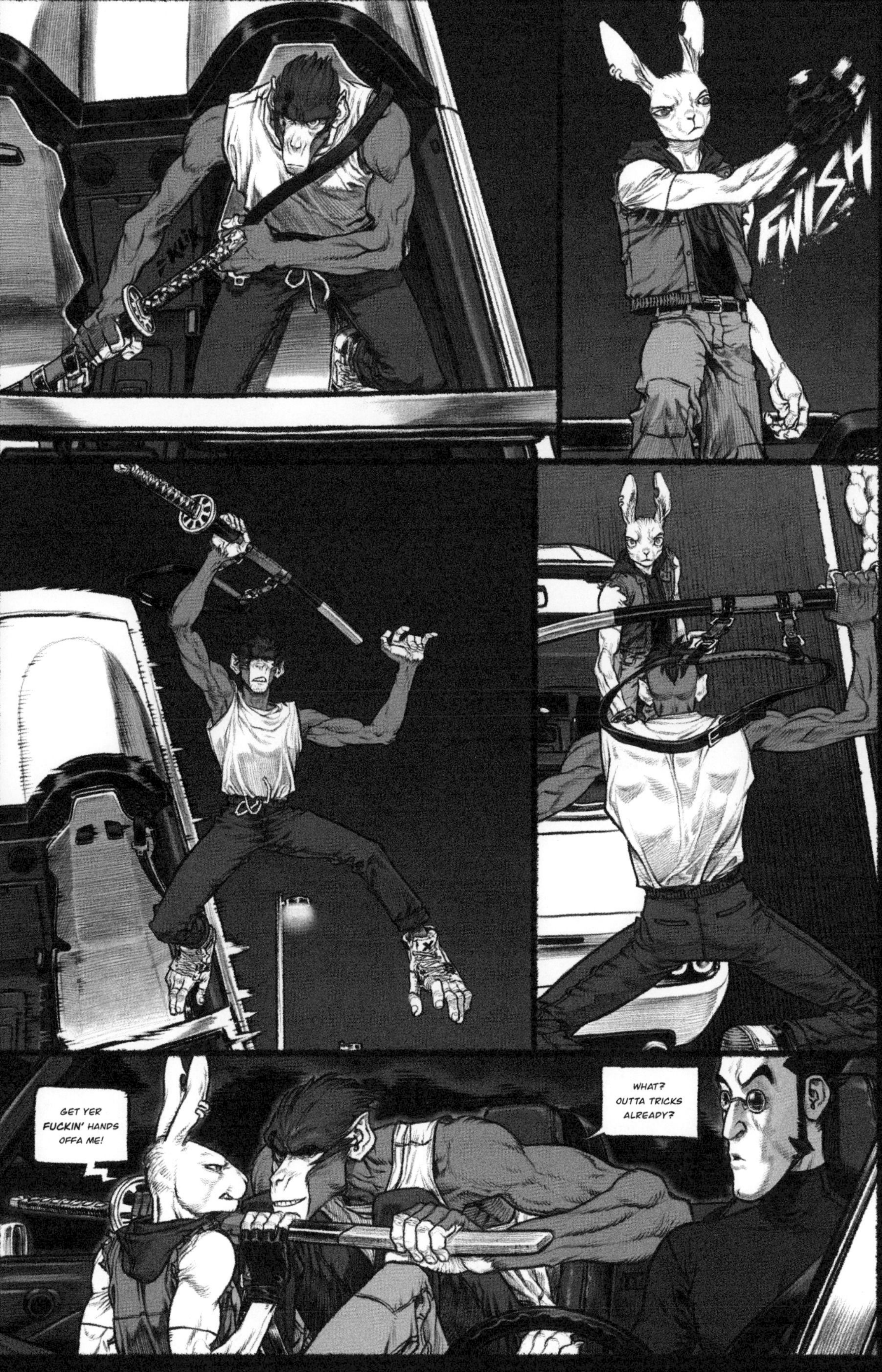
FWISH
GET YER FUCKIN' HANDS OFFA ME!
WHAT? OUTTA TRICKS ALREADY?

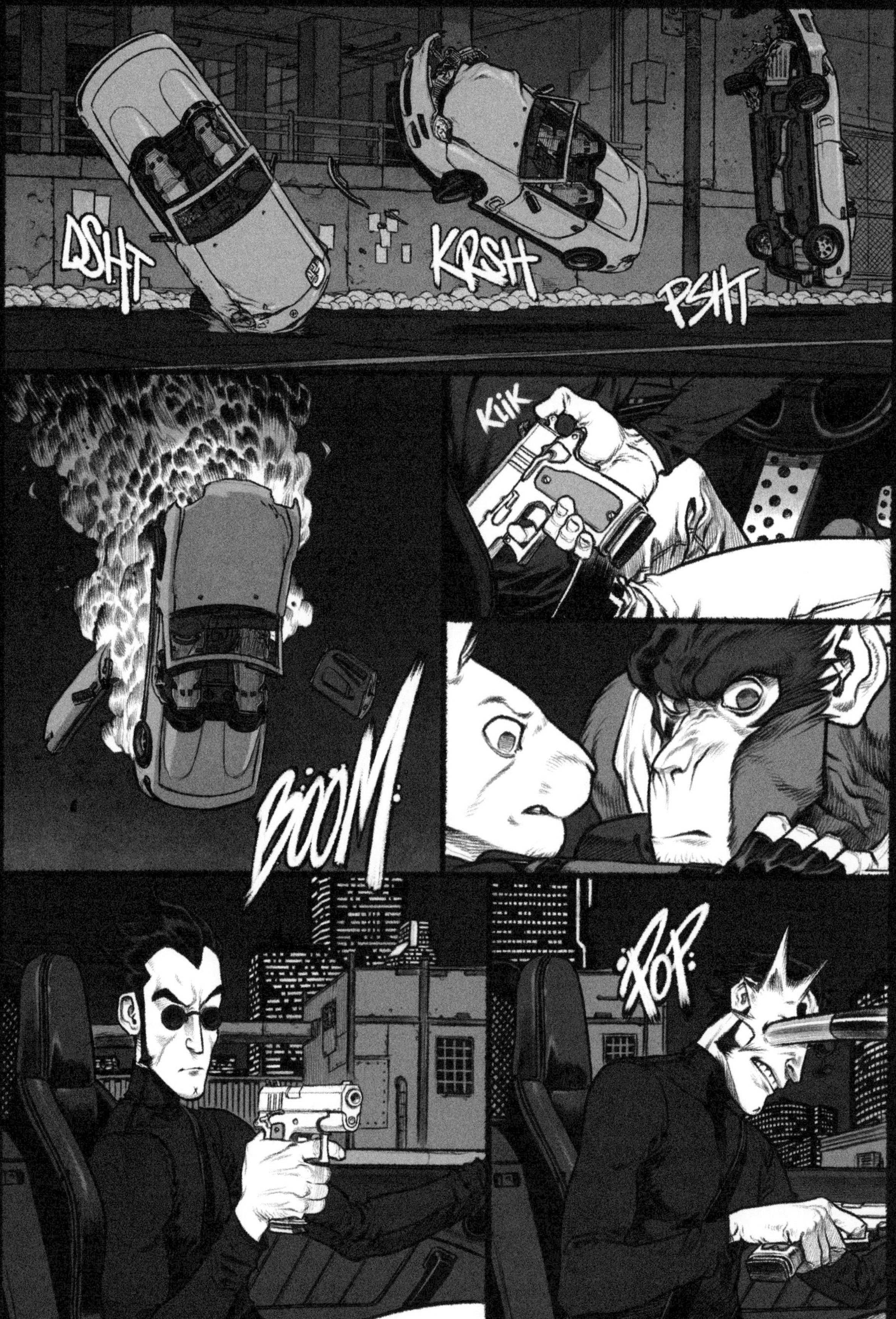
DSHT
KRSH
PSHT
KLIK
BOOM
POP

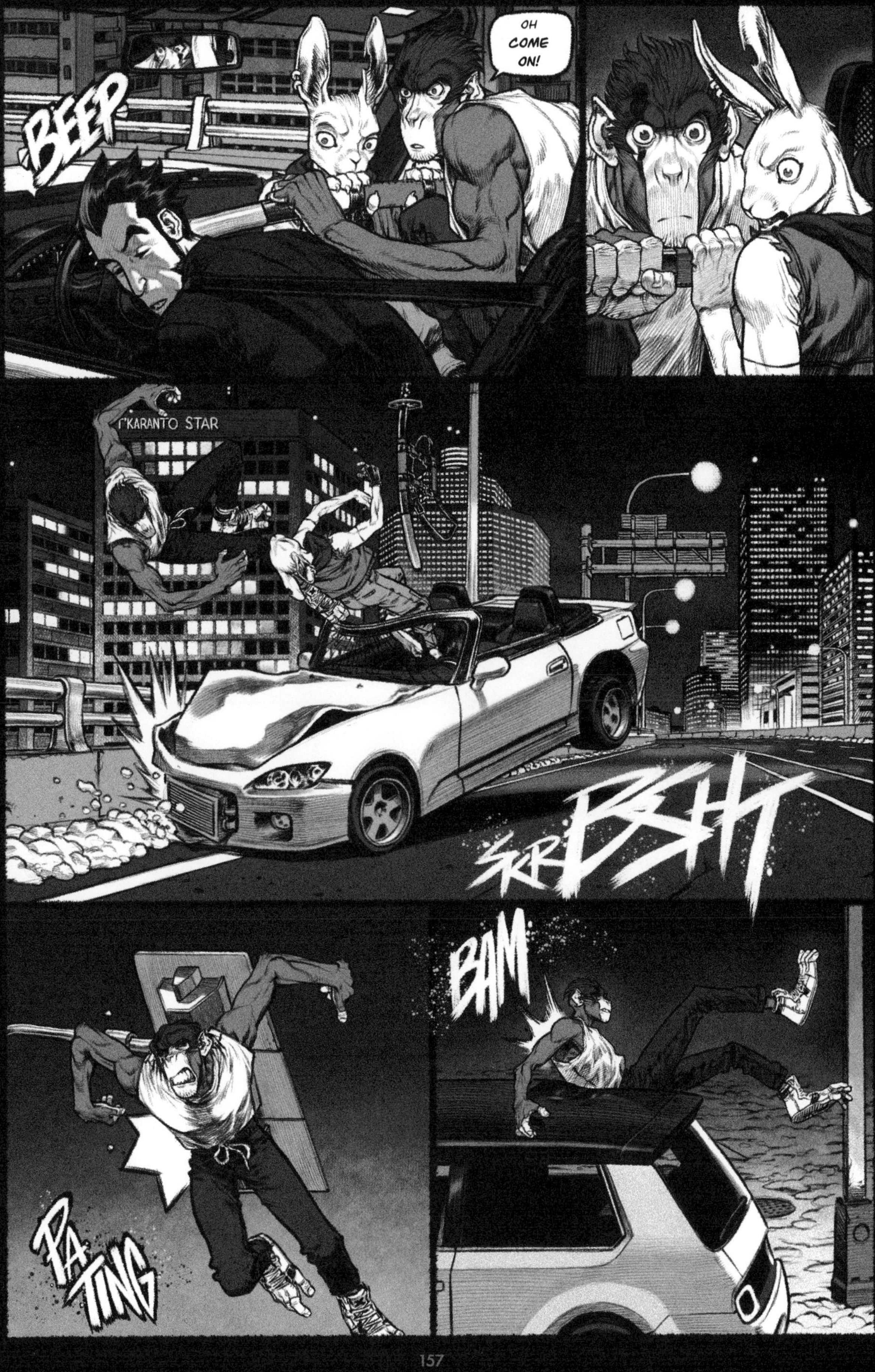
BEEP
OH COME ON!
T'KARANTO STAR
SKR BSHT
BAM
PA TING

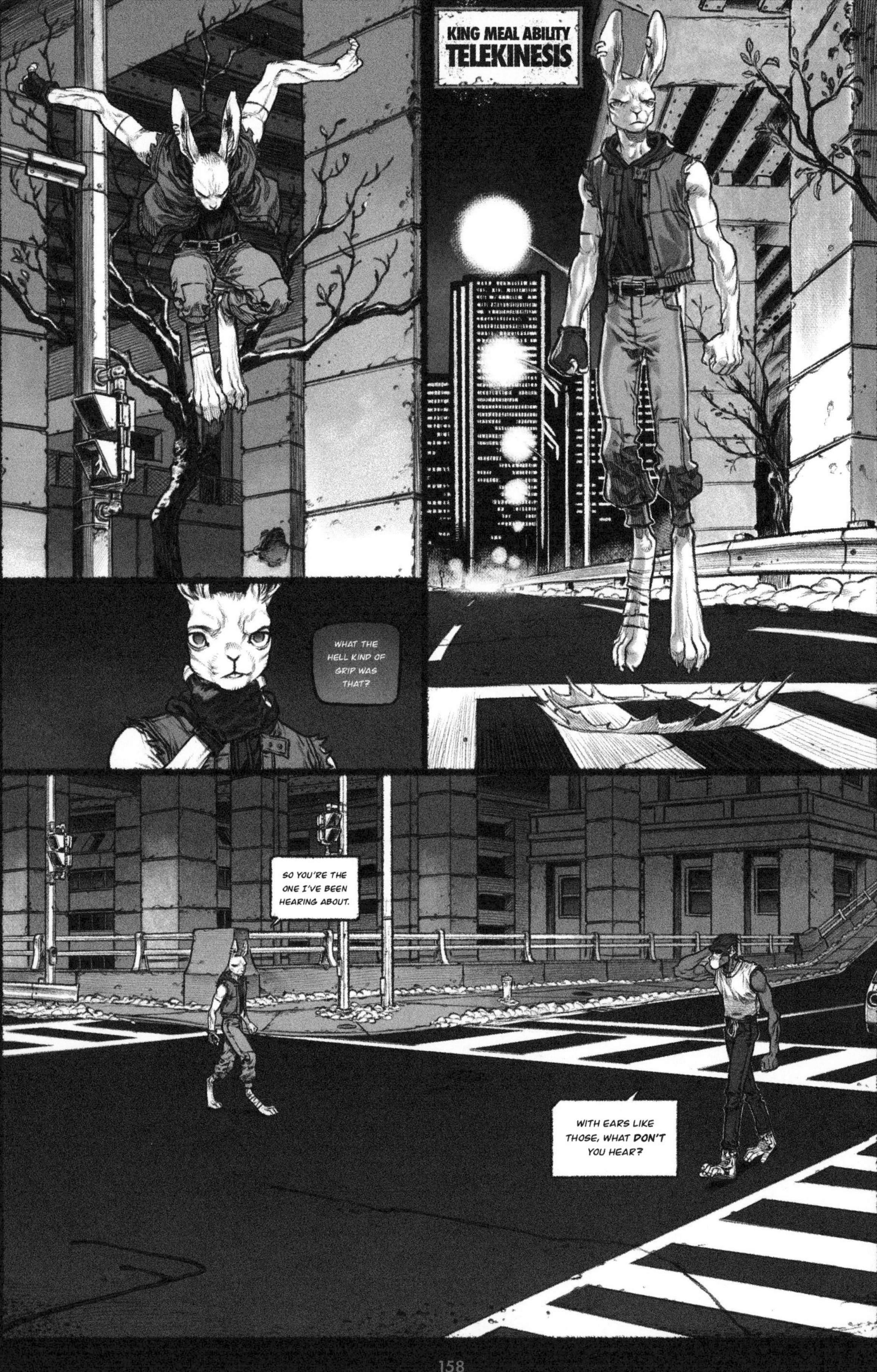

KING MEAL ABILITY
TELEKINESIS
WHAT THE HELL KIND OF GRIP WAS THAT?
SO YOU'RE THE ONE I'VE BEEN HEARING ABOUT.
WITH EARS LIKE THOSE, WHAT DON'T YOU HEAR?

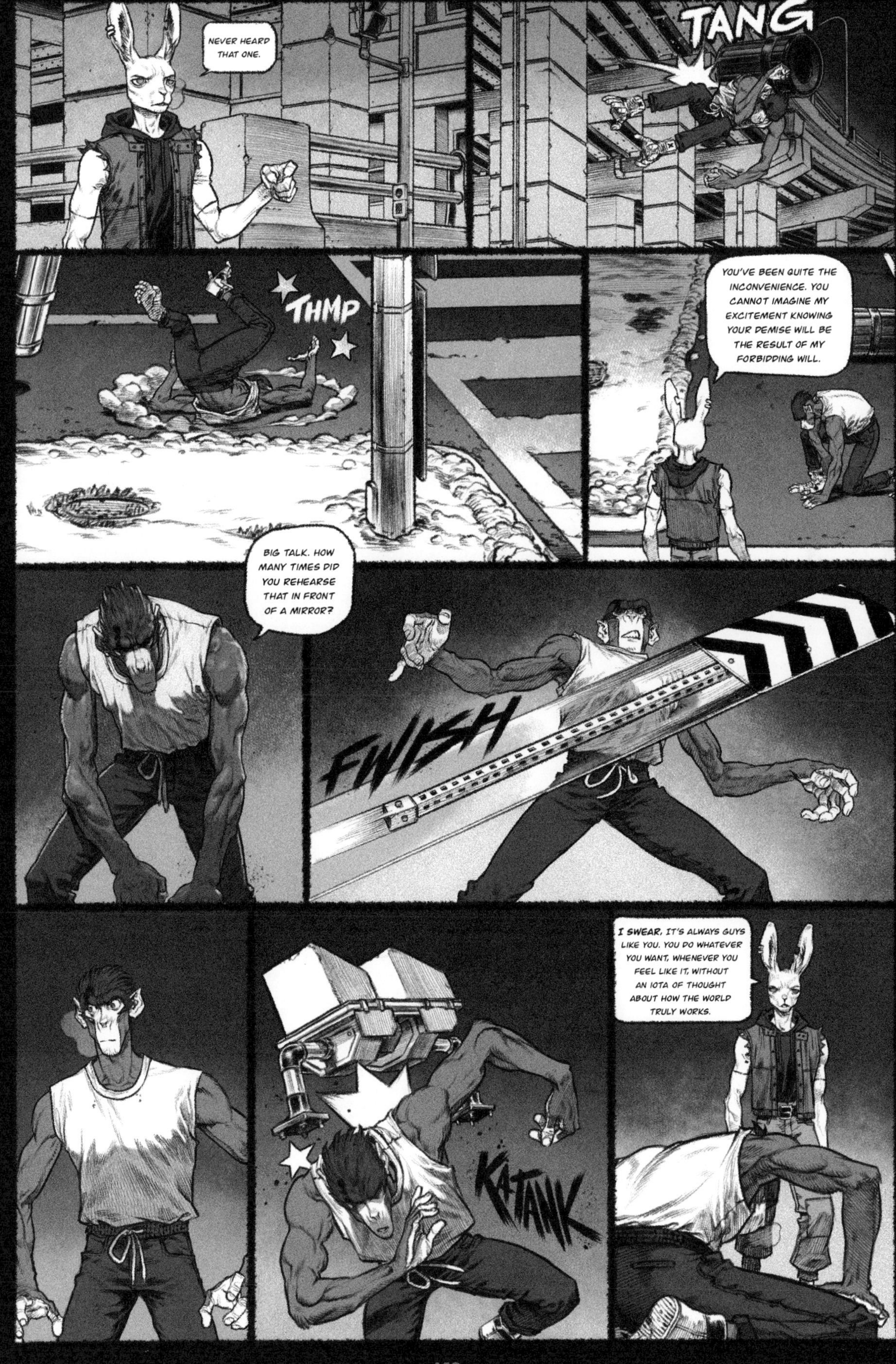
NEVER HEARD THAT ONE.
TANG
THMP
YOU'VE BEEN QUITE THE INCONVENIENCE. YOU CANNOT IMAGINE MY EXCITEMENT KNOWING YOUR DEMISE WILL BE THE RESULT OF MY FORBIDDING WILL.
BIG TALK. HOW MANY TIMES DID YOU REHEARSE THAT IN FRONT OF A MIRROR?
FWISH
KATANK
I SWEAR, IT'S ALWAYS GUYS LIKE YOU. YOU DO WHATEVER YOU WANT, WHENEVER YOU FEEL LIKE IT, WITHOUT AN IOTA OF THOUGHT ABOUT HOW THE WORLD TRULY WORKS.

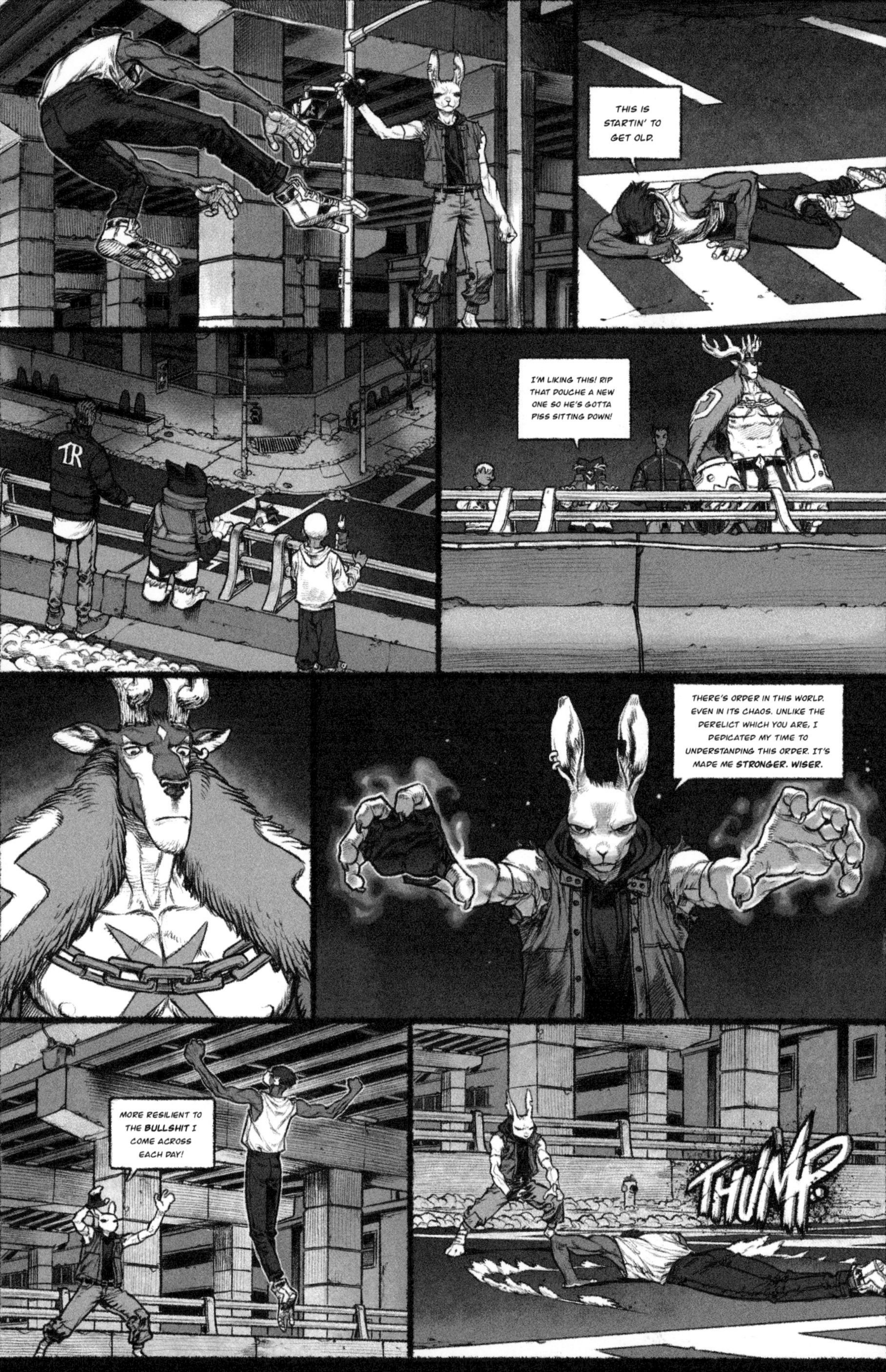
THIS IS STARTIN' TO GET OLD.
I'M LIKING THIS! RIP THAT DOUCHE A NEW ONE SO HE'S GOTTA PISS SITTING DOWN!
THERE'S ORDER IN THIS WORLD. EVEN IN ITS CHAOS. UNLIKE THE DERELICT WHICH YOU ARE, I DEDICATED MY TIME TO UNDERSTANDING THIS ORDER. IT'S MADE ME STRONGER. WISER.
MORE RESILIENT TO THE BULLSHIT I COME ACROSS EACH DAY!
THUMP

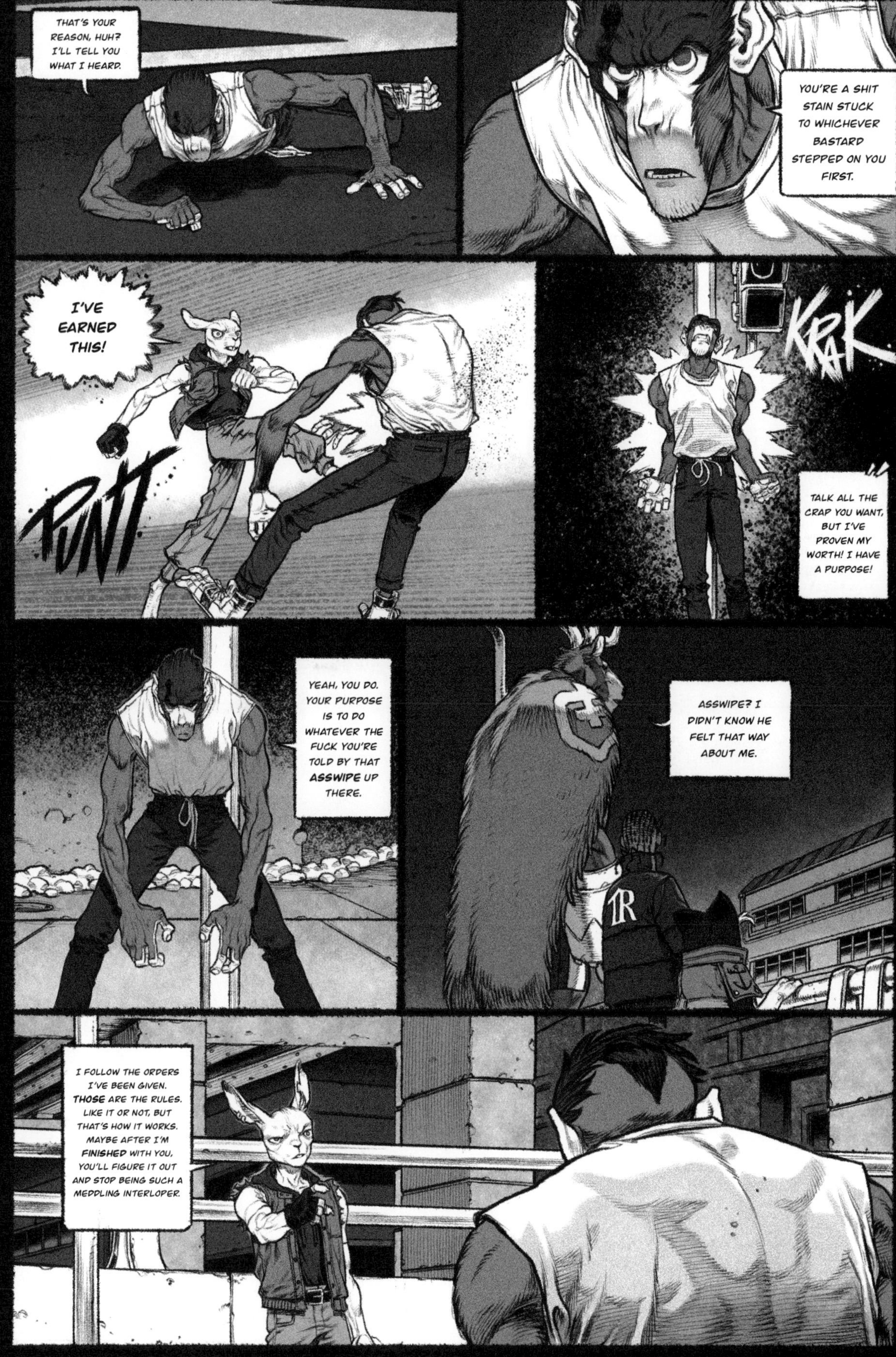
THAT'S YOUR REASON, HUH? I'LL TELL YOU WHAT I HEARD.
YOU'RE A SHIT STAIN STUCK TO WHICHEVER BASTARD STEPPED ON YOU FIRST.
I'VE EARNED THIS!
PUNT
KRAK
TALK ALL THE CRAP YOU WANT, BUT I'VE PROVEN MY WORTH! I HAVE A PURPOSE!
YEAH, YOU DO. YOUR PURPOSE IS TO DO WHATEVER THE FUCK YOU'RE TOLD BY THAT ASSWIPE UP THERE.
ASSWIPE? I DIDN'T KNOW HE FELT THAT WAY ABOUT ME.
I FOLLOW THE ORDERS I'VE BEEN GIVEN. THOSE ARE THE RULES. LIKE IT OR NOT, BUT THAT'S HOW IT WORKS. MAYBE AFTER I'M FINISHED WITH YOU, YOU'LL FIGURE IT OUT AND STOP BEING SUCH A MEDDLING INTERLOPER.

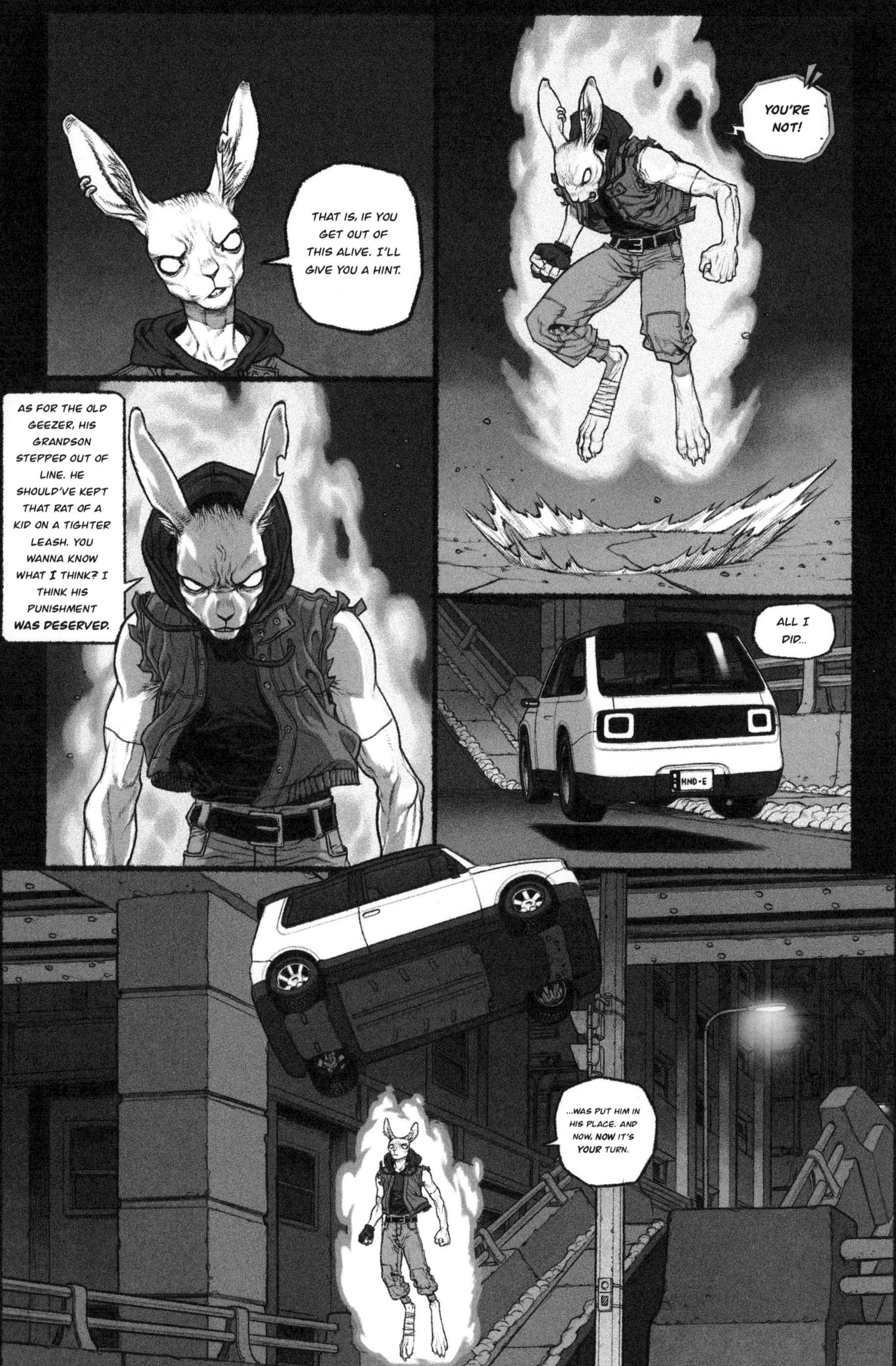
THAT IS, IF YOU GET OUT OF THIS ALIVE. I'LL GIVE YOU A HINT.
YOU'RE NOT!
AS FOR THE OLD GEEZER, HIS GRANDSON STEPPED OUT OF LINE. HE SHOULD'VE KEPT THAT RAT OF A KID ON A TIGHTER LEASH. YOU WANNA KNOW WHAT I THINK? I THINK HIS PUNISHMENT WAS DESERVED.
ALL I DID...
HND-E
...WAS PUT HIM IN HIS PLACE. AND NOW, NOW IT'S YOUR TURN.

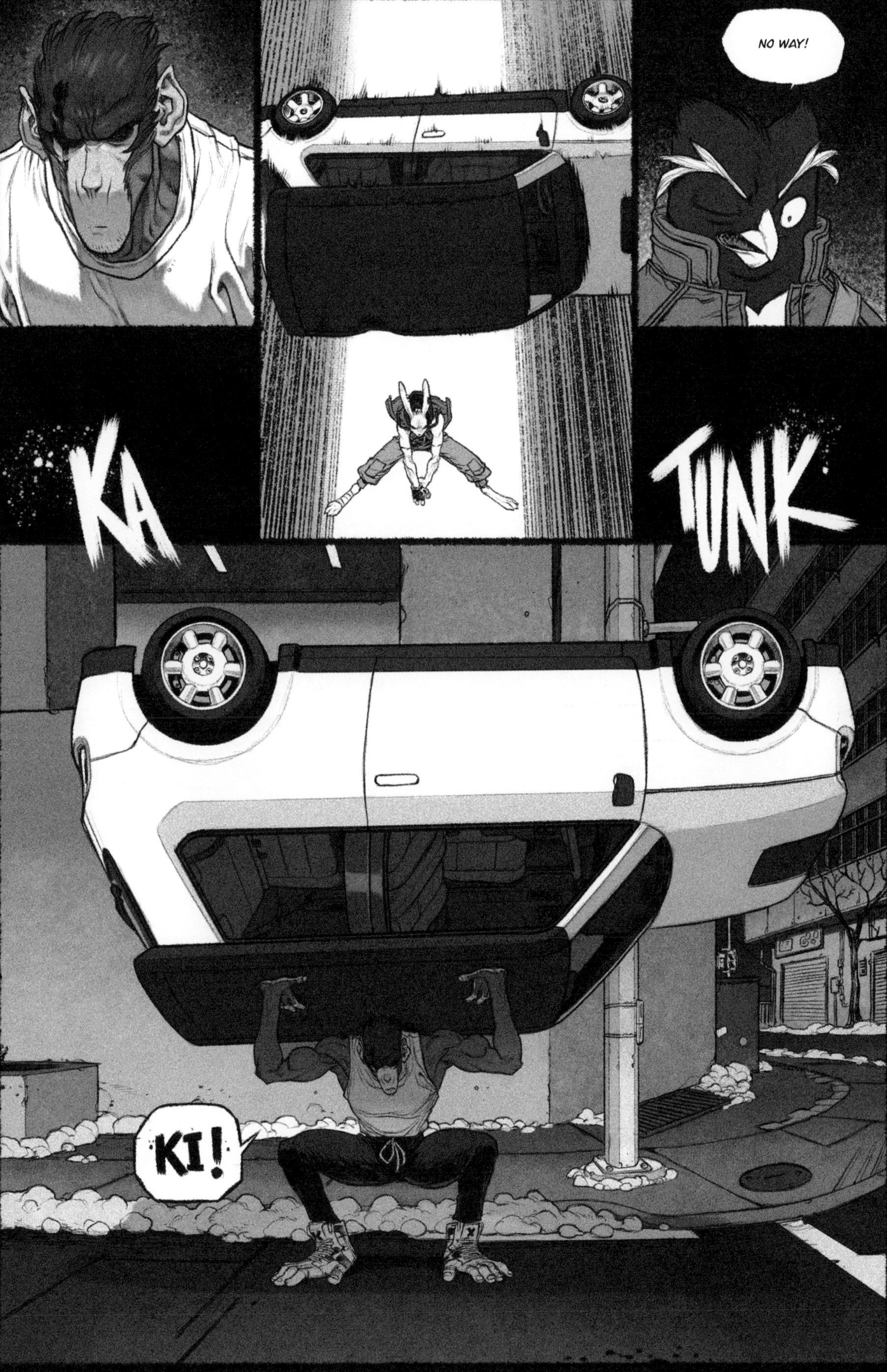
NO WAY!
KA
TUNK
KI!

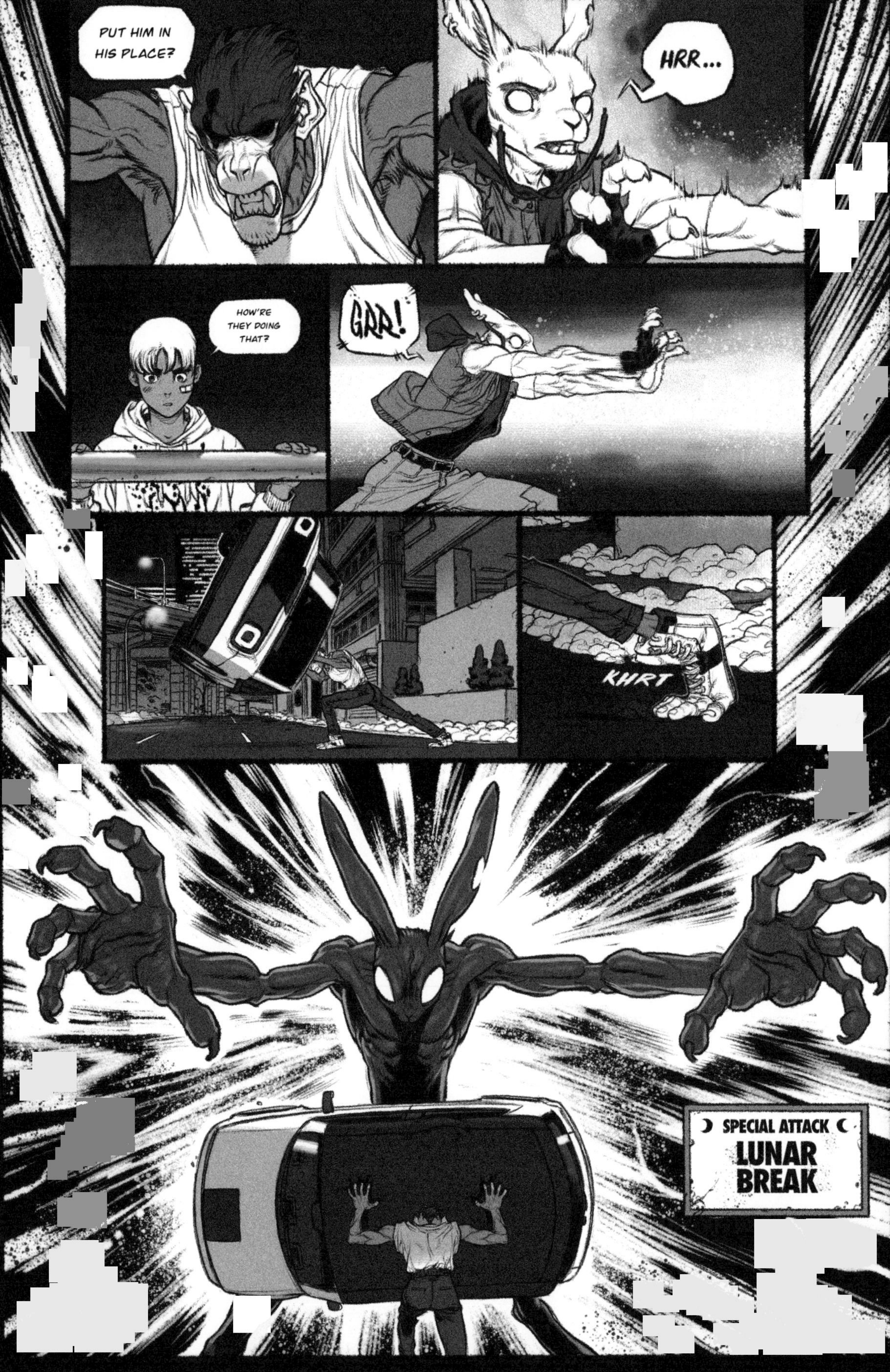
PUT HIM IN HIS PLACE?
HRR...
HOW'RE THEY DOING THAT?
GRR!
KHRT
SPECIAL ATTACK
LUNAR BREAK

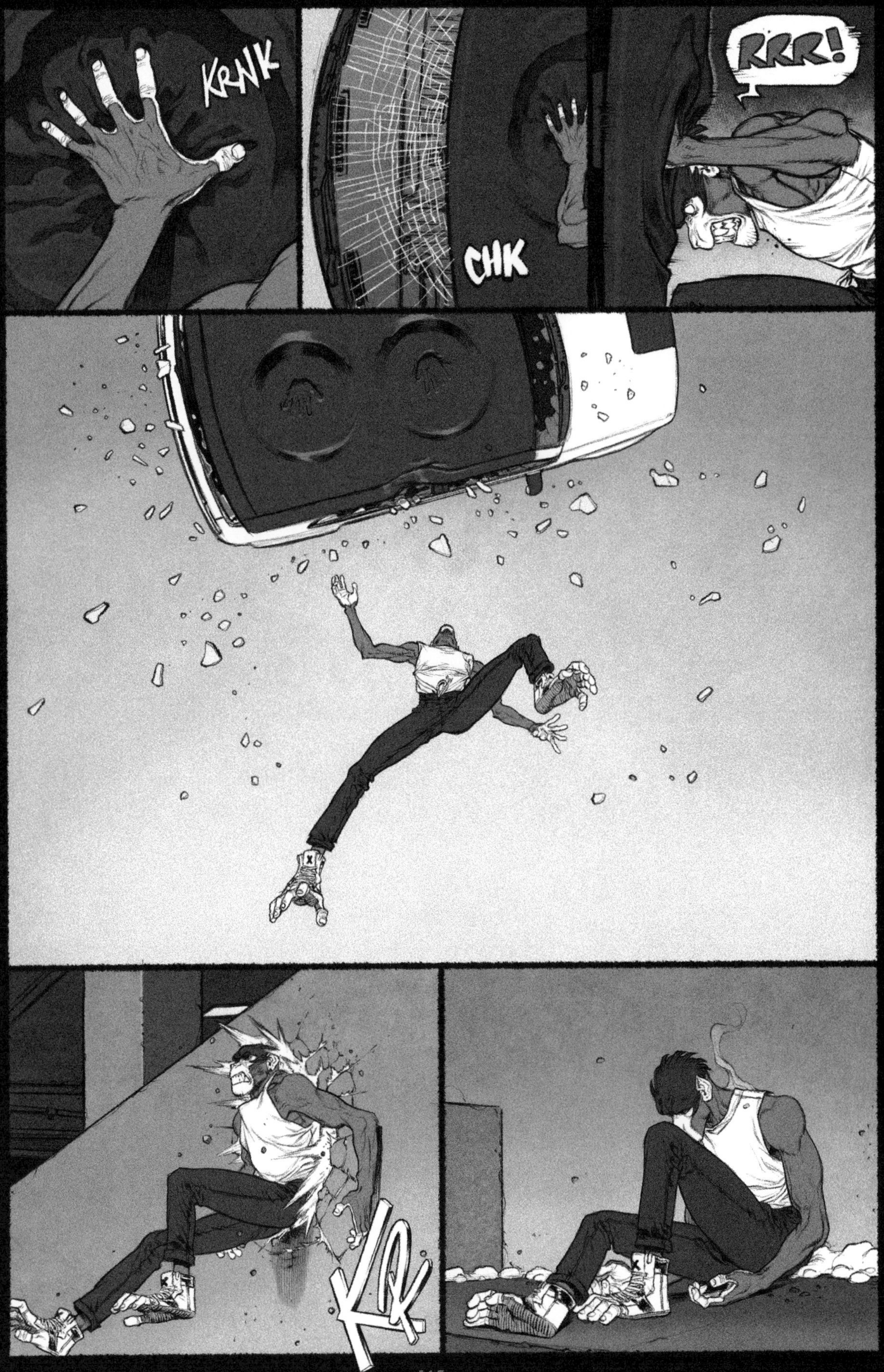
KRNK
CHK
RRR!
KR

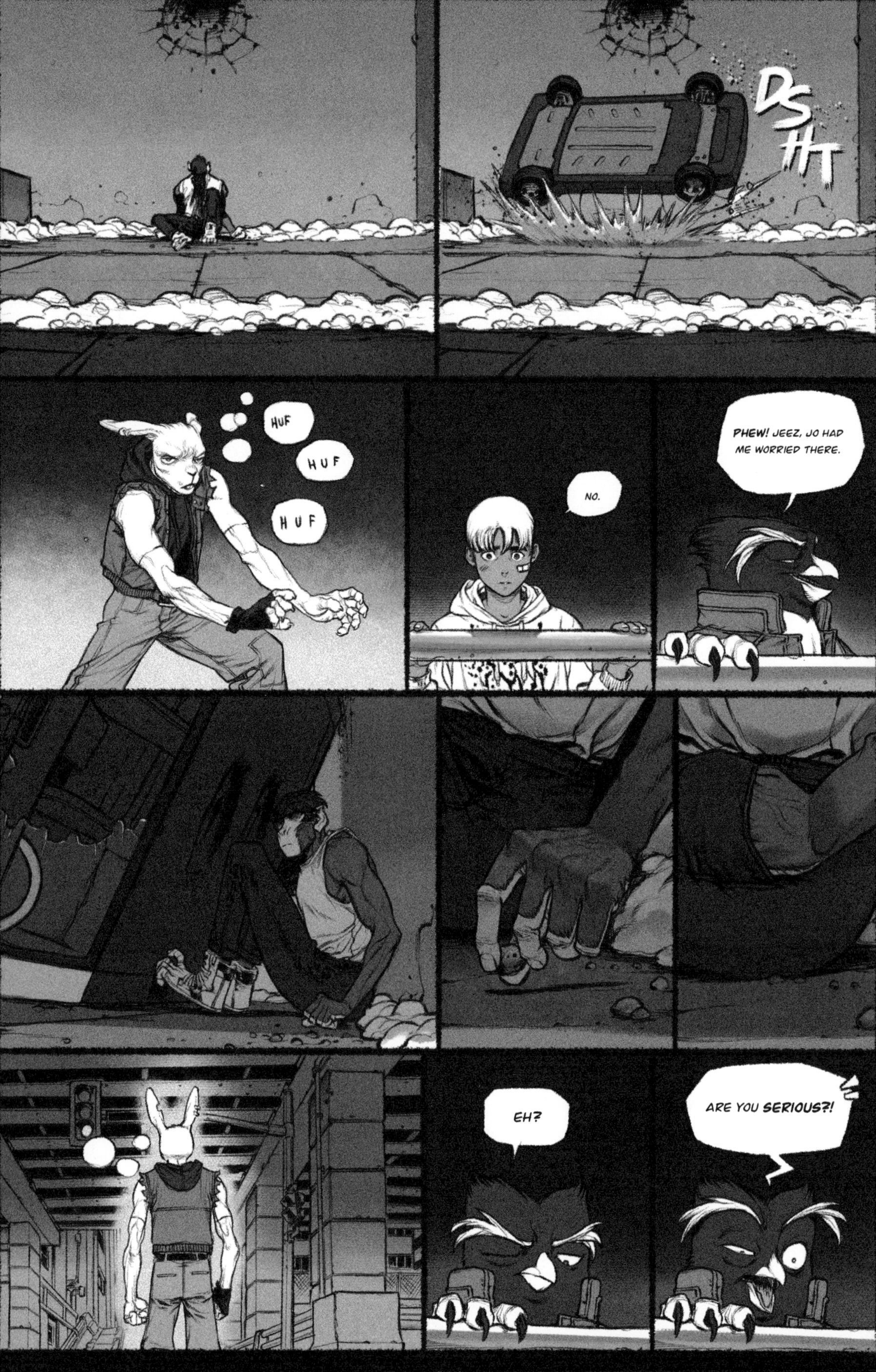
DSHT
HUF
HUF
HUF
NO.
PHEW! JEEZ, JO HAD ME WORRIED THERE.
EH?
ARE YOU SERIOUS?!

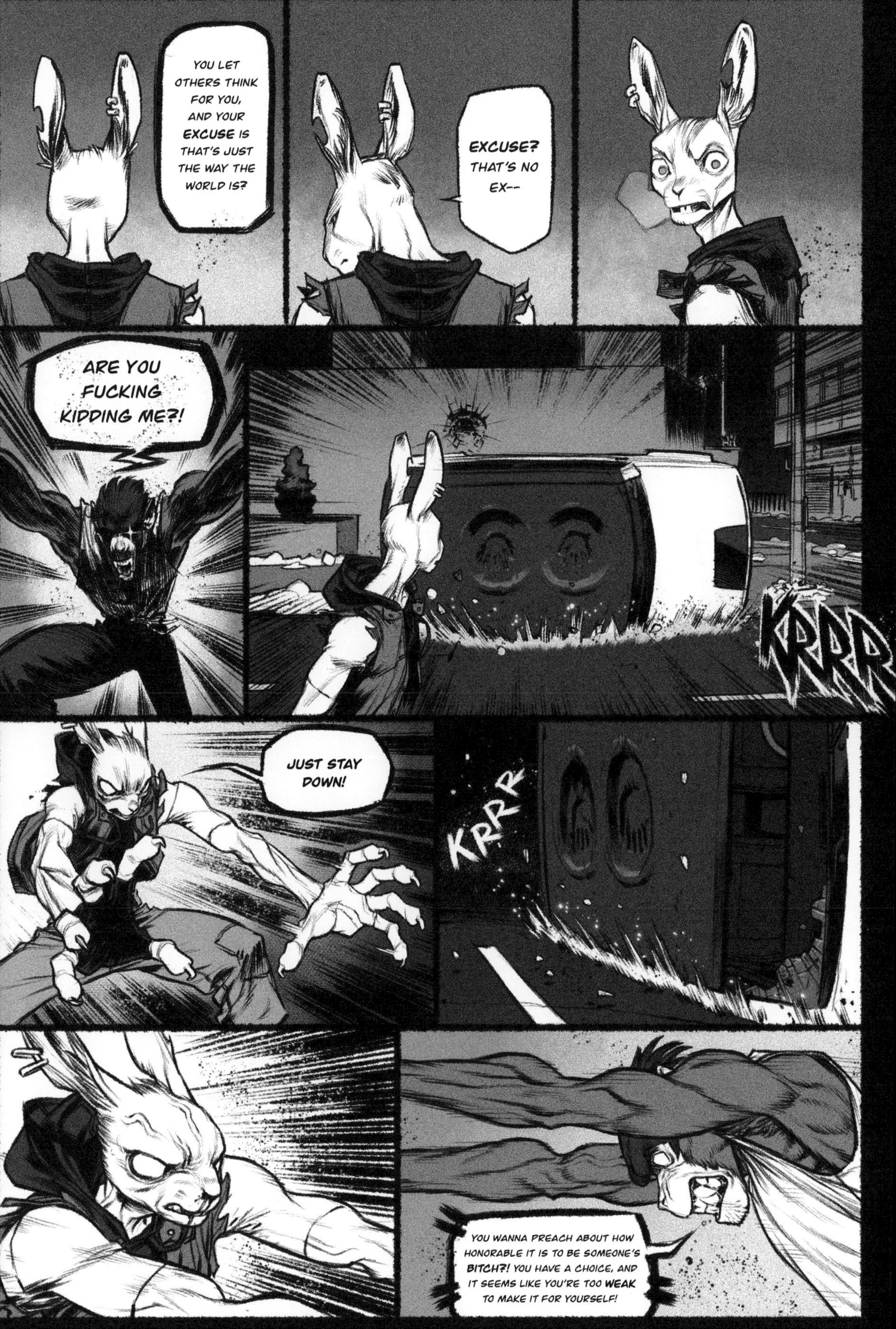
YOU LET OTHERS THINK FOR YOU, AND YOUR EXCUSE IS THAT'S JUST THE WAY THE WORLD IS?
EXCUSE? THAT'S NO EX--
ARE YOU FUCKING KIDDING ME?!
KRRR
JUST STAY DOWN!
KRRR
YOU WANNA PREACH ABOUT HOW HONORABLE IT IS TO BE SOMEONE'S BITCH?! YOU HAVE A CHOICE, AND IT SEEMS LIKE YOU'RE TOO WEAK TO MAKE IT FOR YOURSELF!

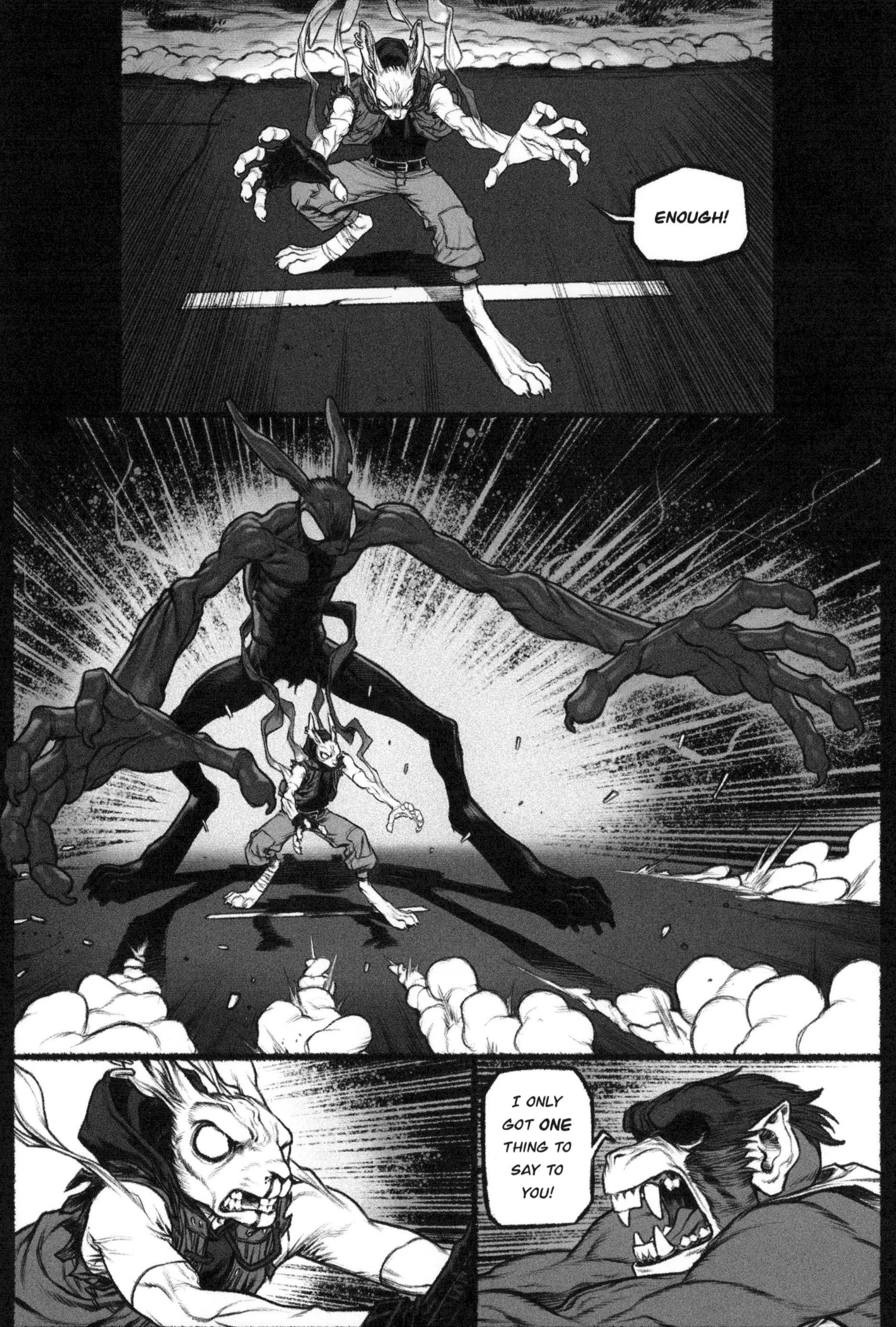
ENOUGH!
I ONLY GOT ONE THING TO SAY TO YOU!

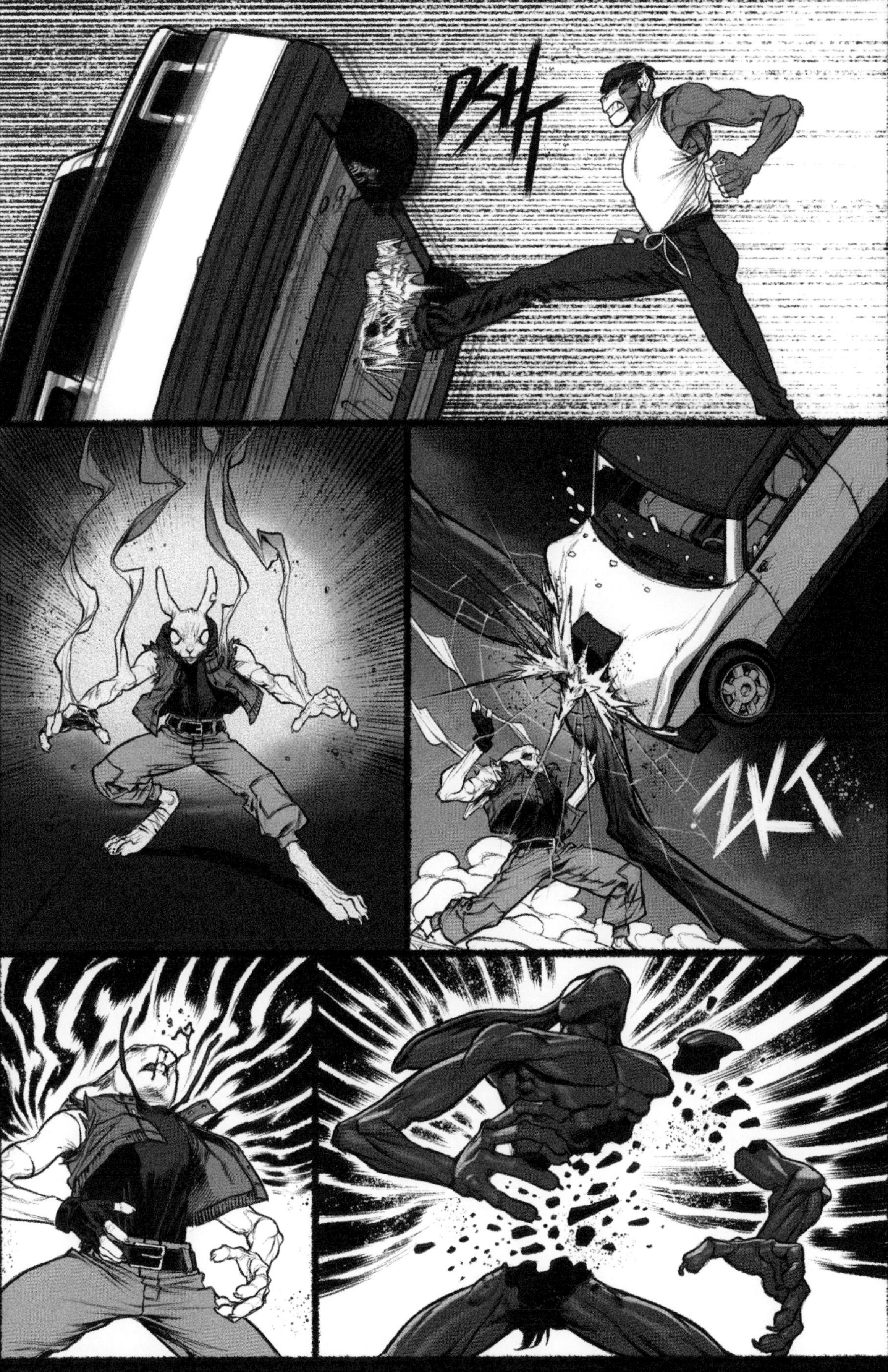
DSHT
ZKT

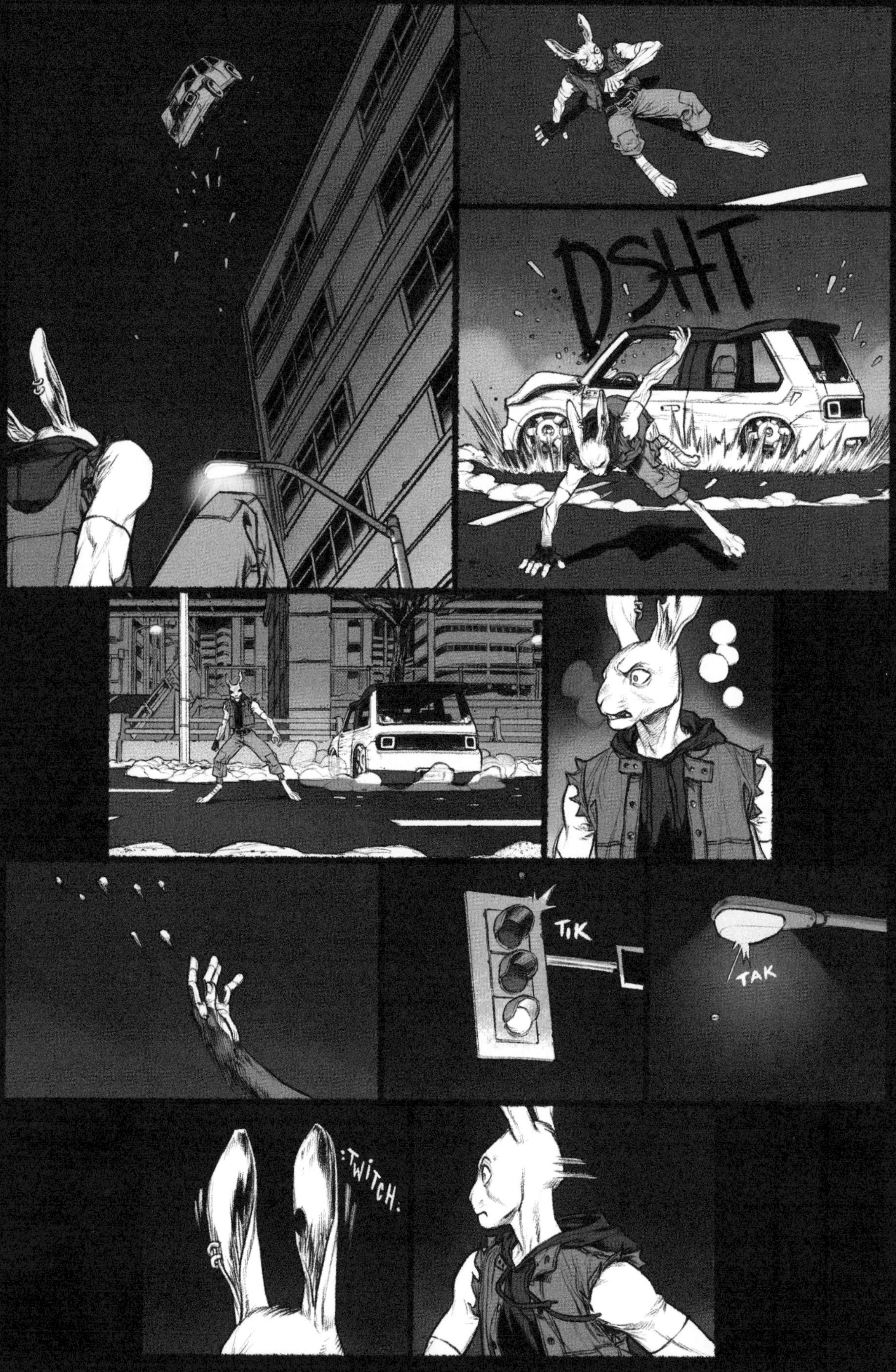
DSHT
TIK
TAK
TWITCH

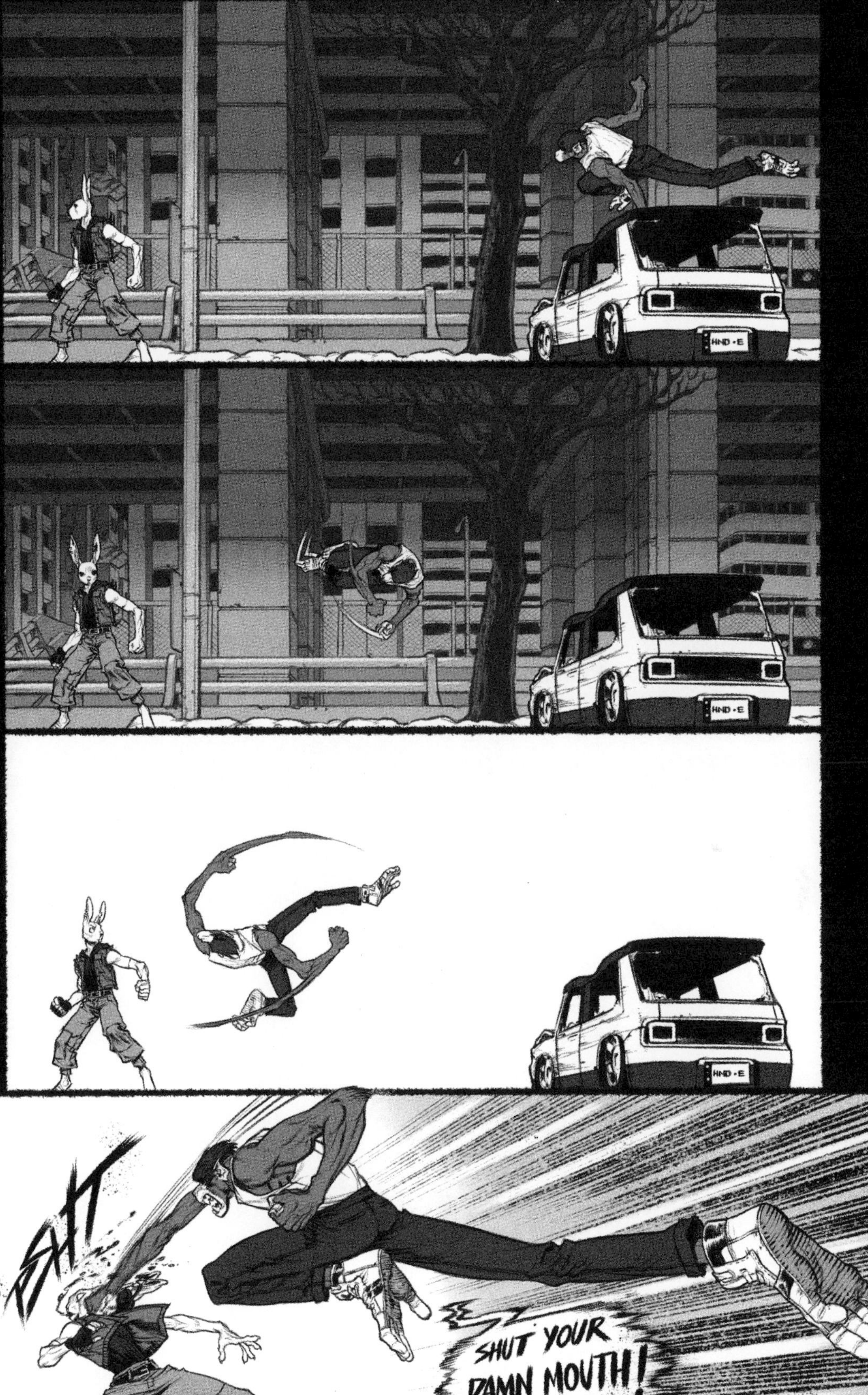
HND-E
HND-E
HND-E
TSHT
SHUT YOUR DAMN MOUTH!

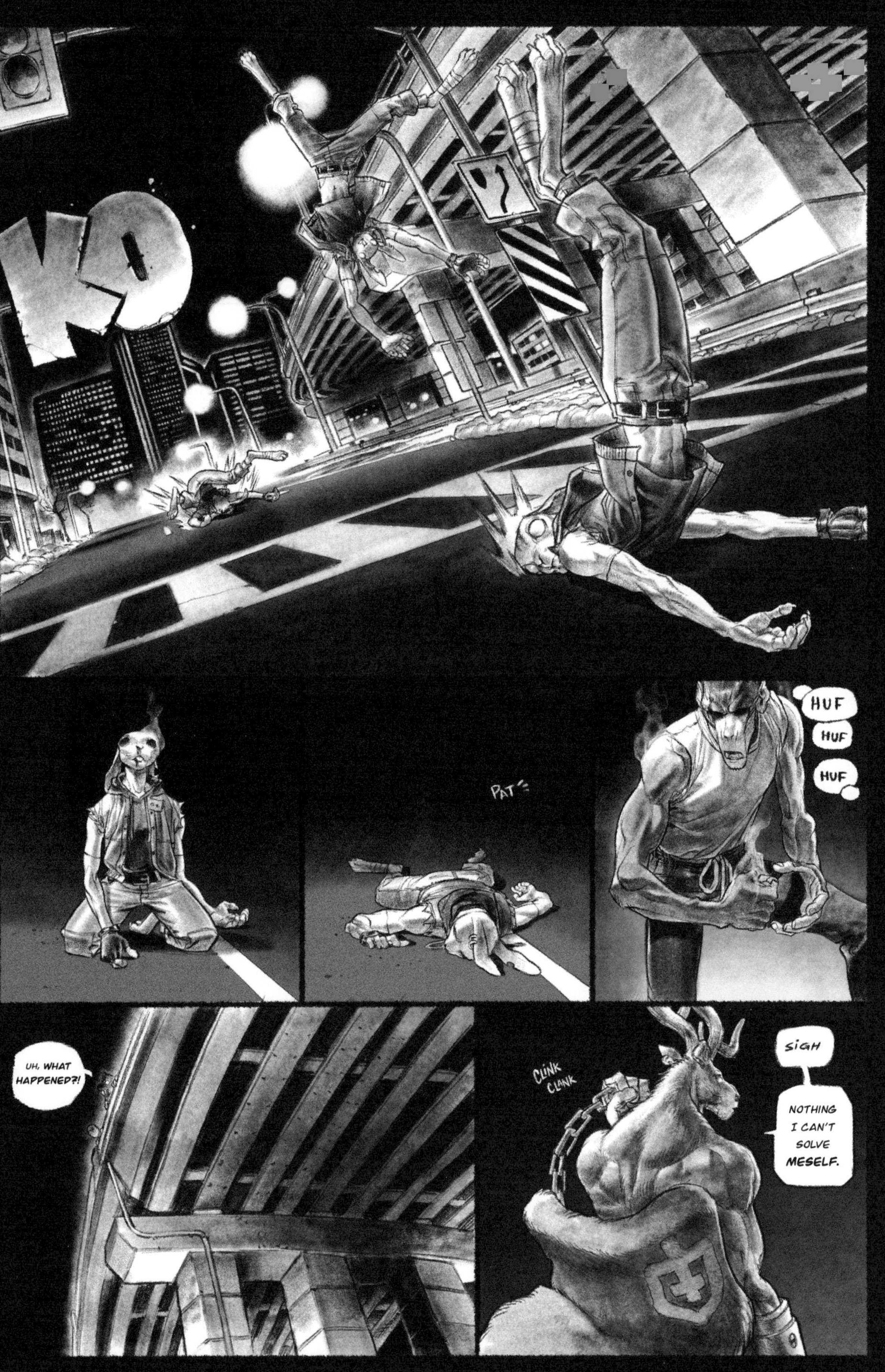
KO
PAT
HUF
HUF
HUF
UH, WHAT HAPPENED?!
CLINK CLANK
SIGH
NOTHING I CAN'T SOLVE MESELF.

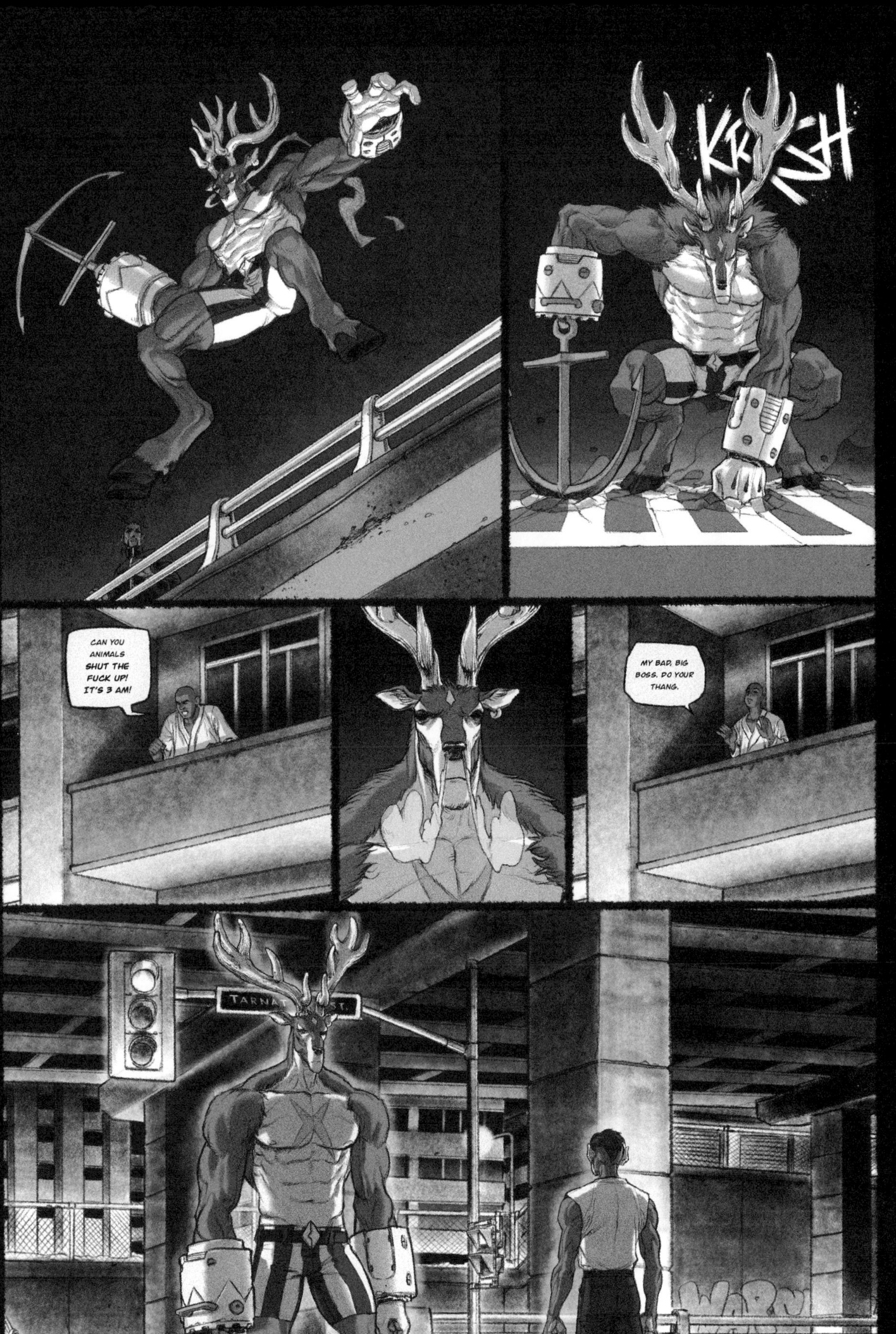
KRRASH
CAN YOU ANIMALS SHUT THE FUCK UP! IT'S 3 AM!
MY BAD, BIG BOSS. DO YOUR THANG.
TARNAT ST.

KINGS OF NOWHERE

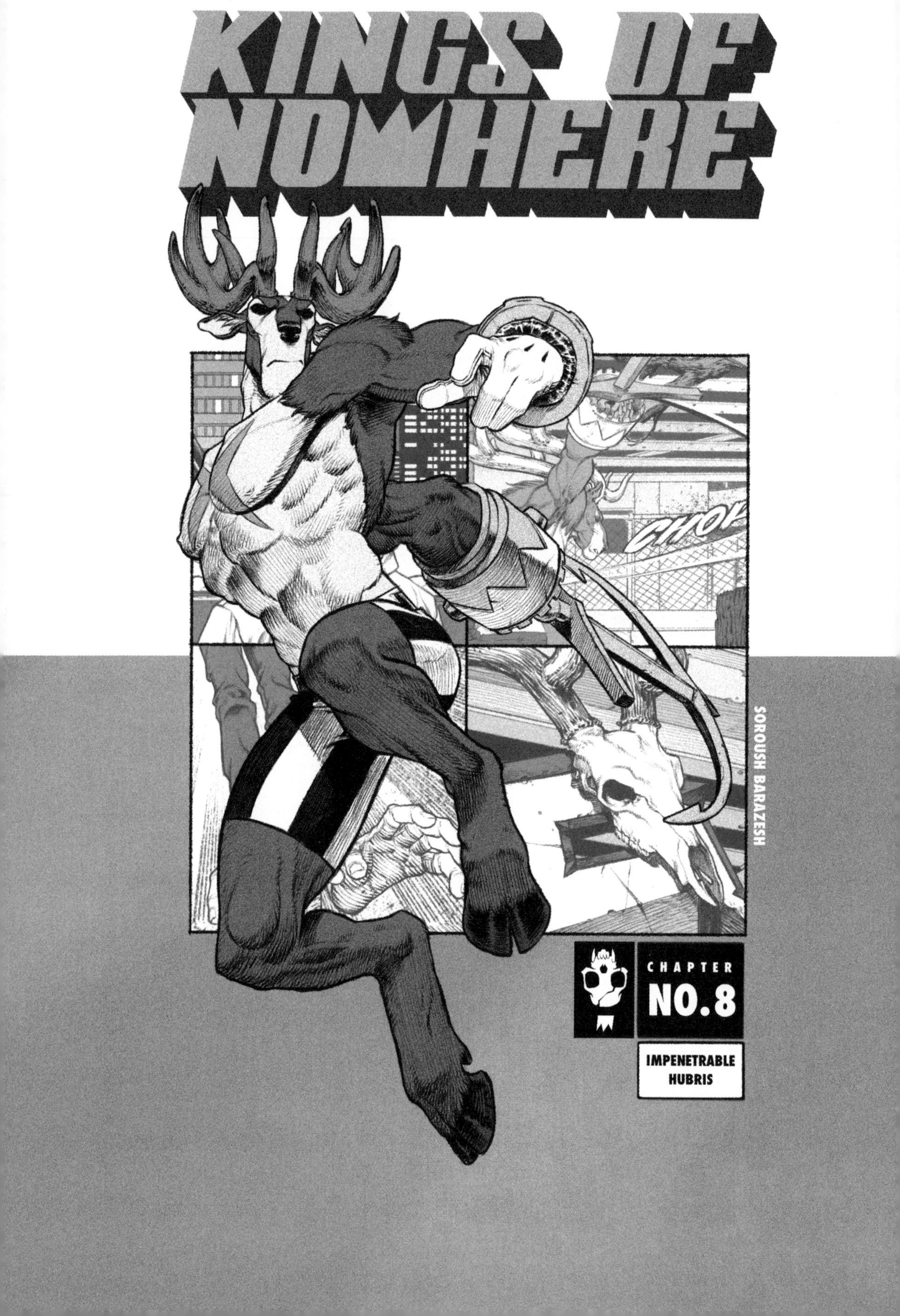
CHOK

SOROUSH BARAZESH

CHAPTER
NO.8

IMPENETRABLE
HUBRIS

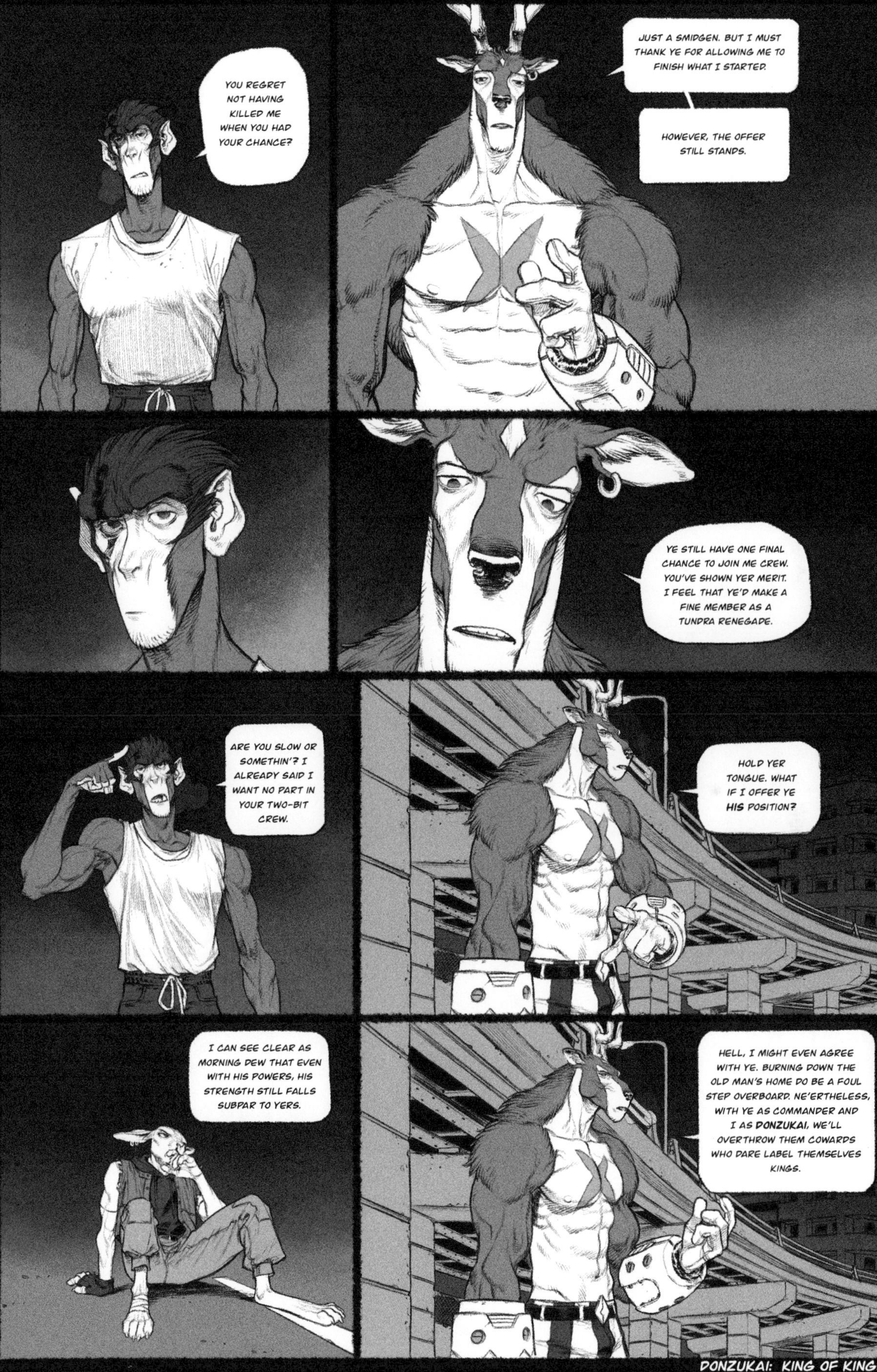
YOU REGRET NOT HAVING KILLED ME WHEN YOU HAD YOUR CHANCE?
JUST A SMIDGEN. BUT I MUST THANK YE FOR ALLOWING ME TO FINISH WHAT I STARTED.
HOWEVER, THE OFFER STILL STANDS.
YE STILL HAVE ONE FINAL CHANCE TO JOIN ME CREW. YOU'VE SHOWN YER MERIT. I FEEL THAT YE'D MAKE A FINE MEMBER AS A TUNDRA RENEGADE.
ARE YOU SLOW OR SOMETHIN'? I ALREADY SAID I WANT NO PART IN YOUR TWO-BIT CREW.
HOLD YER TONGUE. WHAT IF I OFFER YE **HIS** POSITION?
I CAN SEE CLEAR AS MORNING DEW THAT EVEN WITH HIS POWERS, HIS STRENGTH STILL FALLS SUBPAR TO YERS.
HELL, I MIGHT EVEN AGREE WITH YE. BURNING DOWN THE OLD MAN'S HOME DO BE A FOUL STEP OVERBOARD. NE'ERTHELESS, WITH YE AS COMMANDER AND I AS **DONZUKAI**, WE'LL OVERTHROW THEM COWARDS WHO DARE LABEL THEMSELVES KINGS.

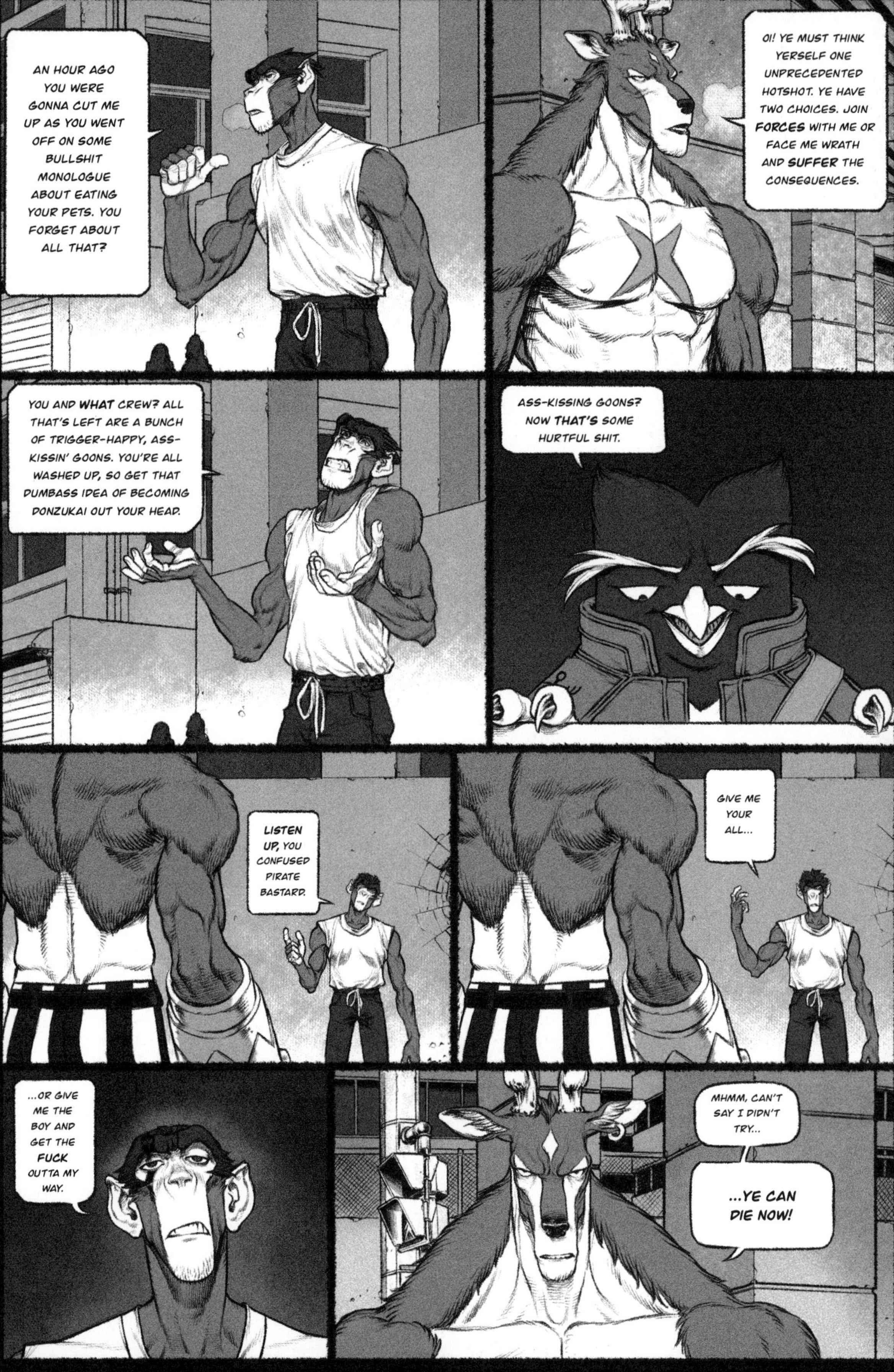
AN HOUR AGO YOU WERE GONNA CUT ME UP AS YOU WENT OFF ON SOME BULLSHIT MONOLOGUE ABOUT EATING YOUR PETS. YOU FORGET ABOUT ALL THAT?
OI! YE MUST THINK YERSELF ONE UNPRECEDENTED HOTSHOT. YE HAVE TWO CHOICES. JOIN FORCES WITH ME OR FACE ME WRATH AND SUFFER THE CONSEQUENCES.
YOU AND WHAT CREW? ALL THAT'S LEFT ARE A BUNCH OF TRIGGER-HAPPY, ASS-KISSIN' GOONS. YOU'RE ALL WASHED UP, SO GET THAT DUMBASS IDEA OF BECOMING DONZUKAI OUT YOUR HEAD.
ASS-KISSING GOONS? NOW THAT'S SOME HURTFUL SHIT.
LISTEN UP, YOU CONFUSED PIRATE BASTARD.
GIVE ME YOUR ALL...
...OR GIVE ME THE BOY AND GET THE FUCK OUTTA MY WAY.
MHMM, CAN'T SAY I DIDN'T TRY...
...YE CAN DIE NOW!

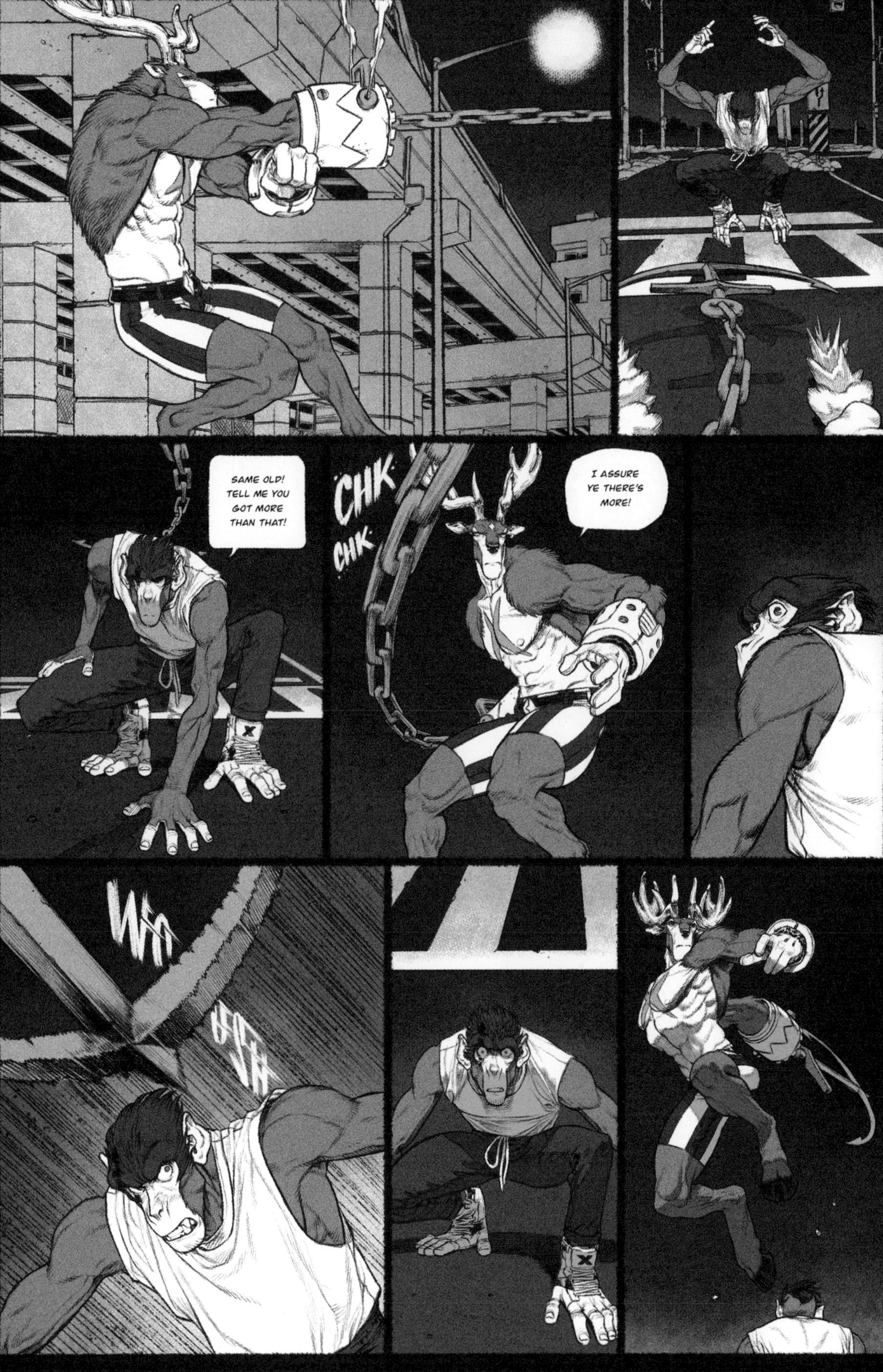

SAME OLD! TELL ME YOU GOT MORE THAN THAT!
CHK
CHK
I ASSURE YE THERE'S MORE!

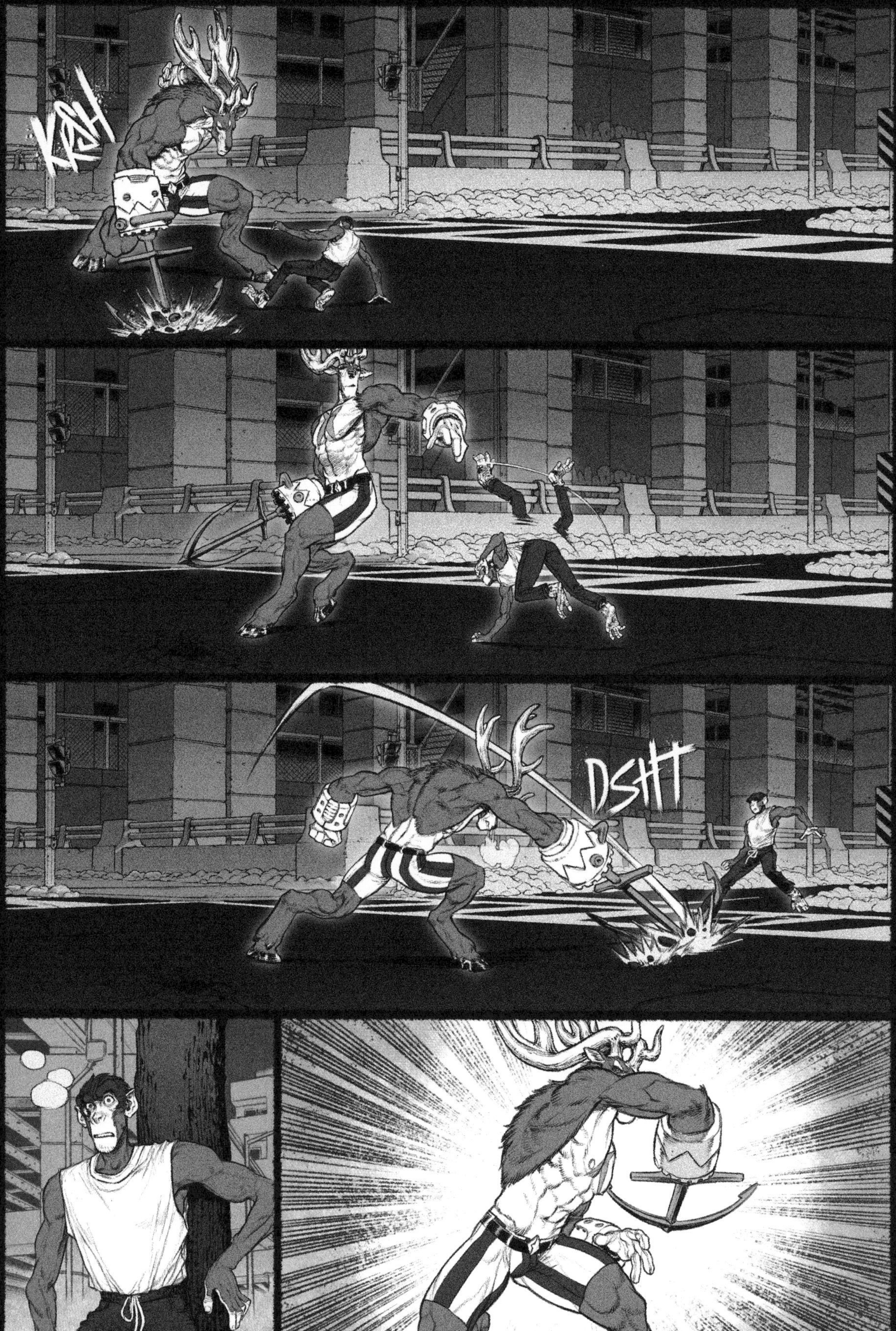
KRSH
DSHT

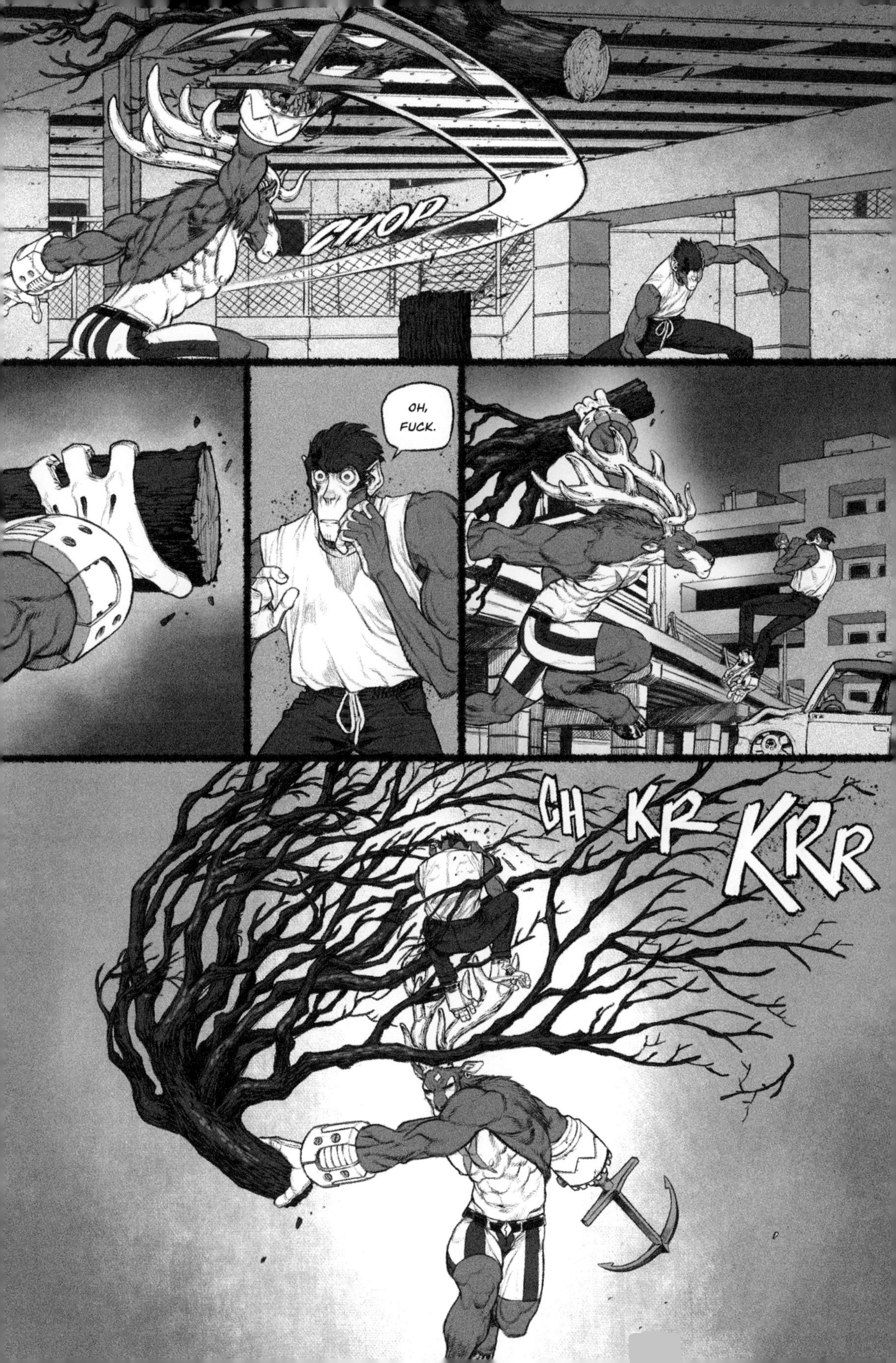
CHOP
OH, FUCK.
CH KR KRR

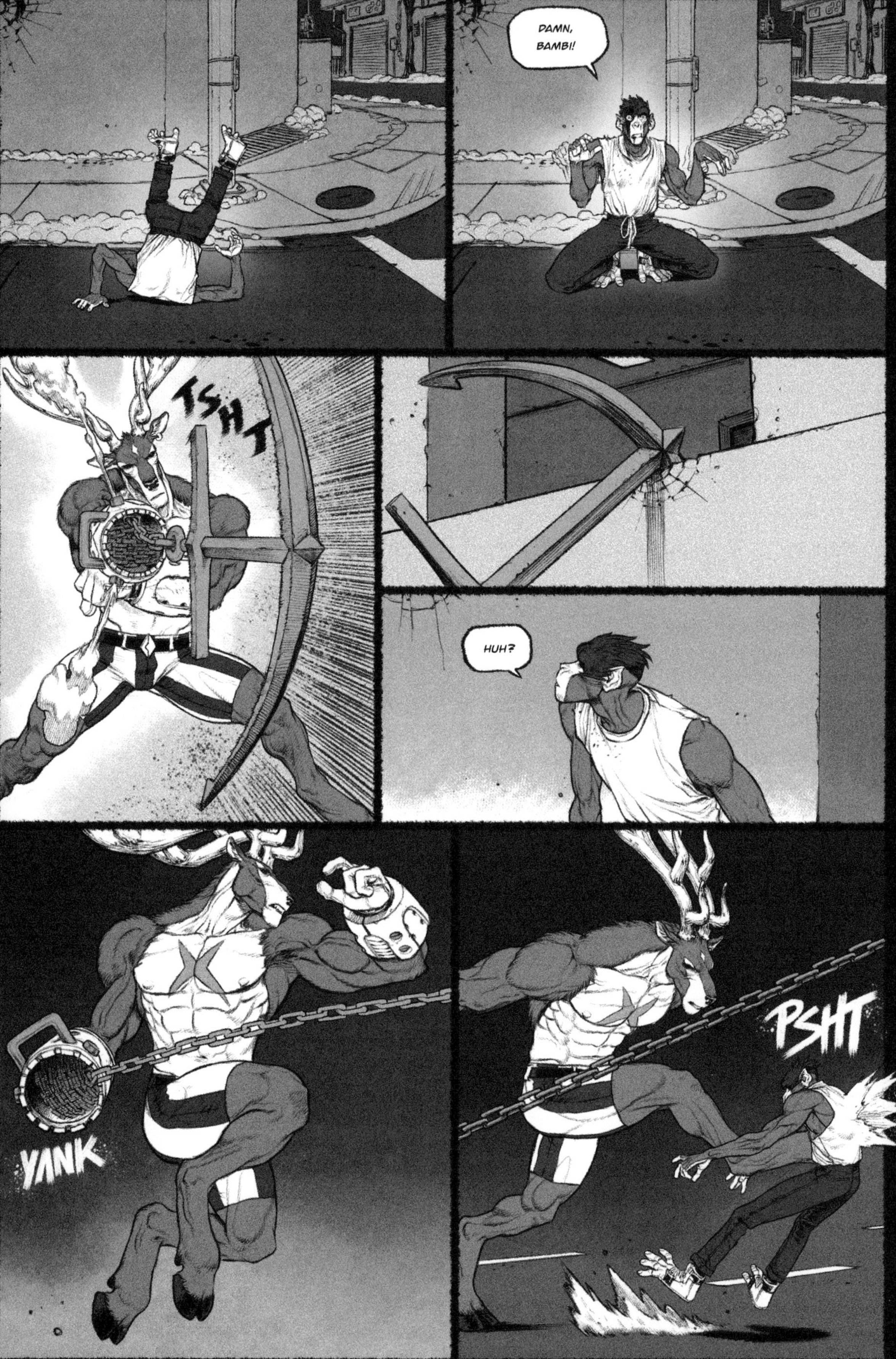
DAMN, BAMBI!
TSHT
HUH?
YANK
PSHT

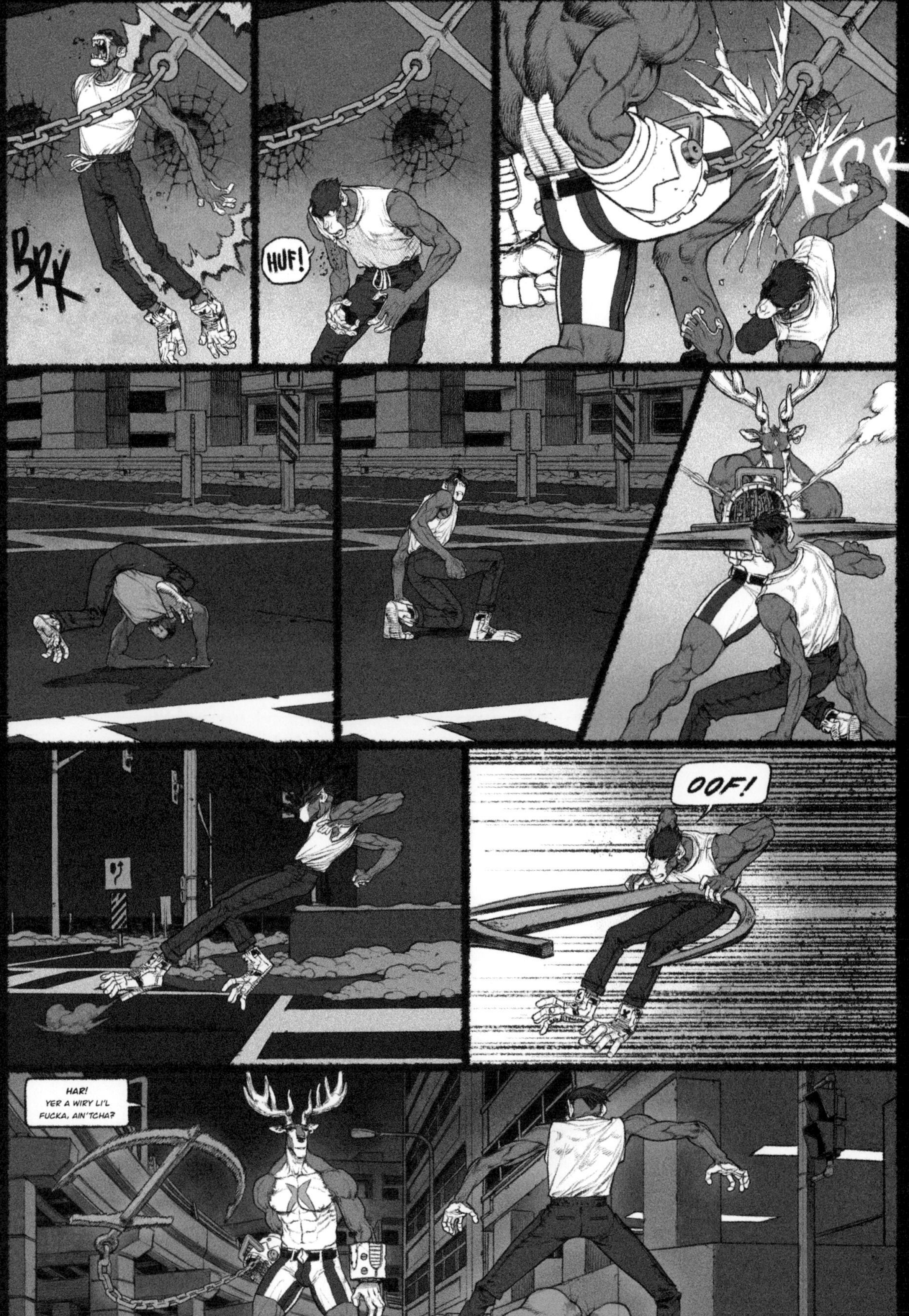
BRK
HUF!
KOR
OOF!
HAR!
YER A WIRY LI'L
FUCKA, AIN'TCHA?

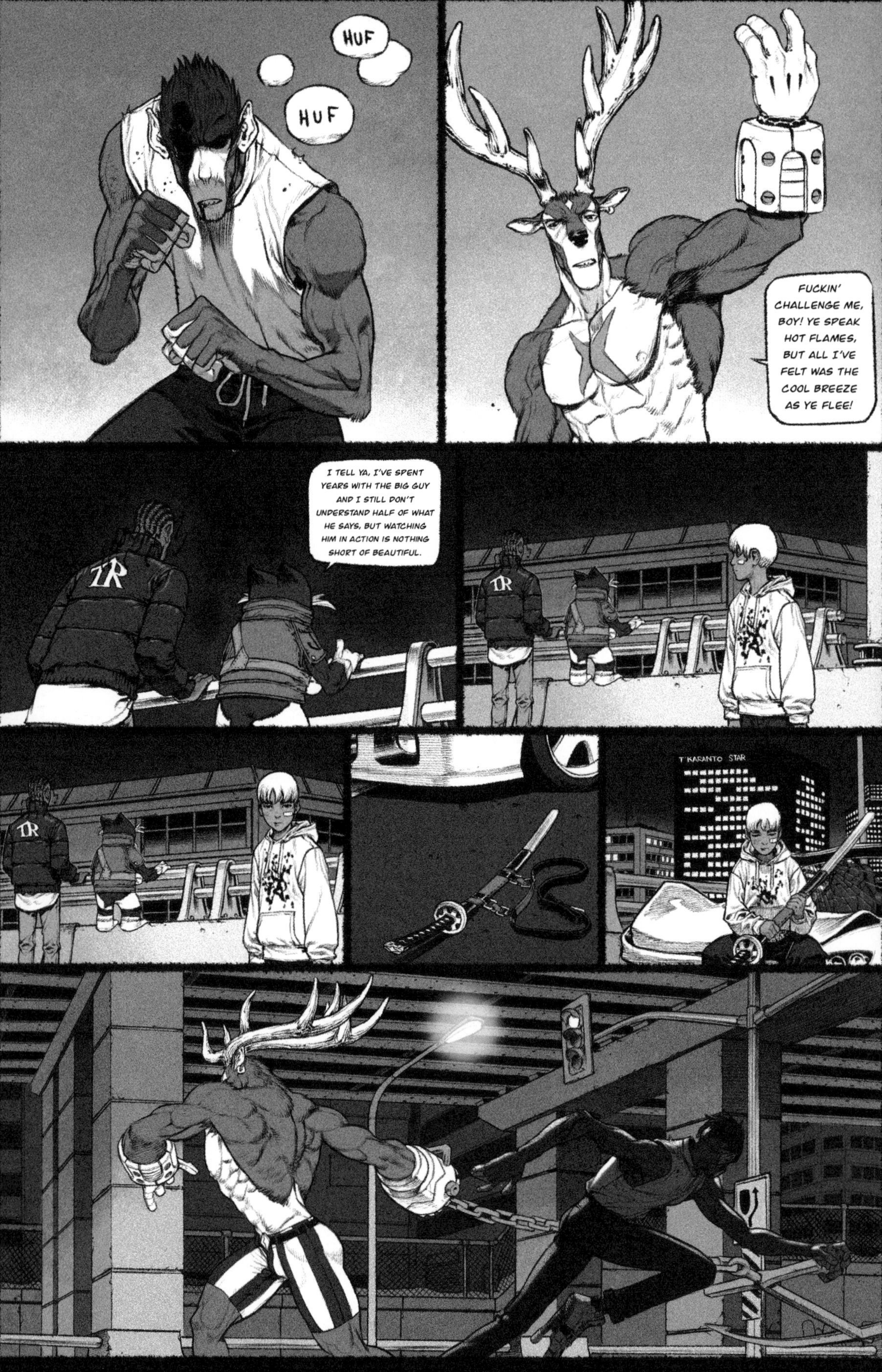
HUF
HUF
FUCKIN' CHALLENGE ME, BOY! YE SPEAK HOT FLAMES, BUT ALL I'VE FELT WAS THE COOL BREEZE AS YE FLEE!
I TELL YA, I'VE SPENT YEARS WITH THE BIG GUY AND I STILL DON'T UNDERSTAND HALF OF WHAT HE SAYS, BUT WATCHING HIM IN ACTION IS NOTHING SHORT OF BEAUTIFUL.
T'KARANTO STAR

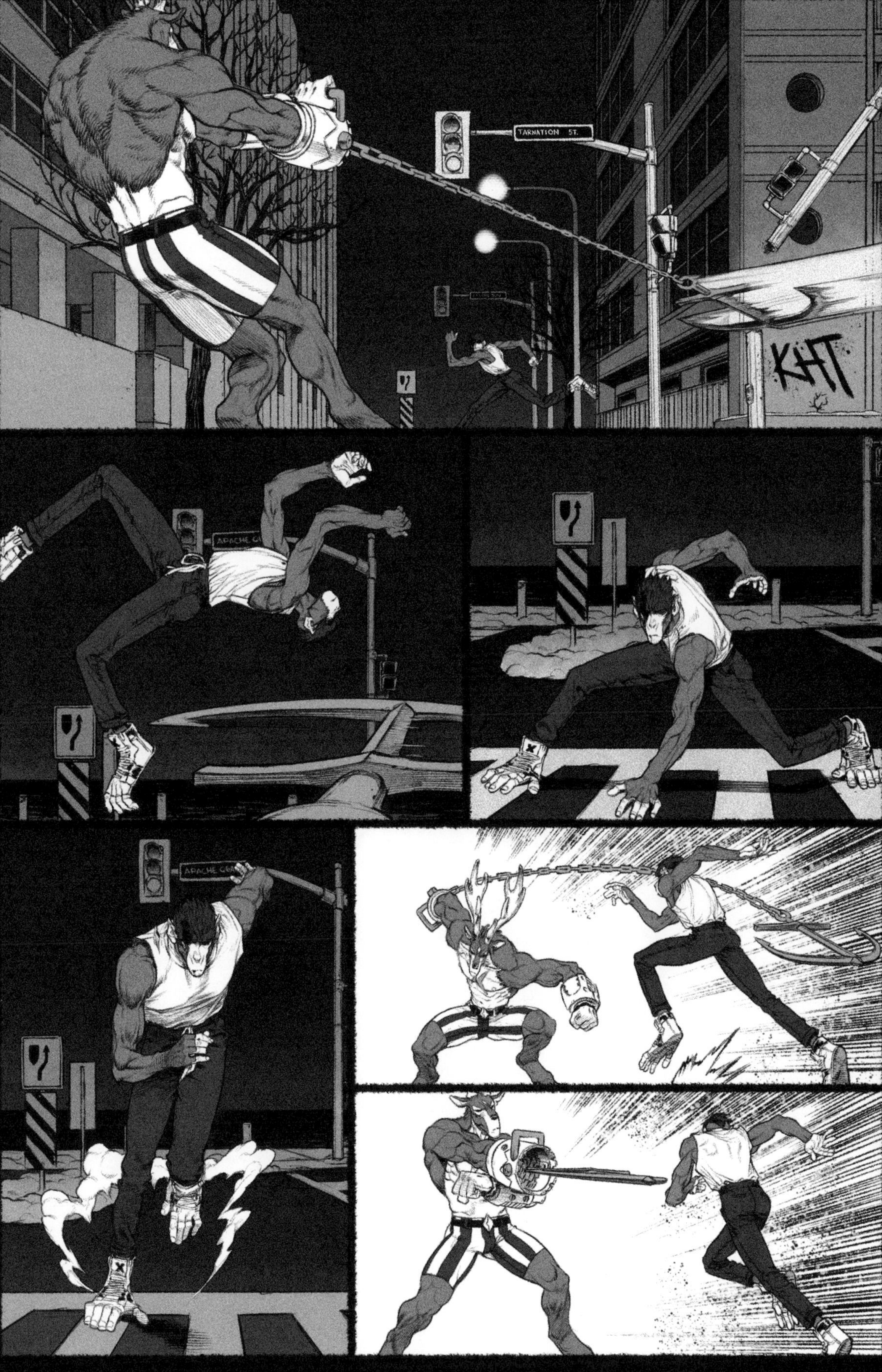
TARNATION ST.
KHT

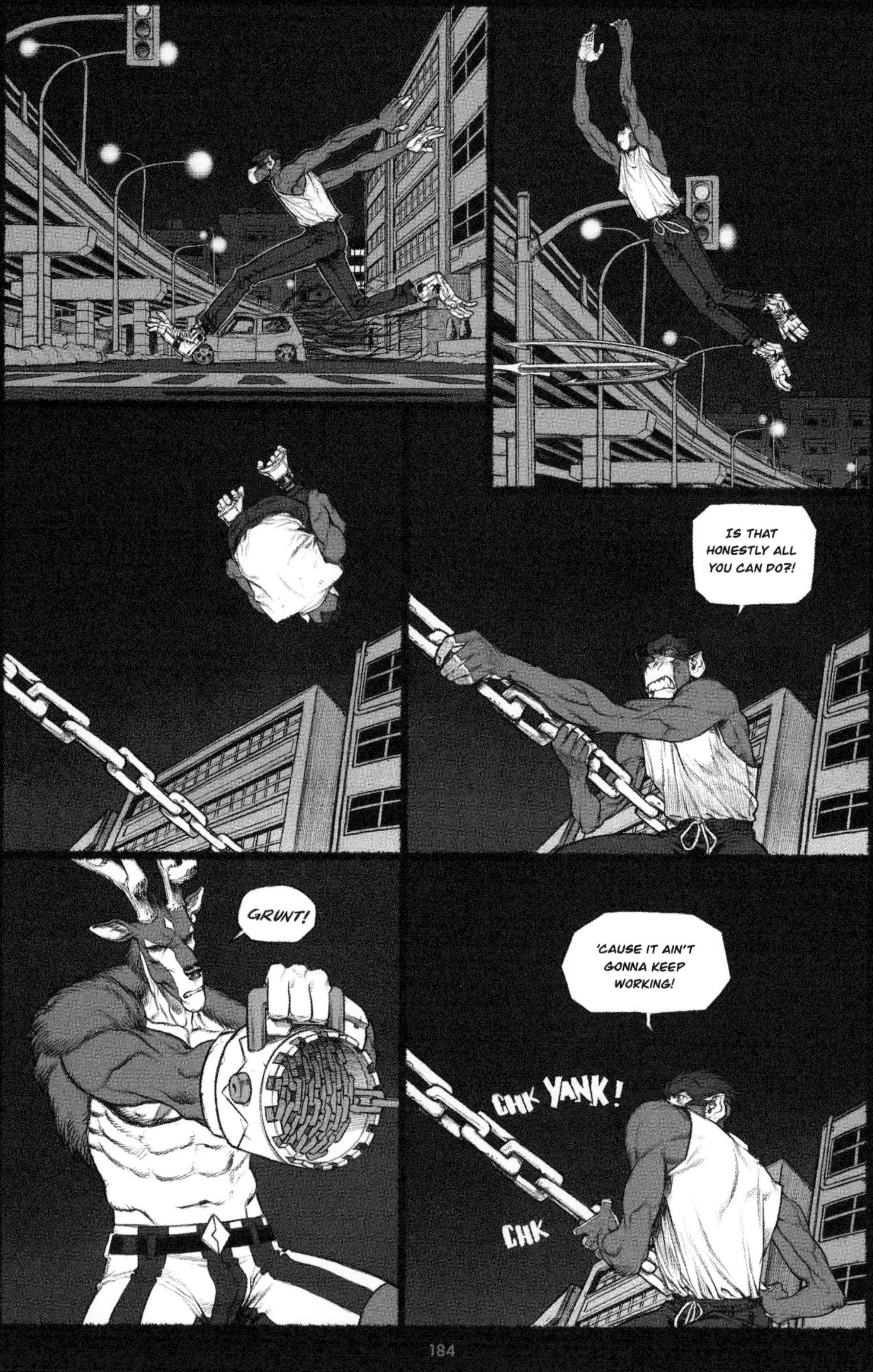
IS THAT HONESTLY ALL YOU CAN DO?!
GRUNT!
'CAUSE IT AIN'T GONNA KEEP WORKING!
CHK YANK!
CHK

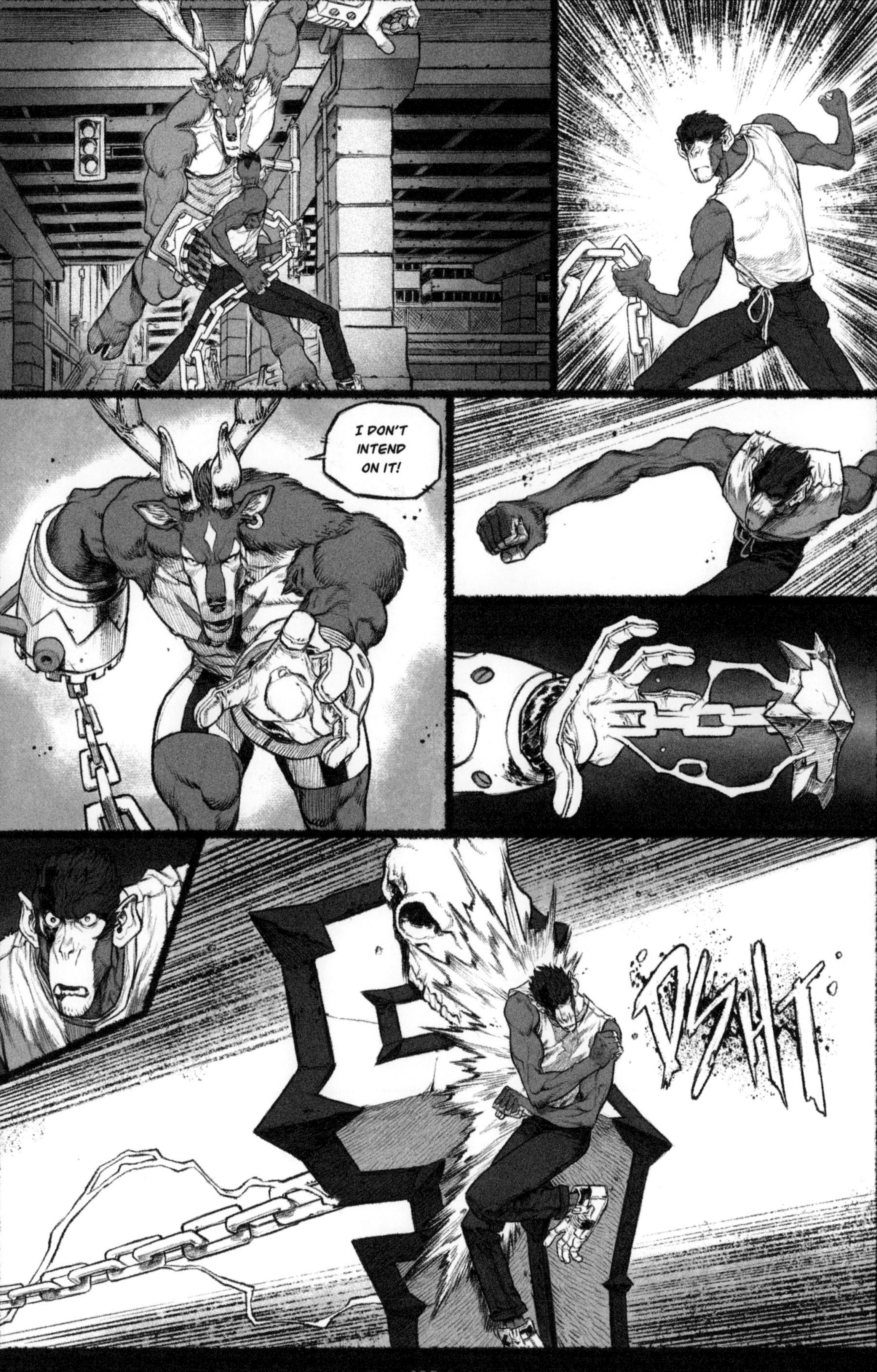
I DON'T INTEND ON IT!
DSHT

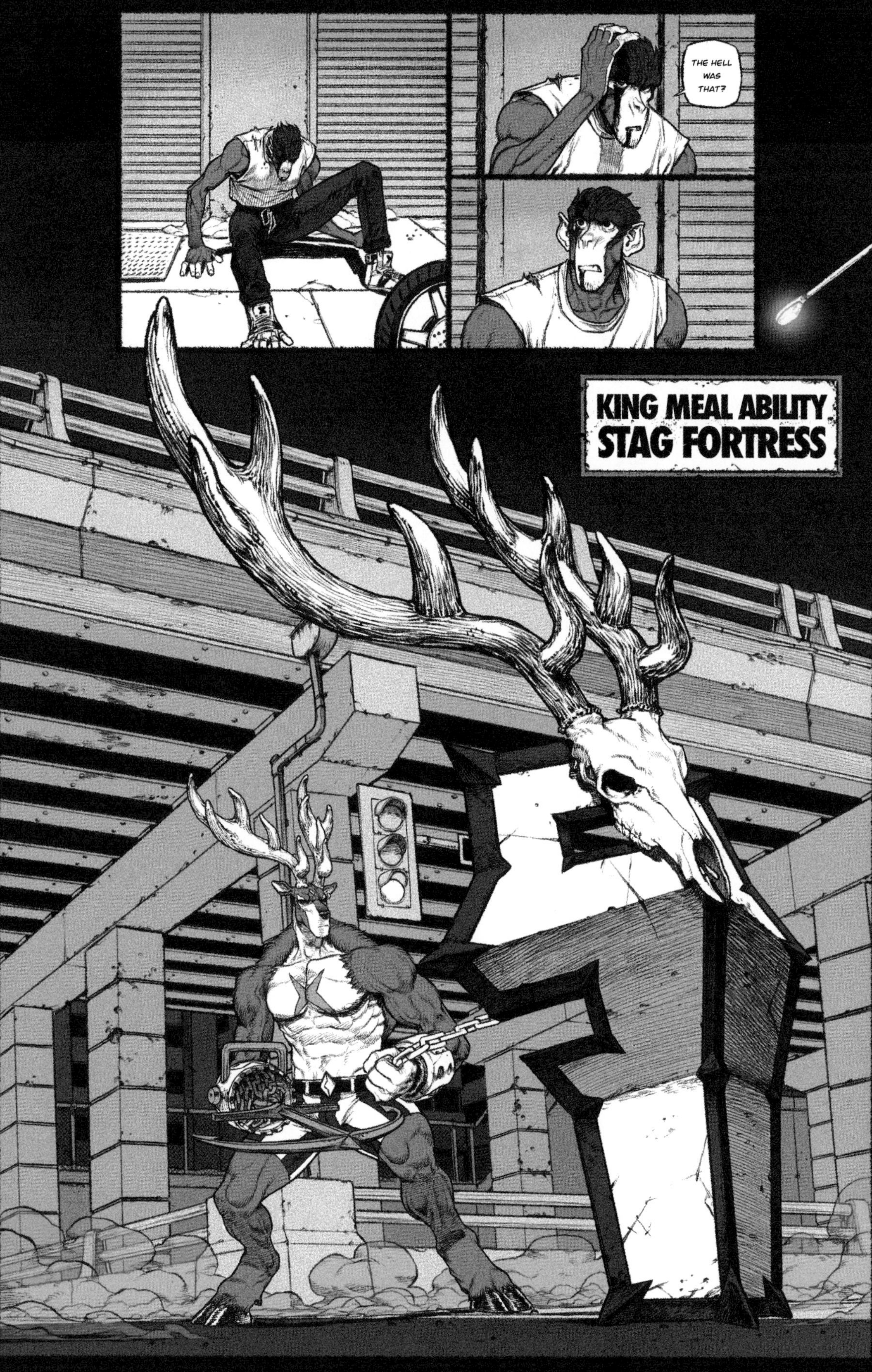
THE HELL WAS THAT?
KING MEAL ABILITY
STAG FORTRESS

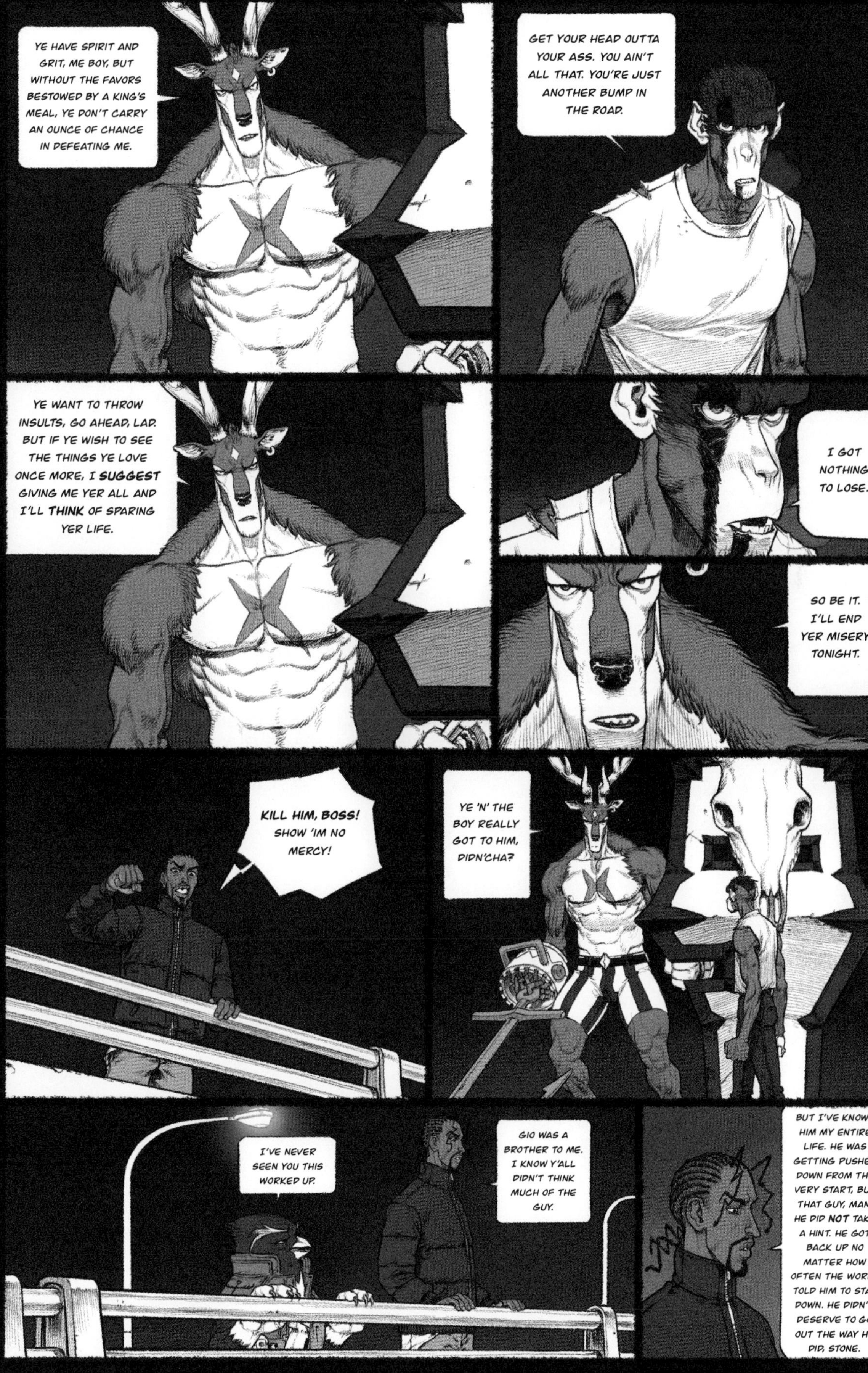
YE HAVE SPIRIT AND GRIT, ME BOY, BUT WITHOUT THE FAVORS BESTOWED BY A KING'S MEAL, YE DON'T CARRY AN OUNCE OF CHANCE IN DEFEATING ME.
GET YOUR HEAD OUTTA YOUR ASS. YOU AIN'T ALL THAT. YOU'RE JUST ANOTHER BUMP IN THE ROAD.
YE WANT TO THROW INSULTS, GO AHEAD, LAD. BUT IF YE WISH TO SEE THE THINGS YE LOVE ONCE MORE, I **SUGGEST** GIVING ME YER ALL AND I'LL **THINK** OF SPARING YER LIFE.
I GOT NOTHING TO LOSE.
SO BE IT. I'LL END YER MISERY TONIGHT.
KILL HIM, BOSS! SHOW 'IM NO MERCY!
YE 'N' THE BOY REALLY GOT TO HIM, DIDN'CHA?
I'VE NEVER SEEN YOU THIS WORKED UP.
GIO WAS A BROTHER TO ME. I KNOW Y'ALL DIDN'T THINK MUCH OF THE GUY.
BUT I'VE KNOWN HIM MY ENTIRE LIFE. HE WAS GETTING PUSHED DOWN FROM THE VERY START, BUT THAT GUY, MAN. HE DID **NOT** TAKE A HINT. HE GOT BACK UP NO MATTER HOW OFTEN THE WORLD TOLD HIM TO STAY DOWN. HE DIDN'T DESERVE TO GO OUT THE WAY HE DID, STONE.

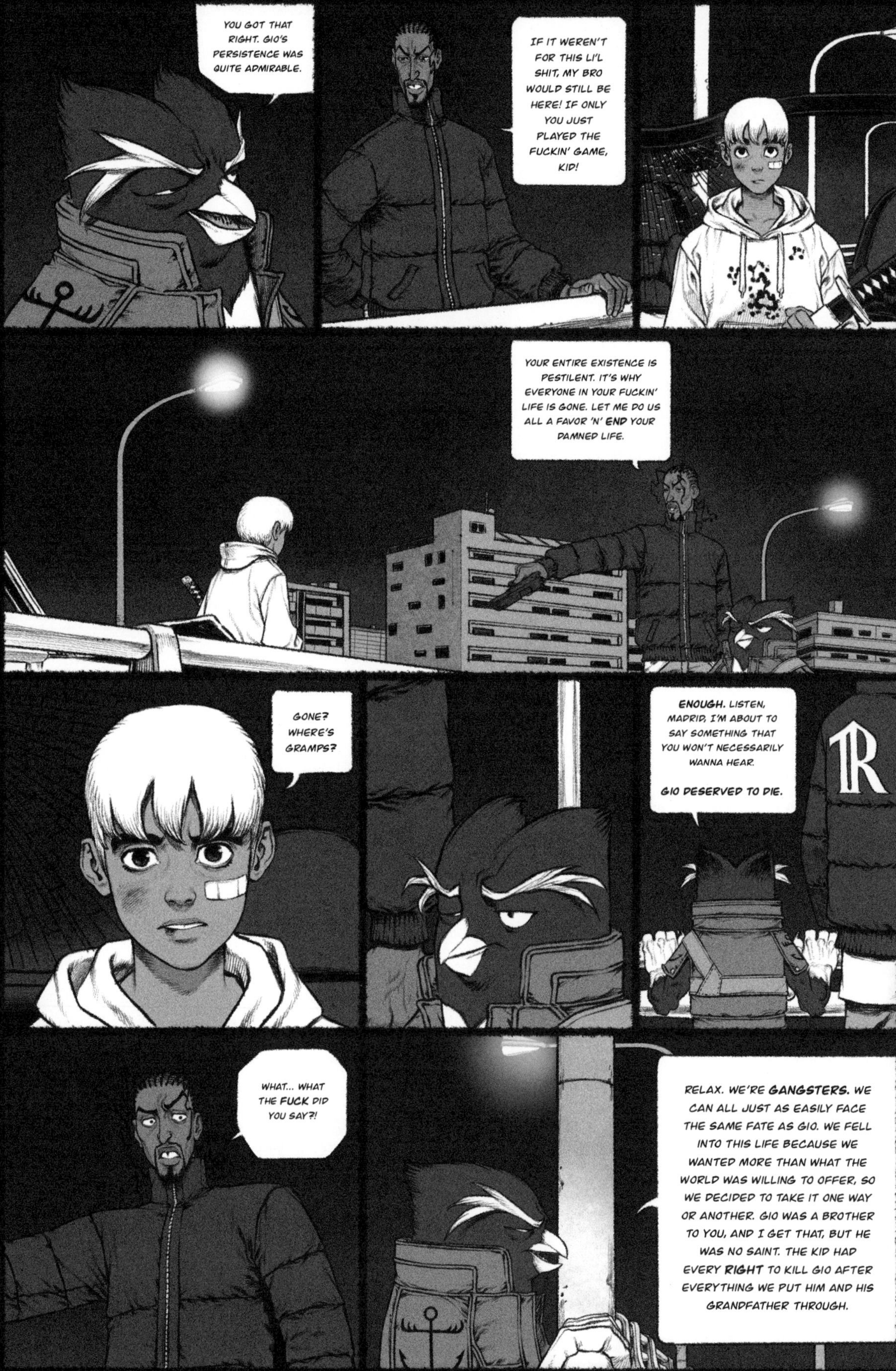
YOU GOT THAT RIGHT. GIO'S PERSISTENCE WAS QUITE ADMIRABLE.
IF IT WEREN'T FOR THIS LI'L SHIT, MY BRO WOULD STILL BE HERE! IF ONLY YOU JUST PLAYED THE FUCKIN' GAME, KID!
YOUR ENTIRE EXISTENCE IS PESTILENT. IT'S WHY EVERYONE IN YOUR FUCKIN' LIFE IS GONE. LET ME DO US ALL A FAVOR 'N' END YOUR DAMNED LIFE.
GONE? WHERE'S GRAMPS?
ENOUGH. LISTEN, MADRID, I'M ABOUT TO SAY SOMETHING THAT YOU WON'T NECESSARILY WANNA HEAR.
GIO DESERVED TO DIE.
WHAT... WHAT THE FUCK DID YOU SAY?!
RELAX. WE'RE GANGSTERS. WE CAN ALL JUST AS EASILY FACE THE SAME FATE AS GIO. WE FELL INTO THIS LIFE BECAUSE WE WANTED MORE THAN WHAT THE WORLD WAS WILLING TO OFFER, SO WE DECIDED TO TAKE IT ONE WAY OR ANOTHER. GIO WAS A BROTHER TO YOU, AND I GET THAT, BUT HE WAS NO SAINT. THE KID HAD EVERY RIGHT TO KILL GIO AFTER EVERYTHING WE PUT HIM AND HIS GRANDFATHER THROUGH.

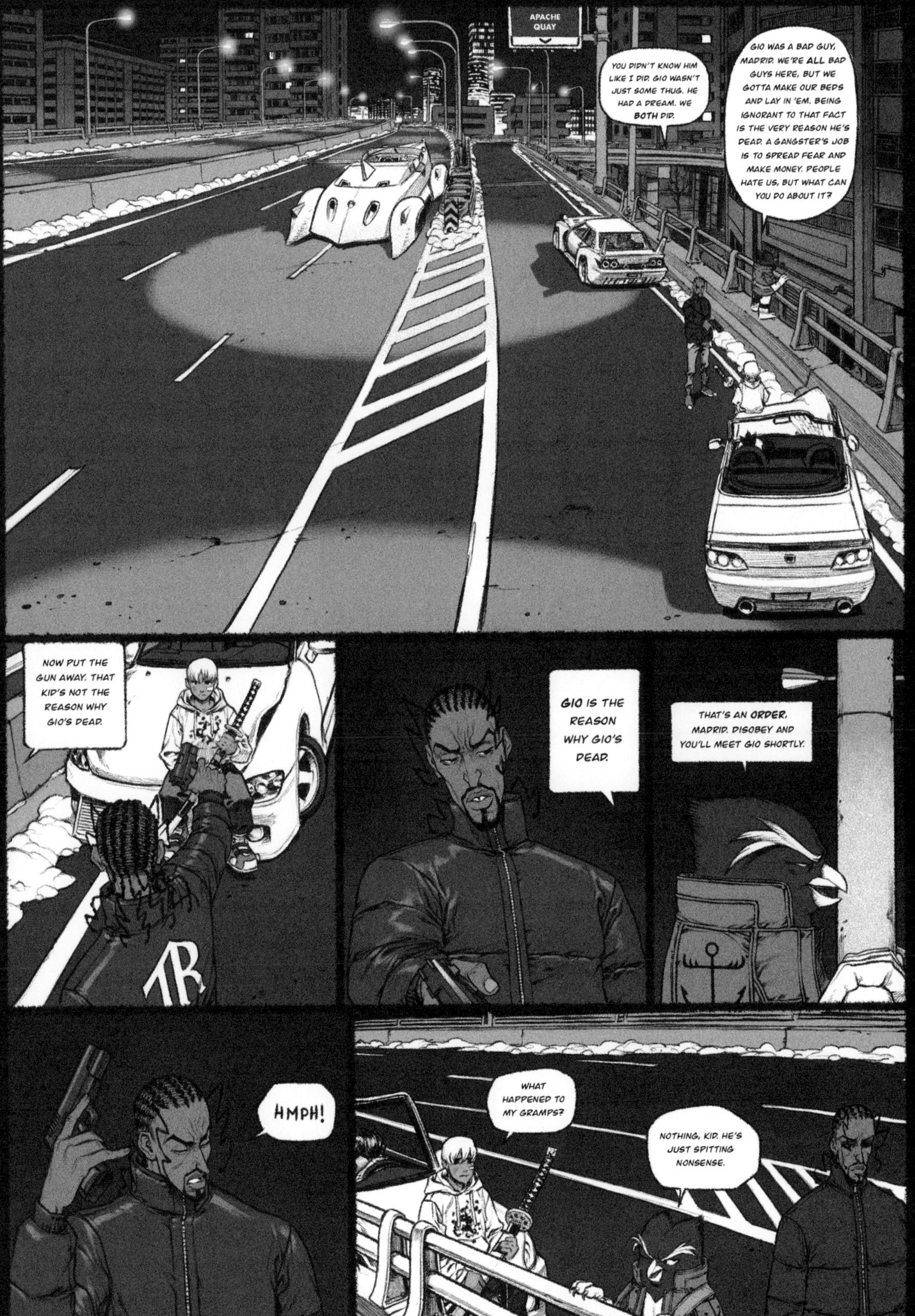
APACHE QUAY
YOU DIDN'T KNOW HIM LIKE I DID. GIO WASN'T JUST SOME THUG. HE HAD A DREAM. WE BOTH DID.
GIO WAS A BAD GUY, MADRID. WE'RE ALL BAD GUYS HERE, BUT WE GOTTA MAKE OUR BEDS AND LAY IN 'EM. BEING IGNORANT TO THAT FACT IS THE VERY REASON HE'S DEAD. A GANGSTER'S JOB IS TO SPREAD FEAR AND MAKE MONEY. PEOPLE HATE US, BUT WHAT CAN YOU DO ABOUT IT?
NOW PUT THE GUN AWAY. THAT KID'S NOT THE REASON WHY GIO'S DEAD.
GIO IS THE REASON WHY GIO'S DEAD.
THAT'S AN ORDER, MADRID. DISOBEY AND YOU'LL MEET GIO SHORTLY.
HMPH!
WHAT HAPPENED TO MY GRAMPS?
NOTHING, KID. HE'S JUST SPITTING NONSENSE.

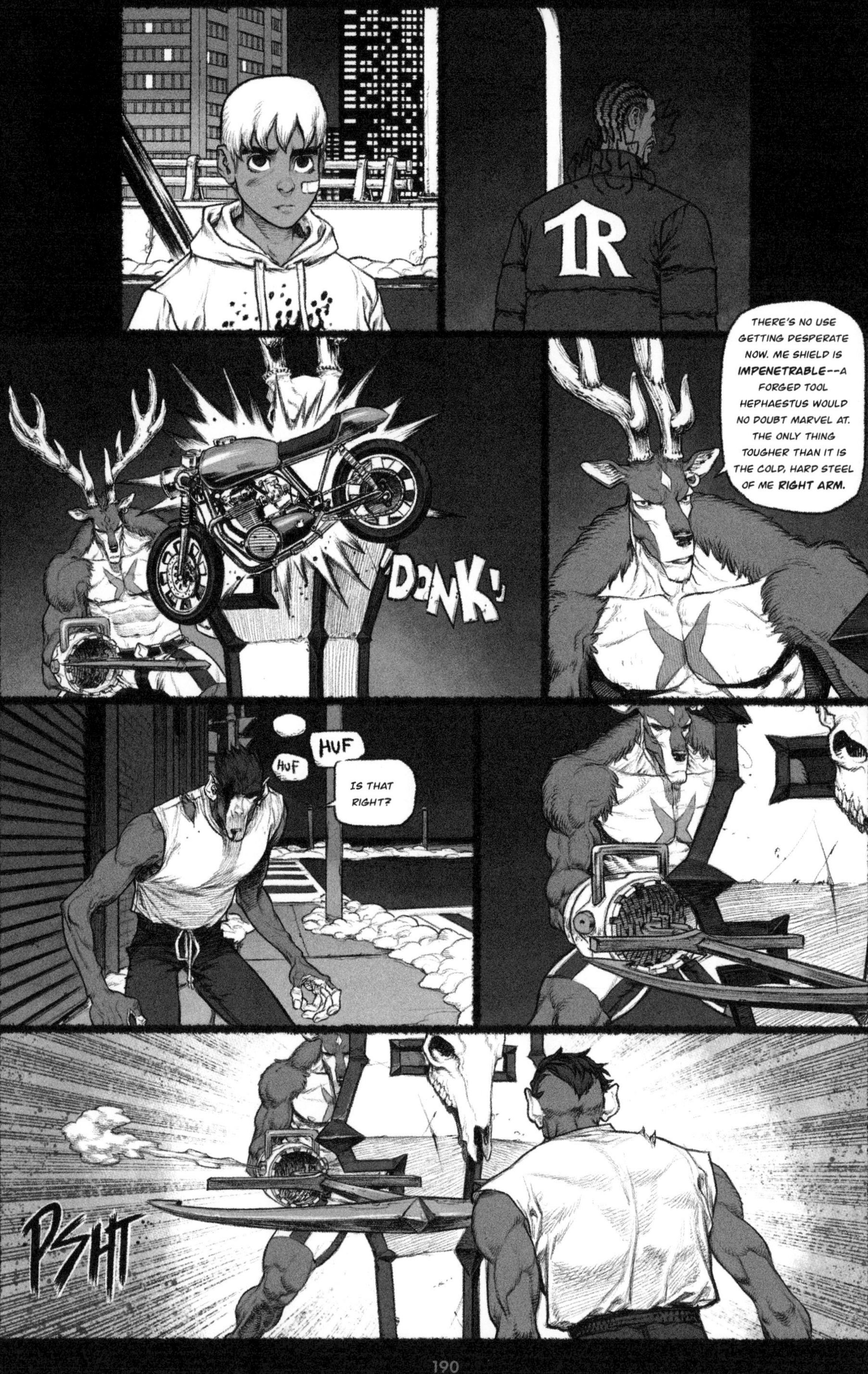
THERE'S NO USE GETTING DESPERATE NOW. ME SHIELD IS **IMPENETRABLE**--A FORGED TOOL HEPHAESTUS WOULD NO DOUBT MARVEL AT. THE ONLY THING TOUGHER THAN IT IS THE COLD, HARD STEEL OF ME **RIGHT ARM.**
DONK!
HUF
HUF
IS THAT RIGHT?
PSHT

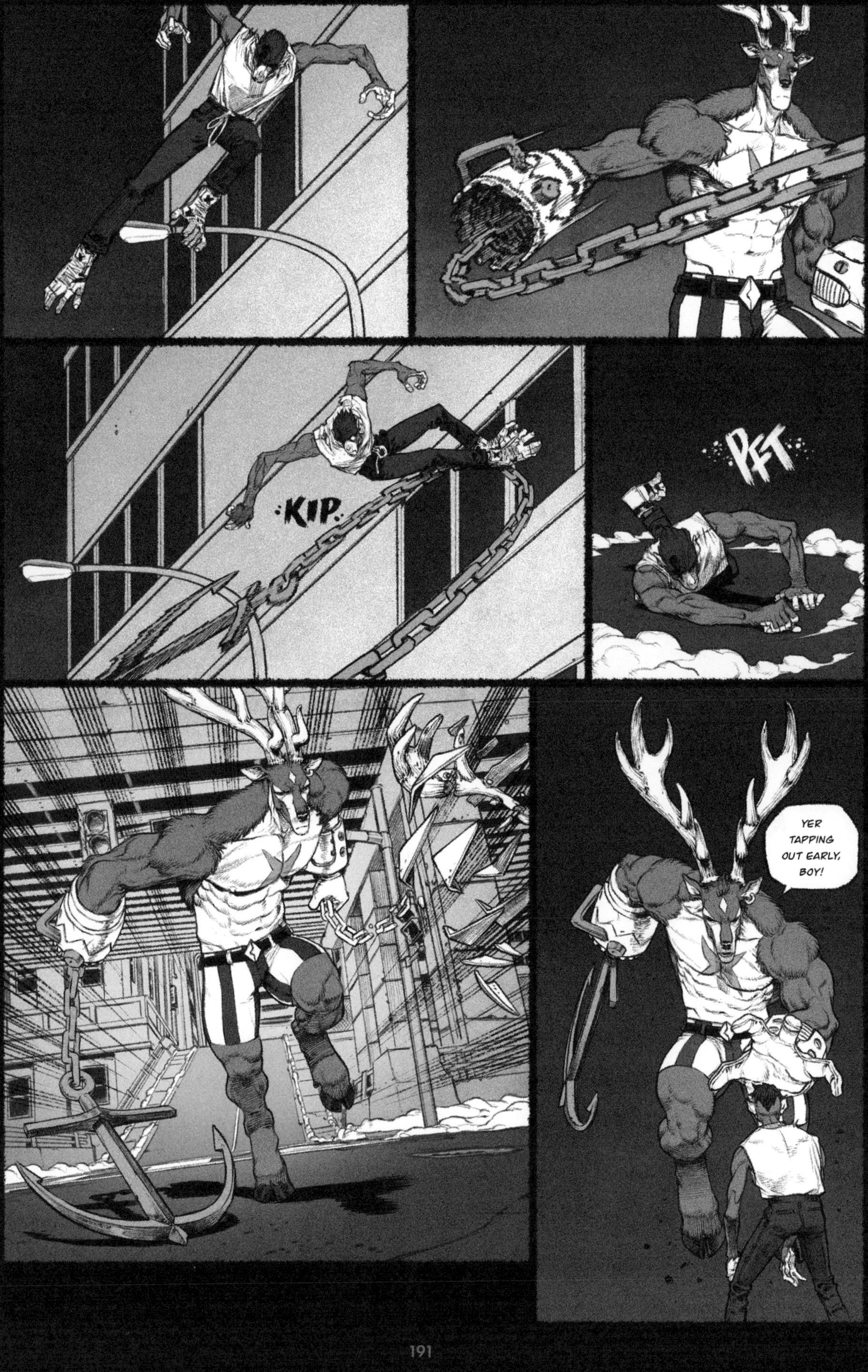
KIP.
PFFT
YER TAPPING OUT EARLY, BOY!

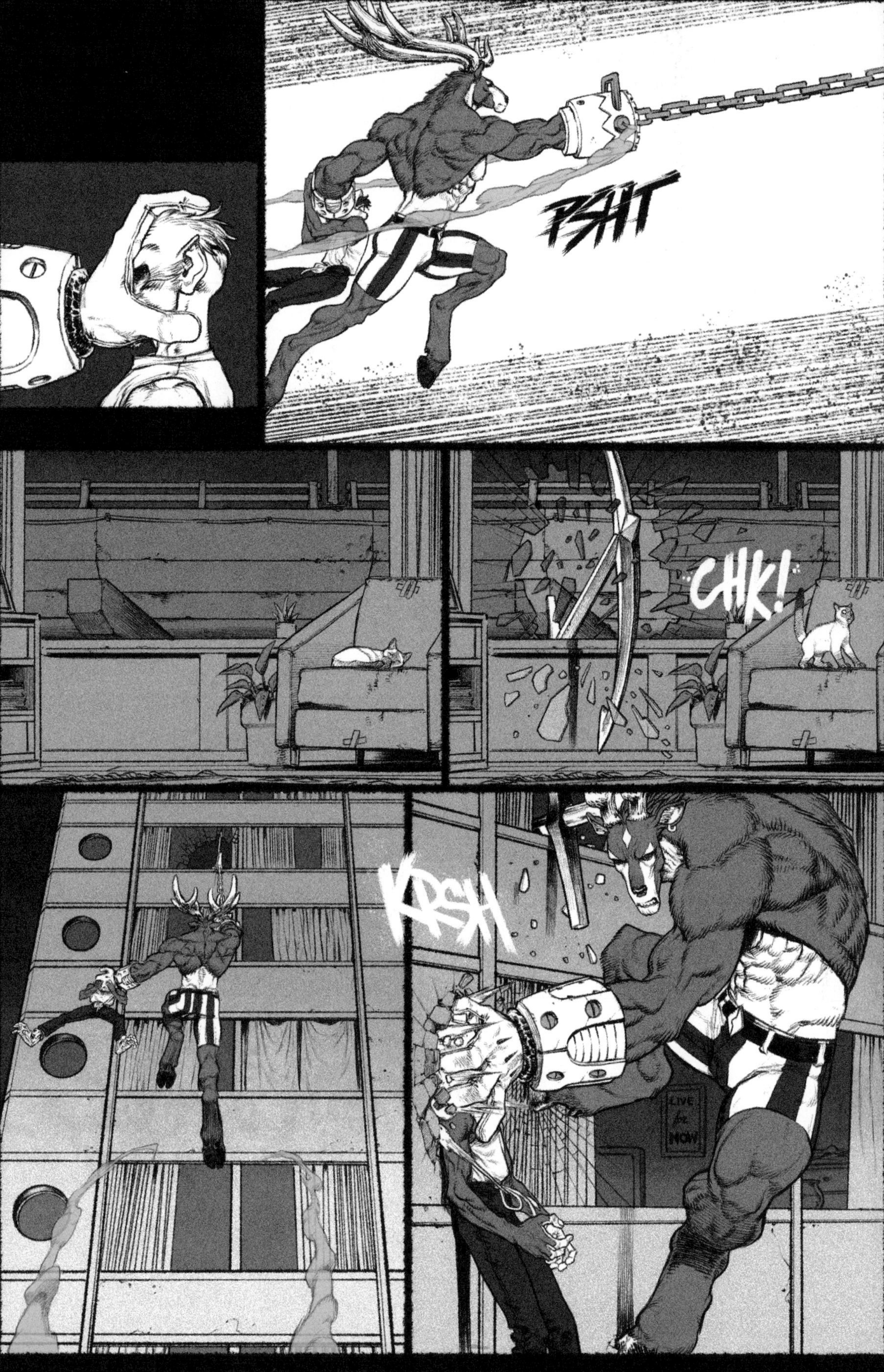
PSHT
CHK!
KRSH
LIVE for NOW

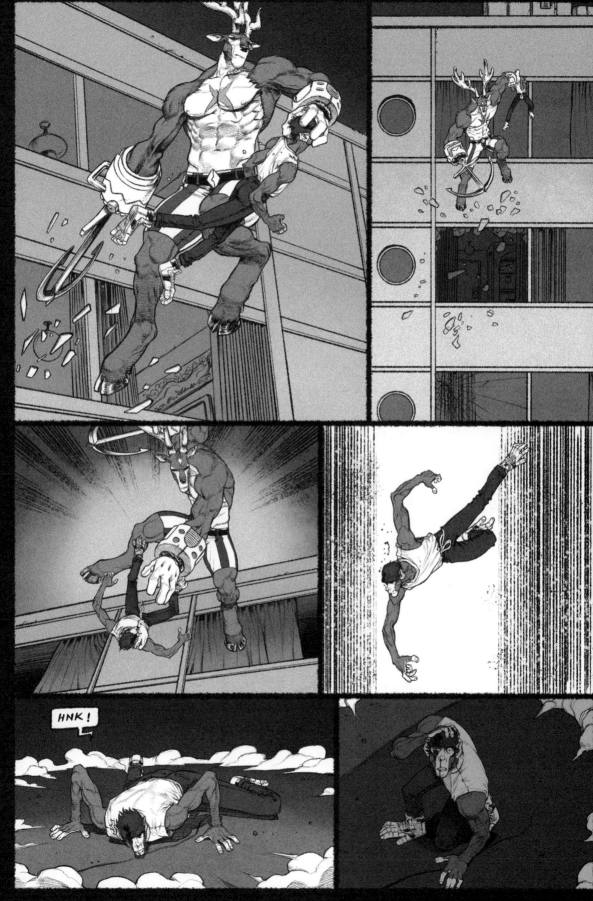

HNK!

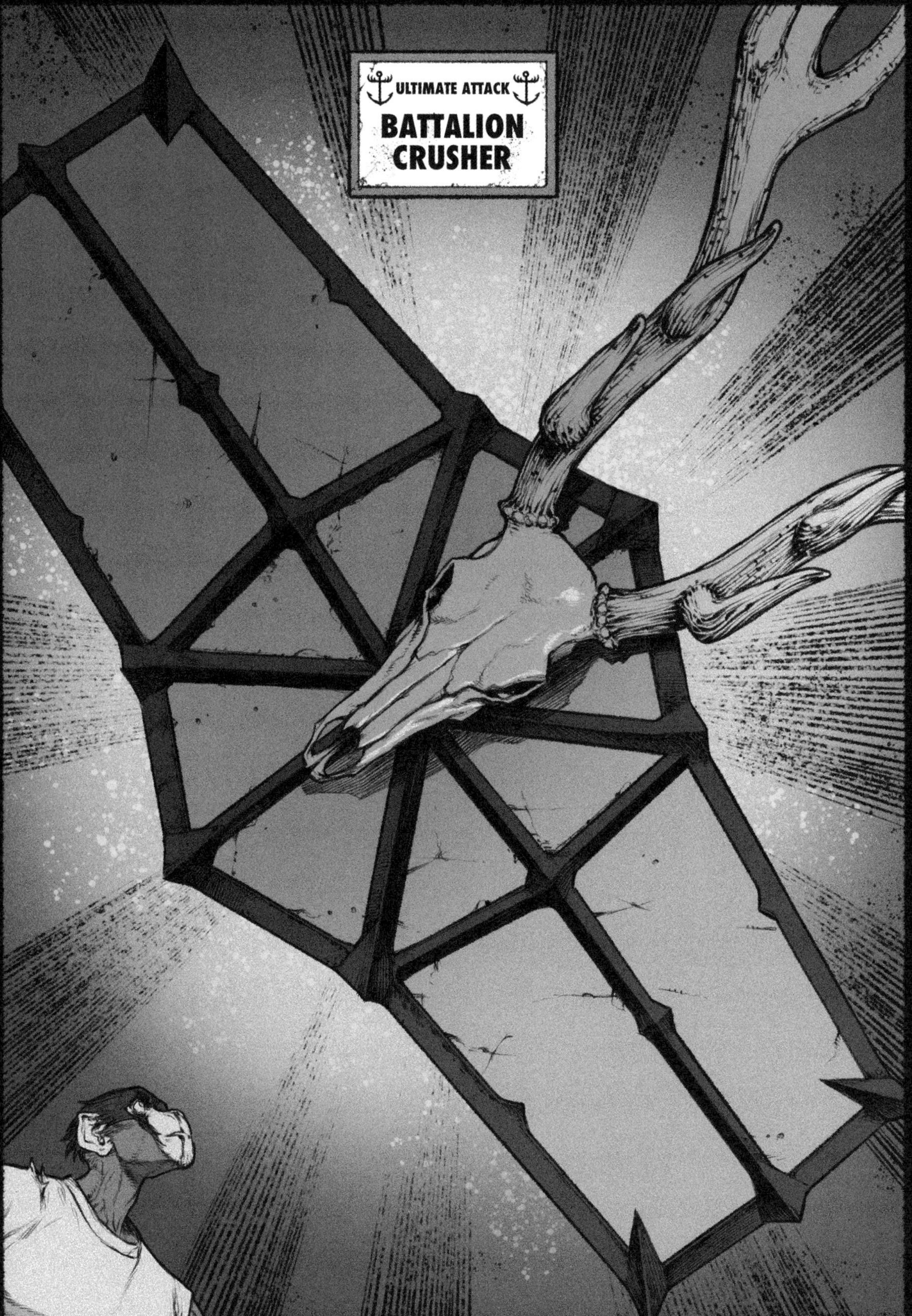
ULTIMATE ATTACK
BATTALION CRUSHER

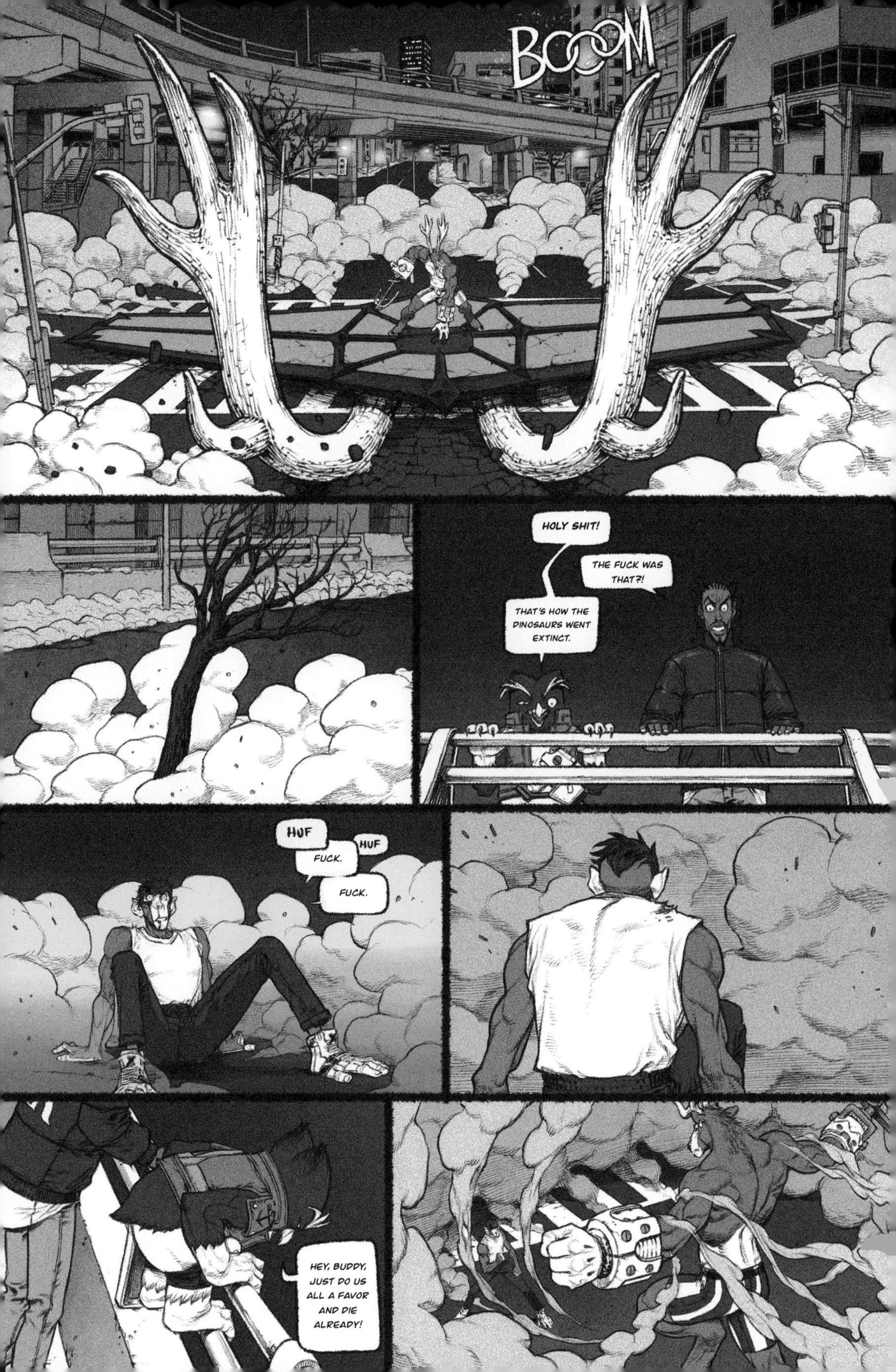
BOOOM
HOLY SHIT!
THE FUCK WAS THAT?!
THAT'S HOW THE DINOSAURS WENT EXTINCT.
HUF
HUF
FUCK.
FUCK.
HEY, BUDDY, JUST DO US ALL A FAVOR AND DIE ALREADY!

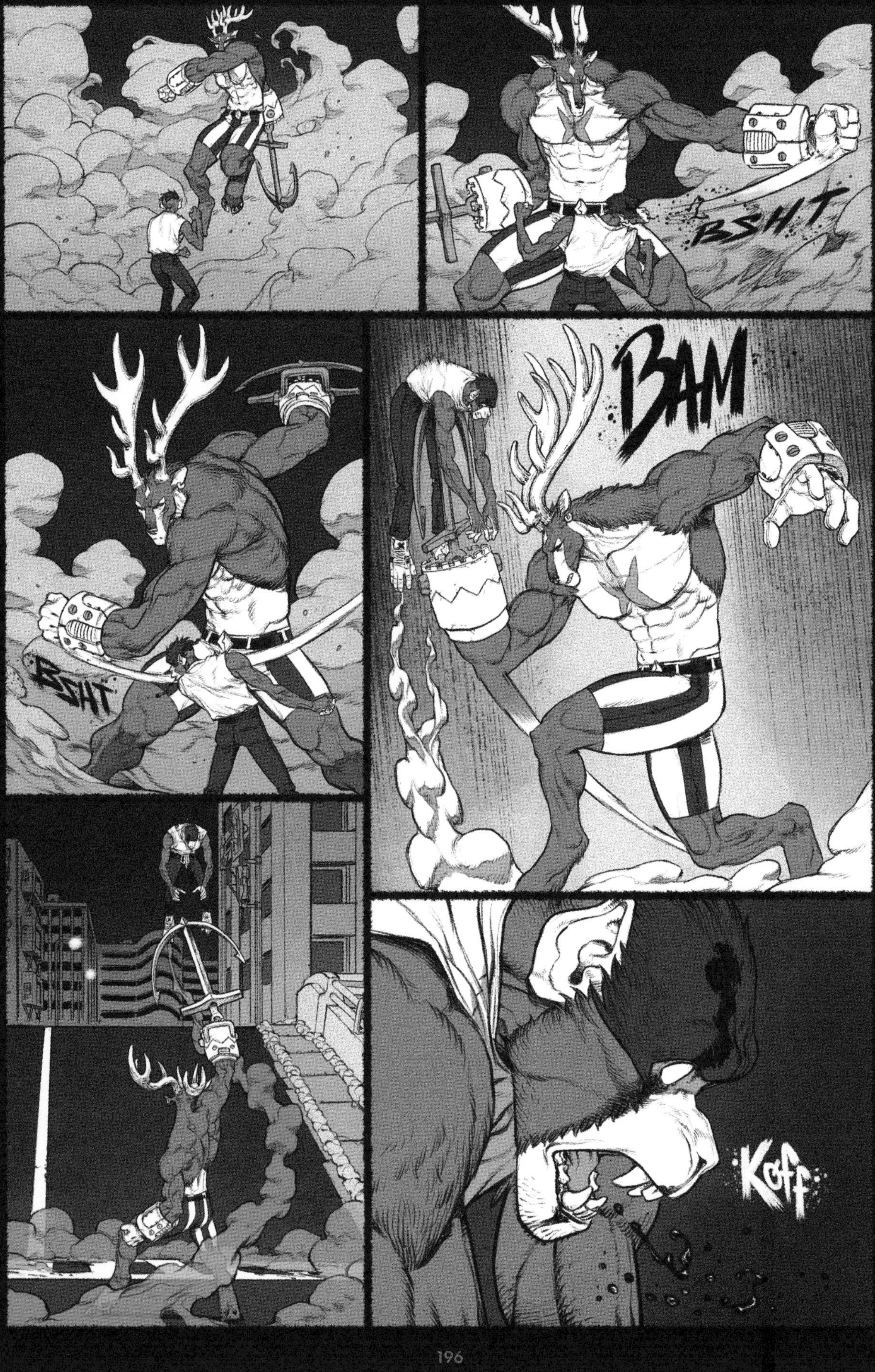
BSHT
BSHT
BAM
Koff

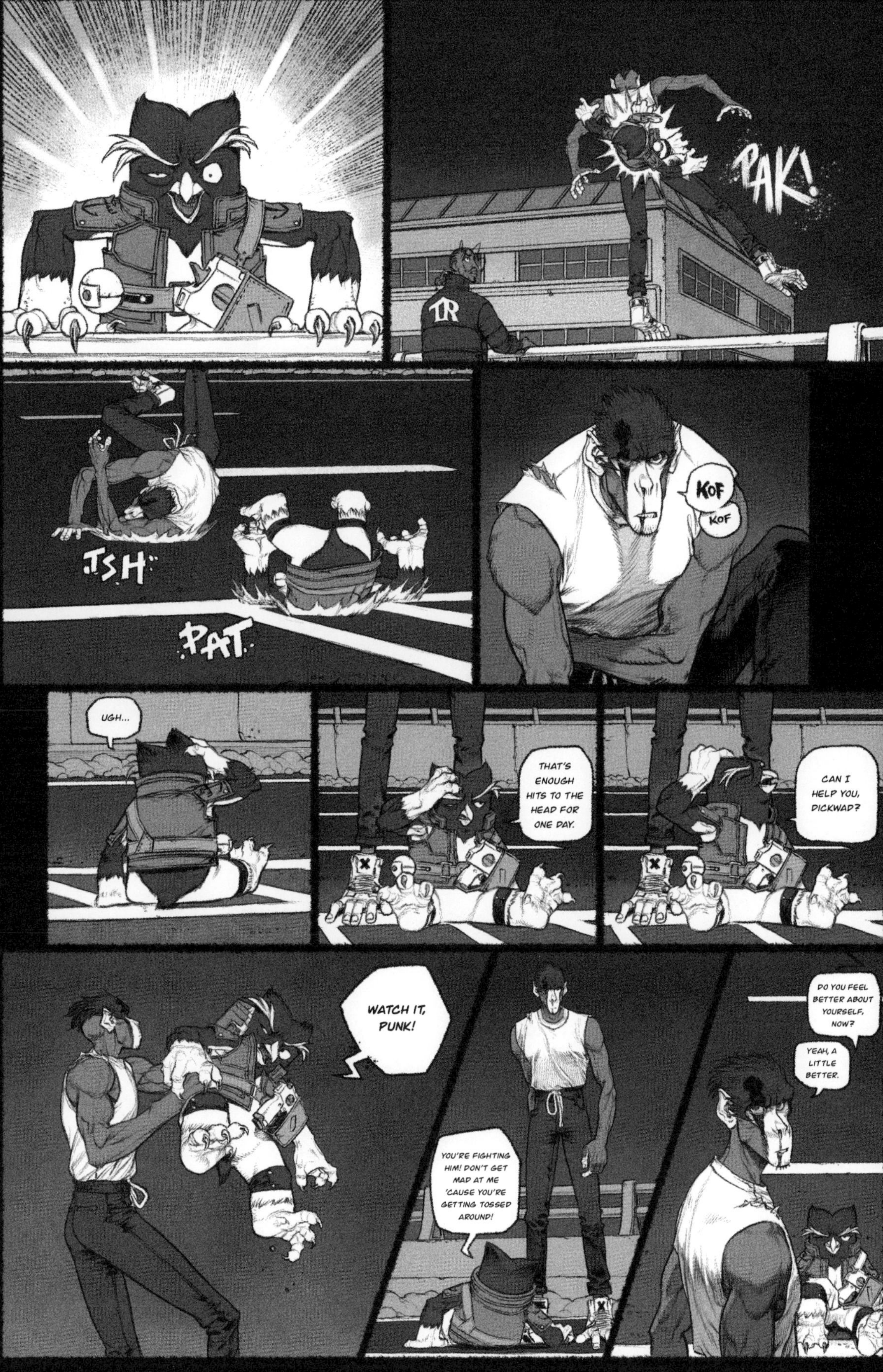
PAK!
TSH
PAT
KOF
KOF
UGH...
THAT'S ENOUGH HITS TO THE HEAD FOR ONE DAY.
CAN I HELP YOU, DICKWAD?
WATCH IT, PUNK!
YOU'RE FIGHTING HIM! DON'T GET MAD AT ME 'CAUSE YOU'RE GETTING TOSSED AROUND!
DO YOU FEEL BETTER ABOUT YOURSELF, NOW?
YEAH, A LITTLE BETTER.

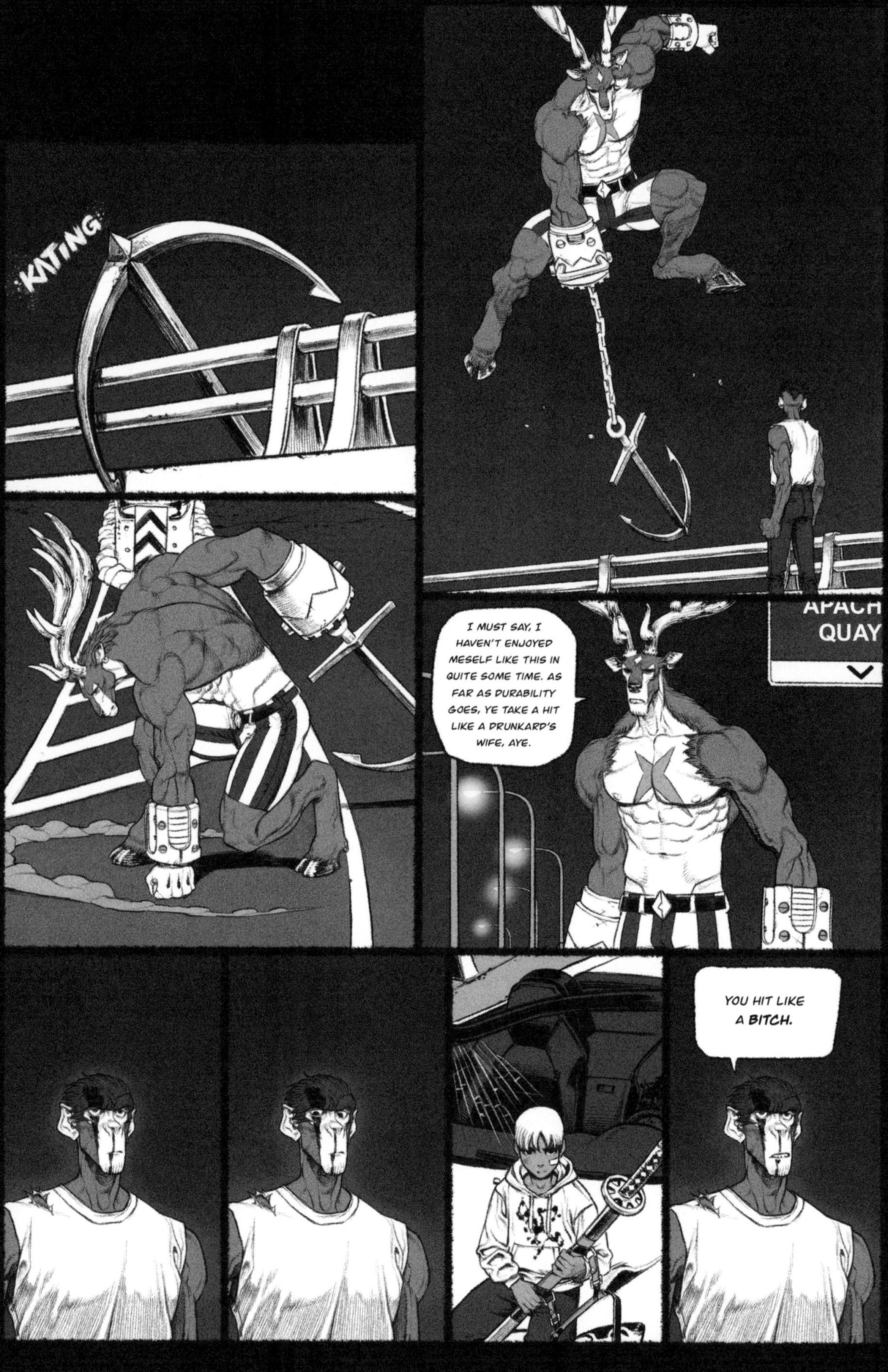
KATING
I MUST SAY, I HAVEN'T ENJOYED MESELF LIKE THIS IN QUITE SOME TIME. AS FAR AS DURABILITY GOES, YE TAKE A HIT LIKE A DRUNKARD'S WIFE, AYE.
APACH
QUAY
YOU HIT LIKE A BITCH.

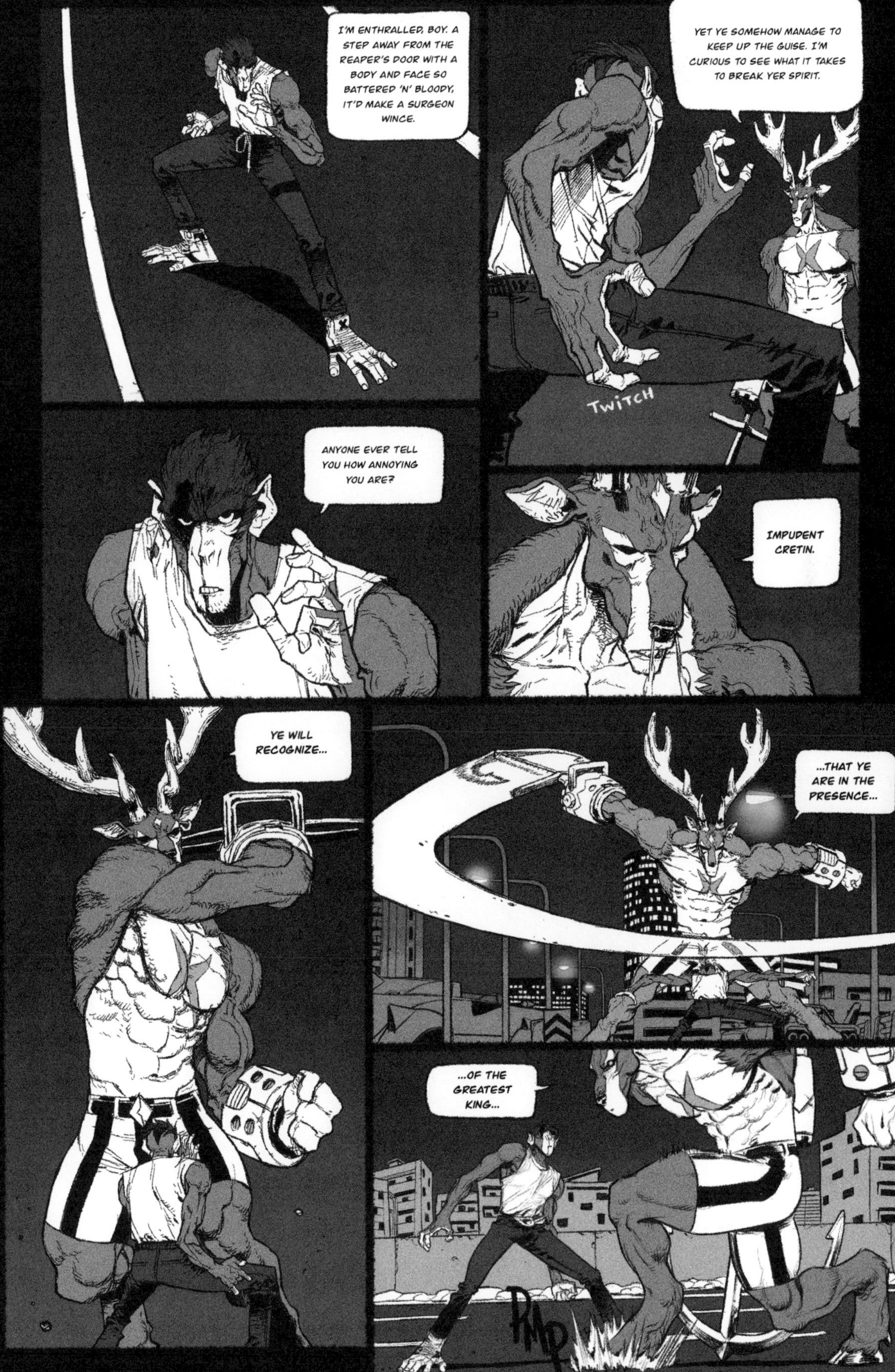
I'M ENTHRALLED, BOY. A STEP AWAY FROM THE REAPER'S DOOR WITH A BODY AND FACE SO BATTERED 'N' BLOODY, IT'D MAKE A SURGEON WINCE.
YET YE SOMEHOW MANAGE TO KEEP UP THE GUISE. I'M CURIOUS TO SEE WHAT IT TAKES TO BREAK YER SPIRIT.
TWITCH
ANYONE EVER TELL YOU HOW ANNOYING YOU ARE?
IMPUDENT CRETIN.
YE WILL RECOGNIZE...
...THAT YE ARE IN THE PRESENCE...
...OF THE GREATEST KING...

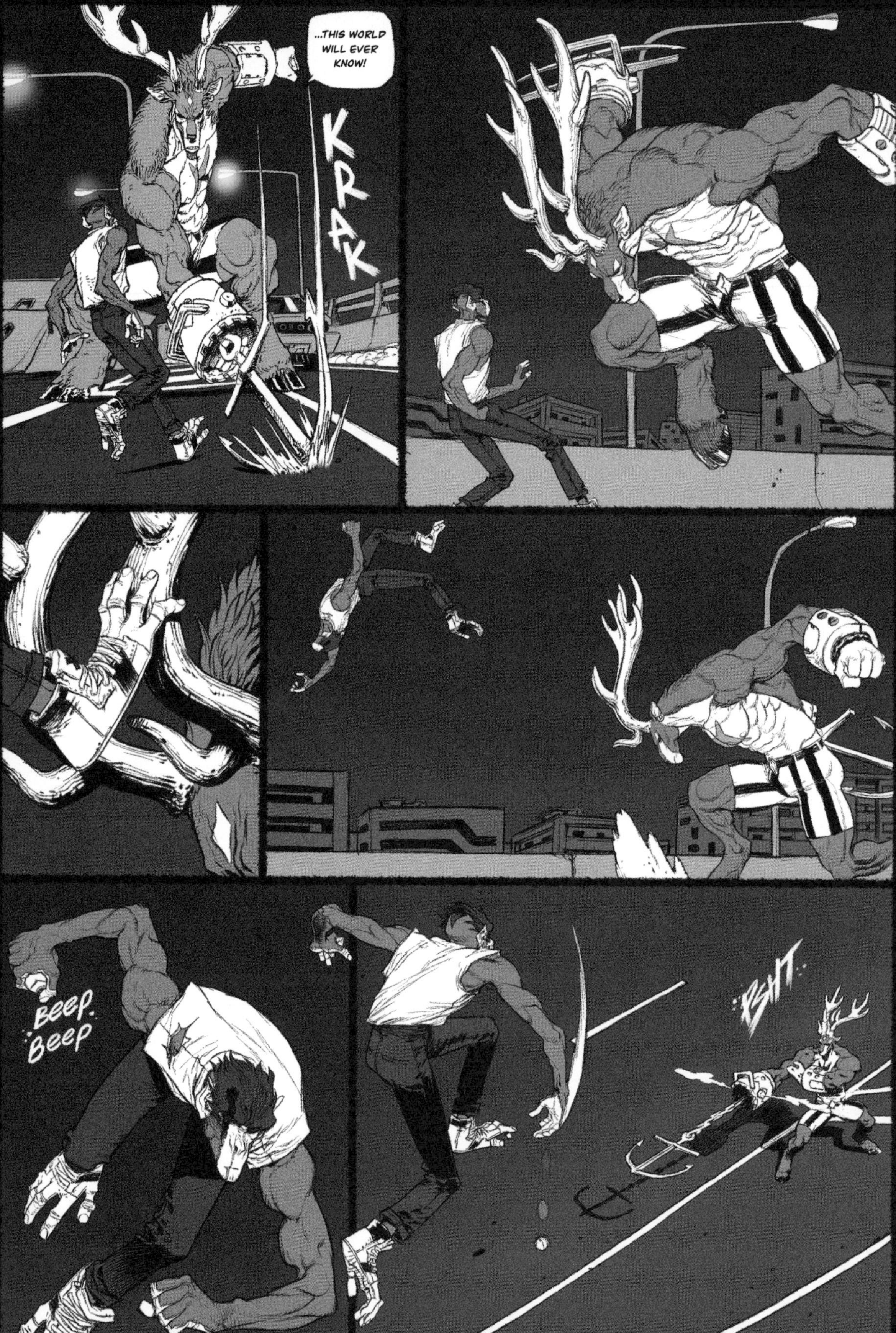
...THIS WORLD WILL EVER KNOW!
KRAK
BEEP BEEP
PSHT

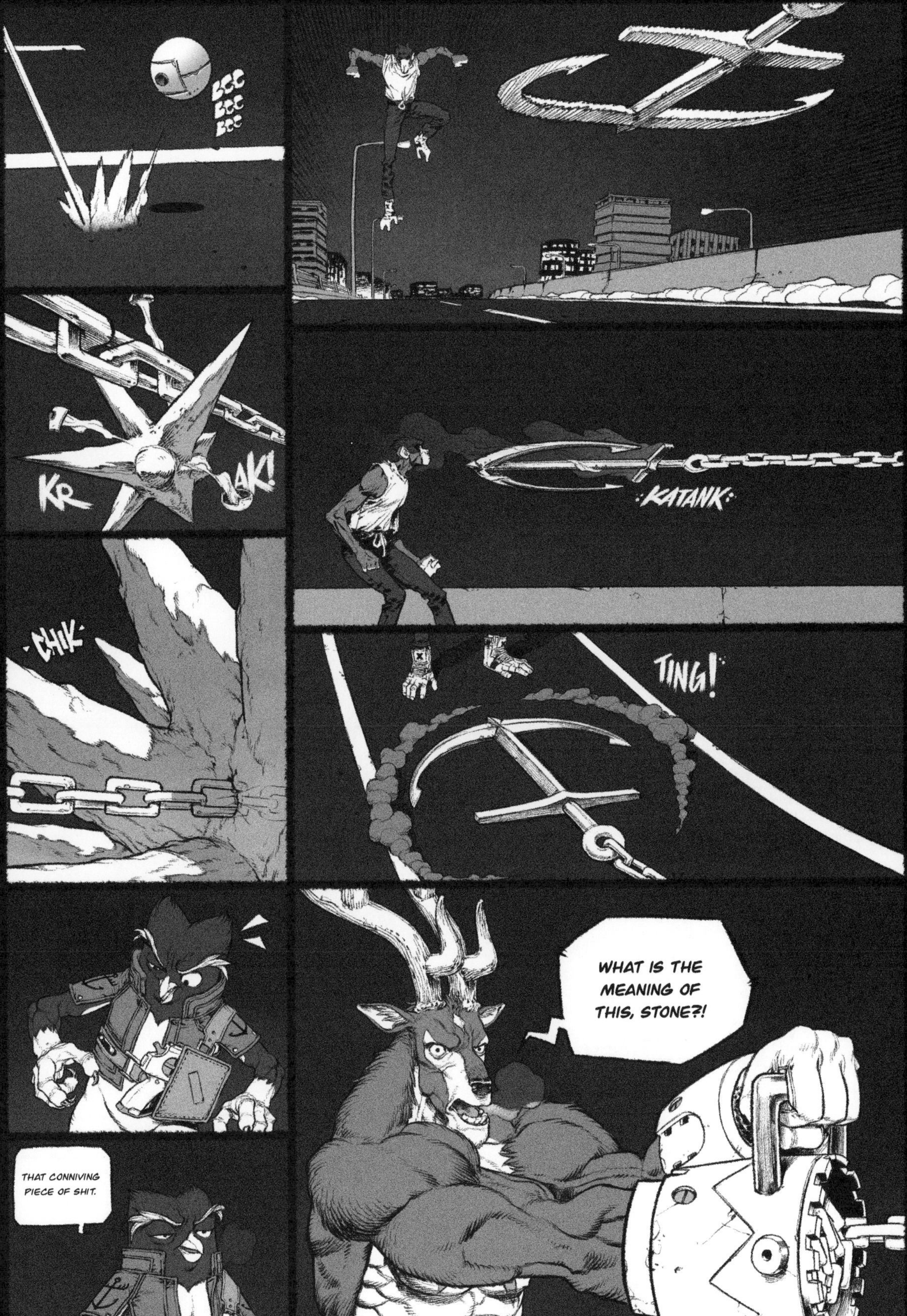
BEE BEE BEE
KR AK!
KATANK
CHIK
TING!
WHAT IS THE MEANING OF THIS, STONE?!
THAT CONNIVING PIECE OF SHIT.

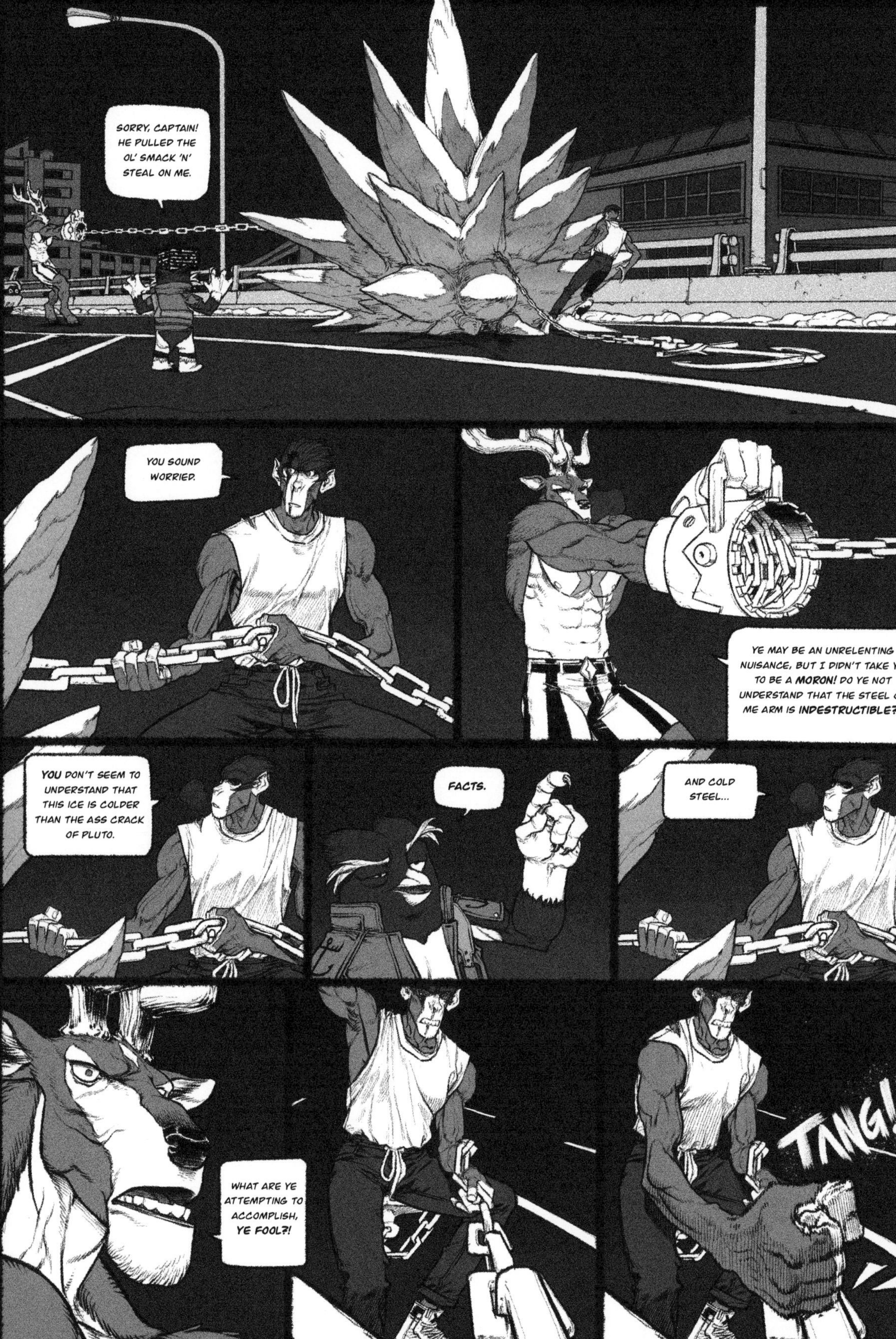
SORRY, CAPTAIN! HE PULLED THE OL' SMACK 'N' STEAL ON ME.
YOU SOUND WORRIED.
YE MAY BE AN UNRELENTING NUISANCE, BUT I DIDN'T TAKE YE TO BE A MORON! DO YE NOT UNDERSTAND THAT THE STEEL OF ME ARM IS INDESTRUCTIBLE?!
YOU DON'T SEEM TO UNDERSTAND THAT THIS ICE IS COLDER THAN THE ASS CRACK OF PLUTO.
FACTS.
AND COLD STEEL...
WHAT ARE YE ATTEMPTING TO ACCOMPLISH, YE FOOL?!
TANG!

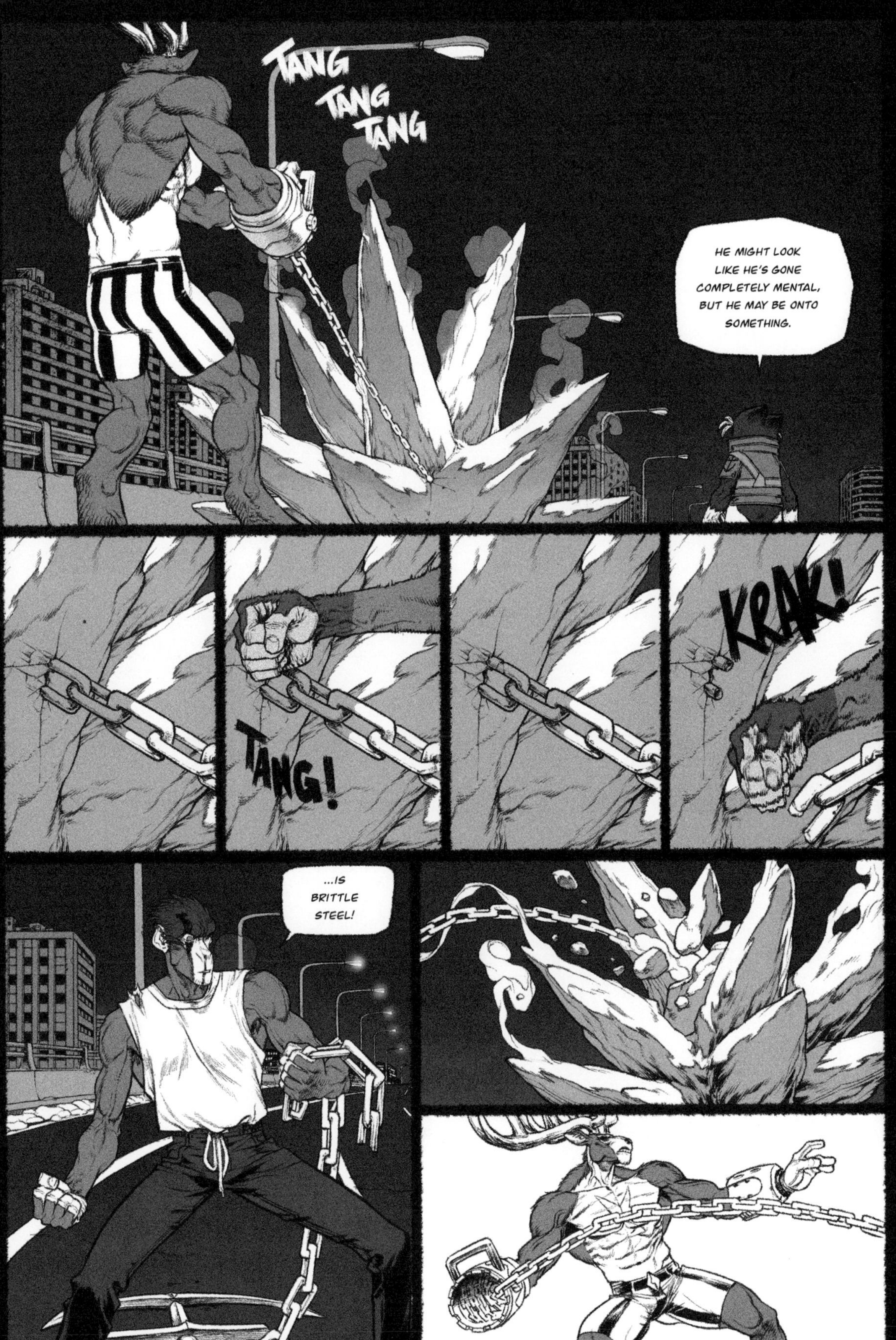
TANG
TANG
TANG
HE MIGHT LOOK LIKE HE'S GONE COMPLETELY MENTAL, BUT HE MAY BE ONTO SOMETHING.
TANG!
KRAK!
...IS BRITTLE STEEL!

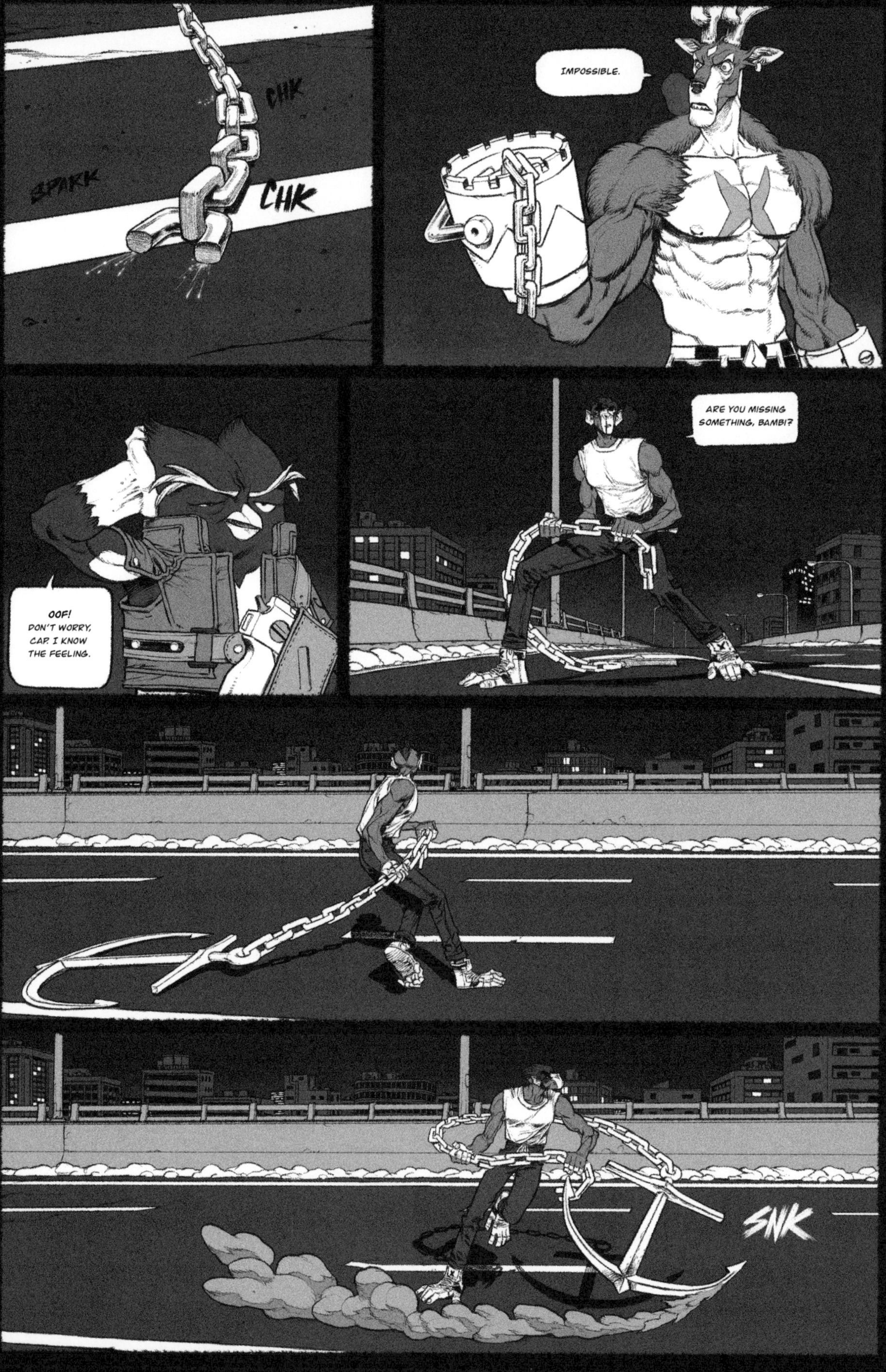
CHK
SPARK
CHK
IMPOSSIBLE.
OOF! DON'T WORRY, CAP. I KNOW THE FEELING.
ARE YOU MISSING SOMETHING, BAMBI?
SNK

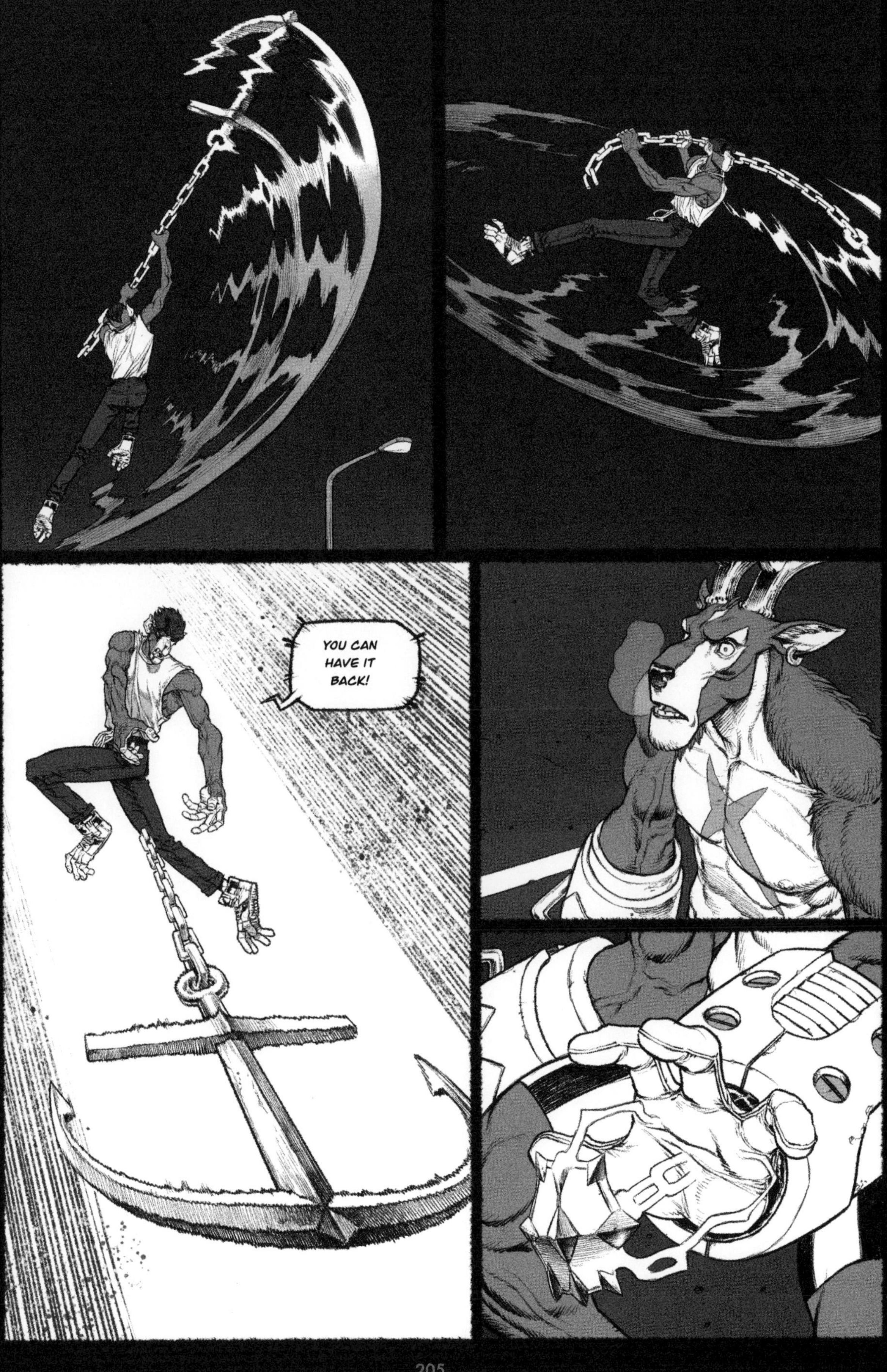
YOU CAN HAVE IT BACK!

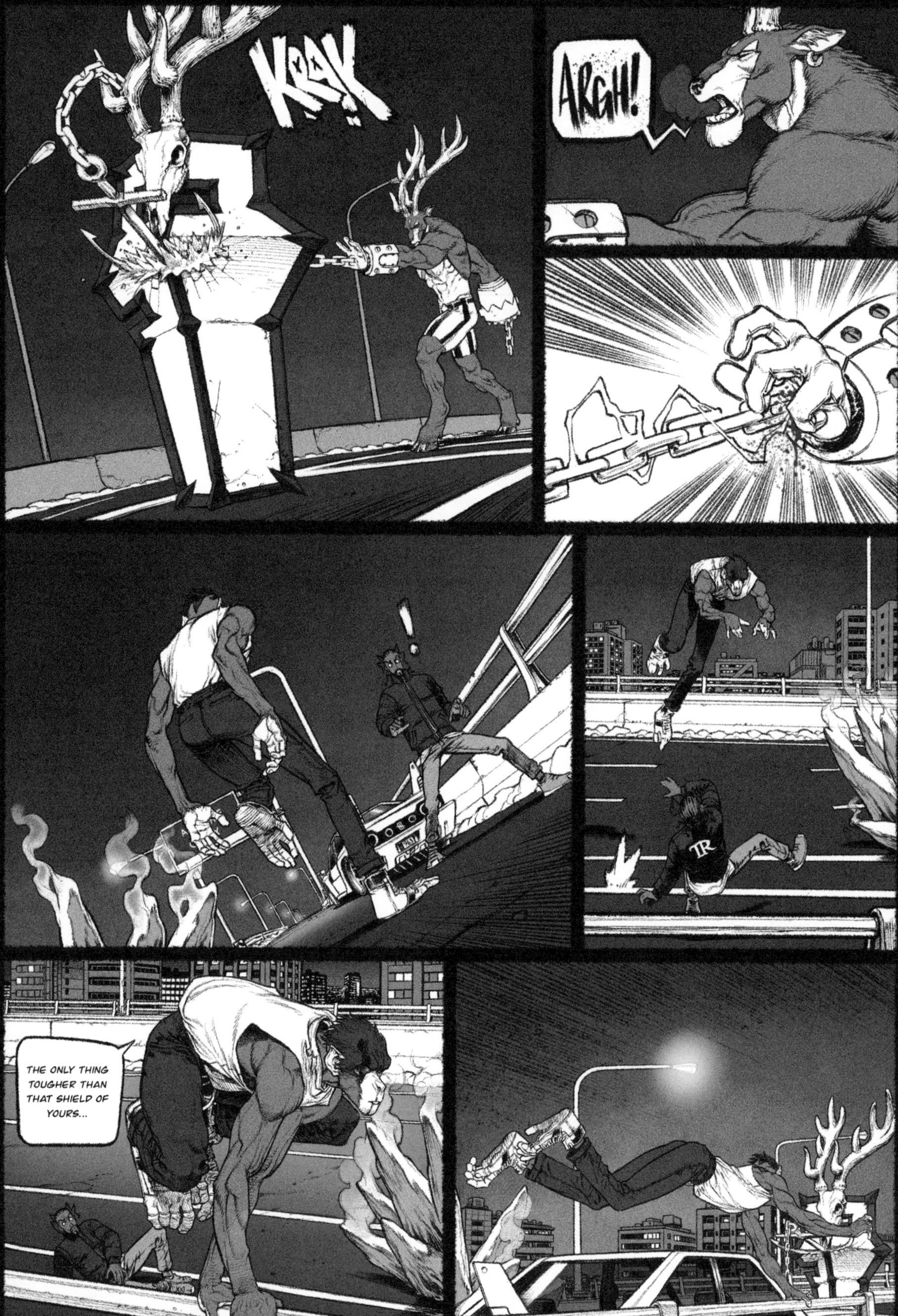
KRAK
ARGH!
!
THE ONLY THING TOUGHER THAN THAT SHIELD OF YOURS...

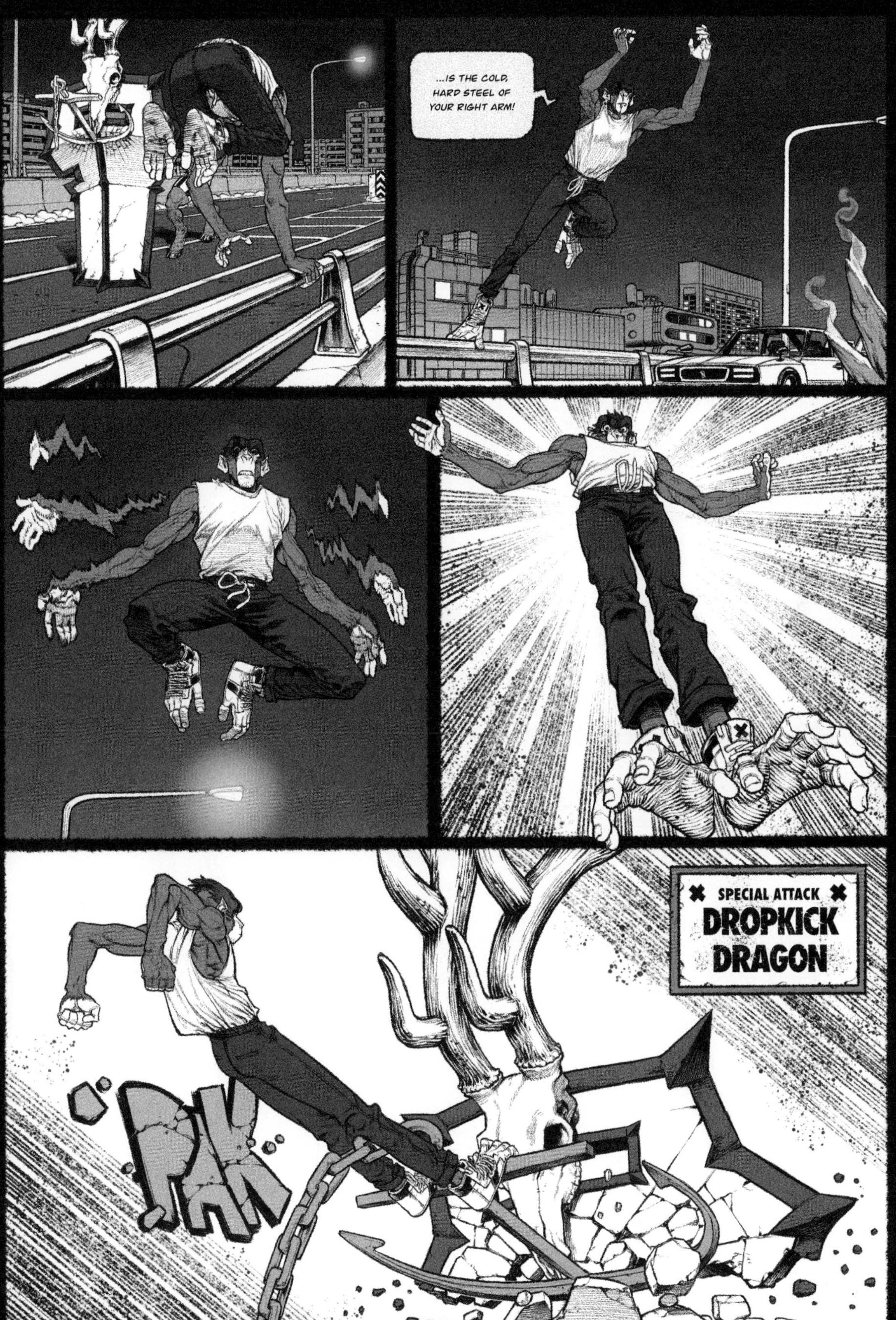
...IS THE COLD, HARD STEEL OF YOUR RIGHT ARM!
SPECIAL ATTACK
DROPKICK DRAGON

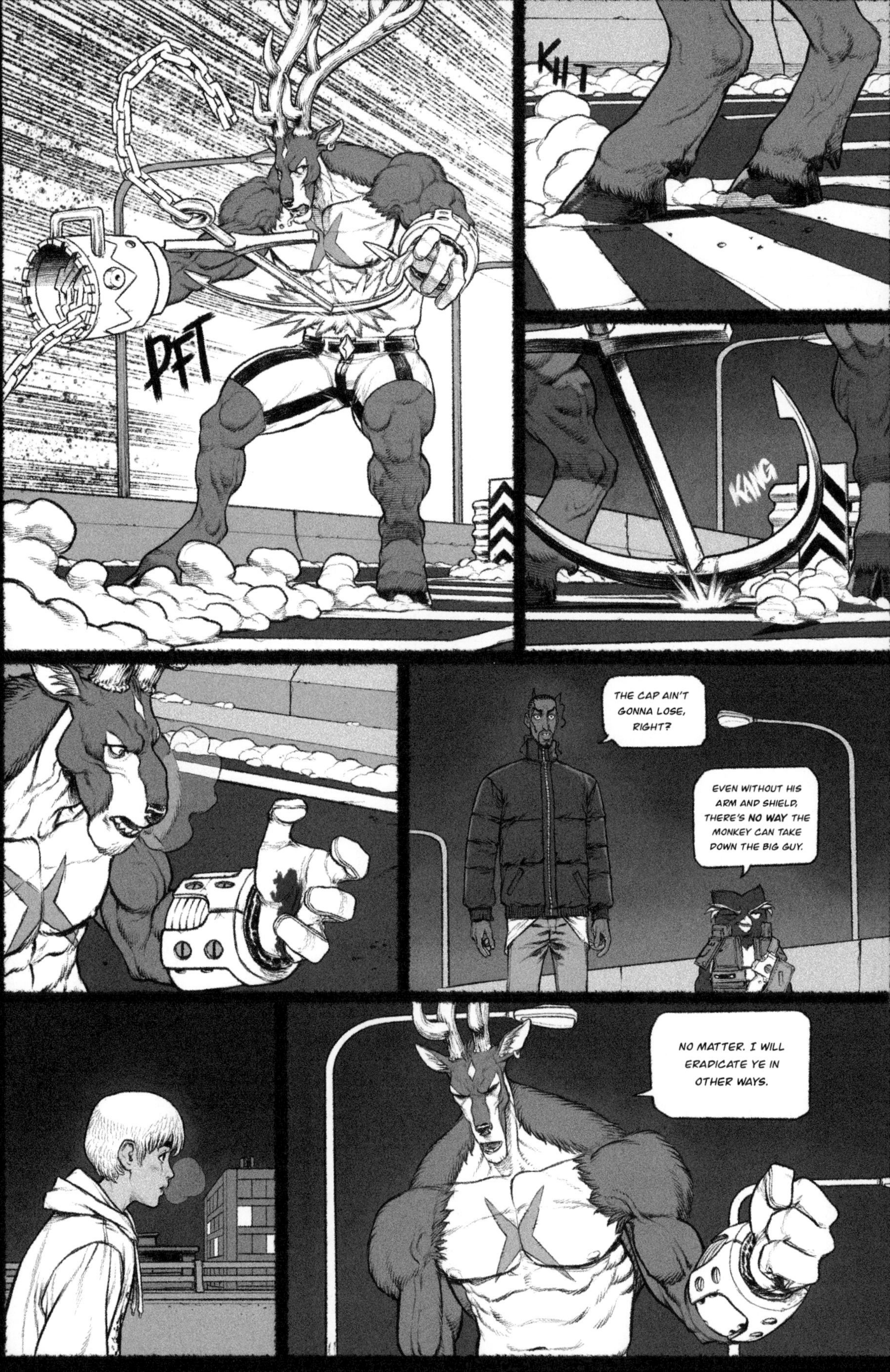
KHT
PFT
KANG
THE CAP AIN'T GONNA LOSE, RIGHT?
EVEN WITHOUT HIS ARM AND SHIELD, THERE'S NO WAY THE MONKEY CAN TAKE DOWN THE BIG GUY.
NO MATTER. I WILL ERADICATE YE IN OTHER WAYS.

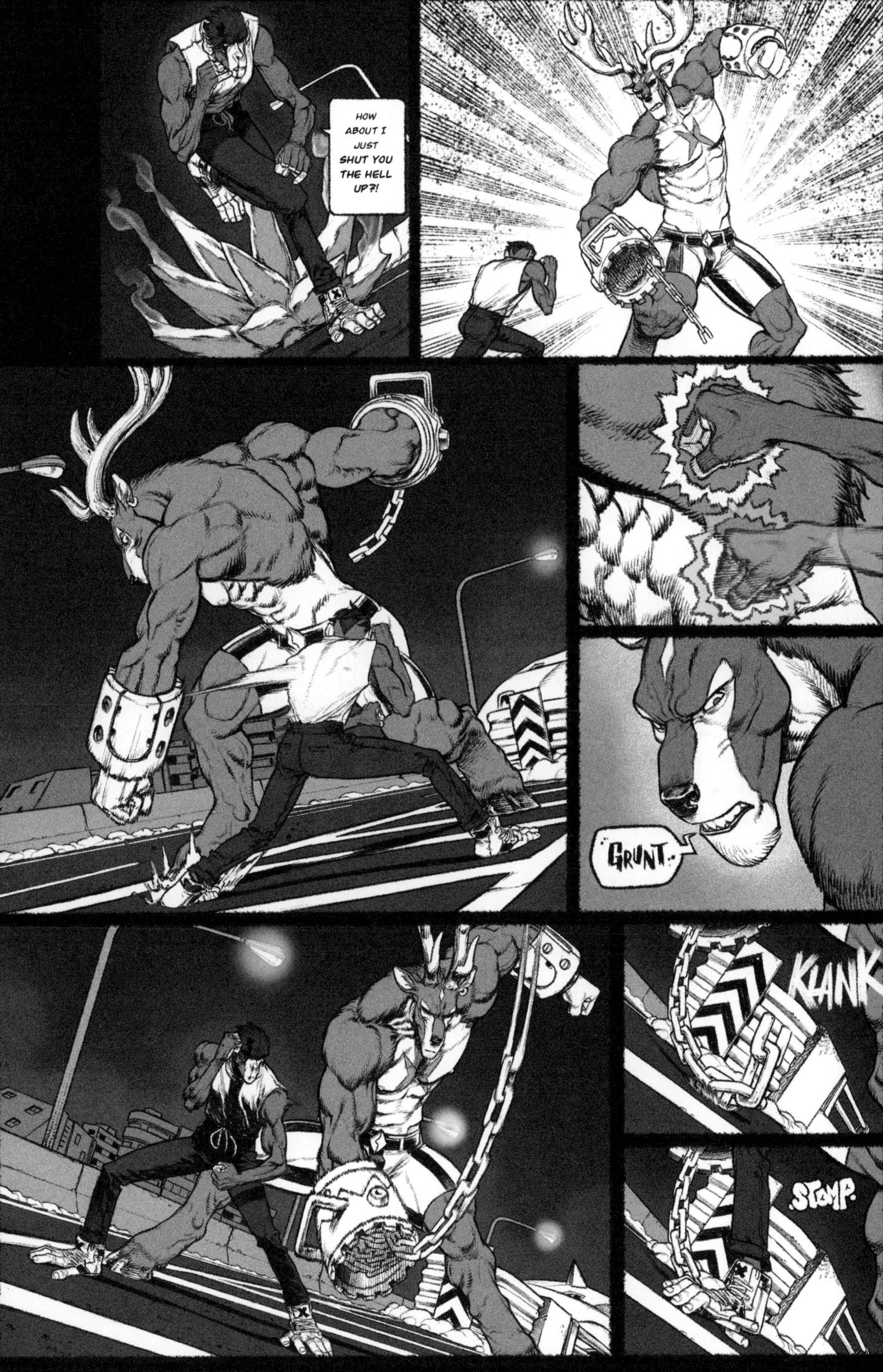
HOW ABOUT I JUST SHUT YOU THE HELL UP?!
GRUNT
KLANK
STOMP

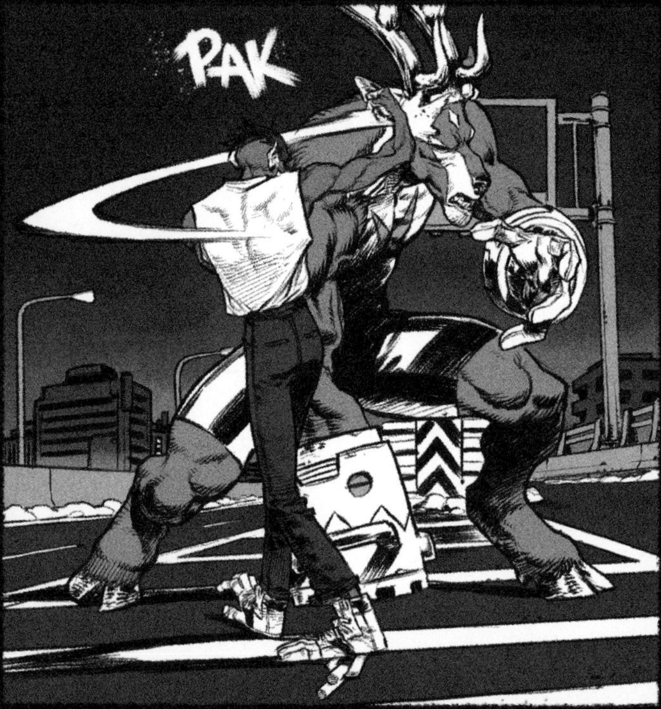
PAK
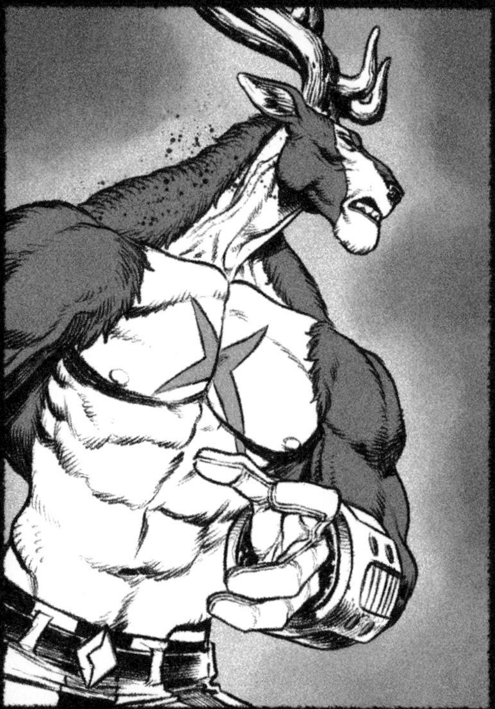
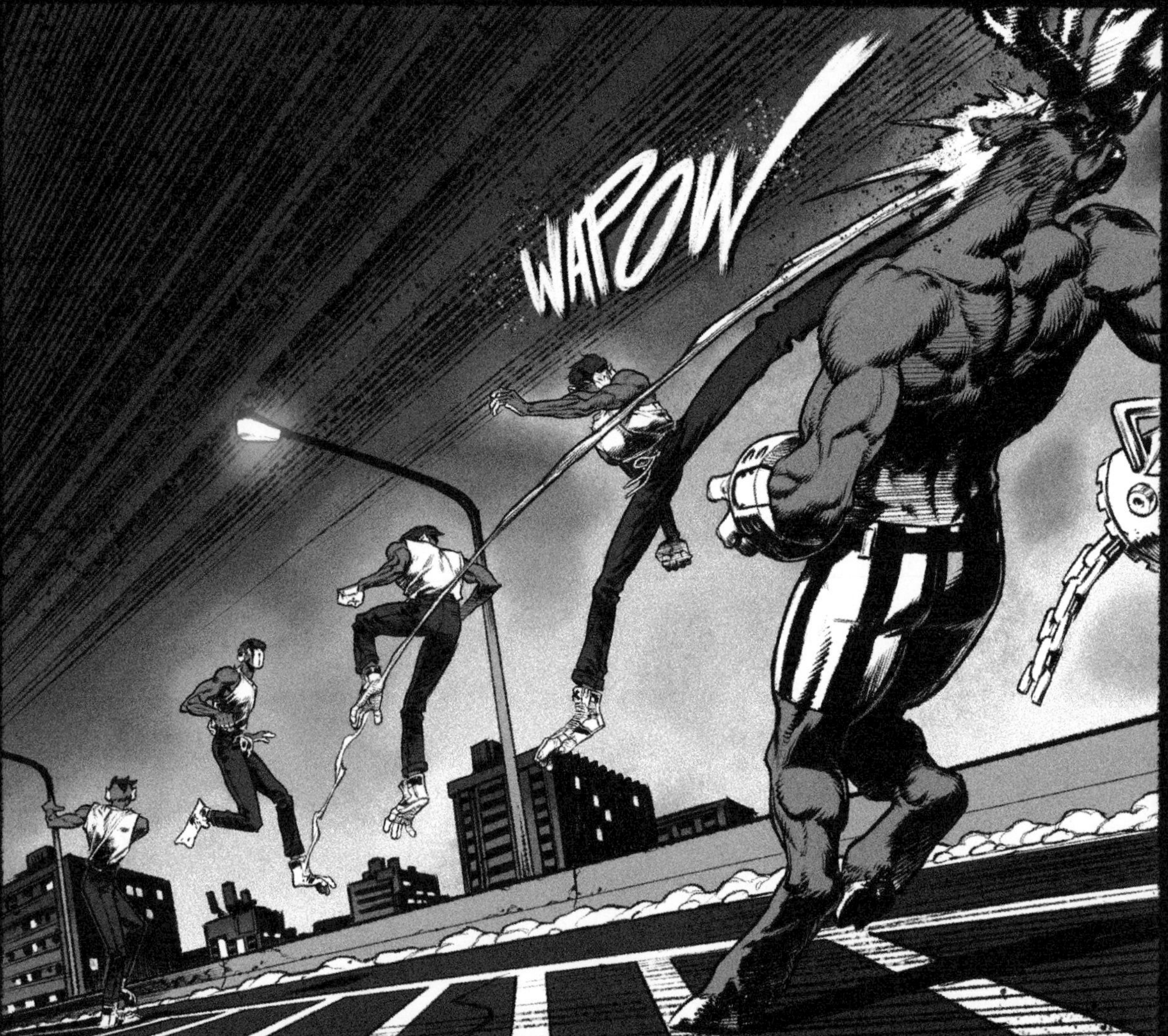
WAPOW

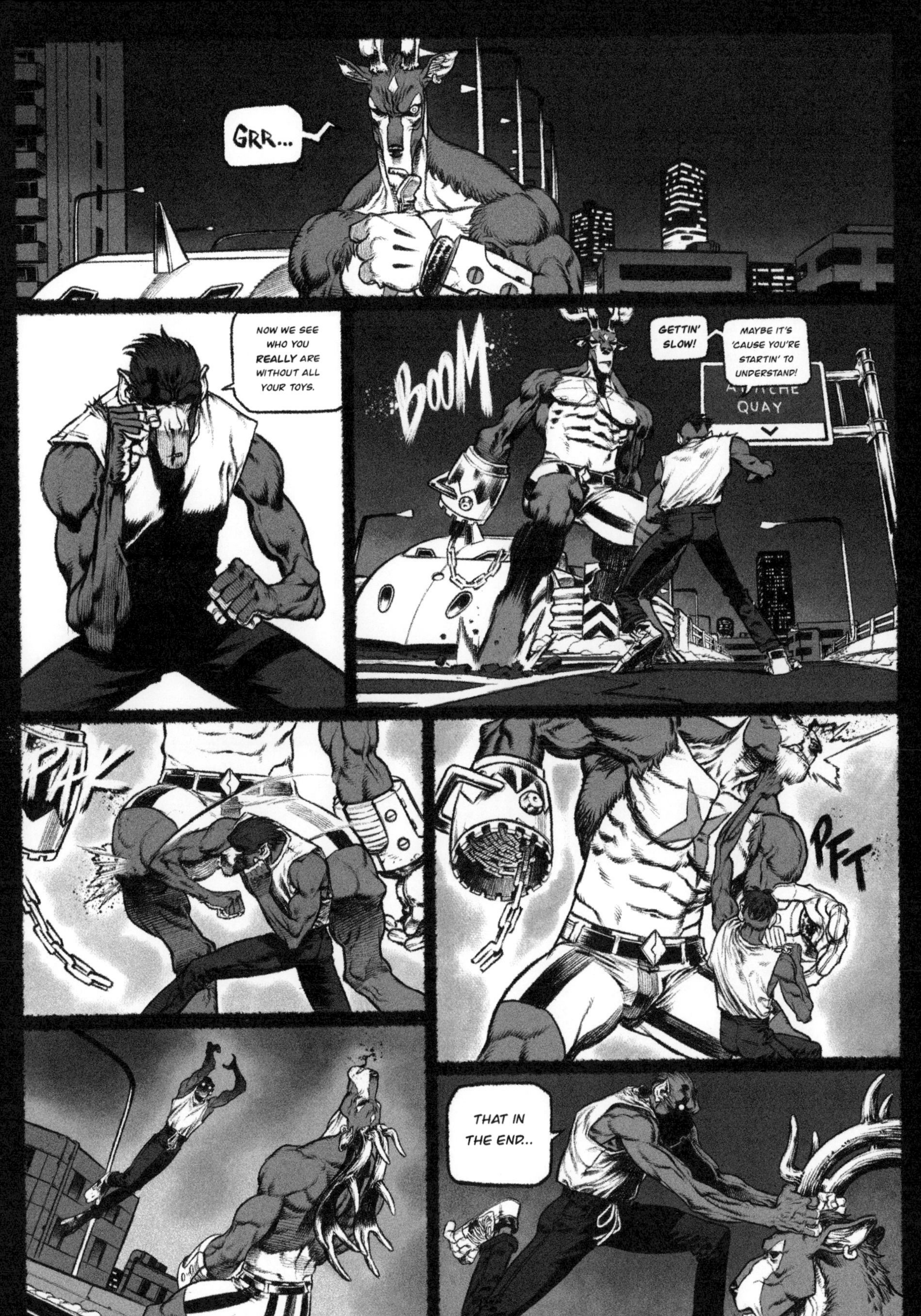
GRR...
NOW WE SEE WHO YOU REALLY ARE WITHOUT ALL YOUR TOYS.
BOOM
GETTIN' SLOW!
MAYBE IT'S 'CAUSE YOU'RE STARTIN' TO UNDERSTAND!
QUAY
PAK
PFFT
THAT IN THE END...

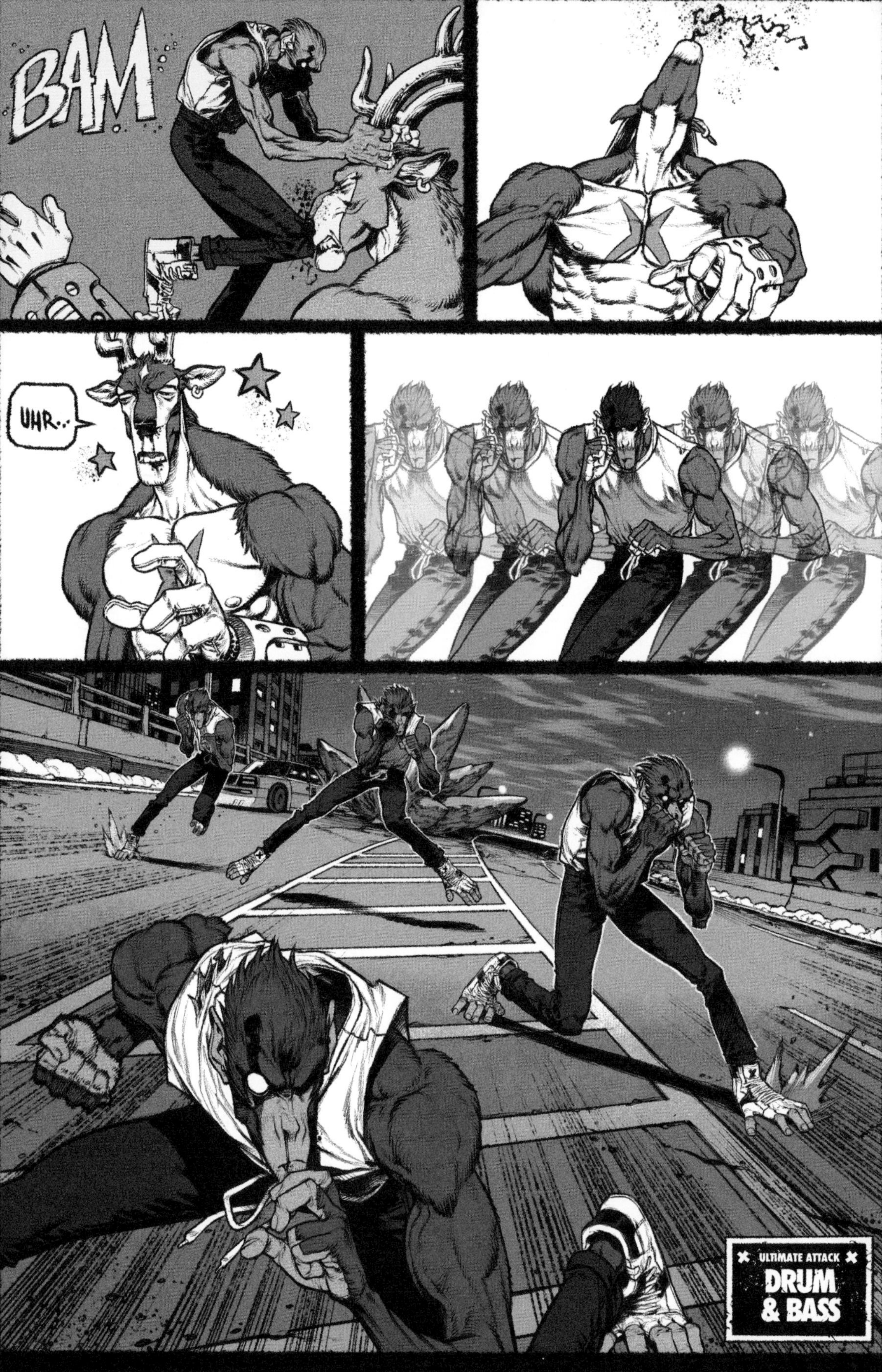
BAM
UHR...
ULTIMATE ATTACK
DRUM & BASS

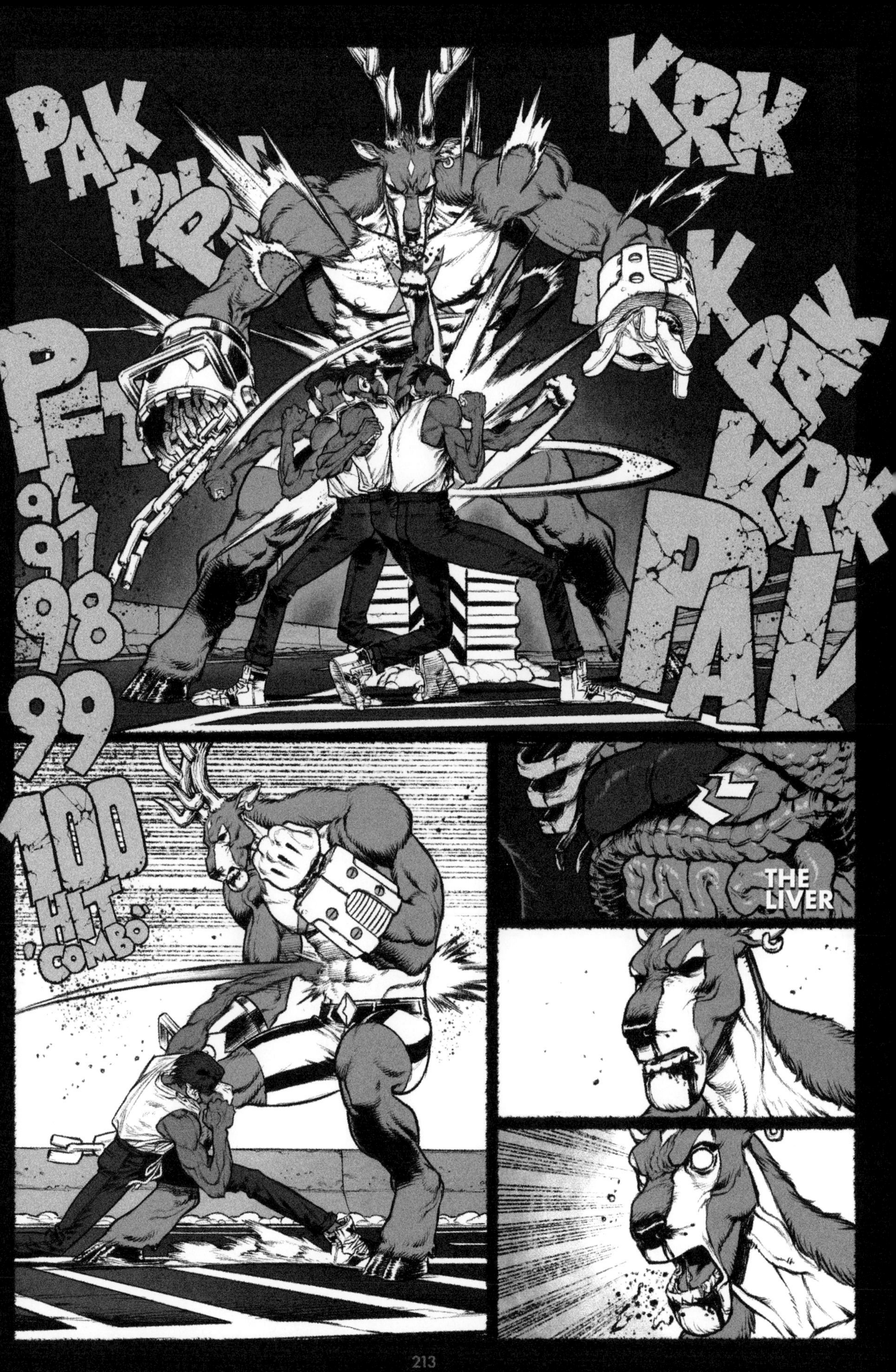
PAK
KRK
PAK
KRK
97
98
99
100 HIT COMBO
THE LIVER

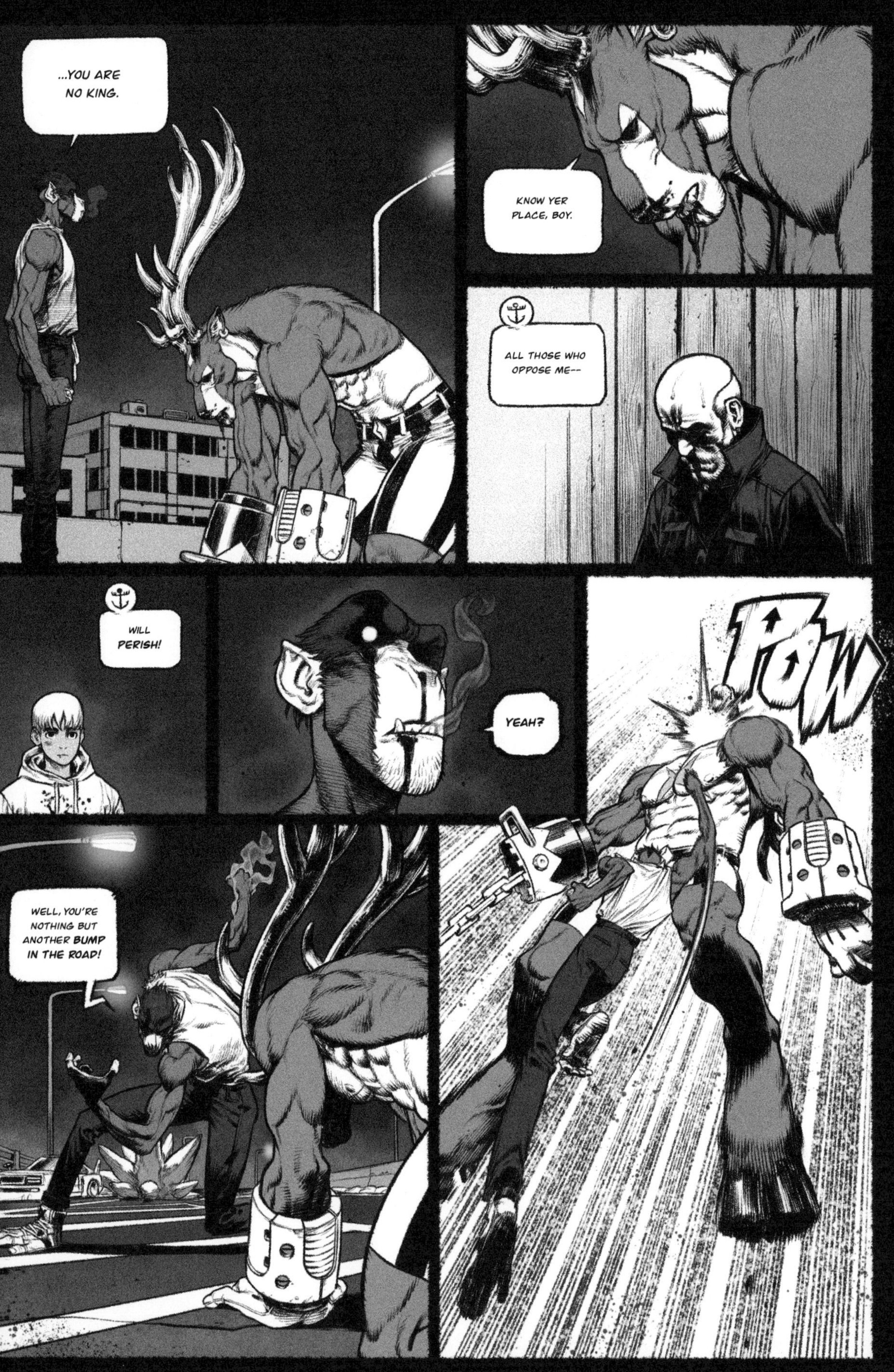
...YOU ARE NO KING.
KNOW YER PLACE, BOY.
ALL THOSE WHO OPPOSE ME--
WILL PERISH!
YEAH?
POW
WELL, YOU'RE NOTHING BUT ANOTHER BUMP IN THE ROAD!

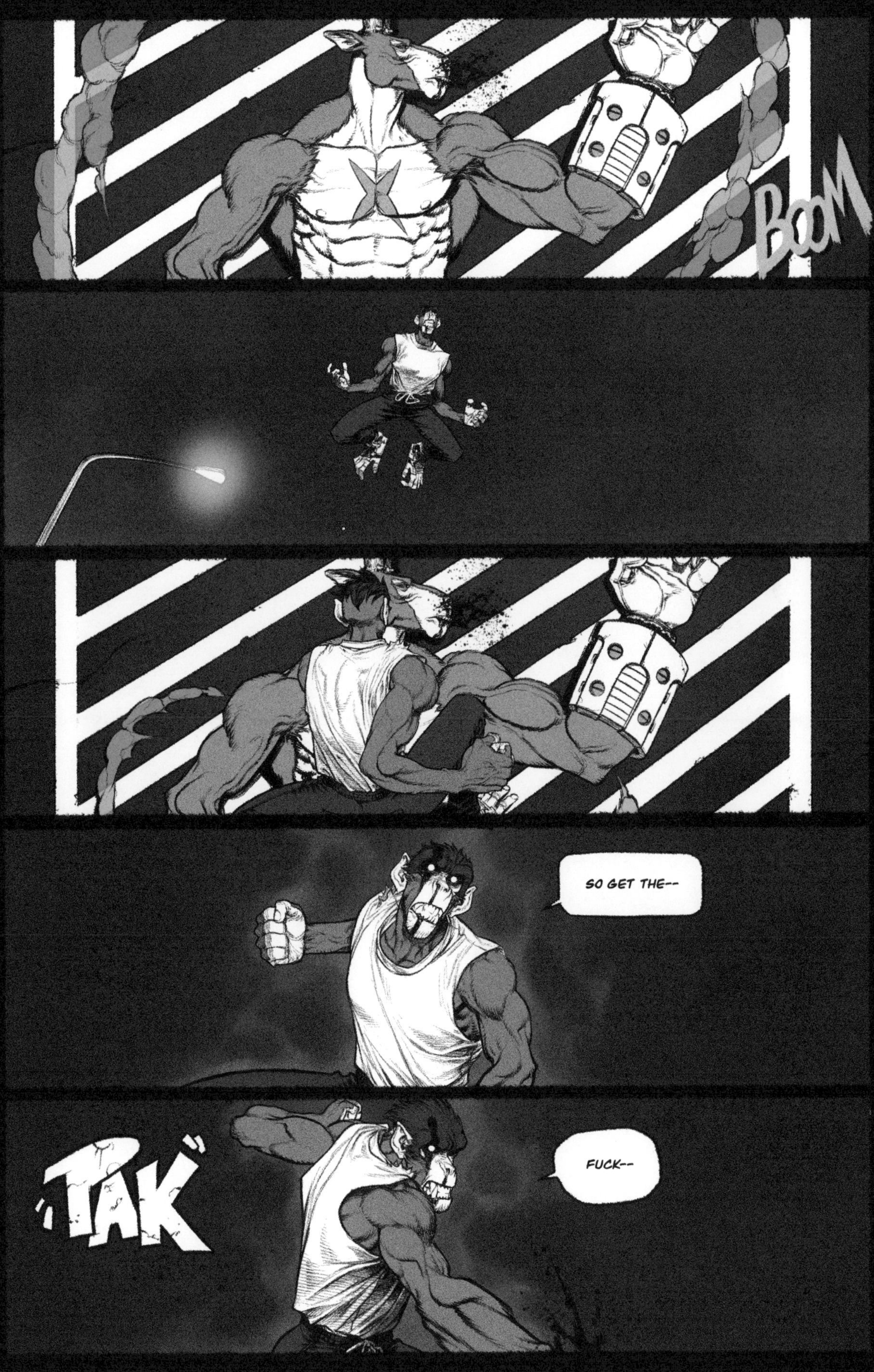
BOOM
SO GET THE--
TAK
FUCK--

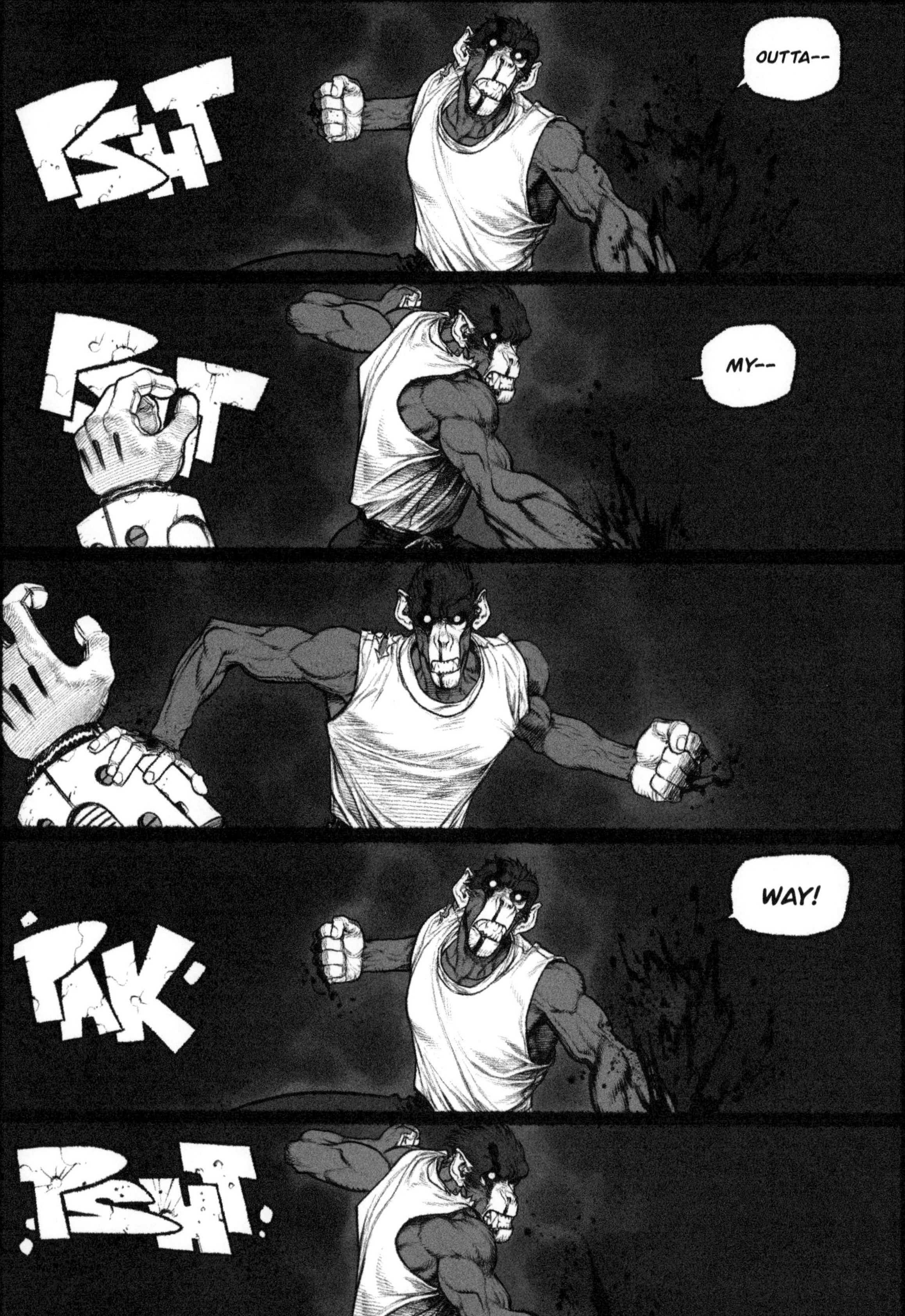
PSHT
OUTTA--
MY--
PAK
WAY!
PSHT

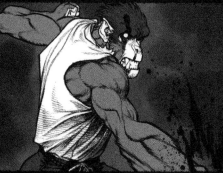

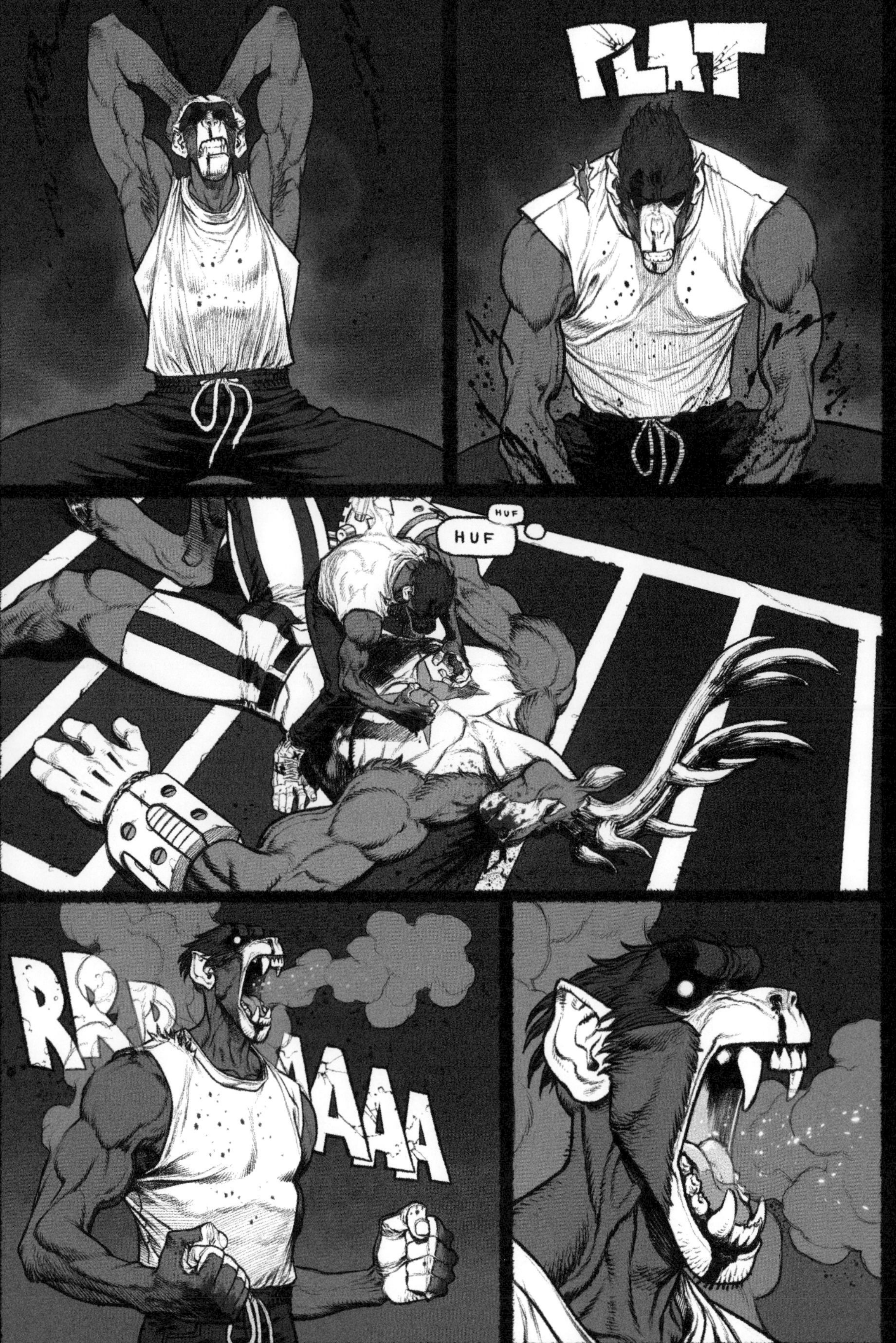

PLAT
HUF
HUF
RRR
AAAA

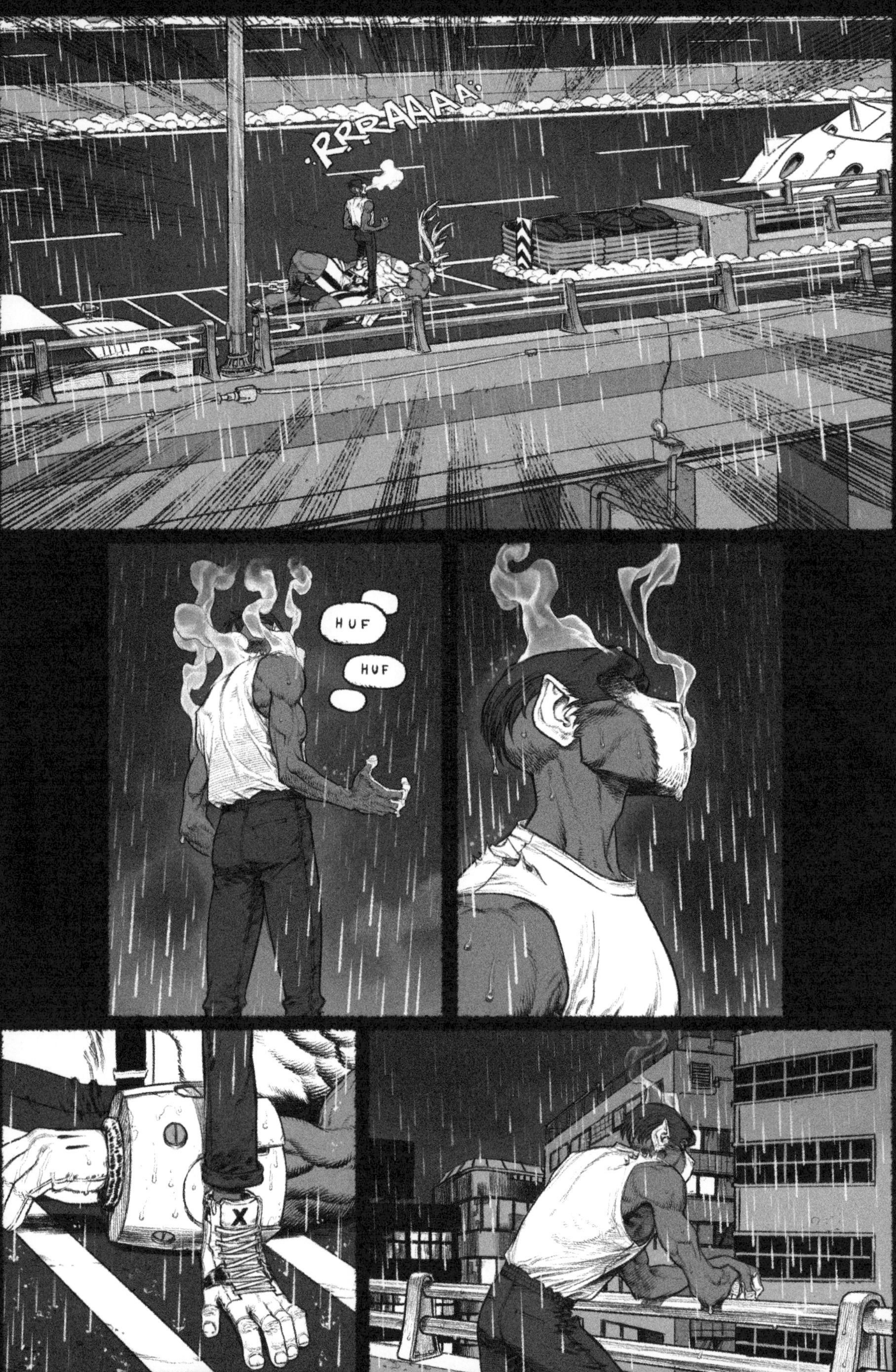
RRRAAAAA
HUF
HUF

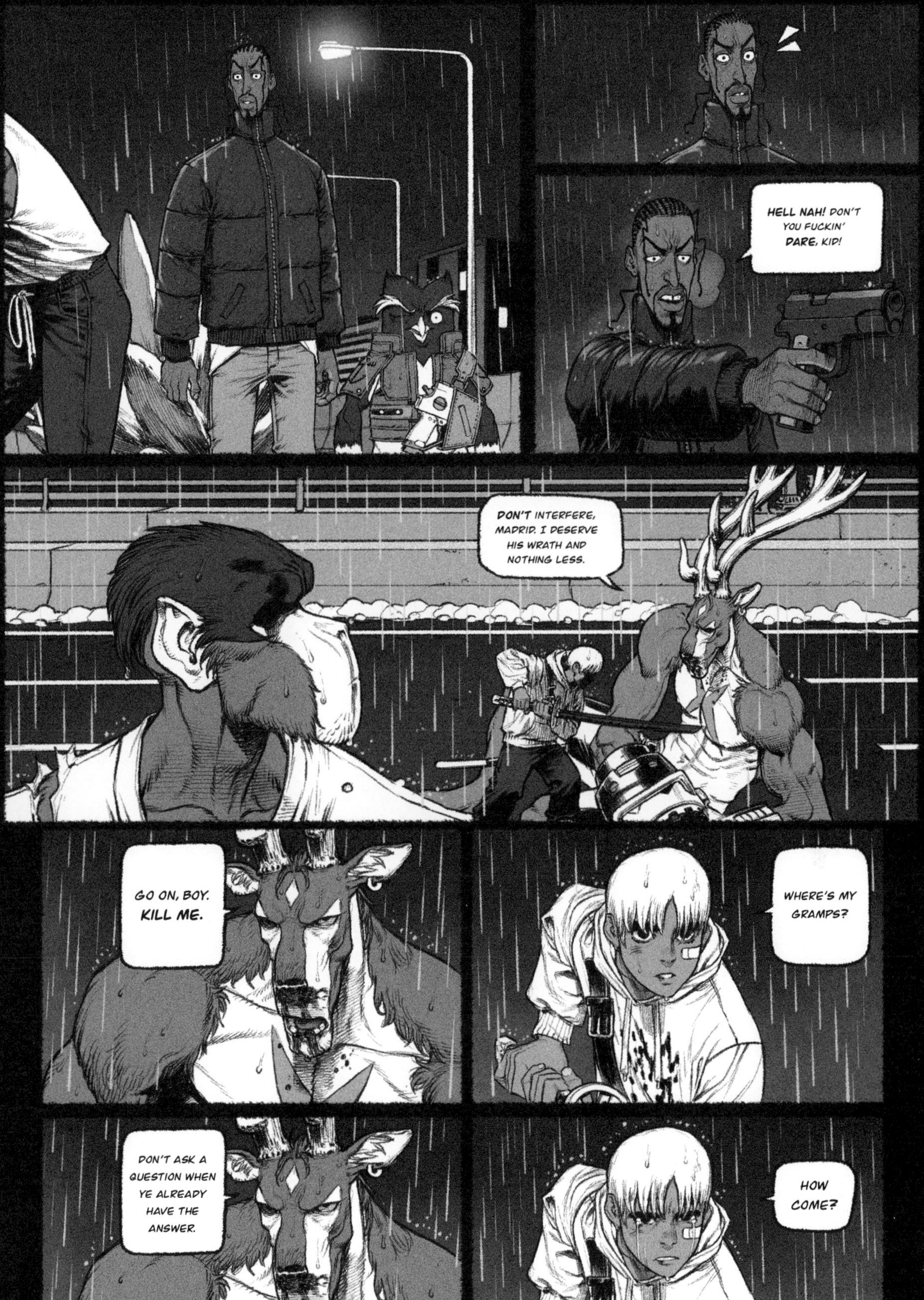
HELL NAH! DON'T YOU FUCKIN' DARE, KID!
DON'T INTERFERE, MADRID. I DESERVE HIS WRATH AND NOTHING LESS.
GO ON, BOY. KILL ME.
WHERE'S MY GRAMPS?
DON'T ASK A QUESTION WHEN YE ALREADY HAVE THE ANSWER.
HOW COME?

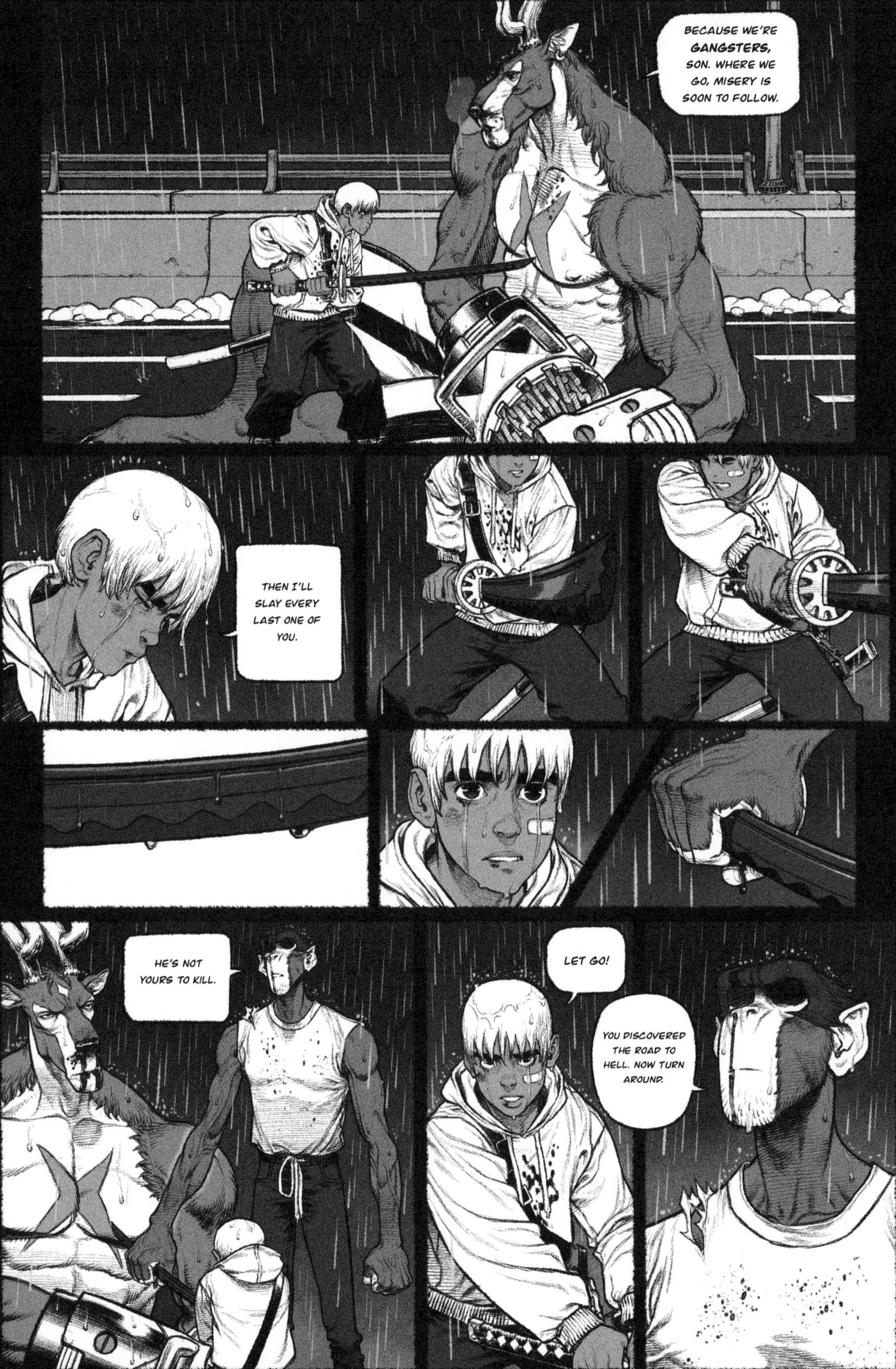
BECAUSE WE'RE GANGSTERS, SON. WHERE WE GO, MISERY IS SOON TO FOLLOW.
THEN I'LL SLAY EVERY LAST ONE OF YOU.
HE'S NOT YOURS TO KILL.
LET GO!
YOU DISCOVERED THE ROAD TO HELL. NOW TURN AROUND.

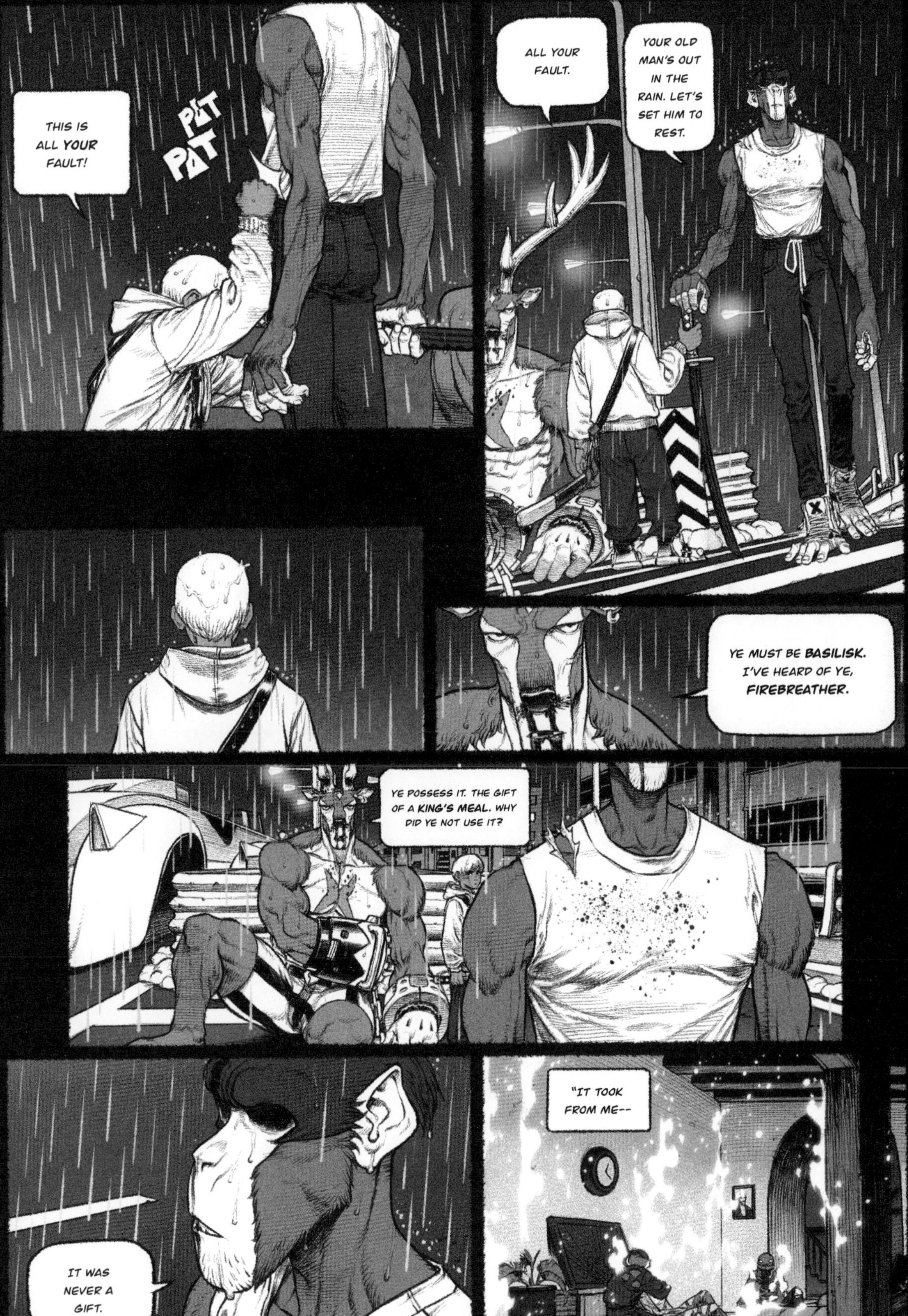
THIS IS ALL YOUR FAULT!
PAT PAT
ALL YOUR FAULT.
YOUR OLD MAN'S OUT IN THE RAIN. LET'S SET HIM TO REST.
YE MUST BE BASILISK. I'VE HEARD OF YE, FIREBREATHER.
YE POSSESS IT. THE GIFT OF A KING'S MEAL. WHY DID YE NOT USE IT?
IT WAS NEVER A GIFT.
"IT TOOK FROM ME--

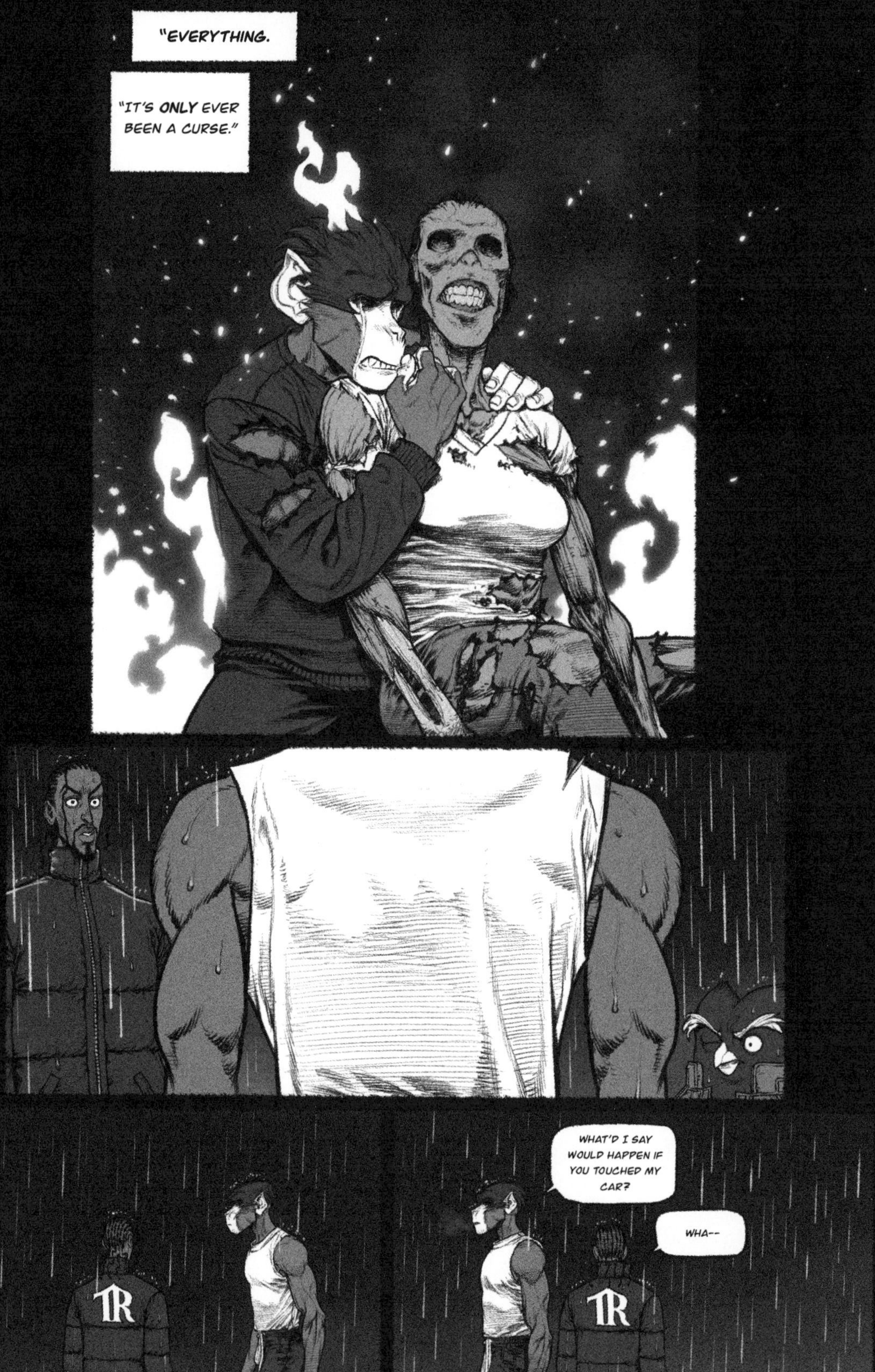
"EVERYTHING.
"IT'S ONLY EVER BEEN A CURSE."
WHAT'D I SAY WOULD HAPPEN IF YOU TOUCHED MY CAR?
WHA--

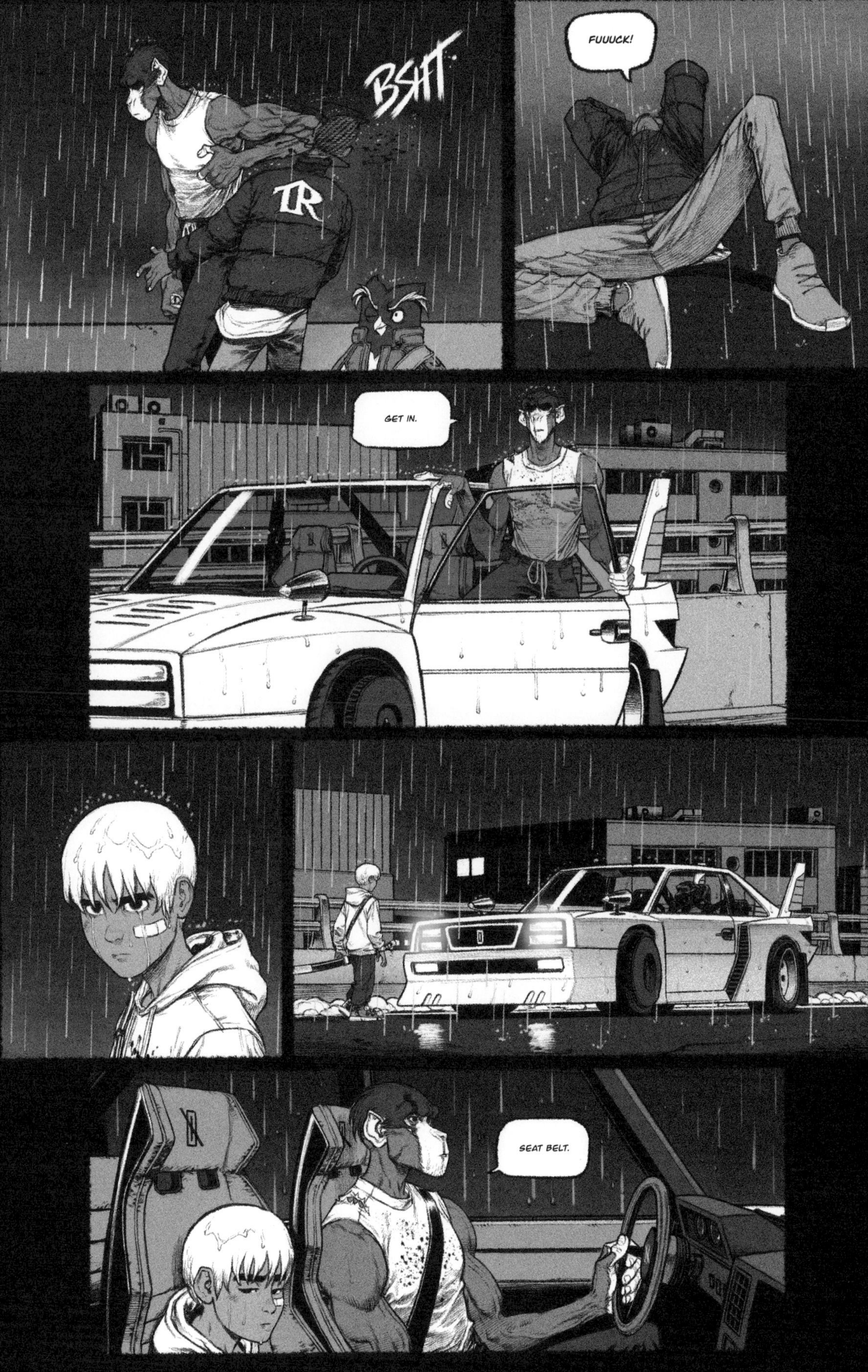
BSHT
FUUUCK!
GET IN.
SEAT BELT.

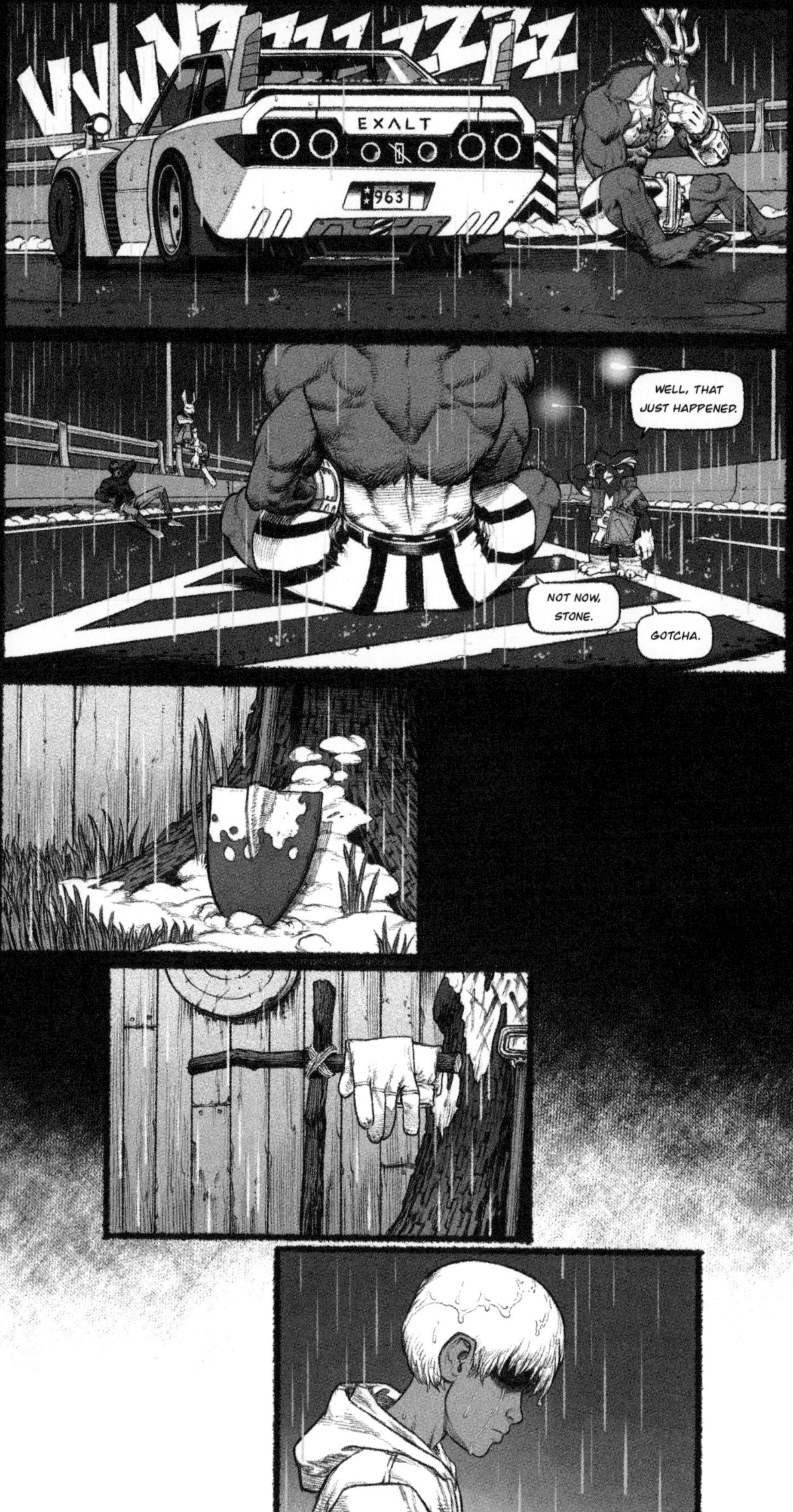
VVVVZZZZZZZz
EXALT
963
WELL, THAT JUST HAPPENED.
NOT NOW, STONE.
GOTCHA.

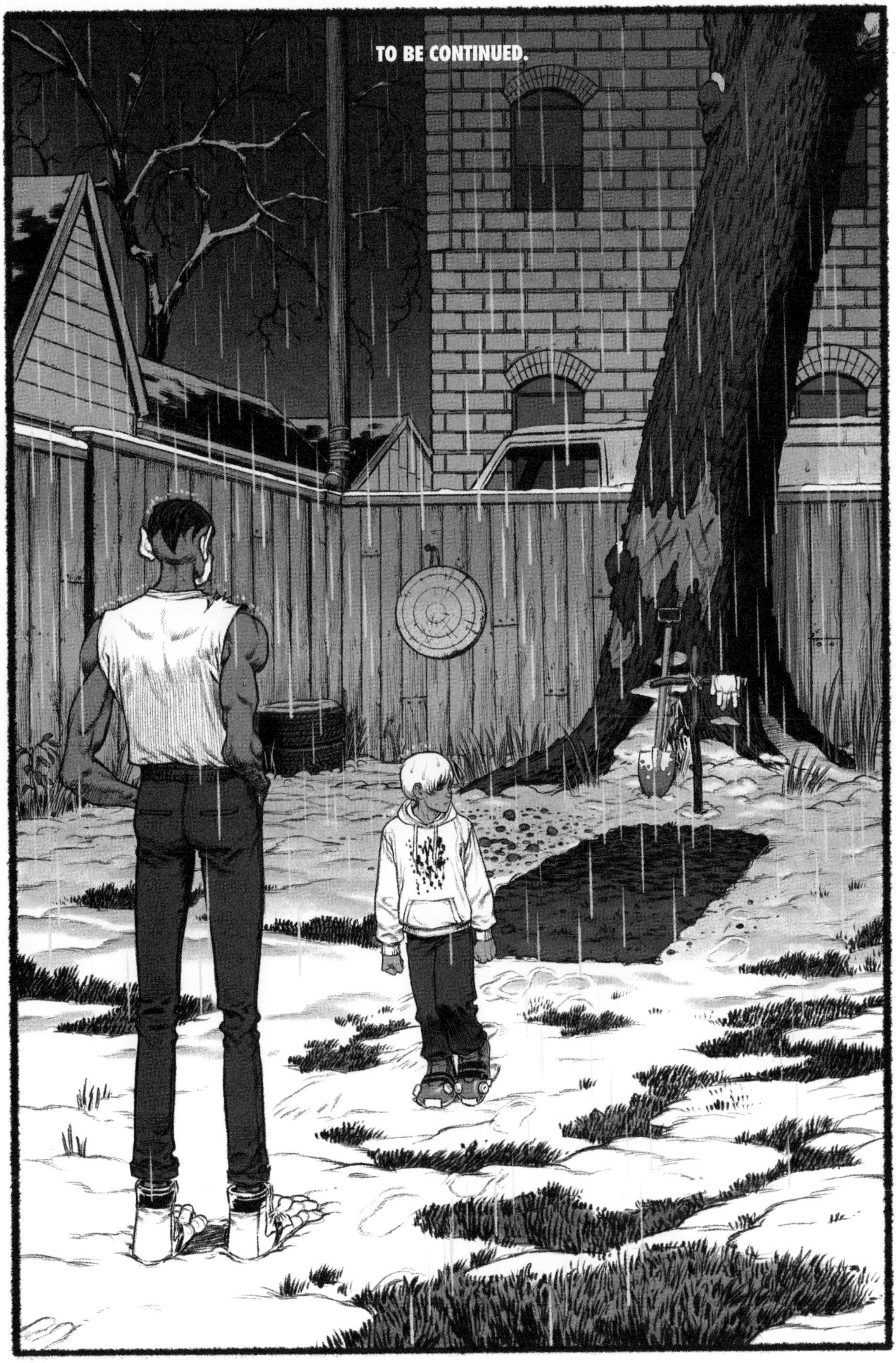
TO BE CONTINUED.

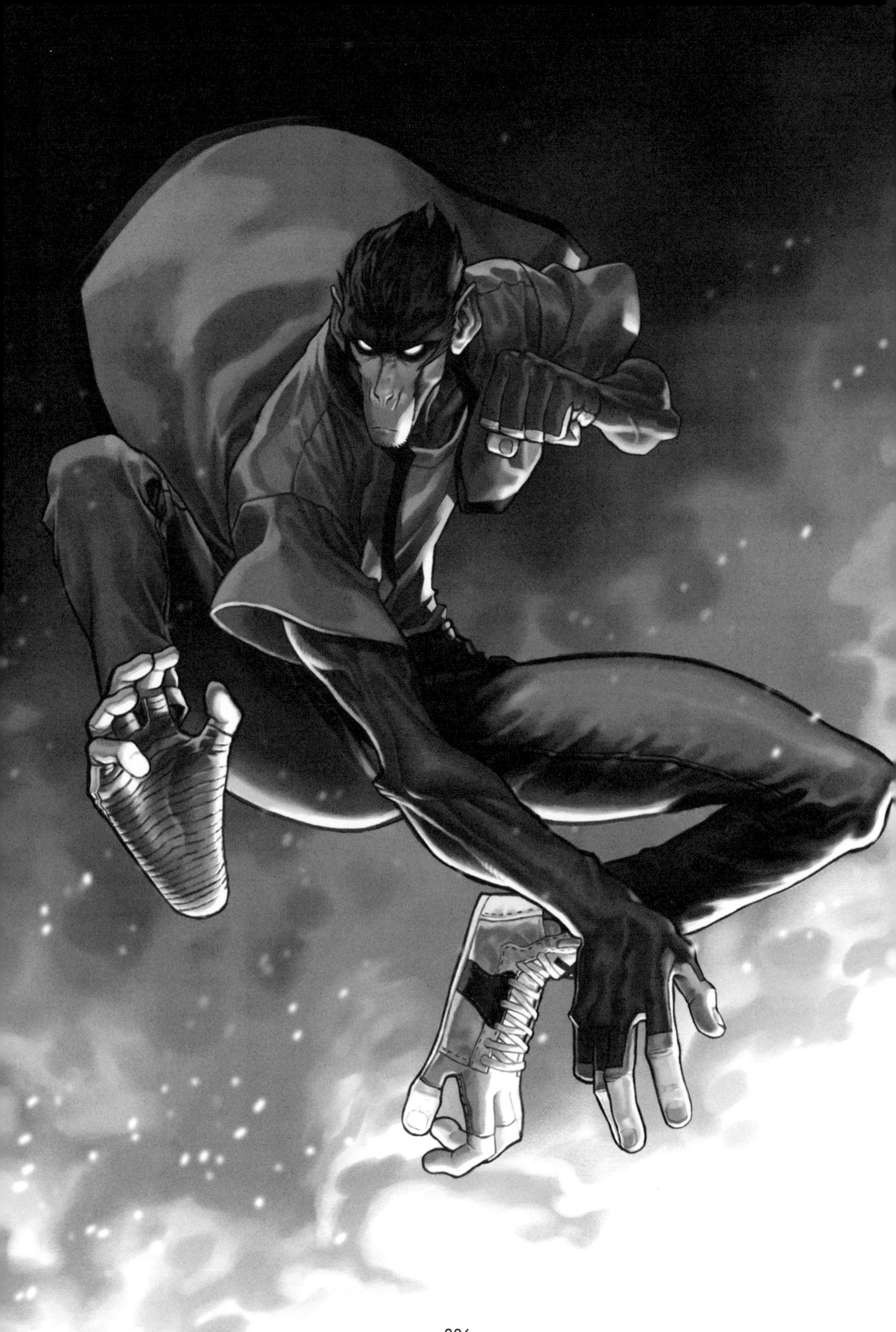

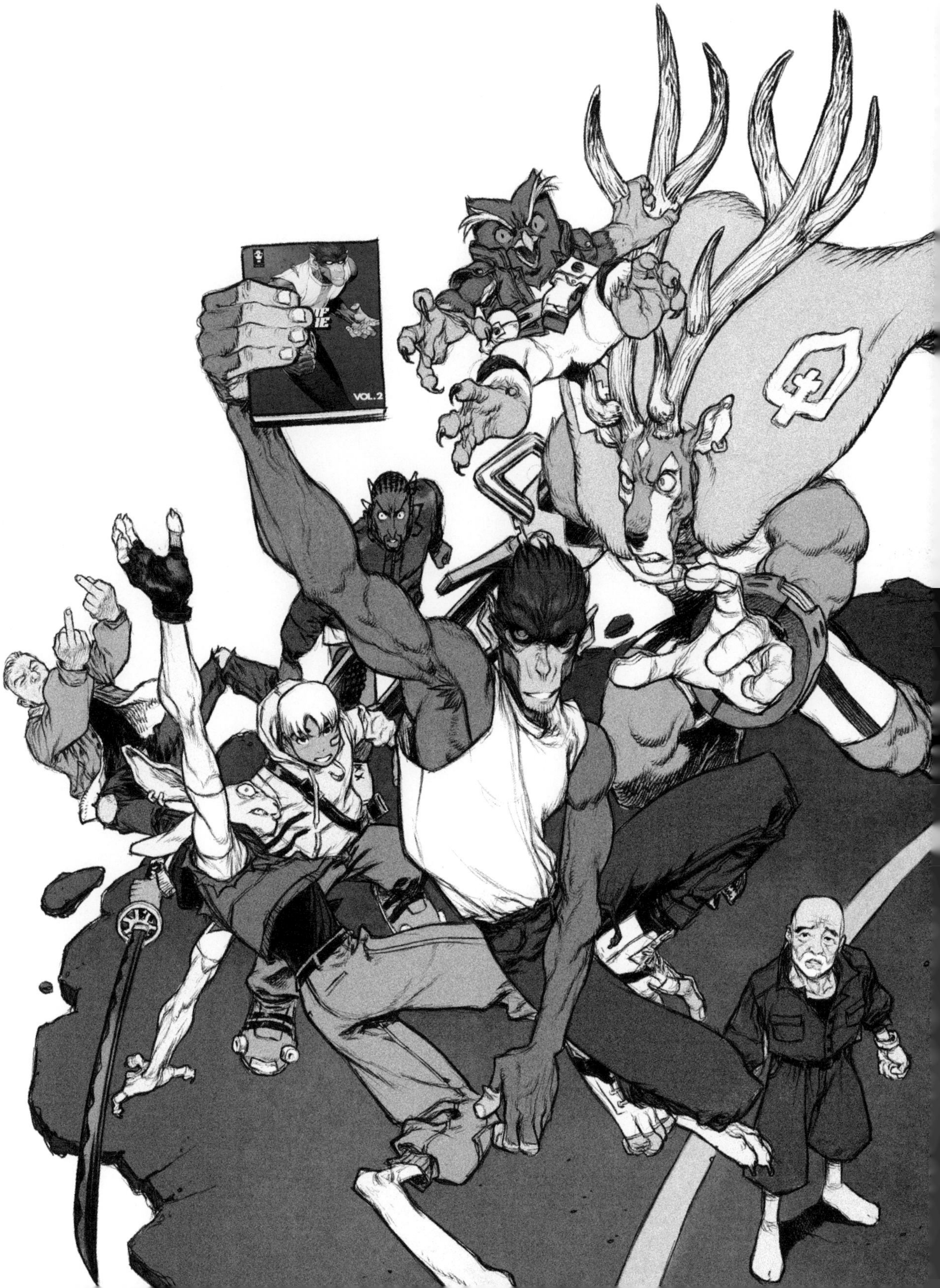
VOL. 2

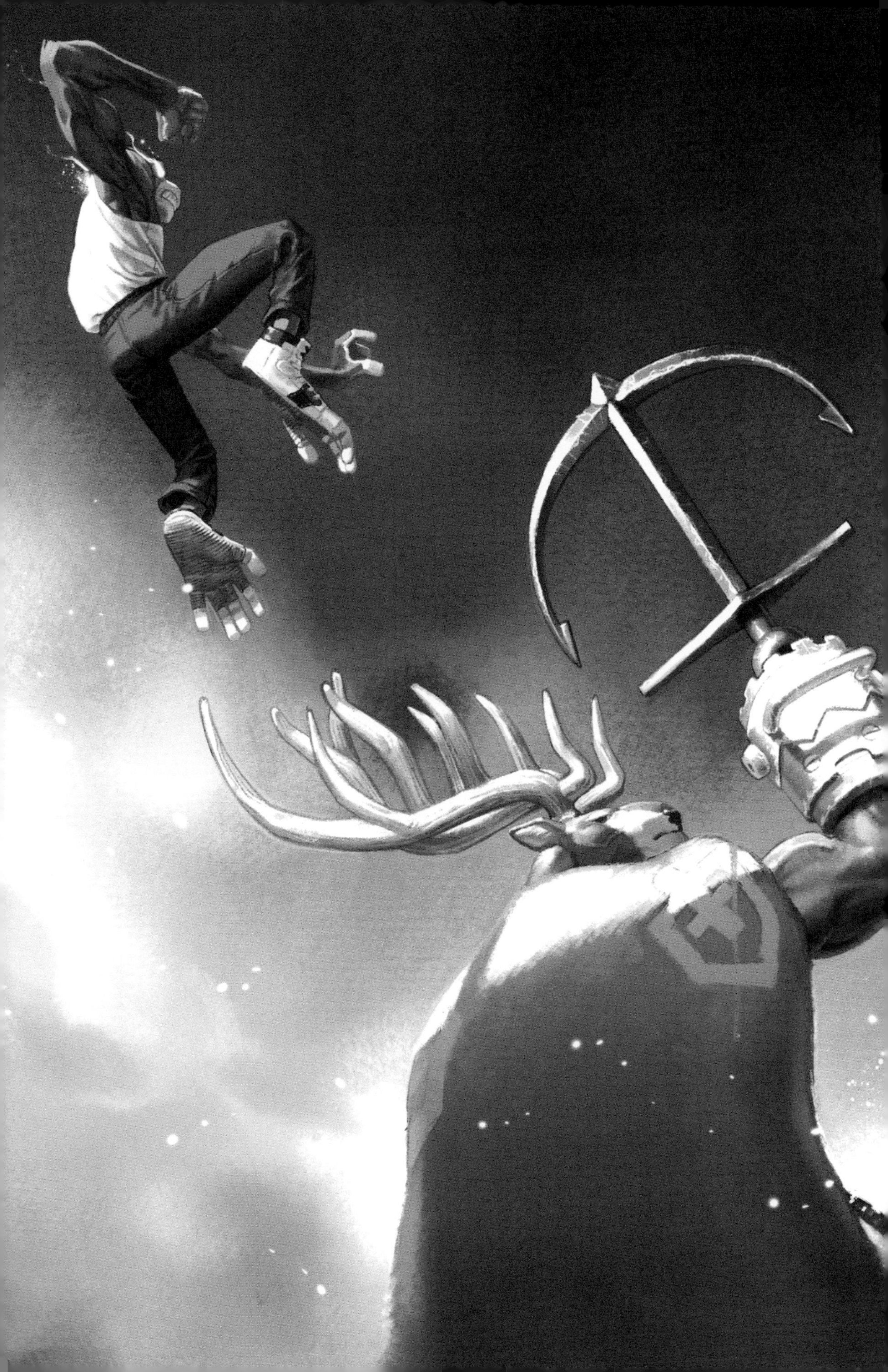

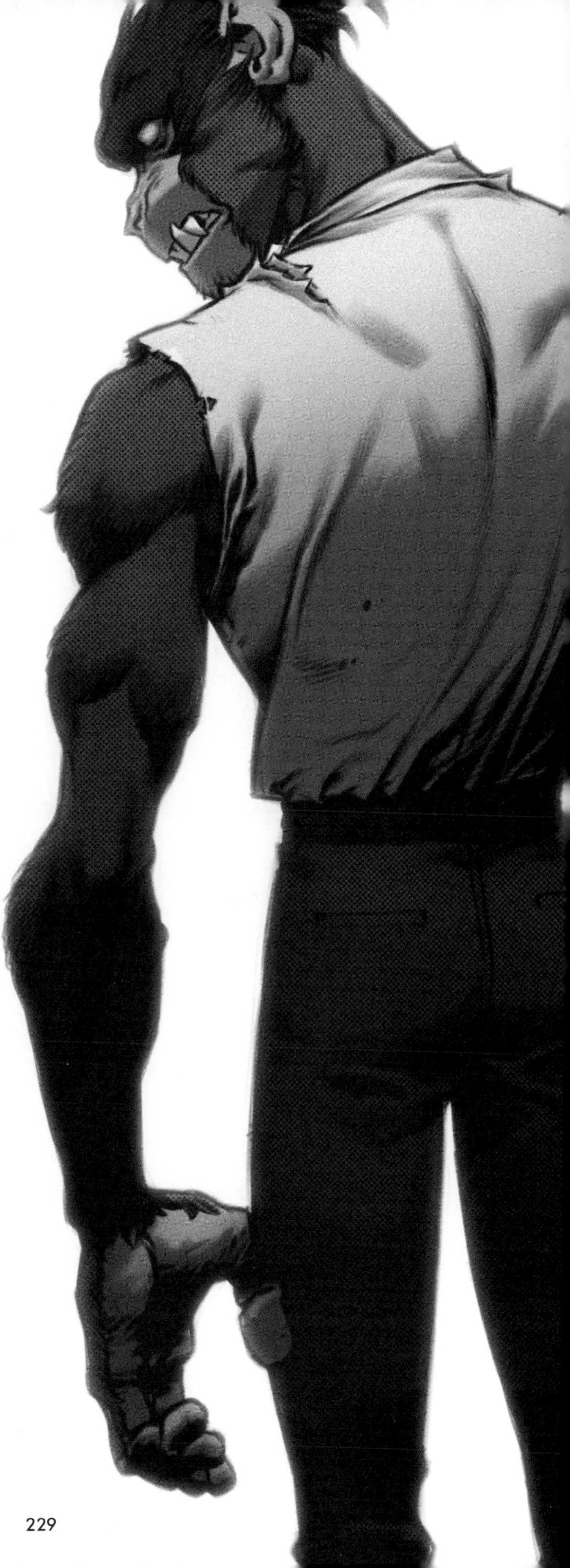

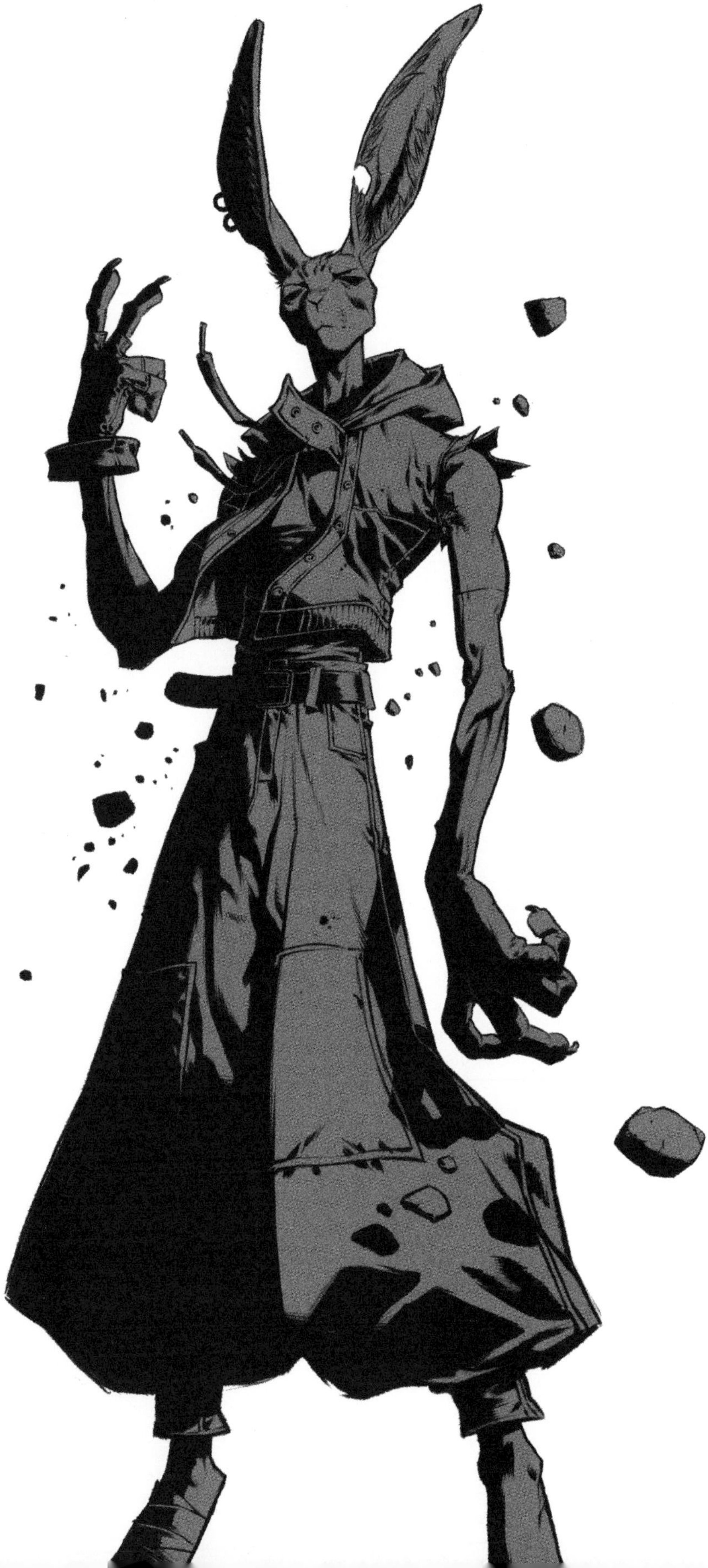

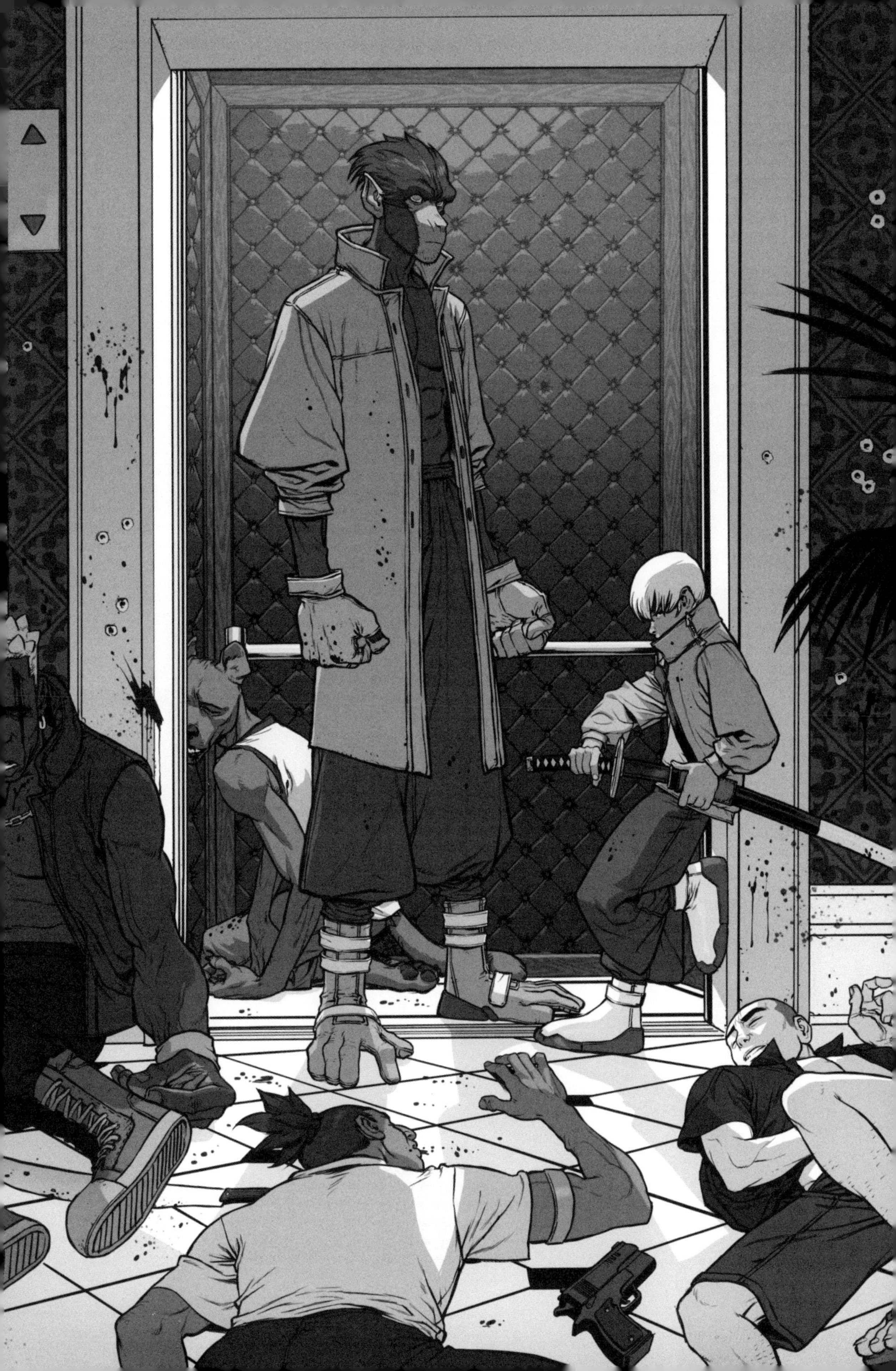

I hope you enjoyed this graphic novel. The story of Bass and Dante is one I've been writing for the past decade. I've swallowed many tough pills while creating this book. In fact, this book was intended to be the first volume of *Kings of Nowhere*—although with a wildly different plot. However, there was always this lingering thought that I could make it better. There was something missing—I just needed time to figure out what. So I decided on having Bili be the main focus of volume 1, because I was much more sure about it, while saving Bass and Dante for volume 2. After completing the first book and seeing the overwhelmingly positive feedback it received, I spent months rewriting and reevaluating my story. My goal was to create a manga this time. Why? My biggest concern with the first book was its length. It took me two years to create 80 colored pages. In the same amount of time, I managed to create over 220 pages by taking on a manga aesthetic. I have been so inspired by fantastic creators such as Takehiko Inoue (*Vagabond*), Katsuhiro Otomo (*Akira*), Makoto Yukimura (*Vinland Saga*), Boichi (*Dr. Stone*), and Kentaro Miura (*Berserk*) that I dream of joining them in the hearts of readers. I wish for *Kings of Nowhere* to echo throughout the halls of comic history. You may be wondering how volumes 1 and 2 correlate. Don't you worry. You'll see soon enough. Volume 3 is going to push my limits even further!

—Roosh

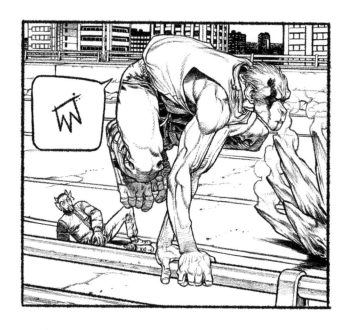